# EMBERS RISING

## THE LAST DRAEGION SAGA
### BOOK TWO

## CINDY L. SELL

AETHER AND ASH PRESS

Book Cover by Maria Spada

Edited by Ellie Owen, Emma O'Connell, and Erynn Snel

ISBN (paperback): 978-1-963768-05-3

ISBN (hardback): 978-1-963768-04-6

ISBN (ebook): 978-1-963768-03-9

1st edition, August 2025

# Author's Note

*The Last Draegion Saga* explores dark themes and situations that some readers may find unsettling, including fantasy battle sequences, trauma and abuse, and persecution of a fictional race. While I'm a firm believer in happy endings, those may be hard-won in these books. Please take care of yourself first and foremost.

For content advisories, please visit my website: www.thelastdraegion.com

See the back of this book for a pantheon guide, translations, and pronunciations.

CONTINENT OF EIDOSINIA
EIDOSINIAN CAPITAL
EIDOSINIAN CITY
ALLIAANSI CITY
NEUTRAL CITY
RUIN
THAUM
JRS
MAUTOR
YORIGEN'S BLUFF
Iceborn Territories
In'Jasuu
Jaiu River
Taaru'Kallii
BRYNN
Mt. Eisekii
NORTHLANDS
STARLIGHT
RU'ISKAAR
AESIN
PENRITH
LIOS'AMA
EOTAARON
Natsa'Kallii
Innixwood
RAVENSPORT
E
KUMA'KIIR
Marduu
Ru'Natha
GIFEVAAR
WILLOWMARSH
BLACKRIDGE
WN'S BREATH
VVIX
SARTON
Sunrise Creek
Palisadic Mountains
Tinturus River
SUNRISE
IDOSINIA
Emerald River
CLYSTERNA
grenti
BELDEN
DOVER'S CLIFF
lands
Illucidine Tributary
Faeflight Mountains
CINTOSH
West
Cintoshi River
FERID
GATE
Denorian
Feridian
Bay
Aivenosian
DENORIA
Desert
Nekri River
MARSH
NOHR
Sea
RYOST
Narisett
Bay
ORTHOVIA
W
E
ean River
BRIGHTON
KEILLIAND
AARILON
S
SAHA
Kjaltemore
IDANIS
DUERWIST
Sea
DUERGUARD
KJESWUER
0        100
LEAGUES
MURENE

For Meg, who never allowed me to settle for 'good enough.'

# THREE THOUSAND YEARS AGO

## BAOKRYN

The god of chaos caressed Baokryn's temple with all the tenderness of the lover he had once been.

His touch burned like acid. Baokryn snarled, straining against him, but his psionic command pinned her to the stone. Her arm twitched around the blade lodged in her elbow. Black blood leaked from a small cut on her opposite bicep—an insignificant wound, but for the soul blight poison it had sent burrowing into her vessel.

Rubble and ruin had claimed the Holy City. Baokryn lay on the shattered steps of the Temple of Saonis, staring up into Anordis's once-beautiful face. Her sword's arcane edge had taken his left eye, and streaks of blood oozed down his lavender cheek. Red stained his white hair and settled into the cracks between his teeth.

Over and over, he stroked her temple. His shadow blotted out the light of encircling flames. "We should have been so much more, Nahariim."

Baokryn scoffed. After all these millennia, the ashen wretch still pined for her prior vessel. "The Traitor never loved you. She used you."

His reedy laughter threaded into her psyche like an echo in a tomb. "How little you know. Would that I had been made the god of love, for love is naught but chaos. Nahariim understood this."

Needles pricked Baokryn's Shield as he sought entrance. She tried to jerk away, but Anordis seized her chin. She was helpless in his grasp, and she choked on her rage as she reached once more for her magic. The flames heeded her call, burning scarlet, but Anordis met her attempts with his greater power, harnessing steel and platinum. He *seized* the flames, dissolved them into misty Aether, and chuckled.

She sagged beneath him.

He'd taken everything. Killed everyone.

*Saolanni forgive me.*

Draegionic power illuminated Anordis's body from within. Silver and bronze. Copper, steel, and cobalt. Even platinum, brass, and titanium comprised the lattice of his Shield, stolen from her people—harvested, rather, for mere *theft* did not encompass the grievousness of his violation. Only gold, Baokryn's power, yet resisted him.

She was the last of a race older than the lesser gods themselves.

And she'd failed them.

The remnants of Xosek's tome dusted Anordis's skin like ash. Her best friend's corpse lay broken at the base of the stairs. Where was Falla, her dragonbond?

Beyond Xosek, Baokryn's own dragonbond, Aliri, fought her way back to consciousness. The gold dragon's foreleg twitched, and her blackened wing convulsed around the lance that had taken her from the sky.

A sob tore from Baokryn's chest.

Anordis's smile was apologetic. "You were supposed to rule beside me."

"That throne wasn't meant for the likes of y—"

His fingers clamped down on her throat. Baokryn jerked again. Heat and pressure built behind her eyes. Instinctively trying to grab his wrist, her arms lurched uselessly against his psionic grapple. Her teeth gritted, but she changed tactics and went limp. If she could coax the darkness closer, banish her soul back to her tome and command Aristyn to destroy it, she could deny Anordis her power forever and give the lesser gods a chance to rally. Surely, they could set aside their differences long enough to defeat him.

"Soon, I shall be the god of all things, and I'll have you to thank for that." Anordis leaned down, his nose brushing hers. "Oh, mighty Bao, you wished so much for others' approval. Look how your self-righteousness has failed you."

Scorching fury bloomed inside her, but Baokryn shoved aside the hurt and let her soul's hold on her vessel slip further. Her eyes closed. She sent one last message for her bookkeeper through their bond, and Aristyn's wordless farewell crested in a wave of sorrow.

Ash, but she prayed this would be enough to safeguard Saolanni, to protect the Greater Throne...

Static skittered across her Shield, and pain pierced her temples. Baokryn jolted back to herself. Sky, stone, smoke. Anordis's hand was gone, and her lungs violently expanded with the urge to scream.

"*Shh. It's alright,* niish amaar. *This will only take a moment.*"

Anordis's voice caressed her from within, his psionic suggestion forcing her to calm. The absence of emotion didn't even allow horror as he breached her Shield and the golden lattice stuttered out. Pain burrowed into her skull, and only instinct made her recoil. There was no fear, no panic, no anger. She was an outsider in her own body.

"*There, you see? Isn't that better?*" Anordis's fingers pressed against her temple. His violet eyes were kind. "*You don't want this power, Bao. You never have. All those people demanding things of you, pressuring you to become more than you are—let me relieve you of it. Let go.*"

Anordis's mind enveloped hers like a warm blanket. He wrapped his psionic presence around her power—and tugged.

Baokryn shuddered. It was like gravity had changed direction, trying to pull her through a keyhole. She resisted, but the soul blight poison had taken hold in her blood. She *should* let go. Let the current ease her pain. Her hold weakened.

No.

She mustn't.

Baokryn fought against the ashen bastard's imperium as Aristyn had taught her.

Anordis's foul poison sprouted thorns and raked through her veins. She screamed again, until his torture eased and the warmth of his mind returned.

"*Let go, Bao.*"

Another tug. Baokryn called to her magic, and fire erupted over her skin. Anordis curled his lip and snuffed it out with a burst of cold, silver magic.

Xosek's magic.

Its familiarity ghosted over Baokryn like a beloved perfume. She should have felt some emotion—relief, hope—but Anordis's psionic hold smothered it.

"*Let go. Let me ease your suffering.*"

Flickers of movement caught Baokryn's eye. The glint of gold, the rasp of scales on stone. And high above, a flash of silver.

"Never," she spat.

The god snarled. *"Then I will take it from you."*

Anordis struck, and Baokryn's existence became agony. Her flames exploded in response, and his stolen silver magic doused them instantly.

Baokryn tried to dissociate, tried to imagine Xosek's pale face, the melodic sound of her voice, the scent of winter in her hair. A glimmering silver thread lingered within Anordis's presence, and Baokryn reached for it. The power that was once Xosek's reached back.

Anordis wrenched it away with a sneer made gruesome by the blood trails on his face. *"Bold of you, wretched fireken, but you only prolong the inevitable."*

The pressure on her mind eased. Movement stirred in Baokryn's peripheral vision, and far above, a distant shape streaked through clouds of smoke. The ground trembled. She dared not reach out to either ally, dared not alert the god to their coming, but her heart lifted.

Anordis grabbed her head in both hands and hot spikes stabbed into her temples. Baokryn's scream broke in her ravaged throat. The tearing sensation returned, as if he meant to rip her very soul from its vessel. On and on it went, until her own heartbeat throbbed within the confines of her skull.

Once more, he banished her flames. A sliver of icy cobalt—that of Zyphanas the Elder—flickered through the god's presence. Baokryn latched onto the magic and *pulled.*

The magic shied from Anordis like oil from water. He was no draegion and had no place wielding her people's magic. It twined around Baokryn's power and snapped free of the god's mind.

Anordis's mental hold on her body slipped. He roared and wrenched her upward. Limbs freed at last, Baokryn drove her thumb into his bleeding eye and braced before he slammed her skull against the stone.

Bright stars exploded in her vision, soon usurped by blood-tinged darkness. The poison in her blood caught fire.

*Ash.* She couldn't breathe. Couldn't see. There was only endless agony, the press of his fingers at her temples, and a tumult of psionic power that blasted her thoughts to shrapnel.

Blood poured from her nose and ears as he tore once more at her soul. Thunder rolled distantly—the call from Baosanni, signaling the death of her vessel—beckoning her toward the Plains of Gray and the tome meant to shelter her soul.

She might have obeyed that summons, but for the brush of Xosek's magic once more. Unruly Xosek, whose only mistake was to believe herself undeserving of honor. Whose sacrifice was perhaps the most honorable of all.

Rage sharpened Baokryn's vision. Her best friend's corpse lay only spans away. Anordis had taken her life, her magic, and destroyed her tome, ensuring her soul could never Shift again.

The god's outline solidified against the haze. His violet eyes gleamed with hunger. *"Give in, Bao. The war is lost."*

As the only remaining draegion on Dessos, Baokryn had one responsibility: to guard their power from hands that sought to use it for destruction. She couldn't forsake that duty any more than she could follow in Nahariim's shadow.

Draegionic threads wove through Anordis's mind, a tapestry within his divine aura. But the weave seemed to weaken as his power reached for hers. Baokryn clenched her teeth.

She would take it back.

For Xosek.

For Saolanni.

For mortalkind itself.

She seized the closest threads of power. Frigid silver and fiery steel came away from that tapestry like saplings torn from the ground.

Anordis jerked back. Baokryn snatched the copper thread in his retreat. Restorative power surged into her vessel as the healer's thread coiled around her, clearing her vision and dulling the throbbing in her head. It forced the knife from her arm and sealed the wound behind it.

"No. *No!*"

Platinum energy exploded from Anordis in misty tendrils, taking the shape of draconic wings. Their savage points plunged toward her as if to skewer her into the steps. Baokryn's Shield flared copper, silver, cobalt, steel, and gold, repelling the attack and scattering Aether over the stone. She shoved onto her elbows as the god's Shield stuttered. Power pulsed inside her veins.

But the soul blight poison still linked her to Anordis. He hammered his will into her vessel and broke her Shield apart.

His fingers dug into her temples and he *seized* her essence again in rending psionic claws. He ripped at her threads of steel and cobalt, but the magic resisted him. As he grappled with them, Baokryn used the copper magic to numb the effects of his poison.

The last threads of draegionic power thrummed across her awareness: titanium, brass, platinum, and bronze, tightly woven within Anordis's psyche. She had only seconds to reclaim them.

Aliri's thunderous roar shuddered through the ground. The gold dragon limped toward them, dragging her mangled wing. Her teeth dripped slaver, and her slitted eyes glowed. Aether coalesced between her jaws, and as Anordis paused to shoot her a mocking smile, Baokryn subtly pulled her own magic closer.

He must have sensed her intent. Anordis's gaze snapped back to her. "You're a fool, Baokryn. You will never—"

She sneered. "You talk too much."

Steel and cobalt snapped back to her. Baokryn summoned all five threads she held, lashed them around the last four affixed to his psyche, and *pulled*.

Like the mighty stone cliffs of Dragon Bay sheering off in a storm, the last of her people's magic broke away from his mind.

Anordis shrieked.

Psionic energy battered her against the ground. Anordis's fingers hooked around her throat. Baokryn reeled from the waves of divine power buffeting her senses.

"Give it back!" he snarled. "*Give it back!*"

Something else had come away with those gleaming threads. Something that was not hers. It lodged inside her like a shard of glass.

Aliri spoke inside her mind. *"Your Shield,* Nashanett.*"*

A streak of silver fell from the sky. Falla's sleek form barely shook the ground in her landing.

"You miserable witch." Anordis's voice trembled. "Give it back! Give it—"

One burst from Baokryn's new Shield blasted the god down the steps. Falla darted forward to block his escape. Aether ignited between Aliri's teeth.

Baokryn threw part of her Shield to protect Falla. As the multicolored lattice swept across the silver's scales, the world erupted in dragon fire.

But when the smoke cleared, Anordis was gone.

# Part One

# CHAPTER ONE

## ALAR

Alar shoved aside a tangle of hanging vines, and stringy white sap stuck to his fingers. He wiped his hand on his trousers with a grimace and stepped over a rotting log.

"Admit it," Daeya called from behind him. "We're lost."

He rolled his eyes and glanced back at her. "We're not lost."

One red-tinted eyebrow lifted, and she jerked her thumb over her shoulder. "That's the same tree we saw an hour ago."

"You can't know that for certain." Alar refused to look at the tree and its much-too-familiar branches, instead keeping his gaze leveled on Daeya while Jack climbed over the log in front of her.

That annoying, endearing, infuriating smile he'd grown to know so well tugged at her lips. She pointed beyond the vines. "Then how do you explain those?"

He followed her gesture to the muddy footprints leading off in the same direction they were traveling. They bore a suspicious resemblance to the tracks stamped in the mud behind them.

Wastelands, she was right. They were going in circles.

*I'm never going to hear the end of this one.*

"Fantastic." Jack wiped his disheveled black hair from his forehead.

Barely containing a groan, Alar turned away from Daeya's widening grin and hoped the heat in his ear tips didn't show. "We just got turned around."

She giggled, pushed the vines aside, and hopped over the log. "That's just an elaborate way of saying we're lost."

Jack rounded on her. "I don't see anything funny about this."

She stopped short, causing Ravlok to stumble into her back.

The monk caught Daeya before she fell and shoved himself between her and Jack. "Back off. She didn't mean anything by it."

Alar gritted his teeth. Ever since their meeting with the supposed goddess of knowledge, Ravlok had taken it upon himself to protect Daeya from the likes of Jack and all her mythological enemies.

Jack thrust a finger at Daeya. "Her people slaughtered an entire village last week, and she pretends nothing happened."

Golden light arced across Daeya's fists. "I don't deny what they did was a travesty, but you seem to forget *your* people destroyed an entire school full of children."

"*Sorcerer* children." Jack spat the word like poison. "Hardly innocent by any stretch of the imagination."

That unnerving light crept upward, reaching beneath Daeya's sleeves. She started forward.

Ravlok stuck out an arm to hold her back. "Don't."

They'd had this argument over and over since leaving Orthovia, and it was doing none of them any good. Alar strode forward, boots crunching through dense underbrush, and placed himself between Jack and Ravlok.

Alar nudged Jack's aura. "Take a walk."

He scowled. "You always take her side."

Ignoring the accusation, Alar pressed harder on Jack's aura to suppress its roiling fury and nodded toward a stand of trees. "We'll camp there for the night. Bring back any game you find."

Jack's mouth twisted beneath his growing beard. "We'd have never gotten lost if Val were here." He turned away. "Strange how you forget who murdered him."

Black anger clouded Alar's vision. He almost, *almost*, seized Jack by his collar, demanded he take the words back, told him he remembered every scar and wrinkle in the face of the man who'd slain his best friend. The Guild soldier had died in a gout of blood, clutching his temples as Alar shredded his mind apart.

Oh, he remembered. He would never allow himself to forget.

But Jack and Val had been close, too, and the younger man was allowed to grieve in his own way.

Alar returned his attention to Daeya, who stood clutching Ravlok's arm with glowing hands. Shimmers rolled off her skin like...

An aura.

Eyes widening, Alar tapped into his aura-sense. For nine aggravating months he'd tried to reach her with his psionics, and here was a spontaneous opening to her mind—

"Agh!" Ravlok jerked away. Smoke curled from his sleeve, and the sable fabric bore the singed imprint of Daeya's palms.

The gold light winked out, and her mouth gaped. "I'm sorry, Rav. I didn't mean to."

Alar shook his head. It hadn't been her aura, just the wavering mirage of dissipating heat. He prodded the space where her mind should be and found it just as impenetrable as it had always been. He sighed. "Are you alright?"

Ravlok examined the new hole in his sleeve. The scent of singed hair was unmistakable. "I'm okay."

Daeya's face fell further. Her green eyes glistened. "I'm so sorry," she repeated. "I don't know what happened."

A familiar shriek split the air.

Paelic, the stalker falcon, settled on a nearby branch in a torrent of beating wings and falling needles. Supposedly the familiar of a forest Guardian whom Ravlok insisted was the goddess of nature, Paelic had been following them for nearly a month. The bird disappeared from time to time, but it always found them again to offer its disapproving opinion whenever Daeya's golden light appeared.

It was happening more frequently. Daeya expertly wielded magic in ways Alar had never seen before, but whatever this new power was, she didn't have control of it.

After acknowledging the bird with a ludicrous nod, Ravlok echoed Alar's thoughts. "It's getting worse," he told her. "You must control your temper. Use the breathing techniques like we've practiced."

"I know." Daeya winced. "I'm trying."

The monk opened his mouth again, probably to assert for the hundredth time that they should have gone to Draeconis with Vortanis, but Alar took Daeya's arm before he could. He was supposed to bring her north to his people as a hostage, if not a new and powerful ally, and none of these gods-crazed lunatics were going to stop him.

Ravlok's jaw snapped shut. "I'll make camp."

As the monk crept away, Alar tugged Daeya's arm and attempted a grin. "Alright, Sorceress, if you're so good at navigating, prove it. Let's head up that rise and figure out where we are."

Normally, a challenge like that would have enlivened her, but the smile she returned was a weak thing. Her solemnity settled like an ache in Alar's chest.

*You're being ridiculous.*

Over the last month, he'd encouraged Daeya's flirting, even reciprocated it, since it seemed to keep her at ease as they headed farther north. But he had to be careful not to allow his feelings to sabotage his mission. His mentor Ashaara would be able to sense if he'd been emotionally compromised, and he'd learned long ago that love and logic were too often mutually exclusive.

Daeya would bounce back to her insufferable good-naturedness soon. She always did.

Alar led the way through the trees, silently cursing the overgrown forest. He wasn't made for the wilderness. No sane person would choose water boiled over a campfire and soggy bedrolls to a tavern with good ale and a soft bed.

Eventually, slick with sweat despite the cold, they emerged at a spot overlooking a steep riverbank. Daeya barely seemed winded next to him. Alar expected a teasing rebuke for his lack of endurance, but she didn't even smirk in his direction.

The sky was awash with shades of purple, red, and orange. Rays of light punched through the forest on the opposite shore, and haloes of color scattered on the rushing water. It had been overcast for most of the day, but now that the setting sun was making an appearance, it was obvious they were facing west instead of east.

Daeya's lips parted with the same wonder she'd had on the plains, in the mountains, and in every swamp and forest between here and Orthovia. With each passing day, she seemed to discover something spectacular in the world beyond the capital.

Waning sunlight streaked her red hair. The rose madder he'd used to dye it weeks ago was fading, and her blonde roots were showing through.

Alar caught himself staring and cleared his throat. "Well?"

"We'll end up back in Fawn's Breath if we cross the river." Daeya nodded to a rocky outcropping where the river curved east. "If we're lucky, we can follow this northeast for a while. Do you know which river this is?"

He cringed. Val would have been aghast at his ignorance. "Depending on how far north we are, it's either the Ru'Natha or the Marduu. Both drain into the Taaru'Kallii. It's enormous, so I know we haven't crossed it yet."

Daeya chuckled.

"What?"

She sat on a rock overlooking the river. "You Syljians"—Daeya said the word delicately, like it was something breakable. After all the times he'd scolded her for using the slur 'blanker,' it seemed his efforts were paying off—"have such funny names for things. Little Snake, Turtle, Thunder River."

"What would you call them? Something Brogrenti?"

"Gods, no." At last, a genuine smile emerged. "That's how you get some vulgar name no one could say with a straight face."

Alar sat beside her. They listened to the river churning along the rocks for a time before Daeya spoke again.

"You're not much of a navigator, are you?"

"Is it that obvious?"

"I'm afraid so."

"Damn." Alar feigned a crestfallen look, and she elbowed him in the ribs. He laughed and gestured toward their surroundings. "Val was always the navigator. He had a sense about these things. Even as children, we never got lost in the woods."

"Was he a Guardian?"

The thought of Val as a pious man—a follower of Caelyn—made Alar snort. "No. He might have prayed to the god of fortune at the dicing table, but not much else."

Though, maybe Val could have been swayed if he'd been the one to speak with the goddesses of nature and knowledge in the same week. He'd always had an easier time accepting things like blind chance or fate.

Daeya's thigh brushed his as she turned to face him. "I really am sorry for what happened to him."

Snakes tangled around his lungs. This wasn't the place for this. He would *not* break down in front of her. "He was Syljian, Daeya."

"I don't care." She seized his hand. "I know he was your friend, and the way he was taken from you"—Daeya winced—"I wouldn't wish it on anyone."

It was almost believable. He curled his fingers around hers.

"Thank you." He should have extracted himself and insisted they get back to camp, but he held her hand a moment longer. A moment wouldn't hurt.

"Will you tell me about him?"

His brows tensed. "What would you want to know?"

"Whatever you want to tell me, I guess. You said you were children together."

"We were." That earnest look on her face was hard to refuse. "Our mothers were friends, so we didn't have much choice. He was a year older, and the architect of most of our mischief."

"Where did you grow up?"

Alar hesitated, studying the little blue veins in the back of her hand. "In the mountains west of Trivvix."

Daeya surely knew about the massacre her people had committed there five years ago. The Battle of Trivvix, the Guild called it, though Alar's friends and family hadn't stood a chance against the Light Paladins and sorcerers who'd slaughtered them in their homes. All because of Leah, the human girl who'd claimed she loved him. At least, until she learned what he was and reported him to the town constable.

Alar stuffed down the surge of anger and hurt that betrayal still caused.

But he wasn't about to tell Daeya about that. There were many things about him she didn't need to know.

"Trivvix," Daeya echoed.

"Yes."

"Is that why you joined the Alliaansi? Because of what happened there?"

"It was. Val lost his mother that day, and I lost my father." Alar allowed himself a twinge of loss. "His father was never in the equation, so Val became an orphan. My mother and I fled to Starlight with him, where he signed up under Cheralach's command. I chose Koraani's."

Daeya chewed her lip. "Odd he'd choose the human."

"Not if you'd known him." One side of his mouth lifted. "Koraani was too rigid. Cheralach was more tolerant of his antics. Val made a terrible soldier, but he had a knack for spy work. He loved causing trouble for the Guild."

She crossed her ankles, heavy-soled boots sinking into the mud. "Sounds like my kind of man."

"He was well-loved." Alar's voice broke. "I'm not looking forward to telling his wife he's gone."

"I'd offer to go with you if I thought it would help."

Scoffing, he shook his head. "I don't think Finn would like that."

"I understand." Daeya squeezed his fingers, then started to withdraw.

"He asked about you," Alar blurted, tightening his grip. He kicked himself as soon as the words left his mouth, and hastily released her.

Daeya's cheeks matched the rosy red of the setting sun. She returned her hand to her lap. "Why?"

There was no escaping the question; he'd dug this hole himself. "He was intrigued by the Guild acolyte who caused clockwork mayhem and destruction."

It had nothing to do with how often Alar talked about her.

Something changed in Daeya's face, and he wished he could see her aura. Reading her body's cues, the tension pulling at her cheeks and pinching the skin around her eyes, he could only guess at the ambiguous emotion plaguing her.

Her gaze strayed across the river. "Can I ask you something?"

A stray lock of hair skated across her cheek. He fought the urge to tuck it behind her ear.

"Of course."

The last shreds of sunlight glinted off her eyes in hues of gold and orange. She frowned at something in the distance.

"When you were posing as Faustus"—the weight of her attention settled on him—"was every part of our friendship a lie?"

His breath caught. It was a question he'd never expected her to ask, especially not in a tone so unaccusing and conversational. Even in disguise, it had been easy to be himself with her, but she was too clever not to assume a distinction between his two personas.

She studied him, her neutral gaze as brittle as glass. The river roared beneath them and coated them with mist.

Saying yes would protect himself, but it would hurt Daeya, whose history of failed friendships stretched long into her past. Denying it, though, even in part, was an admission he wasn't willing to face. He liked her, even felt affection for her, but his duty to his people came first. Admitting his feelings would make him vulnerable, and with that, she could destroy him.

Leah certainly had. In a moment of youthful passion, believing their love was strong enough to rise above the lies and propaganda, Alar had revealed what he was to her. He'd thought she would see him for something more than a blanker. Too many people he loved had died for that mistake.

Seconds ticked by and Daeya's question remained unanswered. Finally, her expression steeled, and she nodded to herself. "I suppose I should have expected that."

His chest constricted. "Daeya—"

"I get it." She rose and turned away, walls slamming up around her. "You were just doing your job."

The words that could have brought her back stuck in his throat. She reached the tree line. Alar willed himself to move, to go after her and tell her the truth.

But he couldn't.

"Daeya."

"We should get back to camp." The smile she gave him was mischievous and teasing, and every bit as fake as Faustus Crex. "Are you coming or not?"

# CHAPTER TWO

## ALIRI

Aliri Aethersworn hadn't cried in over nine hundred years.

Seeing Vortanis again brought a font of joy to her reptilian heart, but the news Tiior's steward carried did much more than that. When the curt announcement left his lips, a curious prickling began behind Aliri's eyes and tightness constricted her golden-scaled chest.

"Baokryn lives."

Shock rippled through the circular chamber. Vortanis strode across the glittering green and blue veins of saphyrum-laced tile. Sunlight poured from the atrium's open window and bathed his white robes as he stepped into the Circle of Nine with his chin held high, dauntless as always in the face of the most powerful among dragonkind.

Dannicus, one of Kythax's brood, trailed in the steward's wake, wearing his humanoid body with its curious three-pronged hook for a left hand.

Murmurs of disbelief echoed off the high ceiling and wall-length murals, swelling to a roar among the nine wyrms and their attendants. Vortanis's platinum-embroidered sleeves snapped upward in a demand for silence.

On the balcony high above the chamber floor, mighty Tiior appeared in a flash of chromatic light. The goddess wore her humanoid body, her dark complexion striped and dotted with sacred tattoos. She stepped into the shadow between two marble columns and placed her hands on the gold-inlaid railing. Aliri dipped her head toward her, and Tiior returned the nod with a faint smile.

Wings folded, claws scraped, and scales creaked as the other wyrms settled on platforms ringing the atrium. Aliri relaxed as well, blinking away tears.

Her former dragonbond lived.

Vortanis continued his account, gesturing once to Dannicus, standing dagger-straight and implacable beside him. He was the one to have identified Baokryn's new vessel, Daeya McVen, a sixteen-year-old sorceress from Eidosinia.

Daeya McVen, who'd refused her calling just as Baokryn had.

Aliri studied the millenneon. Dannicus's copper eyes blazed beneath midnight brows, and the orange stripe tattooed across his nose served as a reminder of his bravery against Anordis's priests four centuries earlier in Denoria. Would that her own son could foster the same prestige as the coppers he so revered. Instead, he'd refused his duty to their family's crown over an infatuation with a lowborn mongrel whose impurity would never be accepted by the Gold Court.

A pang of regret spiked through her, but Aliri forced it aside. Now was not the time to dwell on her wayward *draekhei*.

Across the atrium, Sepheron, Breaker of Armies, lifted his enormous titanium-scaled snout. Even if he hadn't been the largest dragon in the room, he would have cut an imposing figure. "The copper must be mistaken. These signs you speak of are coincidence. Nothing more." His cranial ridges tightened around mirror-like eyes. "The Titanium Court does not recognize the child."

"The Cobalt Court agrees," Deylos said to Sepheron's left. The Lord of Frost's deep voice resonated through the atrium. His cobalt wings flared and light glinted off the ebony membrane beneath. "The epoch of the draegion has passed. We will *not* be enslaved again."

Aliri bristled. She drew herself up to defend her dragonbond, but a fresh stab of pain erupted in the fibers of her mangled wing. Choking back a whimper, she caged her fangs.

*Laangor take this cursed wing.*

"Your grievances are your own, Deylos." Falla, Aliri's closest friend and ally, spoke from the platform to her right, silver scales shimmering. The Heart of Redemption's voice rang as clear and crisp as the crystal bells on winter solstice. "Baokryn was a fair and just queen, as the child will be."

Sepheron growled. "You forget Baokryn was once Nahariim, consort to Chaos, and slayer of Emperor Xavkavhosh—"

Falla's silver lips pulled back in a deadly smile, each tooth as long and sharp as a greatsword. "I do not forget our history, Sepheron, but it appears you do. You once served our queen with honor."

"And I will again, should one worthy of the title return to claim it."

Falla scoffed. Jets of icy flakes swirled before her snout. "Your words are as tenuous as those of a Chaos priest."

Sepheron leaped upright, wings snapping outward. His roar of challenge came with a breath of acrid Aetherial smog. "How dare you—"

Falla rose with an answering hiss. Frost collected on her scales, and she took a step forward, foreclaws curling over her platform.

"Enough." Qiiseraan's command cleaved the air like a whip crack. The platinum Sentinel stepped from beneath Tiior's balcony and gathered magic in waves of radiant light. Her eyes glowed like twin suns. "Or I'll throw you both out of *Saonivhatt*'s hall."

Aliri's wing spasmed again. She tucked it close to her while Falla and Sepheron bared teeth a moment longer. Even after three millennia, their personal feud still lingered.

Vortanis looked between them, unperturbed. "The girl has the Shield. *Saonivhatt* and I both witnessed it. If you won't take the word of your goddess and her steward, I request Daeya McVen be tested to prove her legitimacy."

The very notion that a dragon would distrust Tiior was ludicrous, and was met with affronted growls. Aliri could have applauded Vortanis for forcing an early resolution to the matter. Otherwise, it might have taken decades to reach a decision. The Nine would vote to allow the Test of Flame, and Daeya McVen would prove before all of Draeconis to be what Dannicus claimed.

Tiior remained silent as the discussion continued. She likely already knew the outcome of the proceedings, but she wouldn't personally interfere with the Nine's decision. Tiior insisted the dragons govern Draeconis and make their own choices. Blind obedience, she often said, encouraged the withering of knowledge and the death of accountability.

Aliri stretched her wing in slow, faltering movements, only half listening to the discussion. The sorceress would need a gold dragonbond to align with Baokryn's magic. It was tempting to consider the position for herself, but Aliri nosed it aside. Eleven thousand years old and unable to fly, she was in no shape to train a new draegion. It would have to be a younger dragon from her court, and one known for patience and resilience, especially if Daeya had Baokryn's intractable temperament.

"We have lived peacefully without a *nassshanar* for nearly a millennium." Vorsere's forked tongue slithered over the title as if it tasted sour. "Was it not Baokryn *herssself* who abandoned Draeconis and broke her oath to her dragonbond? I dare not imagine what trouble the child may bring us." The steel wyrm's head snaked toward Vortanis. "Apart from more *senssseless* conflict."

Aliri shot to her feet. Smoke coated her tongue, and shimmers of heat rolled off her golden scales. Her voice rumbled like thunder. "Do not speak of what you do not understand."

"I understand perfectly, Champion." Vorsere placed one foot over her opposite foreleg. Her slitted pupils contracted, revealing irises that mimicked the black and gray striations of her scales. "You served her faithfully for seven *thousssand* years, and she left you when you were no longer of use to her."

An ear-shattering roar exploded from Aliri's chest. She pulled magic from the saphyrum-laced tile, and Aether gathered in the glands beneath her jaw. Black mist swirled between her teeth.

"Aliri!" Qiiseraan warned.

The flash of the Sentinel's power snapped Aliri's jaw shut. Orange flames spewed from between her teeth, and the charry taste of singed Aether filled her mouth. Her wing seized once more, provoking a yelp that echoed through the atrium. Silence followed in its wake.

Aliri panted through the muscle-rending spasms, shame slicing into her like a serrated blade. She never lost herself to passion before the Nine. Such a lapse was unbecoming of a queen. She dropped her gaze from the Circle, but not before Vorsere's smug look of satisfaction dissolved into pity.

It ignited her fervor all over again.

"*Nashanett* did not abandon us." Aliri's claws gouged the stone as she willed her trembling, broken body to straighten and face the rest of her kin. "She left Draeconis to protect us. It's what any of your dragonbonds would have done."

Qiiseraan's winged shadow fell across the two men on the atrium floor. "We will continue this discussion once tempers have cooled. Return upon the fourteenth hour." She spared a maddening expression of sympathy for Aliri. "See Kythax before we reconvene, Champion."

The Copper King would undoubtedly find her as soon as he left his platform. Grateful as she was to Kythax for saving her life from Anordis's poison that day, there had been no end to the healer's incessant mothering for the last three thousand years.

Nevertheless, she bowed in acquiescence. "*Vheth*, Sentinel."

Aliri returned to her antechamber and dismissed her attendants before completing the agonizing transformation back into her humanoid body. It took three times longer than normal to quell her back spasms enough to shift her useless wing.

Falla was waiting for her when Aliri left the chamber and descended to the mezzanine. Her friend was a vision in a backless gown of sleek silver. Loose blonde ringlets framed a strong jaw, and the silver scales arching over her brow complemented intelligent, sky-blue eyes.

"She goads you."

"I know." Aliri fussed with her crimson gown, unable to meet her friend's gaze. For her human likeness, she favored rich russet skin, long polished nails, and wavy chestnut hair. She scratched absently at the tiny golden horns protruding from her forehead.

Falla fell into step beside her. They made for another set of stairs and the palace foyer beyond. "And you let her."

Aliri growled. "I *know*. I made a mistake. I just—"

"—miss Baokryn," Falla finished. The Silver Queen offered an apologetic smile. Her hand was ice against Aliri's skin. "Some may never understand. Breaking your bond was the hardest decision she ever made. You know that."

Three thousand years of guilt crept back into Aliri's thoughts. Her throat tightened. "There is truth in what Vorsere says. I didn't protect her like I should have." For two millennia after the Battle of Vintrios, she'd been forced to watch Baokryn take to the skies without her, searching for Anordis, until he'd finally struck again and mortally wounded her. "Her vessel was corrupted because of me."

Falla's grip turned to steel. She halted at the top of the stairs and spun Aliri to face her. "Stop. You cannot fly this current again. I won't allow it." Her pale eyes hardened. "Chaos shot you both out of the sky. You're fortunate to have lived at all."

She said the last with a twinge of pain and looked away.

Aliri winced. Falla had also lost her dragonbond, Xosek. But while Baokryn had managed to Soul Shift in time, Xosek's tome had been utterly destroyed. Falla had lost not only her dearest friend, but her lover as well.

Claws tore at Aliri's heart and she curled her fingers over Falla's. "I'm sorry—"

"Aliri."

Falla slipped from Aliri's hold and bowed to the owner of that whisper-soft voice. "*Saonivhatt.*"

Aliri stiffened, eyes closing briefly before she turned to face their goddess.

Tiior's platinum skirts flowed behind her like a clear mountain stream. Even smooth-gaited Vortanis lumbered after her by comparison. "We must speak with you."

The goddess's troubled gaze drove Aliri's shame deeper. She bowed her head. "*Saonivhatt*, forgive me—"

Tiior held up a hand. "Peace, *draekhatt*. I know Vorsere struck a nerve. That's not why we're here."

Of course, this must be about the dragonbond. Aliri had already narrowed down the possibilities; one of her fourth cousin's twins might be suited to the challenge.

Vortanis stopped beside Tiior and folded his hands. "It's about your son."

Aliri froze, the twins' names still poised on her tongue.

"Telerion?" Unease seeped into her marrow. "What's happened?"

Tiior glared at Vortanis in silent rebuke before answering. "He is well." She sighed. "We believe he has established a quiescent bond with Daeya McVen. She is on her way to find him as we speak."

Falla's mouth fell open.

Aliri shook her head, trying to process what Tiior was saying. Quiescent bonding was the first step in forging a dragonbond. During sleep, it established the Aetherial and telepathic connections that allowed a dragonbonded pair to communicate over vast distances.

"You're certain it's Telerion?" Aliri asked. Such a commitment from her capricious boy seemed impossible.

Vortanis shifted, as if the prospect was just as unsettling to him. "She asked about him by name and said he'd been speaking to her in her dreams."

"He is too young," Aliri hastened to say. "Too brash. Attempting such a bond could be disastrous." Even deadly.

Falla's hand returned to her arm. "Or perhaps it could be just what he needs. If she gives him purpose..." She searched her face. "Aliri, he's chosen a commitment on his own. Isn't that what you and Mertysian hoped for him?"

Aliri's tiny humanoid heart tried to thunder out of her chest at the thought of her *shavhei*, her mate, whose feelings toward their son had only darkened in the decades since Telerion's banishment. Worse, the Gold Court had recently demanded *vheskhanash*—her abdication—should she and Mertysian fail to produce another heir in the next few centuries.

Desperately, she looked at Tiior. "What have you Seen? What can you tell me?"

Tiior's face fell. "You know how I feel about influencing your choices. But I do have a suggestion, if you will hear it."

If they hadn't been standing in the mezzanine, surrounded by curious passersby, Aliri might have fallen to her knees and kissed her goddess's feet. "Tell me, *Saonivhatt*. I beg you."

Tiior touched Aliri's face. "It would be wise to rescind his exile and encourage him to bring her here."

"Her powers are growing at an unprecedented rate." Vortanis's expression was grave. "She should shelter here in Draeconis while she learns to use them."

He didn't have to explain how the draegion's unfettered might was a danger to everyone and everything. Though draegionic gold—Baokryn's natural color—would manifest first, the other eight colors her soul held would soon follow. It was a wonder Caelyn hadn't tried to confine the girl already.

Aliri nodded. "I will do as you say."

She started to turn, but Falla stopped her. "It's going to be alright. Have faith in them."

Aliri sucked in a breath, and the knife of longing and regret sank to the hilt. Forcing a smile for her oldest friend, she gently extracted herself from Falla's grip.

Faith.

*Vheth*. Faith was what she needed. It had gotten her this far. She ducked into the stairwell and hurried away, ignoring the handsome copper-haired king who rounded the corner after her.

# Chapter Three

## Magnus

Malediction quivered in Magnus's hand.

*Go on,* the voice whispered. *Take it.*

Wracking sobs assailed the sorcerer at his feet. The man scrambled across roots and rocks, his black robe caked with mud. His face was streaked with tears. "Please, don't hurt me."

Magnus crunched through the brush after him. He strained to speak clearly around his scarred vocal cords—the parting gift from his most recent stay in a Guild dungeon. "Did the ones you killed beg to be spared as well?"

"I was just following orders." The man's hand twitched, as if subtly drawing a sigil. "I didn't have a choice."

*Take it, for all they took from you.*

"You are not a victim." Sweltering rage swept through him. Magnus's shadow fell over the sorcerer, and his blade caught a shaft of light. "You are sovereign to your own choices."

Like a cornered innix, the mage's expression twisted. He snarled an incantation. "*Vuurmas.*"

Magnus leaped aside and, as the jet of flame seared the air, drove his sword between the mage's neck and shoulder. He died choking on Malediction's blade.

The voice purred with satisfaction.

Magnus wrenched his weapon out and tossed it away with a grimace. It vanished in a puff of Aetherial mist, splattering fallen leaves with blood.

The sorcerer slumped to the ground. Magnus stepped closer, staring into blue eyes so like his own—like the one that was taken from him.

His empty socket throbbed.

*Take it.*

Those glassy, lifeless orbs seemed to fix on him, and his heart quickened.

*Take his eye.*

He backstepped, his reflection in those perfect eyes moving with him. No, no, he couldn't. What good would it do?

*What is vengeance if not a payment overdue?*

Magnus took another step backward. Cheralach would have never approved of desecrating a corpse. Each beat of Magnus's heart pummeled his temple until pain blotted out his vision.

The voice's presence gripped him like a placating hand on his shoulder. *You must send a message to all who dare harm your people. Show them what happens when they push a compassionate man too far.*

Unmoving, unblinking, the sorcerer continued to stare, taunting him.

*They butchered women and children in the streets. They gutted young and old in their homes. Should they not also know the bitter taste of fear?*

One fist uncurled, reaching for the dagger in his belt loop.

*Send a message.*

Cold steel kissed his palm. Blood pounded in his ears as he stared into the dead man's left eye.

*Take it.*

Grasping the man's hair in his free hand, he lifted the blade—

"Magnus?"

He froze.

The pounding in his head subsided. He blinked his one eye clear.

Startled, Magnus thrust the mage away. Behind him, boots crunched over leaves and came to a stop.

"I heard screaming," Kendi said. "Are you alright?"

There was no way he could explain this to the commander. He wouldn't understand. Magnus hastily sliced off the sorcerer's casting pendant and rose.

"Guild scout." He gestured to the broken tree branch where he'd blasted the sorcerer off his perch. "I took care of it."

Kendi looked from him to the tree, his lavender skin dappled by morning sun. His white braid hung over one shoulder and stray brambles stuck to his cloak. The gashes on his cheek and clavicle were free of bandages today. Without arcane healing, his wounds from the Fawn's Breath massacre would become impressive scars.

The commander's gaze settled on the sorcerer. "*Amaa*, there is something I've been meaning to discuss with you."

That note of caution set Magnus on edge. He pocketed the pendant and his dagger and clasped his hands before him, as Cheralach once had. "What is it?"

Kendi squared his shoulders, opened his mouth, and closed it as if grappling with his desire to cross some invisible line of formality. Finally, Kendi stepped in close and clasped Magnus's shoulder.

"How can I help, *ennii*?"

Son.

Magnus flinched. He'd been thirteen when he left his parents' lice-ridden keallite den in Nohr and followed Cheralach north. The ex-sorcerer had come to regard him as his own son, and for over twenty years, Magnus had never strayed from Cheralach's side. Even when others disbelieved his visions, questioned his mental state—

*Yet he left you to suffer.*

The voice wafted into his mind like smoke. Memories of his torment echoed through him, and he tasted blood on his tongue. Magnus steeled himself. Cheralach hadn't betrayed him. He wouldn't. Whatever secret he'd been guarding, whatever Draeconis was, must have been important. So important that Cheralach had endured torture and let his only son be maimed to keep it from the Guild.

"Magnus?"

Concern etched lines into Kendi's face, and Magnus's chest constricted with emotions he didn't wish to feel. Kendi was as much an uncle to him as Cheralach was a father, but he couldn't replace the man he'd lost.

"There's nothing you can do." He tried to shrug Kendi's hand from his shoulder, but the man's grip tightened.

"There must be something." Kendi's gaze bored into him. "I see you hurting, *ennii*. Orowen says you still won't talk about it."

Magnus's blood pulsed beneath his skin. They'd been talking about him? He waved to the disgusting mass of scar tissue on his face. "I think this goes without explanation, don't you?"

The commander winced. "That's not what I mean. We all know how you and Cheralach felt about violence, yet you've been leading the skirmishes since we left Fawn's Breath. It must be taking a toll on you."

Magnus looked toward the sorcerer. An insect landed on the mage's mouth and crawled along his lower lip. Those dead eyes continued to stare into oblivion, as if awed by the sight of the Gate beyond. At least the pull to remove them no longer plagued him.

Acrid heat rose in Magnus's throat. That he'd even considered such a thing should have sent him running to Orowen for counseling. Only compassion and remorse separated men and women from monsters, and he couldn't lose himself to senseless violence.

He swallowed. "Perhaps you're right."

"You'll find her washing bandages." Kendi's brow smoothed over. "I'll clean this up and finish scouting."

"*Taapad tiik, amii.*" Magnus thanked him and squeezed Kendi's elbow.

"*Ushaar.* Take care of yourself." Pride and sorrow warred in the commander's gentle smile. "Our people look to you now."

*As they should,* the voice whispered.

Bolstered, Magnus followed the game trail through thick undergrowth with his head high, eventually reaching the edge of their circle of defense. Rylan and a pair of new recruits saluted him from the trees.

Naruu, the younger Syljian recruit, called down a greeting. "*Iiren'hyvaa, Amaa.*"

"*Iiren'hyvaa.*" Magnus returned the salute as he passed.

Haphazard tents and animal skins dotted the forest floor. They were strung through the trees and bushes with bits of twine, vines, or woven grass. Humans, Syljians, and Cintoshi with haggard faces and tattered clothing shuffled between them on leaden feet. The shadow of saphyrum sickness brought a deathly pallor to the Syljians' skin and reawakened the simmering dread that had plagued Magnus since Fawn's Breath. Even as conservative as they had been with the saphyrum harvested from their enemies, their supply would run out before they reached Starlight. Silonas willing, the scout he'd just killed would have another bag on him and some rations, too.

As the largest of three cells that had escaped the massacre, this group moved slowest. At fifty strong, it also harbored their most capable mundane fighters. Magnus had sent most of their arcanists ahead in two smaller bands, each containing half the remaining families and orphans, while his own group slowed the sorcerers in their wake. Cook fires hadn't been allowed with Guild patrols nearby, and foraging could only amount to so much this late in the season. They relied on Rylan and his archers to bring in game and used brief magical flames to sear the meat.

He slipped through the camp, returning greetings and stifling the urge to follow them with an encouraging smile. When he smiled, many shied from him. Others offered pitying looks that morphed into grimaces and whispered words the moment he walked away.

He couldn't blame them. Magnus couldn't even look at his reflection in his sword.

Before his imprisonment, he'd been handsome. So handsome, in fact, that it had been a running joke among friends which woman might warm his bed next. He found joy in many dalliances, but taking a wife had never appealed to him. His first love was his work, and even the most doting partners were hard-pressed to compete for his time. Now, he would be lucky to ever have an admiring eye turned his way again.

*But they respect you.*

"It's not respect," he told the voice, his own a whisper as a Cintoshi axe-wielder stepped out of his path, bowed, and hurried away. "It's fear."

*Respect and fear are two means to the same end. You are to lead them, not befriend them.*

He turned over the voice's assertion, troubled by how right it was. The refugees were stirred to action by his presence. They sharpened swords, lowered tents, and packed bedrolls, swiftly breaking camp for today's march. Cheralach would have been proud to see such efficiency.

Magnus followed the sound of the Taaru'Kallii—aptly named for its thunderous rapids—until he reached a rocky outcropping and picked his way down the bank. Orowen sat at the water's edge, rinsing out a bloodstained cloth. Sam stood beside a sack of bandages with her arms crossed.

"I really don't mind helping, Devoted. If it gets your work done faster—"

"Thank you, *neime*, but I don't need help."

Orowen dropped the cloth in a pot over a sheltered fire—permitted at the priestess's insistence—and collected another bandage.

"You just work so hard for all of us," Sam said. "What time did you even wake up this morning?"

A stone shifted under Magnus's boot, drawing the women's attention.

Sam turned, her frown softening as she saluted. "Good morning, *Amaa*."

The tough young soldier had fought beside Magnus during their escape from the Guild dungeon. She was one of few who didn't gawk at him or treat him differently for his scars. At every turn, she responded to him with unwavering loyalty and trust.

Still, this was a conversation best kept private.

He returned the salute. "Good morning, Samara. Why don't you see if Kendi needs help breaking camp? I need to speak with Orowen."

Sam sighed and spared a conflicted look for the priestess, who had admittedly been working harder than anyone to gather herbs, forage for meals, and assist in camp, on top of tending the refugees. Even without magic, Orowen's exceptional healing skills had kept the fleshrot among the survivors to a minimum.

"I'm alright." Orowen twisted the bandage and dunked it again. "Do as *Amaa* says."

Sam's blonde eyebrows tugged inward, then she bowed grudgingly. "Yes, Devoted. *Amaa*." With a final lingering glance, she trudged back up the bank.

Orowen dropped the bandage into the steaming water and stirred it with a stick. "*Ciir, neime?*"

He sat on a stone, sucked in a breath to speak—and coughed violently instead. That ever-present tickle in his throat was like breathing feathers, but coughing turned them to glass.

Orowen studied him as she dunked the next bandage in the river. "Remind me when we return to camp and I will prepare some more frost flower tea to soothe your throat."

He cupped the base of his neck and blinked his stinging eye. "Thank you, Devoted."

The water ran red with old blood. Her expression fell. "I'm sorry I couldn't do more."

Magnus frowned. "You're the only reason any of us are alive today."

Her violet eyes closed briefly, and the dark circles beneath them became more apparent. It seemed saphyrum sickness held her in thrall, too. "I'm the reason so many have died."

That pained admission stunned Magnus into silence. True, many had died in the collapse of the School of High Sorcery—the event that also provoked the Sorcerers' Guild into declaring war and destroying Fawn's Breath. Orowen might have saved them in the dungeon beneath Ryost, but her actions had also unintentionally killed hundreds of others.

She turned and dropped the fabric into the pot. "What did you wish to talk about?"

Magnus blew out the breath he'd been holding. Orowen Evallier was the Anchor of Starlight, High Priestess of Saolanni, and the bastion of hope for the Syljian resistance. Normally, he would find peace and strength in her steady presence. To find her so deeply haunted—he couldn't possibly add to her burdens. He would find another way to deal with his problems.

*She cannot help you. Her goddess has left her.*

Magnus ignored the voice. Saolanni wouldn't abandon her most devout servant.

*Her most devout servant is an oathbreaker.*

He scowled. "Quiet."

Orowen's hand froze as she reached for another bandage. "I beg your pardon?"

His teeth ground together. "Apologies, Devoted. Just some errant thoughts." He grabbed a bandage to assist her. "We will run out of saphyrum before we reach Starlight. I need you to prepare some more herbal remedies for saphyrum sickness."

He plunged his hands into the frigid river and squeezed his frustration out onto the fabric. The current coursed over his wrists and arms, forming swirling eddies in the water's surface.

Orowen pulled her bandage out, folded it, and twisted hard. Ruddy water splashed between her boots. "If we're lucky, we might find some saphflorum still blooming this late in the season."

Magnus nodded. The violet, black-veined flowers mimicked the Aetherial benefits of saphyrum. Even if it didn't provide enough arcane energy to cast from, it could keep their warriors on their feet until they reached the plateau in a few days.

He wrung the bandage out and tossed the stained cloth into the pot.

Orowen stirred the water, and steam curled into the autumn air. "How are you feeling, Magnus?"

*Lost.* He bit down on the word before it could escape. The rift in his chest yawned wider each day. His mentor's absence pulled at him like the Aether itself.

"I'm fine."

"Bottles have a habit of breaking under too much pressure." She lowered her gaze. "I have found that people make poor bottles."

Magnus grabbed another bandage. Orowen's offer of relief was clear; she was willing to listen, if he was willing to share. He wanted to tell her about the voice. About his urges and what the voice was encouraging him to do. How the sickening void widened every time he summoned his sword. How each time he took a life, he slipped further from all that Cheralach had taught him.

Above all, he wanted her to assure him he wasn't going mad.

*And if you are?*

A frown tightened the muscles of his face, straining around his empty socket. If he *was* going mad, then he would be removed from command. He would sever the one connection still tethering him to Cheralach—the one thing he'd been training for since he'd become first officer.

But if there *was* something wrong with him, he *should* be removed from command, at least until he was well again. There was no shame in seeking help, but there was dishonor in negligence. Whatever this was, he owed it to the men and women under his care to know for certain.

The priestess went back to her washing, her expression hard, distant. Magnus drew in a breath. Orowen had decades of experience as a healer; if anyone could help him, it was her.

"Devoted?"

She swiped wisps of hair away from her face. "*Ciir, neime?*"

Magnus balled his fists around the bandage to stop them from shaking. He let the words fall out of his mouth. "I've been hearing a voice inside my head."

For a moment, she seemed not to have heard him. The slightest wrinkle appeared between her eyebrows.

"A voice." She looked up. "What does it say to you?"

"Nonsense, mostly. It's been encouraging me to do some disturbing things of late."

"Intrusive thoughts." Orowen added the bandage to the pot and retrieved the last one from her sack. "That's not unusual, considering everything that's happened."

Hope bloomed in his chest. "It's not?"

"Not at all." The corners of her mouth twitched up in a truer smile. "If you're only hearing the one voice, I'm surprised."

A relieved chuckle raked across his vocal cords. "I thought I was going mad."

Her smile faded. "You have suffered something utterly horrific, Magnus." She reached over and squeezed his knee. "It is simply due to trauma. It will fade with time."

Raw emotion threatened to seal his throat. Magnus took his time washing his bandage, using the motion to compose himself. Trauma—only trauma. But it seemed like something more.

"You're certain?"

She nodded absently, like it truly wasn't a concern.

He let himself relax. If she wasn't worried, then he couldn't be crazy.

Orowen wrung out the last of her cloth and stirred the pot. "I harvested more hops yesterday. I'll bring you some this evening. It should help you rest."

"Thank you, Devoted."

When he rose from the stone, she straightened as well. Her airy voice turned to steel. "First Officer Gibbons."

The gravity behind it froze Magnus mid-step. He lowered his foot back to the bank. "Yes?"

She stared at the pot for a long moment, as if searching for the right words. Worry lines appeared above her white eyebrows, and her lips pinched together. Finally, she clasped her hands in her lap. "I would ask something of you, *Amaa*."

Magnus squared his shoulders. "Of course. Anything."

There was no more hesitation. She spoke calmly, enunciating every word. "When we reach Starlight, I wish to be taken before the council on charges of terrorism, arcane negligence, and mass murder."

# CHAPTER FOUR

## RAVLOK

Ravlok scowled at the page and cursed every letter one by one. Muted twilight illuminated rows of text scribed across the ancient vellum. Some characters were from Monarchal Skriian, with which he wasn't fluent. Some more elaborate symbols were from Tribal Skriian, with which he *also* wasn't fluent. The rest were in no modern script at all.

Tree bark scratched at Ravlok's cloak as he stretched his legs toward the fire. He flexed his toes and the ache in his upper back migrated to a sharp, pinching sensation in his left hip. Wincing, he shifted and resettled the heavy Tome of Eolaan in his lap. It was a blessing he could summon and unsummon it with a word. Hundreds of pages comprised the tome, and Tiior had promised him it would teach him how to protect Daeya in the coming months. Ravlok had studied it daily for weeks.

So far, he'd learned nothing.

He turned the page to find a diagram of an arcane circle and dozens of symbols. Two words stood out from the rest.

"Eh… voss… ess. Zan… rah… klar." He rubbed his forehead, agonizing over an unknown letter in the first word. Then he moved on to the second word, only to find a smaller symbol next to a familiar letter which changed the sound. "No. K… K-har."

Often when he opened the tome, the arrangement of characters and diagrams was different. He sometimes found drawings of nearby plants or an animal he'd recently seen. This circle diagram was the only repeated page, and it showed up after every one of Paelic's outbursts.

Ravlok squinted into the darkening canopy, expecting to see Caelyn's familiar roosting in a nearby tree. Scrawny aspens pierced the sky, and an icy breeze ruffled his black hair. Scents of pine and fir mingled with mud and smoke. The fire snapped in its ring of stones.

There was no sign of the falcon or its mistress.

Thinking of Caelyn might have been a comfort if she were more forthcoming with aid. But if their last meeting was any indication, what the goddess of nature chose to provide would be at her leisure, and only if it aligned with protecting her forests.

At least she'd speak in a language he understood. He scowled at the book. "You would be more helpful if I could actually read you."

The words on the page vanished.

Ravlok blinked.

He rubbed his eyes and blinked again, then tipped the pages toward the fire-light. Still blank.

His breath caught. He touched the vellum where the diagram had been moments before and turned the page.

Blank.

He turned another page, and another, each one pristine and unmarked. Ravlok sagged against the tree and stared at the last empty page, mouth gaping.

*Odes of Ordeolas.* He'd known the book was magical, but to have it withdraw information before his eyes as if he'd offended it…

To Daeya and Alar, the pages had always been blank. What if the tome stopped working for him? How would he help Daeya then? He couldn't keep her safe without knowing what was coming—

*Stop. Breathe.*

Panic wouldn't help him. Ravlok sucked in frosty, smoke-tinged air and let it out. He repeated the meditative breath to a count of six until his heart rate slowed.

Tiior had said the book would open only for him. Not even Daeya could successfully summon it, and no one else could read it. Surely one moment of frustration wouldn't cause it to revoke that privilege.

Ravlok chuckled bitterly and rubbed his face. He must be losing his mind to assign a book such sentience. It wasn't as if it had the fickle temperament of an affronted dragon.

Or perhaps it *was* fitting. If it had truly belonged to Eolaan, there was no telling what sort of strange magic the Mother of Stories might have imbued within these pages. The first dragon created in Tiior's image was rumored to have rivaled the goddess herself for knowledge, and she'd wielded Aether as mightily as the quill.

Ravlok ran his fingers along the back cover, its leather still supple despite its age. Eolaan's tome possessed a wealth of knowledge, but called it forth on a whim, like a well-meaning elder with a wayward memory. Perhaps he could summon information deliberately. But if he couldn't read any of it—

Ravlok stilled.

A magical tome named for the first dragon, given to him by Tiior. The dragon goddess.

*You'll need to learn Ancient Draconic first*, Vortanis had said.

*Of course.*

He might have smacked his forehead if he hadn't been holding the book in both hands.

Ravlok glared at the page. "Why didn't you say so?"

The tome remained blank.

Ravlok scoffed. Learn Ancient Draconic. It sounded so simple, like teaching oneself to use Aivenosian dining tines.

Leather creaked as he shut the tome and hefted it over. This was insanity. But maybe no more insane than talking to an inanimate object, or the fact that his best friend was a real-life dragon rider.

One hand on the front cover, Ravlok closed his eyes and focused on a singular desire: *Teach me Ancient Draconic.*

As if that would be enough.

He peeked through one eyelid, then shut them tighter. *Teach me Ancient Draconic.*

He repeated the thought a third time for good measure, then winced. Specifics were probably best. He thought hard about the oldest language he knew and added, *Using Dessian trade script.*

Partly out of caution, but mostly out of a fear of disappointment, Ravlok repeated his desire until the itch to test his theory worked too far up his back for him to sit still any longer. He cracked the tome open.

Rows of Trade letters appeared, accompanied by Skriian-like symbols. An alphabet. Lightness buoyed him as he turned the page. A row of numbers. On another page, he found tables of common verb conjugations and basic pronouns. Ravlok exhaled as the breadth of this undertaking stretched before him.

He'd been his own tutor in language before. Holed up in a tiny nook behind a secret wall at the courtesy house, he'd learned to read from scraps of parchment and scrolls pilfered from Madame's patrons. He could do this.

Footsteps crunched toward him, and he looked up as Daeya stepped into the light. Alar followed several paces behind her.

"Daeya, I didn't mean—" The psionist paused at the edge of the campsite, glancing toward Ravlok before clamping his mouth shut.

Ravlok closed the tome as Daeya plopped beside him, smelling of Aether and sweat, her proximity warming him even through his cloak.

She tapped the book's cover. "Anything good this time?"

Alar balled his fists and kicked a stone before settling on a log across the fire.

Gone was Daeya's easygoing curiosity, replaced by a tight-lipped smile and eyes too focused. Something had clearly happened between them.

With a pang of guilt, Ravlok silently thanked Silonas for his fortune. Daeya had promised to consider going to Draeconis after the Alliaansi rescued her father and cousin, but an intimate relationship with Alar would jeopardize her willingness to leave. Nor could Ravlok count on Alar to help persuade Daeya that Draeconis was the safest place for her. If anything, he would do the opposite.

Ravlok glanced at her hands, relieved to find no evidence of her losing control. "I think I made it mad."

One eyebrow quirked. "How did you do that?"

Ravlok thumbed the gilded edges. Eager as he was to puzzle out the Ancient Draconic alphabet, his studies would have to wait. "*Asokhovha.*" The book vanished in a puff of shimmering mist. "By being rude, I guess."

"Well, hopefully it doesn't hold a grudge." Daeya tucked an unruly red lock behind her ear and leaned on him, rather than the tree.

Alar viciously snapped more kindling and tossed the pieces into the fire.

Daeya's proximity eased the tension in Ravlok's shoulders. "My penance is relearning the alphabet."

Softer footsteps wrenched his body taut again. Jack entered the circle of firelight, toting a trio of dead rats, a dagger, and a handful of sticks.

Daeya's nose wrinkled. "What is that?"

"Dinner." Jack passed the carcasses to Alar and placed the blade on the log.

Hunger pangs twisted Ravlok's gut. It had been years since he'd eaten rat. Madame had never spared her choicest cuts of meat for her bed warmers, but she'd at least provided bread and wine. Living on Ryost's streets, however, had meant eating whatever food he could steal or trap in back alleys and grain cellars.

Daeya shook her head. "I'm *not* eating that."

Jack drove a stick into the ground beside the fire. "Good." He planted another stick, creating a pair of forks jutting above the flames. "More for the rest of us."

Alar sighed and pulled out his own knife, setting to work butchering one of the rats. Quick, efficient cuts made it clear it wasn't his first. "Wasn't there anything else?"

Jack brushed off his hands and sat, reclaiming his dagger and a second rat. "Nope."

While Daeya continued to complain, Ravlok drew a dagger and reached for the last rat. The Sorcerers' Guild pampered their mages and students beyond measure, but so far she'd taken her new fugitive status in stride. She could hike for hours over rough terrain and nurse blistered feet without complaint. Her protests over sleeping bundled in her cloak on dry ground had ended after a night on rain-soaked leaves. Hard bread, dried meat, and rainwater were a surprisingly easy adjustment for her. She hadn't even pined for an orange in over a week. The rats, however, seemed a step too far.

"It's not bad," he promised. "I'll share mine."

"Surely we still have rations." Daeya reached for her pendant and lifted a hand toward their packs.

"Daeya." Alar's sharp rebuke split the air. "Go get it."

Ravlok sliced down the rat's belly and tossed its entrails into the fire, pointedly ignoring his companions' exchange. Much as he wanted to, he couldn't leap to Daeya's defense every time someone corrected her.

Daeya lowered her hands. Until this evening, her nonchalant use of magic had been the only source of contention between her and Alar. The Guild provided a seemingly endless supply of saphyrum for its mages, but the Alliaansi had no such luxury. For them, Alar had explained more than once, it was a matter of life or death. Their leaders rationed it more strictly than food.

Firelight illuminated her grimace. "I'm sorry."

Alar's expression softened. "I know."

Daeya rose to retrieve her pack, head bowed. She returned with the last strip of salted fish and a waterskin. While the rats roasted on spits and Alar and Jack conferred on their next move, Ravlok offered Daeya a reassuring smile.

Things would get better. Once they reached Starlight and met with the Alli-aansi, they could stock up on supplies, find Telerion, and go to Draeconis.

He just hoped Chaos didn't find them along the way.

# CHAPTER FIVE

## SHEI-GWEN

Guild Councilor Shei-Gwen Mar-Pol was about to commit a crime.

She wiped her sweaty palms on her robe and cursed the streaks left behind. Wearing white to a mine was a crime more reprehensible than stealing saphyrum, but if not for her formal robe, the mages at the checkpoint would have never let her in.

*Stealing saphyrum.* Gwen might have laughed if she hadn't been so anxious. She was a law-abiding citizen of Eidosinia and a devout follower of Delvin, for pity's sake. She followed Guild protocols to the letter, always came prepared for Council, and never took more than her fair share of dessert. But circumstances had left her no choice; Councilor Sarikkian and the healers were counting on her.

Peader, Sarikkian's most trusted acolyte, paused at a three-way fork in the stone. He held up the saphyrum lantern to each rectangular opening, but the light only penetrated a short way into the darkness. His wolf-like snout twitched, then he turned right. "This way, milady."

Gwen sighed and glanced back up the shaft toward the glow from the main catacombs. None of the mages could do anything to her directly, but word of her unsanctioned audit would make it back to Ryost soon. If she didn't move that saphyrum before Gregory's warmongers came to collect it, Eidosinia's healers and all the patients who depended on them would suffer.

"How much farther, Peader?"

"Not far. Don't you smell it?"

Gwen didn't smell anything beyond the sulfuric stench of minerals and rock, but she trusted the Feridian boy. More importantly, *Sarikkian* trusted him, and her mentor had a good sense about people.

Her leather shoes scuffed the ground as Peader led her deeper into the mine. The echoing clangs from the miners' work faded and the tunnel closed in. Gwen focused on the quill-thin veins of blue-green saphyrum lacing the stone. Every now and then, her attention strayed to the stains collecting on her fine cotton robe. Aetherial storms, it was going to take ages to scrub those out.

Minutes later, Peader's lantern finally illuminated the end of the shaft. He stopped before a closed wooden door and sniffed the air again. "Here."

Gwen could smell it now: the metallic tang of Aether, like smelting iron. Eidosinia's second-largest cache of saphyrum lay beyond that door.

The urge to reach for the iron handle was nearly irresistible, but she stuffed it down. Multiple wards guarded this cache, and triggering them would summon mages. It had been hard enough to deny their offer of an escort the first time.

Fortunately, illusion magic was her specialty. "Stand aside."

As Peader obeyed, Gwen pulled saphyric energy from her casting earrings. Static skittered down her arms and white-violet light formed at her fingertips. With small movements of her wrists, she drew an intricate pattern and *pushed* her unmasking sigil toward the vault. Before it struck solid wood, the image of the door wavered. Fractures spiderwebbed along its surface like glass shattering in slow motion. The illusion dissolved, revealing the true entrance—a steel door—behind it.

Embedded within the metal were three glowing wardstones. If her visit had been approved by the Council, they would have given her the access sigils to unlock them. But Sarikkian had urged discretion, and there were ways of defeating even the strongest wards.

*Delvin forgive me.*

Gwen wove a disarming sigil of her own invention. The spell was designed to read the subtle layers inside a wardstone like a pick fitting into a lock. She flicked the light-woven disk toward the first wardstone, and it bounced back to her with several knots and lines rearranged. After memorizing the changes, she dismissed the disk and drew an exact replica of the new pattern as an access sigil. A flick of her wrist, and the first wardstone winked out.

The sight sparked hope, never mind the implications the spell could have for breaking and entering elsewhere. It certainly wasn't a sigil she'd be teaching her students.

She wove two more disarming sigils and their respective keys in quick succession, and a *click* sounded from inside the vault. Peader shifted on his feet and glanced up at her. Gwen reached for the handle, then paused.

"Not a word of this to Olivia, or I'll have your head."

Gwen's partner already had a lackluster opinion of law and order. If she knew Gwen was willing to break into a Guild vault and steal saphyrum for her and the rest of the healers, she'd expect more of the same misconduct in the future.

Gwen's venomless threat provoked a rakish grin from Peader. "I wouldn't dare, Councilor."

His smile steadied her. She nodded curtly, tugged on the handle, and stepped into the room. He followed, closing the door behind them.

The storage chamber was so vast, the sphere of lantern light touched only the nearest wall. Rows of saphyrum barrels marched away into the darkness. Shelving to Gwen's left housed ledgers that tracked the vault's inventory, and loading equipment to her right would allow them to move the heavy barrels safely.

Gwen started for the ledgers. "Contact Sanry and tell him we're in position." She hadn't wanted to involve Olivia's young assistant, but Sanry was the only other magic-adept she trusted who possessed some skill as a Conduit. "He should expect the first rift in ten minutes."

"Yes, Councilor."

She scanned the shelves for the most recent ledger as Peader wove his sigil and passed the coded message through a tiny rift. Unlike Sanry, Peader's Conduit magic was unmatched by others of his rank. The distance he could traverse rivaled even Toby Vika's. Once the boy gained his black robe, Sarikkian planned to appoint him as liaison between the Sorcerers' Guild and their international allies—a move that would reclaim the control Gregory's minions had taken over foreign affairs.

A move that Gwen would throw all her support behind the moment Sarikkian put the motion on the floor.

She shook herself and pulled down the least dusty ledger. Lists and numbers of shipments to satellite schools, abbeys, and infirmaries filled the pages. Gwen located the most recent entries, then grabbed a pumice stone from the scribe's desk. Shipments to the Feridian Sanctuary and Life Coven were determined by their contracts with the Guild, so she couldn't manipulate those numbers. However, a barrel added here and there to other, less static inventories wouldn't draw scrutiny.

As Gwen scraped away the old numbers, Peader positioned a squeaky cart beneath the nearest row of barrels. "Councilor?"

"Now's not the time for second thoughts." She wasn't certain whether that statement was for him or for her.

"It's not that. It's—"

Gwen paused in reaching for a quill. "What's wrong?"

"Someone's coming."

She scowled at the parchment, then the door, as if either might bear a ward she'd missed.

Peader's Feridian hearing was far better than any human's. Several seconds passed before she heard the voices.

"Pretend you're counting barrels."

Peader darted behind the nearest aisle. Gwen grabbed the ledger and a quill, balancing the book under one arm. Powdery pumice streaked the scribe's desk in the shape of the ledger. She grimaced and swiped at it with her sleeve, collecting more grime in the process. Somewhere in the back of her mind, she could hear Olivia snickering.

The door swung open.

"—me handle this." A Cintoshi miner wearing an unflattering gray uniform with a white foreman's insignia on his sleeve entered. A pair of black-robed mages trailed after him—the two who had been guarding the checkpoint when Gwen arrived. "Ah, good morning, Councilor—"

"Twenty-four barrels on this row, milady," Peader called.

"Just a moment, Peader." Gwen silently commended the boy for his timing and made a show of looking annoyed. "Yes, what is it?"

The foreman shrank beneath her glare.

"F-forgive me, Councilor," he stammered, "but your visit is most unexpected."

Gwen lowered the quill and poured all her irritation with Gregory and the Council into her voice. "Well, that's the point of a surprise audit, Mr...."

"Porphis, milady. I—"

"Porphis." Gwen shifted the ledger to one hip and regarded the mages, memorized their faces—one thick and round, the other made of more delicate angles—before returning to the Cintoshi. "Tell me, Mr. Porphis, do you know why there was a dip in production for this mine over the last two quarters?"

Porphis paled beneath a layer of dirt. "No, I can't say I do."

"Why am I not surprised?" She hardened her expression further, and both mages glanced toward the entrance as if seeking an escape. *Good.* "If you can't tell me, I suggest you leave me to conduct my investigation in peace."

The man ran a thick-fingered hand over the braided mass of his beard. "We've had to train new blood at the refinery. I'm sure that would account for the extra losses."

"This unscheduled audit has already put me behind on business this week. I have no intention of being here all afternoon." Genuine irritation warmed the back of her neck. "Save your speculation for when I have finished my task."

Porphis shot a helpless glance at the mages. One of them drew herself up and looked Gwen in the eyes. "Please allow us to assist you, Councilor. We can work faster together."

Gwen clutched the ledger so tightly her fingers ached. "You are in the employ of this mine; that hardly seems like unbiased aid. Who is your superior, Sorceress?"

The girl swallowed. "Councilor Ferren, milady."

Nash Ferren. One of Gregory's biggest supporters, and a dogged advocate for the war effort. That explained the mages' ongoing suspicion. At least there was truth to the dip in production should they investigate her claim.

"I'll send Councilor Ferren word of your generosity, but I'm afraid I must decline. Now leave, or there will be punitive action for your disobedience."

Both mages hastened bows.

"Your command, Councilor."

"Yes, milady."

"Apologies for disturbing you." The foreman fumbled over his apology, and they all lurched toward the exit as if she'd summoned a cloud of scorpion bees.

Gwen drew saphyric energy and Sealed the door behind them.

Peader poked his head out from the aisle, his grin bright against his dark fur. "I thought they were going to wet themselves."

Gwen's shoulders sagged under the weight of pulling rank. She returned the ledger to the scribe's desk. "They'll send others. Let's load what barrels we can on two carts. We'll send them through and do a quick audit of what remains."

*And pray no one notices the missing carts.*

Gwen had done all the necessary calculations for the blind rift last night. Her spellcasting would have to be perfect, or they could lose all their supplies to the

Aether. A poorly cast rift could also harm unsuspecting bystanders, or cause structural damage at the point of egress. Her rift should open on the back lawn of her father's estate a quarter-league away. From there, they could trickle the supplies into the Sanctuary and Life Coven. She'd already spoken with Shavva and Miriam, the directors of both abbeys, and assured them that their saphyrum supplies wouldn't be interrupted by the war. All she'd asked for in exchange was discretion; if she was caught stealing this much saphyrum, it would be a short rope and a long drop rather than sanction and suspension.

Once she and Peader finished loading the carts, Gwen made certain the ledger matched the new numbers. Peader confirmed with Sanry that he was still in position, and Gwen wove the sigil for a Rift Bend, working her mathematical vectors into the spell. Then, with a silent prayer to Silonas, she slashed through the Wall.

Black-violet mist poured into the vault. Wind snapped her robe around the wheels of the cart and pulled the tails of her headscarf toward the rift. She adjusted the protective cloth around her oiled hair and cleared her throat.

Too much time passed. Gwen drummed her fingertips against the cart, noting how its wooden handles had been worn smooth with use. She opened her mouth and closed it twice. Finally, a smaller rift opened beside Peader. A Conduit's sigil shot into his hand.

He studied the white-violet disk for ages. Had she miscalculated? Rifted through a roof? Slashed through a tree and crushed someone? It was only logical that the one time she bent the rules, something terrible would happen.

Impatience nipped at her heels. "Well?"

"The rift worked."

Despite his words, Peader hesitated, and foreboding ripped into Gwen. "What's happened?"

The acolyte's expression turned sheepish. "Olivia says hi."

Four hours later, Gwen stared down into the flooded cellar of Mar-Pol Manor. Rain soaked her scarf and pummeled the surface of the rising pool that had swallowed at least five of the stairs. A fork of lightning split the sky, followed by thunder.

She grimaced. "Delvin curse it."

Olivia Ithenor leaned one moss-green forearm against Gwen's shoulder. Her sharp ear points stuck out from her mass of wet curls. "You know, Shei, I don't think our Lord of Law would approve of what you're doing."

Gwen shot her a sideways glare. "Oh, save it."

"What?" Olivia grinned. "It's not like I mind or anything." She thrust her chin toward Peader, Sanry, and the carts sinking into the ground. "I think it's sweet you'd go through all this trouble for me."

Gwen groaned. If not Delvin, then Caelyn had surely cursed her. They were never going to pull those wheels out of those soggy ruts. Worse, her robe was stained with the evidence of their heist, and her leather slippers were caked with mud.

Olivia took her wrist, squinting down at Gwen's ebony fingers. "Aw, you even got dirt under your nails. Look!"

"Stop that!" Gwen jerked her hand away, and her Aivenosian lover giggled. The sound brought warmth to Gwen's cheeks. Aetherial storms, now she could feel every bit of dirt. "This is serious, Liv."

They both turned back to the stairs. Her father's cellar hadn't been the same since the last cyclone, and it had been raining all week. Groundwater must have forced its way through the foundation. Even if she channeled her water affinity to clear the cellar, it would just fill back up. Flooding wouldn't damage the saphyrum, but moving waterlogged barrels without a firm grasp of telekinetic sigils was going to be a problem.

Olivia whistled. "Well, what do we do now?"

Gwen stifled a retort at her use of 'we' and tried not to shoot Sanry another disapproving look. She couldn't fault the boy for betraying their secret. If he'd seemed even the slightest bit uneasy, Olivia would have picked up on it, and the healer was relentless when she lacked for information.

"I don't know."

Storing the barrels inside the manor would be risky. Her father had been moved to the asylum in Belden years ago, after the blanker attack that had claimed his mind, but her mother kept servants employed at the estate in their absence. Having spent most of her life in service to the Guild, Gwen didn't know the servants well enough to trust them.

"We could store them at the cabin," Olivia suggested.

"No." The word came out sharper than Gwen intended. "No," she repeated more carefully. There was no way she was letting Olivia take that kind of risk. "Maybe I can arrange delivery at the Sanctuary with Shavva and Miriam early."

"There'll be trouble if their inventories don't match," Olivia pointed out. "And this big of an influx will attract notice."

That had been Gwen's concern as well. Not to mention the risks of opening a blind rift inside a building full of Shavva's patients.

Gwen shuddered. With the destruction of the School of High Sorcery still fresh in her mind, she couldn't even consider the possibility. They would have to take the barrels through a side door, or get close enough to rift inside with line of sight.

"If we keep them at the cabin, they'll be much closer to the Sanctuary—"

"*No.*"

It was one thing to store all this stolen saphyrum in her family's home; it was another to store it in the cabin where Olivia practiced illegal healing magic.

"You've warded the cabin yourself." Olivia crossed her arms. "You're telling me you don't trust your own illusions?"

"As careless as you are with visitors?" Gwen shot back. She withdrew a kerchief and dabbed at the water on her brow.

Olivia's green eyes rolled skyward. "Patients, you mean, and I'm *not* careless. I heal only those the Sanctuary can't. They'd be foolish to report me."

"It only takes one unhappy patient or an attentive guard to send you to the gallows."

"Then it's a good thing I have you to protect me, *Councilor.*"

Gwen bristled. Things had always been complicated between them, despite over a decade together, but Olivia's desire to play hero for the non-adepts had only worsened since Gwen's appointment to the Council. Just because she held sway in the Guild now didn't give Olivia the right to defy Delvin himself when it suited her.

Light flashed, and the scent of Aether wafted on the breeze. A Conduit's sigil shot out of a tiny rift beside Peader. He studied the coded message hovering against his palm while Sanry poked his shorter snout over the acolyte's arm. The older Feridian boy tilted the sigil so Sanry could read it and sought Gwen's eyes.

"What is it, Peader?"

He licked his lips. "It's Sarikkian."

She stepped toward him. "What did he say?"

Peader let out a whine, and his ears folded backward. "He says Normos Beck is on his way to Ferid."

"He can't have—" Gwen cut her attention toward the carts, then to the cellar. She snarled and balled her fists. "That bleeding snake."

Of course Gregory would send his whelp to undermine her. Sorcerer Beck was a Rift Walker known for his casting precision. The moment Ferren's mages got word to the Conduits in the north, Gregory must have sent for him. Beck could be here any moment.

Olivia lifted a dark eyebrow. "Who's Normos Beck?"

Delvin take the injustice of it. "Councilor Gregory's favorite pet."

Olivia frowned. "I thought Mardis got rid of that one. Didn't he flee north after the fiasco in Orthovia?"

"No." Thunder rolled overhead, as if to punctuate the 'fiasco' that destroyed the Orthovian port. Gwen scanned the estate, searching for any little-used buildings that could house even one saphyrum cart. "That was his other protégé. The girl."

At least Daeya McVen was long gone by now. Mardis Ulrich's plan to remove Gregory's youngest and most powerful mage had been a stroke of genius. She'd insisted Sarikkian push for McVen's promotion, certain the girl would botch one of her first missions so badly that not even Gregory could stop the vote for expulsion.

Rumors claimed he'd been teaching both McVen and Beck forbidden magic, but there was never enough proof. After reports of McVen using Aetherian magic on the *Breigh Maiden* and in Orthovia, Gwen was certain they'd caught the old bastard. But yet again, Gregory's supporters had insulated him from fault. He'd promised them control over the Council—the freedom to destroy the Alliaansi and expand the Guild's reach into the Northlands regardless of international repercussions—and Gwen feared they were only a few piccara moves from getting it.

Despite McVen's disappearance, Gregory still had one exceedingly powerful sorcerer at his side. Gwen used to watch Normos spar with the other sorcerers, and few compared in raw skill and cunning. Worse, his loyalty to his master was unmatched. He would do everything in his power to further Gregory's agenda, regardless of who suffered for it.

Gwen looked back to Olivia. "Normos is rigid and too smart by half. You'll do no healing outside the Sanctuary while he's here."

"Sure." Olivia scoffed.

Delvin forbid Olivia Ithenor, proud daughter of Aivenosian High Chief Kallen Ithenor, should ever bend to another's directive. "I mean it. If he finds out what you're doing, he *will* execute you."

"Please. You can always—"

"If you get caught, there's nothing within my power that can save you." Gwen clenched her fists. "Not until Sarikkian and I can rally enough support to change that law."

Olivia's expression soured, and Gwen could sense the words she wasn't saying. The Council had already voted to allow the use of magic on rebels and blankers; refusing to allow healing magic for their own people made no sense. The cautionary tales of Noven Ivaeys—the magus who'd maimed and killed his wife with magic—had held them back for too long.

Olivia started to turn away, but Gwen seized her shoulders.

"Promise me you won't be reckless. Promise me, Liv."

Her vehemence, for once, gave Olivia pause. "You really think he's going to be a problem."

"I know he will."

At last, Olivia softened. She stroked Gwen's cheek. "Alright, I promise I'll be careful."

Gwen let out a slow breath, letting Olivia's touch soothe her. She glanced toward the carts, considering. If Olivia stayed away from the cabin while Gregory's minion was here, maybe it *was* the best place for the saphyrum. A few quick calculations could get it there before sunset.

A languid smile stole over Olivia's face, and renewed unease chilled the back of Gwen's neck. "And no sneaking in heals for bumps and bruises when you think the city guard isn't watching."

Olivia leaned in and pinched Gwen's chin. Her grin turned wicked as their noses touched. "You think you know me so well, Councilor?"

Obeying the silent demand, Gwen seized Olivia's waist and kissed her. "Enough to know you're already conspiring against me."

She ignored the glimmer of mischief in Olivia's eyes and turned to Peader and Sanry, who perked up from their own quiet conversation, ears twitching.

"Alright, boys," Gwen said, "let's move these barrels one more time."

# CHAPTER SIX

## DAEYA

*"Nashanett."*

*Leather creaked against Daeya's wrists. She stared upward, counting shapes in the mandalas painted on the ceiling while Gregory's blade cut along her inner thigh. His magic thrummed across her body, each rune binding itself to her with the permanency of muscle and bone.*

Three thousand seventy-three.

Three thousand seventy-four...

*A tug on her mind broke her concentration. She lost count of the shapes and came back to herself, the pain surging. Her teeth sank into her lower lip. She fought to remain still and silent. He hated when she screamed.*

*Webs of magic sewed white-hot agony through her, the enchanted blade like a branding iron. A whimper slipped past her teeth.*

*"Be still, my sweet." Gregory's eyes never lifted from his task. His voice was a caress, a cooling balm against the pain. "It is almost finished."*

*Daeya licked the blood from her lip and refrained from responding, lest it fracture her composure. That would disappoint him, and she hated disappointing him.*

*The tug on her mind grew more insistent.*

*"Wake up, Nashanett."*

*The Councilor's study stank of Aether and blood. A tear slid down her temple and into her ear. She prayed he wouldn't notice.*

*Her eyes fixed on a mandala above her and she resumed counting, trying to slip back into that space of unawareness where pain and fear couldn't go.*

*More tugging. Something was wrong.*

*Gregory's dagger stabbed into her side. Daeya's howl shattered the silence. Darkness spiderwebbed over her vision, inky and scarlet-tinged as she gasped for air. Bleeding gods, what had she done?*

*Black malice stared down at her, violet irises bright with magic. Gregory ripped the dagger out and pressed it to her throat. With his free hand, he wrenched up her bloody shift and exposed three patches of rectangular scarring—remnants of the runes once etched there.*

*"You defy me?"*

*No. No, this wasn't right. He didn't know about that. He couldn't. She pulled against her restraints, fingers tingling with the heat of her new powers. White-gold light swept up her wrists, across her arms and chest. "Councilor, please—"*

*Telerion's voice rolled through her mind like thunder.*

*"Daeya. Wake up!"*

Her eyes snapped open.

Frost-crusted vegetation and campfire embers swam into focus. Pain radiated from her right hip, but as the disorientation of sleep ebbed, so too did the stab of Gregory's dagger. In its place rose the numbing ache of pressure applied too long in one spot.

Wet leaves smoldered beneath her glowing hands.

*Bleeding—*

Daeya grabbed her pendant and barked the incantation to pull the scarlet flames back into her fingertips. She clutched her fists to her chest and breathed in to a count of six. Out again, to another count of six, until the light and tingling heat faded, and she had control once more.

If draegion fire was hot enough to ignite wet leaves, gods only knew how fast she could burn the forest down.

Daeya scanned the campsite, its familiarity bolstering her against the dream. Alar lay against a nearby tree. Ravlok snored softly beside her, his larger frame sheltering her even now from Jack, who slept opposite the ring of stones. The thief muttered something in his sleep and rolled away.

*"Thank you, Telerion."*

Her message carried along the thread-like bond twining between them. Though the dragon didn't respond with words, soothing warmth flowed down her spine like water. Daeya relished the way it steadied her.

She looked to where Gregory's dagger had plunged into her side. Her skin still prickled, but there was sign of neither blood nor blade.

It was only a dream. Her wardstone pressed against her thigh, warm and reassuring. By the time its magic ran out, they should be safe in Starlight.

She dug through layers of clothing to lift her undershirt, skimming her fingertips across the scar tissue on her right hip. The last time Gregory had carved her up, after her return from Belden, the runes had driven her mad with the need to be rid of them. Heedless of the consequences, she'd broken into his study, stolen his ebony blade, and cut with its enchanted edge until she felt like herself again. Not the lethargic shell she'd become.

Daeya let the shirt fall and scrubbed her palms over her face.

She should have known then he didn't have her best interests at heart. But with her father's livelihood at stake, the knowledge would have changed little. Now she could only pray Alar would keep his word and persuade the Alliaansi to extract her father and Murtagh before Gregory made a move on them.

*Alar.*

Gods, had her stupidity no end?

She looked toward the sleeping half-blood, and the ache in her chest redoubled. All the time they spent together, all the teasing and flirting, the way he'd held her hand—

Daeya shoved the hurt down. It was all a lie.

Careful not to disturb Ravlok, she rose to retrieve more logs for the fire. A bitter wind slashed across their camp, making the flames gutter and coals brighten. It blew her own sweaty scent with it. Her nose wrinkled, and she took a tentative sniff under her arm. Daeya recoiled. The musky smell of hard work had never bothered her, but *that* was disgusting.

She hadn't showered in over a month. Neither Jack nor Alar had left her alone long enough for a proper bath, and she wasn't about to explain her runes to them.

The campfire blazed back to life at her coaxing while her companions slept on. She glanced down the game trail leading toward the river, then at her pack. There was a full bar of soap in the corner pouch. If she could just endure the frigid water, she might not smell so much like a corpse.

This was her best chance. The farther north they went, the colder and more miserable it would be. She could take a pot and heat the water with her fire. Alar would never notice that little saphyrum use.

As she rose to retrieve her soap, Jack turned in his sleep and muttered again.

"...Father... no..."

Daeya froze.

"...let him go..."

Should she wake him? He'd likely be angry rather than grateful, but if her companions found her in the throes of a nightmare, she'd want them to wake her.

A few weeks ago, Alar had told her Jack's story. How the Guild took his father, an unlicensed magic-adept, for questioning when Jack was twelve. Days later, the sorcerers returned the man broken and raving like a madman. He'd taken his own life, and the Guild had repossessed his shop for tax evasion, leaving Jack destitute. He joined the Alliaansi not long after.

Guilt tugged her feet toward him.

"...kill... the witch..."

She flinched back, catching a stone in the campfire ring behind her. A log toppled over and fiery embers spiraled upward. Daeya batted at the ones that landed in her hair.

*Idiot.*

That was exactly what they should wake up to: her hair blazing as she danced about the fire like a lunatic. Her eyes flicked toward Alar.

He didn't stir, thank the gods. She resettled her attention on Jack, whose furrowed brow and shallow breathing slowly evened out. After forcing her pounding heart back down her throat, Daeya managed a shaky breath.

He was just dreaming. People said strange things in their dreams all the time. He'd had plenty of chances to slit her throat in her sleep, and he gained nothing by biding his time.

With a cook pot, a spare shirt, and soap in hand, she slipped into the trees. Stark shadows gave way to darkness as black as Aether. She tripped over tree roots, crashing through the undergrowth and disrupting the buzz of insects with her muttered swearing.

"*Luminos.*"

The saphyrum bead in her pendant flared white. She trudged on, the tiny sphere of light casting long shadows ahead.

At least the exertion chased away the cold. By the time she stumbled out of the trees beside the river, Daeya was eager to strip down to her undershirt and trousers. She filled the pot and banished the light spell to speak another incantation.

"*Vuurmas.*"

Scarlet flames danced along her fingertips to heat the cast iron, hotter and stronger than ever. Her magic strained against the confines of her body, demanding *more,* leaving her breathless in her attempts to hold it back.

It was more exhausting than impressive. Tiior had mentioned the god of chaos would covet this magic. Ravlok believed her, but Daeya wasn't convinced. Strong or not, there was no way her fancy-colored fire could overthrow a god. If it were up to her, she'd have given it away just to feel normal again.

Once she'd heated the water to steaming, Daeya removed her sweaty undershirt and gasped as the cold pummeled her. She scrubbed at the filth until her runes shone white in the moonlight, then tugged on her clean shirt and hugged the pot to further warm herself.

*It's worth being clean. It's worth being clean.*

Her teeth chattered hard enough to crack, but Aether take her, at least she smelled like goat's milk and lavender instead of grave dirt. She burrowed under her cloak and closed her eyes, listening to the rush of water while gathering the courage to refill the pot and bathe her lower half.

Somewhere off in the forest, a woman screamed.

"Alar, gods damn you, wake up!"

Alar jolted awake. Jack's fuming silhouette was standing over him. "What is it?"

Ravlok propped himself up on his elbow, wide-eyed. Jack pointed toward him. "The sorceress is gone." He brandished his hand crossbow. "I told you she'd betray us."

*No.*

"She wouldn't."

The words left Alar before he could stop them. He scrambled to his feet and looked over Ravlok.

Daeya's spot was empty.

Ravlok rolled over with a similar disbelief pinching his expression. He patted the leaves, as if he might find her buried beneath them, then stared at Alar. "I'm sure she'll be back."

Jack stormed across the space and gathered his sword. "She can't have gotten far. This time, you'd better listen to me—"

Running footsteps cut him off. Jack dropped his sword and brought his crossbow up. Alar spun, ready to launch a deadly surge of psionic energy into the first enemy to breach the circle of light.

A flash of red hair and a white shirt were his only warning. Daeya crashed through the trees. Jack loosed the bolt as Ravlok cried out, and Daeya dropped to the ground.

"Wastelands!" Heart in his throat, Alar dove forward. He couldn't lose her. Not like this. "Daeya—"

Wild-eyed and winded, she jerked away from him, clutching her arm. "Bleeding bastard," she spat at Jack. Blood seeped from beneath her light-wreathed hand—a glancing shot.

Alar glared at Jack. "Put that away." He crouched beside Daeya, fists buried between his knees to hide their shaking. "You could've killed her."

Jack's aura mimicked the shimmering heat from the campfire. The slightest tremor of satisfaction interrupted that ripple, forming a hollow in Alar's gut. Jack wouldn't shoot her on purpose; he knew how important she was to the Alliaansi.

Ravlok crouched on Daeya's other side and reached for her wounded arm. "Let me see."

"No!" She recoiled. More blood welled between her fingers, saturating her sleeve.

Alar didn't need to see her aura to sense her panic dissolving into fear. "What's wrong, Daeya? What happened?"

"I heard screaming." Her breath came in heaving gasps. She wetted her lips. "A woman. On the other side of the river. I think there were mages."

"What were you doing near the river?" Jack demanded.

*Good question.*

Ravlok's ire shimmered in a halo around him. "Maybe it's none of your business. Look." He gestured toward his side of the camp, where Daeya's satchel lay open. "Her pack was still here. She wasn't going to run."

Tension drained from Alar's muscles. Why hadn't he noticed that?

He rose from his crouch. "It's not important right now."

Jack's fingers dug into Alar's arm. "It's a trap. She had more than enough time to lure her people to us."

"You're insane." Golden light chased away the shadows around Daeya's eyes. "I just went for a bath."

A plausible explanation. The scent of her favored soap lingered beneath woodsmoke and pine.

Alar sighed. He'd entertained Jack's paranoia long enough. "If she planned to betray us, she wouldn't have come back," he told him. "Stay and guard the camp if you want. Ravlok, I need you with me. Daeya..." Alar paused. It was too soon for this. She wasn't ready to fight her own people. "I won't ask you to fight, but if they *are* mages, we could use your help."

Ravlok offered a hand, but Daeya ignored it and rose, still clutching her wound. Though the rosy flush to her cheeks remained, the light at her fingertips faded.

"I can show you where I heard them."

That was a start. It would have to be enough.

"Lead the way."

# Chapter Seven

## Orowen

Orowen sat on a log beside her campfire, hands folded in her lap. She marveled at their stillness, at how easily she'd come to her decision. It brought peace knowing soon she would be held accountable for what she'd done, for how she'd saved so few and condemned so many.

"Devoted, you can't be serious." Kendi was pacing, his feet wearing a path in the underbrush. Magnus stood to the side, arms folded, looking between them as if loath to get involved.

"I must atone for my crimes, Commander." Orowen denied herself the urge to comfort him. He'd only push her away in his anger, and leave her to the misery she deserved. "If I'm not held to the same standards as everyone else, then what good are discipline and honor to our soldiers?"

"You're not a soldier." He continued his silent war on the vegetation. "And this is not the same as a soldier falling out of line. If you follow this path to its end, nothing good will come of it."

Indeed, if the charges stood—and Orowen was certain they would—her fate would be just as all the little lives she'd stolen that day. Her death would be a final measure of penitence for her actions, since Saolanni hadn't forgiven her wickedness and returned her magic.

And why would she? It wasn't the first time she'd caused such catastrophic damage. In the early days of her Aetherian training, long after she and her sister Maralla had proven themselves capable aethermancers, Orowen had brought an entire fortress down on their enemies' heads at the Battle of Ixriia. She'd nearly buried Maralla beneath the rubble, too. After dragging her sister across the blood-slicked wreckage to the only master healer in ten leagues who could help her, Orowen had laid down her sword, sworn off Aetherian magic, and taken up a healer's amulet to ensure such devastation never happened again.

So much for that.

She swallowed and steeled her spine. "I will abide by the council's punishment, whatever they decide."

Kendi stomped across the clearing and dropped to one knee beside her. He took her hand in both of his, the warmth of his skin providing more comfort than she had any right to receive. "Orowen, *nei ama're.* Please. Think about what you're doing. These charges"—he choked on the words—"you could face execution."

All the affection and sorrow he poured into that gesture threatened to seal her throat. But not even a priestess could hide from justice. "If that is to be my fate, then I accept it."

His fingers tightened, and he bowed his head, as if unable to look at her any longer.

It was better this way. Hurting Kendi was the last thing Orowen wanted to do, but she couldn't act as if her transgressions didn't matter. Not even his love could dissolve the guilt and shame that made meditation and prayer impossible. If she didn't face the consequences, it would poison her until the end of her days.

When Kendi looked up again, his gaze caught fire. "Well, I don't." He kissed their joined hands, then rose and turned to Magnus. "I contest the charges and demand there be a trial before a verdict is made."

*Mira's mercy.*

Orowen pinched her eyes shut. The matter was a simple one; she'd destroyed lives and inspired terror with her reckless use of magic. There was no need for a trial. "Kendi, please—"

"It is within his right." Magnus lowered his arms. "I will take this matter before the council, as you requested, but since the commander contests, there must be a chance for others to weigh in."

Orowen glared at him, but Magnus stared back with the same wisdom and resolve he'd been cultivating since Fawn's Breath. It was hard not to let it dull her conviction; Cheralach would have been proud to see him so self-assured. She dropped her gaze. "Yes, *Amaa*."

"Let's finish breaking camp." Magnus turned away, and Kendi fell in behind him. "Most of their troops are behind us now. We'll move faster today."

*Keep your head high.*

The voice seeped into his mind like oil into cloth. Magnus lifted his chin as he walked, and confidence crested in his chest like the rising sun.

*You are in control.*

Orowen and Kendi were over one hundred years his senior, but they'd heeded his command as they once had for Cheralach. His mentor had always said a leader should appear poised and decisive, even when a decision weighed on his mind. The voice had reiterated that lesson after Orowen's disturbing announcement, and again when Kendi stormed into his tent demanding answers. At least for now, Magnus was grateful for its guidance.

Kendi walked beside him now as the sunken-eyed refugees lugged packs and supplies to the edge of camp. The gods themselves wouldn't deny him justice if he lost even one more to the sorcerers' blight.

Kendi tugged his braid in an uncharacteristic show of anxiety. "We can't let her do this."

It was tempting to agree with him. Orowen had saved them all from the Guild dungeon, and while he understood her guilt, throwing her life away for the sorcerers who'd taken his eye and murdered Cheralach was irrational at best. But she'd filed charges with him as first officer, and he would not dishonor Cheralach's memory by interfering with the council's law.

"I must make the report, Commander. You know that."

"But she's not in her right mind. She's grieving. She shouldn't be making decisions like this."

Magnus grimaced. Gods knew he'd made enough decisions in the wrong state of mind. "Then it is for the council to decide."

The commander looked as broken as a new widower. His confession of love for the high priestess had already swept through their ranks like prairie fire.

"You've contested the charges." Magnus softened and put his hand on Kendi's shoulder. "Start gathering witnesses and prepare your argument."

"You're right." Kendi drew himself up. "I'll start with Sam and Rylan. I'm sure they will speak in my favor."

Magnus fought back a smile to avoid frightening the soldiers who bustled past. His scarring tightened. "Anwic and Jessie will, too. You can also count on my testimony. We all know Orowen wouldn't have destroyed that school on purpose."

Kendi squeezed Magnus's arm. "I pray you have a vote in this matter, *ennii*. That seat is yours. I'm certain the council will see that."

Pride pricked Magnus's eye. "I hope so."

"*Amaa!*"

A harried voice broke across the camp, and fighters scattered to allow the young scout through. Naruu slid to a stop in the mud. Twigs and leaves stuck in his thick mop of white hair, and dirt smudged the sharp contours of his cheekbones. His bright lavender eyes illuminated a brighter smile that exposed one snaggled tooth.

Though Magnus represented the council on Cheralach's behalf, Kendi was still in command of the Fifth Legion. He nodded in deference to the commander.

"What is it, Naruu?" Kendi asked.

Naruu pointed up the rise, his grin widening. "Reinforcements, *Amaa*. Come and see."

Someone gave a whoop of joy, and a laugh carried down from the hillside. Excited chatter followed, and soldiers shuffled toward the sounds.

Kendi's open-mouthed expression reflected Magnus's relief. Reinforcements. That meant food, supplies, and an end to the deadly shade of saphyrum sickness. Kendi waved the scout on, and Naruu dashed back up the way he'd come.

When they crested the rise, the sight of so many Alliaansi soldiers took Magnus's breath away. Simple uniforms of forest green stood like shadows against a red and orange carpet of fallen leaves. Faces of many colors turned toward them, their smiles flashing against dappled sunlight.

Those joyful looks faltered as they found Magnus. The closest soldiers recoiled. A hush fell over the celebration.

For a moment, he'd forgotten his horrific appearance.

The ranks parted, and a tiny woman clad in form-fitting leathers stepped out. Taller and fiercer than Orowen, Commander Maralla Evallier's lavender face bore over a dozen warrior's runes. A line of them striped her nose and intersected another over one eye. More runes dotted her forehead and chin. Her white hair toppled over her shoulders in braids adorned with beads and feathers. She paused at the sight of him, then strode up the hill and offered a hand.

Magnus reached for her, only to be tugged down to her level and wrapped in a hug. Her bright laughter was a balm against the ache of pitying stares.

She spoke into his ear. "You look a little worse for wear, *Amaa.*"

His answering laugh was a broken thing, made raw and raspy by the scars in his throat. "What do you mean? I thought I looked rather handsome."

"I'm pleased to see you still have your sense of humor." She pounded his back and pulled away to greet her fellow commander. Once Kendi released her, Maralla gestured to the supply carts. "Anwic said you might need some help out here. We brought food and water, and as much saphyrum as we could carry."

If Kendi's second-in-command had reached Starlight, that meant at least one group of refugees was safe.

"We had one other team ahead of us," Magnus said. "Did they reach the plateau?"

Maralla's smile faded. "*Ciir,* but they lost a few. They veered too far south and encountered Light Paladins outside Willowmarsh."

"Light Paladins?" Kendi spat the words.

Magnus scowled along with him. If the Church's zealots got involved with the war, their training facility in Sarton was perfectly positioned to cut off the Alliaansi's eastern supply chains. "Have you heard from Eris?"

Magnus already suspected her answer. Eris Lathaarios was too proud to ask for help. The crafty Syljian governor fortified her town of Willowmarsh behind stone walls and deep trenches. She used the fork in the river as a moat on two sides, and sentinels patrolled day and night. Willowmarsh remained self-sufficient, taking only what it needed from the supply lines before sending goods downriver to Ru'Iskaar and Starlight.

Maralla shook her head. "*Aon,* but I sent scouts. We should know something in a few days."

Kendi frowned. "How *did* you find us so fast?"

"How do you think?"

The metallic scent of Aether stung Magnus's nose. Cold black mist caressed his nape, and the telltale rush of air followed.

A soft feminine voice came from behind them. "You were a quarter-league from where you should have been, *Amaa.*"

Magnus turned in time with Kendi to see a raven-haired half-Syljian step out of the rift. When it snapped closed, the tree trunks and undergrowth seemed to ripple behind her.

Riisii Evallier's dark eyebrows cinched. Her skin was the palest shade of purple, as if a serious illness had stolen its vibrancy. Maralla's daughter possessed her father's muscular shoulders and discerning violet eyes, though only a hint of her mother's grace. She was an intimidating contrast to her older sister, Anya, whose beauty rivaled Mira herself.

She was also a seer—the most skillful seer the Alliaansi possessed.

Riisii brushed invisible dirt from her leather cuirass and frowned at her knuckles. "I had to adjust my target." Her tone bordered on wistful.

Maralla snorted. "You were close enough, *enniia*."

Riisii turned her hand over to examine her palm, then lowered it, giving her mother an affronted look. "These things matter, *Miaa*." Her gaze shifted to Magnus. "I'm sorry about your eye, *Amaa*. I Saw it too late to warn you."

An involuntary shudder wracked him. Magnus squeezed his remaining eye shut. If his fate had appeared in Riisii's visions, then this atrocity could have been prevented. Cheralach's death could've been prevented.

His fingers curled into fists.

No. No, Riisii's Sight came to her unbidden, just as all seers' visions did. There had been no way of stopping this.

Silence stretched between them as if they expected him to say something, but Magnus didn't trust himself to speak. He had to be confident. Poised and strong.

Kendi took pity on him and turned to Maralla. "Maybe you can talk some sense into your sister."

She barked a laugh. "When have I ever been able to do that?" Maralla held up a hand to stay Riisii as she opened her mouth. "That's not an invitation for an exhaustive list."

The girl sighed and lowered her gaze. "*Ciir, Miaa*."

"She's convinced herself martyrdom is the price for seeing us safely out of Ryost," Kendi said.

Maralla's humor vanished. "What do you mean?"

Kendi beckoned to her and started for the campsite. "I'll explain more on the way. *Iiren'hyvaa, Amaa*."

Magnus returned Kendi's half-hearted salute as he led Maralla away. By the time the two commanders had disappeared through the trees, he'd reclaimed his composure and swallowed the slivers of glass in his throat.

Riisii was studying him with an unnervingly perceptive stare.

*She knows what you are. What you've become.*

Magnus stiffened.

The voice slithered into his mind, flicking at his awareness like a snake's tongue. It was hard to discern it from his own thoughts. His own inner turmoil.

*She could threaten your position. Tell them you're not fit to lead.*

When Riisii stepped into his space, the smell of Aether followed. Magnus's eye socket throbbed. His hand twitched for the knife at his belt.

"You will have your revenge, Magnus Gibbons." Riisii's attention strayed to his hand.

He cursed himself and tried to smooth the gesture into something casual. He hooked his thumb over his belt. "What I want is justice, not revenge."

She nodded, watching him so intently that his skin crawled. Did she See him acting on his intrusive thought? Would she tell anyone he'd considered it? The damage she could do to his reputation would be irreparable.

*Nothing good will come of this.*

*Take it.*

Magnus shoved the impulse aside. He ignored his itching palm and the sword that might have cleaved the seer's head from her shoulders. He had to get away from her. "If that will be all, Riisii—"

"They do not find Draeconis."

*Draeconis.*

Cheralach's killers had been looking for Draeconis.

Sharp pain stabbed into his eye socket. Distantly, he heard screaming. His fingers twisted into his hair, and a groan scraped along his vocal cords.

The smooth, silky voice of his torturer, Nicolas, seeped into his mind: *If he would simply tell me how to find Draeconis, then your torment could end.*

Magnus wavered on his feet, struggling to hold back the searing bile in his stomach. It was too much. It was all too much. Dark shadows closed in; steel glinted.

"Are you alright, *Amaa?*"

The bite of iron, the scent of rot, the taste of blood—

"*Amaa?*"

The world snapped back into focus. Magnus leaned against a white-barked tree, his palms pressed to his forehead. A thorn bush clawed at his trouser leg, and a stray leaf stuck to his sleeve. He lowered his shaking hands.

Naruu stared up at him, white eyebrows drawn inward. Riisii stood behind him, hands clasped, a mask of careful neutrality in place. Magnus caught some curious glances from the other soldiers milling about, but that was all.

No one seemed to have noticed the darkness fraying his mind.

*And you must keep it that way.*

With a deep breath, the lingering tightness in his chest eased. Orowen had said this would pass with time. These voices, these images, were all just a product of his trauma. He wasn't crazy; he just had to be patient with himself.

Naruu offered his waterskin with a lopsided grin. "Riisii said you have a headache. This should help."

The skin was full of wine. Sour, and with a lingering bitterness, but wine nonetheless. Magnus drank deeply.

"*Taapad tiik*," he said, passing the skin back.

"*Ushaar.* The commanders are waiting for you. We're ready to move."

Light speared the thinning canopy and provided weak warmth. The sun seemed higher in the sky than before. How long had he been standing here like this?

Magnus pushed himself away from the tree. His eye found Riisii's, but there were no answers there. Many believed the seer was fae-touched; she certainly hadn't done well during her brief stint in the army. Her unpredictability made her unmanageable to anyone but Tipori, her similarly Sight-gifted father.

*Use that to your advantage.*

The seeds of an idea took root. Riisii wasn't usually wrong about her visions, though they were often as mercurial as the woman herself. Perhaps today was an example of her skills breaking down. A quarter-league off-target could indeed be dangerous on the battlefield. And if she'd failed to predict something as monumental as Cheralach's death...

Riisii stared at him—through him—as if she could See the thoughts in his mind. Magnus turned away and stalked after Naruu, down the slope and back into camp where his people awaited orders.

He would never murder Tipori and Maralla's daughter. But he *would* take Cheralach's seat on the council. He had to ensure the Guild paid for their senseless slaughter, for taking his eye, for the thousands more who would die in this war. If Riisii decided to stand in the way of justice, he could build a defense to discredit anything she said about him.

It wasn't a case of the pot and the kettle, after all.

# CHAPTER EIGHT

## RAVLOK

Screams carried over the river, and Ravlok's hand tightened on the sword still sheathed at his hip. Memories of the dungeon closed in, but the moonlight reflecting off jagged rocks and the breeze knifing through his cloak steadied him. He breathed, willing his mind and body to battle-readiness. He wasn't underground. He wasn't a prisoner.

A flash of magic lit the trees and cut shadows into Alar's grim expression. The psionist hunkered beside Ravlok and peered over a boulder. "Stay low until we know what we're up against."

Though Alar had established a telepathic bond with him moments ago, he spoke aloud for Daeya and Jack. Ravlok glanced at Daeya, wishing she'd allowed him to treat her wound before tying it with that dirty strip of cloth. Shavaan forbid she end up with fleshrot and need her arm amputated.

Maybe Daeya was right; he *was* becoming a mother hen.

"It's probably a scouting party." Alar reached into a blue velvet sack—Daeya's old Guild-issued saphyrum bag—and withdrew a bead. He reached across Ravlok and placed it in her hand. "The river's too wide here. You'll have to Bend us across."

Daeya rolled the bead once between her fingers, and paused. "I can't."

"Why not?" Alar asked.

"I could take you, maybe, but Rav and Jack don't have magic."

Of course, she wasn't supposed to use magic on non-adepts.

Jack scoffed. "*Now* you'll let that stop you."

"I've *never* used magic on—"

Another shriek split the night, punching through Ravlok's wall of calm. Daeya shrank against him. Alar turned to her again, his face darkening with the makings of some razor-edged remark.

Ravlok tried to direct his thoughts toward him. *"You can't ask her to betray the most basic Guild principles. They fought an entire war over this."*

The response inside his head was immediate. *"Any of the others would do it."*

Jack thrust his crossbow toward the screams. "Seems like that's a rule of convenience for you sorcerers. Destroy a town? Sure. Save a few civilians? Oh no, let's damn them to rape and murder instead."

Daeya winced, and Ravlok put his arm around her. He met Alar's gaze through the mist. *"You know she's not like the others."* He wasn't sure how well his exasperation would translate telepathically. *"That's why she's here with us. If you asked me to betray my beliefs, I would push back just as hard. Maybe harder."*

Alar's reluctance and understanding passed through their link as easily as if they were Ravlok's own. He was still marveling at the sensation when another scream tore across the water.

"See?" Jack's teeth flashed. "We could've killed the bastards by now."

Rather than punch him square in the face, Ravlok tightened his hold on Daeya. She tucked herself under his arm.

"Alright." Alar turned to Jack. "I can't lift more than one of you at a time. I'll send you over first. Go sit on that rock."

"You can't be serious."

"I am." Alar's tone bordered on dangerous. "Go. We're wasting time."

Jack stalked over to the rock Alar indicated. No sooner had he sat down than the stone lifted free of the ground. A grunt escaped Alar as he guided it over the wide river. Once Jack stepped off on the other side, Alar tugged the stone back across the water.

Ravlok gave Daeya's uninjured arm a squeeze. "Are you alright?"

She avoided his gaze. "I'm fine."

"Ravlok," Alar prompted.

Cries raked through the trees, chilling Ravlok down to his boots.

"Bleeding Aether." Daeya extracted herself and rose. "I'll take you across. If Ravlok follows us, I won't be able to stop him."

She side-eyed Ravlok with meaningful intent, and he dipped his chin in acknowledgment. If the workaround cleared her conscience, that was good enough for him.

Satisfied, Alar nodded and released the rock. Ravlok rested his palm against his sword while Daeya began to chant. She traced a bright sigil, then sliced into the Aetherial Wall with a downward sweep of her hand. A second slash of light appeared beside Jack.

Air and mist swept Ravlok's hair toward the void. With no further warning, Daeya seized Alar's cloak and yanked him into the rift. In the same movement, Ravlok grabbed his shoulder, uttered a prayer to Silonas, and took three quick steps forward.

The rift *pushed*, then *pulled*. He met resistance, like the straight-line winds of a storm, and myriad grays streaked his vision. A jolt of alarm shot through him, but the fear didn't fully form before he burst through that resistance as if it were wet parchment. Ravlok lurched out of the exit rift with the acrid taste of metal coating his tongue. His skin crawled and wind pulled at his back, as if the Aether might suck him back in. Orowen's rift and tons of fractured stone flashed before his eyes.

But they weren't in the dungeon. Ravlok breathed to calm his galloping heart. He wasn't about to careen into the void like one of those unfortunate soldiers.

Alar doubled over, gripping his knees.

Daeya didn't wait for him to recover. She dismissed the rift with a flick of her wrist. "If we can see their magic, they can see mine. Come on."

The distant quality to her voice made Ravlok's chest tighten. He let go of Alar and reached for her. "You got us this far. You don't have to go any farther."

Moonlight reflected off the whites of her eyes. Ravlok searched her expression, and her uncertainty tugged at him.

A woman's whimpered plea and a man's low cackle carried toward them. Cries of terror and the sharp tearing of fabric followed. Daeya shrugged Ravlok off with a scowl and darted into the trees.

"Daeya!" Alar hissed, lurching forward on unsteady feet.

Stunned, Ravlok stared at the branches swaying in Daeya's wake. The bright glow of a campfire passed in and out of view, silhouetting her slight frame in short bursts.

*"Follow her. I'll send Jack around to flank them."* Alar's irritation prickled the hair on the back of Ravlok's neck. *"And start praying to your gods we aren't facing a whole squadron."*

Ravlok drew his sword and slipped after Daeya. He called upon Silonas's fortune and Tiior's wisdom, praying either boon might reach Daeya before she did something stupid. In the same breath, he reconsidered his promise to Tiior. Perhaps protecting Daeya from Anordis was too ambitious an endeavor when protecting her from herself was challenge enough.

As if to affirm his doubts, fire bolts shot through the campsite up ahead. Ravlok hurried forward until a flash of gold lit the forest, and a familiar screech glued his boots to the dirt. Alar paused as well, uttering more lamentations as he looked up, searching for the falcon.

That golden light—Daeya's light—brightened until it resembled the midday sun. Fire swirled around her like ribbons. Mages in varying states of dress were weaving sigils with hasty sweeps of their hands, their attention trained on the sorceress. Shouts and orders rose above the thundering river.

Eyes watering, Ravlok followed Alar's gaze upward. Paelic's huge form swooped across the treetops. Caelyn's familiar shimmered white with her magic.

Lightning *cracked*, accompanied by renewed cries of alarm. A fire flared in its wake, halfway up a tree and belching smoke.

"Get her!"

"Gods be damned."

"Counter-orbs, now!"

"Bleeding Chaos!"

The encampment exploded into a cacophony of frenzied movement and hasty incantations. One black-robed mage stumbled away from the site, loose trousers fisted in one hand. He hit the ground not five paces from Alar, bleeding from his eyes and nose.

"Ravlok," Alar said aloud.

His urgency propelled Ravlok forward, even as his mind retreated from the chaos of light and sound. An odd numbness overcame him, and he lowered his sword. Twin splashes of scarlet bloomed in the smoky haze, illuminating Daeya's silhouette.

Alar wasn't looking toward Daeya, or the remaining mages forming up around her. Nor was he looking at the dead man at their feet. "Which god did you pray to?"

An odd question from a man who didn't believe in gods, despite meeting both Tiior and Caelyn face-to-face only weeks ago. Because they didn't come at mortals' every whim, because they allowed his people to suffer, Alar refused to acknowledge their divinity. Ravlok had mostly accepted that. He no longer tried to explain free will or accountability; he simply allowed him to think what he wanted. If only Alar would show him the same courtesy.

Ravlok braced himself. "Tiior and Silonas. Why?"

For once, Alar didn't brandish his blasphemous wit. "I think you attracted the wrong one."

Those twin scarlet plumes brightened, and more orange ribbons twirled through the smoke.

"What do you mean?"

Alar nodded to a stand of trees where a sleek black shadow stalked toward the fire.

Ravlok's mouth went dry. No normal animal would run *toward* the fire. The shadow coalesced into the shape of a wolf. Caelyn's second familiar darted between two trees, ears flat, eyes gleaming in the firelight, magic shimmering white at ear tips, paws, and tail.

And she was heading straight for Daeya.

Figures darted toward them through the smoke. Two women and a child, all Syljian. Alar caught one of them. She screamed, clutching the shreds of her torn white shift. Ravlok stepped into the other woman's path.

"Peace! *Teshiiqar.*" He said the word first in the trade tongue, then Aivenosian, hoping it was close enough to Syljian for her to understand.

The young woman clung to the boy in her arms, her entire body shaking. Blood oozed from a gash on her face, and her upper half was bare. The child was little better off, with a fat lip and spell burns across his torso. All three looked half-starved and pale.

Her companion went eerily calm under Alar's touch. He rattled off instructions in their native tongue, then she nodded and shook herself, as if coming out of a stupor.

Ravlok spoke to the younger woman in his slowest and clearest Trade. "You're safe now. We're with the Alliaansi."

She shifted the child against her hip and threw herself into Ravlok's arms.

Alar barked something else and waved the women toward the river.

Ravlok gasped in smoky air as the woman released him. She said nothing, only wiped her eyes and hurried to obey. Telltale bloodstains marred the back of her shift. He adjusted his grip on his sword with deadly purpose and turned back.

He'd lost sight of Corra. His gaze flitted between trees and shadows. He had to warn Daeya—

Scarlet heat struck him like a hammer. Ravlok staggered back and shielded his face. Smoldering embers peppered his travel leathers and seared his palm. His sword slipped from his hand and clattered to rest beside his boot. He dared a glance over his upraised arm.

Scarlet fire engulfed the forest. Bushes snapped and hissed. The trees stood like pillars of fire, and leaves and branches fell as scarlet rain.

Sweat slicked his body, his eyes and lungs burning. The path ahead was clear now, and smoke billowed through a gaping hole in the forest canopy.

Daeya knelt at the heart of the inferno, her body glowing like a beacon.

# CHAPTER NINE

## DAEYA

Daeya crashed through the trees on her way to the mages' campsite, low-hanging branches tearing at her sleeves. Anger warmed her against the late autumn chill, and her pulse beat away the pain in her shoulder.

She'd defied a Guild decree to get Ravlok across the water. That knowledge lodged like a stone in her chest. It was inevitable, really, now that she'd left her people, her home, in favor of her enemies who historically had no qualms about such barbarism—

She slid to a stop at the edge of the camp, and all the fear and outrage welling inside her spilled over.

Ransacked supplies littered the grass. A cloak hung from a nearby branch, and a woman's skirt had been stomped into the dirt near Daeya's feet. She stared down at the red patches marring the fabric. And the victims...

Daeya lifted her eyes to the black-robed mages she'd once called brothers. The half-dozen men looked up from their broken conquests and stared at her in confusion.

She summoned magic. Her first fire bolt slammed into a mage atop a glassy-eyed Syljian, knocking him sideways. Her second struck his companion, who held the woman's wrists in a knuckle-white grip. The third bolt met a counter-orb and exploded in a shower of light and black-violet mist. Daeya snarled and pivoted toward the orb's source, the taste of ash on her tongue.

A resonating chuckle came from a sandy-haired mage with arms like tree trunks and shoulders as broad as Murtagh's.

"What's this, now?" The mage hefted himself off a log near the fire and sauntered closer, eyeing Daeya up and down. White-violet static arced over his fingertips.

Ribbons of fire twisted around her, flowing like rivulets into her palms. Golden light formed a brilliant web across her skin like the shattered crust of a lava stream, a protective lattice. She placed herself between the closest woman and the lightning savant.

The Guild taught its students to distrust blankers. From her earliest memories, her instructors spoon-fed her their own versions of the Schism, the Saphyrum War, and the Blood Crusades. They'd reiterated the danger of Syljian masterminds a thousand times by the time she'd cast her first spell. But throughout her training, they'd never encouraged her to brutalize and maim women or children. It wasn't a matter of race or allegiance. The goddess Mira had made a race to match each lesser god's likeness; it was no fault of the Syljians that she'd made them in Anordis's image.

Jack's accusation burned hotter than any draegion flame. If she'd been willing to take them across the river sooner, there would have been more time to defend these people. Maybe she could've stopped them. Maybe the women wouldn't have been violated.

Maybe the child lying face-down near the gnarlwood tree would still be alive.

Daeya's rage mounted. She sidestepped a lash of the mage's lightning, and a tree burst into flames behind her. Her lips stretched taut across her teeth. More fire. More power for her to use.

"Get her!"

A wolf-faced Feridian charged her. With a twitch of Daeya's fingers, the fire in the tree became a whip. It lashed across his snout and set his fur ablaze. He dropped to the ground, howling and grabbing fistfuls of leaves to smother the embers.

A second Syljian woman darted for the first. A third woman, not much older than Daeya herself, clutched the tattered remnants of her shift and tried to reach for something—*another child*—behind a fallen log. Bleeding Aether, that boy couldn't be more than two or three years old. He clutched his guardian and buried his face in her neck.

Daeya's skin burned with raw energy. Her tears evaporated seconds after they slipped down her cheeks.

A water savant called upon his magic. Daeya hurled a stream of scarlet death into his sphere of frost. The ice burst into a cloud of steam that scorched his hands and face.

"Gods be damned." A Cintoshi mage scrambled backward.

Daeya glanced down at the women, their owl-eyed stares a mixture of awe and fear. She scoured her memory for the right verb in Syljian and thrust her chin toward the tree line. "*Iviist'ruh.*"

Go.

The women understood. They scrambled after their companion and the child. Daeya channeled magic and wove a double-layered spell of protection for them.

"Counter-orbs, now!"

Black-violet orbs streaked across the clearing. Her sigil exploded into motes of light. Daeya spun, scowling, and lashed out with her flames.

"Bleeding Chaos!"

Sorcerers scattered. Daeya tried the protection spell again, but another counter-orb fractured her half-formed sigil. Two spheres of lightning struck her abdomen, sending her sprawling. Her golden lattice deflected the spheres, but they still hammered the breath from her and scorched her shirt.

One of the women stumbled and hit the ground. The lightning savant darted for her, hauled her up by her hair, and held her before him like a shield. She screamed as his lightning blackened her skin. The other women stared, their horrified faces lit by the magic wracking their companion's body.

"Come now, blanker-lover." He adjusted his grip on the woman and sneered at Daeya. "You wouldn't want me to break this one's pretty neck would you?"

The other mages crept closer, flanking their friend.

Daeya snapped at the two women with the child. "*Iviist'ruh!* Gods damn you, get out of here!"

The Cintoshi mage started after them, but the lightning savant held up his free hand. "Let them go. We've found a better prize." His smile was pure malice. "Daeya McVen, your Councilor's been looking for you."

Of course he knew her name. It would have been surprising if he hadn't, for all the records she'd shattered in the sparring ring and her prolific advancement through the Guild ranks.

The thought of Gregory cut through her poise like a scythe. He'd threatened to destroy her da's livelihood if she ever ran from him again. If he discovered she'd attacked her own people, there was no telling what he might do to him. Her eyes strayed to the blackened form of the Feridian on the ground. The mage's chest didn't rise.

Her breath seized in her throat.

"You'll come back to camp with us, nice and easy." The lightning savant gave the Syljian's head a shake. She whimpered, trying to pry his grip from her hair. "And maybe we'll let this one live, since you seem so fond of the creatures."

This wasn't right. None of this was right. There was no fear of psionics in this man's heart.

Daeya shifted one foot behind the other. Scanning the clearing and the other mages surrounding her, she licked her lips. "Let us go peacefully, and I won't burn you all to ash."

The leader-apparent laughed. "She talks a big game, doesn't she?"

The others grew in confidence, laughing along with him, and Daeya tightened her grip on her bead. She'd taken in enough fire energy to obliterate the campsite. Her every muscle sang with power like a plucked harp string. More rivulets of flame poured off the campfire and the tree, swirling around her in a wavering haze.

She kept him talking as she plotted the map of a final sigil that could save the woman. "If you know who I am, then you know what I can do. Don't test me."

Another round of laughter. At the leader's signal, gleaming spheres of fire, lightning, and frost coalesced at the mages' fingertips. The Cintoshi lifted empty hands, likely an air savant preparing to steal her breath.

Daeya's magic responded to the threat of its own accord. The bead cracked between her fingers. Twin scarlet orbs erupted from her palms, and heat drained from her face. A desperate noise escaped her as she grappled to contain that power, but it was as hopeless as trying to stop an avalanche.

"Last chance," she warned, her voice strained. Her hold on the immense font of magic slipped further.

"You can't fight all of us at once—"

A crossbow bolt sprouted from the lightning savant's throat. His two nearest allies spun in surprise, and the woman darted free. Daeya began to trace a fire ward to protect her, but the air inside her lungs left her in a rush, crushed out by a force so great she feared her ribs would crack. Then a sphere of—something, gods knew what—struck her chest. All the power she'd been holding back exploded.

Scarlet light filled her vision. Her body spasmed, and she pawed at her torso until the crushing weight on her ribcage lessened. She raked in a super-heated breath.

The light dimmed to near-darkness, despite the pulse of magic electrifying her skin. A distant pressure on her right knee suggested she was no longer standing. She blinked away bloody haloes and recoiled as two white-violet eyes swam into focus. They floated toward her through the fiery haze until a shadow took form behind them.

Her glowing fingers sank into the embers littering the ground. She shoved back to her feet and stared into the face of a nightmare creature silhouetted in iridescent white. Behind it, black mist billowed outward, obscuring the flames. Brilliant light pierced that scarlet-tinged darkness, morphing into the shape of a towering, olive-skinned woman wrapped in vines and carrying a staff of carved wood.

When the woman spoke, her thunderous command shook Daeya to her core: "Seize her."

The wolf lunged for Daeya's throat.

# CHAPTER TEN

## ALAR

Alar's psionic blast should have shattered the wolf's mind before its teeth closed on Daeya's arm. Instead, the creature only yelped and released her. Its black tail fanned the flames as it circled away to come at her again.

Not even on the darkest night in the Wastelands would he allow it. Daeya was *his* to protect, as long as his people needed her.

He *seized* the nearest log in a crushing telekinetic hold and hurled it at the wolf. Pinned beneath it, the wolf scrabbled. Its spine should have been pulverized. Alar hammered his will into the creature. Its howl reverberated through air and Aether, but its mind remained intact, still bent on shredding Daeya apart.

Caelyn's face twisted, her sneer a savage slash of red. "This is not your fight, boy."

Roots sprouted from the ground and ripped the log from Alar's psionic grip. Agony spiked behind his eyes. Only Ravlok's hand beneath his arm kept him upright.

The wolf rose, mouth dripping slaver, eyes shining with eerie arcane light. It stalked toward Daeya, and she stepped back, attempting a battle mage's defensive stance. Her skin glowed so brightly that Alar could barely make out the tatters of her white shirt.

More roots and vines thrust upward, lashing across Daeya's ankles and arms. Red fire exploded from her and turned her bonds to ash.

Alar shook off Ravlok and stepped farther into the clearing, against his better judgment. Already, his clothes were drenched in sweat. "Call your creature off, Caelyn. There's no need for this."

If the goddess was surprised that he knew her name, she didn't show it. Daeya, however, shot him a wide-eyed look.

"You're right; there isn't." Caelyn swept her staff toward the sky and summoned storm clouds. Lightning forked and thunder crashed. Torrential sheets of rain struggled to pummel the flames into submission, and steam curled upward. Caelyn waved her staff again and a gust carried away smoke and mist. "If the draegion is as concerned for the safety of our world as she should be, she will come with me voluntarily."

"I'm not going anywhere with you," Daeya spat.

The wolf's ears and lips pulled back. Alar wasn't stupid enough to place himself between it and Daeya's flaming hands. He looked toward Caelyn. "We discussed this with Tiior already. She's coming with me."

"Tiior is a fool if she thinks I'm going to let that blight roam free in my forests." Lightning flashed, and it was all Alar could do not to recoil from her display of power. Caelyn gestured to the fire still raging around them. "You see the destruction she has caused. It will take centuries for this land to recover."

He smirked, despite his fear. She had a knack for hyperbole. "It shouldn't be that hard for a god of nature to regrow a few trees."

*"Alar, that's probably not wise."* Ravlok's shock rippled through their telepathic connection.

Caelyn planted her staff in the steaming coals. "You know nothing, impotent whelp. Draegion magic poisons the soil. It is an affront to nature."

Thunder crashed as if to punctuate her statement, and the hair on Alar's arms stood on end.

Ravlok appeared at his side. "You would take her to Draeconis? Where she can learn to control this power?"

As if anticipating his thoughts on the matter, Ravlok squeezed his shoulder. Alar held his tongue, nails biting into his palms.

Caelyn barked a laugh. "Draeconis? No. The last thing I would see returned to this world are the dragons who nearly tore it apart."

Ravlok's unease trickled into their connection. Alar shared a glance with him, then shook his rain-soaked hair free of his cheeks. "Where, then?"

Her focus returned to Daeya. "Dromas."

The Aivenosian prison island, said to be the most impenetrable magical fortress in the world. It harbored only the most dangerous arcanists—those who couldn't be killed or contained by ordinary means—whose very existence threatened life on Dessos.

He followed Ravlok's gaze to Daeya, who stared open-mouthed at Caelyn.

"Dromas?" Daeya looked down at her hands, still wreathed in red flames, then closed her fists to smother them.

Alar approached, keeping a healthy distance from the wolf, and took her rain-soaked sleeve. "Daeya—"

Her intense violet stare froze any further sound from his throat. For that split second, she almost looked part-Syljian herself, if not for the rose madder in her hair. A bare patch of glowing skin shone through a hole in her shirt. When he dragged his gaze down to it, Daeya wrenched away from him. She pulled the shreds of cloth together and folded her arms over them.

Wastelands, if he could just touch her aura and take her fear away. But with her new tendency to spontaneously combust, he was stuck trying to placate her in the most inefficient way.

"Hey, easy. It's just me." Alar winced, not sure where he was going with that. She still wasn't speaking to him after his blunder by the river. Maybe he should have let Ravlok do this. "It's okay."

"I don't want to go to Dromas." Rain plastered her hair to her shoulders, and the pitiful way she looked between him and Ravlok made his chest hurt. "Please, Alar, I can control it. I just need to find Telerion."

It was like she'd struck him. Suddenly all his misgivings about being vulnerable with her seemed so petty. She'd asked about Val; she'd even offered to go with him to speak with Finn. She *cared* how he felt, and all she'd asked for in return was reassurance that he cared for her, too. And now, at the sight of her shaking, on the verge of tears, begging him not to send her away—

It was too much for him.

Before he could stop himself, Alar wrenched her into a hug. He breathed in the smell of her rain-soaked hair as she buried her face in his chest. His throat tightened and he pressed his lips to her ear. "I won't let her take you, I promise."

Her golden light faded, and her taut muscles relaxed. The softness of her against him constricted his throat further.

He glared over the top of Daeya's head at Caelyn. "She's not going with you."

The wolf bared its teeth again, matching its master's deadly scowl. Ravlok strode forward, placing himself before the beast. The next fork of lightning reflected off his sword.

Caelyn's grip tightened on her staff. "You would doom your people, setting her loose among them."

Alar's bitter laugh cut through the pounding rain. "Funny, now you're concerned about my people. Where were you these last two centuries while the sorcerers slaughtered them?"

"Your insolence is tiresome, child. War and suffering are my brothers' domains."

An insult and an evasion. Alar might have spontaneously combusted himself. "You have worshippers on both sides of the mountains. Seems like any goddess who cared about her followers would want to stop one from systematically eliminating another."

"Oh, I have long pondered the possibilities if I were to exert my will upon your fleeting mortal existence. If people cared for nature as they care for killing each other, my domain would be the most perfect one of all."

"Then make it so."

The way she smiled sent a chill down his spine. "To intervene in mortal affairs is to disallow free will," she said. "But should you wish to be my servants, I would gladly make it so."

Slaves.

Alar shuddered. She would make them slaves.

Ravlok shifted on his feet. His aura shivered before settling back into that steady hum of awareness. "You speak of mortals' free will, but forcing Daeya to go to Dromas violates that creed."

"She is no *mortal*."

Lightning cracked overhead, and Alar flinched. Water flowed over the tops of his boots.

Daeya stiffened and lifted her head.

Ravlok lowered his sword. The wolf padded forward and stopped, its nose mere handspans from the soft organs in his belly. Still, strength imbued his every word. "Mortal or not, you would imprison her on Dromas against her will. But just as war and suffering are not your domains, neither are law and justice."

Alar's eyes widened. *"Clever, Ravlok."*

Weeks ago, Caelyn had refused to take them any closer to Delvin's city, Orthovia, than the surrounding forest. She'd brushed the god of law off like he was of no more consequence than a fruit gnat, but her avoidance of him seemed to suggest their relationship was more complicated than that.

She twisted her staff, studying them.

Ravlok's satisfaction rolled across Alar's telepathic link like wind across the plains. "Maybe before you take her to Dromas," the monk said, "we should hear what Delvin has to say."

Caelyn's stare might have turned them all to stone. Her wolf familiar closed its mouth and retreated to her side. "Seek Delvin's ear if you must, servant of Ordeolas, but he is hard of hearing these days. Some say he's abandoned his followers. He's grown weak, his power sapped by his counterpart, who grows stronger every day." She straightened to her full, intimidating height and fixed her eyes on Daeya. "Anordis will surely see the Greater Throne if *that* abomination continues to walk free."

Daeya glared around Alar's bicep, looking for all the world like she might argue, only to shiver and tuck herself back into his cloak.

A wave of Caelyn's staff dispersed the storm. All around them, the terrain lay soggy and scorched. Black mist roiled upward around the goddess's feet, and she stepped into the rift. The wolf turned to follow.

As the rift closed behind her, Caelyn's voice carried across the clearing one final time. "When you come to your senses, you know how to find me."

# INTERLUDE I

## GREGORY

Frosty autumn air whistled through a gap in the Guild command tent. Oiled canvas burgeoned then went limp in rhythmic waves, as if sighing with every breath of northern wind. Outside, sorcerers and guards spoke in low voices, giving the tent a wide berth. They all knew better than to disturb Lucius Gregory before breakfast.

A small stove kept the space warm even on the coldest mornings. Saphyrum lanterns banished the gloom. He'd arranged them strategically to avoid casting shadows over the battle map and carved figurines atop the oak table. A bottle of Rillion's finest vintage sat beside the map, and the crystal goblet he held still had a ring of spell-born frost around its edge.

The accommodations were subpar for Gregory's tastes. He'd hunted blankers—no, *one* blanker—across the continent for years during his youth, and he'd seen more than his fair share of unfortunate sleeping arrangements. In those days, he'd foregone comfort for efficiency and utility. Back then, his sole focus was on bringing one man to justice. Nothing else had mattered.

Nothing until Addy.

His jaw twitched. A smiling face. Beautiful blonde ringlets. Perfect sky-blue eyes. His hand tightened around the fine crystal. Gregory sipped his wine and waited for the stab of guilt—of remorse, of failure—to pass.

These days, he preferred to have a proper roof over his head, a comfortable chair, a sturdy desk, and a bed that didn't smell like sheep. Instead, he was out here in the Northlands, waiting for Councilor Blake's scouts to report in from the blanker city of Beigaare.

He set the goblet down and picked up the newest figurine from its velvet-lined box. The woodcarver's rendering was taken from Gregory's own accounting, not from any scouting attempts into Starlight itself. No, that was too dangerous. One never knew when a mastermind could supplant the memories of one's followers and turn them into double agents for the Alliaansi, and the risk was too high inside the largest blanker stronghold in the world.

Cheralach's replacement, the new governor of Starlight, was well-known to him. Tipori, he called himself now.

Gregory smirked.

Mercy. A ludicrous name for a man such as he. Even so, Tipori was a man of rare charisma, and one Gregory respected in his own way. They both had complicated histories best left forgotten, and the shaky truce they'd reached years ago still stood to this day.

Pity that Tipori chose to side with the masterminds and northern blankers, rather than listen to reason. He was once one of the most powerful men in the world, but his love for Maralla Evallier and that soft-headed poet had ruined him.

Gregory turned the figurine toward the light. Its nose was too straight, the eyes too narrow, and the ears without the proper tapering, but it would do.

He set the piece over the raised spot designating Starlight Plateau. Tipori had strengthened Cheralach's defenses since he'd joined the Alliaansi twenty years ago. If the fools on the Guild Council had listened sooner, they could have eradicated this problem with ease. But as it was, standing over two hundred spans above the forest floor, surrounded by well-trained sentries, physical traps, and rift wards, Starlight was impenetrable by any army, magical or otherwise, that Gregory currently had at his disposal.

However, the Alliaansi still needed food. The Light Paladins stationed at Sarton had spent the last two weeks routing Alliaansi scouts and tracking blankers through the mountains. If they could shatter the last of their supply chains before winter, they could starve the population out by spring.

Voices drew his attention. Blake's scouts. It was about time.

Boots scraped against hard-packed dirt, followed by an annoyed grumble at the second fastening that too often stuck. Morning sunlight poured into the tent, and Gregory reached for his wine.

Cameron Vika—not one of the incompetent fools under Blake's command—stepped inside. The sorceress shook out her windblown curls and let the canvas flop closed. It blew against her legs, but she didn't seem to notice.

She bowed. "Councilor."

Perhaps he'd been too quick to assume her competency. Gregory sipped his wine and waited.

Cameron hesitated. When a loud snap accompanied the next gust of wind, her expression turned sheepish. "Right. Apologies, sir."

She refastened the flap and returned to the table, her confidence fading. She twisted a plain gold band around her left ring finger—a nervous habit developed after the School's collapse. Fear for her lover, no doubt. He'd ensured Killian Cendaire would survive the incident, only because her death would have rendered Cameron useless.

"I hope you're not bringing me another report of your failure, Sorceress."

A bright pink flush stained her cheeks. It might have been endearing on another young face. "No, Councilor. I think I found her—or her trail, at least."

His annoyance vanished. "Tell me."

"I was tracing Aetherial anomalies, as you requested. There was one strong enough to shake the ground up by Sorumei's Bluff." Cameron imparted the information with little fanfare. Gregory favored her for her deductive reasoning and investigative skills, but her knack for brevity also had its allure. "I followed it to the northern bank of the Little Snake and found Councilor Ferren's missing patrol. They were..."

Based on that harrowed look, Gregory could guess what she'd found.

Destruction.

Desolation.

Daeya's powers would overwhelm her without a stronger force to contain them. His source assured him a dragonbond would temper her chaotic nature, but true control would take more. That was why he needed to find Draeconis. Cheralach had known the location, but Gregory's imbecilic minions had killed him before they could extract the information.

The longer he dallied in finding the realm of dragons, the longer this war would last. The more innocents would fall to blanker psionics.

Cameron's incessant twisting of that ring made his jaw tense. "Stop that."

She inhaled sharply, then lowered her hands. "I'm sorry, Councilor. It was just…"

Gregory indulged her unease. He rounded the table and took her by the shoulders.

"It was shocking, I'm certain." He kept his tone measured and sympathetic. If he could drive the sword home now, there would be no room for doubt about what must be done. "You understand why she bears those runes."

When Cameron looked up, her expression was pained. Blue eyes so like Addy's met his, and for the briefest heartbeat, he couldn't breathe.

"Yes." It came out a whisper.

He squeezed her shoulders. "Do not lose sight of that. She will answer for what she has done. You have my word."

"Thank you, Councilor."

Gregory turned away to retrieve a clean goblet and poured more wine. Cameron took the offered glass and sipped delicately while he considered their next move. There were only a few ways over the mountains still navigable this time of year. Trivvix and Sarton guarded the easiest passes. Sarton was closer to Daeya's last-known location, but according to Normos's last report, she had friends among the blankers. They would know the Northlands better than she did.

Gregory leaned against the table, examining the map. There were only two blanker cities close to the Little Snake River near Sorumei's Bluff: Kuma'Kiir and Starlight.

"When, exactly, did you feel the anomaly?"

"Shavasday, sir."

Shavasday. Six days ago. Enough time to take shelter beneath Starlight's rift wards. He considered the options, cursing himself for sending his only Walker to deal with Sarikkian's dog.

Cameron corrected the piece he'd placed to a spot a few fingerspans downriver. One side of Gregory's mouth lifted. Precision was key.

"The ash blow obscured their tracks," she said, "but if I had to guess, I'd say they were headed for Starlight."

"We don't have the means to penetrate the city." Not yet.

They both studied the map again. Then, as he gazed at the figurine of Starlight's new half-blood governor, Gregory's lips tugged into a true smile.

"What are you thinking, Councilor?"

"I am thinking"—Gregory drummed his fingers on the table—"perhaps it's time I send a message to an old friend."

# Part Two

# CHAPTER ELEVEN

## NORMOS

The city of Ferid wasn't made with humans in mind. Normos Beck found himself having to duck beneath the squat pear trees and vine-laden pergolas flanking the road. He grumbled as another pair of Feridians skirted around him, their wolf-like heads passing perfectly beneath the branches.

Normos sighed. At least he wouldn't have to be here long. Once he'd secured the saphyrum and dealt with Councilor Mar-Pol, he could return north to help with the war. He wouldn't miss the moment when Aon'In and Starlight fell, when the blankers finally paid for killing hundreds of children and destroying the only home he'd ever known.

Branches snapped behind him. "I hate this place," Joss Vika groused. "These bleeding half-pint dwarves and dog-faced gremlins can't trim their gods-forsaken trees any higher? It's like they've never seen a ladder."

Normos turned to his wretched companion but jerked back, narrowly avoiding another branch. His secret healing spells had long since reformed his broken nose, but he didn't wish to repeat that experience. He shoved the branch aside. "If you're going to spew that vitriol, do it somewhere far away from me."

Gregory wouldn't tolerate that kind of talk. No civilized person would.

Joss paused in the middle of breaking a branch. He seemed oblivious to the half-dozen locals glaring from the market stalls along the road. "What crawled up your arse and died this morning?"

Normos's face twitched. Gods, the man was insufferable, but Gregory had designed this assignment as punishment for his mistakes in Orthovia. He had no choice but to bear it. "You're disgusting."

The branch snapped off in Joss's hand, and he plucked a red-bellied pear from it. "You're not much to look at yourself."

Normos rolled his eyes. He ducked away through the trees and under a chest-high pergola that smelled of autumn foliage and old wood. A carriage passed by, riding higher than the branches over his head, and behind it walked two humans and a long-legged Aivenosian. All three eyed him with amusement, and when a frown tugged at Normos's mouth, the Aivenosian stifled her giggles and pointed upward.

Toward open sky.

*Of course.*

Another carriage trundled by, followed by more humans. Ignoring the heat rising in his cheeks, Normos stepped into the street and took a moment to stretch the kinks out of his back.

Joss followed, tossing and catching the pear. "Too much traffic in this town. City council ought to do something about these bleeding useless streets."

Normos side-stepped to avoid a passing cart, but Joss didn't bother to move. He forced the driver to steer his horse around him, almost smashing into another carriage. As civilians shook their fists and cursed each other, Normos closed his eyes and tried to fight off the pulsing ache in his temples.

It was tempting to pull from the casting chain around his neck and draw a tiny healing sigil to numb the pain, but sorcerers were not to squander their talent on such spells. Only weak adepts with no elemental affinity or divination skills practiced healing.

And Joss would be too eager to tell Gregory that Normos had been using inferior magic again.

Normos rubbed his temples. He just had to endure breakfast with the Life Coven director and lunch at the Sanctuary, then he could find a secluded place to deal with the growing pressure behind his eyes.

His destination was still half a league away. Normos observed the passing carts and wagons, then left Joss standing in the eastbound lane.

"Hey, where are you going?"

Normos leaped onto the side of a carriage, holding fast to the handrail.

"Normos!"

Despite the pain the movement brought, he bade him farewell with a wave and a smirk. Joss soon passed out of sight, and the pressure between Normos's ears eased a fraction.

Unfortunate that he'd never told Joss where the director wished to meet. Though he could confer with his brother Toby and find Normos easily through Aethersight, Joss wouldn't trouble himself. He'd saunter back to the inn, drink himself into a stupor, and find some courtesan to attend him.

Normos had done him a favor, really, and saved the Life Coven's director from having to endure the cretin's attention along with it. Rumors claimed Miriam Serrasiva was the most beautiful human in the world, and Joss's unabashed crudeness knew no limits. The healers' new saphyrum restrictions were already going to upset her. Normos didn't need harassment charges compounding his problems.

He rode to the edge of town and stepped off the carriage as it turned from Quayside Bridge. Normos continued on foot toward the rolling hills that sheltered the Life Coven, where followers of Mira practiced.

Bare trees ringed by fallen ochre leaves dotted the landscape. A sloping plain jutted up against the coastline, and white sails hung like puffy clouds in the southern harbor. Normos slowed as he reached a bridge built of gray stone.

Ferid was a favored port for Aivenosian ships whose captains avoided the larger Eidosinian cities. A catastrophic earthquake had altered the Cintoshi River's course many years ago and left the town ringed with water. Bridges such as this one had sprung up to cross it once the land had settled. The road beyond was a winding path of grass flanked by wagon trenches.

His black robe brushed his ankles as he breathed in the bayside breeze and reveled in the crunch of grass beneath his boots. He'd foregone hiring his own carriage for this fleeting sense of freedom. The open air dulled his headache.

But a short Walk through the Aether would put him right at the Life Coven's doorstep. He must be timely. Gregory wanted expedient results, and Normos couldn't disappoint him again.

He summoned magic and wove his sigil, envisioning the Life Coven and the landmarks surrounding it. Black mist and white-violet light engulfed him, sending him careening through the Aether in streaks of sky blue and gold. The pounding in his head worsened at the sudden jolt that spat him out on the road in front of a sprawling, two-story estate.

His stomach churned, but not from the Aether. He didn't get sick anymore when he Walked.

Only when he Walked off-target.

Twelve spans off. Mira's mercy, how had he missed? His hands trembled, and a cold sweat broke over his body. Normos lurched forward, across the road and up the walk to reach the door he'd been aiming for.

Inferior magic or not, he hastily drew two healing sigils over his palm. One for tranquility, one a balm against nausea and pain. He slipped his hand under his shirt, pressed both sigils to his chest—

—and breathed.

His humorless chuckle mingled with birdsong and the distant roar of surf. He listened until the tremors subsided. Thank the gods Gregory wasn't here to see this.

Normos mounted the steps, crossed the small veranda, and knocked on the oaken door.

A Cintoshi woman greeted him. She wore the white and gold robes of a priestess of Mira, and clay beads of the same colors hung from her braided beard. Her eyebrows swept upward and lifted even higher as she looked up, up, until her gray eyes met his. "Well, you're a big fella, aren't you? The Guild grows you boys well these days."

"Good morning, priestess." He dipped his chin. "My name is Normos Beck. I'm here to see Lady Serrasiva."

Her smile exposed a gap between two teeth. "Ah! Yes, come in. Milady mentioned another representative from Ryost would be stopping by."

*Another?*

Mar-Pol.

Normos fought the urge to growl. She must have gotten to them first.

The priestess turned, and he followed her into the foyer, then down a narrow hallway. He fidgeted with the hem of his sleeve, struggling to match his long-legged stride to the short Cintoshi's unhurried gait.

The journey gave him too long to think. Honestly, it was hard to disagree with Mar-Pol. So many people depended on the healers, but they also relied on mages to protect them. If the Alliaansi were bold enough to plant spies in the Guild—if they could brazenly destroy an entire school—Eidosinia would be much safer once they were eradicated. The redirection of the healers' saphyrum to aid the Guild army would only be temporary, and then life in Ferid could return to normal.

A baby cried down the hall. Normos's steps faltered. A woman's panicked voice soon shushed it, delving into quiet song.

His shoulders relaxed, and he allowed himself a smile. Better to think of new life, of Mira's creation, than of devastation. "A new mother?"

The priestess threw a roguish look over her shoulder. "Oh, she's a mess, that one, but she'll learn fast. The good ones always do."

Normos eyed the door as they passed, his smile fading. He'd never known his mother. His magic had manifested at the orphanage in Watersgate, and the Guild had taken him in before his first birthday. Gregory had overseen his training from his earliest memories, and Normos was forever indebted to him for nurturing his potential.

They entered a communal dining room with four tables, eight rows of chairs, and a blazing hearth that defied the creeping autumn cold. The priestess frowned, then steered him into a kitchen to wait.

"Forgive me, Sorcerer. I thought she'd be—"

A cry echoed across the estate. Normos's hands twitched upward defensively, but he paused when the priestess spun, smiling.

"Yzara must be giving birth. Mira's work never rests, you understand. Milady is probably with her now."

Her rush of excitement was contagious. Normos laughed and waved her on. "Go, please. I wouldn't dream of standing between you and the goddess's work."

"Oh, you are a dear, aren't you?" She backed toward the opposite door, gesturing as she went. "Help yourself to whatever you'd like from the pantry. I'll send milady down shortly."

The door closed behind her. Normos's stomach rumbled, but even with permission, it was improper to rummage through the cabinets. He spotted a basket of pears on the counter, groaned—because of course there would be pears—and took two before retreating to the dining hall.

Mira's work indeed waited for no one. He'd likely be delayed a while, but he was here, doing as instructed. Everything else rested in the goddess's hands now.

Normos sat beside the hearth, careful to keep his elbows free of the table as he ate. He studied the crystal chandeliers, the prismatic sunlight, the crown molding, and the coffered ceiling. Inevitably, he found himself staring into the flames.

A shiver passed through him.

He'd struggled to heal the burns Daeya's fire had caused that day on the docks. Several patches of flesh on his left side were still numb to the touch. The eerie, unnatural change in her element had made it hotter, fiercer, and it had devoured the port in minutes. Her fire might have taken the entire city had there not been enough water savants at the embassy to hold it back. Not even the fire savants could draw upon those flames without triple-layered protection spells, and some of them had still sustained horrible burns.

Daeya McVen was powerful. Admittedly more so than he. Three times, their mentor had issued Normos the challenge to eliminate her or be replaced, knowing he was too weak, too sentimental, to carry out the task. It was Gregory's way of chastising Normos for his inadequacies, as if he needed more proof that he would never measure up to the Guild's star prodigy.

Yet, for all that Gregory had invested in the ungrateful brat, she'd turned out to be in league with a blanker spy.

Normos still couldn't believe it. Growing up, she'd been like a sister to him. They used to sit together at breakfast, share strawberry tarts, and sneak out on the roof at night to watch the stars. She'd been the first to learn about his desire to study healing magic and, at least until being second-best no longer suited her, she'd allowed him to practice on her scrapes and bruises. Her irrational fear of the Guild infirmary had been a boon for him for years until she'd told Gregory what he was up to.

That betrayal still stung, after all these years.

Even so, she'd never been the type to murder children. The spy she'd been harboring for months must have imperiumed her. Normos had argued as much, but their mentor wouldn't hear it. Despite all the protocols for dealing with sorcerers who fell prey to psionics, Gregory still pursued her as if Daeya could return to his side once they found her.

"Good morning, Sorcerer Beck."

Normos started. A woman stood before him, tawny-skinned, dark-haired, and wreathed in sunlight. He clambered to his feet. "My deepest apologies, my lady. I didn't hear you come in."

She clasped her hands before her gold-embroidered robe. "I'm told I am light on my feet. *My* apologies for keeping you waiting. I'm Director Serrasiva."

Mira's mercy, but the rumors weren't wrong. Her midnight brows framed golden eyes, and her full lips curved into a perfect smile. She stood of a height with him even in her flat-soled sandals. He couldn't place her ethnicity, but he guessed she must have ties to southern Skriia or Rillion.

Normos tried to speak, then cleared his throat and tried again. "Sorcerer Beck—I mean, I suppose you already know my name."

Her grin widened. "Yes, I suppose I do. Please, sit."

His chair squealed against the tile when he attempted to adjust it. Normos cringed, and the director laughed. She let the chair across from him squeak just as loudly before seating herself.

"The pears are lovely this time of year, aren't they?"

If his face got any hotter, it would surely burst into flame. Normos swept the remnants of the cursed fruit into his lap. Gods be good, he had to get a hold of himself. "There are none better in all of Eidosinia," he forced out.

"Caelyn's work never fails to impress." Those golden eyes sharpened. "But you didn't come to talk about pears, did you?"

"No, I'm afraid not."

"I suppose the war was bound to reach us eventually." She frowned. "I already spoke with Councilor Shei-Gwen Mar-Pol. She assured me there would be no interruption in our supply."

Of course she had, the impulsive wretch.

He didn't want to do this. He really, really didn't. "I'm sorry to say she spoke preemptively. We need as much saphyrum as we can spare on the front lines. I'm certain you, as a follower of Mira, were just as devastated by the School's destruction as we were. We must make certain this doesn't happen again."

"How far back are you cutting our supply, Sorcerer?"

Normos did his best not to wince. "I've been ordered to cut off the supply entirely, my lady."

"Entirely," she echoed.

"Yes. You will be allowed to keep your current inventory. It should last at least a year. If we can end this matter quickly, you won't even notice the interruption."

"I see. And when your mages come to the Sanctuary for healing? What then?"

That brought Normos to his next point. "They will be treated elsewhere. The Council has requested twelve of your best healers to be sent north immediately. Four to Sarton, four to Trivvix, and four to the encampment south of Kuma'Kiir. They should be ready to leave by month's end."

"And by 'requested,' I assume you mean 'drafted,'" she said with a bite of venom.

Normos hardened his expression; he must be uncompromising in this. "Volunteers are always welcome, but the Guild must have the numbers regardless."

The priestess closed her eyes as if to steady herself. When she opened them again, her calmness was that of the eye of a storm.

"I know this isn't the news you wanted to hear." Normos reached for her hand. "I promise your supply will be restored and your people returned as soon as possible."

As he made to withdraw, she seized his wrist. "You're a gods-fearing man, Sorcerer."

A statement, not a question.

"Well, yes—"

She withdrew a small medallion from her robe and placed it in his palm. She closed his fingers around it, the thin gold chain hanging from their joined hands.

"The goddess has heard your prayers. She will accept you, should you choose a different path than the one chosen for you."

Normos jerked to his feet, his chair falling backward and striking the floor. He kept reflexive hold of the medallion and looked down to find a dove and holly branch stamped into its surface. The symbol of Mira, patron goddess of mothers, midwives, and artists. His gaze flicked upward, alighting on Serrasiva's unnervingly perceptive stare. "How do you know those things about me?"

Miriam Serrasiva rose and rounded the table. She incanted, drawing a golden sigil in the shape of the pantheon's twelve-pointed star. She pressed the spell into his chest.

Dizzying warmth flooded him. Normos gasped. The dull, ever-present ache in his temples vanished, and the medallion glowed softly in his hand.

"Choose life, Normos Beck." Her eyes shone with the same golden light. She blinked twice and it was gone. "Choose love."

❧

Normos left the Life Coven in a fog, trembling fingers clutching the medallion. After trudging down the road for a time, he stopped at the same stone bridge and stared at the clouds.

How did Serrasiva know he was secretly praying to Mira for guidance? Had she seen him casting on the front walk? Or perhaps she'd seen him in town when he'd slipped away last night to quell an oncoming headache.

Whatever the case, he had to be more careful. Normos uncurled his fingers from the medallion and smoothed his thumb over the holly branch in the dove's beak.

He should get rid of this. Gregory would know he'd been practicing healing arts if he found it in his possession. No good would come of it if Joss or Toby caught him with it either. They could use it to discredit him, advance themselves in the Councilor's hierarchy, and Normos would no more stand to be replaced by one of the Vikas than by Daeya McVen.

Ever the obedient mage, the disciplined student, Normos strode to the middle of the bridge and held the medallion over the water. The chain dangled from his grip, glinting as it caught the light. His fingers relaxed around it; the chain slipped and swung from his hand.

His arm trembled.

It was the dutiful thing. The honest thing.

That which was expected of him.

But he couldn't.

With the utmost care, he slipped the chain around his neck and tucked the medallion under his shirt. Warm metal pressed against his skin, over the spot where the heat from the priestess's sigil still lingered.

# Chapter Twelve

## Shei-Gwen

Firelight bathed Gwen and Olivia's third-story flat in hues of gold. It was a far more appealing effect than the stark white-violet of the saphyrum lanterns that normally lit Gwen's Guild apartment, and it was less wasteful.

However, the lighting was the only homemaking decision on which they agreed. A disjointed arrangement of practical and flamboyant furnishings littered the combined sitting and dining room. Their bedroom was a mess of furs and throws on one side, and neatly arranged stationery and scrolls on the other. But despite their opposing tastes, it was home.

"I signed up for the draft this afternoon," Olivia announced at dinner.

Gwen choked on her braised pork, silverware clattering to the table. "You what?"

"Shavva was asking for volunteers." Olivia shrugged. "I could use a little adventure."

"Adventure?" Gwen dabbed her mouth and chucked her napkin down beside her half-eaten meal. The absurdity. The audacity. Aetherial storms, did she think this was a game? "Just what in Delvin's name do you think that's going to accomplish?"

Olivia leaned back and folded her arms. "You can't just go off to war and expect me to stay here."

"I'm *trained* for war, Livvie. You're not."

"I thought you'd want me with you." She lifted her chin and kicked a dirty boot up on the chair.

Gwen shoved her foot back down. "Don't do that. That's not what this is about, and you know it." She jabbed her finger into the table. "I want you to stay safe. That means not traipsing across some battlefield littered with aethermancers and blankers."

Olivia sighed. "Here we go. Tell me again how the aethermancers will kidnap me for my healing skills, and the blankers will steal all my precious secrets."

Wine turned to vinegar in Gwen's stomach. "You saw what those foul creatures did to my father."

Olivia's scowl faded. Of course, she remembered. The day the sheepherder had found Gwen's father on the valley pass—all his wares stolen, covered in his own excrement, and gibbering like a madman—their lives had changed forever. He was in large part the reason Gwen supported Olivia's use of magic on non-adepts. When the Sanctuary healers refused to offer her father arcane medicine, only Olivia's secret healing had made him well enough to earn a place at Belden Abbey. It had been worth the risk of magic maiming or killing him when his only other alternative would have been a fortified facility for psionic experimentation run by Light Paladins.

Olivia picked at the straps of her scandalous outfit—strips of green leather shaped like vines that wrapped her ample breasts but otherwise left her torso bare. "How is he, anyway?"

Gwen swallowed her emotion and reached for her wine. "He still can't remember my name."

"What happened to him was a tragedy, Shei—"

"Yes, and I don't want it to happen to you."

"—but they're not all like that."

"*Don't* get all sympathetic on me." That placating healer's tone grated. It was bad enough Olivia healed anyone regardless of their affiliation with the Alliaansi, but the blankers themselves? Gwen couldn't bear it. "Really, is it such a crime that I care about your welfare?"

Olivia glared at her. "No, but I'd prefer if you did it in a way that makes me feel less like an incompetent child."

"Then stop acting like one. Stay. Here."

Olivia stabbed her fork into her salad several times, then shoved the purple-veined seffa leaves into her mouth. Gwen expected her to let the garlic oil drip off her lips and onto her clothes, but at the last moment Olivia's emerald tongue darted out to catch it.

Gods, why couldn't she use a napkin?

As if reading her thoughts, Olivia smirked and wiped her mouth with an elegant flourish. "No. It's too late, in any case. Your friend Sorcerer Beck already added me to the Guild payroll."

Warmth drained from Gwen's face. Gregory's minion had arrived in Ferid a few days ago, but they'd yet to cross paths. "When did you speak to him?"

Olivia speared more leaves and a ripe red pomitto. "At the Sanctuary. He met Shavva for lunch. Can't say I was fond of the other void-addled twits, but he seemed nice enough."

"He had others with him?"

"Mhmm. Both went by Sorcerer Vika. One was a Conduit like Peader. He kept sending messages at the table and pissing Shavva off. They—" Olivia paused. "What's wrong?"

Appetite forgotten, Gwen sagged back in her chair. "Stay away from those two, Liv. Especially the taller one."

There had been many complaints about Joss Vika from the female students under her care, but as close to Gregory as he was, any evidence rolled off him like water.

Olivia studied Gwen, then finished off her salad and stood. Her emerald lips twitched upward as she reached one arm behind her back. "I know what will ease your mind."

Gwen scoffed. "Really—"

The straps crisscrossing Olivia's chest slipped free, and Gwen's protest died on her tongue.

That sly uplifting of Olivia's mouth became a full-blown smirk. "That's better."

Static scrambled Gwen's thoughts as one by one, Olivia disarmed herself of two small daggers and four razor-edged throwing stars. Each clattered to the table, and then the lower half of her outfit hit the floor.

Heat pooled in Gwen's belly, her bodice suddenly grown tight.

"You've been working too hard." Olivia leaned over the arms of Gwen's chair and let their noses touch. "You haven't even taken time for prayer."

It was true. Whether for lack of time or avoidance of guilt, Gwen hadn't visited Delvin's shrine all week. Not that kneeling in some temple and praying for justice to prevail could fix anything. Her country was broken, its people made lawless and its leadership a well of corruption. It was hard to find faith when even she had stepped outside the bounds of order for the healers' sake. In that regard, Gwen was no better than the rest of the Council.

Olivia claimed her mouth in a kiss so firm she forced Gwen's head backward. She climbed into her lap, and Gwen welcomed her distraction. But even as her lover nipped a trail down her neck, Gwen's thoughts strayed back to their predicament. Guild payroll or not, she could see Olivia removed from the draft. Mental unrest or unfitness to serve would be reason enough, though undermining her came with its own consequences.

If nothing else, Gwen had to stress the dangers of getting involved with Gregory's minions. "Just because a person seems nice doesn't mean you can trust him."

Olivia folded inward with a groan, resting her head on Gwen's shoulder. "Shavaan help me, your mental calisthenics are exhausting."

A firm push on Olivia's sternum brought their gazes level again. "What you're doing carries serious risks. I need you to understand that."

"I do understand." Warm hands cupped Gwen's cheeks. "Now, come to bed."

"I—" Gwen glanced toward their bedroom, worry still gnawing at her. Olivia couldn't help healing all of Mira's creation. If she slipped up even once out there, she wouldn't get the chance to be kidnapped by blankers. Normos Beck would see her to the gallows himself.

Olivia growled. "You're impossible."

She climbed off Gwen's lap and retreated to the hearth. Gwen winced, but found herself unable to rise from the chair.

Things had been simpler before her promotion, when they both entertained dreams of changing the world. Of Gwen ushering her country into a new era of prosperity, and Olivia saving lives regardless of her patients' magical aptitude. Now, Olivia clung to those dreams, while Gwen knew just how impossible that future was.

Olivia jabbed at the glowing coals with a poker. Gwen squeezed the arms of her chair until her hands ached, still fighting some invisible weight that kept her pinned. Only one truth still persevered despite the insurmountable setbacks they had endured in the last year. She voiced it with all the conviction and strength she possessed.

"I love you."

Olivia's violent motions stilled. After a long look into the hearth, she lobbed a gentle smile over her shoulder. "I love you, too."

The simple phrase negated whatever binding spell had taken hold. No matter what challenges they faced, they'd always done so together. Gwen left her spot at the table and extracted the poker from Olivia's grip. With tender insistence, she pulled her woman close and kissed her, pressing their curves flush.

"I know I can't stop you," Gwen whispered between kisses. "But I wish you'd reconsider."

Olivia caught Gwen's lip between her teeth. "Isn't there something you'd rather be doing?"

"Yes."

This time, Gwen didn't hesitate. She ceded ground as Olivia guided her backward and through the bedroom door, their mouths still locked in sensual combat. When Gwen's calves struck the bedframe, she hooked her arms around Olivia's waist. They tumbled onto the mattress, and for the first time in weeks, Gwen didn't think of politics.

Creaking floorboards roused her from sleep.

Gwen groped blindly for Olivia only to find warm sheets beside her. A slender figure moved through the open doorway to their dining room, familiar dark waves tumbling down its back.

"What is it?"

Olivia paused in reaching for her boots. "I won't be gone long. Go back to sleep."

Gwen's grogginess evaporated. She pushed herself upright. "Where are you going?"

"Sara's husband's having chest pains again. I'm meeting him at first bell."

Gwen might have launched out of bed if her legs hadn't been tangled in the sheets. She extracted herself from the covers. "Seriously?"

"What?"

She knew what. Two carts full of stolen saphyrum hidden beside the cabin was what.

Gwen was on her feet and striding toward her, hackles raised. "We talked about this. It's not safe."

"This is my job, Shei." Olivia spoke like she was placating an irrational patient. "No one else will see him. At least no one with the skills to treat him."

Her tone only fanned the flames of Gwen's annoyance. Gwen circled around her and planted herself before the door. "You promised me you wouldn't heal outside the Sanctuary while Gregory's minions were here."

"No, I promised I'd be careful."

Gwen's fists balled at her sides. "Gods curse the semantics—what if a guard sees you? They'll follow you to the cabin and find that saphyrum there. You'll be complicit in its theft."

Olivia returned a calm and collected gaze. "Chest pains are serious. I have to go."

There was no stopping her. There never was, but Gwen couldn't just step aside. Not when it could get Olivia killed.

Though if she didn't, the man relying on Olivia's healing magic could die instead. If it had been her father, she would have never dreamed of stopping her.

Delvin forgive her for what she was about to do.

"Then I'll go with you."

Olivia started to throw up her hands, but paused. "You will?"

"I can get you out of town with a cloaking spell." Gwen strode to her closet and pulled down a set of smallclothes. She made a face at the drab trousers she would have to wear.

"You're serious." Olivia drifted to her side as Gwen dressed. "You really want to come?"

"If you insist on risking your life, the least I can do is make sure my mistake doesn't get you hanged."

"Ensuring the healers' supply line wasn't a mistake."

"Nevertheless, I—"

"Councilor!"

Sharp knocking cut her off. Gwen started, and Olivia spun toward the door.

"Councilor Mar-Pol!"

"Peader." What in Delvin's name was he doing up at this hour?

Brows furrowing, Gwen glanced toward the clock tower outside a nearby window, but fog obscured its face.

More pounding rattled the door. "Councilor!"

At Olivia's questioning glance, Gwen nodded. "Let him in."

The Feridian boy practically tumbled into the flat. He bent at the waist as if he'd run the whole way, tongue lolling out of his snout. He was still wearing his sleep clothes. "Councilor, I have... a message... from Sarikkian."

Olivia led him to a chair at the dinner table while Gwen closed and locked the door behind him.

"What's happened?" Gwen asked, pacing back to the table.

Peader didn't reach for the satchel slung over his shoulder. Whatever his message was, Sarikkian hadn't entrusted it to parchment.

"He found something... when they were clearing wreckage from the School."

Gwen shared a look with Olivia. Cleaning up after the Alliaansi attack was an enormous undertaking even with magic. Many of their strongest mages had volunteered to assist. Sarikkian, Councilor Ignab, and many from Councilor Blake's team were among them.

*Out with it*, Gwen wanted to demand, but she forced herself to patience.

Peader wrung his furry hands. "He says it wasn't a rift that collapsed the west wing."

Gooseflesh swept down her back. "What do you mean? Blake's mages confirmed it was a warped rift."

"The rift never reached the outer walls. It couldn't have brought the entire structure down." The boy licked his snout free of nervous saliva. "He said we shouldn't return to Ryost until he sorts this out. Th-the evidence, milady, it's unbelievable. I was sure I'd just read the message wrong but I checked it twice..."

As Peader floundered with his report, Gwen reached for the nearest chair and guided herself into it. Sarikkian said they shouldn't return to Ryost? She'd planned to call the Council over the healers' affairs as soon as possible.

"Start at the beginning, Peader." Gwen clasped his hand. "What did he find?"

# CHAPTER THIRTEEN

## RAVLOK

The sun's last rays died over the Northlands, and any trace of warmth went with them. Ravlok's breath formed clouds before his face, but he was careful not to huddle too close to the flames. The last thing he needed, despite multiple urges to the contrary, was to set the fickle tome in his lap on fire.

Daeya was already asleep beside him. Their hard march through increasingly rocky terrain had taken its toll. Their new companion, Helenia, had braided Daeya's hair after the Syljian fashion—thin, tight plaits left to tumble around her face—and her ruddy locks obscured the warrior's runes Sessiri had playfully drawn on her cheeks with mud.

Both older women had taken well to his friend in the days since their rescue, and their easy acceptance spurred hope. If they could trust a sorceress, perhaps the rest of the Alliaansi could as well.

Careful not to wake her, Ravlok pushed those braids away from her cheeks and tucked her thrice-mended cloak a little tighter.

Their other companions, the youngest woman, Niam, and her little brother, Ezra, slept soundly between Sessiri and Helenia on Ravlok's other side. Jack was off scouting the route ahead, and Alar sat on a stone with his dagger in hand, carving a spear tip from an ash branch.

The steady rasp of blade against bark might have lulled Ravlok into sleep if he could only allow himself to rest. But Daeya's control had slipped again today, and even absent Paelic's flesh-prickling shrieks, Ravlok still scanned every tree and shadow waiting for Caelyn to reappear.

He was under no illusion that the goddess would give up on whisking Daeya away to Dromas. His threat to involve Delvin would only keep her away for so long, especially since his prayers to the god of justice had fallen exactly where she'd predicted: on deaf ears.

It was hubris, to think he suddenly deserved a straight answer from the gods. Just because Tiior and Caelyn had appeared to him didn't mean the rest of them would, too. Still, if Delvin was the protection Daeya needed, Ravlok would blot out the stars with incense and fill every altar with offerings until his prayers were heeded.

A flash of white-gold caught the corner of his vision, and Daeya murmured something low and guttural. He started, shifting the tome to reach for her.

"Shh. You're okay."

His touch seemed to steady her. The iron tang of Aether coating his tongue was gone as quickly as it had come, and the scent of burning dissolved into campfire smoke. Daeya mumbled something else and her eyelids fluttered. Ravlok kept one hand on her until she nestled further into her cloak.

He sat back, letting his shoulders sag. The closer they got to the In'Jasuu—the Shattered Mountains—the more disturbed her rest became. Telerion called to her in her dreams, she said. Pity that she couldn't just follow that call to the dragon and forgo Alar showing them the way. But her father came first in her mind, and not even the fury of a goddess could sway her from helping him.

Ravlok smiled despite himself; Angus McVen was a fortunate man.

He glanced at Alar. He had paused in his spear-making to observe Daeya, but his attention shifted as if he sensed Ravlok's eyes on him.

Ravlok ignored his contemplative frown and returned to his studies.

"*Khas... asor... mevhak...* dash?" He paused at a symbol with no equivalent in the Dessian trade alphabet and turned back to a phonetic guide he'd summoned and bookmarked with a leaf. He scanned the list of monastic runes until he found one that closely matched the unknown letter. "No. *Dhash.*"

Asking the book to translate itself had only resulted in more blank pages, as if Eolaan's tome were appalled by such a menial task. Fortunately, many of the letters that hadn't found their way into the Dessian alphabet had near-exact replicas in the ancient runes used by Ordeolas's monks. He'd puzzled out most of the Draconic alphabet in a matter of days and moved on to common exceptions to the phonetic sounds.

"Do you really think that's helping?"

Ravlok looked up to find Alar studying him from beneath furrowed brows. He straightened and stilled his aura, willing calm into tense muscles. "I do."

"What have you learned so far?"

It sounded like genuine curiosity, but Ravlok knew better. Even though Alar had taken Daeya's situation more seriously since she'd nearly burned the forest down, he still refused to acknowledge the importance of taking her to Draeconis. Ravlok's jaw worked around his admission—that he'd been deciphering a dead language and hadn't actually learned anything else—and glared down at what was an unequivocally blank page.

His hands curled around the cantankerous tome as he fought the urge to groan. *You're not helping, Eolaan.*

Alar returned to his whittling. "That's what I thought."

Ravlok scowled. "Tiior said the tome would have answers."

"Then where are they?" Alar didn't look up from his spear. "You've been muttering over that book for weeks."

It was like being cast adrift in a sea of his own doubts. After all, he had a history of over-preparing for a job, only to fail when it counted. In the Corvallis Manor heist—the last job he'd done for Laerin, which had landed him in jail—he'd focused so much on details like locks and security schedules that he'd missed the glaringly obvious wardstones on the way out. Perhaps it *was* wasted effort trying to learn the Draconic alphabet.

Then again, if he hadn't broken his leg in the pitfall trap, he'd have never met Yonfé. He'd have never joined the monastery, and he certainly wouldn't have met Daeya.

*A wise man knows the difference,* Yonfé once said, *between the futility of persistence and persistence despite hardship.*

Unfortunately, Ravlok wasn't a wise man.

He set his jaw. There was little he wouldn't do for Daeya. He knew how the acolytes scorned her for her talent; it was much the same as how the other bed warmers at Madame's were jealous of Ravlok's letters. He and Daeya had bonded over being outcasts in the year he'd trained her in hand-to-hand, daggers, sword, and staff. She was more family to him than his own mother or siblings.

"And if it takes weeks more, I will do it for her."

Alar hummed noncommittally. "In the meantime, I'll make sure she stays rooted in reality."

Ravlok bristled. "Like the reality that she'll not be imprisoned the moment we get to Starlight?"

That concern had been eating at him since they'd crossed the border. Despite defecting from the Guild, Daeya was still a sorceress, and they were still at war.

Firelight danced across Alar's face. He lowered the spear again. "As long as she tells the truth, she has nothing to worry about."

"Assuming they believe her."

"We can ensure her honesty."

"We can only..." Ravlok's eyes narrowed at the 'we' that wasn't meant for him. "You mean the masterminds."

No confirmation was needed; Alar's expression spoke volumes.

"You know she won't submit to that." A chill unrelated to the temperature numbed Ravlok from within. "You weren't even going to tell her, were you?"

"It's standard procedure. My mentor will know in moments that she can be trusted, and Daeya will never know she was touched by psionics."

Ravlok opened and closed his mouth so many times he had to swallow to wet his tongue. "You need to warn her."

"There's no need to frighten her." Alar scoffed. "It's not like it's an imperium."

Ravlok pounced on the slight hitch in Alar's speech. "You said you couldn't read her. What if no one else can either?"

"My mentor is the strongest mastermind on the continent. Believe me, she can read her."

"But—"

"You want to help her family, don't you? This is the quickest way to do that." Alar gestured dismissively toward the book. "Much faster than that, anyway."

Every argument Ravlok could make was as frost to the flame against that truth. Even if he could translate the entire book in the span of days, it still wouldn't provide Daeya with the resources or allies needed to mount a rescue.

Unless the dragon could be enough. The threat of burning an entire Guild city down was surely worth negotiating for the release of a blacksmith and his nephew. And it solved Ravlok's other concerns. Alar had all but admitted his people would only trust Daeya if they could read her mind. What would happen if they couldn't? Kendi and Orowen might speak on Daeya's behalf, but what if that didn't sway the rest of them? It wasn't worth sticking around, anticipating what they might do to her...

The snap of the fire grew in Ravlok's awareness until it drowned out the sound of his misgivings. His aura stilled again, quelling his emotions, but he couldn't remember directing a conscious effort toward it.

What had they even been discussing?

*Return to the book. Study and stay out of the way. That's the best way to help her now.*

Ravlok found himself staring down at the circle diagram where the blank page and lists of letters had been moments before. He blinked away the film over his thoughts.

Helping Daeya. That's what it was. And studying.

Alar was still watching him with an intensity not unlike Caelyn's wolf familiar. Ravlok kept his eyes on Eolaan's tome to avoid it. Fatigue dug its claws in, but he had to read a little more before bedding down.

Time slipped by, and Ravlok kept reading, kept translating, until more of the symbols around the diagram made sense. The longer he stared at the text, the more root words he could identify.

*Usokhar,* 'partner.' *Khevas,* meaning 'sleep,' seen in fae tales that took place in Khevasria, the realm of dreams. And *moru*—'with' or 'join.'

Beside him, Daeya mumbled something low and guttural in her sleep.

He didn't realize his mouth was hanging open until his teeth ached from the cold. What he wouldn't give for a quill and ink, or even a piece of coal—though Tiior only knew how the tome would react if he tried to tear out a page or write in it himself.

*A bond forged in the realm of dreams.*

This was it.

This was the breakthrough he'd been praying for.

# Chapter Fourteen

## Orowen

The wooden lift creaked upward through a channel in the cliff face. It rose on a system of chains and pulleys, the ticking of gears high above them reverberating through the platform at Orowen's feet.

"Have you heard from Anya?" she asked her sister.

Maralla's grin dazzled even in shadow as she turned from the spectacular view of the forest a hundred spans below. "A bird arrived from her last week. She's pregnant."

It was hard to feel gloomy when faced with that smile. Maralla's eldest daughter and her mate had been trying to conceive for years, and Syljian pregnancy was a miracle without adequate access to saphyrum.

Orowen returned the smile. "Congratulations, *ne'miaa*."

Kendi lifted an eyebrow, holding on to the chain supporting one corner of the platform. "You're too young to be *ne'miaa*, Commander."

Maralla snorted. "Don't say that in front of Tipori. He's been begging me for another child."

Behind them, Sam giggled. "Already?"

"*Ciir.*"

Orowen's grin widened. "What does Damiir think about that?"

Maralla had birthed Damiir's first son three years ago, and even that had been a source of long debate in their unusual family. Though Tipori and Maralla had many childbearing years left, their human husband Damiir was in his early fifties now.

Maralla's nose wrinkled. "He's been no help at all, of course. Last week, he said he missed having a baby in our bed."

To her own surprise, Orowen chuckled. Joy felt so peculiar after its long absence. "I suppose I won't prescribe any more contraceptive tea."

Her sister's glare could have curdled milk.

The lift wobbled to a halt at the top of the platform, and their group filed off into a hollow carved in the side of the plateau. A narrow tunnel wound around the freight shaft to the next lift.

Maralla linked arms with Orowen and leaned in conspiratorially. "I suspect my mates will have their hands full soon. Riisii says Anya is moving back home, and Zakaari is going to meet someone."

"Zakaari?" Her oldest nephew was a handsome boy with a long history of promiscuity despite being only seventeen. Orowen glanced toward Riisii at the front of their group. "Did she say who?"

"*Aon.* You know how she is. No one can ask her a question and expect a straight answer."

Such was the nature of a seer, especially one as talented as Riisii. Still, the thought of who might finally tame Zakaari Evallier occupied Orowen enough that the last two lift rides passed by in a blur.

"It's so good to see you happy again, Devoted." Sam met them with a smile, and settled down between Magnus and Rylan in the wagon that would take them through the cliffside town of Lios'ama and into the city of Starlight.

A subtle shift occurred in her companions' demeanors. The weight of all their eyes sobered Orowen, a reminder that something catastrophic had happened, that she'd started a war with a more powerful nation, and now they were all likely to die.

She swallowed hard.

"Orowen," Kendi murmured, taking her hand in his. "Please don't be so hard on yourself."

She gave his fingers a squeeze and looked out across the sprawl of tents leading into the city, but couldn't shake the melancholy a second time.

The tents gave way to small dwellings made of wood and thatch and bigger buildings made of stone. People of all races crowded the roads. Starlight's main street ran from the Temple of Life to the central square. The wagon bounced along the cobbled stretch and stopped outside the council hall. Orowen waited until the others had disembarked before reaching for Kendi's hand and climbing down herself.

Riisii stared down the road at the Temple, tilting her head.

Orowen paused. "Is something wrong?"

"No, Aunt Wen." The seer blinked furiously and smiled. "The fire will be an accident."

Orowen nodded, took a step, then paused again when she processed the words. "What fire, *neime*?"

Riisii didn't seem to hear her. She strode toward the one-story building after the others, humming an unfamiliar tune.

Unlike her father, who Saw only seconds or minutes into the future, Riisii's Foresight could predict events weeks or months in advance, often giving them time to sidestep disasters with careful planning. Orowen would suggest more attention be paid to the Temple candles, incense, and braziers in the coming weeks.

"I worry about that girl." Kendi watched Riisii trail Maralla and Magnus into the council hall. "I worry about all you Evallier women."

He looked about to say more, but the moment passed, and Orowen thanked the pantheon for his silence. They'd already said all there was to say. Now their leaders would decide her fate.

The council hall was one long room built after the Skriian tribal style, with a fire pit running its length and vents in the roof to disperse the smoke. The air was thick with the scent of burning wood and animal skins. A door to one side led to their largest saphyrum cache. On the other side was the audience chamber, equipped with a few dozen rows of chairs. Three men occupied the head table, one bored, one calm, one irritated.

Old Jerinoch Bevausecc banged his pipe against the tabletop and mumbled to himself as he packed more dohanni into the bowl.

Tipori's vulpine features were as fine as ever, though new streaks of gray lightened his dark beard and shoulder-length hair. His saphyrum earring glinted in the firelight as his violet gaze slid from Maralla to Orowen and back, no doubt communicating with his wife in a way only those married nearly forty years could.

Koraani drummed his fingers on the table, his lavender skin drawn taut over smooth cheekbones and a triangular jaw. In the seventeen years since his sister Nerimoria's disappearance, his joy had grown thin, and his time as an Alliaansi leader had only thickened his spite.

Both chairs flanking the trio sat empty. One would have been Cheralach's; the other belonged to Nemaala. But because the former Astenpori matriarch spent most of her time looking after Aon'In, her absence today was no surprise. Koraani's mate Ashaara, and Damiir, with his scribe's quill and ink, stood on opposing sides of the head table.

There was a moment of silence as Orowen's companions took seats in the audience. Magnus stood before the council, and Kendi took a position to Magnus's left. Orowen remained standing at the back of the room, her hands clasped over her tattered dress.

Koraani stared openly at Magnus for a long moment. Orowen finally exhaled when he sat back, forgoing commentary on the state of the man's face.

"Well, on with it." Jerinoch lit his pipe with a nearby candle and puffed a smoke ring. He coughed and pounded his chest. "We've already heard the story a dozen ways. I would hear it from you, First Officer Gibbons. How did my brother die?"

Magnus bowed his head, then recounted the events of the last two months. Their failed supply run and capture, Cheralach's death and Magnus's disfigurement, the destruction of the School, Alar's search for the Guild student from Cheralach's visions, and their flight from Fawn's Breath.

At the end of Magnus's report, Tipori broke the heavy silence. "We are fortunate you've all returned safely."

Koraani nodded. "I think we can all agree war with the sorcerers was inevitable."

"That debate is a nonissue." Tipori looked back at Magnus. "Until we can hold an election for Cheralach's seat, First Officer, are you prepared to step into his role?"

"Yes, *Amaa*. And the governor's seat as well, if necessary."

Bold of him. Orowen didn't hide her surprise. Magnus truly was intent upon following in Cheralach's footsteps.

"You're a little late for that," Jerinoch said. "Tipori's already filled that seat."

Magnus inclined his head. "Understood, *Amaa*."

Tipori's look to him was something akin to an apology. He straightened. "I know preparing for war takes precedence. There will be plenty of discussion over how to protect our cities with so few resources. But I also want to prepare a vigil to honor those lost to us in Ryost and Fawn's Breath. I think it will give us all some closure."

A wonderful idea. Orowen nearly voiced an offer to assist with preparations at the Temple before Tipori's gaze found hers. He seemed to look *through* her for a moment, the way Riisii had stared at the Temple. Then his face crumpled.

Magnus cleared his throat. "There's one other matter that should be addressed, *Amaa*."

Tipori had Seen it coming. A sour taste flooded Orowen's mouth. Maralla turned in her seat, her eyes pleading for Orowen to reconsider, to turn her course, before Magnus could utter the words that would condemn her to the sword.

Perhaps she *was* being foolish—

*Charlatan...*

Her own inner voice, forbidding and intrusive, slipped down her spine like ice. *Oathbreaker...*

Orowen steeled her resolve. This was the right course. This must be done.

"Orowen wishes to be charged for her part in the School of High Sorcery's collapse." Magnus motioned to Kendi. "Commander Emaaris wishes to contest those charges and force a trial."

Jerinoch's pipe went slack against his teeth. Tipori lowered his head.

Koraani's face twitched into a mask of rage. "That is ridiculous. We don't have time for this."

An expected response, and one she'd prepared for. Orowen strode into the long aisle between chairs. "*Amaa*, if I may speak."

Jerinoch took his pipe from his mouth. "I should hope you'd care to explain yourself, Devoted."

"I broke my oath as a healer and opened an Aetherian rift beneath the Guild's school. I did this knowing the repercussions. I provoked the attack on Fawn's Breath. Because of me, hundreds of people have died." She held up a hand when Kendi tried to interject. "If I were a soldier in our army, would you not bring the full weight of Alliaansi law down on my head?"

"The circumstances were not as black and white as the priestess makes them seem," Kendi argued. "I have witnesses ready to give their testimony—"

"This is not a tribunal, Commander." Koraani beckoned to Ashaara. A sleek pelt of white innix fur trailed behind the mastermind as she glided to her mate's side. "We will know your thoughts and put this matter to rest."

Orowen hadn't prepared for Ashaara, but planning wouldn't have helped anyway. A mastermind as skilled as she could expose lies and extract truth with no more than a glance.

Ashaara's stormy gaze settled on her. Her violet eyes slanted inward toward a thin nose, and her chin and cheekbones were sharper than Tipori's axes. She wore her white hair in a high tail flowing freely down her back rather than in traditional Syljian braids.

She might have been intimidating to anyone who hadn't grown up with her in Astenpor. Orowen stood firm, expecting to feel the mastermind's presence wading through her thoughts at any moment.

But after a mere six heartbeats, Ashaara looked at Koraani. "The priestess is drowning in her guilt. She still suffers Mage's Folly and believes Saolanni has left her for breaking her oath. By seeking punishment, she hopes to atone and regain her power."

All the heat left Orowen's body.

Jerinoch puffed his pipe, and smoke rolled out of his mouth. "Well, you know better than any of us that Mage's Folly takes time to heal. The gods wouldn't take your magic, Devoted. That's preposterous."

With her innermost thoughts laid bare before the council, Orowen's composure slipped. "My assertions still stand," she snapped, curling her fists. "I'm the reason this war began, and I must be held accountable."

"No one blames you, Devoted." Sam spoke up, rising from her seat.

Rylan rose, too, his hand resting on Sam's chair. "We know you would've never done it on purpose. You're the reason we made it out of Ryost alive."

"You didn't start anything the sorcerers wouldn't have themselves," Tipori agreed. "They've been seeking a path to war with us for years."

A stone settled in Orowen's chest. She looked from one earnest face to the next, fighting back the mounting urge to scream. How easily they could overlook the detestable thing she had done. It was like Ixriia in so many ways, only back then, her penance had been easier. She'd killed soldiers in war, not innocent children. She'd been given the chance to turn her course, to focus her efforts on saving lives, not taking them, and she'd squandered it.

Blood pounded in her temples.

The war had begun with her. Perhaps it could end with her as well.

"If the Alliaansi leadership will not hold me accountable," Orowen spoke slowly, enunciating every word, "perhaps the Sorcerers' Guild will."

The room erupted into chaos.

Chairs scraped and voices rose and something fell into the fire pit, sending up swirling embers. Maralla shot out of her seat and stormed down the aisle. "Don't you dare."

Tipori and Koraani were also on their feet. Even Jerinoch rose, hands braced on the table. The tiniest sliver of grim satisfaction flickered through Orowen's awareness at Tipori's surprise. It wasn't often anyone could catch her brother-in-law off guard.

Maralla seized her arms. "Have you lost your scabbing mind?"

Orowen stared beyond her sister's fury, ignoring the cacophony of protests from the audience. She nearly lost her nerve when Kendi turned to her, staggering as if she'd struck him. His look of horror crumbled into one of betrayal.

It gutted her. Without healing magic, it seemed she could only hurt the ones she loved.

Tainted. She was tainted. How cruel she must be to have strung him along like a prisoner tied to a fast-moving cart. A more merciful heart would cut him loose. Eyes burning, Orowen tore her gaze from his.

Tipori strode around the table with a quick glance toward Riisii. "Orowen," he said, as if trying to pacify a wild mare, "do you really believe the Guild will stop the fighting if you turn yourself in?"

Maralla's grip on her tightened. "Think, *neime*. They're more likely to kill you before you ever reach one of the mages in power."

Their words stuck fast to Orowen's web of doubt. But if she could explain it was all an accident...

No, they were right. Too much blood had been shed already. The mages wouldn't just call off their invasion and pull back over the mountains. Orowen clamped her mouth shut around the pained noise forming in her throat. There was no way to spare her people.

Kendi started toward her, but Magnus stopped him with a hand on his arm and turned to Tipori. "Our laws are clear. If Kendi contests the charges Orowen has submitted, I would rather try her here than see her executed by the Guild."

"There's no need for a trial," Koraani said.

Orowen gaped. "But *Amaa*—"

"We have heard the accounts." Koraani lowered himself back into his seat. "You acted in the defense of others while fleeing an enemy prison. A prison in which an Alliaansi leader was dismembered and executed without cause. Others have corroborated this story. That is enough to acquit you of all charges."

Orowen shook her head. Only her sister's steady hands kept her legs from buckling. *Please*, she wanted to beg. *You don't understand.*

No amount of prayer had alleviated her guilt. She'd knelt at Mira's altar until her knees bled. She'd burned incense in Saolanni's name until the smoke left her lungs raw. She needed this—*needed* to be punished.

"We are at war, *neime*." The patient look Tipori leveled on her was maddening. Orowen's fingers hooked into claws. Mira's mercy, she could have torn out her own hair. "We must focus our efforts on survival, and we'll need every healer we have."

"I have no magic!"

*And I'm nothing without it.*

The knot in her throat tore loose with a vicious sob. Distantly, Orowen felt Maralla's arms wrap around her. She clung to her even as she glared past her at Tipori, at Koraani, pleading with Magnus and Jerinoch to speak in her favor.

This was her last chance to atone. Her last chance to appeal to Saolanni and redeem herself in her goddess's eyes. If this didn't work, she... she didn't know what else to do.

Once more, Kendi started for her, but Tipori stepped into his path. He strode down the aisle toward them. "It will return. You must be patient."

Orowen scowled. "Does your Sight tell you that, or is it just wishful thinking?"

Ever the portrait of control, Tipori remained steadfast. "In the meantime, your students still expect to learn from you. You're confined to the Temple and Havensguard until further notice. There will be guards posted to ensure you comply."

He thought she was a danger to herself. Her hands closed on Maralla's leathers and tears seared trails down her face.

Saolanni's grace, he was probably right.

Maralla cupped the back of her head. "We are here for you. You're going to get through this, *ru'toriia*."

Little sister. Maralla always knew just where to strike.

As Orowen collapsed into the nearest chair, Kendi finally broke free of the attempts to stay him. He was at her side and seizing her in a fierce hug within seconds.

She didn't deserve him. She didn't deserve any of them.

Orowen might have buried her face in shame, if not for Kendi's near-crushing hold on her.

Koraani cleared his throat. "If there's nothing else—"

"There is one more thing." Riisii's soft voice drew an annoyed glance from Koraani, but she wasn't looking at him. She was smiling at her father.

"What is it, *enniia*?" Tipori's brows furrowed.

Riisii's grin widened. "The sorceress has arrived."

# CHAPTER FIFTEEN

## DAEYA

"Again, Yaya. Again!"

Daeya's arms and lower back ached from lifting two-year-old Ezra, but she couldn't resist that enormous grin. Breathing a laugh, she slipped her hands under the boy's arms. "Alright, alright. Last time, though, or you'll break Yaya."

The boy squealed his delight. Daeya counted down from three in Syljian. "*Taas... viio... nuu!*"

She hoisted him high, his chubby cheeks framed by blue sky and evergreens. Ezra screamed, clutching his hands to his belly, legs flying free as Daeya spun him around. When she set him back on the hard-packed ground, he wobbled and reached his arms up. "Again! Again!"

Her arm twinged from Jack's crossbow bolt. She had avoided exposing her runes for this long, despite the near-encounter with Alar. The last thing she needed was to rip that injury open and face more demands to let someone treat it.

With an apologetic smile, she ruffled the boy's white curls. "No more, *ru'amii.*"

Ezra whined, earning a scathing look from his sister, Niam, and aggrieved groans from their neighbors, Sessiri and Helenia.

Daeya caught Alar's smirk and stepped over a downed branch to reach his side. His hand found hers, and lightness fluttered through her.

Things had been different between them in the days since they'd rescued Ezra and the others. Alar was softer, more affectionate, and quicker to laugh. He was also kinder to Ravlok, despite the monk's steady retreat into his tome. In return, Daeya polished up on her Syljian, and did her best to learn the customs that would help her fit in among his people.

Alar nodded toward Starlight Plateau in the distance. "You think you're ready?"

She eyed the three deep channels cut into the cliffside. Rift wards guarded the plateau from invaders, so the wooden lifts were the only means of access.

They had come into view early this morning—the only time in the last several days Ravlok had looked up from his tome with any real interest. His distraction was a familiar comfort; back in Ryost, he would get lost in books for hours at a time, and she often had to remind him to eat.

He'd been eager to explain the marvel of Duerwisti engineering. As the spools turned, one lift went up and another came down, with freight or ballast placed in the center channel. The two outside channels carried people, and the entire system was powered by winches that were turned by mules. A pair of spools dotted the cliff face every thirty spans or so, and none sat idle for more than a few minutes. Traffic on and off the plateau, it seemed, was more organized than the rumors claimed.

Daeya looked back at Alar and brushed a lock of hair behind his ear. "*Ciir.*"

His cheeks darkened. Whether from her touch or the way the Syljian affirmation came off her tongue, it was hard to say.

Behind them, Jack groaned and spat on the ground. Daeya suppressed a grin, and Alar's expression soured. He said nothing more until they reached the lifts a while later. When the forest opened onto a section of rock-strewn grassland, he released her hand and turned to the rest of their group.

"I'll need to send word to the council before I can bring Daeya up. You're all welcome to go ahead of us. There will be others at the top who can help you find refuge."

"*Taapad tiik*, Alar." Helenia still spoke around a split lip, but the herbal salve Ravlok had made for her burns helped her move easier. She squeezed Daeya's arm. "And thank you, *amii*. We are in your debt."

"No." Daeya mirrored Helenia's gesture. "There's no score between us." It was the least she could do after her people ran them out of Fawn's Breath.

*Her people.*

They weren't her people anymore.

Helenia arched a rune-lined eyebrow. "Well, if you're ever in need, I hope you think of me."

She pulled away, and Sessiri took her place. Shorter than Daeya by only a fingerspan or two, Sessiri leaned in until their foreheads touched. "*Saonis taob'ruh tiik doros.*"

Gods give you wisdom. A common farewell among the Syljians. Daeya pulled back and fumbled the expected response, 'Gods guide your steel.'

"*Saonis evas'ruh tiik nalii.*"

"*Naali,*" Sessiri corrected, drawing out the 'a' sound. "*Nalii* means sheep, and I'm afraid I don't have any of those."

Daeya's cheeks warmed. "Apologies."

"You'll get it. You already speak Syljian better than Alar."

"Hey." Alar feigned offense.

Sessiri stepped away with a wink, and Niam brought Ezra in for a hug. "No go, Yaya."

"We'll see each other again," Daeya reassured him. "Be good for your sister."

She spared a tender smile for Niam, who had been mistreated most of all by the sorcerers. What little remorse Daeya might have felt for killing them had dissolved after she'd found Niam half-frozen by the river, desperately trying to scrub all traces of their abuse away.

Niam didn't smile in return. The solemn-faced older girl seemed to have gone mute as well. She only dipped her chin, stared into Daeya's eyes for a moment, and hurried after the others.

Daeya's jaw tightened. Those men had gotten what they deserved. She might have known kindness from some of her instructors—Master Ulrich, Rizzy Tallion—but they couldn't all be blind to the ways the Guild mistreated others. Worse, they were complicit, if they knew and yet still allowed such things to happen. Between the massacre at Fawn's Breath and the brutality she'd witnessed in the forest, she would never ally herself with the Guild again.

Three approaching soldiers peeled off to address the refugees. The other two approached Alar, speaking Syljian.

As they conversed, Daeya elbowed Ravlok. "I heard you speaking Draconic last night."

He snapped out of his examination of the cliff lifts. "You actually recognized it?"

She nodded. In truth, she'd marveled both at her ability to understand him and how fast he was picking the language up. "But don't ask me how I know it. I've only heard it in my dreams."

"From Telerion."

"Yes."

"I think I understand why you've been dreaming of him. There was something in the book." Growing ever more animated, Ravlok opened his tome and flipped to a blank page. He drew a circle with his finger and looked up at her, attempting to balance the massive book on one arm. "I keep seeing this symbol repeated." He pointed to something else Daeya couldn't see. "This word here appears to be the ancient root for 'dream' in the Dessian trade tongue. And this one"—he gestured to another blank spot—"means 'connection' or 'bond.'"

He looked up at her expectantly.

Daeya frowned. "Dream bond?"

"Exactly. Whatever bond you're supposed to make with him, I think you might have already started it." He lowered his voice, glancing toward Jack and Alar before adding, "That should help us find him."

A hollow formed in Daeya's stomach. The tug from Telerion had grown stronger as they moved north and lessened again when they turned east and crossed the Taaru'Kallii. Proximity must be a factor, and they could certainly use that to track him down, but it sounded like Ravlok was suggesting they abandon their companions.

"Rav, Alar said he would help us. He showed us the Three Sisters, and he said the mountain we need isn't far from Starlight. We can trust him."

The excitement drained from Ravlok's face. "I'm not so sure, Daeya."

"He knows how important it is." She was careful to keep her voice even. Ravlok wanted her to go to Draeconis so badly, he must have forgotten why she'd agreed to meet Alar's people in the first place. "As soon as we speak to the Alliaansi about my family, he'll take us there."

Ravlok didn't look convinced. He'd been so certain weeks ago. The only difference now was Caelyn's warning—and, she supposed, Jack's troubling dreams. The thief had never mentioned them, but the dark circles under his eyes suggested they hadn't gone away, and he'd been spending more time away from camp at night. She'd tried to talk to him about it once while he was frantically rummaging through his pack, but he'd snapped at her to mind her business before resuming his search for... something. She hadn't bothered to ask what.

Daeya sighed. She couldn't be upset with Ravlok. Not when it was such a blessing that he cared at all. "Remember, you asked me to believe him in Orthovia. Master Ulrich told me to trust him." She nudged him in the ribs. "And two of the smartest people I know can't be wrong."

Ravlok winced. "I pray you're right."

The soldiers departed with Alar's message, and the sun was high in the southern sky before they returned. Daeya sat up from where she'd settled beside Ravlok, who was practicing Draconic while she translated or corrected his pronunciation.

"Koraani's pissed," the shorter soldier said. He thrust his cleft chin toward Daeya and brandished the flimsiest pair of silver manacles she'd ever seen. "He says she's not entering the city unless she's spellbound."

Alar scowled. "No."

His curt response shocked the soldiers. Gods, it surprised Daeya, too. She pushed herself to her feet. Ravlok banished his tome in a puff of black mist and followed suit. As they approached, the taller soldier studied her from beneath graying eyebrows, setting her on edge.

"She came here willingly, not as a prisoner," Alar said.

"That's the problem." The older soldier shrugged. "She came here willingly. Who says she's not a spy?"

"She's not a spy," Ravlok snapped. "The sorcerers turned on her and tried to have her executed."

"Where is Commander Emaaris?" Alar asked. "He sent us to retrieve her. I'm sure he can clear this up."

Both men straightened. The manacles clinked in the younger one's hands. "He's the one who suggested binding her. Koraani wasn't going to allow her in at all."

Daeya tilted her head, examining the spellbinders. How could they think those dainty scraps of metal could hold her? Even if the chain hadn't looked like it would break under the slightest pressure, she doubted the lock would stand up to a pick.

The argument continued; the soldiers kept stealing glances at her, as if expecting her to shoot off fire bolts at any moment. Daeya gnawed her lip while Ravlok sidled closer to her—close enough to act if the men tried to bind her by force. The possibility sent a jolt through her. If she was taken prisoner, their leaders might refuse to hear any requests regarding her father or Murtagh.

Maybe a show of good faith could buy their trust.

"...then send for Orowen," Alar was saying. "She can—"

"Orowen's not allowed off the plateau," the older man cut in. "She's confined to the Temple and Havensguard until Tipori says otherwise."

"What? Why?"

Ravlok paled. "What happened?"

Orowen—the healer whose absence Alar had lamented when Daeya refused to let him or Ravlok treat her wound. Orowen, he'd grumbled, would have known the right thing to say.

The soldier shrugged. "All I know is she's not allowed to leave the Temple unless it's to return home or attend council."

Alar rubbed his temples. "This is insanity—"

"I'll wear them."

Heads snapped toward Daeya.

She nodded toward the spellbinders. "If it will put their minds at ease, I'll wear them. I'm not here to spy." She met the older soldier's gaze. "I'm here to request refuge for my family. If this is what I have to do to secure it, then I will."

The man's face didn't soften. His eyes flicked toward Alar. "Do I have your leave, psionist?"

Alar's face twitched. "By all means."

The soldier took the binders from his companion and approached Daeya. She held out her wrists, and the rings snapped closed. Dainty as they looked, the metal weighed cold and heavy against her skin. Arcane scrollwork encircled each cuff. She didn't feel any different, but if these worked the same as Guild binders, they would impart a steady trickle of saphyric energy. Not enough to be useful, but enough to prevent her from channeling it outward to cast spells.

Satisfied, the soldier reached for her elbow. Alar stepped between them. "I'll take her from here."

Without waiting for a response, he tugged Daeya forward and shouldered past the guards. Ravlok and Jack fell in behind them.

"I'm sorry about this." Alar's expression remained dark as they strode toward the lifts. "You won't be spellbound long, I promise."

A worker on the rock face shouted for the closest lift to lower. Alar offered his hand to help her onto the platform, and their lift lurched upward. Daeya rested her bound hands on the guardrail for balance.

Beside her, Ravlok gripped one of the overhead chains and tugged on his beard. He looked increasingly troubled as the trees shrank below them.

Ravlok had heard much about the tent cities of Starlight. Travelers passing through the monastery always painted the bleakest images of the place. They spoke of hundreds of refugees huddled in crates and lean-tos, barely surviving against the bitter cold. The god Laangor featured heavily in their stories of sickness, fleshrot, and famine. Hopeless tales of children fighting over scraps and moth-eaten blankets always led to days full of prayer and meditation.

On those days, tithes were collected for Silonas to inspire good fortune. Stories were told to honor Tiior and encourage wisdom. Incense was burned in Delvin's name as a call for justice to prevail—a prayer normally intended as a slight against Starlight's leadership.

But seeing the tents in person, the stories couldn't be any further from the truth.

There were no lean-tos or crates, but massive communal tents made from dozens of animal hides stitched together. Sloped sides and circular profiles provided a buffer against wind from every direction, and flues allowed for braziers or cook fires inside them. Each tent housed between ten and twenty refugees.

The people were dirty, and the dull pallor of saphyrum sickness afflicted many, but no one appeared to be starving or deathly ill. Most were even in good spirits, offering smiles and waves to Alar as their wagon trundled toward Starlight.

Alar returned the waves and emptied Daeya's bag of saphyrum into the hands of three dozen Syljians, whose coloring improved within seconds of receiving the beads. Though others were obviously disappointed, they didn't swarm the cart begging for more, nor did they fight over the spoils once the wagon rolled on.

Tents gave way to communal houses, and those gave way to squat stone buildings. The tallest among them were still unimpressive by Ryost's standards, but the craftsmanship was remarkable for a city not quite thirty years old. Starlight was founded by the late Cheralach Bevausecc shortly after he joined forces with Nerimoria Alliaar and orchestrated the single largest exodus of Syljian and Eidosinian refugees from Guild territory.

Daeya, taking in every detail with wide eyes and parted lips, seemed just as impressed as he.

Alar tossed them a grin. "Welcome to Starlight."

"How is this possible?" Daeya asked Alar. "That stonework is masterful."

He shrugged. "We have connections."

Connections, indeed. Ravlok had recognized the markings on Daeya's spell-binders. Despite Alar's promises—and he'd made a lot of them recently—the Alliaansi wouldn't be removing those anytime soon. From his far-flung studies of all things arcane, Ravlok knew Rillanese slave binders when he saw them. Designed by master artificers, they were said to be inescapable. His hand itched to put that claim to the test.

Regardless of Kendi and Orowen's good intentions, Daeya had just been taken hostage.

Why hadn't he warned her about this? Had his studies of the tome been so all-consuming that he hadn't realized the very real danger he'd put her in?

Some guardian he was shaping up to be. Maybe Madame was right; no matter how many books and scrolls he stole, no son of a courtesan was meant to rise beyond his next patron's bed.

His fists clenched in his lap as if to seize the thought before it could take root. Eyes closing, he breathed in.

*You would not allow a man with muddy boots into your home,* Yonfé's voice rose in him with the gentle warmth of the morning sun, *so why allow him to tread with muddy boots through your mind?*

Thoughts of Madame had plagued him recently, a little voice in his head whispering untruths that only meditation and strict control of his aura could stave off. Even after all these years—after all his work with Yonfé to move past her cruel lessons—she could still make him doubt his worth.

His fingers relaxed as he breathed out and opened his eyes, but the tension in his shoulders didn't abate.

Daeya glanced at him, her awe faltering. "What's wrong, Rav?"

*We shouldn't be here. You should be in Draeconis, far from people who would harm or imprison you. Far from Alar, who's clearly been using your heart to his advantage.*

He was sure of it now, but he had no proof. Only Alar's fake smiles that dissolved the moment Daeya looked away, and a constant itch in Ravlok's mind that something wasn't as it should be.

"Nothing."

"I thought monks weren't supposed to lie."

The hurt in her voice sobered him. He'd never made a habit of lying to her. It wasn't even like she'd blame him for the disaster they drew closer to with every turn of the wagon's wheels. Ravlok squeezed her knee. "We'll talk later." He glanced at Alar, who was watching them closely. "Just you and I."

Assuming she wasn't locked in a cell somewhere.

The wagon stopped beside a one-story building. Ravlok leaped down and assisted Daeya off the seat. Alar climbed down after her, still eyeing them, until the building's door swung open.

A Syljian woman stepped out. Her tapered ears arched away from her head, which tilted with a look reminiscent of the vulpine shixxies they'd encountered throughout the Northlands. Well-muscled for one so slight, her balance and easy gait suggested a familiarity with martial arts.

"Riisii," Alar said in greeting.

Riisii walked right past him. She stopped before Daeya and bowed. "Hello, dragon rider."

Ravlok's pack slipped from his fingers.

The woman caught the strap before it hit the cobbles. She held it out for him.

Stunned, Ravlok fumbled with the strap twice before retrieving it. "Thank you."

Riisii's attention never left Daeya. The trade language flowed off her tongue with flawless precision. "The council is anxious to meet you. I'm afraid they won't be very hospitable at first, but in most futures, you forgive them. I cannot wait for you to find Telerion."

Daeya recoiled, and Ravlok stepped closer to her, unsure whether to place himself between her and the Syljian. They had all agreed not to mention dragons or draegion to the Alliaansi right away. Since dragons were believed extinct and dragon riders were supposedly a fae tale, associating her with them wouldn't garner any favors.

Alar lifted a hand, but it didn't stem the excitable stream burbling from Riisii's mouth.

"Don't worry. I haven't told anyone else. In most futures, they don't believe me anyway. But *Peiaa* will believe you, when you're ready to tell him." She frowned. "At least, he's supposed to."

Ravlok's brows furrowed. "How did you—"

"Oh, I See things," Riisii broke in with a smile. Her amusement vanished like quicksilver. She seemed to stare past them for a moment, then shook her head. The smile returned. "Lots of things. Have you translated the ritual yet?"

Ravlok blinked. Who *was* this woman? "What ritual?"

"You have the book, don't you?"

"I—" He might have asked what book she meant, but the answer was obvious. "Yes."

"Oh, good." The crease in her forehead smoothed over. "Hurry up, will you? That becomes important."

Ravlok rubbed the back of his neck, feeling chastised, but unsure why. "I'll get right on that. I think."

"Excellent."

Alar stepped closer. "Daeya, Ravlok, this is—"

Riisii pivoted on her heel and slapped him in the face.

Alar's head snapped sideways. He cupped his cheek. "Agh! What was that for?"

Riisii shook out her hand and flexed her fingers. "You'll know once you've done it, but I won't be there to witness it. Now, if you don't mind, Koraani is getting impatient."

She turned and strode back toward the meeting hall, humming a disjointed melody. Ravlok stared after her, wondering what in Ordeolas's name just happened.

Jack stepped around the wagon to join them. "Nothing like a visit from Starlight's resident lunatic."

Eccentric or not, the sound of Riisii's palm cracking across Alar's face had been so satisfying that she'd instantly bought Ravlok's affection. Whatever Alar was about to do, Ravlok was sure he'd deserve that.

"She's not normally so violent," Alar grumbled, still rubbing his cheek.

"She's a seer?" Daeya asked.

"Yes, and a good one. Some would say too good. She Sees so many futures, they often get confused."

"She didn't seem confused to me," Ravlok said, earning a scowl from Jack.

Daeya stared after her. "That must make predicting the future hard."

"Trying to alter it is worse," Alar said. "These days, she just lets things happen as they will."

Riisii opened the door to the meeting hall and beckoned to them.

"Well, come on." Alar sighed and started for the door. "Let's get this over with."

# Chapter Sixteen

## Alar

The council hall smelled of woodsmoke and dohanni, and its warmth was stifling after so long in the autumn chill. Alar shed his cloak by the door, then strode along the fire trench to the head table, guiding Daeya by one arm.

Magnus sat in Cheralach's old seat beside Jerinoch. Nemaala's place on Koraani's other side was empty. A sizable audience had gathered in the chairs flanking the aisle, Kendi and Orowen among them. Jack dropped into a seat beside them. Ravlok remained pinned to Daeya's back.

Orowen, pale-faced and red-eyed, wiped her cheeks with a kerchief and gave Alar an encouraging nod as he led both Eidosinians to the front of the room.

Ashaara's voice spilled into his mind like water over rock. *"Welcome home, apprentice."*

*"It's good to be home, Amaa."*

The mastermind stepped out of the smoke, her dagger-sharp gaze on Daeya. *"What have you brought us?"*

Alar's stomach clenched. He released Daeya's elbow and she glanced at him uncertainly, but he kept his expression hard and his gaze trained forward.

*"An asset,"* he answered. *"This is Councilor Lucius Gregory's star pupil."*

He clasped his hands, only half-listening to Tipori make introductions while Ashaara sifted through his thoughts. Whisper-soft as her presence was, Alar shivered. It had been a long while since a mastermind's touch had laid his thoughts bare.

Koraani drummed his fingers on the table and side-eyed Tipori. "I think we can dispense with these pleasantries, *ashaan*. I would know why Alar insisted on bringing an enemy into our home."

"First Officer Gibbons said they sent him to find the girl in my brother's visions." Jerinoch gestured toward Magnus with his pipe. "Isn't that right, my boy?"

"Yes." Magnus studied Daeya, his single eye narrowing. "How old are you, child?"

Alar had never explained the visions to her, but Ravlok had drawn parallels between them and Tiior's involvement more than once. Despite Alar's gentle pressure on the monk's mind, steering him away from more treacherous decisions of late, he'd allowed Ravlok to at least make Daeya aware of them.

Daeya shifted, spellbinders clinking. "Sixteen, sir."

Magnus nodded to the rest of the council. "She matches the description Cheralach gave Orowen."

*"She will fetch a handsome price."* Ashaara's approval lapped at Alar's awareness. *"Well done."*

"The question remains," Tipori said, "what are we to do with her?" His focus shifted to the audience. "Devoted, it's my understanding Cheralach's visions were never interpreted clearly. Is that correct?"

Orowen's voice broke on her first attempt to speak. She cleared her throat. "*Ciir, Amaa.* I believe he withheld much of what he saw from me."

Alar swallowed. "Visions aside, *Amaa*, I have promised her safety here in Starlight. She's agreed to join our cause." His response was as much for his mentor as the others.

Koraani's fingers stilled on the tabletop. "A promise that wasn't yours to make. Nor was Cheralach's mission sanctioned by this council. The lack of discipline the fool has inspired is appalling."

Daeya's shoulders stiffened. Conflicting emotions stormed across Ravlok's aura, and a chair scraped behind them. Alar dared a look over his shoulder to find Kendi pulling a red-faced Sam back down in her seat. The commander murmured something into her ear.

Tipori frowned. "It's true, Cheralach did act without our approval. But he was also a free man, able to do as he chose."

"And he chose to waste our troops and resources." Koraani scoffed. "Tell me, why would a sorceress want to join the Alliaansi?"

Jerinoch smirked. "I could think of a few reasons."

Alar reminded himself to breathe. Despite Jerinoch's facetious nature, his support would be vital. As a former Guild sorcerer himself, his contribution to the Alliaansi could sway the others to Daeya's side.

"Her peers tried to have her executed," Alar told them. "Her mentor also threatened harm to her father if she disobeyed him."

Ashaara's curiosity was piqued. She spoke aloud this time. "And yet, she is here. Why?"

Alar hadn't been bluffing that night he told Ravlok the masterminds could ensure Daeya's honesty. Ashaara should have slipped through her wards and known her inside and out by now. But if she was asking questions...

Unease coiled in his gut.

"They gave me no choice." Daeya lifted her eyes from the floor. "It was come here, or hang in the gallows under false charges."

"And what were the charges?" Tipori asked.

"Use of Aetherian magic and consorting with the Alliaansi."

His eyebrows rose. "A pity they were false. Another Aetherian could be of use to us."

As an Aetherian himself, Tipori would surely test her for potential later. He glanced toward Riisii, then leaned back in his chair, as if the proceedings no longer interested him. The expansion of his aura, however, suggested awareness. Expectation.

He was baiting her.

Alar would have given anything for a telepathic link with Daeya to warn her, but he could only watch as she stepped forward, right into Tipori's trap.

"I'm the youngest mage in Guild history." She straightened. "The strongest in Lucius Gregory's entourage. Before my rival framed me for crimes I didn't commit, I was expected to replace him as Gregory's right hand. I *can* be of use to you."

Tipori's aura pulsed with triumph. He nodded for her to continue. Alar clutched his hands to steady them. A precarious line existed between Daeya proving herself an asset and rendering herself a threat.

"I have knowledge that can help the Alliaansi win the war."

Magnus regarded her warily, and Jerinoch paused in tamping his dohanni. A dangerous gleam appeared in Koraani's eyes.

Warmth drained from Alar's face. Only one thing followed that look.

"Oh?" Jerinoch made a show of searching for something, patting down the front of his tunic. "Pray tell, before the wolves sink their teeth into you."

*Wastelands.*

Daeya's tone didn't falter. "Supply lines. Saphyrum storehouses. Secret mines."

Alar closed his eyes. Even though he wasn't a pious man, he prayed then. For all the good it would do, he prayed for Daeya to stop talking. If Ashaara couldn't slip through her wards, there was only one other option. They had to be sure.

"I know troop maneuvers, battle strategies, even the techniques employed in forging their weapons and armor."

"Daeya..." Ravlok warned. He shot an accusing glare at Alar that rivaled the sun for heat.

*Cursed, bleeding Wastelands.*

Koraani rose from his chair, gaze leveled on Ashaara.

Alar reached out to her. "Amaa, *I would speak with you.*"

"Any information I have is yours," Daeya went on. "All I ask in exchange is refuge for my father, Angus McVen, and my cousin Murtagh. They live in Ryost, and I'm afraid my being here has put them in grave danger."

Ironic, really, the things that came out of her mouth.

*"What troubles you, apprentice?"*

*"I know she can't be touched by psionics, but—"*

*"Anyone can be touched by psionics."* Ashaara's amusement was a cooling draft across his fraying nerves. *"You know this."*

*"She is enchanted somehow."* Alar had hoped Tipori's enhanced spellbinders would dampen whatever arcane anomaly kept him from seeing Daeya's aura, but they'd made no difference. He had to be extremely careful now. *"I couldn't slip past her wards."*

*"Any mental ward can be broken with pressure applied in the right place."*

*"I didn't want to hurt her. Respectfully, Amaa, I would caution against using psionics. She wants to help."*

Annoyance rippled across their connection. *"I did not train you to be an idealistic fool. If she is warded, there is a reason. You have been deceived."*

*"No. I know her. She's being truthful."* Alar gritted his teeth. "Amaa, *this isn't the way.*"

*"She is a* bashiin, *and a sorceress."*

Fast as a viper, Ashaara struck. Her mind shattered the walls he'd built around his feelings like a bolt fired through glass. Alar gasped, the twin needle points at his temples blurring his vision. The truth of his feelings flowed out of him like blood from a wound.

Daeya looked back at him, brows furrowing.

*"You care for her."* Ashaara's disappointment seeped into his bones.

There was no sense denying it. *"I do."*

*"Then you have been compromised."* Ashaara turned to Koraani. "Shall I take her here?"

Alar bristled. He spoke aloud, no longer able to contain himself. "She killed six of her own people to save ours last week. Three women and a child came into the city ahead of us this morning. Speak with them. They will vouch for her."

Ashaara touched Koraani's temple, establishing a mental link in preparation. With her psychic imperium of Daeya, she could transfer any of Daeya's memories to Koraani as she viewed them.

"There is no need," Koraani said. "We will see the truth of that in her memories."

Tipori scowled. "That isn't necessary. Her request seems reasonable."

"We do not have the resources to send another team into Ryost," Koraani snapped. "We will take what we need from her."

As if finally realizing what was about to happen, Daeya stepped back. "Now, wait a minute—"

"No!" Ravlok started for her, but Ashaara's telekinesis snared him mid-step, staying Alar's own urge to reach for Daeya.

Tipori abandoned his chair, his aura roiling with an air of menace so potent that Alar tasted Aether on his tongue. "Riisii, send for Zakaari. Have him find these newcomers. I would hear from them. Ashaara, release him."

Ravlok bared his teeth, straining against the mastermind's hold.

"Ashaara—"

Ashaara wafted away from Tipori, her eyes bright with excitement. Daeya shrank from her, backing right into Alar's chest. His hands closed on her shoulders.

"She doesn't answer to your command," Koraani reminded Tipori.

"This city is *my* jurisdiction. The refugees here are mine to protect."

"The sorceress is not a refugee. She is a prisoner of war."

"Alar..." Daeya pressed against him. "Please."

More knots formed in Alar's stomach, but there was nothing he could do. This precaution had kept them safe from spies for decades. "Daeya, listen to me. They're not going to let you out of this room unless they know for certain you mean us no harm—"

"You know I don't!" she sobbed.

"I know that." He forced his sympathy down and made a decision. Daeya had trusted him until now. She'd formed an attachment—one that he shared despite his attempts to curb it. He could use that to ease the trauma of an imperium. "But they don't. It's just to protect everyone."

Ashaara's presence breezed against his thoughts. Alar made no attempt to hide his intentions. The mastermind stopped three paces away, her eyes locked on his. *"You think you are ready?"*

His grip on Daeya turned possessive. *"If it's an imperium you want, then I will do it."*

*"There are risks."*

He didn't allow his resolve to waver. He knew the risks: nausea, dizziness, memory loss, and bleeding from the eyes or nose. More severely, if his hold on her wasn't absolute and she resisted him, he could fracture her mind. But Riisii's prophesying suggested Daeya walked out of here with her mind intact. The phantom sting of her palm against his face arose as the seer departed.

*"I accept the risks."*

*"Very well."* Ashaara folded her arms. *"Proceed."*

Steadying himself, Alar pressed his lips to Daeya's ear. "If you don't want her to do this, you have to let me inside your mind. I need you to lower your wards."

She turned in his arms to face him. "I didn't even know I had wards." Her voice strained around her tears. "Please, don't do this."

"I have to."

Her chains clinked as she pressed her hands flat against his chest. "There are things you shouldn't see. Not like this."

It wasn't surprising. As close as he'd allowed her to become, Alar still held his own secrets; of course she'd do the same.

He looked away. The audience's auras overlapped to form a singular quivering mass of anticipation. Rylan and Kendi had taken hold of Ravlok, who looked on in helpless rage.

Alar reclaimed his composure and looked back down at Daeya. "Do these things compromise you?"

"No. But you'll hate them. Because I hate them."

Curious. Alar drew a measured breath and let it out. "You can explain later. For now, let's just get through this."

Eyes glistening, Daeya bowed her head.

It was as close to consent as he was going to get. Alar wrapped one arm around her waist and lifted the other, placing three fingers against her temple. "Don't be afraid."

Her eyes fluttered closed, and for a moment, he worried she might faint. Then her face became granite. She bit her lip and went deathly still. Alar pressed inward.

But, as always, there was nothing where her mind should be. Not even a glimmer of an aura, the flicker of a thought, a twitch of emotional resonance. He pressed harder, and her muscles tensed beneath his fingers.

"Relax, Daeya. Relax your mind. Just let me in."

Her expression smoothed. Her body softened against his. Still nothing. Alar closed his eyes and delved deeper. He summoned his strength and *pushed* on that space.

He might as well have chucked a pebble into a rift.

Ashaara's mind brushed his, searching. A tremor of curiosity vibrated through her. *"All wards have seams. Go to the heart of the void, and you will find it."*

After a moment to orient himself, Alar obeyed. He spiraled down into the void.

Darkness engulfed him. A rift flashed before his mind, Val's body scraping stone as it sank into the mist, his voice echoing as if from beyond the grave: *Tell Finn I love her.*

Alar's heart seized in his throat—

*"Focus."*

Ashaara's stern rebuke wrenched him back. Something zinged across his senses, like flint against steel.

*"There. There, you have it."*

Daeya gasped.

Alar passed over that spot again, and his entire perception listed. Sparks scorched a trail across his awareness.

"Stop." Daeya tried to push him away. "That hurts."

He paused. "I'm—" *Sorry*, he meant to say.

*"The ward. Take it down."*

"It's hurting her."

*"Take it down,"* Ashaara growled, *"or I will."*

Indecision wrenched at him. He removed his hand from Daeya's temple and blinked his vision back into focus. "Daeya, please don't fight this."

"Let go!"

She struggled against him, and he tightened his grip. "I can't. This has to happen—"

"No, it doesn't," Tipori broke in. "Alar, stand down."

Ashaara's glare could have melted steel. *Take her, Alar.*

Alar's gaze flicked toward Koraani. At his commander's nod, he gave Tipori an apologetic look. He reached for Daeya's temple.

She slapped his fingers away. "No. I've been hurt enough"—Daeya planted her hands on his chest—"and this is *wrong*."

With all her strength, she shoved him backward.

Ashaara lunged.

Ravlok threw off Rylan and Kendi, too late. Ashaara seized Daeya's head in her hands.

Daeya *screamed.*

It happened so fast that Alar had barely righted himself before it was over.

Ashaara stumbled away, clutching her own temples. Shock reverberated across their psionic bond, strong enough to rattle Alar's teeth, if his jaw hadn't fallen to the floor. For nearly five years, he'd studied under Ashaara, and never once had she failed an imperium. Gasps and murmurs erupted from the audience. Men and women rose from their seats.

Heaving breaths blew through Daeya's teeth. She hastened toward Ravlok, her gallant defender. A sour taste coated Alar's tongue. Her violent struggle was still a phantom pressure against his skin, and sickness twisted his gut.

What had he done?

Ashaara stared, her aura wavering with barely restrained fury. "What manner of magic is this?" She crept forward like a chaagra with cornered prey. "There has never been a ward I could not break."

Daeya glared back, palms raised as if to cast despite the chain swinging from her binders. "Until now, I guess."

"You insolent brat—"

Tipori's voice cracked the air like thunder. "Enough!"

Alar flinched. The concussive force of the Aetherian's rage rippled outward like an earthquake, shaking the walls and floor. It left Alar's hair standing on end.

Tipori's molten gaze leveled on Koraani. "Recall your mastermind before I throw her out of my city."

Koraani hesitated, then called Ashaara off with a jerk of his chin. Even he wouldn't jeopardize their allegiance with the Alliaansi's wealthiest benefactor.

Ashaara's gaze swept Daeya from head to toe one last time. Ravlok stepped between them, glowering, as if his posturing could intimidate a mastermind. Alar felt a nagging sense that he should do something, but his feet remained rooted to the floor.

Tipori's deadly expression lingered until Ashaara returned to the shadows. Then his attention flicked toward the door, which opened and closed with a blast of frigid air. "Zakaari." He beckoned to his son. "Please bring our new guests before the council."

Alar ignored the appearance of Starlight's resident courtesan and tried to catch Daeya's eyes. She avoided him, of course, all too content to keep Ravlok between them. The monk's hand came to rest on her lower back, and a prickling sensation skittered across Alar's neck.

Ravlok tucked Daeya close and glared at him. Their telepathic link had long been severed, or Alar might have tried to explain himself. It was his duty as a psionist, not some sadistic desire to cause her pain, that had made him push her so hard. Still, guilt gnawed at him. He would speak to them as soon as this meeting was over.

Sessiri and Helenia trailed Zakaari to the front of the room, and behind them came Riisii.

Zakaari was a beardless reflection of his father, though he shared his older sister's pale lavender complexion. Overdressed in pristine cotton, black wool, and gray wolf's fur, his attire could have funded an entire night of drinking for his obnoxious little harem. Zakaari swiped his windblown black hair from his tapered ears with one flamboyant gesture and winked at a young woman in the audience as he passed by. The arrogance in his violet eyes was just as grating as it was unearned.

Helenia's steps faltered as she took in the state of the council hall. A solemn determination sobered Sessiri. Both women's auras clung to their skin. Wary.

Tipori strode to the floor's center and addressed the newcomers. "*Iiren'hyvaa, amiien.* My apologies for interrupting your afternoon." He went on to request a full accounting of their encounter with the mages.

Their story was much the same as the one Alar had already heard. They'd been running from the Guild since Fawn's Breath, and they were separated from their band of refugees by sorcerers scouting near Kuma'Kiir. They'd been sitting by their campfire when the mages attacked. The men had bound them and helped themselves to their supplies and their bodies until Daeya skidded into camp.

Tipori's aura simmered, but he kept his face a mask while they spoke. Alar paid close attention to the way he stilled at their recounting of Daeya's magic.

Magnus leaned forward as the women described the blood-red flames that devoured everything in their path. Jerinoch remained at ease, leaning back and puffing his pipe. Koraani observed the proceedings with a mixture of skepticism and disdain.

"So, to be clear," Tipori said, "you would trust this girl among our people, even knowing she is a sorceress?"

Helenia spared a tender look for Daeya. "*Ciir.*"

Sessiri nodded. "Without question. She's been nothing but kind to us and the young ones in our care."

Tipori inclined his head. "Thank you, again, *amiien*. You're free to go." As they bowed and departed, he shifted his attention to Daeya. "You have my sincerest apologies, Sorceress. The way we have conducted ourselves today is inexcusable."

Daeya peered out from around Ravlok. Alar's hands curled at his sides, his palms sweaty. Her distrust wasn't unwarranted, but surely she was smart enough to see he'd had no choice in how things had unfolded.

Tipori's expression softened. "Is there anything more you would like to add to their account?"

Her voice was small but firm. "No."

Nodding again, Tipori beckoned to her. "Step forward, please."

Ravlok bristled as if he might protest, but after some hesitation, Daeya obeyed. Alar smothered the urge to reach for her, ignoring the ache in his chest.

"You're welcome among our people. I extend to you the same protection and amenities as any other refugee." Tipori's gaze swept the audience as he made his decree.

Alar also studied those gathered, expecting another round of protests. Fortunately, no one spoke. Perhaps they knew better.

Tipori gestured toward the binders on Daeya's wrists. She hesitated, but he smiled and repeated the gesture as if coaxing a feral cat to milk. "It's alright."

Metal clinked against metal as Daeya lifted her binders.

Magnus rose sharply. "Don't remove those."

Tipori paused, fingers poised over the cuffs. "Why not?"

"For once, I agree with the *bashiin*," Koraani said. "The girl admits she served under Gregory. If her wards are that strong, she must a spy."

"Bleeding Aether, I'm not a spy!"

But they couldn't prove it. Alar had hoped his accounting would have been enough to secure her place here, but he should have expected Koraani and Ashaara—the two most harmed by the humans—to demand more.

Daeya looked back at Tipori. "Look, I appreciate what you're trying to do, but I'm not staying here. I'll find somewhere else for my family."

Koraani chuckled humorlessly. "You think we're going to let you leave?"

"You're insane if you think you can keep me here."

"We are more than capable—"

"If I may propose an alternative," Magnus broke in. "Allow her to remain in Starlight, spellbound, while we assess her motivations. At the end of a trial period, she may earn full rights as an Alliaansi citizen and refuge for her family."

"Let her prove her worth." Jerinoch tongued the end of his pipe. "I like it."

"There's room in Havensguard for her, and her companion." Magnus nodded toward Ravlok.

Alar would have rather she stayed with him in Baani'anii, Koraani's communal house, but Cheralach's house was still better than the pits. At least in Havensguard, he could have Sam and Orowen look after her.

Reluctantly, Tipori lowered his arm. "How long?"

"Well, First Officer?" Jerinoch asked. "It was your idea."

Only a parting of his lips betrayed Magnus's uncertainty. "Four months."

"Four *months*?"

Daeya's outburst earned another cutting glare from Koraani. "Make it six."

"No! My father doesn't have that kind of time."

"With two conditions." Tipori held up a hand to silence her, then pinned Alar with a hard stare. "No one touches her mind again without her permission and explicit consent from me. Zakaari will be assigned as escort until the trial has ended."

"What?" Zakaari's attention snapped from the woman in the crowd to his father. "*Peiaa*, I have other duties—"

"Which you so often neglect." Tipori's tone was dismissive. "I don't suspect one spellbound sorceress should give you trouble, *ennii*."

"That's not fair. Why not Riisii?"

"Because Riisii is needed elsewhere."

Alar's face twitched. Zakaari's outrage might have been comical if he'd been assigned any other task than babysitting Daeya.

"I have conditions as well," Koraani said. "If she starts trouble, the trial ends immediately, and Ashaara may attempt to break her wards again."

Jerinoch snorted. "So you can have your minions antagonize her, Koraani? I think not."

"If she causes trouble, she will be subject to the same laws as any Starlight citizen." Tipori addressed their audience. "And there will be ten lashes for anyone attempting to sabotage her trial. Make it known."

Murmurs of assent followed. As the meeting neared its end, Alar uprooted his boots and closed the distance between himself and Daeya. He reached for her arm. "I will escort them to Havensguard—"

She shied from him. "*Don't* touch me."

The words seared him like a fire bolt.

Tipori spoke an incantation, and the chain between her spellbinders turned to mist. He stepped before Alar, giving his back to Daeya. "Zakaari will take them. Perhaps Sam can see them settled. The council needs you after we adjourn."

Alar wanted to protest, to reach for her, but the message in Tipori's dagger-edged stare was clear: back off.

He swallowed. Later. They would speak later. He had to make her understand that duty came first. Sullenly, he nodded. "Yes, *Amaa*."

# Chapter Seventeen

## Magnus

Magnus lowered himself back into his seat, letting the familiar herbal scent of dohanni ease the pounding in his head.

Blood-red flames. Aetherian potential. Wards the most powerful mastermind on the continent couldn't break. The girl posed too great a threat to allow her to go free in Starlight, and Tipori's boy was too immature to be trusted with their people's safety. At least in Cheralach's house—*his* house—Magnus could have his people keep a close watch on her.

*She will be of use to us. Do not let her leave the city, and keep her bound.* The voice whispered its reassurance, and the throbbing in his eye socket eased.

"There are no idle hands in Starlight," Tipori said to the Eidosinians. He gestured to his husband, who stood to Magnus's left. "Once you're settled, Damiir will find jobs for you."

Kendi raised his arm, and Tipori acknowledged him. "Yes, Commander?"

"Ravlok here proved himself resourceful during our escape from Ryost. If he is willing, I request he be assigned to my command."

The monk looked torn. "I've sworn to protect Daeya, Commander."

"She is safe here," Tipori assured him. "And we need all the fighters we can get. I would urge you to consider it in the coming days."

Ravlok's conflicted expression didn't ease, but he nodded. "I'll consider it."

"Thank you." Tipori returned the nod. "Zakaari, see them to Havensguard. Alar, Kendi, Maralla, please see us after council. If there's nothing else—" He paused. "This meeting is adjourned."

Their audience shuffled out, and the sorceress trailed Zakaari and Ravlok into the early afternoon light. Chairs were drawn around the head table, and by the time the last civilians departed, the war council had assembled. Riisii, Damiir, and Ashaara remained standing; everyone else took seats at the table.

Maralla rolled out a crinkled map of the Northlands with lines drawn and redrawn to designate the changes in the borders of the Alliaansi lands over time. A large portion of the continent north of the Palisadics fell under their protection now, save for a strip of tundra ruled by the Iceborn raiders to the northeast and another strip of coastline populated by horned Mautori to the northwest.

Two mugs, a sheathed dagger, and a cracked scrying mirror weighed down the corners. Maralla marked several locations around the map with clay beads.

"Most of my scouts have reported in," she began. "Black beads designate the known enemy encampments." There were three of those: one west of Trivvix, one northeast of Sarton, and one west of Fawn's Breath. She placed a smaller black bead due south of Kuma'Kiir. "Based on Sessiri and Helenia's account, there could be a fourth encampment somewhere around here."

She gestured to several beads farther north and northwest of the Guild camps. "Purple is for cities under our control where no Guild activity has been found yet." Those included Zeo'Taaron and Aon'In—the Alliaansi's oldest and best-defended western cities—as well as Starlight. "They're overflowing with refugees."

She placed two red beads on top of Kuma'Kiir and Beigaare, and a smaller yellow bead beside Willowmarsh. "Red are the cities that have reported Guild spies inside their walls, or larger patrols on their outskirts. They're the likeliest targets for the Guild's next major offensive." She nodded toward the last bead, grimacing. "Yellow designates the one place from which none of my scouts have returned."

Magnus studied the map and the hundreds of leagues separating those red and yellow beads. The problem was clear. "Their greater numbers are working against us."

"And still no word from Eris?" Kendi asked.

Maralla shook her head.

"*Aon*," Ashaara confirmed.

Maralla withdrew a handful of coppers and placed three leading north from Sarton to Willowmarsh. Four more nestled in strategic passes over the mountains. "Light Paladins were reported by the refugees who veered too far south on their way to Starlight." She waved toward the coppers. "I suspect the Church is to blame for decimating our supply lines."

"Could they have taken Willowmarsh without our knowing?" Alar asked.

"Possible." Koraani leaned over the map. "But not probable unless they've laid siege."

"Eris's city is well-defended. A siege that quiet and on that kind of scale would have been in the works for weeks, if not months." Tipori looked up from the map. "But our shipment from them is past due. We can't rule it out."

Kendi tugged on his braid. "We need to get in there and see what's going on. Blow open our supply route again. If they cut us off there before winter, Starlight will starve."

"With the bulk of their sorcerers near Kuma'Kiir," Magnus said, "and more patrols near Beigaare, we'll be spread too thinly to deal with them all. We will have to choose our battles with care."

Koraani nodded. "And allocate saphyrum appropriately. If we slough off too much for our warriors and the supply lines cannot be restored, we risk our civilians."

Tipori tapped his thumb on the table. "Starlight's saphyrum cache is nearly empty. How does Aon'In fare?"

"No better," Koraani said. "They descend upon us like carrion raptors."

A pained silence claimed the table. After years of pushing for war, Koraani had finally gotten what he wanted. But just as Cheralach had always cautioned, it was never wise to wish for violence. Magnus stared at the map, eyeing that yellow bead over Willowmarsh.

*Kill them.*

Tipori broke the silence with a growl. "An order from Rillion would take over four months to reach us by ship. Ferid is our only other option. We'll need to reach out to our contact there." He sighed. "What we need is another Walker."

An unreadable emotion flickered across Riisii's face. Though she could Walk, the intensity of her Foresight made her less precise. She couldn't do it reliably enough to transport other people or supplies beyond what she could carry.

"Our new resident sorceress may know something." Jerinoch tapped his pipe on the table, scattering ashes into the air. He patted his clothes, searching for his dohanni pouch. "Why not ask her?"

Koraani sneered, but it was Alar who answered. "We should."

"You're sure we can trust any intel she gives us?" Maralla asked.

"Yes. Though I'm sure she would be more willing to cooperate if you could send a team to extract her father. He's a blacksmith—the one who makes most of the Guild's steel."

*Foxhollow.*

Magnus frowned.

*Nettlesbane.*

While the others strategized over the girl, he turned his attention toward the voice.

*Xiranthesium. Merisander. Poppy wine.*

A list of medicinal painkillers and toxic plants. What was he supposed to do with those?

*When the time is right, I will tell you.*

"Riisii," Maralla said. "*Enniia*, what futures have you Seen surrounding the girl?"

*Stop her.* The voice's whisper turned urgent. *You must stop her. She will ruin you.*

Magnus started, spurred to action but uncertain how to respond. He followed the council's collective gaze to the woman at the end of the table.

Riisii's forehead creased in concentration. "I have Seen..."

*She will take everything from you.*

Palms pressed against the table, Magnus couldn't move. Couldn't breathe. How? How was he to stop her Sight?

Riisii's frown deepened.

*Stop her. Stop. Her. STOP HER.*

A distraction would only delay her, and he couldn't affect the Aether without calling attention to himself. He balled his fists, tensing to rise—

The voice stopped.

Cold swept through Magnus. A cavernous void opened inside him, pulling at the nerves behind his eye sockets. His vision wavered, as if from an Aetherial warp. It pulled from the corners of his sight, converging on Riisii like ripples in a pond reversed in time.

Riisii's eyes rolled back. Her body spasmed once, then began to shake.

Damiir caught her before she hit the floor. "Riisii!"

Tipori scowled at his wife as they both shoved away from the table. "Silonas slay us, Maralla, you know that's not safe for her!"

"C... c... c..." Froth bubbled out of Riisii's mouth. She convulsed in Damiir's arms, staring glassy-eyed at the ceiling.

Maralla knelt beside her daughter. "I didn't mean for her to look. I just wondered if she'd Seen anything."

Tipori knelt on Riisii's other side, placing a hand on her forehead. "We're here, *enniia*. You're safe."

"C... c... c..."

Maralla took Kendi's offered handkerchief and wiped her daughter's mouth. "It's alright, Riisii. You're going to be fine."

Magnus slowly uncurled his hands. He stayed rooted to his chair, mouth gaping. The seer continued to shake. With Maralla's help, Tipori carefully turned her onto her side, her head on Damiir's thigh.

Had he done this? Had he hurt her?

*No, Magnus.* The voice returned, soft and placating. *I have helped you.*

Warmth returned to his fingertips. Whatever hollow chasm there had been inside his mind, he felt whole again.

*This way, there is no need for violence. The seer will be fine, and your secrets are safe.*

His taut muscles turned to soft clay. Fatigue settled into his bones, and his eye grew heavy-lidded. All around him, his companions reclaimed their seats, one by one. Minutes passed before Riisii's seizure abated.

She stared up at Damiir, chest heaving. "*Haalii.*"

"I'm here, honey bee." He tucked a lock of hair behind her tapered ear.

Tipori retrieved his cloak from a nearby hook and laid it over Riisii. He returned to the table, his expression grim. "I must see my daughter to the Temple. Alar, I'm afraid Koraani is right; we don't have the troops to retrieve the blacksmith right now. But if the sorceress really wants to help us, she will work with us to bolster our saphyrum stores. If we can secure an opening sooner, we'll revisit her request."

Alar nodded once. "I'll make sure she knows what's at stake."

To Maralla, Tipori asked, "How soon can the Fourth Legion be prepared to march to Kuma'Kiir?"

Maralla rose from Riisii's side. "A week. Two at the latest."

"See it done." Tipori took her by the chin and kissed her. Then he bent to hoist Riisii up and kissed Damiir where he knelt. "We should be home for dinner."

"You'd better."

Tipori departed, backing out the door with Riisii in his arms.

"The Fifth should stay behind to defend Starlight. The First will guard Aon'In," Koraani decided. He turned to Ashaara. "Send a message to Nemaala. Tell her to send the Second Legion to defend Beigaare. Perhaps a portion of the Third can march from Zeo'Taaron to aid Maralla."

"*Ciir, Amaa.*"

Kendi gestured to the map. "That just leaves Willowmarsh."

Jerinoch nudged the yellow bead with his pipe. "It's possible the city is already lost. With Paladins involved, we ought to send human or Cintoshi scouts to investigate."

*Kill them.*

Magnus's sword hand itched. He picked up the bead and rolled it between his fingers. "I'll go."

Kendi looked sharply at him. "You should rest, *Amaa*. You've just suffered serious trauma."

*The enemy doesn't rest.*

"The enemy doesn't rest, Commander." Magnus replaced the bead on the map. "I'll take Rylan with me. We'll be there and back before solstice."

"It's settled, then." Jerinoch clapped Magnus on the back. "And not to worry, my boy. I'll motion to make you official when you return."

Magnus had to remind himself not to smile. No need to terrify his companions with such a grisly sight. Even so, his lips tightened. "Thank you, *Amaa*."

Koraani studied him for a long moment before nodding. "*Ciir*. You have earned it."

Support from Koraani was the last thing Magnus expected. But as he turned to look at him, Magnus found approval not just on Koraani's face, but Maralla's and Damiir's as well.

Pride shone in Kendi's eyes. "Indeed, he has."

# CHAPTER EIGHTEEN

## DAEYA

Every step Daeya took away from the Alliaansi council hall buried the blade in her back a little deeper. Heat seared her cheeks even as the north wind nipped at her nose and ears. The mastermind's touch still needled at her temples.

*That* was a feeling she would never forget.

"I should have listened to you, Rav." Brambles clawed up her throat. "We should have gone with Vortanis."

Ravlok, gods bless him, didn't rub her stupidity in her face. He walked beside her down the dusty street, following her surly new bodyguard. "This isn't your fault. Alar made a lot of promises he had no business making. Even one of the elders said so."

Koraani. Daeya scoffed. If she ever saw that Aethershite again, it would be too soon.

"But if anyone is to blame—I asked you to trust him. He fooled me, too."

"Can you two walk any slower?" The half-blood, Zakaari, glared at them over his shoulder.

Daeya stopped in the street and folded her arms. "Yes actually, I can. How's this?"

Zakaari sighed and turned to face her. "Very funny. Now, if you're done being a petulant child, let's move on."

"Petulant?" Daeya laughed. "That's a pretty big word for you, isn't it?"

His eyes narrowed. Shadows cut his already chiseled features into razor edges. "Only as big as your head, apparently."

Ravlok started to speak, but Daeya had tolerated these blankers and their bad attitudes long enough. This once, she was going to push back.

"What if I were to stand here all afternoon?"

"Then I guess I know where to find you."

"Your father charged you with babysitting me. You'd really risk pissing him off by letting the scary sorceress wander free in his city?"

The boy snorted. "You're not that scary. Especially not while wearing slave binders."

"You—" Daeya looked down her wrists.

Rillanese. That was the language inscribed on the manacles.

"No comment, Sorceress?" Zakaari chuckled. "Good. Now, come."

Her teeth clicked shut, and she drew her cloak tighter. Ravlok put his arm around her, glaring at the half-blood's back as they made to follow once more.

"Ravlok!"

A small figure darted toward them. Blonde hair, strong shoulders, and a smile as wide as the Taaru'Kallii.

Ravlok lit up. "Sam!"

Daeya stepped aside as the woman rushed him and threw her arms around his neck.

Ravlok staggered, returning the embrace fiercely. Daeya loosened her death grip on her cloak. It was rare to meet a person whose overly friendly touch didn't cause Ravlok to recoil.

"I knew you'd be alright." Sam pulled back and looked him over. "I just knew it."

"It's so good to see you." Ravlok beamed, his hands lingering on her waist.

Rarer still was a woman he would hold like that. Daeya caught Ravlok's gaze and lifted both eyebrows. An introduction was absolutely in order.

Ravlok's cheeks darkened. He cleared his throat and carefully extracted himself. "Daeya, this is Sam. We"—they shared a glance—"escaped prison together."

Daeya's breath hitched. That meant Sam would have been there when the School collapsed. She bowed to hide the lapse in her smile. "It's a pleasure."

"Likewise." Sam offered her hand. "Any friend of Ravlok's is a friend of mine."

It was the first show of kindness since their arrival that didn't feel tainted by ulterior motives. Daeya numbly shook her hand. "Thank you, Sam."

"I was there in council." Sam winced. "I'm sorry about what happened. That's not normally how we do things around here."

"I shouldn't have expected anything else." Daeya shrugged. "Asking them to trust a sorceress *is* sort of ridiculous."

"Starlight's founder was a sorcerer. Jerinoch was, too. Many of us have forgotten that. In time, I think they'll forget you were, as well."

Unlikely. Gods willing, she wouldn't be here that long.

Zakaari stalked back toward them, scowling. "At this rate, we'll be lucky to reach Havensguard by dinner."

Sam glared back. "Piss off, Ari. Why are you in such a hurry?"

The half-blood folded his arms. A feline smirk stole over his face. "If you must know, I have a date tonight."

"Seriously? Does she know about the other three?"

His grin soured. "Of course she does. I always make that clear from the start."

Daeya shared a look with Ravlok. She could see why Zakaari might have an unsavory reputation. His strong features and perfectly tapered ear points might have been handsome on anyone but this pig-headed arse.

Sam slipped an arm through hers—a gesture Daeya found oddly comforting, despite having only just met the woman. "Well, don't let us keep you. I can take them from here."

The hardness in Zakaari's expression dissolved like snow in summer. "Thank the gods. You're a peach, Sam." He backed down the street, pausing briefly to scan their surroundings. For his elders, probably; gods forbid he get caught running off. His violet gaze returned to Daeya. "I don't have to tell you to stay put, do I?"

Her urge to rebel was as instinctive as breathing. But before she could bite back, Sam placed herself between them.

"She's not a dog, you damned codnopper. If she wants to go anywhere, I'll send for you, and you'd better not be late."

"Certainly." Zakaari gave Sam a mocking bow. When he straightened, he tipped an invisible hat toward Daeya. "Until tomorrow, my lady."

Daeya bristled. She watched him retreat into the midday sun, cursing her ill luck and every stupid decision she'd ever made.

"Come on, Daeya." Sam tugged her arm. "Your hands are freezing, and Ravlok, you stink." If Ravlok could have turned any redder, he'd have rivaled a pomitto. "It's baths and soup for both of you as soon as we get home."

Home.

Daeya swallowed hard. This place was no more home to her than the Sorcerers' Towers. Home was where Da was. Da, who had no idea what danger she'd put him in. Left to the mercy of the same sorcerers who'd brutally raped three women, murdered a child, and incinerated an entire village, he could already be rotting in a cell somewhere.

Daeya had little hope the Alliaansi were any better at keeping promises than Alar was. Even if she gave them what information she had, they would weigh every move she made against her and inevitably decide Da wasn't worth the risk.

"Hey, cheer up." Sam nudged Daeya's bolt wound, forcing a gasp from between her teeth. The woman stopped short, her face crumpling. "Oh gods, you're injured. I'm so sorry. Do you need a healer?"

"No."

"Yes." Ravlok's hard stare brooked no argument. "Has Orowen regained her magic?"

"No. I'm afraid Orowen isn't well. She…" Sam paused, like she wanted to say more, but thought better of it. "There are other skilled healers at the Temple, trained by Orowen herself."

"I don't need a healer," Daeya insisted, trying to keep her rising panic at bay. Ashaara and Alar thought there were wards around her mind. Gregory would have no doubt made psionic resistance a priority among the dozens of so-called channeling wards and spell runes he'd carved into her. If nothing else landed her in prison, her scars certainly would. "It's just sore. There's no need to waste saphyrum on me."

Surely that would be enough of a deterrent. Only hours ago, she'd witnessed how a single bead could rejuvenate the refugees in the tent cities in a matter of moments.

"It's not a waste if you're in pain," Sam shot back. "It's the least we can do after—"

"Please. I'm cold and hungry, and I need a bath. I just want to get to wherever we're supposed to stay."

Sam looked her over, then sighed, keeping their arms linked as she guided them down the street. "Alright. But if you change your mind, promise me you'll say something?"

Daeya breathed a sigh. "I will. I promise."

Havensguard wasn't the calm, quiet haven its name implied, but an enormous communal house packed with people. Humans, Syljians, half-bloods, Cintoshi, and even a few thin-boned Duerguardians filled the three wings of the two-story structure. Children tumbled across the wooden floors and threadbare rugs, wrestling for toy wagons and carved horses. A dog barked, and an older child chased a chicken down one hallway. The smell of baking bread and seasoned meat made Daeya's mouth water.

Sam ducked a flying tiffleball as she closed the door behind them. Two wide-eyed Cintoshi boys screeched to a stop in the foyer, paling when they saw her. News traveled quickly as others darted off into the left and right corridors. Echoes of "Sam's home!" and "Hide the honey sticks!" filtered through the house.

Sam put her hands on her hips. "Berric, Fimros, how many times have I said we don't throw things in this house?"

"Sorry, Samara," the children muttered in unison. They peered around her, clearly more concerned with the ball that had rolled to a stop in one corner.

"Gods, at least take it outside." She shooed them off, and the boys darted after their ball. When she looked back at Daeya and Ravlok, she was grinning. "I hope you don't mind a little noise."

Daeya gazed around at the destruction. Tiny feathers drifted down from the open loft overhead. She plucked one off her cloak and let it flutter to the ground. Despite her misgivings, the sight of so many children let some light into her heart. She didn't fight the smile as a human and two Syljians came tearing down the hallway after another chicken. Their bare feet squeaked on the polished wood. The bird darted under a table.

Sam glowered at the children. "Why are the chickens out of the coop, Gentrii?"

"Sam!" The younger pair hugged her legs while the oldest Syljian blanched.

"Uh, well, Jessie wanted eggs for dinner, but Patch got out while I was checking the nests."

"That dog, I swear." Sam rubbed her temples. She hugged each of the children, then waved them off as well. Cupping her hands over her mouth, she called, "That's right, Sam's home! I expect clean rooms and floors that shine like mirrors by curfew tonight!"

Gasps and squeals erupted, and sounds of scrambling and furniture scraping followed.

"This is what I get for leaving Finn in charge." Sam glared at the chicken under the table. "I'll deal with you later."

She beckoned Daeya and Ravlok upstairs, past rows of doors to a room near the end of the hall. A side staircase led back down to the lower floor on their left, and a large window overlooked the city in front of them.

Sam slammed her weight against the door twice. It scraped against the top of the frame before popping free. "You'll have to share this room with Jessie and me, but I don't snore much. It's her you'll have to worry about."

It was smaller than Daeya's private suite in the Towers. Two bunks piled high with furs flanked the dirty window, and an unlit brazier stood between the beds. On their left was a closet full of simple tunics, fur cloaks, and surprisingly ornate dresses, and on the right was the washroom equipped with a shallow steel tub and a chamber pot.

No plumbing, then. Bleeding Aether, what she wouldn't give for a shower.

While Sam set about lighting candles, Daeya stepped toward the right-hand bunk and sat. Straw crinkled beneath her. It wasn't the down mattress she'd slept on for much of her life, but it outclassed mud and leaves. Her fingers sifted through white and brown speckled furs, beneath which lay a stained linen sheet.

Daeya grimaced as her mind drew its own morbid conclusions about the stains. "Whose bunk was this?"

Sam looked up from lighting the brazier. "My friend Perron. Willaarios slept above him." The lightheartedness in her face faded. "They were killed outside Ryost."

Of course they'd have been killed by sorcerers. Daeya fidgeted with the metal binder on her wrist. "I'm sorry."

With a one-shouldered shrug, Sam went back to fanning the coals. "Thanks."

Daeya shot Ravlok a wordless plea. He took pity on her and sat, slinging his satchel to the floor. He cupped her knee, and with his touch, the tension in her body bled away like night before the dawn.

"Sam, maybe you could explain more about what's expected of us here," Ravlok suggested.

Sam sat back on her heels. "I'll add you both to the rotation of chores this week. Laundry, cleaning, kitchen duty, that sort of thing. The children do most of the housework while the adults tend to jobs around the city. Once you're settled, Damiir will assign yours."

She rose, brushed off her trousers, and sat on her bunk facing them. "We have breakfast at eighth hour, lunch at noon, and dinner around seventeenth. Don't be late or you'll be eating in the garden with the dogs."

Daeya's temples throbbed harder as she attempted to convert Sam's twenty-four-hour times to Eidosinia's six-bell system. Eighth hour would be third bell, noon was fourth, and seventeenth hour was an hour past fifth bell.

"Our house volunteers in the tent cities on Saosday and Shavasday mornings. You'll want warmer furs and better boots for those days."

Daeya and Ravlok both looked down at the state of their attire. Ravlok's boots had holes in the toes and scorch marks from the fires. The edges of Daeya's cloak were frayed beyond mending, and she'd cut rough squares from the garment to patch the holes in her tunic.

"I suppose we do look a little ragged, don't we?" Ravlok remarked.

"Just a little."

Laughter fluttered out of Daeya's chest. Between the patches on her clothes, the grime clinging to her skin, and the faded rose madder in her hair, it was a wonder anyone believed she'd once belonged to the Sorcerers' Guild.

Sam's quizzical look only prompted more laughter, and Ravlok soon joined her. Their mirth eventually won Sam over, too.

Daeya sniffed and wiped her eyes. "It's been a bad few weeks for us all, I guess."

"Agreed."

Sam's smile was a beautiful thing. Daeya could see how she'd caught Ravlok's attention. The soldier was all muscle, save for a few subtle womanly curves, and her concern for strangers suggested a pureness of heart that might have rivaled Ravlok's own.

Sam picked at a hole in her trousers. "We play games some nights, and sometimes Wilfau brings the children's choir over to sing. Other nights, we sit around and tell stories. I hope you'll both join us tonight."

Ravlok stilled beneath Sam's meaningful stare.

Oh, Mira help the poor monk. Daeya laughed again and elbowed him in the ribs. "*He* wouldn't miss it. I'll make sure he bathes first."

Sam giggled and returned to her feet. "Please do." She wiped her hands on her trousers, then started for the corridor. "I'll send up some soup and fresh clothes."

Rising himself, Ravlok stammered his thanks. Once she'd gone, he pushed the ill-fitting door closed behind her and leaned against it with a sigh.

Bleeding Aether, was that steam coming out of his ears?

"I never thought I'd see the day." Daeya studied her friend with new eyes. "My Ravlok in love."

"It's not like that," he hastened to say. He rubbed the back of his neck, more out of sorts than she'd seen him since they'd gotten caught riding Yonfé's king tortoise through the Halls of Reflection. He shuffled back to sit at her side. "You know how I feel about those things."

The reminder of Ravlok's past sobered her. Born in a courtesy house to a woman who didn't want him, sired by a man he'd never met, Ravlok had been required to service patrons who preferred boys in exchange for room and board. Many of them had been unkind, and the mistress of the manor had treated him terribly. For a long time, he'd struggled to trust anyone, and he still didn't engage in intimacy, even though monks of his order weren't sworn to celibacy.

Daeya leaned against him, shoulder to shoulder. "I think you should try. Not everyone is as awful as Madame."

He fidgeted. "I know."

"And who knows, Sam could be just the person for you."

"Sam is wonderful." His smile didn't reach his eyes. "But I don't think of her that way. I'm not ready. I may never be."

His pain lay bare as a physical wound, and all thoughts of shoving them in a room together until they figured things out vanished. Daeya reached for him, and he wrapped his arms around her with the sort of desperation only thoughts of bleeding Madame could provoke.

Gods, if she ever got that woman alone, she'd tear out her vile heart.

"You don't have to do anything you don't want to," she told him. "And if anyone tries to make you, I'll send Telerion to eat them."

Ravlok's broken laugh shook them both. He pulled back, but kept hold of her shoulders. "That's no idle threat coming from you."

"Damn right." Daeya gave his beard a tug and grinned when he batted her hand. "You want me to talk to Sam? Let her down for you?"

He drew in a long breath, then shook his head. "No, I'll handle it."

He rested his elbows on his knees and scrubbed his hands through his hair. "What are we going to do, Daeya?"

She let him change the subject and pulled a fur over their laps. "I don't know. I thought this was the answer. Now it seems we're both trapped here."

Daeya fingered her star pendant and the bead nestled in its setting. The binders' steady, albeit useless, trickle of magic made her feel more awake, like drinking copperthorn tea. Pulling on her bead heightened the effect, sharpened her focus, and made her heart beat faster, but the binders prevented her from directing the energy outward.

Ravlok glanced at her, then hooked his foot through his satchel strap to pull it closer. He sifted through the pockets until he found his lock picks. "Let me see one of those binders."

Daeya offered her wrist, and Ravlok worked the tiny lock for several moments until something snapped and he gave a triumphant hoot.

Only, the binder didn't pop open.

Ravlok's grin faltered. He held up the pick—or rather, *half* the pick. The other half tumbled out of the lock and skittered across the floor.

Daeya stared at it. "I take it that wasn't supposed to happen?"

"No. That definitely wasn't the result I was hoping for." He let the broken pick fall and put his face in his hands.

Tentatively, she touched his arm. "Rav?"

"I should have never brought you here," he mumbled through his fingers.

"You can't blame yourself for this." When he didn't move, she socked his bicep. "Hey, we're going to get out of here."

Ravlok lowered his arms. "This war will escalate further in six months. I'll bet they decide you're easier to manage in slave binders and extend your trial indefinitely."

He was right. Even if her bodyguard had other things on his mind, others would be watching her, awaiting a mistake grievous enough to warrant locking her away or sending her back to Ashaara.

Daeya frowned at the cracks in the wood floor.

An idea took shape—a way they could covertly scout for a way out. The Alliaansi might be watching the treacherous sorceress, but maybe they wouldn't watch a common soldier.

"I know that look," Ravlok said. "You're plotting something."

"Is it that obvious?"

"Well, let's hear it."

"You're not going to like it."

He groaned. "Daeya..."

She adopted her winningest smile. "I think you should join the army."

# CHAPTER NINETEEN

## OROWEN

It was a shallow cut, no more than three fingerspans long, and barely enough to warrant the saphyrum needed to close it. Orowen clutched the bead and tried to pull the gods' magic into her casting hand. A trickle of light formed at her fingertips. It wasn't the first time she'd gotten this far, but she'd failed to surpass this point four times already this afternoon.

She focused harder. Her arm shook as she tried to will the magic into something usable.

It should have been easy. It was one of the first healing sigils she'd ever learned. So easy, and yet impossible.

Her tendril of light winked out.

Five times. An uncanny stillness overcame her. The Temple grew quiet, despite the ringing in her ears. Incense twirled through the shafts of light dappling the infirmary beds.

Five times the point of failure. A miserable sound forced itself from between her teeth.

Her patient, seven-year-old Haana, looked up. "Are you okay, Devoted?"

The girl's brown eyes were so innocent and trusting.

*Charlatan...*

Orowen didn't deserve that trust. Not anymore.

She took a shaky breath. There was no space for doubt between her and her patient. Orowen attempted a smile. "I'm fine, *neime*. Just tired." She scanned the sea of mostly unoccupied beds and beckoned to Bren, a white-robed human wearing a red sash around his neck. The acolyte of Shavaan set down a stack of towels and hurried over.

"Yes, Devoted?"

Orowen wiped the wound on Haana's palm again. "Bren, would you be a dear and heal Haana's wound, please?"

The fourteen-year-old leaned over Orowen's shoulder, examining the wound. "Sure."

Effortlessly, Bren channeled magic from his casting amulet. He drew a sigil of healing and guided it over the cut. Smoky ribbons of light penetrated the tissue, sealing it from the inside out.

Haana keened with delight and wiggled her fingers.

Bren smiled, teeth gleaming against his dark lips. "How does that feel, Haana?"

"It doesn't even hurt at all. Thank you, Bren!"

Haana's forceful hug nearly knocked the acolyte over. Bren laughed and steadied himself against the back of Orowen's chair. "Of course, *ru'amii*."

The girl gave Orowen a squeeze and a peck on the cheek, then scurried off through the rows of cots and disappeared into the sunny afternoon.

Bren watched her go, tucking his hands into his robe. Orowen had trained him in the healing arts since he was Haana's age; Saolanni's light shone so well in him, and Shavaan's gift was strong. Only a few months separated Bren from completing all the rites of priesthood and taking the Oath of Saonis—a healer's declaration of service to the gods.

*Oathbreaker...*

A telltale sting warmed her eyes. Gods willing, he would honor his goddess far better than she had.

Bren turned back to her, his joy fading. "That wasn't just a training exercise, was it, Devoted?"

He wasn't only a talented healer, but a perceptive one as well.

Orowen blinked rapidly and stood. "No, *neime*, it wasn't."

"So, the rumors are true? You've really lost your magic?"

Her outburst in the council hall this morning had reached the Temple acolytes long before she'd convinced her new guard to escort her to work, rather than to Havensguard to rest. Like all the others, Bren was seeking reassurance that all would be well, that her magic would return in time. Orowen wanted to give that to him. She readied the lie, as she had half a dozen times already.

Bren took her hand instead. "'We cannot hurry the seed, nor hasten a flower to bloom. The Mother always provides, but in her own time,'" he said, quoting the Book of Life. "Your magic will return, Devoted." He squeezed her fingers. "Likely when you need it most."

Orowen shoved aside her impulse to scoff at the purity of the child's thoughts. She patted his arm. "Well said, *neime*."

Bren beamed. Light haloed his beaded black faelocks, and for a moment, the acolyte's silhouette seemed to glow.

The illusion broke when the Temple doors burst open.

"Orowen!"

She leaned around Bren to find Tipori carrying Riisii in his arms. Her niece was deathly pale, and her head rested against her father's shoulder. Spurred into motion, Orowen rushed to pull the linens back on the nearest bed. Tipori laid Riisii down and helped her straighten out.

Riisii's forehead was cool beneath her palm. Orowen examined her pupils. "What happened?"

"She tried to predict the future." Tipori fussed with the blanket. "It sent her into another seizure."

"No, I didn't." Riisii's tone was indignant, but her violet eyes remained glassy.

Tipori opened his mouth to argue, but Orowen shot him a warning look. She checked Riisii's pulse, then felt under her jaw for swelling.

"What were you trying to do, *neime*?"

"*Miaa* asked me what I Saw." The words came slowly, distantly. Riisii stared up at the rafters. "But I can't remember." Her gaze drifted, as if searching for answers in places only she could see. "I had it. Just a moment ago. Then he did something."

Orowen and Tipori shared a glance.

"Who did something?" Tipori asked.

"It was important."

Unease spider-walked down Orowen's spine.

"It was important." Riisii's expression crumbled further. "It was important. It was important, and he *stole* it from me." She raked her fingers through her dark hair.

Alarmed, Orowen grasped Riisii's shoulder. "Easy. Easy, *neime*. Deep breaths." Aside to Bren, she said, "Prepare some passionflower root with lemon."

"Right away, Devoted." Bren bowed and hurried off.

She sat beside Riisii, coaching her through a breathing exercise. This, at least, Orowen could do without magic.

Once Bren returned with the potion, she patted Riisii's hands and pulled Tipori aside, into the shadow of a nearby column.

"How long did it last this time?"

Tipori didn't take his eyes off his daughter until Orowen touched his wrist. "A few minutes. Maralla asked her about the sorceress. Apparently, Riisii's Seen some things about her future, but she couldn't get anything out before the seizure started."

"Did anything out of the ordinary happen before the seizure began? Any injuries or dietary changes in the last week?"

"I felt a ripple in the Wall." Tipori's frown deepened. "I know your patients' privacy is important to you, but I don't think that matters to Cheralach now. I need to know about his visions." A shade darkened his eyes. "I need to know if this sorceress is a threat to my daughter."

Of course, that would be his priority. The Aetherian would level mountains and topple kingdoms to protect Maralla, Damiir, and their children.

Orowen sighed, rubbing her forearms. "I don't think Cheralach would have gone looking for her if he thought she meant to harm us. He said she was in danger, and that proves true with her story about the false charges. He was sure her fate and ours were intertwined."

"But he never explained how or why?"

"No." She was convinced now that Cheralach had known about the School and what she would have to do to get them out. There was so much he'd refused to explain, and so much she wished she'd asked. "He did mention red flames. The ones the refugees reported in council match the ones rumored to have destroyed the Orthovian port. And, Tipori..." Orowen considered how best to put this. "Riisii said something about a fire, lit by accident, here at the Temple."

He looked sharply at her. "When?"

"This morning, before the meeting. She didn't say when it would take place or who would start it."

Tipori nodded. "I'll tell Damiir not to assign the sorceress any duties at the Temple."

"Devoted?" Bren's voice reclaimed Orowen's attention.

Riisii sat on the cot, her cup forgotten in her lap. She seemed to stare *through* the column in front of her.

Tipori sat beside her, taking the cup before it spilled. "What do you See, *enniia*?"

Orowen approached more carefully. Riisii's pupils dilated until they left only a hairsbreadth of violet around their edges. She'd witnessed hundreds of episodes of Riisii's Foresight, and pupil dilation to that degree wasn't normal. She glanced toward Bren to request a seeking sigil—one used to diagnose unseen injuries and ailments.

Riisii's sudden, gut-wrenching cry lifted every hair on the back of Orowen's neck.

"Nothing," Riisii sobbed. "I can't See anything." She searched the rafters once more. "He's taken my eyes from me."

"Who?" Tipori's hands clenched the bed linens, as if he might shred the man responsible apart. "Who, Riisii?"

Her haunted eyes leveled once more on the column, her voice a whisper.

"Chaos."

# CHAPTER TWENTY

## ALAR

Alar pinched the bridge of his nose. "Open the door, Ravlok."

"No." The monk stood in the sliver of space between the door and its frame, refusing to allow him even a glimpse into their bedroom. "She doesn't want to see you."

If the situation had been any more dramatic, Alar might have mistaken them all for Duerwisti stage performers. One woman didn't want to see him, while another—Val's wife, Finn—had been only a few steps behind him since the war council that morning.

He wasn't ready to face Finn, so he'd done his best to be everywhere she wasn't. He'd even steered her away from Havensguard with a psionic suggestion to ensure their paths didn't cross while he spoke with Daeya. Just being in his friends' communal home was challenge enough when every room, alcove, and shadow reminded him of Val.

Still, he needed to make at least one thing right.

"It's not like I had a choice in the matter," Alar pointed out. "Surely you both see that."

Ravlok only glowered. "You could have said no. You should've at least warned her what they might do."

It was hard to tell if he remembered demanding that already. Alar had become familiar enough with the flow of Ravlok's thoughts to sense when they turned treacherous. All week, he'd been guiding him back to his tome, keeping him distracted so that if anyone could benefit from Daeya's alliance with a dragon, it would be the Alliaansi. "The results would have been the same."

"No. We would have gone to Draeconis, like we should have in the first place." Ravlok glanced back into the room, then scowled and lowered his voice. "I hope you realize you've broken every promise you've ever made to her in a single day."

Damn him. Damn the bastard.

Even if it was an exaggeration, Alar sucked in a breath. Ravlok began to close the door, but Alar slammed his palm flat against the wood. "That's exactly why I'm here."

He braced the door as Ravlok pressed harder, but Alar was no match for him in a test of physical strength. Summoning his psionics, Alar *pushed*, flinging the handle out of Ravlok's grasp. It banged against the wall, and the monk stared in shock.

Alar shoved past him, but Daeya wasn't in the room. He paused, brows tensing, until the sound of splashing water drew his attention to the closed door on his right. He stepped toward it. "The council has proposed an alternative for your father."

Ravlok inserted himself between Alar and the washroom, bristling. "You need to leave."

Did he really think he stood a chance against a psionist? Alar clenched his teeth. There was no way he was going to let his posturing intimidate him. "Don't do something you'll regret, monk."

"Don't you dare threaten him," Daeya warned from behind the door. Another slosh of water followed.

At least he'd gotten her attention. Alar met Ravlok's gaze, triumphant, then called over the monk's shoulder, "Come out, Daeya. I just want to talk."

"To the Wastelands with you."

He barely restrained the urge to roll his eyes. "Please. This is important."

Ravlok's aura roiled, distorting the wood grain behind him. "Get out."

He was determined to make this impossible. Alar could sense him readying for a fight, his aura drawing taut as a bowstring. Subtly, he felt along the fringes of that aura and applied pressure. Just enough to make Ravlok more amenable, but not enough to extinguish his anger completely. That would have been too suspicious, and Daeya might not forgive him for manipulating Ravlok's emotions more than necessary.

"Let me make this right." He wove the words into Ravlok's psyche as he spoke them. "She needs to hear this."

The monk hesitated just long enough. Behind him, the door creaked open. Daeya's hair was freshly washed, and water streaked her tawny, bell-sleeved blouse. She looked so much like any other Starlight citizen in her oversized shirt and fur-trimmed leggings that Alar forgot his practiced speech entirely.

Daeya's glare was far more frightening than Ravlok's. "You have thirty seconds. One, two, three..."

Alar scrambled to regain his stride, blurting out the first words that came to mind. "If you tell them how to get more saphyrum, they'll help your father sooner."

She stopped counting.

Alar tried not to wince. That wasn't exactly what Tipori had said. "As long as they have an opening to do so."

Daeya thrust a finger at him. "Don't think I don't see what they're doing. You brought me here as a hostage, not a refugee. They'll take whatever information I give them and leave my father in ruin."

Cursed Wastelands, was she taking intolerability lessons from the monk?

"I tried to help you," Alar snapped. "There are some things I can't control—"

"Like me." She folded her arms. "And it eats at you, doesn't it?"

He refused to entertain her intuition, gesturing toward her spellbinders instead. "If I could have read your thoughts, none of this would have been necessary."

"Then let them read yours."

This time, Alar did wince. "I did." *Sort of.*

"Aethershite."

Now wasn't the time to explain that his feelings for her had compromised his judgment. He wouldn't have that conversation while she was angry. She'd use it to tear his heart out.

"What about mine?" Ravlok asked. "Would that get them to remove her binders? My memories can prove she no longer allies herself with the Guild."

"No. Sessiri and Helenia's testimony kept her out of the pits, but the council's decision to keep her bound is nonnegotiable." Alar shifted his focus back to

Daeya. "Even if my memories could sway them, you admitted there were things I didn't know."

"Then I suppose I'll play their game and pray they're more honorable than you."

That stone struck Alar's defenses so hard, he grunted with the impact. Mortified, he channeled the pain into fury and sneered. "I see the Guild did a stellar job of teaching you gratitude."

"*Gratitude?*" Her eyes widened. "I'm wearing *slave binders*, Alar. If I wanted to be a slave, I would have stayed with Gregory."

Alar searched her face, uncertain how to respond.

She didn't give him the chance. "You've said your piece. Now, please leave."

He should apologize. He'd made a mistake; he couldn't leave things like this. "Daeya—"

"For the gods' sakes, *leave!*"

Her face contorted with such agony that Alar stepped back. "Alright. Alright, I'm going."

Ravlok followed him to the door, while Daeya fixed Alar with a scowl so deadly she might have been a dragon herself.

They'd been fine this morning. He could still feel the softness of her hands against his, her curves against his chest, the warmth of her in his arms. He'd been so sure he could make her understand, but now the rift between them felt wider than ever. Alar straightened and slammed up his defenses, resolved not to let his blunder in Trivvix repeat itself.

But she wasn't Leah. She'd already accepted what he was and shown him affection anyway. She just needed time. He would give her space, if that's what she wanted. There would be time to reconcile when she felt better.

Alar turned on his heel and fled the room.

Ravlok didn't mean to slam the door, but gods help him if it didn't relieve some of the pressure in his chest. Too bad he hadn't caught Alar's backside on the way out.

His breath rasped through his teeth. How had he not seen this coming? How could he have so blatantly handed Daeya over to her enemies? Had he been so desperate to prove himself a worthy caretaker—studying the book, learning Draconic—that he'd missed all the signs that could have steered them away from this course?

Had Alar manipulated him? Ravlok bristled at the thought. He'd felt that same itch in his mind only moments ago. It certainly could have been the psionist influencing his thoughts. Even as his fingers curled into fists, he almost hoped that was the case, or this inadvertent betrayal was entirely his own fault.

He turned back to Daeya, an apology poised on his lips, but she pivoted for the window, clutching her pantheon star pendant in a white-knuckled fist.

The rejection stung, but Ravlok squared his shoulders against the urge to wilt. In moments like this, when she refused physical comfort and her tears threatened, he'd learned it was best to let her come to him.

He returned to his spot on the floor and summoned the Tome of Eolaan. His hands shook as he opened it to the page with the circle diagram and reached for his quill, nearly spilling ink onto the parchment beside him.

He threw himself into the work, the scratch of the quill grating and accusatory in the silence. With Daeya's help, he'd puzzled out many of the simpler symbols and committed them to memory. Now that he had quills, parchment, and ink again, it was time to finish the translation.

"Ay... vosh... ess. Zav... rak... har."

"*Aivhoshess Xavrakhar.*"

Daeya's pronunciation flowed from one sibilant sound to the next. Ravlok looked up. She was still staring out the window, her pale face illuminated by midday sun. Her damp locks soaked the back of her blouse.

He no longer questioned how she knew these things. When gods walked among them and a book gave him the silent treatment for cursing its ill-mannered pages, the least of his concerns was how his best friend spoke Ancient Draconic. "What does it mean?"

She turned from the window, brows furrowed, and as if she hadn't heard him at all, asked, "Should I tell them about Telerion?"

Ravlok lowered his quill. Her thoughts must have turned to her father again. She always hugged her elbows like that when she was worried. "No. Remember, we decided they'll either think you're crazy or use him to control you further."

"Their seer said Tipori would believe me. They think saphyrum will keep them going, but they won't last long against the Guild. A single dragon can shatter entire legions. Telerion could turn the tide of this war and drive the sorcerers back over the mountains. Our combined strength is the best bargaining coin I have."

Of all the Alliaansi leaders, Tipori seemed most willing to give Daeya a chance. Even Magnus, who had stepped in and offered a solution when Tipori and Koraani butted heads, insisted on keeping her spellbound. And Jerinoch seemed too busy getting high to care at all.

"What happened to me joining the army and finding a way out?"

"I'm not discounting it. I'm just..." She gestured helplessly. "I'm running out of time, Rav. Da and Murtagh could've already paid the price for my disappearance. I have no way to know if they're okay."

Her desperation made Ravlok's chest ache. He relented with a nod. "If you think it's worth telling them, then I support you." He attempted a grin. "Since the seer already knows, maybe you can ask her how to approach him."

"That's not a bad idea." Daeya turned back to the window. Sunlight caught her blonde roots and reflected off the faded red in her hair. "It means Ritual of Ascension."

Ravlok's eyes snapped back to the parchment.

A ritual. *The* ritual? The one Riisii had mentioned?

It couldn't be a coincidence. Each time the diagram appeared, he'd been worried about Daeya's power and the repercussions if she were to lose control of it. Had the tome been trying to give him the solution all along?

Beneath the smattering of symbols already translated, he'd written their equivalent in Eidosinian. The seemingly random words weren't random at all, but a list of components and instructions for the ritual they needed.

Ravlok barked a laugh at the absurdity. The utter relief.

Daeya looked back at him, frowning.

He put his face in his hands. Gods help him, he'd been so obtuse. Somewhere out there, Vortanis and Tiior were surely laughing at him.

Daeya stepped from the window. "What is it?"

"I need—" Ravlok wheezed another laugh and waved to the parchment. "I need you to translate these. If you can."

She sat cross-legged beside him and reached for the parchment. Her eyes roamed the script, then she retrieved the quill. "Well, first of all, that's not the right symbol for this." She added the tiniest mark to the parchment. It looked like an ink spot on the tome's page, but it changed the entire shape of the symbol on the transcription. Daeya winked. "No wonder you were having trouble reading this."

She swept through the symbols in moments, correcting his transcription and adding the proper translations in between fits of giggles.

"If only I could've written this down sooner," Ravlok lamented.

"In your defense, quill and parchment aren't normally considered survival tools."

"A poor oversight on my part." One he wouldn't make again.

Daeya hugged her knees. "So, this ritual—what does it do?"

A good question. He turned the page and scanned the next few lines of ancient symbols. Then he reached for a sheet of fresh parchment from the stack. "I'm not sure yet. I'll need you to translate more of this."

Within half an hour, they'd decoded much of the next page. It left him with more questions than before. The structure of Ancient Draconic made some passages ambiguous in Eidosinian and contradictory in the Dessian trade tongue. Daeya also marked several words with multiple meanings, which changed the text in subtle ways.

He frowned at one passage, which contained a word that repeated several times throughout the ritual. It meant either 'sibling' or 'chosen,' and it seemed imperative to the ritual's success.

Ravlok read it aloud in a way that made the most sense. "'A sibling's sacrifice to Ascendant divine. Across ages and echoes, their souls will align.'"

"Mm. If it's a sacrifice it wants, it's not going to get it." She leaned against the bunk. "I don't have any siblings. Just Murtagh, and he's not even related by blood."

Ravlok lingered on the second translation. "Maybe it's metaphorical. A lot of these old texts are known for being hyperbolic."

Or it meant someone she was close to. Someone chosen, or a volunteer.

Icy stillness settled over him.

"Why do I even need to ascend? I'm not a bleeding bird."

Ravlok shoved his foreboding aside. "But you're a dragon queen."

"No, Vortanis said *Baokryn* was a dragon queen." She sighed. "Do I look like a queen to you?"

He made a show of appraising her from her messy hair to her blistered toes. Then he adjusted the collar of her blouse. "Maybe a homeless one."

That at least got her to smirk. "A queen with no kingdom and a crown of air. How the great dragons of Draeconis will tremble." She pushed herself to her feet and returned to the window. "You really believe all this?"

"I do."

"Why?"

Ravlok placed the tome beside him and rested his elbows on his knees. "Because I have faith."

"It's hard to have faith these days." She frowned. "That's probably ridiculous to you, isn't it?"

Ravlok chuckled. "One god shows up to train you. Another god wants to send you to a magical prison, and still you don't believe a third would seek an ancient power you possess to command dragons? I don't see what's so ridiculous."

Lightness crept back into her eyes. "Alright, when you put it that way."

He uncrossed his legs and rose to join her. Following her gaze out the window, across the rooftops, and into the expanse of cloudless sky, Ravlok said, "There can be no faith without doubt. Only blind obedience, which is the enemy of free will. I choose to have faith in Tiior, and she chose to have faith in you. Combined with everything I've seen you do..." He turned to face her. "Daeya, that is enough for me. Whatever your destiny is, I would follow you anywhere."

She hugged her elbows. "My destiny is my own."

"It is. *You* decide what's right for you. Not even the gods can change that."

"Thank you." Daeya's eyes brimmed with tears. "I really needed to hear that."

Ravlok cuffed her shoulder. "That said, I still reserve the right to tell you when you're being an idiot."

She laughed in earnest, knocking loose a pair of tears. "That's fair."

"We can save the ritual talk for later if you want."

Daeya wiped her face with her sleeve. "I'm not doing it if it requires sacrificing anyone I like."

Dread itched along Ravlok's spine once more, but he banished it with a shake of his head. "I'm sure that part isn't literal. I'll do some more research to be sure. But I do think it will help you. It's shown up every time you've struggled with your power."

Daeya rewarded him with a grudging nod. "You're the scholar."

"We'll need to gather supplies." Ravlok retrieved the parchment and scanned the list. "Some of these should grow in the area. If the winter frost hasn't already killed them, I can find them when I'm scouting. A few might have to come from Orowen, and I have no idea where we're going to get talotiba mushrooms this late in the season."

"A local herbalist might have some dried ones."

"Good idea. I can ask Sam later."

"Only one problem." Daeya tapped a finger against one spellbinder.

Of course, that would complicate things. Even if Ravlok joined the army and scouted their way out, she still wouldn't have her magic after they escaped, nor were there any major cities between here and the In'Jasuu where they might find a blacksmith.

"Well, we can wait the full six months and hope they honor their word." Ravlok had fully expected her sour look. "You could also try to persuade them to remove them sooner."

"Alar said that was nonnegotiable."

"Alar said a lot of things."

It sounded sharper than he intended, but Daeya didn't flinch.

"Or"—he glanced toward the door and lowered his voice—"I can steal the key."

"Tipori spoke an incantation to make the chain disappear. He was going to cast a spell to remove them." Daeya fidgeted with the hem of her sleeve. "What if there is no key?"

"Is that possible?"

"I don't know. But there's magic to them, that's for sure."

He took Daeya's wrists and studied the locks again. Each was smaller than an apple seed, and not deep enough for a traditional set of tumblers. But if they were meant to only be removed by magic, why would they have keyholes?

"There has to be a key." Ravlok released her. "The question is who's most likely to have it."

Daeya's sigh fogged the window. "My gold's on Tipori, or one of his minions."

"Maybe his son?" If he'd put the key in Zakaari's hands, that would be a blessing from Silonas himself.

"They didn't pass anything off in the council hall." She looked thoughtful. "But maybe I can get him to tell me where it is. We should also talk to the seer. Find out what she knows."

"That seems wise."

"Especially if she's Seen us trying to escape."

"She said the ritual was important. Maybe she'll help us."

"At this point, I'm willing to try anything."

Daeya turned and paced the length of the room like a caged chaagra. Ravlok settled back beside his tome with his notes in his lap.

He scanned Daeya's translation, dipping his quill to scrawl his own notes alongside hers, making a list of the items that should be easy to acquire from Orowen. The rhythm of Daeya's steps became a background lull while Ravlok worked.

His eyes snagged on that one line again. The lie he'd told her tasted sour on his tongue.

A sibling's sacrifice. Or, using the secondary translation, one who chooses to sacrifice.

There weren't many people Ravlok would trust with Daeya's welfare, especially not after Alar's deception. If Caelyn wanted her imprisoned on Dromas, then whatever power Daeya possessed had only begun to manifest. This ritual was important. Not only had the seer said so, Ravlok could feel it in his bones.

The spellbinders might have bought them time. He'd caught no flashes of light or arcs of flame skittering across Daeya's fingertips since they'd arrived. But Tiior only knew what would happen once the binders came off.

Sam's vegetable soup roiled in his stomach. Ravlok tightened his grip on the quill. There was still more to translate. He could be misinterpreting it. He swallowed hard, buried his misgivings beneath a layer of dutiful iron, and dipped the quill once more.

# Chapter Twenty-One

## Alar

Alar strode down the west wing hallway, past the dining room, and between rows of bedrooms and offices. He avoided Jack, who looked up from his conversation with Anwic in the kitchen as he passed. Both men's auras were lost in a flurry of activity as Sam directed the older children in skinning turnips and potatoes.

Afternoon sunlight poured in from the side exit, promising a reprieve from his melancholy mood. He would visit his mother before retreating to Baani'anii to bathe and meditate. She was always cross with him when he didn't stop to see her as soon as he arrived. He could return here tomorrow and speak to Sam and Orowen about Daeya.

His hand was only fingerspans from the door when a choked female voice stopped him cold.

"You bastard."

Grief and shame seized him so unexpectedly that he had to steady himself against the doorframe. "Finn."

"I should have heard it from you."

His psionic suggestion must have worn off. He could maybe use it again, talk her down then slip out the door and bury himself in tasks for Koraani and Ashaara.

But no. There was no escaping this.

Alar turned. The warrior woman's fur-clad shoulders quivered, and tear streaks gleamed on her cheeks. Though she was a little taller than Daeya, Finn still had to look up to meet his gaze. She did so with silent fury, her soft features contrasting with that razor-edged stare. A pair of runes on her left cheekbone blazed white against her lavender skin. She'd cut her hair short since Alar had last seen her, and kinky white fuzz stuck out in every direction.

Her winter cloak trailed the ground as she stalked closer. "You promised you'd keep him safe."

Another promise broken. Ravlok's accusation clung to him like pitch.

"I know." Alar's throat tightened. It was too soon. He couldn't do this. He backstepped, groping blindly for the door handle. "I'm sorry." He braced for a slap as she closed the distance.

But Finn didn't hit him. She slung her arms around him, instead. "Take it from me," she sobbed into his chest. "It's unbearable."

Her anguish sent him reeling. "H-he told me to tell you he loves you." Wastelands, he had to keep it together. "He—"

"You promised me. *He* promised."

He shuddered. They couldn't do this here.

Alar dragged her down the corridor and into an unoccupied office. He kicked the door closed and finally allowed himself to return the embrace with a ferocity that would have been mortifying in front of anyone else.

Her scent, so much like Val's—that of pine needles, fall rain, and forest herbs—undid him. A ragged sob tore through him, followed by another, and another. "I'm sorry. I'm so sorry."

Her fists balled in his cloak.

"We were so close to getting out." If Orowen had acted only moments sooner. If Kendi hadn't taken a dagger. If *someone* had been there to help Val. "I shouldn't have left his side."

Finn trembled. "I can't live without him. Gods, it hurts too much."

"I know." He held her tighter. It was like someone was carving out his heart with a serrated knife. "I know it does."

A pained gasp drove her to her knees. Alar sagged to the floor with her, as if the rift that had swallowed Val might drag them both down after him. Finn rested her forehead against him, both palms flat against his chest. Their auras overlapped, amplifying Alar's sickening grief until his shoulders shook and no number of calming mantras or deep breathing could restore his composure.

He'd been a fool to ever let Val get so close. Love was the greatest weakness of a man, and Alar had allowed his attachment to make him vulnerable. No mastermind would have made that mistake. Ashaara was right; he'd been compromised, and not just by his affection for Daeya. The agony of Val's loss would haunt him forever.

"Take it from me," Finn said again. Her damp eyes settled on him. "I want you to make it stop."

"Finn, I can't—"

Her fist came down hard on his chest. "Don't scabbing lie to me. I know you can!"

Alar caught her wrist before she could hit him again. "A psionic suggestion is only temporary." As soon as he released her aura, the crushing grief would return.

"I know there's a way. Ashaara has done it. Please. I can't"—her expression twisted—"I can't bear this."

Alar let go of her wrist, and she slumped against him. He wanted nothing more than to ease her grief. He *could* if he dulled the memory of her loss—a technique that mimicked the passage of time—but he wasn't practiced in that skill. Ashaara would say it wasn't worth the saphyric energy.

Still, if it was within his power to relieve Finn's suffering, then why shouldn't he?

It wasn't a decision she should make in the throes of her grief. He *squeezed* her aura, compressing the tumultuous emotions as tightly as he could. His temples throbbed with the effort. "What you're asking is risky."

"I don't care."

"Val would."

"He wouldn't want me to suffer, either."

That was indisputable. "You're right. I... I'm willing to try. I can make it seem as if time has deadened the sting, but it will never truly stop hurting."

Finn hiccupped and wiped her face. With her aura suppressed, words came more easily. "Do what you have to. Please."

He nodded and let his psionic hold slip. Finn shuddered as her emotion returned. Alar came away from her aura with the slightest tremor in his limbs. It was the sort of mental fatigue that left him physically drained, like he'd spent the last several hours levitating boulders.

Finn hugged her elbows and doubled over. Titanic waves of grief rolled off her, threatening to drown them both. Alar shuttered himself off from the emotion and stroked her hair.

"Finn, listen to me." When she didn't look up, he grasped her jaw and lifted until he could see her face. "I need you to think of Val for me. Think about the moment you learned he was gone, and focus on that memory while I work. Can you do that?"

She nodded, still clutching her stomach.

A fresh surge of remorse overcame him. He'd failed to be there for Val, but he would take care of Finn. He had to.

Alar shoved down all his sorrow and pain and locked them away. He let go of her and crossed his legs, gesturing for her to do the same. Once she mirrored him, Alar placed three fingers on her temple.

"It's going to feel like I'm chipping away at your thoughts. Don't try to stop it." He offered his other hand for her to hold, and she took it without hesitating. "If it starts to hurt, squeeze my hand. Alright?"

Finn nodded. "I trust you, Alar."

Her words steadied him. "You have the memory?"

"*Ciir.*"

"Hold on to it."

Alar slipped into the river of Finn's thoughts and immediately lost himself among the rapids—the shock of chilling disbelief, brief flickers of hope doused by pain and rage, the cascade of sorrow. The bottomless void of despair poised to swallow her whole.

He shied from those black thoughts, the implications of them clear. If left to her own whims, Finn might indeed choose not to live the rest of her life without Val.

He waded upstream through the river to the memory's source. Other eddies fed into the flow of her thoughts: Magnus, Orowen, Kendi, each with an imprint that was as familiar to him as his own. Finn must have been in the council hall when his companions gave their report. And there, winding further upstream, was the current of worry that had steadily eroded away at the banks of her mind.

Val.

His imprint—the collective memories, thoughts, and emotions surrounding their life together—and all the love and anguish that coursed through it made Alar falter. For the briefest moment, he could see his friend smiling in a memory Finn must have revisited often. Val's eyes shone with affection for his wife, his hands sifting into her hair as he leaned down to kiss her. Alar felt the warmth of him on her lips, tasted the coolness of Val's favored mint on her tongue. His teasing voice echoed in her mind: *I'll be home as soon as I can. I promise.*

Like he'd stepped into soft silt, the imprint dragged Alar under. Despair flooded his lungs as he fought to regain his footing. He thrashed his way back to the surface and distantly felt Finn's hand tighten on his. Gasping, Alar pulled back.

*"I'm sorry."* He spoke directly into her mind.

*"It's alright."* Her hand relaxed. *"I know you loved him, too."*

Alar swallowed hard. Indeed, Val had been a brother to him, but he couldn't let his own misery interfere. *"Remember, focus on that memory."*

Acknowledgment rippled through their psionic connection. All around him, the river of her thoughts churned and crashed. Alar stood at its heart, still and silent.

He felt along the fringes of Finn's mind and *squeezed*, compressing the channel to encourage the river to flow faster. The swifter current blunted the jagged edges of the memory, eroding them.

Finn's hand relaxed further. Her breathing fell into rhythm with his.

Alar loosened his hold, slowing the flow of her thoughts. He dipped his hands into the river, searching until he found Val's imprint again. He let its current flow over his fingers, relishing the memory of his friend as Finn saw him: compassionate, quirky, impulsive. Over time, that imprint would fade and make any thought of him less likely to reopen these wounds.

*"Alar? What's wrong?"*

Alar could see Val's lopsided grin, hear the playfulness in his voice, feel the warmth of his skin. To muddy his imprint when it flowed as crisp and clear as a mountain stream would be like poisoning a well, or drowning a friend.

But if he didn't do this, Finn might follow the stream of her thoughts to its dark conclusion. He took a steadying breath. *"It's alright. I'm almost done."*

Uncertainty reverberated through their connection, and Alar stiffened. This required a delicate touch, or else he risked damaging other parts of Finn's mind. He met her tremors of uncertainty with an equal and opposite wave of psionic energy that rendered her mind blank—still and empty of feeling—for the time it would take him to work. He directed another psionic burst along the edges of Val's imprint, attempting to scatter small portions of the stream and blend it with the current of her thoughts.

Except the imprint remained undisturbed, its edges as stark as a midday shadow. He frowned. With how strong Finn's connection with Val had been, perhaps it needed more. He sent a stronger burst into the stream, but its fringes only misted.

*"What are you doing?"*

The artificial peace he'd created for her wavered under ripples of alarm. He had to keep her calm. *"Relax, Finn. Please."*

*"Tell me what you're doing. That felt..."* She hesitated. *"...wrong."*

Alar didn't have time to explain to her. There were only seconds before she regained her full awareness. He studied Val's imprint, seeking any sign of weakness.

*"It's alright."* He directed another wave of psionic energy to blank her feelings. *"Just trust me. You're going to feel better when I'm done."*

*"I..."* In a voice as flat as any subject Ashaara had ever imperiumed, Finn said, *"I trust you. I'll feel better when you're done."*

Alar sank his hands into the river and delivered a final, firm blast of psionic energy. Like a long-dormant geyser, the stream of Val's imprint burgeoned beneath that psionic pulse. It reached a state of maximum pressure.

And exploded.

Finn's sharp cry snapped Alar's awareness back into his body. Blood poured freely from her nose.

*No.*

He snagged her sleeve to keep her upright. "Finn?"

She slumped against him, eyes rolling back.

"Finn!" Alar dove into her mind. Jagged cracks appeared in her psyche, and the river overflowed.

*No, no, no, no.*

Bleeding Wastelands, what had he done?

Alar *seized* those pieces of her mind, then struggled to hoist her body up. He spun for the door and wrenched it open. The sun blinded him as he shouldered his way out of Havensguard.

He started toward the Temple of Life at a lumbering jog, but his footsteps faltered. Taking her there wouldn't do any good. No healer could fix this. It was beyond even Orowen.

He needed Ashaara.

Straining his mental capacity to its limit, he split his attention between holding Finn's mind together and reaching out to his mentor. Ashaara's psionic range was much wider than his. Even without line of sight, she would hear him from anywhere in Starlight.

*"Amaa, I need your help."* He made no effort to sound calm or collected.

Ashaara's response came swiftly. *"Baani'anii."*

Dust swirled as he spun back around. His arms shook beneath Finn's weight. Pain spiked into his temples as her mind tore further. A thin rivulet of blood leaked out of one eye.

First Val, now Finn. The full force of his guilt nearly brought Alar to his knees. "Hang on, Finn. Just hang on."

Starlight's citizens parted for him, shouting demands to clear the way. A Syljian man with white braids tied into a topknot hurried toward him, reaching for Finn. "Here, let me—"

"Get out of my way!"

Another man—this one human—dashed up the front steps of Koraani's communal house. He held the door for them, and Alar lost his feet on the threshold.

An invisible force caught him before he struck the tile. Alar stiffened in Ashaara's telekinetic hold as she appeared through a gap in the gathering crowd.

For Finn, Alar wasn't above begging. "Help me, *Amaa*. Please."

Ashaara slipped through his mental shields like smoke while lowering him to the floor. Alar opened his mind to her completely, letting the events of the past half hour spill forth in a jumble of thoughts and images.

She clicked her tongue. Her disappointment was sharp as a scalpel. *"Your feelings cripple you."* Ashaara turned on her heel and started for the nearest hallway. *"Bring her."*

Her hold on his body fell away, but bone-weary fatigue kept him pinned to the floor. "I can't—"

*"You can, and you will."* Ashaara threw an ambivalent look over her shoulder. *"Channel your feelings into something useful. Hold her mind intact if you wish to save her."*

Alar bowed his head, cheeks burning. More aware now of all the faces gawking at him, he spoke telepathically this time. *"Yes, Amaa."*

When he returned his attention to Finn, he found several significant tears in her mind already mended. He relaxed his death grip on those portions and exhaled in a rush. Ashaara's methods might be vicious, but she wouldn't let Finn die to prove a point.

He got his legs under him. Aching heat stretched across his eyes, and he abandoned all pretense before the collective attention of Baani'anii in favor of bracing Finn's mind and putting one foot before the other.

They reached Ashaara's sparsely furnished quarters—her true home was in Aon'In—and the door swung closed behind him. Alar followed her silent gesture and placed Finn on the bed. Ashaara dragged over a chair from a nearby table.

"Grief this sharp embeds itself too deeply within an imprint to dull its blade," Ashaara said aloud. She closed her eyes and placed her thumbs along Finn's temples, letting her first and second fingers rest against her cheekbones. Ashaara's mental touch slipped in over Alar's and gripped the fragments in a vise-like hold. "And often you cannot separate the emotion from a person's mind without removing the imprint itself. Release her."

Alar obeyed, staggering from the loss of tension like he'd released a bowstring with too heavy a draw. He took a moment to compose himself and wipe his face before sitting beside Finn. His hands still shook, but the sickening knot in his chest loosened. She was going to be okay.

Likely hearing his unspoken thoughts, Ashaara opened one eye. "She is not safe yet. You would do well to pay attention."

It was like he was a child again, being scolded for eating dessert before dinner. "Apologies, *Amaa*."

"Come. Observe."

Alar reached up to touch his mentor's temple with three fingers and closed his eyes.

Ashaara's mind wasn't just one river between two banks, like most mortals, but a sweeping delta of branching forks that flowed into an endless ocean. Hers was the product of two hundred years of immersive study in psionics and countless imperiums, and while it was disorienting for Alar, Ashaara could navigate it in a matter of seconds.

She guided him into a rivulet with banks that had sloughed off in jagged chunks. Alar recognized Finn's imprint, though the river of her thoughts was murky and stagnant. Ashaara's imprint permeated every span of this space.

*"Fixing a mind that has been broken is no task for a psionist. You will not do this on your own."*

*"Yes, Amaa."* As he observed, Finn's mind reformed under Ashaara's touch. *"You've used an imperium for this?"*

*"Ciir. I must, to retain her memories. I will return them to her when I am finished."*

The channel narrowed, deepened. *"She will still have all her memories and faculties?"*

*"There will be some loss, but I have preserved what imprints remain. Her faculties are all intact."*

Eroded banks reformed with steeply sloping sides. Alar turned her response over, and winced at the implication that not all imprints had survived. *"Does Val's imprint remain?"*

*"Aon. His imprint is beyond repair."*

Her curt reply stung, though his mind remained entrenched in Ashaara's, far from the awareness of his body. *"She won't remember him at all?"*

Annoyance rippled through his mentor. *"You know the answer to that question."*

He did. He *did*, and it provoked such a crippling wave of guilt that his psionic tether to Ashaara began to fray. He'd done this. He'd broken Finn's last connection to Val. Now there was truly nothing left of his dearest friend.

Feather-light pressure on his aura snuffed out his emotions like fingertips to a candlewick. *"Focus."*

Alar had no choice but to obey. The *absence* she fabricated inside him forced the command deep into his psyche, and he absorbed the remaining steps of her demonstration in crisp detail. The banks hugged the river of Finn's thoughts, encouraging it to flow faster and smoother. Within minutes, it was as if no trauma had occurred at all.

A surge of psionic energy staggered him as Ashaara transplanted the entire stream back into Finn. An identical imprint remained behind, forming a new fork in the ever-expanding delta of her mind. Then she cast Alar out as if she were batting away a fly.

He blinked his eyes clear. Ashaara's psionic suggestion eased, and his emotions returned in force. He bowed his head, sniffed, and swallowed, trying to regain his composure.

To assure himself Finn was really alright, Alar placed the back of his hand on her forehead and observed the gentle rise and fall of her chest. The blood on her upper lip and cheeks was almost dry.

"I was just trying to help her." His voice cracked.

Ashaara shrugged. "You did."

Her nonchalance shattered something inside him. "I destroyed her memory of him!"

Ashaara's expression remained perfectly, maddeningly smooth.

His fists curled into the bedspread and all his grief and anger came pouring out in gut-wrenching sobs.

She waited, watching him.

He made no attempt to hide his tears. "Her husband died, and now she won't even know his name."

"Tell me what you set out to do for her." Her voice lowered, but it wasn't soft or placating like a healer's. It was cool and matter-of-fact, like Wilfau speaking to an enraged child.

"I just wanted to ease her grief."

"And you think you failed."

His chest clenched around another sob. "Of course I failed."

"Why do you believe this?"

"Because I nearly killed her!"

Ashaara leaned back in her chair and crossed one leg over the other. "She will yet live."

"Thanks to you." The words shouldn't have been as bitter as they were. Alar rubbed his chest as if that could stop its aching. "She will never forgive me for this."

"You have erased the source of her grief."

"But that wasn't mine to take!"

"What was it she said when she came to you? What did she ask you to do?"

"She—" Alar hesitated. Ashaara wasn't asking out of curiosity; she would have seen the events in his mind. "She asked me to take it from her."

"*Ciir.*" She folded her hands in her lap. "She asked you to take her grief from her. You informed her of the possible dangers, and she persisted. She begged you to take away her pain, and you did. She will never suffer the loss of her lover again. In this, you did not fail."

"Then why do I feel like I've done something terrible?"

For the first time, Ashaara softened. She didn't reach for him, but her left hand slid forward along her thigh, as if she considered it. "Our work is never easy, apprentice. You desire to fix others so they do not feel pain as you have."

He knew better than to deny it. She knew him better than anyone.

"Your compassion is admirable, but it is misguided. You cannot fix everyone. Pain and grief are as much a part of life as breath and blood. Even if you *can* stop others from feeling those things, it doesn't mean you should."

Some of the bone-crushing pressure lifted from his chest. "Then what do I do?"

He couldn't just let the people he cared for suffer. Could he?

Fading sunlight set her white hair ablaze. The trio of runes that ran from the middle of her lower lip to her chin seemed to glow faintly against her darker skin.

"You must learn to control your feelings, Alar. Love, grief, anger—these will not serve you. They will master you—cripple you—if you allow them."

He frowned, sensing the subtle shift in her meaning. "But don't you love Koraani?"

One corner of her mouth lifted. "I enjoy his company, but if I must ever choose between my mate and duty, it will not be a difficult choice." Her smile faded. "My skills keep our people safe. Our survival is more important than any partner I may have."

Her admission wasn't as unexpected as Alar would have liked. Ashaara had been there at the Coup of Vale's Hollow. She'd watched the Crystal Towers of Astenpor fall. She'd lived through the Blood Crusades, the Massacre of Sessia, and countless other battles that had shattered their people over and over again.

How petty and inconsequential she must find his problems, then. His love for Leah had blinded him; his caring for Finn and Val had brought him here. His affection for Daeya could yet endanger them all.

Ashaara nodded toward Finn. "I must commend you, mistakes aside. Your growth in Ryost has exceeded my expectations. Should you wish to study the imperium more formally, I will assist you."

Alar's attention had strayed toward Finn as well, but it snapped back to Ashaara at the promise of advancement. A psionist's first imperium was the equivalent of a sorcerer earning a black robe. Once completed, he would be a mastermind in earnest.

"Yes." An eager note lifted his voice. He would have been a fool to refuse. "I would be honored."

"Good." Ashaara rose and withdrew a saphyrum bead from her pocket. She crossed the floor to her meditation circle—a ring of candles surrounding a bear-skin rug. "We will begin tomorrow."

Though her promise was also a dismissal, Alar looked toward Finn and opened his mouth.

"Her mind will need time to stabilize," Ashaara said. "She will be safe here tonight."

Alar rose and bowed to his mentor. "Thank you, *Amaa*."

A taper floated up from the nearby table and drifted toward her. From wick to wick it moved, lighting each candle in the circle. Then she plucked it from the air and tucked it into the candelabra beside her.

"I would caution you against further relations with the sorceress." Shadows painted the sharp hollows of her cheeks. "I need no seer to see she will prove a traitor."

Alar squared his shoulders. "With all due respect, *Amaa*, I think you're wrong."

She frowned. "You believe her dragon will serve us."

"I—" Alar might have laughed. Of course she knew about the dragon. Though he'd shielded his thoughts, she'd probably read Ravlok's mind the moment they entered the council hall. But why had she not told the others?

"Her power troubles me," she said, answering his unspoken question. "Her wards more so. The others would leap at the chance to gain a dragon on our side, but if she proves untrustworthy, it would be as the innix to the lamb."

Alar shifted from one foot to the other. There was no way to sway her. Not with his feelings for Daeya compromising his judgment. "She will be an asset. I'm sure of it."

"She has six months to prove it." Ashaara's gaze softened only as much as a blunted dagger's edge. "For once, I pray I am wrong."

# CHAPTER TWENTY-TWO

## OROWEN

Once Riisii's condition had stabilized, Orowen sent her home to the Evalliers' garden villa with orders to rest. She spent the rest of her afternoon flitting from one task to the next, trying to outrun her treacherous thoughts.

She'd strayed into a Temple alcove some time ago, but when exactly she couldn't remember. The ache in her legs and lower back was telling enough. Stars pierced the blanket of night on the eastern horizon, and the last of the day's light was swiftly fading. Orowen shook herself and turned from the window, adjusting her hold on a bundle of soiled linens. She dropped it in the laundry basket and reached for a fresh stack of folded cloth.

She didn't know what to make of her niece's declaration—that Anordis, the god of chaos, had somehow stolen her Foresight. Given Orowen's experience with Chaos priests, it wasn't impossible to believe. She and Maralla had chased the last sect of Anordis's twisted clergy out of Aon'In over forty years ago. Back then, when she'd been a master healer, she might have leaped at the chance to oust any zealot who dared harm them in the name of the divine.

But without her magic, she could no more remove such a threat than she could seal a tiny cut on a seven-year-old's hand.

The day's events tugged at Orowen's eyelids, and she lugged her limbs back to the unmade bed as if they were unwieldy bags of sand. There were still herbs to grind, bandages to boil, and cots to strip. Anything to keep her mind from wandering. Anything to distract her from the void of despair yawning ever wider in her chest.

Her hands trembled as she went through the motions of dressing the bed, smoothing the fabric, tucking the corners with first too much tension, then not enough.

It wasn't enough. It was never enough. It was—

"I thought I'd find you here, Devoted."

Orowen started, nearly knocking over the bedside lantern as she whirled. "*Saonis miraar.*"

Kendi winced and held up placating hands. "Apologies. I didn't mean to frighten you."

She hadn't even heard the door open. Orowen dropped to the cot, her heart still galloping against her ribcage, and the corner of the sheet she'd been working on popped free. She choked on a sob—on the futility of all her wasted effort.

"Oh, *neime.* Here." Kendi shooed her off the cot, then folded and tucked the corner easily.

The simple task pried the hollow between her lungs even wider. No magic, no way to atone, and now she couldn't even make a bed properly.

"There, now, all—" Whatever lightness he'd forced into his tone vanished. "What's wrong?"

*Everything.*

"I..." Emotion crowded up against her vocal cords. "I just..."

Her knees nearly buckled, and Kendi tugged her into his arms. More sobs shook Orowen's entire body. Blessed Mother, was she glad for sending most of the acolytes home early. The few who remained politely ignored them or changed course to give them space. She buried her face in his cloak.

"Come home, *nei ama're.*" His command was quiet but firm. "It's past time for you to rest."

"I can't. I *can't*, Kendi. I'll only see them—"

Rest meant nightmares of little faces crushed by rubble. Bodies broken by fallen beams. Tiny fingers bloodied in their attempts to dig themselves out. Voices gone hoarse from crying, too weak to call for help.

"Then ask one of your acolytes to prepare a sedative sigil." Kendi tilted her face up to meet his. "I'll stay with you here, if you feel safer in your goddess's house."

As if she deserved to stay here in Saolanni's house.

*Oathbreaker...*

The urge to bolt for the doors came so suddenly, she jerked in Kendi's arms. He held fast, as if he'd anticipated it. He didn't wait for Orowen's assent, but swept her off her feet and carried her toward the back hallway of private rooms. He paused at the threshold, and Orowen half-heartedly indicated one she knew to be unoccupied. He didn't put her down until they'd made it inside and he'd kicked the door closed.

The heaviness in her limbs redoubled, as if her fatigue had been two steps behind her all evening, waiting for the moment she slowed enough to acknowledge it.

Kendi turned her around, his fingers seeking the stays to her robe. "I know you were disappointed by the council's decision today," he said, working the ties loose, "but I have an idea, if you'll entertain it."

His knack for understatement was a thing of legend. 'Disappointment' was reserved for missing the last sweet roll at breakfast, losing a friendly wager at the dicing table, or knowing one's injury would make performing the amaariana at solstice more difficult. No, Orowen wasn't disappointed by the council's decision to deny her only remaining path to atonement. She was devastated.

And he, complicit in their denial. It was all she could do to swallow the hurt, much less respond in the too-long beat that followed.

Kendi sighed. The last tie came loose, and her robe went slack at the shoulders. Orowen let her attention linger on the sparse furniture in the tiny room—the bed, the table, the chair—as he slipped the robe down her arms. He hung it over the chair and spun her to face him.

Sweet Kendi, who had always cared for her, waited for her, set aside his deepest desires for her—the man she had hurt repeatedly with her refusals, her excuses, her hesitations, and yet kept coming back to...

*A prisoner tied to a fast-moving cart.*

It was a far more accurate description for him than any bard's song about love. For years, she'd prayed he'd find another and fulfill his want for a family and a life free of heartache—things she couldn't give him. Instead, she'd let him in at her weakest moment and now he would suffer again on her behalf. She wouldn't let a patient keep self-harming, and yet she practically sharpened the knife for him.

She should cut him free of her. For good this time, so he could have what he so desired with someone who wasn't tainted. Someone worthy of him.

Kendi opened his mouth to speak, but closed it, his brows furrowing.

Orowen tried to school herself into neutrality, but banishing the tension in her expression was about as feasible as commanding the stars. "*Neime*, I don't think we should—"

"No." He scowled. "Don't you dare."

"But—"

He kissed her. Roughly, desperately, he kissed her, shaking his head and cupping both her cheeks. "No. I know that look, and I won't hear it. Not again."

"But we shouldn't—"

Orowen's desire to protest eroded the longer his lips smothered hers, the tighter he held her, until she was kissing him back. She should have stopped him, should have steeled her resolve, should have demanded he leave, but her selfish heart couldn't bear it. Not when it threatened to tear itself in half the moment he released her.

"You always do this when you're scared," Kendi whispered between kisses. His warm hands found their way beneath her clothes and held her close. "You push me away like you think it'll make me stop loving you, but it won't work. Do you hear me?"

She sobbed against his lips, and heat blazed across her ear tips. She nodded.

"I love you." Kendi unhooked his cloak and let it fall. He lifted her once more and carried her to bed. "A hundred thousand times, I love you, and that's never going to change."

She clung to him, seeking skin beneath the insufferable tangle of fabric. When her back struck the mattress, she tugged him down on top of her. "I don't deserve you."

"Yes, you do. If I have to spend the rest of my life helping you believe you're worthy of love, I will do it."

Tears welled and slipped down Orowen's temples.

"I know you're hurting." He propped himself on one elbow and brushed the hair from her face. "You're so strong, *nei ama're*, but sometimes even high priestesses need help. I would rather hold you while you cry than let you suffer alone."

How could she argue with that? She cupped his cheek, and he rolled to the side, pulling her with him. Her head came to rest on his shoulder. Orowen burrowed into his warmth and let more tears fall.

She shouldn't encourage this, but no matter how many times she circled back to her unworthiness, her heart refused to scrabble for its freedom—for his sake, and for hers. How selfish, how cruel she must be to think this could end any other way than it always did: with heartbreak.

Sometime later, between spurts of fitful dozing, Orowen jolted awake to the sound of crumbling stone. Light filtered through an overhead window, and sand clung to the corners of her eyes.

Dawn. Mira's mercy, she hadn't meant to fall asleep. Exhaustion still hooked into her muscles, but there was nothing for it. She had incense to light, bedding to wash, prayers to—

"Your mind never stops working, does it?"

The teasing humor in Kendi's voice brought sheepish warmth to her cheeks. "No, I suppose it doesn't."

He folded one arm behind his head, tapered ears flattened against the pillow. "I have an idea I'd like you to consider."

He'd said the same thing hours ago. Orowen rubbed her face and grasped at patience. "What is it?"

"Reaffirmation."

She frowned. "Renewing my vows?"

"*Ciir.*"

Reaffirmation was common for those who left the faith and returned. It involved months of study, reflection, and prayer, followed by a vow of service not unlike the one she'd taken as a junior priestess. In her younger days, when her mistakes hadn't affected so many, she might have considered it. But now, as a high priestess, such a thing felt dishonest. Her oath wasn't some simple promise she could mend by picking up the pieces and swearing to do better. She'd already taken her second chance after Ixriia.

"I haven't strayed from my faith, *neime*. I broke a sacred vow."

"A distinction I think you make in error. I'm sure you're not the first to break the Oath of Saonis. What do other priests do when they make a mistake?"

Little faces. Little bodies. Tiny hands.

Knees bloody from praying. Her throat raw from smoke.

Unable to hold his gaze any longer, Orowen looked down. "They seek absolution."

She left out that those few who'd broken the oath in decades past were normally dismissed from the clergy in disgrace. If she were made to leave Saolanni's service, she would have nothing. *Be* nothing, save for a charlatan and a child-murderer.

To have left her Aetherian studies behind only to cause more destruction as a healer—perhaps that was what she deserved. It was a fate worse than death, after all. But as the highest ranking priestess in the Northlands, her acolytes were no more likely to condemn her than the Alliaansi council was. Nor could she cast herself into exile now that she was bound to the Temple and Havensguard. Unless she petitioned the council again—

"Stop." Kendi touched her chin. "It's like watching you drown yourself."

Her anger struck like a viper. "Forgive me if my feelings have inconvenienced you."

Steadfast as always, Kendi didn't flinch. "I know you've sought forgiveness from your goddess. But it's been my experience that the gods don't often respond in ways we would like. If the world is telling you that you don't need to be punished, that's likely all the answer you'll get."

Just as the coals of her anger ignited, frustration and shame snuffed them out. "It's not enough."

Kendi stroked her hair. "When we speak as a nation, we employ an ambassador to represent us. If you make it part of your reaffirmation to seek absolution from your fellow clergy, as representatives of the gods, maybe that would be enough."

It would never be enough. None of her priestesses held the murders against her; they weren't affected directly by what she'd done. It was too easy, the gift of absolution too hollow, to feel true.

The conflict must have shown on her face. Kendi blew out a long-suffering breath. "Just think on it. Please."

A refusal balanced on her tongue, but Orowen squashed it with the press of her lips. She'd tried everything else. Perhaps studying Saolanni's teachings and walking the path to priesthood again would be as much a lesson to her as her acolytes.

When she'd taken her oath after Ixriia, she'd emerged from the year-long period of temple confinement and prayer with a renewed perspective on life, untainted by the bitterness and despair that studying Aetherian war tactics had brought. Choosing to save lives instead of take them had been the most impactful decision of her young life. Perhaps it could be so again. As for absolution, there was no harm in trying.

Orowen picked at the hem of her shift. "I will consider it."

Kendi pulled her close, kissing her firmly. "That's good enough for me. Now lie down. I can see you're still exhausted." When she tried to voice all the things that couldn't wait for her to rest, he pressed his finger to her lips. "None of that. Lie down. I'll call for a sedative sigil and be right back."

Orowen tracked him across the room. He tossed a final, pointed look over his shoulder, and she grudgingly settled against the pillow.

Sleep pulled her under before the door swung closed behind him.

# CHAPTER TWENTY-THREE

## RAVLOK

Storytime in Havensguard's common room could have made even the rowdiest of Eidosinia's performing theaters look dull by comparison. Children and adults piled atop sagging couches, creaky chairs, and threadbare rugs to hear the silly tales of Magus Anastemar Crom and his magical quill. They argued over which of Maralla Evallier's epic victories against Father Durn's Light Paladins was most impressive. They listened raptly to a poetic tale of the doomed lovers Sillana Silversbane and Prince Ionus Vhelak, heir to the Skriian throne.

Ravlok endured three rounds of cups and cobbles against Jerinoch before the old man lamented his losses and shuffled off for more snacks, his ever-present dohanni pipe between his teeth. He stumbled twice over the children's dog, Patch, and nearly leaped onto the dining table when three boys came tearing after the animal with a ball tied to a rope.

Daeya would have loved every minute of this.

Ravlok swiped Jerinoch's coins into his pocket and began to clear the cups of ale from the table. The weight of Alliaansi silver bolstered him. If he and

Daeya were going to escape into the Northlands, carrying something other than Eidosinian currency would work to their advantage.

Someone clapped him on the shoulder.

He started, and Rylan laughed. The archer had shaved his beard and trimmed his hair since council this morning, and the dark circles under his eyes were already fading. "No need to tidy up, *amii*." He reached for the stones beside the cups and nodded to Jessie, who sauntered into view with another pitcher of ale. "We can take it from here."

"Sam's in the kitchen." Jessie winked. "She was worried you wouldn't come. Where's your friend?"

Daeya had stayed behind under the guise of going to bed early, but it was likely she'd be pacing their new room until she'd worn a path in the floor.

"She wasn't feeling well." Ravlok tapped his temple, alluding to her encounter with Ashaara this morning.

"Mm." Jessie grimaced.

"Bad day for psionics, I guess," Rylan remarked, tossing and catching one of the smooth stones.

Ravlok didn't stick around to interpret the look that passed between them. There'd been whispers of an incident involving Alar this afternoon. Ravlok could have pressed his new friends for details, but he had enough on his mind already.

Further translation of the Ritual of Ascension had confirmed Ravlok's interpretation of the ambiguous phrase. He'd banished the tome with his notes inside it to keep Daeya out of them. If she discovered the true cost of her ascension, she would never agree to it.

Truthfully, Ravlok wasn't so sure about it himself.

*A sibling's sacrifice to Ascendant divine.*

A sibling, or one choosing to sacrifice. If Daeya's ascension was an act of divinity, how could he not choose to make himself the sacrifice? He'd sworn to Tiior herself that he would protect Daeya, but he hadn't known it could come to this. He wasn't ready to—

Ravlok balled his fists.

Now wasn't the time to spiral. He would read the ritual again to be certain.

Wading through the crowd, narrowly dodging the return of Patch and his pursuers, Ravlok ventured toward the kitchen in search of Sam.

Dear Sam.

Ravlok swiped at his wrinkled clothes to no avail. He'd been pondering what to say to her all afternoon. He'd never had to explain his inadequacies before. Not like this. Yonfé and Daeya had coaxed and pried the information out of him, but Sam deserved a real explanation.

It wasn't that he didn't desire her companionship. He just couldn't give her the physical intimacy expected of him in a romantic relationship. Even after Yonfé's lessons on inner healing and self-acceptance, it was the one thing Madame had taken from him that Ravlok would never get back.

Dusty paw prints trailed across the dining room. Ravlok followed them to the kitchen entryway and paused open-mouthed.

Flour wafted through the air, coating the counter and half a dozen residents in white. More paw prints evinced some kind of struggle, and a sack lay overturned on the floor.

Sam stood over a pan of sweet rolls and wiped bare a stripe of skin across her face. Four suspicious circles of grease adorned the vacant spots beside the remaining pastries. "Next solstice, we're having puppy stew."

Seated at the table, Jerinoch chortled and stuffed more dohanni into his pipe. "Oh, you adore that mangy mongrel. Reminds me of Cheralach when we were boys. Fleas and all."

The corner of Sam's mouth lifted grudgingly. She shooed away her help and moved to right the flour bag. "*Amaa* didn't steal pastries when no one was looking."

"Ha! That's what you think. My brother would have bartered his place in the Afterlife for a slice of orange cream cake."

Ravlok hurried forward to help Sam heft the sack against the cabinet, and she offered him a tired smile, running a hand through her hair. "Thank you."

"My pleasure." Ravlok stopped himself from brushing away the flour in Sam's blonde hair. He could be that friendly with Daeya, but Sam might mistake the gesture for something more.

A gnarled hand swiped something off the table, and Ravlok turned. Jerinoch froze, but the appearance of a fifth circle of grease on the pan gave the old man away. He pressed a finger to his lips.

The tension in Ravlok's chest released like a snapped thread, and he laughed. Sam followed his gaze, brows furrowing.

Jerinoch tucked his pilfered prize into the folds of his cloak. "And don't forget that time he traded four clean socks for my last strawberry tart," he deflected.

"You mean the strawberry tart you stole from Kendi." Sam snatched the tray and set it on another counter out of his reach.

Jerinoch huffed and shoved away from the table, sticking his pipe between his teeth. "They were fine socks," he mumbled. He shook a finger at Ravlok, his pipe bobbing with every word. "All those coins I let you swindle, and you can't let an old man eat his sweet rolls in peace. You should be ashamed of yourself."

Ravlok hesitated, uncertain whether to take the rebuke in stride or rib him back. After all, his days of swindling his opponents at games of chance were long past.

Sam came to his rescue and grabbed a nearby towel to snap Jerinoch's backside as he made for the door. "They're bad for your blood, *old man*."

Jerinoch tossed a crude gesture over his shoulder and lumbered away, muttering about pastries and injustice.

Of all the people who could lead Starlight… Ravlok shook his head. The stories always glorified his brother's heroics, but rarely mentioned Jerinoch's. He was starting to understand why. "He's quite the character, isn't he?"

Sam's smile faded. "He misses Cheralach something awful." At Ravlok's questioning glance, she added, "They were always picking fights with each other. Jer's been snipping at everyone since we got home."

He was trying to find an outlet for his grief. Of course he was—who wouldn't be out of sorts? "Does he have anyone else?"

"He and Tipori are close. He'll be alright. It's just…" She shrugged. "I worry for him. They've been inseparable for so long."

Something about the way she said it pierced through Ravlok's own inner turmoil. For the last year, he and Daeya had been inseparable too. If he followed through with the ritual, she would never forgive him.

"Anyway." Sam brushed his arm in an awkward attempt at lightness. "I'm glad you came down."

All at once, the more immediate issue kicked Ravlok square in the chest. He fumbled for any response—

"I'm glad I did, too."

—and cursed himself.

Her cheeks darkened, and she looked down. They stood in silence as kitchen attendants and children bustled around them. Sam wrung the towel, and Ravlok fidgeted with a coin inside his pocket.

She studied him from beneath her lashes, her eyes a dusky silver in the lantern light. He had to say something. He had to explain why this couldn't happen before he made things worse.

They opened their mouths at the same time:

"Do you want to—"

"I need to tell you something."

Ravlok grimaced.

Sam leaned away from him, not quite in full retreat, though her gaze shuttered. "You're not interested."

Tiior help him. "It's not what you think."

"It's Daeya, isn't it?"

"No." He shook his head and offered his hand. "No. Just—can we go somewhere else? I owe you an explanation."

Her frown deepened.

"Please, Sam."

Finally, she sighed and took his hand. "Alright."

He squeezed her fingers, then looked between the dining hall and the corridor, considering. Their own room wouldn't be private enough, and he didn't know the layout of the communal house well enough to lead her away.

Sam rolled her eyes and tugged him toward the corridor. "Come on."

Heat seared his cheeks, though it cooled again at the tiniest flash of a smile from Sam. Maybe her friendship wasn't entirely lost to him. He steadied his aura with a breath and braced himself for the conversation to come.

Sam escorted him to a room equipped with three mismatched chairs, a sturdy desk, and a low table surrounded by tattered cushions. Scribbles covered one wall near the table. Apparently, the children who frequented this space had imaginations far bigger than parchment could contain.

Ravlok pulled out a chair for Sam, then sat across from her. She let him take her hand again, but her gaze weighed heavy. All of his carefully crafted explanations were as smoke to the wind. He grappled for words.

"If it could be anyone," he ventured, "it would be you."

Sam's lips parted.

"You're so fierce. You're loyal and kind. Anyone would be fortunate to know you that way." The words tumbled out of him with all the finesse of a drunken poet, and he cringed. "But Sam, I'm..."

Ravlok studied their joined hands to anchor himself. Hers were strong and callused, yet with slender fingers and glossy nails. Nothing like Madame's patrons. He tried, *he tried*, to imagine Sam's touch elsewhere—his arms, his chest. But the memory of weathered palms scraping his skin sent a shiver down his back.

Ravlok focused on real sensations: stark shadows from the oil lanterns, pressure from the chair beneath him, the far-off din of voices. He breathed again, and the violent tremors in his aura calmed to an unsteady ripple.

"I was raised in a courtesy house." He swallowed. "And because of that, I've never been able to…" Gods help him, what was he even trying to say? "I can't—"

"Ravlok, stop."

The strength in Sam's voice snapped his attention toward her like she'd yanked him by a string. Her jaw worked, and when she spoke again, a new ferocity overcame her. "If you're trying to tell me you've been a victim, then you don't have to explain anything else."

Relief. Overwhelming relief cooled the fire in Ravlok's veins.

His elbows came to rest on his knees, and though he kept hold of Sam, he bowed his head. "Thank you."

"Don't thank me." She gripped his shoulder. "Thank *you* for trusting me enough to tell me. I'm sorry that happened to you."

Ravlok blinked back a sting. "I guess I still have some healing to do."

"Honestly, I wish it *had* been Daeya now." Sam smiled. "At least then I'd have a chance."

He managed a weak chuckle. "She encouraged me to pursue you. I've no doubt she would have invented a reason to lock us in a closet together."

Sam's laughter was bright and melodic, provoking a longing so intense that it forced Ravlok to reconsider, albeit briefly. Maybe Sam *was* the woman for him. He'd never known someone more compassionate, more beautiful, more selfless, and yet still willing to stand up for herself and others. Tentatively, he reached out to cup her cheek.

Sam stilled.

They studied one another again, each second stretching into a long moment of possibility. He could try to kiss her. He could try to hold her like a lover would. But even as he considered those things, nausea welled, images long-suppressed arose, and Ravlok couldn't breathe.

He released her, and the images slipped away. "I wish I could," he choked out, "but it wouldn't be fair to you."

"No, I suppose it wouldn't." Her eyes glistened, but that protective fierceness rose again. "But we'll still be friends."

Pressure once more built behind Ravlok's eyes. "Yes."

She squeezed his knee, then sat back. "I guess it makes sense now. I remember how you shied from Jessie. No man has ever looked at her as clinically as you did."

Ravlok's face flushed. Jessie's injuries had placed her in compromising positions multiple times in their flight from Ryost. He'd seen more of her than he ever needed to. "A dungeon is hardly the place for such thoughts."

"True. But you don't look at Daeya that way. I really thought—" She shook her head. "Especially after I saw her and Alar in the council hall. How you defended her."

"They were close." He tried not to bristle. "Long enough to get her here anyway."

"Alar has always taken his job a little too seriously. I'm sorry Daeya got caught in the crossfire."

"It's not your fault." *It's mine.*

Sam tapped the table, looking for all the world like she'd heard the part he didn't say. She rose and beckoned to him. "It's been a long day. How about we take our minds off everything for a while?"

He tipped his head to the side and stood as well. "That seems wise."

"I know just the thing."

Hours later, after they'd cleaned up the sitting room and shooed all the children—including Jerinoch—off to bed, Ravlok linked arms with Sam and heaved his weary legs up the stairs.

"So, a monk and a sorceress." Sam giggled, stumbling over her feet. "How does that sort of friendship come about?"

Ravlok steadied her with an arm against the wall. She smelled strongly of Jerinoch's dohanni. Tiior knew he did, too. "We were study partners."

"Study partners?"

Nodding streaked the stairwell with moonlit grays and lantern light—a distracting combination that required a hard jab with Sam's elbow to correct. "Well, study-adjacent. She was looking for trouble. I was looking for answers."

Sam blinked owlishly at him as they turned along the switchback and staggered to the second floor. "Answers to what?"

It would have been easier to list the answers he *wasn't* looking for. "Military history. Political unrest. Magical ap-approp"—his brows pinched and he tried the word again—"appropriation."

She echoed his stammering amidst a fit of laughter, but never managed to say the word. "I thought you didn't have magic."

The reminder stung only distantly. Ravlok stared down the corridor to their room, as if by gazing long enough at the shape of the window etched in moonlight across the floor, he could see into the past. "I don't. I've always wanted it, though."

Thus had the goddess of knowledge granted him a semi-sentient tome with an attitude problem and a terrible sense of humor. The verdict was still out on whether it was a blessing or a curse.

His quest for arcane aptitude was the reason he and Daeya had met in the first place. She'd sold him half a bag of Guild-issued saphyrum at a rate far cheaper than he could have purchased from Laerin's crew. She was going on a trip, she'd said, and wouldn't be needing it anymore. Because saphyrum was impossible for non-adepts to procure legally, he'd jumped at the chance.

"Daeya was trying to teach you magic?"

"She might have, if I'd asked." Why *had* he never asked before? He chuckled, and the sound tasted bitter. "But no, she just liked breaking into the restricted archives. She would help me search for scrolls and books, then lie on the table and eat oranges while I studied."

"The sorceress knows how to study."

"Top of her class."

Ravlok grinned again, but his mind soon wandered. About two months after their first meeting, he'd gotten caught with Daeya's saphyrum. He'd been attempting to channel magic from a bead and hadn't heard the library doors open. Rizzidigus Tallion might have thrown him in prison for stealing from a senior acolyte, but Daeya had swept in out of nowhere—he hadn't even realized she'd returned—and thanked him for finding it. She'd deflected the Councilor's son and taken the blame for misplacing the beads—a mistake that, Ravlok learned later, had earned her a brutal switching and a month of cleaning latrines. At the time, he hadn't even known her name.

No one had ever taken the fall for him before. Daeya could have let him rot in prison until his crimes caught up with him, but she hadn't.

"She looked out for me, too," he murmured. "Even before I taught her to spar, I knew she wasn't like the other sorcerers."

They stopped outside their room. Sam's expression was thoughtful. "Do you think Daeya and I could be friends?"

Lightness nearly lifted Ravlok off the ground. "I think she would love that."

Tiior knew Daeya was in desperate need of friends. Especially if he couldn't find a way out of Starlight, and the ritual left her without...

Ravlok shivered.

Sam nodded emphatically. "It's settled, then."

And with no further preamble, she shoved open the door and stepped inside. The screech of wood made Ravlok wince.

As Sam stumbled to her bunk, movement from the other bed caught Ravlok's eye. A rush of air from blankets thrown back, a small figure bolting upright, the flash of brazier light glinting off metal—

"Rav?"

"It's alright, Daeya. I'm here."

Her sigh dropped the outline of her shoulders several fingerspans. "Bleeding Aether."

Ravlok went to her, staggering across the wavering shadows. Caelyn's wrath, where did Jerinoch get that stuff?

He dropped gracelessly beside Daeya, and she folded herself into his arms with the ease of familiarity, of deep, irrevocable affection. Ravlok breathed her in, and the full force of his guilt struck him as Sam rolled away.

He couldn't be what she needed, but he could be for Daeya. It was better this way, staying uninvolved, if he truly had to follow through on his promise.

The Ritual of Ascension would change her, but both the tome and Riisii confirmed it was the way forward. He swallowed against the sand in his throat and held her tighter. Daeya was a better friend than he could have ever prayed for. He would do anything to see her become the person she was meant to be.

So, if it was a sacrifice the ritual needed, a sacrifice it would get.

# CHAPTER TWENTY-FOUR

## NORMOS

Not fifteen minutes into breakfast at the Tipsy Tankard, and Normos was already fed up with everything. The sausages were under-spiced, the eggs were overcooked, the company left much to be desired, and Shei-Gwen Mar-Pol was late.

"She's a pretty thing, isn't she, Normos?"

Normos shoved Joss's elbow off the table. "We're not here to ogle the wait-staff."

Over a week had passed since his meeting with the Life Coven director and Shavva, the Sanctuary's high priestess. He'd secured all twelve healers, reviewed the Ferid mine's ledgers, and prepared for three convoys to transport Gregory's inventory north. The first had left earlier this morning, bound for Sarton and escorted by Toby. Joss and Normos would escort the second and third convoys to Trivvix on Silonasday, two days from now. While he wasn't thrilled to be stuck with Joss for the next few months, he could at least ensure both remaining convoys got to their destinations safely.

Joss leaned back on two legs of his seat. He leered at their waitress's backside while she bent to retrieve the coins he'd tossed on the floor.

It still wasn't clear what Gregory saw in the oldest Vika brother. His family wasn't wealthy, and Joss was far less useful than either of his siblings. Normos kicked Joss's chair and threw him off balance. "Mind your manners, pig."

Joss flailed and knocked over his wine glass. "Scabbing Chaos, man. What's your problem?"

"I can think of at least two. I'm not sure who's worse: you or Gwen Mar-Pol."

Joss ignored him. "Wastelands. Now I need another drink." He swiped wine off his black robe and snapped his fingers at the nearest server. After demanding another drink, he sniffed and claimed the dry chair to Normos's left. "You know she's not coming, right?"

*Joss,* Normos decided, picking at his food. *Joss is worse.*

He was glad for whatever magic Miriam had used on him. Despite his constant state of annoyance, he hadn't experienced any more headaches.

Normos brushed his knuckles over the medallion beneath his clothes. "She'll be here."

Everything had gone smoothly this week, save for one thing. During his visit to the saphyrum mine, Councilor Ferren's mages reiterated their reports that Gwen Mar-Pol had audited inventory in the southeastern cache and refused all aid, save for one Feridian acolyte she'd brought with her. While looking over her paperwork, Normos had noted an odd uniformity to the ledger pages that previous books lacked. The columns and script were too perfect, and Normos planned to confront Mar-Pol about them this morning. Her response to his request for a meeting had suggested she wanted to discuss something with him as well.

Joss sipped a new glass of wine, his elbow on the table while he lounged in his seat. Normos's face twitched. Gregory would have been appalled at such slovenly posture.

"You know"—Joss crossed one ankle over his knee—"I rather like that Aivenosian healer. What was her name? Ollie? Olive?"

"Olivia." Normos's fingers tightened around his glass. Olivia Ithenor was the only healer who had volunteered for the position. A curious sort, scandalously dressed and with a regrettable taste for ale rather than wine, but she came with stellar recommendations from Shavva.

"Yeah, Olivia." Joss lingered on her name, letting it roll off his tongue.

Normos resolved to speak with Olivia about Joss before they ventured north.

He sat back and looked around the tavern. It wasn't the sort of upscale establishment he frequented with Gregory, but the glassware and linens were clean, and the wooden floors didn't squeak much. There was only one fist-sized hole in the wall near the bar and a single crack in the front window. Still, he missed the capital, where he could have a properly seared steak and at least one beverage that didn't taste faintly of pears.

"Well, look who it is." Joss rapped his knuckles against Normos's arm and motioned to the door that swung open to admit Councilor Mar-Pol. "By Delvin, you were right. For once, anyway."

Normos bristled. "Touch me again and I'll make you regret waking up this morning."

Joss laughed. "I always do when I wake up without a woman on my cock. I'm taking applications if you want to give it a go."

Ah, there was his headache. The dull throb behind his temples returned in force. "Your ill-bred vulgarity bespeaks your lack of intellect."

"Those were some pretty big words, there. Don't hurt yourself with those." Joss turned in his seat. "Councilor! Good morning."

Gwen grimaced, but straightened her spine as the tavern's patrons glanced toward her. This far outside the capital, seeing a Guild Councilor was an affair all its own. Her tangerine skirts snapped at her ankles with each purposeful stride toward Normos's table.

"Sorcerers."

Clipped and impatient as always.

Normos pushed his plate away and folded his hands. "Good morning, Councilor. Thank you for meeting us."

She remained standing. Far be it from Normos to offer the senior-ranking sorceress a seat.

"I hope you have a good reason for causing so much trouble, Sorcerer Beck. You've gotten the healers all aflutter with your preposterous statements."

The ferocity of her opening move didn't sway him. There was only one person in the world whose anger Normos feared. "I'm afraid I only carry out the orders, Councilor. These decisions were made to ensure a swift end to the controversy up north."

"The war, you mean. Let's call it what it is, shall we?" Gwen leaned over the table, her black hair a lion's mane about her head. "And I'm not sure why you think you know more about the Council's decisions than I do. War or not, citizens travel from all over Eidosinia to receive treatment here. It's folly to take the healers' supplies away from them."

Normos shrugged. "I agree with you."

"If—" Gwen paused, her eyes narrowing. "You do?"

He dipped his chin in a show of deference. Best to let her think she had the upper hand. "Of course. That's why I have an important question for you."

Gwen smoothed her skirts and sank down into the chair opposite him. Wary. "I'm listening."

Normos adjusted his silverware into parallel lines, letting her steep in suspense long enough that her guardedness crumbled into annoyance. It was a technique he'd learned from Gregory, meant to maintain the advantage in any negotiation with a passionate opponent. Once her impatience reached its peak, Mar-Pol would be so unbalanced that any surprise could elicit reactions Normos could use.

She reached that point within seconds. "Stop toying with me—"

Normos struck. "Why did you amend the inventory ledgers?"

Joss's eyebrows shot up. He rested his chin in his hand.

Gwen's ire flickered into shock before she could wrench her expression back under control. "What are you insinuating, Sorcerer?"

Casually, calmly, Normos presented the facts, from his inquiries with the foreman to his own investigation of the mine's inventory. He kept his voice low to avoid drawing attention. Gwen's hands curled into fists and slid into her lap.

When Normos finished, he took a sip of wine. "So, I ask you again, why did you amend the ledgers?"

As Gwen floundered for a response, Joss cackled and pounded the table. "Oh, this is delightful. Wait until Gregory hears this."

For once, Joss's presence proved useful. Gwen stood abruptly and thrust a finger into his face.

"You'll tell him nothing because there's nothing to report. I was investigating a dip in supply, which proved to be a nonissue." She shoved her chair back into place and glared at Normos. "And whatever oddity you think you found in those ledgers is simply a manifestation of a paranoid mind."

Her performance might have cowed a lesser mage, but it didn't convince Normos. He'd had time to consider her motivations. Gwen Mar-Pol's advocacy for the Sanctuary and Life Coven was unmatched in the Council. With the war threatening their saphyrum supply, her loyalty to the healers had come into conflict with her duty to the Guild.

"By my estimation"—Normos set his glass down—"between ten and twenty barrels are missing. I suspect I'll discover the exact number as a surplus in the Sanctuary storehouse."

Something unreadable passed over Gwen's face. She shook her head and laughed. "Audit the Sanctuary if you must, but you'll find nothing amiss."

Her candor might have been genuine, or she could have been calling his bluff. Either way, there was no time for him to audit both the Sanctuary and the Life Coven before Silonasday. Not by himself. Even less plausible was a search of every property in Ferid. He glanced at Joss, considering.

There were other mages in the city that he could call upon, but that would draw Ferren's mages away from the mines. Perhaps the threat of action would be enough.

"I hope you're right, Councilor. We will conduct audits of both locations and search the city. I will enact the full weight of Guild law upon anyone found in possession of undocumented saphyrum. That is, unless you'd like to tell me where you've hidden it. Then we can skip this nonsense, and you can return the barrels without further marring your reputation."

Gwen's teeth flashed against her dark lips. "You overstep, Sorcerer. I could have you censured and relieved of duty for this. You have no evidence to support a search and seizure of any property in this city."

Joss popped a sliver of overcooked bacon into his mouth and crunched noisily.

Normos pushed himself up and met her eye-to-eye across the table. "I invite you to try, Councilor. I'm simply upholding the law."

"The law as only one man sees it," she spat. "You're a marionette on the high shelf, Normos Beck, and it's a long fall to the ground. Shavaan have mercy on you when he cuts you loose."

Fortunately, Gwen didn't stick around to witness how her accusation punched straight through his defenses. Normos flattened the barb forming on his tongue. Even if she was unworthy of her position, it would be uncouth to insult her.

She stormed out of the tavern. The door banged shut behind her.

Joss whistled. "You sure know how to rile the ladies, Beck. Gods damn me, it never gets old." He swung his arm out for a congratulatory thump on the back.

Normos dodged it, still simmering as he watched Gwen retreat through the window. His medallion brushed his bare skin, steadying him against a storm of conflicting emotions.

"Finish your breakfast." Normos flagged down a waitress and pressed several coins into her hand. "We have work to do."

The audits revealed nothing.

Every barrel in the healers' inventory had been carefully recorded in Miriam's own ledger. Normos had worked tirelessly to finish the audit of the Life Coven's supply. Then he'd helped Joss and Ferren's mages finish the larger audit at the Sanctuary.

On Tiiorsday evening, the night before the convoys were scheduled to leave, Joss retired to their flat for dinner, and Normos relished the chance to eat alone at the Moon and Meadery, whose cook knew how to properly marinade cloisterfish with lemon zest and garlic.

Frost collected on the window beside him, and heavy clouds threatened the season's first snow. Ferid's city guard didn't enforce a curfew, so the street saw ample traffic. Most people hurried home ahead of the storm, dressed sensibly in furs. Others, like Normos, lingered in the taverns and shops, loath to venture into the cold. He'd tipped his waitress well enough that she'd allowed him to remain after closing time, and only she, the bartender, and a pair of Feridian patrons remained.

Frustrated by his failure to find the missing barrels, Normos sipped his wine and stared out at the guttering street lanterns. Three blew out as he watched.

The candle on his table flickered, and a shadow fell across his empty plate. He looked up to find his waitress placing some kind of crumbly dessert before him, her smile baring one gold tooth.

"Slice of pear cobbler for you, Sorcerer."

Normos stifled his groan. More pears. But he wasn't about to ruin the thoughtful gesture by refusing. He reached into his pocket for an extra coin. "Thank you, Sara."

She waved him off and collected his other plate. "Keep your money. It's on the house. How was the fish?"

Normos slipped the coin into her pocket anyway and chuckled at her sour look. "It was perfect. If you don't mind me saying so, I don't think you charge enough for it."

"Ah, well." Sara's cheeks reddened. "We do well enough. Money isn't everything, my nana always said."

"Your nana was wise."

"She was, at that." Sara stacked his dirty silverware, then put her hand on one ample hip. "Can I get you anything else? More wine? Some bread?"

"No, thank you. I'll only be a few minutes more." He lifted his glass toward the snowflakes spiraling down outside. "I'm summoning my courage to brave the cold."

Her laugh shook her entire body. "I can see why. You're such a thin lad." She pinched his shoulder as if testing it for substance. "You wouldn't last long out there." She started toward the bar. "Don't let that go to waste, now. It's the best pear cobbler you'll ever have."

Sara backed through the swinging doors with her dishes. She spared a look of motherly admonishment for him, then disappeared into the kitchen.

Resigned, Normos set his wine down and retrieved his spoon.

It *was* the best cobbler he had ever tasted. It had the perfect balance of sweet and piquant flavors. His eyes closed on the first bite, and his opinion of Feridian pears took a sharp turn for the better. He set to with gusto, savoring every bite.

A sharp cry and a shattering dish froze the spoon halfway to his mouth.

The sound came from beyond the kitchen doors. The tavern's other two patrons started, their attention darting toward him.

"Help! Oh gods, somebody help!" Sara's voice.

Normos shot to his feet, and his spoon clattered to the floor. He stormed across the inn, black robe snapping, preparing himself for every possibility, from common thieves to Alliaansi invaders. He pushed through the swinging doors, channeling white-violet lightning in one hand and palming a dagger with the other.

He drew up short at the sight that greeted him. Sara knelt beside the bartender, who lay clutching his chest and staring at the ceiling.

"It's his heart again. Laangor's weakened his heart!" Sara tried to haul the bartender up, only to stumble beneath his weight. "I've got to get him to Oran Osa. She'll help him."

In Aivenosian folklore, Oran Osa—or Mother Bear—was a fae spirit who could cure any malady from a patient who was pure of heart.

Normos growled. Leave it to some mortal to spin the tale into an illegal enterprise and profit off the fae spirit's name. He'd encountered illicit magic-users before. They were always poorly trained, unhinged sorts who cast worthless spells in exchange for drug money or favors. If this alleged Oran Osa practiced nearby, it was a wonder they hadn't seen more arcane maimings here in Ferid.

Sara tugged on the bartender's upper body, lifting him halfway through panic alone before they both collapsed. Her knees cracked against the floor. She stared up at Normos through her tears. "Please, help me, Sorcerer. I can't let him die."

His feet were leaden as he closed the distance and knelt, checking the man's pulse. It feathered erratically under his fingers. Normos studied the rapid rise and fall of his chest.

While he was no healer in truth, Normos had learned much from his secret studies—enough to know heart problems were rarely cured by mundane herbs.

Sara's lip trembled and more tears fell. "He's all I have. Please."

"He's your husband?"

She nodded, sniffling.

Normos knew the basic healing sigils, but he wasn't skilled enough for this. He could Walk the man to the Sanctuary faster than they could ride by carriage. But before he could Walk him anywhere, he had to know. "Does he have magic?"

Sara shook her head. "No, but Oran Osa will see him. She helped him just days ago."

His teeth gritted. Use of magic was forbidden on non-adepts unless they allied with the Alliaansi and threatened the Eidosinian way of life. It was part of the treaty on which the Guild was founded after the Great Schism nearly two centuries ago—the sorcerers' promise that such catastrophic arcane war should never touch their people again.

That included arcane healing, for Magus Noven Ivaeys had started the Schism himself with a healer's sigil that had mutilated and killed his wife, Princess Ourelia Eioden.

"Please, Sorcerer."

Normos clutched the medallion beneath his shirt. The penalty for repeated magic use on a non-adept was execution, and harboring an illegal magic-user demanded the same penalties. Sara was so distraught over her husband's condition, she probably didn't realize the consequences of what she was asking.

If he took them to Oran Osa, it could lead to the arrest of a potentially dangerous criminal. Gregory would reward such vigilance, and Normos would be lauded a hero. But that would also require him to arrest Sara for not reporting Oran Osa sooner. She could end up at the gallows herself.

The thought made his stomach turn. He could walk away from this. He *should* walk away, both to protect himself and to protect Sara. Her husband was likely lost to her already. But if the man was dying, an untrained healer's magic wasn't going to make his situation worse. Perhaps he could school Sara on the right things to say *and* apprehend the magic-user.

"Please. I beg you."

Her tears gutted him, and a tremor passed through his hand. If there was a chance this so-called Oran Osa could save the man, could he really ignore this woman's plea? Then again, if the healer performed a miracle, was he prepared to reward her with a noose?

Gregory would expect him to be uncompromising. Practical. Ruthless.

*Choose life,* Miriam had said. *Choose love.*

He couldn't Walk them through the Aether, but he could see them into a wagon and escort them safely wherever they needed to go. As for what happened from there...

Normos looked up at Sara. "Where do you wish to take him?"

# CHAPTER TWENTY-FIVE

## NORMOS

Snow fell thicker the farther outside of Ferid the wagon went. Flakes swirled through leafless branches and collected on sodden ground. Normos's breath clouded before his nose, and he shivered but refused to complain. He wouldn't be the first to break the solemn silence.

Sara turned onto a narrow track between trees. Normos rode in the back with her husband, Vincert, keeping the wool blanket pinned beneath his boots. Occasionally, he leaned down to brush snow from the bartender's chest.

The scent of Aether offset the crisp air with a tinge of iron. When Sara finally pulled her horse to a stop, Normos lifted his eyes from the dying man's face and looked around.

It seemed like any other part of the forest: overcast and dark amidst silhouettes of low bushes and bare trees. The lanterns hanging from the coach hooks swayed, casting long shadows. Sara secured the reins and leaped down from the driver's seat.

Normos rose from the wooden bench. "Where are we?"

Rather than answer, she put her thumb and forefinger to her lips and whistled a short-short-long pattern three times—the night lark's call, just as in the Oran Osa fae tales. Normos let out a humorless chuckle. Whoever this charlatan was, she'd gone to great lengths to reproduce the Aivenosian myth.

Sara unlatched the creaky tailgate, keeping her eyes trained on a stand of trees. "She has to be here. She has to."

They waited. The rise and fall of Vincert's ribs was nearly invisible under the blanket. Clouds of vapor blew in irregular intervals from his nose.

Sara signaled once more. Normos touched the medallion resting against his sternum. He drew it out of his shirt and ran his thumb over the holly branch. The metal held its warmth even against the bitter cold. This far from the city, far from witnesses who could be his undoing, he considered—

But no. Magus Ivaeys had been a trained caster as well, and his magic had still acted unpredictably. It carried too much risk.

Sara's relieved sob drew his attention upward. The image of the trees wavered, then vanished into motes of light and black-violet mist.

Nestled behind a waist-high wall, surrounded by snow-dusted flowerbeds, sat a stone cottage. Circular windows flanked the door and glowed with warmth. A trail of smoke distorted the skeletal branches behind the chimney. Ivy grew along the walls, flowing up from the ground as if nature might swallow the structure whole. Wide stones half-buried in the snow formed a path to the door, which opened upon a small figure silhouetted by firelight.

An illusion of this size would have been generated by wardstones ringing the area. Normos scanned the ground, locating the bare patches in the snow where the wardstones still warmed the soil. And beyond the stones, illuminated by the light from the cabin, were two carts wrapped in canvas. Normos squinted into the snowfall, eyeing the curved shape of barrels beneath the canvas.

*Gods be good.*

His sudden bark of laughter startled Sara.

The figure at the door hesitated. "Sara? What's happened?" A boy's voice.

Normos rubbed his forehead, barely holding himself together at the sheer absurdity of his bumbling discovery. He recognized the work of master illusionist, Shei-Gwen Mar-Pol. No wonder she wasn't worried about the Sanctuary's or Life Coven's inventories; she'd hidden the barrels here, in a place he would have never found on his own.

"It's Vincert again." Sara spared an uncertain look at Normos. "His heart is failing. He needs Oran Osa."

The boy shook his head. "You shouldn't have brought him here."

"But she said to come back if he had trouble." Sara's tears returned. "He's dying, Sanry!"

"Not him." The boy thrust an accusing finger at Normos. "*Him.*"

"Oh." Sara stiffened, finally realizing her mistake. "Oh no."

Normos crouched on the tailgate and tucked the blanket more tightly around Vincert. There was still a man's life hanging in the balance; he could address their crimes later.

"Sorcerer—" Sara began.

He kept his tone casual. "I could use a hand here."

A much taller figure appeared in the doorway, and a familiar Aivenosian accent carried across the yard. "Sweet Shavaan."

Sara shuffled out of Olivia Ithenor's way as she strode toward the wagon.

Ludicrous. This entire night couldn't possibly get any more absurd. Normos made room for her at the tailgate. "Oran Osa, I presume?"

Olivia nodded, curt and businesslike, as if she wasn't about to commit a hanging offense. "Help me get him inside."

Normos didn't dwell on the circumstances any longer. With Olivia's help, he carried Vincert down the path and into the single-room cottage. Sara and Sanry followed.

A padded table stood next to a shelf laden with herbs and potions. Olivia set to work, summoning saphyric energy and shaping her seeking sigil with practiced ease.

This presented a new layer of complication. Olivia was one of Ferid's best healers, not some keallite addict selling useless spells for her next sniff. To rob not only the Sanctuary but also his own retinue of such skill due to illicit magic use seemed folly. There was also the very real possibility that she *could* save Vincert.

Normos found himself hoping, despite his misgivings, that she would. He also prayed to Mira that he wouldn't have to cart out more than one mutilated corpse if her spells went the way of Magus Ivaeys's.

Ignoring the heated stare from the Feridian boy, Sanry, Normos kept his own expression neutral for Sara's sake. Still, he chose his position carefully before the door, ensuring everyone stayed inside until this situation resolved.

Sanry paced the worn rug before the hearth and scratched the back of his furry neck. Sara sat on the winged sofa, glancing toward Normos as if she might speak. Then she put her face in her hands.

After a few tense seconds, Olivia's seeking sigil faded. "His heart's not pushing blood. Come, Sorcerer, I need your help."

What little warmth he'd reclaimed from the ride left him. The echoes of Gregory's last painful correction made Normos shudder. "I can't—"

Olivia scowled. "You brought him this far. I can save him, but I need your help. Now come."

"He's just waiting to arrest us all," Sanry snapped.

"Quiet." Olivia beckoned to Normos again. "You wear Mira's medallion. That means life has value to you. We don't have time to argue the legality of this situation. Just help me."

His hand closed around the medallion. Gregory wasn't here. Even if Normos aided the healer in some non-magical way, he could always deny it. He took an uncertain step forward. "What do you need?"

"I need you to perform chest compressions while I ready some supplies." She beckoned one final time, and Normos crossed the floor to her side. Olivia positioned his hands on Vincert's chest. She demonstrated the steady, rhythmic push she needed. "This will force blood through his heart."

Normos took over. "Like this?"

"Yes, just like that. Keep doing that."

The motion quickly grew tiresome, but Normos pressed on despite the ache in his arms.

Olivia returned with a few salves and large leaves. "Every living being has a little magic," she explained as she applied a paste to the leaves. "It's a tiny jolt that keeps our hearts beating and our organs working in harmony." She pressed one leaf above Normos's hands. The salve had a floral scent. "Sometimes, when that magic falls out of rhythm"—she gestured for him to step aside and applied the second leaf—"we need only deliver a jolt of our own to set things right again."

Olivia caged her fingers over the leaves. The scent of Aether filled his nostrils as she pulled from her casting bracelet.

"Hold his wrists."

Normos obeyed, his attention rapt.

White-violet static shot from her fingertips, jolting the man's body upward. Normos started, clenching Vincert's wrists harder, but remained riveted by Olivia's deft control of their shared element. As a battle mage, Normos only concerned himself with how *much* power he could channel, not how little.

Olivia withdrew. "Check his pulse."

He placed two fingers over a pulse point. The erratic fluttering he'd felt before had given way to a strong, slightly elevated beat.

Normos looked up at Olivia. "Much better."

A smile slid across her lips. She waved him off and checked for herself. "You checked it before."

Warmth suffused his cheeks. "I did."

"They don't teach you that in the Guild." She peeled off the leaves. "Let's get him comfortable. Sara, he'll need to stay off his feet for several days. I'll leave a list of herbs for you and have Sanry check in while I'm gone."

Normos winced. Now came the distasteful part. "Olivia—"

"Is this when you tell me saving his life was wrong and I'm to be executed for what I've done?"

"What you're doing out here is extremely dangerous."

She sighed. "Now you sound like Gwen."

Gwen. Normos didn't bother to suppress his groan. Of course Mar-Pol knew what Olivia was doing. Gregory was going to love this; he'd been looking for a way to unseat her ever since she'd risen to her Council chair.

"It's not just that you're hiding it." Surely, she knew this. "Using magic to heal non-adepts is forbidden for a reason. You can't tell me the Aivenosians weren't affected by the Schism and Princess Eioden's murder—"

The healer's long-suffering amusement vanished. "Noven Ivaeys didn't murder his wife," she snapped. "He tried to save her from a deadly illness, and his enemies used his failure against him. They didn't want magic being used on the weak and mundane. They wanted to keep it all to themselves, and they used King Eioden's grief to do it."

Mira's mercy, was he really hearing this? If Normos sounded like Gwen, then Olivia sounded like the gods-cursed magi who'd sided with Ivaeys during the Schism.

Olivia shook her head. "You've been lied to your entire life, Normos Beck. You just refuse to see it."

He was *not* going to debate this heresy with her, no matter how she tried to needle him. Normos stepped backward until he leaned against the closest wall. "Every living being has a little magic." He tested her assertion on his tongue, hoping to diffuse this saph-bomb before it exploded. "If that's true, why can't everyone use it?"

Olivia paused in cleaning the salve from Vincert's skin. Her expression softened. "Some mages are stronger with magic than others, right?"

"Right." Immediately, he could see where she was going with this.

"Not everyone's magic is strong enough to use as mages do." She finished wiping off the salve and covered Vincert with the blanket. "But we all have it. Down to the last little ant and leaf, 'we are all created with Saolanni's light and Mira's love.'"

Normos sagged under the weight of that simple truth, quoted from the Book of Life.

Quiet shuffling and the sound of the crackling hearth filled the room. Even if Olivia could explain away her infraction—even if it made sense despite everything he'd been taught—the argument wouldn't hold up when he inevitably had to report this.

Normos's brows furrowed. The Guild's recent decree allowed for magic use against people suspected of conspiring with the blankers. It never stated what kinds of magic.

"You suspected he was an Alliaansi rebel," he tried.

Three pairs of eyes settled on him. He wetted his lips and smoothed the lapels of his robe. "You used magic on him to keep him alive for my interview, but I found no evidence of traitorous activities and released him."

Olivia snorted. "Whatever you have to say to convince yourself."

"You obviously don't understand the gravity of this situation. Not only have you broken Eidosinian law by healing this man, but you're also harboring several thousand gold's worth of undocumented saphyrum. I could have you sent off to the gallows by morning."

"But you won't."

Shock reverberated through him. Certainly, it was the last thing he wanted to do, but he had to uphold the law. Who in the gods' names did this healer think she was?

Olivia returned her salves to the shelf. "You need me up north. I'm the only healer who volunteered to go with you, and"—she nodded toward his medallion—"I can teach you how to use that."

Normos spluttered, hastily tucking the symbol beneath his shirt. He'd always wanted a formal teacher in the healing arts—to see babies born and children grow and wounds mend—but that wasn't who he was meant to be.

"Did Mar-Pol ask you to store that saphyrum here?" he asked instead.

"No. I insisted." Olivia measured doses of dried herbs and packed them in parchment, then placed them in an oiled skin. "She was going to hide it elsewhere, but the last storm flooded the cellar at Mar-Pol Manor." She chuckled, rounding the table to approach the hearth. "She's so overbearing, it's a miracle I've managed to keep the Oran Osa legacy going in this town." Olivia glanced over her shoulder as she passed the herbs to Sara. "Has she talked to you yet? About the School?"

The sudden turn in their conversation left Normos blinking. Mar-Pol *did* say she had something to discuss with him yesterday. They'd never gotten that far before she'd stormed out of the tavern.

"What about the School?" Even the thought of it made his blood simmer.

Olivia ignored him while she gave instructions to Sara regarding Vincert's herbs. Sanry crept across the cottage, sizing up Normos with his large, wolf-like eyes. The pup barely reached his beltline, so he climbed a chair next to Vincert to better look Normos in the face.

"The healers need that saphyrum more than the Guild does." He licked his short snout and growled. "You sorcerers always take everything from us."

"Sanry!" Sara gasped.

Sanry's hands balled into fists. "It's not right."

The accusation struck Normos like a stone. Unrest was a side effect of war, but this clearly had been brewing long before the Alliaansi's attack. The Guild strictly monitored saphyrum distribution to keep it out of black markets and untrained hands. But Olivia's control of her element had just saved a man's life. She'd not mutilated him or caused some horrific accident.

And if magic existed in them all, didn't that warrant some consideration?

Normos regarded Sanry with a seriousness that made the boy's bravado falter. "What do you suggest I do with it?"

Sanry shot an uneasy look at Olivia, who arched an eyebrow and offered no assistance. The boy puffed out his little chest. "I think you should leave it here. I'll keep it safe, and make sure it gets to the healers who need it."

"So, you think I should defy my superiors?" Normos tilted his head. Gutsy, this boy. "You think I should trust you not to sell it? You could make quite the fortune."

Sanry scowled. "I wouldn't do that."

Gutsy, but not the best actor. The thought to sell it might not have occurred to him before, but the slightest hesitation and the way his eyes darted toward the door suggested he was considering it now.

To report the theft would considerably delay the journey north. Gregory expected timeliness. And taking Oran Osa north would effectively staunch her illegal practice without condemning a talented healer to death. As for Gwen Mar-Pol's involvement, he could always report her for amending the ledgers later.

Normos looked beyond the boy to Olivia. "I cannot allow that saphyrum to remain here," he told her. "I will see it removed from the premises and added to the Sanctuary inventory, where it will be easily accessible to the healers." He smirked. "Have Gwen amend the ledgers, since she's so adept at that."

Sanry gripped the back of his chair, his tail swishing.

Olivia's guardedness evaporated. She echoed Normos's smirk. "She did say you were too smart by half."

He straightened and steeled his features into solemnity once more. "Now, what do you know about the School?"

# Chapter Twenty-Six

## Shei-Gwen

Gwen was half-asleep, a book on early Eidosinian building techniques drooping against her chest, when the door to her flat flew open. Startling awake, she shot to her feet, silk nightgown askew, and fell smoothly into a caster's stance. The book hit the floor.

Normos Beck strode into her flat like a scowling blond specter, his black robe crusted with snowflakes that immediately melted in the warmth. "We need to talk."

Gwen's surprise shifted into open fury. She drew upon her casting earrings and frigid arcs of blue-violet light snapped between her fingers. "Have you any idea what time it is? How dare you barge into my home—"

A flash of green skin followed shortly behind Normos. "It's alright, Shei. He's with me."

"Livvie?" She looked between them as Olivia shut and locked the door. "What's going on?"

Normos started forward, only to stop as the magic crackled in Gwen's hand. He lifted placating palms. "What makes you think the School's collapse was an inside job?"

Whatever she'd expected him to say, it wasn't that. Even more unexpected was the pain in his eyes and the absence of derision in his tone, as if he believed there could be truth to it.

Cautiously, maintaining her casting stance, Gwen side-stepped toward the linen robe slung over the desk chair. Normos remembered himself and looked away while she dressed. Once she'd cinched the sash around her waist, she crossed her arms and glared at Olivia. "You don't know how to keep your mouth shut, do you? Where did you even find him?"

"He found me, technically. And he moved your saphyrum."

Aetherial storms. It would be the noose for them both. Gwen spun toward Normos. "How did you—"

"He got lucky." Olivia snorted. "Old Vincert's heart finally gave out. Normos helped Sara bring him to Oran Osa."

Gwen's breath caught in her throat. He hadn't run to Gregory yet? He was a Walker, true, but even he couldn't have Walked that distance twice in one night. Not without suffering Mage's Folly.

For once, Normos abandoned his stuffy formality. "I know why you did it. I promise it's safe and in the healers' hands."

Sweet Shavaan, she needed to sit before she collapsed. Gwen sagged into the seat beside the table. Was he trying to lower her guard and get her to admit what she'd done? Not even the Jurists in Orthovia would demand more proof than what he'd already gathered.

It was as if Delvin himself was giving her a chance to fix this.

"You gave the healers more saphyrum." She took care choosing her words, as if implicating him in the crime might force him to reconsider a hasty report. "Why?"

Normos hesitated. The sod.

Olivia answered for him. "Because he wants to be a healer."

"No!"

His vehement denial made them both jump. Gwen shared a glance with Olivia, then stared at Gregory's frazzled right hand.

Redness bloomed in his cheeks "I mean, no. I was only preparing the healers for the extended delay in their shipments."

Gwen straightened in her chair. His Councilor had such a poor opinion of healers; Gregory would have never approved a surplus shipment, not even to discredit her.

Olivia rolled her eyes. "Sure, that's why you were drooling over my herbs and healing sigils a few hours ago. You just wear Mira's casting amulet as a trinket."

Normos glared back and shook his head. His arm twitched at his side, as if he meant to reach for something, but stopped himself. "Praying to Mira doesn't mean I want to be a healer."

"Could have fooled me."

Gwen studied the younger mage more closely. Normos wore a casting chain like a collar around his neck. Even if he was the most devout follower of Mira in the world, he would have no use for a healer's amulet. Its sparing imbuement of saphyrum wouldn't allow for the kind of power a battle mage could channel. Maybe Olivia was right, Normos *did* want to be a healer, and wouldn't Gregory love that?

"Let me see it. The amulet."

"It's none of your business," he snapped. "Now, was the School's attack an inside job or not?"

Gwen scowled. "Watch your tone, Sorcerer." She'd be Chaos-sworn if he thought she would bend to such disrespect.

At last, Normos seemed to remember he held the lower rank. He dropped his gaze. "Councilor, please," he said. "I need to know."

That was more deference than she got from Olivia, anyway, and Gwen knew Normos wasn't the type to let things go. She would have to give him something or risk his pursuit of information elsewhere. He would take word back to his Councilor, and that would have its own repercussions if certain factors held true.

She had to stall Gregory catching wind of this. She had to pull Normos into her confidence, even if she kept him at arm's length. It was the only way that didn't see her or Olivia hang as early as tomorrow.

Gwen sighed. "It's under investigation."

"Tell me."

An earnest request, not laced with venom or suspicion. She wetted her lips. "There was structural damage found on site that couldn't have been caused by a rift."

She watched him as he absorbed the information—the way his mouth went slack and his eyes widened. Either he hadn't known, or he was an excellent actor.

Gwen rose from her chair and moved to stand before him. She'd given this enough thought in the days since Sarikkian had ordered them to stay away from Ryost. There were only two possibilities that could explain the evidence they'd gathered so far.

"Normos." She attempted a candor that couldn't quite loosen the knot between her shoulder blades. "Has Gregory been having nosebleeds lately?"

He would know the signs of psychic imperium as well as she. "No," he said. "No complaints of headaches or burst blood vessels either. I'm certain his wards are still intact."

Gwen nodded. "What about others? Councilor Blake? Councilor Ferren?"

"I don't know." He frowned. "You think the blankers could've gotten to them?"

"If it's not blankers"—her chest tightened and she turned away—"the alternative is much worse."

"What are you saying?"

The edge in his voice made her hesitate. Of course, he was smart enough to immediately recognize the only other option, but to vocalize it was to breathe life into the possibility.

Gwen touched a hand to her throat and stared into the hearth. "There are many on the Council who've pushed for war for years." She left out the fact that Gregory himself had spearheaded the movement against the Alliaansi for over two decades. "What if they didn't want to wait any longer?"

She let the implications go unsaid. A tragedy manufactured to topple all argument. An event that left no other recourse but war.

"That's outrageous," Normos spat. "What evidence could possibly support our own people destroying our School?"

Gwen breathed out, uncertain how far to push him. She needed him on her side, yes, but his sense of morality might not outweigh his loyalty to Gregory. If Normos scurried off to report on their findings before Sarikkian could fortify their argument beyond reasonable doubt—whether blankers had forced the Councilors' hands or not—this entire investigation could fall apart. There would be no justice served. No answers found. And it would give Gregory and his allies time to retaliate.

She closed her eyes. Trusting Normos with their findings was tantamount to abetting espionage. But he'd secreted away a healer's amulet. He'd come here instead of reporting her and Olivia to other authorities. If she could make him understand the seriousness of their predicament, maybe he could be convinced to exercise discretion. Even a few more days would give Sarikkian more time to act.

"It wasn't the rift that collapsed the building," she said quietly. "We think it might have been a distraction."

Boards creaked behind her as the sorcerer adjusted his footing.

Gwen swallowed once and turned back to him. "A debris crew found clean diagonal breaks on the piers holding up a section of the west wing's second floor. They could've only been caused by magic. Several support beams were also burned through to collapse the floors above them."

Normos's hands balled into fists. "The blankers must have gotten inside the wards. It's not that hard to do."

Certainly, it wasn't. The entire building was warded against rifts originating from outside the towers—allowing students to practice Rift Bending and Walking from within the safety of their halls—but it didn't stop intruders from strolling in the front door.

His lip curled. "One of them cozied right up to McVen under Gregory's nose. Maybe she burned the beams."

Gwen had considered that as well, but McVen would have been on a boat bound for Keilliad at the time. Still, that did lean toward the possibility of blanker involvement. The destruction in Orthovia also correlated with her arrival, and Normos himself had reported the presence of a mastermind there. "If you believe McVen was compromised, Gregory could be, too. That spy would have had access to his office. With him. Alone."

Normos uttered something under his breath that sounded suspiciously like a swear. Gwen raised an eyebrow, and he cringed.

He ran a hand through his hair. "This is insanity."

"I know." She gazed back at him, certain now of her course. Taking a deep breath, she came out with the rest of it. "The crew that found the sabotage disappeared shortly after they reported their findings to Councilor Blake's mages. None of their families have seen them, and no bodies have been found."

"An entire crew?"

Gwen nodded. "Six men and two women."

"Gods have mercy."

It didn't take a mathematician to solve that equation. A rift could just as easily dispose of a few bodies as it could a chunk of stone.

Normos paced toward the hearth. Light reflected off his pale features, and his shoulders rose and fell with labored breaths. It was hard to tell whether the chill creeping into the room was real or imagined, but Gwen shivered nonetheless.

"Blake's mages wanted to cover this up," he mused, echoing her conclusion.

"Hers aren't the only ones." While Olivia collected more logs and stoked the fire, Gwen paced to Normos's side. "When Sarikkian went to investigate the site, the whole area was cloaked by illusion magic. Inside the wards, he found Councilor Ignab's mages hurling the evidence into the Aether."

"It has to be blankers." Normos's entire body quivered as he wrestled with his denial. "We're talking nearly a third of the Council involved in this. They wouldn't murder our own children to start a war with the Alliaansi. I won't believe that."

Unless they assumed only the most grievous blow against the Guild would align all thirteen Council members against the Alliaansi. Not to mention, the blankers' motives for striking the School made no sense. They needed resources and farmland more than they needed to draw the ire of the Eidosinian army.

"I don't want to think they would, but if even one of them has been imperiumed, they're a threat to the rest of us. We need to know for certain." The image of her father soiled and raving on the side of a mountain returned to her in force. Gwen looked away, distracting herself from the tug of grief. If masterminds *were* involved—if they'd made thralls of anyone in a Guild seat of power—the entire provocation of war could be a ruse to lure them into a trap up north, just like the slaughter of Vale's Hollow. There were too many variables. Too many uncertainties. "That's why I'm going north with you."

Normos was looking at Olivia when Gwen returned her attention to them. He nodded, his brows furrowing. "Good idea." Softer, he added, "I'm perhaps too close to him to look at this objectively."

His admission earned a wide-eyed look from Olivia. Gwen's acknowledgment was more subtle, barely more than a nod. Maybe Gregory's lapdog wasn't as blindly obedient as she'd thought. Still, she would proceed with caution.

"Go home. Get some rest," she told him, "but say nothing to Joss. I don't trust that Aether-addled moron any farther than I could rift him."

Normos barked a humorless laugh. "It seems we agree on something after all, Councilor." He managed a bow for Gwen and bade Olivia farewell. "Good night, my lady."

Olivia straightened. "Until the morrow, Sorcerer."

# CHAPTER TWENTY-SEVEN

## DAEYA

Sam pushed a basket into Daeya's chest and waved a dough-crusted hand toward the garden door. Puffs of flour stirred in the morning air as she returned to her biscuit cutter. "Jessie needs onions for the children's eggs. Can you get them for her? They're in the south bed, next to the fence. Half a dozen should do."

Daeya tucked the basket into the crook of her elbow. "Of course."

She dodged a flying spice jar on her way through the swarm of children, then donned a wool cloak before ducking out into the crisp mid-autumn morning. Wet manure and evergreen usurped the smell of baking bread and spiced sausage.

Daeya's nose wrinkled, and she glanced back toward the kitchen. Sam's hastily barked orders and Jerinoch's wheezing laughter filtered through the door. The window framed the Alliaansi elder, who was stuffing his pipe and leaning on the counter while older children scurried by with baskets of fruit.

After being on the road for over a month with her comparably muted companions, the busy household of Havensguard had been an overwhelming, though not unwelcome, change of pace over the last week. Her blisters had blisters and her muscles ached, but it was a good pain that only manual labor and contributing to the communal home could provide.

Daeya passed beneath the apple tree and reached up to snag a fruit from a low-hanging branch. She'd held out hope for an orange or two, but they were too far north for the tropical fruit to keep. Strawberries had also been in her prayers, but she hadn't seen any since they crossed the border.

Apples would do just as well; they were far better than salted meat and forest rat. She bit into it and savored the tangy zing as she made her way across the yard to the onion patch.

Holding the apple between her teeth, Daeya knelt and wiggled the first two onions out by the greens. Their roots gave way with quiet snaps, and she shook the dirt off into the bed. She pulled out four more and placed them in her basket. Then she pulled the apple from her mouth and bit into it with a sigh.

Ravlok had left her before breakfast, responding to a summons from Commander Emaaris. He'd been training under the commander all week, and every morning was a battle to get him out the door. Constant questions—would she be alright without him? Did she want him to stay? Was she sure she felt safe in this house alone?

His concern was endearing, but if she had to hear one more word about the ritual or her gods-cursed destiny, she might use that book of his for kindling.

While Ravlok was away, Daeya was never alone. She helped in the kitchen, played with the children, and even smoked dohanni with Jerinoch a few times. She also tried with varying success to avoid the one-eyed man.

Magnus gave her the creeps. Though he'd advocated for her trial period in council, that eye of his seemed to follow wherever she went, like he was weighing her every move using a metric known only to him, just waiting for something to tip the scale. Sam assured her Magnus was one of the kindest people in Starlight, but he'd been tortured by Guild mages, and Daeya was all too aware of the resentment that could breed.

Mercifully, he was leaving for Willowmarsh today, so she wouldn't have to endure him for a few months.

She took another bite of the apple and tipped her chin into a light wind that, for once, didn't make her cheeks sting. Between the busy house and Ravlok's near-suffocating concern, Daeya savored this rare opportunity to be alone.

The shuffle of approaching boots must have been masked by her chewing. It wasn't until she noted a change in the wind that she turned.

A Syljian man stood behind her, his posture predatory. Instinctual saphyric flares drove Daeya to her feet. His scowl charged the air and forced her back a step. Her foot caught in the basket and the onions spilled out.

He was tall for a Syljian, though not as tall as Alar. A fresh scar traveled the curve of his cheekbone, and his white hair was close-cropped in the style of a soldier.

"For all the trouble you've caused, *bashiin*, you sure don't look like much."

Daeya's face twitched. Their resident Normos, then. His derogatory slur for humans might have had teeth if she hadn't spent the last several years being called worse. She'd been lucky to avoid most of the venomous stares in the Alliaansi community so far, but of course one would eventually find her out here.

Alone.

Daeya dropped her apple into the grass. She shifted one foot forward, one foot back, like Ravlok had taught her. One look at the man's biceps straining at the sleeves of his tunic and the easy way he held himself told her she was outmatched. She clenched her jaw, then reminded herself to relax, careful not to hold her breath or roll her ankle on a bleeding onion.

"What do you want?"

The bastard chuckled. "I thought I'd get a look at the reason why Cheralach Bevausecc was tortured to death in a Guild prison."

A cold finger scraped down Daeya's spine. So it was vengeance he wanted.

Fighting this man was out of the question. If he didn't beat the Aether out of her, he could claim she'd started it, and the Alliaansi leadership would take his word over hers.

She glanced toward the kitchen door, cursing the distance. He was obviously stronger, but Daeya might be faster.

"I had nothing to do with the Deserter's death." Her feet crunched into the onion greens as she tried to sidle around him.

"Oh, but you did." He stepped into her path. "His visions of you lured him to Ryost. *You* were all he could think about as we traveled south."

Shards of ice shot into her core. "What?" Alar had never mentioned that before. "You mean he was looking for me?"

"*Ciir.*" He took another step, and another; Daeya ceded ground with mounting dread. "He should have never been at that drop point. He died because of *you*."

The man made a grab for her. Daeya ducked under his arm, driving an elbow into him as she passed. Onions and basket forgotten, she darted for the door.

His foot caught her ankle and sent her sprawling. A jutting root scraped her palm. Daeya scrambled to get back up, but the weight of his knee against her spine drove her to the dirt.

Air wheezed from her lungs. His strong hands pinned her shoulders. She clawed at the ground, trying to fling dirt backward into his face. Rage and panic lent her strength, and she forced herself upright, only to be shoved back down.

"Bleeding blanker—"

Footsteps crunched through the grass, and a pair of black boots came into view. The newcomer snarled in Syljian, his speech so fast that Daeya couldn't understand what he said. But the weight on her back disappeared, and a body struck the ground beside her.

Zakaari knelt over her attacker, his hand wrapped around the man's throat. Her bodyguard's ear tips quivered, and he hissed into the man's face, "You're blocking the view, *amii*."

Stunned, Daeya pushed herself up, then settled on her backside facing the men. She'd only seen Zakaari once in the last few days, when she'd requested a trip to the herbalist. There hadn't been time for false pleasantries, much less an attempt to pry information from him about his father's keys before he'd rushed off afterward with the same excuse—a date—and the customary warning to stay where he left her.

The man drove his fingers into Zakaari's elbow. "Get off me, *ashaan*."

Half-blood. Apparently not even their own people were spared from derogatory names. Daeya might have scoffed if her lungs weren't protesting every breath. Her hand settled over the bolt wound in her arm. Gods, at this rate, it was never going to heal.

Zakaari released him and stepped backward toward Daeya, placing himself between them. "Maybe you missed the governor's decree, Anwic. The sorceress is off-limits."

The man, Anwic, curled his lip and leaped nimbly to his feet, as if he hadn't just been choke-slammed into the ground. "Your father is a fool, Zakaari."

"I'd wager a hundred gold you couldn't say that to his face."

The slightest wavering of air around Zakaari's fingertips and the scent of hot iron reached Daeya.

So, Tipori's son was an aethermancer.

She struggled back to her feet, subtly testing her ankle for damage. Anwic's eyes darted toward her. Then he spat on the ground, turned on his heel, and fled.

Zakaari didn't spare a look for her. He bent to collect the onions and place them back in the basket.

She pulled the cloak tighter around her shoulders. "You... saved me."

"Your powers of observation are stunning to behold."

Heat rose in her cheeks, and she looked down sharply.

"You alright?" He sounded more irritated than concerned.

Still holding her arm, and with a new ache in her spine, Daeya nodded. "I'm fine."

"You don't look fine." Zakaari held out the basket and flicked a clump of dirt from her hair. "Do you need a healer?"

What was with these people and their healers?

"No." Daeya took the basket, wringing the handle. She gestured toward the disturbed grass and grappled for what more to say. "Thank you for that."

"Yeah, well..." He shrugged. "Don't make a habit of needing rescued."

It might have been a quip, but Zakaari didn't smile. Daeya didn't either. The implication that she couldn't defend herself was ludicrous. They'd spellbound her for just that purpose.

"I'll try not to." Bleeding Aether, she could've plucked the tension between them like a harp.

Rolling his eyes, Zakaari started for the house. "Come on. Damiir is waiting for you."

Right, her new career path. She'd forgotten Damiir was visiting today. Daeya fell in beside him. "Who was that, anyway?"

"Anwic. Kendi's second."

"Commander Emaaris?" Daeya's steps faltered. "That arse is his second-in-command?"

That meant Ravlok was his subordinate.

"*Ciir*, that's what I said." Zakaari shot her an impatient look. "Don't worry. He's a real bastard. He deserves what's coming to him."

"What's that?"

"Ten lashes. And probably another ten when I tell my father he assaulted you."

Her breath quickened as she zipped through all the 'accidents' that might befall Ravlok if Anwic got a hold of him. The endless number of ways he could exact vengeance for Cheralach.

"Please don't," she blurted.

Zakaari paused, his hand halfway to the door handle. "Why not?"

"It'll only make him hate me more."

A fine crease appeared in Zakaari's forehead. "If we don't make an example of him, more people will try to hurt you. Surely you're not stupid enough to think he's the only one who doesn't want you here."

*As if I want to be here myself.* "Because of Cheralach?"

Just as quickly as it appeared, that crease vanished; it was hard to guess the emotion that replaced it. "*Ciir.*"

"Because he was having visions of me?"

Slowly, Zakaari nodded.

She pressed harder. "What can you tell me? What did he see?"

"I don't know."

Zakaari tugged open the door, and the scent and heat of the kitchen wafted over them. Daeya stood her ground and folded her arms.

"Really? This again?" His growl was almost lost to the din.

"Please." Alar had been keeping more secrets from her. Daeya was determined to get answers however she could. "I think I deserve to know."

His exasperation ebbed the longer they stared at each other across the stone walkway. Finally, Zakaari sighed. "That's a question for Orowen." He held up a hand to stop her next request at her lips. "Damiir first. My father also wants to speak with you. I'll take you to her after that. Deal?"

It was a start, at least. "Deal."

He gestured to the open door with a flourish. "After you, Sorceress."

Daeya passed the basket of onions off on Jessie and excused herself before following Zakaari out of the kitchen. They dodged children in the hallway, Patch in the foyer, and some sort of spined lizard in the common room that skittered under a sofa to hide from the boy chasing it.

Zakaari ruffled the lad's white hair as they passed. "Better catch him before he rifts away, *ru'amii.*"

The boy's eyes widened, and he dove under the sofa with such fervor that Daeya couldn't stifle her grin.

Zakaari's boots squeaked to a halt, and he did a double take as she drew up alongside him.

Her amusement faltered. "What?"

"Nothing." Still, he regarded her a moment more. "I'm just surprised you can smile."

"Is there something wrong with me smiling?"

"Not at all."

He met her narrow-eyed stare with a roguish grin and turned away. Three young girls darted into the space Zakaari left. Daeya sidestepped to avoid one of them crashing into her. The girl giggled her apology and kept running, dragged along by one of her friends.

They passed through the sitting room, and Zakaari waved her into an office several rooms down from the foyer. He closed the door and flopped into a chair before a large desk.

In the only other chair sat the same brown-skinned Rillanese man Daeya had seen in council. He shot Zakaari a look that rode a fine line between annoyance and amusement before rising and extending a hand.

"Sorceress, thank you for coming." His palm was unusually silky against Daeya's. Clearly not a swordsman. His brown eyes held a similar softness, and though he was surely in his fifties, he bore a full head of wavy black hair that faded to gray only at his temples. When he released her, he made a motion to shoo Zakaari out of the chair. "Please, sit."

The sight of the desk curdled something inside her. No bleeding way was she sitting there.

She planted her feet and clasped her hands. "I'd prefer to stand, if it's all the same to you."

Zakaari, who'd risen halfway at the man's gesture, slumped back down. "Best not argue, *haalii*. She could teach Anya a thing or two about being stubborn."

"That's quite alright. This shouldn't take long." The man returned to his chair. "You may remember, my name is Damiir. Tipori asked me to find a job for you." He reached for a quill and dipped it into an inkwell. "Now, do you have any skills that might aid me in placing you?"

"Well," Daeya began, "I can cast a mean fireball and weave a six-layered sigil of protection. I can craft a counter-orb capable of shattering a four-layered ward, and I can Bend up to half a league if I have line of sight."

Damiir's quill tip paused above his scroll, and Zakaari started laughing. Despite her attempts to keep a straight face, a smile crept across Daeya's lips.

Damiir's mouth twitched before he wiped off his quill and set it down. He laced his fingers and looked at her over his knuckles. "Alright, point taken. But I'm certain you have other interests outside of your magic. What did you do in your free time?"

"My studies didn't allow for much free time."

Zakaari snorted. "Well, that explains some things."

Damiir shot him a warning look, then sighed and opened his hands in a gesture of surrender. "Daeya—may I call you Daeya?"

She shrugged. "I suppose that is my name."

His gaze sharpened. "Unless you want to dig latrines in the tent cities for the next six months, I would encourage your cooperation."

A shovel would make an excellent bludgeon in a pinch, but there were better ways to secure weapons. Daeya bit her lip. "I know a little about blacksmithing. My da taught me."

"That could be useful. What else?"

"I worked in the Guild nursery."

"You're good with children?"

"They seem to like me well enough." She'd loved volunteering in the nursery—one of the few breaks Gregory had allowed from her training.

Damiir picked his quill back up. "We can always use more hands in the orphanage." He scrawled several notes. "I'll ask our blacksmith if he needs another apprentice. For now, let's start with three shifts at the orphanage and see how you like it."

"See how I like it?"

"Indeed." Damiir looked up from his notes. His features smoothed over, and the knowing look he gave her reminded her of Master Ulrich. "You're not a prisoner, Daeya. You have choices up here. We want you to feel safe and welcome in our city."

Zakaari mumbled something under his breath in a different language. Damiir looked between them, his dark eyes calculating, then he responded to Zakaari in the same tongue.

Heat swept across Daeya's chest. They were talking about the attack. They had to be. "I may be wrong, but isn't it generally considered rude to exclude someone from a conversation?"

Damiir pushed away from the desk and stood. "Please forgive us, Sorceress. I won't keep you any longer." He nodded toward Zakaari. "Ari can see you to Wilfau for further instruction."

She scowled. "Now, hang on—"

"I'm supposed to take her to *Peiaa* after this." Zakaari stood and stretched, twisting his back to elicit several audible pops. "And she's asked to see Orowen."

"*Peiaa* took your sister back to Orowen before dawn. They're both still at the Temple."

That gave Zakaari pause. "She had another episode?"

Damiir winced. "She was carving into her bedroom wall with a knife."

Daeya frowned as he rounded the table. She still hadn't spoken to Zakaari's sister about her visions. Riisii had been confined to her home and unable to receive visitors since they'd arrived last week.

Damiir squeezed Zakaari's shoulder. "Promise me you'll see your *miaa* tonight. Her troops march in a few days, and you'll regret not making the time."

"I will," Zakaari promised.

Daeya began to protest again, but Damiir stopped her with a look. "Attacks against you will not be tolerated. We will ensure Anwic has no further chance to harm you."

Her thoughts flitted back to Ravlok. "Please, there's no need—"

"It's not up for debate."

With no other outlet for her anger, Daeya whirled on Zakaari. "You shouldn't have told him anything. I could've handled it myself."

"Yeah, I could see how well you handled yourself."

Her fists balled. She turned back to Damiir. "You can't just protect me, then. My friend Ravlok just joined your army under Anwic. If he can't get to me, he'll have every chance to hurt him."

Damiir's eyebrows rose. Even Zakaari's haughty smirk faltered.

"Your friend is safe, Daeya," Damiir said. "Tipori will remove Anwic from command immediately. Assaulting a refugee will see him imprisoned as well. We take these things very seriously. I assure you it will not happen again."

Imprisonment just for attacking her? That was insane. The Guild would have never done such a thing. How many of Anwic's companions might be incensed by his treatment? What would they do to retaliate?

Her nails dug into her palms.

Damiir softened. "This is going to get easier. Just give it time."

Pressure mounted behind her eyes, and she squeezed them shut. She wouldn't cry in front of these people. She would *not* show them weakness.

Damiir bade them farewell and departed. Zakaari hung back, glancing between her and the door as if he'd rather be anywhere else in the world.

She scoffed. Who could blame him, anyway?

"Are—" He cringed. "Is there anything I can do?"

Daeya shook her head, still battling for control.

"I'm sorry I told him. I thought—"

"I get it," she croaked. And she did. She truly did. In his own unusual way, Zakaari was trying to help her. Maybe when it no longer felt like he'd tried to bash her ribs in with a hammer, she'd appreciate it more.

"Right." He raked a hand through his hair. "Hey, why don't I get us some breakfast? We can eat in here, away from all the noise."

Breakfast. She chuckled bitterly, knocking her tears loose. She'd forgotten all about breakfast. As if in answer, her stomach grumbled.

"Right," he said again, sidling toward the door. "I'll, uh, I'll be right back."

# CHAPTER TWENTY-EIGHT

## OROWEN

Orowen poured two steaming cups of cider and set the kettle aside. Scents of apple and cinnamon wafted up from the mugs, and she breathed in, preparing herself for the encounter to come.

Riisii paced the Temple floor, clutching her hair and shaking her head. "It was important. It was important. It was important..."

Her ravings had only worsened over the last week. Orowen wasn't certain the girl would accept being admitted to a private room in the Temple, but it was the safest option, especially with this new development of carving into walls.

She picked up a mug and turned back to her niece. "Riisii, would you have a drink with me?"

"It was important. I know it was important. He's taken it. He's taken it from me, and now I can't See..."

Eight white-robed acolytes hovered in a loose circle around them. They were not to intervene, but to remain close in case Riisii's episode escalated or triggered another seizure. Tipori stood among them, hands folded. If not for the whiteness in his knuckles, Orowen might have believed her brother-in-law's stoic façade.

Bren leaned close and whispered, "Should we sedate her or something?"

"No," Orowen replied. "Right now, we need to keep her calm and listen to what she has to say. If your seeking sigils found nothing amiss, then there's little healing magic that can help. We may yet need psionics"—she tried not to wince at the thought of trying once more to convince Tipori to let a mastermind anywhere near his daughter—"but for now, just watch closely."

"Yes, Devoted."

Orowen approached Riisii with the mug. She waited until the girl completed her circuit of the long aisle between a row of beds and columns and started back.

"It was important. It was important, that's why he took it. He doesn't want me to See..."

"Riisii." She hardened her tone just enough that Riisii's eyes flicked upward. She blinked several times, seeming to stare past Orowen.

Then Riisii's face crumpled. "I can't See, *haaliia*. I can't See. I can't—"

"I know, *neime*. I hear you. Please, will you sit and talk with me? I want to help."

Riisii followed her gesture to the closest bed and sat heavily, putting her face in her hands. "He wants inside. He wants inside my mind. He can't have it. He can't..."

Orowen's chest tightened. *That* was a disturbing new addition, and far too similar to the ravings she'd heard long ago in a poppy den full of Chaos priests. She abandoned the mug on the table beside the bed, careful not to let the tremor in her hands show. She sat next to Riisii and cupped her knee.

"Who wants inside your mind, Riisii?"

"Chaos."

At least that was consistent. "Is he saying something to you?"

"*Ciir.*"

"What is he saying?"

Riisii lowered her hands and stared into the rafters. "He says my mind is weak. That he wants to help me. But I don't want him to."

Mira's mercy, it *was* happening again.

Tipori moved in Orowen's periphery, his expression dark. If he trembled any harder, the walls of Saolanni's temple would quake. "Your mind is not weak. Whoever is doing this to you will answer for it."

Orowen shook off her chills and cut a sharp look in his direction. Tipori's brows knitted, head turning aside as he visibly restrained himself.

"He took my eyes." Riisii's fearful gaze settled on her father. "He can't have my mind, too."

Orowen squeezed her knee. "You're safe here, *neime*." It took a force of will to keep her voice steady. "He can't make you do anything you don't want to do. Do you understand?"

"He took my eyes. He took my *eyes*!"

"I hear you. *Haaliia*'s going to fix it, but it may take time." She was careful not to wince. "You Saw something last week in the council hall. Do you remember that, Riisii?"

Riisii went pale. Her voice edged higher, bordering on hysterics. "*Ciir*. It was important. It was important, and I can't remember. He took it. He—"

"Is there anything at all you can remember?"

"He was there."

"Chaos was?"

"*Ciir*."

Tipori bristled. "In the council hall?"

"Tipori." Orowen so rarely used a stern voice that three of her acolytes jumped. "I'll dismiss you if I must."

He expelled a sigh and retrieved his façade with a nod. "Apologies, Devoted."

She waited a few moments more, allowing him to calm further before returning her attention to Riisii.

"It was important. It was—" Riisii straightened. "The bookkeeper's ritual." As quickly as her moment of clarity appeared, it dissolved. She clutched her head, her posture wilting. "No. No, that's not right. Before that, in the garden."

"What about the garden?" Starlight had several gardens, but Orowen refrained from naming any of them in case she unintentionally influenced Riisii's thoughts. "What can you remember?"

"I…" Riisii's eyes danced as if searching for answers in the tile. Then she bent double with a snarl, her hands clawing into her hair. "I can't remember! It was important—"

"It's alright. Give yourself time." Orowen rubbed slow circles over Riisii's back. "Perhaps a little rest will help you remember. Can Bren use a sedative sigil to help you sleep?"

Still holding her head, Riisii nodded.

"Thank you, *neime*." With one last squeeze of Riisii's knee, Orowen rose and beckoned to Bren. "Escort Riisii to a private room and help her get comfortable."

Bren bowed, his dark faelocks tumbling over one shoulder. "Yes, Devoted."

"Thank you. I'll be along soon." Orowen caught Tipori's eyes and tipped her chin toward an alcove.

He followed her there, his eyes reflecting light from a candle on the altar. "Her mind should have been warded against psionic attacks. What's happening to her?"

"You know wards can be broken." Orowen kept her voice low. "I still want Ashaara to examine her—"

"Absolutely not."

She lifted her hand to stay Tipori's protests. "She will know if someone's trying to imperium Riisii. But *neime*..." Orowen hesitated. "I'm almost inclined to believe her."

Tipori's mouth pressed into a line. "What, that Chaos is trying to possess my daughter? You know how ridiculous that sounds."

"*Ciir*, I do." Orowen steeled herself with a calming breath. "But everything she's describing echoes the experience of an acolyte in Chaos's clergy. The lore claims he was the first mastermind, and that in his quest for power, he abandoned his corporeal form, and now resides only in the minds of his followers."

"And why would he target Riisii? She's never shown interest in the gods."

Orowen drew another steadying breath. She had to approach this very carefully. "Some believe Chaos preys on those who have experienced deep psychological trauma. It's said he promises strength when theirs falters." She paused again, before deciding that she helped no one by holding back information. "Her history could make her susceptible."

Tipori stiffened. Rillion was always a sensitive subject for her brother-in-law. Though he'd left his past behind him, the slavers' nation had still left its share of scars on his family.

"You've fought Chaos priests before. It started like this?"

"*Ciir*. Maralla and I chased a sect out of Aon'In many years ago." She gripped her wrists beneath her sleeves. "If Chaos priests have returned, we may see more of this cropping up all over the community."

"Of course it would be now of all times." Tipori rubbed his face. "How do we fight this? Surely, you're not insinuating we fight a god."

"No, of course not. But rooting out the sect's members will be key. They often act more irrationally than normal, and some are prone to fits of violence."

"So, we'll ask the community to report any unusual behavior." Tipori made a flippant gesture. "What else?"

"She said something important happens in a garden. Perhaps post security around all the gardens in Starlight to deter whatever she Saw."

"Consider it done."

"*Peiaa?*"

Orowen turned at the sound of her nephew's voice. Zakaari weaved through the infirmary beds as the Temple doors swung closed. Daeya trailed behind him with a slight limp. Streaks of dirt peppered her front and a fresh scrape marred her cheek.

Orowen started. "*Saonis miraar.* What happened?"

"Anwic happened," Zakaari said. "But she's being stubborn and refuses healing."

"What do you mean, 'Anwic happened'?" Tipori demanded.

Zakaari glanced back at the sorceress. "Do you want to tell him, or should I?"

Daeya sighed. "I'll tell him." She addressed Tipori with all the care of a fisherman testing the thickness of ice in a pond. "Anwic attacked me in the garden outside Havensguard. It's really no big deal. He was just trying to scare me."

A garden. Orowen shared a glance with Tipori. Could that be one mystery solved? It felt too easy.

"I know what I saw." Zakaari glowered at Daeya. "If I hadn't shown up, he'd have beaten you bloody."

Anwic, of all people—Orowen could have kicked herself. As angry as he'd been that Cheralach's visions had led them to a sorceress, she should have seen this coming. Still, volatile as he was, Anwic had never been provoked to such violence before. It wasn't too big a leap to assume he'd been compromised.

"You saw the attack?" Tipori asked his son.

"*Ciir.* I pulled him off her."

He swore in Rillanese. "I want him detained immediately."

While Tipori waved over an acolyte to deliver orders to Kendi, Orowen studied the girl Cheralach had given his life trying to rescue. She was short for a human, not even as tall as Zakaari, but Orowen still had to look up to meet her green eyes. Light glinted off her white-blonde roots while the rest of her reddish locks framed a feminine jaw and delicate chin.

A sense of familiarity tugged at Orowen. "Are you certain you won't accept healing from one of my acolytes? Several are human if that would make you more comfortable."

Daeya blinked. "It-it's not that. It's just—you don't need to waste saphyrum on me."

"That is thoughtful of you, but I think it's worth a sigil to see you well again."

Something flickered in Daeya's expression. Panic, maybe, or fear. The poor thing was so unnerved, Orowen had to fight the urge to reach for her.

"I'll be alright. It's just a few bruises."

Zakaari groaned. "Gods, just let her heal you."

Daeya came to life with a glare. "I said no."

"You're impossible—"

"It's alright, *neime*. She doesn't have to." Orowen offered her a smile. "But if you change your mind, Saolanni's doors are always open."

That sense of familiarity tugged at Orowen again when Daeya attempted a half-hearted smile in return. "Thank you."

The acolyte bearing Tipori's message dashed out the door. Tipori reclaimed his spot in the tight circle they'd formed and addressed Daeya. "Did Anwic say or do anything strange before or after he attacked you?"

She shrugged. "I don't really know what's strange for him, but he said your leader, Cheralach, died on my behalf." She leveled her gaze on Orowen. "Zakaari said you could tell me what he meant by that."

Orowen grew still. "Alar didn't tell you about the visions?" As the words left her mouth, she knew the answer. Alar had put little stock in them from the beginning.

"No." Daeya hugged her arms. "He kept a lot of things to himself."

"As he does," Tipori groused.

"You will have all the answers I can provide," Orowen promised. That conversation was bound to be a lengthy one, and something that should be addressed carefully. She glanced toward the private rooms, considering. "I have a patient who requires my attention, and my next few days will be busy helping the Fourth Legion prepare to march. I can find you in Havensguard after the memorial. Would that be alright?"

"Sure, whenever you have the time."

"And I will see to Anwic's punishment personally." The anger had never truly left Tipori's voice. "Your poor treatment in my city ends now. You have my word."

Alarm shot across the girl's face. Before she could speak, Zakaari placed a hand on her shoulder. "Don't worry. I told you he would handle this. For the sake of all that is divine, just let him. Please."

It was clear the pair had spoken of this at length already. Orowen waited out the heartbeats as the sorceress came to terms with it and nodded. Relief smoothed

Zakaari's lilac features, and Orowen smirked. She couldn't remember the last time her nephew asked so nicely for anything.

Zakaari caught her gaze and looked away quickly, but a rare darkening of his cheeks gave him away. Orowen's smile edged wider.

He jerked his thumb toward Daeya. "You wanted to see her, *Peiaa*?"

"*Ciir*. Has Damiir found you?"

As Daeya nodded, Zakaari explained, "He assigned her to Wilfau, and maybe Clem if he wants another apprentice."

The Cintoshi blacksmith didn't trust sorcerers, and he'd never warmed to Cheralach or Jerinoch despite their defection from the Guild nearly thirty years ago. Truly, he could hold a grudge better than Koraani.

"The blacksmith will say no." Tipori echoed Orowen's thoughts. "But we always need help with the children. In addition, I want to assess your skill with magic and martial arts."

He'd spoken of his interest in testing the girl for Aetherian potential. Orowen shifted on her feet, trying to ignore the echoes of soldiers' screams and splitting stone. She dared not look at her hands, lest she see the blood beneath her nails.

Her sister's blood. Children's blood.

Daeya frowned. "Isn't that going to be sort of pointless? With the binders and all."

"The binders are of no consequence," Tipori said. "I can remove them or replace them with a word. If you're in agreement, we can begin after the memorial."

"I guess. It's not like I have anything better to do."

"We should also discuss the information you have on the Guild's saphyrum stores. You're free to report in council, or we can meet privately, and I will report on your behalf."

Daeya's expression darkened, and for a third time, familiarity yanked at Orowen, delaying the sickening spiral into the black rift of her thoughts. She'd seen that look before—one both brazen and stubborn, bowing to no one. She blinked her eyes clear, certain she was seeing things.

Until Daeya folded her arms and leaned back on one foot. That tilt of her head, the set of her mouth, and the haughty narrowing of her eyes. The twelve-pointed pendant around her neck caught the light, and all the air in the room got sucked out through a rift.

*It can't be.*

"I'm not telling you anything until arrangements have been made for my family."

*Saonis miraar*, she even sounded like...

Orowen shook herself.

Zakaari sidled away from Daeya, muttering, "Oh, now you've done it."

Tipori fixed the sorceress with a molten stare. "Getting Angus and Murtagh McVen out of Eidosinia will take time and resources we don't have. I'm asking you to help us. If we can procure what we need, I have a contact in Ryost who can see your family north sooner than the Alliaansi can. But that contact doesn't work for free."

"Neither will I." Daeya stood firmly. "Even a thousand barrels of saphyrum won't give you an edge in this war, and I think you know it. Why else would you be so nice to me? You need me as much as I need you."

It was akin to watching the tide turn, the way his sternness eroded. Echoes of his ire lingered like ripples in the sand, but there was no substance to them.

In its place emerged the barest hint of appreciation. The smallest fraction of a smile. "You want to make a deal."

"Yes."

"Alright. Name your terms, Sorceress."

"I want eyes on my father and cousin. I want weekly reports of their welfare, guaranteed passage north for them by spring, and a promise of immediate extraction if the sorcerers make a move on them."

Orowen didn't realize she was grinning until her cheeks began to ache. She gathered the panels of her white robe together and tucked her hands into her sleeves. How many years had it been? Seventeen? Cheralach believed the girl to be about sixteen. It was possible, even probable, given the last conversation she had with Neri before she disappeared. And that pendant, crafted by a master jeweler whose work was renowned throughout Astenpor...

She couldn't take her eyes off that necklace.

"Monthly reports," Tipori amended, "with the understanding that disruptions in communication may occur. Passage north by spring, or when the worst of the snow has passed, to guarantee my people's safety. And immediate extraction is contingent upon you and your friend acting on your best behavior." He fixed her with a knowing look. "That means no stealing my keys or trying to sneak off."

Color rose in Daeya's cheeks. The girl's likeness was so uncanny that it stole Orowen's breath. A telling sting took root behind her eyes, but she blinked it away. Best not get ahead of herself.

"In exchange," Tipori continued, "you will provide comprehensive knowledge of every Guild supply line and storage cache to the best of your ability. I want tactics, bases, weapons, every scrap of information you have. You will also adhere to a training schedule in magic and weapons." At Daeya's confused frown, he added, "I'll not see your potential squandered on mundane tasks while you're here."

She nodded, her arms loosening from around her midsection. "That seems fair."

"And"—Tipori held up one finger—"upon delivery of your family, you will swear your allegiance to the Alliaansi."

He was pushing her, testing her negotiation skills. Orowen's brows lifted.

Daeya had gotten Tipori's attention. Her brother-in-law wasn't known for taking many students, but he dedicated himself to the few he had. He also used every teaching moment given to him to build the best warriors and strategists the Alliaansi possessed. A better future for the young sorceress couldn't have been fabricated by Silonas himself.

Orowen swallowed back her emotion.

Perceptive as always, Zakaari's brows furrowed in silent question. She gave him the barest shake of her head. Now was not the time.

Daeya latched on to the last of Tipori's terms with a grimace. "If by 'allegiance' you mean remaining in Starlight, I'm afraid I can't do that. I won't be bound to anyone's will but my own."

A spark lit Tipori's violet eyes. "You would be free to come and go as you wish. By allegiance, I mean you accept a place among us, and should we call upon you to fight beside us, you will do so with honor." He extended his hand to Daeya. "Do we have a deal?"

Daeya stared at Tipori's fingers for several heartbeats. When she finally reached up and clasped her palm against his, all the tension in Orowen's shoulders vanished. Even Zakaari sighed, his expression caught somewhere between relief and astonishment.

Daeya's attention remained on Tipori. "Deal."

Tipori released her. "Now, if you'll excuse us, Orowen and I have more business to discuss. I'll send word when I have news of your family."

"Thank you, Tipori." Daeya bowed, the softness in her face returning.

"It is my pleasure."

Zakaari turned with Daeya toward the door, still studying the girl from beneath furrowed brows.

Tipori called after him, "*Ennii.*"

"*Ciir, Peiaa?*"

"If you witness any more outbursts or strange behavior among our citizens, report to me or Orowen immediately. I'll speak with our community leaders this evening to discuss specifically what we're looking for."

"Of course."

Tipori stepped closer to Orowen and folded his hands as the pair departed. "Should we be worried her arrival and the appearance of these Chaos zealots seem to coincide?"

Orowen cleared her throat and drew herself up. "*Aon*. I think she was meant to be here."

Tipori glanced at her. "Copper for your thoughts?"

She considered telling him. Neri had been Tipori's first friend in Starlight when he and Damiir had arrived with Maralla years ago. He'd been just as devastated by Neri's disappearance.

Still, Orowen held back. "Right now, it's just a feeling. I'll tell you when I know more."

He nodded, but the way he hesitated could have written tomes on the art of subtlety. "Devoted."

Not today. She didn't want to do this today. Orowen stifled a groan, returned to the bed where Riisii had been sitting, and started stripping the sheets. If she ignored him long enough, maybe something would call him away.

Tipori came to stand on the bed's opposite side. "Have you given thought to Kendi's suggestion?"

Reaffirmation. Of course she had. She'd even been studying alongside Bren and the other acolytes. But she still couldn't call forth magic in any useful way. Even if she made absolution a part of the ritual to reaffirm her oath, her healers would grant it too easily for it to mean anything.

Tipori seemed to read her silence as denial and sighed. "Self-flagellation, I can understand. You feel responsible for what happened; that, I understand as well." He tugged the sheet free when it caught on one corner. "But what you're doing is self-destructive, and we're all worried for you."

She poured all her ill feelings into a single glare. "Then you should have granted my request for atonement."

He didn't flinch. Didn't blink. Saolanni's grace, the man was even more stalwart than Kendi. "If Chaos priests have really infiltrated Starlight, we're going to need you."

*Charlatan. Oathbreaker.*

The admission wrenched jagged holes in Orowen's armor. Saolanni's light was further from her now than ever. How could he expect her to do more?

She rolled up the sheet and turned away. "I have no magic to fight them with."

"But your magic has returned."

That drew her up short. Orowen looked back to find Tipori's hard gaze on her. She could only stare as he rounded the bed and took hold of her shoulders.

"I've seen you pull light from your beads. That means Mage's Folly isn't your problem." He touched the runes along her temple, his callused fingertips gentle. "Whatever stops you is up here, and here." He tapped the space over her left breast.

Hope sparked, albeit grudgingly, as if loath to pierce the veil of misery shrouding her heart. There *was* a trickle of magic seeping into the void between her and her goddess, but like the meager flow of saphyrum from a set of spellbinders, there was little she could do with it.

The realization staggered her. She'd built her own fortress to keep the world out; of course it would block Saolanni's light as well. Maybe Kendi was right. Maybe renewing her vow—the ultimate show of vulnerability before her goddess—would prove to Saolanni and herself that she was worthy.

"We all see you, *toriia*." Tipori planted a kiss on top of her head. "You don't have to be strong all the time."

The warmth of his affection brought renewed tears to her eyes.

"Have dinner with Kendi tonight. That's an order." Tipori released her. "You know he won't let you avoid him forever."

Orowen chuckled despite herself, and wiped her cheeks. It had been hard to face Kendi since she'd tried to break things off. It was Silonas's fortune that the man was so stubborn.

"*Ciir, Amaa*," she forced out.

Tipori winked. "That's better."

She relaxed her hold on the balled sheet and nodded toward the private rooms where Riisii would be staying. "I should go relieve Bren."

"Maralla will be along to check on her soon."

Orowen nodded, distrusting her voice any further. That spark of hope blazed brighter as she dropped the sheet in a nearby basket. She left the infirmary without looking back.

# CHAPTER TWENTY-NINE

## DAEYA

Four months.

Daeya kicked a pebble down the road and pulled her cloak tighter. At least four months was better than six. Maybe with updates on her father's wellbeing, she'd feel less like she'd failed him at every turn.

She felt along the spider-silk threads that made up her delicate bond with Telerion. *"I'm going to need you if this falls through."*

As always, the dragon didn't acknowledge her. He only responded in her dreams, and the spellbinders seemed to limit her connection with him. The bond was still in place, at least. She hoped he hadn't given up on her taking the Test.

Daeya gnawed her lip and pointedly ignored the sidelong glances Zakaari kept throwing her way. She had other problems, like how Tipori knew about their plans to steal the key to her binders. Had Riisii Seen it and warned him? If so, what else had she Seen? If not, maybe their room was spelled with surveillance sigils.

The Alliaansi could have an arcanist like Toby Vika, whose Aethersight allowed him to spy on others from leagues away, but Alar said Starlight Plateau was warded against Aetherial travel. That would block Aethersight as well. Not to mention, if someone had been listening in on her conversations with Ravlok, the Alliaansi would surely have more questions for her.

Whatever the case, it was better to make Tipori an ally than an enemy.

"That was pretty impressive, what you did back there."

Daeya's attention snapped toward Zakaari. Certain he was about to poke fun at her, she readied her own biting reply, but all he did was grimace and look away. The silence stretched between them, broken only by the scuff of boots and distant chatter of others along the road.

Finally, her curiosity won her over. "What was?"

He shot her a wary glance before letting his expression soften. "Seeing you stand up to my father. Most people wouldn't dare."

"Why? Because he's an Aetherian?"

She stopped herself from saying Tipori likely wasn't even half as strong as the only other Aetherian she knew. When she'd met Vortanis, Tiior's servant, the very air had tasted of metal. Not only was he the right hand of a goddess, he'd enchanted their wardstones—a long and difficult spell for most sorcerers—with a flick of his wrist.

"Partly, *ciir*. But also because of, well"—Zakaari shrugged—"who he is."

She raised an eyebrow. "And who is he?"

"He's…" His face tensed, and he shook his head as if he were annoyed with her again. "Never mind."

Daeya frowned. He'd been kind enough at breakfast, allowing her time to compose herself and avoiding all talk of Anwic or her current predicament. But it was as if her presence was a personal grievance. "You know, I'm sure if you tell your leadership how insufferable I am, they'll take pity and reassign you."

He looked taken aback. "What?"

*Bleeding Aether. The playing dumb routine.*

"It's obvious you'd rather be anywhere else. Believe me, I don't want to be here either. But at least you can do something about your situation."

"I…" Zakaari scowled. "You're really charming, you know that? You must have tons of friends at home."

His words stung swiftly, precisely, like a switch to the back of her thighs.

It must have shown on her face. Zakaari's glare vanished. He stopped in the middle of the street and reached for her. "Look, I didn't mean—"

A flash of lavender caught Daeya's eyes. A tiny Syljian woman ducked under Zakaari's bicep and put her head on his chest, giggling. "Hey Ari. Did you miss me?"

Daeya used the distraction to clear her throat and steel her spine. No way was she going to crack out here in the open.

Zakaari blinked at the woman, whose crown of white braids barely reached his shoulder. "Cirra."

"Of course, you missed me. Who's this?" Cirra's eyes were a soft periwinkle, but the way they sliced over her set Daeya on edge.

"This is Daeya McVen." Zakaari let Cirra wrap his arm more tightly around her as he spoke. "McVen, this is Cirra Nevallia."

"A pleasure." Daeya kept her tone neutral.

"*A pleasure*," Cirra mocked in Syljian, giggling again. She leaned into Zakaari. "This is the sorceress everyone's been talking about?"

Zakaari switched from Trade to Syljian, likely assuming Daeya wouldn't understand them. But even if she didn't speak it perfectly, her comprehension lacked for nothing.

"She is, and she's had a bad enough morning already. There's no need to be rude."

"Please. You just feel sorry for her hair. It looks like someone used it to polish a rusty sword." Cirra slipped her arms around Zakaari's neck and tugged him down, seizing his mouth in a kiss.

Bile rose in Daeya's throat. She rolled her eyes and looked away while Cirra devoured Zakaari's face. It dragged on for a small eternity, eliciting mixed looks of amusement and disgust from passersby. Daeya was just contemplating whether she could find the route back to Havensguard on her own when Zakaari pried his mouth from Cirra's.

He sucked in air like a man drowning. "*Neime—*"

Cirra seized his collar and brushed her nose against his. "When you're done with the carrion feeder, you know where to find me."

"I do," he agreed breathlessly.

Cirra gave Daeya another sweeping glance doused in smug satisfaction.

Daeya faked a pleasant smile in return. "*Saonis taob'ruh tiik doros.*"

She carefully enunciated each syllable of the Syljian farewell she'd learned from Sessiri and Helenia, her own smugness stretching her smile wider when Cirra's mouth fell open.

Cirra recovered slowly, as if steeped in sap. Her face pinched and her nose turned upward. "*Gesuu'bashiin*," she purred.

Zakaari glared at her. Cirra didn't seem to notice. She sauntered away, her white fur cloak whipping behind her.

Daeya shook off the insult. "She seems lovely."

"I'm so sorry about her."

His quick apology left her blinking. She'd been prepared for him to defend his partner. Instead, he narrowed the distance he'd kept between them as if closing ranks. It brought Daeya comfort, even if she'd never admit it.

They crossed an intersection, avoiding the spray from hooves and wagon wheels. Recognizing the nearby cobbler's shop and the row of vendors along the street, Daeya counted seven blocks separating them from the rows of communal houses.

"I really didn't mean to hurt your feelings."

What she should have said was 'thank you,' but what came out was, "I'm a carrion feeder. I don't have feelings."

Zakaari regarded her uncertainly until she tossed him another look—this one full of mischief—and his smile twitched to life. "Now I know that's not true."

Wind caught Daeya's cloak and blew it against Zakaari's legs, calling attention to how close they were. He didn't seem to mind, and she welcomed his added warmth. Her boot caught another stone and sent it skittering across the street.

"Are all your partners so delightful?"

Zakaari actually shuddered. "No. I've tried for a while with Cirra, but it's not working."

Daeya snorted. "Good luck telling her that."

"I'll make sure you're unbound for that encounter. You owe me one, after all."

"It's true." She studied him, tipping her head. "If I ever have a chance to settle that debt, I will."

He regarded her in turn. "I'll hold you to it, McVen."

The rest of their trek to Havensguard was made in less awkward silence. They stopped beside the front gate.

"We'll go see Wilfau after midday meal. You can stay out of trouble until then, right?"

She turned to walk backward toward the door. "I make no promises."

Zakaari chuckled. "You really are impossible."

Zakaari's instinct to wait until after lunch to visit the orphanage was a good one. When they arrived, the place looked like a study from Phan Lu Zho's potato period. Creamed potatoes painted the main hall from the baseboards to the rafters. Handprints smeared the windows, and most of the children under ten had streaks of potato in their hair.

Daeya cringed. The Guild nursery was always busy, but it was never as disastrous as this.

The orphanage director, Wilfau, was every bit the blustery middle-aged woman Daeya had feared. She was squat and stout for a Syljian, as if the pressures of rearing so many children had manifested as a weight on her shoulders that had compressed her over the years. She wore her white hair in a braid so tight that it pulled at her temples. Frazzled shorter strands stuck out in curly poofs that haloed her pointed ears. One white rune adorned the corners of each eye, and another adorned the cleft in her chin.

Wilfau took one look at Daeya and clicked her tongue. "I suppose I shouldn't have expected much. You at least know your letters, I hope?"

Daeya fought the urge to glance toward the door, where Zakaari had just made his hasty exit. "Yes, I can read."

"Good." She snagged the collar of a passing Cintoshi boy. "Kalvus can show you to the library. Reshelve the books and return the scrolls to their cases. I'm sure you can find something to dust or sweep in there. Just stay out of my way and don't let the children eat the parchment."

Daeya gestured toward the abstract potato drawings on a nearby table leg. "Would you like help cleaning up first? I'm quite handy with a bucket and a rag."

"Let go, *Amaa*!" Kalvus extracted himself from Wilfau with an indignant whine. He dodged her attempt to swipe his brown hair into any semblance of uniformity and used his stubby fingers to ruffle it again. Daeya bit down on a laugh, certain it would only incense Wilfau further.

"If I wanted your help, girl, I'd have asked for it. Now go on, and don't let me see you again until your shift is over." Her words were punctuated by the sound of shattering pottery, and Wilfau spun so fast that Daeya braced for a blow. "Errin, Ersev, if that was you, I swear to *saonis* I'll have you mucking stables for a week!"

An insistent tug on her cloak pulled Daeya's attention from the skitter of children trying to flee deeper into the house.

"Come on." Kalvus shot a wary look toward Wilfau as she stalked toward the source of the crash. "Best be far away when she catches 'em."

Daeya let him pull her toward a side passage. As they retreated from the main hall, the random streaks of potato tapered off until she only had to sidestep piccara chips and abandoned toys. The noise lessened, too. By the time the library door closed behind them, Daeya might have mistaken the quiet space for a little-used study chamber in the bowels of the Guild archives.

The smell of dust and old parchment permeated the room, and five walls of the oddly shaped nook were lined with bookshelves. The last housed a shelf filled with tattered scrolls and dusty scroll cases. More empty cases littered the floor.

Tables and chairs of varying heights were scattered atop a stained brown rug. A few chairs lay overturned and books covered every surface, open or closed, face up or face down. If the dust hadn't tipped her off, Kalvus's roaming gaze alone could have confirmed the space was almost never used. Ravlok would have been scandalized.

It gave Daeya an idea.

She turned to Kalvus. "Are there towels or scrap clothes I can use for dusting?"

"Yeah, I can bring you some. I don't know why you'd bother, though. Most of us can't read."

Daeya had guessed as much. "It's not hard. I could teach you if you like."

He cringed and backed toward the door. "I don't think I'd be any good."

"No one is, at first. It's like learning to sew or wield a sword. It takes practice." When he still looked uncertain, Daeya eased up. "Just think on it. I imagine I'll be here a while." She gestured dismissively at the mess.

Kalvus nodded. "Alright."

He left briefly to retrieve a stack of rags, then departed again, leaving Daeya alone with echoes of laughter and indignant screams filtering through the walls of the tiny library.

She got to work righting chairs, collecting books, and wiping tables. The scrolls were a disaster she'd tackle another day, but the books would receive a thorough cleaning before she returned them to the shelves. Wilfau might have tucked her away to keep her out of sight, but that didn't mean Daeya wouldn't give her task proper attention. Every child deserved to read, and they needed a suitable place to do it.

She was just starting on the first stack of books when the door squeaked open. A familiar figure slipped into the room.

Daeya beamed. "Niam."

The Syljian girl started like a frightened ullopie, nearly dropping the book she was carrying. Then her shoulders caved and she breathed a sigh. Still mute, it seemed, but reading Niam's body language was easy enough.

"Apologies. I didn't mean to scare you."

Niam glanced back toward the door.

"You can stay if you want." Daeya waved her rag toward the stack of books. "I'm just on cleaning duty."

Niam looked down at her book, then toward one shelf. She slipped across the floor on silent feet and replaced the tome. When she turned, the uneasy flush in her cheeks had faded.

Daeya patted the empty chair beside her. "No pressure."

The girl's mouth worked as if it had forgotten how to smile. She crossed the rug and sat, her eyes straying to her lap.

In the brief time they'd traveled together, Daeya had learned that yes or no questions were easiest for Niam. She pulled the first book closer and wiped the cover free of dust. After turning it over and wiping down the back and spine, she set it aside to start a new stack.

"So," Daeya ventured, "are they treating you well, here?"

Niam nodded without hesitating. Her quick response brought cooling relief.

Daeya took another book off the stack. "And Ezra? Is he liking it?"

Another nod. Seconds passed before Niam reached across the table. She touched Daeya's wrist and fixed her with a steady look.

Daeya paused. It took her a moment to interpret Niam's frown as a question. "You're asking if I'm alright?"

Niam's fingers wrapped her wrist when she nodded this time and pointed to the scrape on Daeya's cheek.

"I'm fine." Self-consciously, Daeya touched the wound. It was still swollen from Anwic's attack. "But I'll not lie to you. I wish I hadn't come here."

Niam's head tilted. An offer of a listening ear.

The chance to open up and just be *heard* rather than offered advice was too great a gift to ignore. So, Daeya told her. She left out the parts about dragons, destiny, and draegion, but she told her about Da and Murtagh. How she'd nearly been executed by her own people. How her mentor had lied to her, manipulated her, and broken the most fundamental principles of the Guild's creed. How she felt cast adrift up here, where her only Alliaansi ally had taken her hostage. How she'd thought she and Alar had something special until he betrayed her and ditched her among strangers.

At some point, Niam picked up a rag and helped her clean and reshelve the stray books. They straightened the tables and cleaned the scroll cases. By the time Daeya's retelling was done, they'd begun tidying the loose scrolls.

"I guess I *am* getting to see more of the world." Daeya held the next scroll case open. "I can't be upset about that."

Niam tucked a scroll inside, then Daeya capped it and set it on the shelf. A feather-light touch on her shoulder drew her attention. When she turned, she found herself wrapped in Niam's arms.

It took only a beat to return her embrace. Daeya's throat constricted. "Thank you."

Niam pulled back and cupped Daeya's cheeks. No words were needed for the look she gave her—the essence of understanding, patience, and affection.

The door creaked open, and a tiny white-haired boy peered around it.

"Ezra!" Daeya knelt and beckoned to the toddler.

"Yaya!" He dashed forward and flung himself into her arms.

Daeya squeezed the boy, heedless of whatever stickiness covered his hands. He smelled faintly of syrup. "It's so good to see you, Ez."

He wiggled out of her arms, pointed at the scrolls, and patted his chest. "Yaya, read me?"

"You don't want to read those boring old scrolls." She chuckled. "How about a storybook?"

Nodding eagerly, he rushed over to the nearest shelf. "*Ciir!*"

While Ezra strained to pull out the largest tome he could reach, two more faces—one Syljian, one human—appeared in the doorway. Niam glanced at Daeya, lips twitching, before going to assist her brother.

Daeya smiled at the two newcomers. "Do you girls want to hear a story, too?"

They exchanged an uncertain look before pushing the door wider. Daeya sat cross-legged on the rug. Niam helped Ezra carry over a tome with cracked leather binding—a collection of children's stories, many Daeya had memorized.

"Oh, this one is perfect, Ez. Good choice."

She patted the space in front of her and all three children clamored over to sit. Niam chose a chair at the closest table.

Daeya thumbed through the crackling parchment and looked up when she settled on a page. "Alright, this is the story of the little boy who found a faery girl's enchanted slipper in the forest..."

She carried on in the Dessian trade tongue to ensure all the Alliaansi children understood her. Her excitement proved contagious as the two older girls leaned forward with knobby elbows on their knees. Daeya varied her vocal inflection for the dialogue and made sweeping gestures to illustrate the action. If she'd had her magic, she could have formed illusions to act out the story. It was only a minor loss, however, and one the children would never know they'd missed.

The door creaked again, and Kalvus appeared, perhaps drawn by the laughter elicited by the boy in the story tumbling headfirst into a vat of meadberry pudding. The Cintoshi boy settled in a chair beside Niam. Three others crept in after him and found places on the floor.

"...in exchange for returning her slipper, the faery girl gave the boy a very special mirror. Does anyone know what it was?"

"Was it a scrying mirror?" a copper-haired human boy asked.

"Of a sort." Daeya swept her growing audience with an appraising look. "Any other guesses?"

A Syljian girl with a sprinkling of white freckles across her nose raised her hand. "It was the Mirror of Yearning."

Daeya grinned. "It was, indeed. Do you know what it did?" The girl shook her head. Daeya leaned forward and lowered her voice, as if telling them all a great secret. "Some say the Mirror of Yearning can show you the path to your heart's deepest desire."

Their eyes bugged and the older children broke into delighted chatter about what they might ask the mirror for. Ezra grew restless and climbed into Niam's lap. Daeya started to close the book, but a lavender hand on her knee stopped her.

Intelligent violet eyes implored her from beneath a tangle of curly white hair. The boy was maybe eight or nine, and he had a large chunk missing from one pointed ear. "Could you tell us another one?"

A chorus of agreement rose, and the sound brought a wave of joy so potent that Daeya's eyes warmed. She raised her hands in surrender. "Alright, alright. Another one. Let's see..."

Pages crinkled as Daeya searched the tome. When she looked up again, she found three more children sneaking into the library. The two boys cast furtive glances around the room, and the girl froze when she caught Daeya watching them.

"It's alright." She waved them over. "Come, have a seat."

"Come on, Seb, she was just about to start another one," Kalvus said.

The trio shared wary looks and settled on the rug closer to the door. Daeya didn't let her attention linger on them long, lest she scare them off.

Another figure appeared in the doorway. This one squat and round and wearing a scowl that morphed into quiet astonishment. Daeya was careful to avoid Wilfau's gaze. "Has anyone ever heard the story of how Illustria Stormflight calmed a cyclone at sea?"

Hands shot up and excited voices cried out. Wilfau leaned against the doorframe and folded her arms.

"The legends say she was the strongest air savant in the world, but she wasn't always that way. She had to grow and learn and *listen*." Daeya touched the open page. "This is the story of Illustria and a very stubborn pair of goats."

Gasps and giggles were stifled behind hands or shushed by others. Daeya pressed a finger to her lips and waited for their attention. Some of her younger audience fidgeted, only to be pulled into the laps of older children to stay their wiggling. Once the room was quiet, Daeya began the tale.

"It all started one Saosday morning, when Illustria ran out of milk for her oats..."

Out of the corner of her eye, she caught a curious tightness in Wilfau's plump cheeks. It wasn't quite a smile—not yet—but Daeya counted it as a win just the same.

# CHAPTER THIRTY

## ALAR

Finn recovered slowly over the course of twelve days, and Alar stayed close to help her heal. At first, they remained in his room in Baani'anii, where Ashaara performed intensive psionic therapy to assure the integrity of Finn's restructured mind. Once the danger had passed, Ashaara instructed Alar in the administration of her therapy and approved Finn's return to Havensguard.

Alar stood at the window inside Finn's bedroom, looking out over the dusty street. He sighed and adjusted the sheer curtains for the fifth time in an hour. The Fourth Legion paraded by outside, marching toward the outskirts for the Fawn's Breath's memorial and their official send-off—the Alliaansi's first true acknowledgment of the war.

"You make a better door than a window, Alar."

Finn might have lost her memory of Val, but her wit was as sharp as ever. Alar turned from the cheering civilians and multicolored flags to find her sitting on the bed she'd shared with her husband, her back propped against the carved headboard. A side table held a few candles and a small sketch of Val that Alar had requested from Jessie.

He'd referenced that sketch often in conversations with Finn, using stories to fill the gaps in her memories. Val had been such an integral part of her life for the last four years that losing his imprint had blurred most of that time. She could remember major events and other people, but whenever she tried to recall her husband, she explained it was like a shadow of a face she knew she should recall.

Alar pointedly avoided Val's uncanny charcoal likeness and fixed his attention on Finn. "Are you sure you want to attend the ceremony? No one will blame you if you want to stay here."

She smirked and smoothed the tawny blanket over her lap. "Are you sure it's not you who wants to skip the memorial?"

Trumpets and drums sounded in the distance. Alar glanced back out the window. "Truthfully, it's the last place I want to be."

"I think it would be good for you."

He folded his arms. "You sound like my mother."

Alar had taken only a few hours away from Finn to visit his mother, whose interrogation of him over Daeya had been too much to endure. He wasn't ready to define who Daeya was to him, especially with Ashaara's advice weighing on his mind.

"I may not remember him, *nei amii*, but I do remember you. You'd just as soon pretend none of this happened, but you know when you leave this room, you'll be faced with questions." She tilted her head. "And I bet your meeting with Koraani yesterday was about a new mission. One you probably volunteered for, knowing it would take you away long enough that people forget they saw you carrying me through the street with blood on my face."

Alar's jaw twitched. His meeting with Koraani and Ashaara *had* been a discussion regarding information Daeya had provided over the Guild supply caches. Koraani wanted to organize strike teams to secure them, and Ashaara agreed Alar should go along to practice his imperium on enemy troops.

He opened his mouth.

Finn scowled. "Save it."

His teeth clicked shut, and he swallowed the lie like a stone. "I'm sorry."

She threw the blanket off and stood, wobbling at first, but Alar knew better than to assist her. Finn was more likely to part his head from his shoulders with her sword than accept his aid. He remained beside the window, careful not to block her view.

"You've apologized more to me in the last week than you have in your entire life. *Stop.*" Despite the dark blood vessels still marring the whites of her eyes, Finn's gaze was as sharp as ever. She shuffled to the window. "For Mira's sake, I'm fine."

Alar winced. "How can you forgive me after what I've taken from you?"

"You think I should be angry?"

"Yes. Of course you should."

"Is that what you want?"

"If—"

Finn pressed on with all the savage frankness Val had loved about her. She jabbed a finger into his chest. "You want me to scream, cry, and rage at you. Demand that you leave so you have an excuse to run away from the feelings that frighten you so much. Is that it?"

He felt like a toad being dissected in a healer's first year anatomy lesson.

Anger seeped into him, but he willed his mind to calm. He couldn't allow her insight to unsettle him. He would be a mastermind soon—the Alliaansi's most powerful line of defense—and he had to hold himself to a higher standard. One worthy of Ashaara's mentorship.

"Maybe I would be angrier if I thought you did it to hurt me. I know going out there and facing everyone isn't going to be easy, but we can't hide in here forever. The memorial is a good place to start. People will be grieving, not fishing for gossip."

Alar scoffed. "This is Starlight. Only Guild acolytes gossip more."

She smacked his arm. "I'm trying to be serious here."

"It's not a good look on you."

"Alar!" Finn barked a laugh. "Really."

To see her smiling that way, it was almost like the last few months had never happened. Like Val would walk in any moment with one of his enormous grins and chastise him for flirting with his wife.

It provoked a stab of longing, and Alar looked away.

"We should go to the service." The humor in her voice faded. "You should talk about him. Remember him, and celebrate him. I want to do it with you. I want to hear more of his stories and get to know the man I married again. Will you help me do that?"

She clasped his arm, and her touch sent a jolt through him. Closing his eyes, he placed his hand over hers. "I would do anything to give him back to you."

"Thank you." Finn squeezed his bicep, then started for her dresser to change.

Alar resumed his vigil at the window. White-robed master healers wearing gold and red sashes came next in the parade, amulets flashing in the sunlight. During war council this week, which Ashaara still demanded he attend between caring for Finn and studying the imperium, the Alliaansi had agreed to send their best healers, save Orowen, with the Fourth Legion. That left mostly acolytes and junior healers to attend the wounded in Starlight, but the council deemed them adept enough to handle any minor ailments or broken bones that might occur.

"So." The rustle of cloth and the whisper of a dagger into a sheath accompanied Finn's voice. "When do I get to meet your sorceress friend?"

"I'm sure you'll meet her soon enough. You live in the same house."

"But the proper thing would be to introduce us."

Alar's laughter sounded empty even to his own ears. "You're schooling me on what is proper? Don't you use a dagger in lieu of a dinner knife?"

"This isn't about me, you lack-livered ape." She appeared again, dressed in tight leather trimmed with fur. "Have you even spoken to her recently? I heard Zakaari pulled her out of a brawl with Anwic the other day."

Alar didn't bother to hide his distaste. "He did."

Finn leaned against the opposite side of the window casing and folded her arms. "Did you check on her at all?"

"I asked Orowen and Sam. They said she's fine." He didn't offer further explanation. Anything else would lead to an argument or unsolicited advice, and he was in no mood for either. He'd seen Daeya at breakfast yesterday and a few times in council, but it was impossible to get to her without the monk biting at his heels.

Discerning eyes studied him. "You're avoiding her, aren't you?"

"I've had other pressing matters."

"You don't get to use me as an excuse."

"Ashaara has needed me in council. My duty to our people comes first."

"If you care about her, you need to talk to her."

His eyes strayed back out the window, catching a flash of green from a war banner.

He cared. Wastelands, he cared so much that he was willing to overlook all the glaring signs of her potential deception—her upbringing, her prior allegiances, how even Ashaara couldn't reach her with psionics. But he'd been hasty with his heart before, and that had gotten his own father and dozens of others killed.

"She's still angry with me." Part truth, part deflection, all to avoid an admission that he was in over his head and trying not to drown.

"Because you tried to breach her wards?"

"I only did what was asked of me," he snapped. "To protect us all."

Finn didn't flinch. "I'm not the one you have to convince." She held his gaze. "When do you leave?"

Alar hesitated. "Tomorrow."

Her expression darkened. "You were going to leave without saying goodbye. That's foolish, Alar. She deserves better."

"I don't remember asking for your opinion."

"If you think she's upset now, imagine how it'll be when you disappear without a trace for months and she's stuck here with people she doesn't know."

The tightness in his face eased a fraction. He could have argued Ravlok would be with her, and she was getting along with Sam, but that wasn't the point.

"You brought her this far," Finn continued. "You wouldn't have done that if you thought she'd hurt us. Don't ruin your chance at happiness because you have doubts." She nodded toward the door. "Go. Talk to her."

His jaw worked as he mulled things over. He should at least tell Daeya he was leaving. He might have a job to do, but it wouldn't hurt to reassure her she would be alright here without him.

Ravlok would be with the Fifth Legion, preparing for the memorial crowds. There was no better time than now to catch Daeya alone.

Alar nodded and turned for the door. "Alright. This shouldn't take long. I'll meet you downstairs in a few minutes."

Alar stood before the ill-fitting door to Daeya's room, psychically nudging the stragglers in the second-floor hallway to move along. If he was going to speak with her, he refused to have spectators waiting around for another shred of gossip. Alar lifted and lowered his hand twice, then adjusted his cloak and cleared his throat.

He was being ridiculous again.

It was just Daeya. They might not have a psionic connection, but he'd spent months getting to know her at the School. Finn was right; Daeya would want to know where he was going and when he might return. He owed her that much.

At last, he mustered the courage to knock. Moments later, after a barrage of muttered swearing and three forceful tugs on the handle, she opened the door.

"Hi."

Daeya froze. "Alar."

Not long ago, when he was posing as Guild Initiate Faustus Crex, she would have greeted him with a smile and yanked him inside by his arm. She would have slipped into the slightest Brogrenti lilt in her excitement and ushered him to sit, demanding he tell her all about his endeavors since she'd last seen him.

Cursed Wastelands, he shouldn't have left Finn's room. He glanced around to dispel some of the tension in his chest, only to find more people coming up the stairs behind him. "May I come in?"

A full three seconds passed before she stepped aside. "Sure."

The room was a mess of Sam and Jessie's belongings, but Daeya's scent permeated the space. In the time since they'd ventured north, it had morphed from citrus and smoke into something earthy and sweet.

Blue and red paint speckled her hands, likely from her shift at the orphanage this afternoon, and her high-collared shirt bore mud stains from pitching new dwellings in the tent cities this morning. Wilfau and Sam were keeping her busy, and whatever free time she had remaining would soon succumb to Tipori's tutelage.

He tried to close the door quietly, but it stuck against the frame, scraped free with more pressure, and slammed home hard enough to make Alar wince.

"Sorry."

Daeya twisted the hem of her shirt. "It's fine."

He nodded toward her bed. "Can we sit? I think we need to talk."

She sighed. Some of the tension ebbed from her posture, but she remained standing. "I don't want more of the same excuses."

"I just want to help you understand."

She glanced toward the washroom, as if seeking an escape. It cracked something in Alar's carefully crafted mask. Acid coated his tongue. "Is this how it's going to be between us?"

Her green eyes snapped back to his face. Alar braced himself for the storm that would follow.

But her voice was surprisingly steady. "I don't want to fight with you."

"Then don't." Encouraged, Alar reached for her, but she leaned away. He cringed. "Daeya, my intention was never to hurt you. But when my people's safety is called into question, I have to do my job. Please, try to see it from our perspective."

"You said we would find help for my father and then you'd show me the way to the mountain. Instead, I'm a hostage in a city where half the people would gladly see my head on a pike. Forgive me if I have a little trouble sympathizing with you."

"They've agreed to help you. It's just going to take more time than we hoped."

That seemed to mollify her some. Her fingers unclenched and curled again, looser this time.

Seeing his opening, Alar pressed on with news of his assignment. "I'm still going to take you to the mountain, but I have to secure saphyrum for my people first. They're sending me to act on your information. By the time I get back, much of your trial will have elapsed. Telerion's waited this long. What's a few more months?"

"You're..." Her ire dissolved. "You're leaving?"

"It's my duty." Alar tried to look apologetic as he stepped toward her. She didn't flinch away this time. She even leaned in when he brushed her cheek. "But you'll be safe with Ravlok and Sam. Just keep doing what the council asks. I'll be back before you know it."

Eyes glistening, Daeya leaped forward and threw her arms around him.

Rocked by the force of her body against his, Alar blinked into space for a moment before wrapping his arms loosely around her in turn. Ashaara's advice stuck in the back of his throat. He breathed in Daeya's scent and held her tighter. Her body fit against his without gaps or discomfort, like she was made for him, and the thought produced such a vicious stab of agony that he scowled into her hair.

How could he just give this up?

"Alar, I..."

She looked up, eyes searching. He tried to smooth his expression into something softer, something she would want to see, but the anger at being made to choose refused to surrender.

Sniffing once, Daeya pulled away and squared her shoulders. "Just don't do anything stupid."

"I am the steward of caution." He touched her chin this time, relishing the feel of her skin against his. "I'm coming back. I promise."

"You'd better." Softening some, she reached for her cloak on a nearby hook. "Are you going to the memorial, too? We can go together—"

He grimaced. "I don't think that's a good idea."

"Why?"

"You said yourself half this city would see your head on a pike." He pulled her hand from the cloak to interlace their fingers. "The memorial is for Fawn's Breath. That's no place for a sorceress."

Daeya wilted and looked down. "I guess I hadn't thought of it like that."

"I think it's best if you stay inside tonight. There'll be happier occasions for you to attend." Alar released her. "Word is Tipori still plans to celebrate winter solstice."

Steeling her expression, she nodded. "That will be good for morale."

"It will." Alar's gaze lingered on her lips before flicking back up. "I won't be back in time, but I'm sure Sam would take you."

She nodded once more, her voice strained. "I'll ask."

Alar wouldn't make this worse by reaching for her. Daeya was one of the strongest women he knew. She would be okay. His own useless emotion crept into his throat, and he wrenched the door open with a screech of wood. Finn was waiting downstairs and sunset would be upon them soon.

Daeya held the door for him. Her eyes wandered anywhere but his face.

Much as his chest constricted at the sight, Alar didn't acknowledge the single, silent tear that she hastily wiped away. He couldn't. If he took her into his arms even for a moment, he didn't think he would ever let her go. Duty came first, and his heart couldn't be allowed to interfere with rational decisions. He wouldn't disappoint Ashaara again.

"Farewell, Daeya." He summoned the last of his crumbling willpower, turned, and walked away.

Daeya closed the door firmly behind him.

# CHAPTER THIRTY-ONE

## DAEYA

The northern wind teased Daeya's hair off her cheeks. Cold stone pressed against the seat of her trousers as she shifted on the parapet surrounding the orphanage roof.

Far below, Starlight's citizens congregated around a dais on which Tipori, Koraani, Jerinoch, and Maralla stood. Behind them, an enormous bier had been piled high with wreaths of late-blooming wildflowers, artwork, farewell letters, and countless other mementos for the dead. From this distance, Ravlok, Sam, and Jessie were lost among the columns of dark leather, spears, and shields saluting the parading Fourth Legion.

Even if Alar believed she shouldn't bear witness to this ceremony, Daeya couldn't stop herself. If not out of mingled shame and curiosity, then a sense of duty that someone once allied with the Guild should bear witness to their enemies' pain.

Commander Evallier's troops would leave at first light to reinforce the city of Kuma'Kiir, which had been besieged by Guild forces. Winter's approach would slow the legion's march, but the Alliaansi council hoped the early snow would also force the sorcerers to shelter in place.

Rumors whispered that Councilor Gregory led that siege. Daeya had cautioned the council not to underestimate the old sorcerer, though her warning might have fallen on deaf ears if not for Tipori's agreement. He, at least, seemed willing to overlook her former allegiance, as did Jerinoch. It probably helped that Jerinoch and his brother Cheralach had once been Guild defectors, too—something Jerinoch reminded the others of often.

Daeya had spent the last few mornings divulging every secret Guild route and supply cache she could remember, as well as standard practices for moving saphyrum. While some of these details weren't commonly shared with Guild students, she'd nosed around Gregory's office and listened in on conversations enough to know more than she should.

She held off mentioning Telerion.

A stronger wind whipped icy needles into her cheeks. Down on the dais, Tipori's husband Damiir turned his back to shield the torch he held. Once the last members of the Fourth Legion marched to the front of the crowd, the Fifth began distributing tiny white sticks, barely visible as more torches ignited against the encroaching night.

"What are you doing up here?"

Daeya whipped toward that silky baritone, jaw tight. She'd broken one of the first rules of her so-called trial by sneaking out. Zakaari was likely to report her infraction to his father, and Tiior only knew what might happen to her then.

She approached her answer carefully. "I just wanted to watch the memorial."

Zakaari frowned, though he seemed more curious than angry. He came to stand beside her and leaned against the parapet. Between the faintest touch of torchlight and the bright glow of a rising moon, Daeya could make out the strong shape of his jaw and pointed ears.

"Hard to see from up here. Why aren't you with the rest of Havensguard?"

Daeya side-eyed him, expecting a jest. Surely, he would feel the same way Alar did about her presence.

But when his seriousness didn't abate, she sighed and looked toward the dais, where Koraani was speaking, his voice amplified by air savants.

"Alar said it wasn't my place."

"He said what?"

The incredulity in his tone caught her off guard. She tried to save face with a shrug. "I didn't want to intrude, but it felt disrespectful not to attend."

"You lost people, too, didn't you? At the School?"

Daeya fidgeted with a hole in her mitten. She'd been trying not to think about the School for some time, but the images spawned from her nightmares—bodies crushed under blood-spattered stone—came flooding back in a rush. "I don't see what that has to do with anything." Her response tasted bitter.

Zakaari hoisted himself onto the parapet and swung his legs over the roof beside her. "This memorial isn't just for our people, McVen. You have every right to be here."

"What do you mean?"

"*Peiaa* insisted we include the students who died at the School. He thought you might appreciate the chance to mourn them."

"He..."

Words escaped her. For a long time, she couldn't wrap her mind around the idea. Tipori had included sorcerer children in the Alliaansi's eulogy—for her?

She blinked hard against a sudden sting. Had Alar known Tipori planned to do that? Surely he wouldn't have tried to exclude her if he had.

Or maybe he would.

Gods, if she only knew where their friendship stood. Less than an hour ago, she'd taken comfort in his arms and nearly confessed her feelings for him, but the anger in his distant gaze had stayed her tongue. Perhaps it was best he'd left with nothing more than a farewell.

Daeya forced those thoughts aside. "I'm sure that went over well with the rest of the leadership." It was hard to dull the combative edge in her tone.

His eyes reflected the moonlight. A rare softness smoothed the sharper planes of his face. "It was an accident. No matter how the Guild wants to frame it, it should have never happened."

His sincerity stole her breath. Daeya's ribs ached as she battled for a response. He truly seemed to care, and that was more than she should have expected from anyone up here. "Thank you."

The night brightened in the distance, drawing her gaze from the intensity in his stare. Tiny flickers of light spread around the circle. Candles, it seemed, had been distributed to every attendee, and fire passed from wick to wick, eventually reaching the edges of the crowd. A melodic hum carried on the air.

"We normally share stories of those who have gone beyond the Gate at their memorial," Zakaari told her. "Is there anyone you want to talk about?"

Her feet hung over the two-story drop, heels bumping against the stone. Talking with Niam a few days ago had helped her process all the hypocrisies she'd lived by for years, but she'd kept her feelings about the School buried. Everyone, Ravlok and Sam included, swore it was an accident, and she had no reason not to believe them.

Still, the thought of all those children crushed under a mountain of stone provoked pain so intense that her voice cracked under the pressure. "I'm not sure how many of those I knew were lost, but the nursery was beneath that rubble. I worked there for a while."

"You have my condolences." Zakaari hesitated. "*Haaliia* was devastated about the children. Kendi says she barely sleeps anymore."

It took Daeya a beat to recognize the Syljian word for aunt and that Zakaari meant Orowen. Rumors swirled around the Devoted of Saolanni and her involvement in the School's collapse, particularly one outlandish story about the priestess *requesting* to be executed because she'd warped the Aether in their escape. But she didn't seem like the kind of woman who would deliberately kill innocents.

"She wouldn't lose sleep over it if she'd hurt them on purpose." Daeya licked her chapped lips. "Whatever part she played, I don't hold it against her."

"I'm sure she'd love to hear that from you," Zakaari said.

Daeya nodded. She would see Orowen to discuss Cheralach's visions later tonight. Maybe they could speak then.

Below them, Koraani ceded the dais to Tipori, whose voice rumbled over the crowd like distant thunder. There was true power behind his words, and the crowd grew still. Even Zakaari sat a little straighter. She might have teased him if she hadn't done the same herself.

"...and as we move forward into these uncertain times," Tipori said, "we must all remember our goal is not to destroy our enemies, but to protect our allies. We don't go to war because we hate those who stand against us. We march because we love the ones who stand beside us..."

Nerves flitted about Daeya's stomach. Spurred by the Aetherian's words, the urge to move—to act—became almost irresistible. The memory of Niam's battered face, of Ezra, Sessiri, Helenia, all those spell-burned bodies coated in ash might have been motivation enough. But Alar's betrayal had forced her position here into flux; the information she would have given freely instead had become piccara chips to be played strategically in a game for her father's life. She wanted to fight, but not until all her pieces had been returned to her side of the board.

Daeya cemented her hands on the stone and huffed a laugh. "Your father's very good at this."

Zakaari's brows quirked. "You have no idea."

"...so, look around, all of you. Embrace your loved ones. Your brothers and sisters in arms." Tipori reached for Damiir's torch and passed it to their wife. Before he relinquished it completely to Maralla, he cupped her face. "And know that each and every one of them is worth fighting for."

Shouts and cheers roared across the plateau as Tipori dipped his head to capture Maralla's mouth with his. All around them, others embraced with a similar fervor, and soon the entire circle seemed to exchange its solemnity for passion. Boots stamped the ground and weapons clanged against shields. Torches and candles shimmered as the crowd waved them about. Starlight's outskirts glowed with thousands of tiny flames, as if the stars overhead were only faint reflections of those on the ground.

The beauty of it left Daeya breathless. So many people, all brought together in companionship and mourning. Even the wind couldn't snuff out the fire as people of every race and magical aptitude sheltered together, holding true against a coming storm.

Such camaraderie would have never existed among the Guild mages.

On the dais, Damiir stepped up to kiss Maralla, and the three embraced so tightly that the commander vanished between her two husbands. Warmth spilled into Daeya's cheeks, and she averted her gaze as if the display wasn't meant for her to see.

She found Zakaari studying her.

He shook himself and cleared his throat. "I, um..."

Daeya's eyes widened. "Don't even think about it."

"I wasn't!"

"Mhmm."

He let out a full-bellied laugh and elbowed her ribs. "Come on, McVen. Don't tell me you haven't thought about it."

"I assure you I haven't." Even so, her lips tugged upward.

Zakaari shrugged. "Your loss, Sorceress."

"Oh, how will I ever live with myself?"

Torchbearers surrounded the bier of flowers. Tipori took the stage again. "Lastly, *nei amiien*, we ask you to pray for those who died in the tragedy that befell the School of High Sorcery in Eidosinia."

Daeya expected the eddies of dissent that traveled through the crowd. She braced for them, hands tightening on the parapet.

"Now, I know there are those among us who believe the Guild got what it deserved. But let me remind you, the Alliaansi don't condone taking the lives of children. I understand if you cannot find it in your hearts to pray for your enemies. But wiser hearts will pray for the children who were too young to choose a side."

Dissent and disgust, Daeya had expected. What she didn't expect were the louder calls of approval. The candles and torches lifted high in support of Tipori's request. The outpouring of assent that drowned out the opposition.

It wasn't until Zakaari touched her cheek that she realized she was crying.

A deft swipe of his thumb caught a tear tracing its way down her face. "You alright?"

A sob wracked her, pressing her cheek more firmly into his hand. Mortified, she pulled away and wiped her face.

It took her two tries to get the words out. "I guess I'm just surprised. The Guild would have never done anything like this for you."

For once, his smile was free of arrogance. "You're not alone out here. There *are* people who care."

The sound of one voice singing cut through the din.

Damiir's voice. And gods, was it beautiful.

He sang in Syljian, each note soft and airy yet clear as a mountain stream, flowing from one syllable to the next. The song was a prayer to Yasuo the Gatekeeper, and to Baosanni, asking that the souls of those who died would pass through the Plains of Gray and beyond the Gate to find peace in the Afterlife. Daeya let the music cascade over her.

Very softly, Zakaari's voice lifted in perfect harmony beside her.

Her attention drifted toward him. His eyes were closed and he looked at peace, lost in the song. As other voices joined in, the torchbearers set fire to the bier, and by the time the prayer ended, smoke blotted out the stars.

Zakaari broke the silence that followed. "I hope this helps ease your loss."

"Thank you." She frowned, studying him. "What about you? Did you lose anyone?"

"A few friends." His feigned nonchalance almost disguised the wistfulness in his tone. "And I was fond of Cheralach."

"I'm sorry." Daeya fought the urge to reach for him; not everyone appreciated physical comfort like she did. "I only know what the Guild taught me, but the way people mourn him here, he must have been really remarkable."

"He built all of this for us." Zakaari's sweeping gesture encompassed only the circle below them, but Daeya understood his meaning. Cheralach was largely the reason that thousands of Syljians had fled Eidosinia safely over the last three decades. "He and my parents were close. When I was little, he would bring oranges over the border for me and my sisters."

It had been too long since she'd tasted the sweet tang of a Ryostian orange. "Now that's a good man. I'd do bad things for an orange right now."

His smile turned mischievous. "Is that so?"

Daeya immediately regretted her choice of words. "Now, whatever you're thinking—"

"What, you don't trust me? I saved your life, remember."

"It's not like you'll ever let me forget."

Zakaari barked a laugh. "You're right; I won't."

With that, he shoved himself off the roof.

"Zakaari!"

Daeya's cry of alarm was punctuated by a white-violet burst of magic that slowed Zakaari's fall before his legs could splinter on the ground. He landed primly in a crouch and shook his hair out of his eyes.

Moonlight reflected off his teeth as he rose, grinning. "Do you want an orange or not?"

Gods, but did she. "You're insane!"

"Maybe." Magic rippled the air around his uplifted hands. "Jump."

It was impossible to say which of them was crazier: Zakaari, for suggesting the idea, or Daeya herself, for considering it. "You're bluffing."

"I'm not."

Before she knew it, she'd pushed herself into a crouch on the parapet. Her heart hammered in her throat.

"Come on." Light swirled in tiny ribbons around his hands. "Jump."

The drop seemed much farther than it had seconds ago. Daeya tried to swallow, but her mouth had gone dry. "I don't have my magic."

"I know. I'll catch you."

Whatever spell he'd summoned wasn't one Daeya recognized. Aethermancers rarely used sigils or incantations to direct the flow of saphyric energy, opting for faster, though less precise use of the Aether. If she hadn't seen him slow his own fall without the proper sigils prepared, she wouldn't have believed it was possible.

"Jump, Daeya."

Her first name on his lips sent shockwaves all the way to her fingertips. The familiarity in his tone harbored both challenge and promise, as if putting her trust in him would fundamentally alter everything.

This was stupid. So incredibly stupid. The thrill set every part of her alight. Daeya's boots scraped against the stone. She adjusted her cloak around her shoulders, leveraged her weight between both feet—

And jumped.

Wind slashed at her hair and cheeks, tore at her cloak, and ripped the scream right out of her throat. As the ground rushed up to meet her, Zakaari's magic flashed, and a tightening sensation not unlike a warm embrace surrounded her middle. Her fall slowed, giving her stomach a chance to catch up with the rest of her. Glowing palms still upraised, Zakaari reached for her and gently hoisted her out of the air.

Daeya's knees were shaking when her feet touched the ground. She clung to his forearms, laughing with tears streaking upward across her temples.

His strong hands steadied her. "I can't believe you did that."

"You—" Daeya's jaw fell to the ground. "You thought I was going to chicken out, didn't you?"

"Of course I did! What woman in her right mind would leap off a building?"

"You're such an arse!" She smacked his shoulder with enough force to rock him backwards, but he only laughed harder.

Mirth quickly doused all traces of her outrage, and by the time they both regained the ability to breathe, they'd rounded the orphanage to the road that would take them back to the center of town.

Zakaari's arm still wrapped her waist, supporting her jellied legs. "And you called me insane."

"You were very convincing."

"Look, I know I'm irresistible, but you can't blame me for your breakneck antics."

"I suppose I can't argue with that."

Caught off guard by her agreement, Zakaari's gaze snapped toward her.

Before his ego could inflate any more, she winked. "After all, Mira meant to slay hearts when she made you."

He knuckled the top of her head. "You're alright, McVen."

They stumbled down the road together. Soft light from distant fires spilled across the landscape. To their right stood storage sheds and outbuildings filled with summer grain and root vegetables. A stone path on their left led into a nearby garden.

Daeya leaned against Zakaari, her hands tucked into her cloak. "So, I take it there aren't any oranges after all?"

"I'd say you've earned one, wouldn't you? Come on."

He steered her onto the garden path. They wandered through twisting turns flanked by barren plots and bushes until they reached a wooden bridge arching over a manmade creek bed. Zakaari released her and started across, then offered his hand on the slope downward.

She took it with a smirk. "Such a gentleman."

That lopsided grin appeared without fail. He mock-bowed. "Anything for you, my lady."

Arm-in-arm, he escorted her through more empty flowerbeds and under a wide trellis covered in woody plant growth. It meandered with the garden path until it opened upon an iron gate set into the low stone wall.

Daeya paused, staring at the villa beyond.

Built of light-colored stone with a low-pitched roof, a squat turret, and dozens of gleaming arched windows, the villa had to be the only one of its kind in all of Starlight. The sprawling veranda extended into the courtyard, and even in the moonlight, the wide steps appeared stark white, as if freshly scrubbed clean. A peaked awning sheltered the front door, and clay pots on either side overflowed with dried vegetation. It could've easily rivaled any of the nicest homes in Ryost.

Zakaari leaned close. "Can you believe my father claims this is modest living?"

She shook her head. Her da lived in a three-room flat beside his smithy. *That* was modest living. "I can't fathom what he considers immodest."

"I can't either." He flipped the latch on the gate. "Your oranges await."

Inside the villa, the furnishings were simple in design, yet made from some of the finest wood and leather she'd ever seen. Zakaari deposited her on a smooth-backed sofa, tossed a few logs and kindling into the hearth, and disappeared into the kitchen. He returned with a bowl full of oranges and a strange, spiny thing that resembled a Duerguardian cactus.

He plucked an orange from the bowl and tossed it to her. "Have you ever had a spike melon?"

She caught it, and immediately tore off her gloves to sink her nails into the peel. "I don't think so." Sweet-smelling mist wafted into the air. "Is it native to the north?"

"No, it's from Rillion." Zakaari produced a knife and turned the odd fruit on its side. He sliced off the spiky top to reveal a bright yellow interior, then cut into the spike melon to remove both the prickly skin and hard white core. "It's one of my favorites."

"How did you manage to bring that all the way from Rillion?" The journey was over four months by ship with fair winds.

"We have connections."

Daeya rolled her eyes. She'd heard that all too often when it came to the Evallier family. Many claimed Tipori himself funded all the building and military operations in Starlight.

"Here, try this."

Daeya shifted her orange peel into her lap and took the yellow fruit. Zakaari waited, watching intently as she lifted it to her lips.

Sweet and tangy flavors exploded across her tongue, and her eyes blew wide. "Bleeding Aether."

Zakaari's face lit up. "You like it?"

She nodded, chewed, and swallowed. "It's delicious."

"I hoped you would." He offered another piece. "It's sort of like an orange."

"I'm not saying it's better," Daeya finished off the first slice and pinched the second between her forefinger and thumb, "but I would also accept this the next time you ask me to leap off a roof."

"I'll keep that in mind."

Daeya returned his smile. She became acutely aware of the sliver of leather between them, and static skittered across her skin. Zakaari's brows furrowed, as if he'd felt it too. His lips parted as if he might speak, only no sound came out.

A knock came at the door.

He straightened abruptly. "Excuse me."

"Sure."

Daeya shook off the awkward feeling he'd left her with and popped an orange slice into her mouth. Zakaari disappeared around the corner, and a door opened. Female voices carried through the foyer.

"Hey, Ari, I thought you were coming to Cirra's."

"Yeah, where were you tonight? We waited for you at the memorial."

"Cirra and I aren't seeing each other anymore. And I was there. I just..." Zakaari hesitated. "...had a friend who needed someone."

*A friend.*

Warmth bloomed in Daeya's chest. She exhaled sharply and looked down into her lap. But it was just a deflection on his part. His assignment to her had garnered enough gossip already. Tiior only knew how his friends would tease him if they saw her here with him.

"Oh, well, it's not just Cirra. It's all of Baani'anii. Marduu is bringing Mautori ale."

"Sophii—"

"Come on, Ari. Please?"

"We'll make it worth your while."

Zakaari let out a long-suffering sigh. "Let me think about it."

The girls squealed and departed with eager farewell. By the time the door closed and Zakaari returned to the sitting room, Daeya had finished off her orange and deposited the peel on the table. She rose from the couch and turned to face him.

He winced. "Sorry about that."

"It's alright. You should go with them."

"Do you want to go?"

Daeya grimaced. "I don't think Koraani would appreciate me in his house." And gods help her if she saw Alar there, too.

"Koraani's an overgrown child. The only reason his strike team has any leads on saphyrum is because of you."

Zakaari's vehement response felt almost defensive. It warmed her in an entirely new sort of way. Still, she shook her head.

"I'll have plenty more opportunities to piss him off. I'm supposed to meet with Orowen anyway."

"You're sure you'll be alright?"

She tilted her head, as if considering, then nodded toward the bowl of fruit. "If I can take a few more of those, I might make it through the night."

Zakaari grinned and thrust two more oranges at her. "Alright, McVen, let's get you home."

# CHAPTER THIRTY-TWO

## OROWEN

Orowen hadn't seen the inside of Havensguard in months. She turned a slow circle in the common room, taking in the worn rug and couches stained by paint-covered hands and child-sized feet. Wooden toys were haphazardly stuffed into two large chests, both so full that neither lid would close. A dusty tiffleball, a forgotten spoon, and several stray piccara chips littered the floor.

The evidence of joy, and of Sam's dogged attempt to maintain order, teased a smile from Orowen's lips. Much as she'd dreaded coming home, certain Cheralach's absence would make everything more real, a feeling of quiet anticipation muted her sorrow.

Tonight, Orowen might finally put to rest a seventeen-year-long search for answers and welcome one of their lost children home.

Her smile widened as Kendi eyed the well-loved settee with its sagging cushions and one corner held up by a stack of books.

"Why don't you borrow a few chairs from the dining hall, *neime*?" she suggested.

Kendi's relief smoothed every line in his face. "Excellent idea."

He pecked her cheek and started for the room in question, only to swear and sidestep as a startled kitten shot through the doorway.

Laughter caught Orowen wholly unprepared. Knees creaking, she bent to coax the gray-speckled creature from under the settee. Wide green eyes regarded her as she tapped her fingers on the rug. After a long moment, the kitten crept out and sniffed at her. Orowen's world narrowed to the soft glide of fur beneath her fingers as the creature arched into her hand and spun around for more.

"There, now, it's alright. I know Kendi has big, scary feet, doesn't he?" She chuckled and scratched along the kitten's spine, cooing at Caelyn's tiny creation. Kendi gave an exaggerated sour look, then resumed course and returned with two chairs to place beside the hearth.

Orowen scooped the kitten up and sat. It settled bonelessly against her thighs and purred its contentment into her woolen cassock.

Kendi sat beside her, his smile bright. "She feels safe with you."

"Because she is."

The words left her mouth before she could second-guess them, before grief and self-loathing could deaden the surge of joy that such a tiny creature's trust brought. Orowen clung to the sensation, refusing to let doubt strip away something so pure.

Kendi squeezed her knee. "That she is, *nei ama're.*"

Having demanded a place among Orowen's escort for the memorial, rather than at the head of the Fifth Legion, Kendi hadn't left her side since before the ceremony began. Despite the embarrassment of her tears, Orowen felt stones lighter after sharing her burden with him.

The front door opened, admitting her nephew and Daeya. Orowen's anticipation redoubled, but she continued stroking the kitten's downy fur to ground herself. Cries of merriment rode in on the air behind them. The sounds bolstered her. In the morning, her sister would lead the Fourth Legion in the march for Kuma'Kiir. Tomorrow, there would be time for nervousness, fears, and tearful goodbyes, but tonight was for celebration, remembrance, and reunion.

Neither young one seemed to notice them right away. Zakaari hesitated at the door, an unusual diffidence pulling his chin and shoulders inward. "I'll see you tomorrow?"

Orowen's hand stilled on the kitten's back. Beside her, Kendi's brows lifted so high, they nearly scraped his hairline.

"Right—for council?" Daeya breathed.

"Right." Zakaari glanced out the door, then back at Daeya. "Night, McVen."

"Night."

They lingered at the threshold so long that when Kendi cleared his throat, both children jumped.

"*Iiren'norvaa, enniien.*" He chortled his 'good evening' through a knowing smirk.

Orowen whacked him with the back of her hand. "Gadfly," she murmured.

His expression was that of a meddling uncle: smug and unapologetic.

Daeya's cheeks flushed scarlet, and Zakaari's ear tips darkened. Both hastened greetings.

"Good evening."

"*Iiren'norvaa, Amaa. Haaliia.*"

Zakaari fumbled for more to say, then turned to flee, nearly colliding with Sam and Ravlok, who appeared in the doorway behind them.

Orowen hid her mirth behind her palm. Mira's mercy, she'd never seen her nephew so out of sorts.

"Your date can stand to wait a little longer, Ari," Sam called after him. She shook her head. "Gods, you think he'd learn after Sophii's father chased him out of the toolshed with a hay fork."

Ravlok shot a bewildered glance out the door, then looked Daeya over with the protective scrutiny of an older brother. "Are you okay?"

She gathered her cloak tighter, her cheeks a match for summer strawberries. "Yes, I'm fine."

Kendi's shoulders were still shaking when the newcomers joined them before the hearth. Startled by Sam and Ravlok's creaking leathers, the kitten bolted from Orowen's lap. Sam slumped into the sofa cushions beside her. Ravlok and Daeya sat across from them, the monk eyeing the stack of books holding up the settee with no small amount of distress.

They exchanged pleasantries briefly before an appropriate break in the conversation prompted Orowen to speak. "Well, I know you've been anxious to hear more about Cheralach's visions—"

"Actually," Daeya broke in, "there's something I wanted to say to you first."

Like snowflakes before the sun, Orowen's lightness evaporated.

She knew. Daeya knew what she'd done. Of course, it was only a matter of time.

Orowen folded her hands in her lap. The sorceress had only recently defected from the Guild. The School's destruction would have affected her most deeply.

She wouldn't deflect or run from this; she deserved every damning word the young woman could muster. "I would hear anything you have to say, Daeya."

Daeya twisted the hem of her cloak in her fingers. "I understand you were responsible for the rift that destroyed the School. People say that it warped and did more damage than you intended."

"*Ciir*, that is correct."

Daeya glanced toward Ravlok. "I've also heard you asked to be punished for it."

*Charlatan.*

Nausea rose, but Orowen choked it down. "As is only prudent."

When Daeya looked back at her, Orowen braced for venom and anger. She expected tearful fury, or explosive rage, or scathing admonishment. All things she'd earned for defying her faith.

*Oathbreaker.*

Her hands tightened in her lap. Her heart pounded in her ears as the sickening wave of grief poised to crash over her once more.

"I know I can't speak for the families of those children, but I really wanted to say..." Daeya grimaced. "Well, to me it's clear that you're not at fault for what happened."

Everything stopped.

Hands, heart, and throat remained clenched. At first, only a high-pitched ringing registered in Orowen's ears. Then the crackle of the hearth returned, and the couch creaked beside her, and cloth rasped against the cushions.

"Come again?"

"You've been nothing but kind to me since I arrived," Daeya said. "You concerned yourself with my comfort and agreed to meet with me when you owed me nothing. I can tell you feel remorse, and it's obvious what happened *was* an accident."

Was this really happening? Tentative yearning welled inside her, but Orowen forced it back. Kendi must have put her up to this, or perhaps Tipori and Maralla. But when she glanced at him, Kendi was watching Daeya with a similar bafflement, his brows knitted.

"None of you should have been held captive in the first place," Daeya added. "You were just trying to help the people you love."

To hear it from her fellow Alliaansi didn't move Orowen much. But to hear it from a sorceress, who'd likely lost many dear to her in the collapse, made all the difference.

Words were so long in coming for Orowen that Daeya looked down and adjusted her cloak. "I hope that eases your mind a little."

*A little.* Daeya offered forgiveness in its purest form, unburdened by obligations or demands. It helped so much more than a little.

There were so many preparations to be made, studies to attend, and prayers to recite before Orowen could retake the Oath of Saonis. But with a source of true absolution at hand, she could pour all her efforts into reaffirming her faith. She owed it to her goddess, her people, herself, to reclaim her position as high priestess and thereby restore her magic.

"Thank you." Orowen cleared the frog from her throat. "That means more than you can ever know."

Ever the opportunist, Kendi studied Daeya with a sudden shrewdness that could only mean he was up to something. Orowen reached for his hand, but despite her warning squeeze, he shoved onward. "Orowen is planning to reaffirm her oath to Saolanni in a few months' time."

Goodness, no, it was asking too much, too soon. "Kendi—"

"Would you be willing to take part in her ceremony for absolution?"

Orowen gritted her teeth. "Please don't think you have to—"

"I'd love to."

The girl offered a smile that was equal parts sympathy and warmth—a familiar smile that provoked such a staggering urge to embrace her that Orowen gripped Kendi's hand hard to keep herself in her seat.

She floundered for the right way to express her deepest gratitude. "It is fated by the gods themselves, I think, that you're here with us now."

Daeya snorted a laugh. "I don't know about all that."

It was like looking into the past, truly. Orowen suppressed her tearful smile. "I have a story I would like to share with you, in addition to answering your questions about Cheralach. Would you oblige me?"

"Sure."

Orowen closed her eyes. There was a slim chance she was wrong about all this. But the visions, the timing, the necklace—one of only two specially crafted by Sedryn Alliaar for his children—all fit too perfectly to be coincidence.

Seventeen years. Would that she'd invited Koraani to sit in on this. But Neri's brother had never worked through his anger surrounding his sister's disappearance. It was best to be certain before involving him.

"Cheralach never told me everything he saw in his visions," Orowen began, "but there were a few things he saw repeatedly in the months before we left for Ryost." She smoothed the white fabric of her cassock across her lap. "He spoke of an event that would change the course of our people's future. He insisted he had to find a young woman—that she was in danger, and needed our help. He brought together his most trusted allies and told us who he sought: a girl with white hair, green eyes, and an exceptional gift with magic. He said you would be about sixteen."

"So, he did come looking for me." Daeya's tone held the ring of guilt.

"You're the reason he went to Ryost, *ciir*." Orowen leaned forward. "But you're not the reason he died. This, I need you to understand, before I say anything more."

Daeya cast an uneasy look at Ravlok.

He squeezed her knee. "You know you're not. Anwic was just trying to hurt you."

Ravlok had been furious that day he heard about Anwic's attack. Only Orowen's reassurance that Anwic had already been detained kept the monk from barricading himself and Daeya in their quarters and never coming out again.

When Daeya nodded, he settled back in the cushions, placated for the moment.

Orowen sat back as well. "I never asked myself how he knew how old you would be."

Daeya looked sharply at her. Firelight caught the pendant around her neck and reflected off the whites of her eyes.

"I assumed he was simply guessing," Orowen said. "But when you came to visit me at the Temple, I realized he knew much more about you than I thought."

"What do you mean?"

"I will tell you, but first, the story."

Kendi shifted beside her, looking curiously between them. Sam doffed her cloak and the top layer of her leathers and crossed an ankle over one knee.

"Seventeen years ago, the commander of the Alliaansi's First Legion and twelve of her best warriors went missing." Orowen remembered that morning clearly, from the devastation on Koraani's face to the exact placement of Neri's favorite book on her bedside table. "There was no sign of struggle. No notes left. No ransoms demanded. We scoured the forests for them and found nothing. We even had our arcanists look into the Aether, but it was as if they'd vanished. Months passed, and we began to think the worst.

"Her brother, Koraani, was beside himself. For three years, he sent out patrols, long after the rest of us had given up hope. But the one person who never searched—never gave in to the panic and fear—was her husband."

Kendi's eyes widened. "Gods be."

The youngsters each gave him curious frowns.

"Commander?" Sam asked.

"My apologies." He waved Orowen on. "Please, continue."

Even so, his lips pressed into a line, as if he was already piecing things together.

"Koraani believed his brother-in-law knew what happened to his sister. Her husband's lack of concern drove others to think he'd harmed her. But those who knew him best were certain he would never do such a thing."

A phantom chill passed through her at that. Even now, animosity still lingered between Baani'anii and Havensguard.

"The commander and her husband had been planning a family for some time. They came to the Temple often for blessings and prayed to Mira every day that she would grant them a child. This went on for years with no answers from the gods."

Orowen met Daeya's stare with quiet confidence.

"But one day, a few weeks before she disappeared, the commander came to the garden sanctuary. She kissed my cheek and thanked me for all my help. She said the gods had finally answered—that they had chosen them for something very special. Something she couldn't talk about, but she asked me to pray for them."

Kendi nodded sagely. "I remember that day. You were so worried for her."

"I was," Orowen admitted. "The pressures of trying to conceive a child for as long as they did start to affect the mind after a time. It eats at you until it's all you can think about. Every ache, every twinge, starts to mean something more than it does." She'd known those fears herself in the years it took to accept the damage the Light Paladin had done to her lower abdomen. The fact that she would never bear children was the kind of suffering Orowen wouldn't wish on anyone. "I feared for her and offered what advice I could. That was the last time she set foot in Saolanni's garden."

"So, what happened?" Daeya asked.

This was where Orowen's story had pieces missing. Where a final confirmation would allow everything to fall into place. She gestured toward Daeya. "That is a beautiful necklace you wear. Can you tell me where you got it?"

The sharp deviation took Daeya aback. Her hand closed protectively over the pendant. "What does that have to do with anything?"

Saolanni's grace, if she had a copper for every time she'd witnessed that same short fuse. "It's alright, Daeya. No one's going to take it from you. Did your mother give it to you?"

Sam leaned forward now, staring at Daeya. Ravlok's gaze shifted from one face to another, calculations ticking away behind his expression.

Daeya's fingers slowly uncurled and returned to her lap. The pendant swung gently against her high-necked blouse. "It was my birth mother's."

Orowen's heart skipped against her ribs. Drawing breath was suddenly like trying to suck air through wet cloth. "What can you tell me of her?"

Daeya's attention strayed toward Ravlok again. He nodded encouragingly. "I never really knew her. Da said she was very sick when she showed up on his farm with me. She died not long afterward."

Kendi's grip tightened on Orowen's hand, as if he intuited how, even after all this time, that news would sting.

"Did…" Orowen closed her eyes, willing her composure back into place. "Did your da happen to get her name?"

She nodded. "He said her name was Neri."

"Neri." To hear her say it aloud was like watching the clouds part after years without sun. "Short for Nerimoria."

"No way." Sam's mouth fell open. "But if she's Neri's daughter, wouldn't she be—"

Orowen held up a hand. "One thing at a time, *neime.* Let us all process this."

Kendi sat back, chair creaking. He looked thoughtful as he stroked his chin. "I can see her now in your face. Your nose. Your chin."

"You all knew my mother." Daeya frowned. "How is that possible? You say she's Koraani's sister; that means she's Syljian. I'm not. Da would have told me."

"She was Syljian, but her husband was human." Gods knew what a shock this must be. "It's a gamble what half-blood offspring look like."

"I'm not," Daeya repeated. "I'd never have survived in Ryost this long. Not with the Church and the Light Paladins so close. They would have sensed me long before now."

Ravlok touched her knee again. "Not if whatever wards you against psionics also blocks their aura tracing."

"That's…" Daeya's attention fixed on a point on the floor. She rose from the couch and began to pace.

Orowen tracked her movements, so like the feral pacing her mother was once prone to. The resemblance between Neri and Daeya was like a peek through time. "I know this must come as a shock to you—"

Daeya whirled on her. "What was her husband's name?"

Orowen flinched.

Kendi's hand tightened on hers again. "We can see that you're upset," he said to Daeya. "Perhaps that should be addressed another time."

Like a lioness, Daeya stalked forward, teeth bared and bristling. Ravlok rose to catch her by the shoulders, but she stopped a full span shy of him and stared at Orowen. "What. Was. His. Name?"

The visions. The timing. The necklace. Knowledge that would change everything and nothing.

Orowen patted Kendi's hand and extracted herself, rising to meet the girl eye-to-eye. "You're certain you're ready to know?"

Daeya's entire face twisted around her answer. "Yes."

Orowen stepped around Ravlok and cupped the girl's cheeks. "Your father's name was Cheralach Bevausecc."

Cheralach.

The Deserter. Syljian sympathizer. Guild betrayer. Founder of Starlight. Alli-aansi leader.

Her *father*.

And her mother, Nerimoria. A Syljian. Commander of the First Legion. Ko-raani Alliaar's sister.

They had prayed for her conception in this very city. They'd *wanted* her.

Daeya pulled herself from the priestess's touch and turned away. She wrapped her arms around herself, staring through the windows, out into the night.

That made her one of them. A half-blood. Why had Da never told her? That he'd kept such an important secret from her—gods, it was like half her heart had been ripped out. She pressed her hand against her chest as if pressure alone could stop its aching.

Gregory knew.

The bastard *knew*.

The wards. The runes. The secrets, the isolation, the threats—all of it, a means of control. All while *he knew what she was.* All this time, he'd warned her to keep the runes covered so no one would question whether her blood was pure. Ironic, really, that she'd believed him, believed in her humanity and perpetuated his lie so her torture could continue.

How many wards had it taken to hide her in plain sight of the Light Paladins? Out of the hundreds he'd carved into her under the guise of channeling magic, making her stronger, protecting her...

In a sick, twisted way, she supposed he had.

The hypocrisy shouldn't have surprised her. After all, he'd betrayed the very foundations of Guild doctrine just because it suited him. But somehow, *somehow*, she'd been caught off guard by this.

Never again.

Her teeth clamped down on her lip. Her nails dug into her upper arms, the sharp pinpricks of pain a conduit for the rage that mounted like an inferno inside her. The desire to set the world aflame was so potent that the taste of ash coated her tongue. Had she access to magic, she might have done it.

A memory, fleeting and evanescent, stirred at the thought. A flicker of scarlet flame, the flash of golden scales, the scent of acrid smoke.

A city burning. The smell of death.

Daeya rubbed her face.

"I know this is a lot to accept," Orowen said behind her. "Just know we are here for you in whatever way you need."

"Daeya?" A warm hand gripped her shoulder. The smell of leather and sweat overpowered Ravlok's signature scent of old parchment. "Let's go back to our room. I can give you some privacy if you want."

She shook her head and clasped his hand. The last thing she wanted was to be alone. She sniffed and turned back to Orowen.

Cheralach had come for her. He'd seen her in his visions, sensed that she was in danger, and came to rescue her—*his daughter*. But one thing still didn't make sense.

"Why was my mother in Eidosinia when I was born? Why wasn't Cheralach with her?"

Orowen's lips parted. She lifted one hand, but let it fall. "I don't know, *neime*. I wish I did."

"He should have protected her." Daeya's fists clenched. "He should have protected *me*."

Instead, he'd left her to the whims of a sorcerer who'd exploited her, manipulated her, *tortured her* for most of her childhood. If Cheralach had been there, how much of her life could have been different? How much pain would she have never suffered?

Would her birth mother still be alive?

Sam and Kendi shared a conflicted look. Ravlok stayed close, the heat of his body warming her.

A maddening expression of implacable calm smoothed the worry lines on Orowen's face. "I assure you, he would have never abandoned your mother if he'd thought she was in danger. He loved Neri with all his heart, and he loved you just the same."

The priestess's confidence dulled some of Daeya's anger, but didn't banish it completely. She fought against the emotion pinching her throat shut.

Ravlok addressed Orowen. "You said twelve of Neri's best warriors disappeared at the same time. Is it possible Cheralach sent them away and didn't tell anyone?"

Orowen nodded. "Truthfully, it's the only conclusion that makes sense."

"Why would he do that?" Sam asked.

"Only the gods know, now," Kendi said. "*Amaa* always had a reason for every-thing he did. I'm sure this was no different."

Ravlok scratched his beard, his expression thoughtful. He looked like he was about to say something wise, something that would set Daeya's mind at ease the way he always did, but all that came out was, "He came looking for you. That counts for something, doesn't it?"

It did. She didn't want it to, but it did. A man who'd prayed for her existence wouldn't send her away on a whim. A man who didn't want her wouldn't traverse hundreds of leagues through enemy territory to get to her. She was misdirecting her fury onto a man she would never know. It was better to focus on the now—on the man who had truly wronged her.

No, Cheralach didn't deserve her anger. Nor did Angus, for his lie of omission. There was only one man in the world who deserved to burn for all this treachery. For all the suffering he'd caused not just her, but everyone in this city who had lost someone to the Guild. The reason the Alliaansi had hosted a mass funeral only hours ago.

Gregory's betrayal far outpaced even Alar's and Ashaara's attempts to break her wards. If she needed any more reason to fight, this single, inarguable truth provided all the kindling necessary.

Daeya looked from Sam to Kendi and Orowen—her parents' people—and found the reason for her presence here.

They needed her, even if they didn't know it yet. Her draegion magic could give the Alliaansi the edge they needed in this war. Once her family's safety was assured, once she built their trust and regained her magic, she would reveal her connection to Telerion and bring to bear whatever power she possessed to drive the Guild back.

And, when she came face-to-face with Gregory again, he would answer for every lie he'd ever told her.

# INTERLUDE II

## GREGORY

Snow had fallen overnight. By midmorning, the worst of it had been scooped away, but a thin layer still crunched under Gregory's boots as he returned to his tent.

The snow and Starlight's defenses had created a weeks-long hindrance in sending his message. None of his Conduits could penetrate the Aetherial wards surrounding the city, and procuring a bird trained to fly the distance had proven equally insurmountable. He would have to send a warded scroll on horseback with strict instructions to deliver it only into Tipori Evallier's hands.

Of course, the likelihood of the messenger returning from enemy territory was slim. Gregory would send a common soldier or two to spare his mages.

Winter's approach would delay the extermination efforts and tax the Guild's saphyrum stores, but the fires of vengeance from the destruction of the School and the Orthovian port still raged hot enough to keep his troops warm. If the Alliaansi made no offensive moves by early spring, a new attack could be manufactured to stoke those flames.

His cloak brushed the snowdrifts as he walked. He frowned and tugged the white wool closer.

Unacceptable. He would see these paths widened immediately.

A flash of blue robes drew his eye.

Acolytes darted through the snow, faces flushed, wearing wide grins and thick blue mittens. The younger acolyte, a girl of about fourteen, spun toward her pursuer, blonde curls whirling. She flung a snowball and hit the black-haired boy solidly in the chest. He roared with laughter, bent to scoop up a fistful of snow, and hurled it at her retreating back.

Gregory's lips parted. It took him back through the years to another girl with blonde curls dusted with snow. A pair of blue eyes so clear and perfect that they reflected the winter sky in all its beauty. Her smile as bright as the illusions he'd once drawn to bring her favorite stories to life.

How she'd loved the snow. She used to climb the tree beside the front walk and wait there just to rain snowballs on his head. She would sled down the embankment behind their home at the expense of many a Saosday dress. And her mother—how she would rage at him for all the time their daughter spent away from her studies, building snow forts with him and facing off on the estate lawn.

Long ago when things were perfect. Before everything changed. Before *he* robbed him of *her*.

*Oh, Adelaide, my sweet.*

Grief sank its blades into him with a pain so acute that it stopped him in his tracks. He stared past the young ones while they played. A slight tremor began in his hands, and he stiffened his fingers to stay them. Cold knifed at his exposed skin, but he didn't turn up his collar against the wind. His anger was more than enough warmth for him. His vision sharpened, honing in on the two acolytes at play.

"Stop that nonsense at once!"

Both students froze. The girl's arm was poised to launch another snowball; she lowered it, cheeks reddening. The boy opened his mouth to stammer an excuse, but Gregory made a curt gesture with the blade of his hand.

"It appears you both need something to occupy your time." He waved toward the drifted snow near his feet. "See these pathways widened by fourth bell."

They both wilted.

"Yes, Councilor."

"Right away, sir."

He waited, glowering, until the pair scurried off. Then he resumed his course, breathing out a plume of vapor. The towering command tent rose out of the drifts before him like a slumbering dragon.

*Soon, very soon.*

By the time his message reached the plateau, everything would be in position. The deal he expected to make with Tipori was one the half-blood couldn't refuse. Then all these years of planning would finally come to fruition.

*I will see justice done for you, Addy. No power in this world shall keep me from it.*

# Part Three

# CHAPTER THIRTY-THREE

## ALIRI

The goddess's voice whispered from every corner of the forest: "I hope you've come to take that vile creature out of my domain."

Wind knifed through the snow-crusted evergreens, and Aliri stiffened.

Falla spun, the dappled sunlight reflecting off her golden ringlets. Even though Aliri's breath fogged before her nose, her friend wore only a sleeveless blouse and silk skirt. The Silver Queen needed no cloak to ward against the coming winter.

Vorsere's steel-and-black-striped irises cut toward a shadow slipping between the trees. She hissed, painted black lips curling, stark against her ash-gray skin. Even in her bipedal form, the Steel Queen wore four pairs of needle-sharp fangs, and two scaly frills flared outward in place of her ears.

As one, they fell into formation with their backs to each other. Vorsere might have been an unwelcome companion on this journey, but she was still an ally.

The shadow materialized into the form of a wolf. Corra paced into the clearing, her lips curling back from her teeth.

Corra's counterpart, Paelic, was watching them from the sky. Aliri ignored the stab of jealousy for the falcon's wings.

The godling familiars had been tracking Aliri and her companions ever since Vortanis had Walked them out of Draeconis. Her keen senses had picked up their presence hours ago. She'd hoped to find her *draekhei* before Caelyn got involved, but Telerion still wouldn't answer her telepathic summons, and their search through the mountains between Mautor and Starlight Plateau had been treacherous at best.

The goddess of nature bore no love for their kind or the draegion. Aliri scanned the forest behind Corra. She saw no other sign of Caelyn, but she spoke carefully into the midmorning air. "We come wingless and intend to harm no leaf, *Saonivhatt*. It is another of our kind we seek. Perhaps you have seen him and can hasten us on our course."

Vorsere snorted. "You're a fool if you think the witch-queen will help us."

Corra growled and snapped her jaws.

A blast of frigid air swirled around them like a cyclone. Aliri tucked her chin and shielded her eyes.

An attempt at provocation. She steadied her nerves and let her inner fires warm her.

The wind died. Snow crunched somewhere to her right, and Aliri lowered her arm.

Caelyn stopped five paces from Falla and planted her staff. "Does your all-knowing mistress plan to ignore the obvious threat to our world, then? Anordis could be closing in on the Shard as we speak, and it seems my brethren are content to do nothing."

To turn fully toward the goddess would put the wolf at Aliri's back. Her companions moved with her, shifting their formation so Vorsere squared off with Corra. *Saonis* help her if she came to regret that.

"Tiior sent us to retrieve the girl and her prospective dragonbond." Aliri kept her hands before her, spreading her fingers to show she wore no claws. "They are to return with us to Draeconis, where she will complete the Test of Flame and learn control. The Shard will be safe, *Saonivhatt*. Chaos will never gain the Greater Throne."

Caelyn scoffed. "My brother has breached Tiior's realm twice before." Her fingers drummed against her staff. "Better she be contained in Dromas, where she can live out her days surrounded by walls impregnable even to him."

"You would have her imprisoned? Isolated for all time?" Aliri's eyes widened. "No child deserves that fate."

"The Traitor only bears a child's face," Caelyn hissed. "Or have you forgotten the destruction your dragonbond's former vessel wrought?"

Aliri winced. She'd been but a centureon at the time, but she remembered the destruction of Corridae and the betrayal that led to the fall of the Draegion Empire. Baokryn's prior vessel, the Traitor, Nahariim, had been far too ambitious, and her thirst for power had driven her right into Anordis's arms. Even millennia later, after Soul Shifting into a new vessel and becoming Baokryn, she had still struggled with the remnants of Nahariim's desire.

"She is not the same person," Aliri argued, "and has not been for over seven thousand years."

"Ah, that's right. Baokryn the Elder, *Nashanett* and Shardbearer, would have never destroyed an entire city. Oh wait," Caelyn sneered, "who was it that created the Wastelands surrounding our dear Vintrios?"

Aliri bristled. "Mistakes were made, yes, but—"

"And she's once more reduced to a sniveling girl." The goddess glanced toward Vorsere. "Surely, you would not be ruled by a child-queen, dragonbond of Raoghys the Wise. Your master would be appalled."

Vorsere's snarl startled birds into flight. "Keep his name out of your mouth, witch-queen."

"Vorsere," Falla warned. She looked toward Caelyn. "We waste precious time. I implore you, *Saonivhatt*, either help us or step aside."

"To pander to the draegion is folly." Caelyn's knuckles were white against her staff. "If you truly want to keep her from Anordis, then we must remove her from all chance of his influence. Bring her to Dromas. It is the only way her story ends without bloodshed."

Aliri suppressed the urge to bare her teeth. She had failed Baokryn twice. She would not fail this new vessel. Daeya McVen, soon to be Daeya the Younger, wouldn't be sentenced to eternity in exile for the circumstances of her birth.

"The girl isn't going to Dromas," she growled. "We will complete our task with or without your help, but if you wish us gone sooner, I humbly request your aid in finding my son, Telerion."

Caelyn lifted her chin. "Can you not commune with him yourself, Aliri Aethersworn?" Her tone was so thickly layered with ice that even Falla could have gotten frostburn. "Or did my brother's lance shrivel more than just your useless wing?"

Aliri trembled with the effort of her restraint. Her Aether glands warmed in her throat until the heat became smoke, and twin puffs blew out of her nostrils. "He ignores my call."

Caelyn threw her head back and laughed. "The child draegion who doesn't listen to reason, and the wyrmling who ignores his elder's summons. Even Silonas couldn't write a better formula for disaster."

Corra gave a final growl and trotted across the snow to settle at her mistress's feet. The goddess reached out, and her moss-green skin turned to old oak bark. Paelic shot out of the trees, stretched his talons, and alighted on her arm.

Caelyn turned toward the trees, whose bare branches parted for her as she approached. "Come. The gold roosts in the caverns of Mount Eisekii. If it gets you out of my domain faster, I will take you to him."

# CHAPTER THIRTY-FOUR

## MAGNUS

The nauseating scrape of metal against bone vibrated through Magnus's palm as Malediction parted the Light Paladin's sword arm from his shoulder, and his weapon clattered to the creek bed. Jets of arterial blood splashed across the Paladin's white and gray vestments. Magnus drove his blade into the man's throat.

*Yes. Kill them.*

Another Paladin threw a shaft of brilliant, crackling light from the opposite shore. Magnus channeled saphyrum from a stolen bracelet and infused his sword's edge with Aether. Black-violet mist trailed in Malediction's wake as he swung at the arcane lance. The sword connected, and light shattered in a blinding arc.

*Kill them. Kill them!*

Magnus withdrew one hand from Malediction's hilt, punched through the Wall, and flames erupted in his palm. He hurled the fireball across the creek, but the Paladin spun aside. Steam belched from where the fireball struck the ground.

Steel rasped as the Paladin drew his sword. Magnus leaped over the body and charged to meet him.

Their weapons clashed. The Paladin fought viciously, utilizing the higher ground along the bank. His movements were disciplined and well-practiced, far superior to any sorcerer or mundane Guild soldier. Light Paladins combined the best of both professions, making them savage opponents capable of matching an aethermancer in both martial skill and battle magic.

Magnus parried a slash aimed for his left flank and pulled more saphyric energy, which Malediction greedily consumed. Aetherial mist poured from the blade, lightening its weight while lending incredible force behind his next swing. The Paladin responded in kind, and white runes illuminated the length of his sword's fuller. When their weapons met again, the force that should have shattered his opponent's steel instead traveled up the length of Magnus's arms to his shoulders.

Unaccustomed to such power, he staggered. His foot slipped on a submerged rock, and he crashed to one knee.

A deadly mistake.

Cold stabbed into him. The creek rose to mid-thigh and turned his weary muscles to ice. Light and steel streaked toward him. He barely got his sword up to block. Malediction went flying. It exploded into Aetherial mist before it hit the water.

Magnus reached into the Aether, but too slowly. Metal flashed, and his opponent swept his weapon in an arc. Time seemed to slow as Magnus's death hurtled toward him. He looked into his killer's face and roared, hands *pushing* the Aether he'd gathered—

An arrow sprouted from the Paladin's neck. Bright red feathers stirred in the breeze.

The man's arms went slack, but his sword carried through its swing. Magnus allowed himself to fall forward, palms slapping hard against the muddy bank. With no weight behind the attack, the sword stuck in his wool tunic, then splashed into the creek. The Paladin's body collapsed, and his eyes stared unseeing into the sky.

Magnus crawled forward, pulling himself out of the stream. The bite of northern air usurped the sting of icy water, and he rolled onto his back, breath coming in painful, ragged gasps.

Alive.

*"Amaa!"*

Rylan's voice carried from the far bank. His footsteps labored in the water, slowed as they reached the deeper center, and quickened again until they reached Magnus. Windswept blond hair and a bearded frown obscured a portion of the blue sky.

"Are you alright, *Amaa*?"

"Good shot," Magnus croaked. He forced himself upright and blinked as the world righted itself. "Quite dramatic of you, waiting until the last moment."

Rylan's frown flipped on its head, like they were boys again, rummaging through the military surplus bins for old bows to repair. "Jerinoch would say my timing was impeccable."

A chuckle rumbled through Magnus, and he swallowed against the ever-present ache in his throat. "I'm in your debt."

"I accept payment in wine and bowstrings." Rylan shouldered his bow and helped him up, eyes sweeping their surroundings. "Someone will have heard all that."

"These two were sentries." Magnus flicked mud from his sleeves. "Scout ahead. I'll relieve them of their saphyrum and meet you on the rise."

"Yes, *Amaa*." With a curt nod, Rylan climbed the bank and darted off into the trees.

Magnus waited until the red-fletched arrows in Rylan's quiver disappeared, then crouched beside the Paladin.

*Take it.*

He paused in reaching for the golden chain around the Paladin's neck. Magnus tilted his head, studying the dead man's face. He lingered on the unmarred whites of those eyes, so unlike his own, yet much as they'd been only months ago. Much as they should be now.

Whisper-soft, yet insistent, the voice caressed his mind.

*Take it.*

The Paladin had been a handsome man. Those eyes had likely aided him in many a midnight tryst. Soft pools of gold flecked with red and tan, warm and alluring even in death.

*Wasted now.*

Why should a corpse get to keep such lovely eyes?

Magnus frowned. He abandoned the chain and pried down one of the man's eyelids. Red veins spiderwebbed away from those amber irises and disappeared behind the flesh.

*Cut it out.*

The thought didn't startle him as it had before. Much worse had been done to the Syljian scouts they'd found last night. The sight of them would haunt Magnus forever. Maralla's missing men and women had been nailed to the trees in an arc around the Paladins' newly occupied territory as a warning to any who dared breach the perimeter.

Pain spiked behind his eye socket. He rubbed at the sunken scar with the back of his hand.

This man was probably one of the bastards who'd driven those nails. He'd persecuted Magnus's allies and prayed for their extinction. He would have killed him, all while hiding a soul as black as Aether behind that handsome face. Those lovely eyes.

It was an injustice. A deception.

*One that must be righted.*

Yes.

*Take it.*

He drew the blade from his boot. Beads of water clung to the metal, and its wooden grip fit perfectly to the contours of his fingers.

Magnus's focus narrowed. With one hand, he pried the eyelids apart, and with the other, he tucked the point of his knife against the pink tissue beside the corpse's nose. Blood pressed out of that spot like water from a sponge. Red tears streaked the man's cheek. Magnus met resistance from the stiff muscles, and he cut them away, digging in with his blade. Still holding the lids wide, he pushed above and below the eye while leveraging the knife.

The eye bulged, but didn't pop out. Magnus gritted his teeth. Determined now, he wedged his dagger as far into the socket as possible and pitched the point toward the man's ear.

The eye turned and slipped from his grip. Growling, Magnus tried to hook his fingers around it, but its slimy surface was partially obstructed by bone. He pried the eye up, found purchase, and pulled.

A thick strand of tissue still held it fast. Magnus hacked through, and it came free with a satisfying snap.

*Good. Very good.*

The voice's satisfaction sent an echoing hum of delight into Magnus's core. He reveled in the sensation, his prize held up in triumph. It wasn't enough, that feeling. He needed more. Nothing would sate his desire faster than taking the bastard's other pretty eyeball. Then, he would be nothing but an ugly, gruesome wretch.

Just as the Guild had made him.

The sticky fluid between Magnus's fingers and the chill of cooling blood drew him back to himself. He looked down at the eye and recoiled. A strangled cry of horror burst forth, and he flung it away. It bounced off a rock and rolled to a stop facing him. The grisly tail of the nerve bundle trailed in the mud.

Magnus frantically wiped his hands on his tunic, but the drying fluid between his fingers became glue. He dropped his knife and submerged his hands in the creek, scrubbing furiously. Gods, he would never get them clean enough. No. No, he shouldn't have—

A feeling far colder than the icy creek seeped into him.

What had he done?

*You've given them something to fear.*

The voice steadied him. He kept scrubbing, but slowed.

*This is to be the fate of our enemies. It is our answer to their brutality. A much kinder one than they deserve.*

But it was wrong.

*There is no right or wrong in war. Only action or reaction, strike or counter. You can defeat your enemy by simply making them fear what you are—what you can do.*

His hands stung with the biting chill. He flicked off the water and tucked his fingers under his armpits. He still had to collect the Paladin's saphyrum.

That bloody eye stared back at him in silent accusation.

*Do not fret, my friend. You save lives this way.*

How? That didn't make sense.

*Fewer will wish to fight you if they fear the outcome.*

The tightness in Magnus's chest lessened. Cheralach had once said something similar. He'd believed presenting a strong front to the enemy empowered those in the back to rise up. All the better when that front wasn't shields and spears, but cunning and calculated leadership that settled conflict before it dissolved to violence. The will of a united people was a true force to be reckoned with.

Magnus stripped the Paladin of his saphyrum-laced amulet and other beads, careful not to linger overlong on that yawning hole in his face. He collected his dagger and returned to his feet, bracing himself for the cold trek across the creek to the other body.

*If the opposition believes you could be anywhere, watching their every move, you compromise their belief in victory. But such a reputation takes time and consistency to build.*

He turned the body of the one-armed Paladin over with his boot. This man had blue eyes. Eyes like his. As they used to be.

*Take it.*

Magnus shuddered.

*Do not be a coward. Be strong.* Take *it.*

The hand holding his dagger twitched upward. Magnus sank to one knee beside the body.

*Give them something to fear.*

He stabbed down into the corpse's face and set to work.

# CHAPTER THIRTY-FIVE

## MAGNUS

Willowmarsh had been taken.

Pikes speared corpses in regular intervals along the blackened city walls, and the victims' pallid skin sparkled with frost in the morning sun. There were over a hundred of them—humans, Syljians, half-bloods, and Cintoshi alike.

Quivering rage heated Magnus to his core.

*Such savagery*, the voice whispered.

His breath fogged, and he adjusted his elbows against the ice-crusted detritus.

*Such wickedness.*

He willed himself to stillness.

Inside the walls, far below the rise where he and Rylan lay, the snowy grounds of Willowmarsh Commons crawled with white-robed Light Paladins. Blue-robed Guild acolytes sifted through buildings whose inner rooms had been blown wide like some grim caricature of a child's dollhouse. Rifts stood open near those buildings, and whatever the sorcerers couldn't salvage was thrown into the Aether. At the city gates, mages ushered in carts and wagons full of supplies.

Wind howled into the valley and whipped the canvas free from one wagon. The mages guarding it shouted for a halt. One sorcerer stilled the air with a warding sigil, while others moved into defensive stances with their hands raised, as if readying to cast.

Magnus frowned.

The canvas went slack under the mage's sigil, exposing several steel-plated boxes. A crossed-out flame symbol adorned the lids—the mark used for saphyric flares. With that many in one shipment, the cause of the char marks on the city walls and extensive damage to the buildings was no longer a mystery.

Saph-bombs.

Foreboding ripped a chasm in Magnus's stomach. There was only one other village between here and Starlight, and it hardly warranted that much killing power.

All the crates in those wagons combined couldn't destabilize Starlight Plateau, but they could destroy the cliff lifts. Without those mechanisms to move supplies and troops, the Alliaansi would be forced to lower their Aether wards to allow rift travel, leaving them vulnerable to the enemy's Benders and Walkers as well.

The first mage refastened the canvas, then pounded the wagon to signal the driver on her way.

"I don't see Eris or her officers among the dead." Rylan's spyglass pointed toward the piked corpses. "They could still be alive in there."

"They would be valuable for prisoner exchanges." Magnus beckoned for the spyglass. He neglected to remind his friend that Eris Lathaarios would have rather died than become a prisoner of war.

"The jailhouse is on the north side of city hall. If they haven't been moved, that's where they'll be." Rylan scowled at the long procession of green-and-gold-liveried troops ferrying across the river to the city gates. "What I wouldn't give for a water affinity."

Magnus huffed his agreement. One well-placed wave could sink the entire retinue and all those supplies, too. He turned the spyglass on the river, the muscles around his missing eye twitching, as if trying to close for a better view. He breathed out, forcing himself to relax.

On the foremost ferry stood a towering, light-skinned Paladin with a clean-shaven jaw and an extra gold stripe on his high collar. His bejeweled greatsword glinted in the sun, and steel gauntlets flashed with a pure white saphyric inlay, marking him as one of the Enlightened's esteemed Archephs—or high priests. This one bore a familiar, stylized rose on his breastplate.

Magnus scowled.

Elfred Roseheart. Also known as Roseheart the Reaper, Elfred was a direct descendant of Father Durn Roseheart, founder of the Church of the Enlightened. It was said Elfred had inherited his great-grandfather's skill with aura tracing, and few Syljians who saw him face-to-face ever lived to speak about it. He'd killed so many of Magnus's friends over the years.

*Kill him.*

Magnus's palm itched. His fingers opened and closed in the shape of his sword hilt.

"What's wrong?" Rylan asked.

Magnus returned the spyglass and pointed. "The Reaper is here."

Rylan peered through the spyglass and swore. "That's why none of our scouts have gotten through."

Sourness leached into Magnus's gut. Supplies running north from Sarton were always funneled down Natsa'Kallii through Willowmarsh. Their only other options were trekking barrels and crates through steep mountains and dense forest or hiring sailors to deliver them by ship to Brynn or Aesin. Even then, overseas orders took months to fill.

"Caelyn burn me." Rylan lowered his spyglass. "What do we do?"

Magnus studied the Guild-infested land below them, drumming his scarred fingers against the ground.

*Kill them all.*

"All the saphyrum in the world won't help us if we can't blow open this supply route again." His attention strayed to the wagons passing through the city gates, then leveled on Rylan. "How's your hand at wiring explosives?"

Not long after their scouts discovered the eyeless bodies near the stream, Light Paladins and mages spewed forth from the city gates, directed by a fuming Elfred Roseheart and an old sorcerer dressed in the white and gold robes of a Guild Councilor.

Sparser troops made slipping into Willowmarsh through a breach in the wall much simpler. After scouting out the storehouse where the flares were unloaded, Magnus and Rylan crept down to the chandlery to fill satchels with candles and rolls of string. Ironic that one of the few buildings left untouched by fire would be a candlemaker's shop.

They used a guard change as a distraction to journey farther into the city, looking for Eris.

Magnus darted from a half-destroyed bakery wall to a row of merchants' shops. He crossed another snow-packed street, then crouched in an alley near the city hall. Wood chilled his back, and the stolen amulet pattered a rhythm against his breastbone.

Two younger Paladins flanked the building's oaken doors. They scanned their surroundings, hands curled around their sword hilts.

*An attentiveness borne of fear. They know what you've done.*

Rylan settled into the shadows beside him. "Should I draw their attention?"

"No. We don't want to announce ourselves until the flares are in place." Magnus nodded toward an abandoned row of vegetable stalls. "Let's check the security on the north side."

"Yes, *Amaa*."

Magnus stuck to the sodden ground whenever possible, and Rylan's weak earth affinity erased their tracks behind them. They paused beside a wall while three sorcerers passed. A red-haired mage laughed uproariously at something another said, and their blonde companion scowled. Magnus flexed his hand.

"I can't believe you. Two bodies found with their eyes removed, and you think they'll stop there?" The sorceress glowered at the others. "Has Councilor Tallion even bothered to tighten security near the break in the wall?"

"Oh, lighten up, Cam. Tal has it under control." The redhead clapped the woman on her shoulder. "Not all of us are as uptight as Gregory."

She slapped his hand away. "There are Alliaansi out there, and they'll be coming for the prisoners. You lot mess this up, and Gregory will have your heads."

The other mage snickered. "I'd like to see the old bastard try."

They continued down the street, still bickering. Heartened by the confirmation of prisoners, Magnus shared a look with Rylan, and found his brow furrowed.

"Their eyes removed?"

Magnus hesitated. Rylan wouldn't approve of what he'd done. He would report him to the council, suggest Magnus wasn't fit to lead, that he shouldn't follow in Cheralach's footsteps—

*You sent a message.*

"I sent a message." His words cracked on mingled uncertainty and relief.

If the voice had encouraged him to perform such an act, surely it would guide him through this. Magnus winced at the needle-sharp pain in his throat, and his eye socket throbbed once.

*Speak with confidence, and he will follow you.*

Rylan grimaced. "*Amaa*, that's—"

"Gruesome, I know." Magnus forced himself to hold Rylan's gaze. He tapped into his reservoir of deep-seated anger and drew it up like water from a well. "But they put our people on pikes, *amii*. Our women and children suffered excruciating pain before they died of exposure outside our own city. What I've done is but a fraction of what our enemies deserve."

Apprehension slowly dissolved from Rylan's face, his expression transforming into something fierce. "You're right."

Whatever reservations Magnus had over the voice's disturbing suggestion caved at that. If one of Kendi and Cheralach's most trusted scouts saw merit in such a message, then perhaps it was but another necessary evil. One that could save lives if their enemies heeded it. It was merciful, in a way.

Magnus nodded to himself. "It gives them something to fear."

"It's long past time they start to fear something," Rylan agreed.

Magnus glanced around the wall. The path to the jailhouse behind the city hall was clear.

He chased his shadow across the slushy road with Rylan at his heels and took shelter behind a felled tree. Peering through its shattered branches, Magnus examined the north side of the jailhouse. Wooden steps led to an unguarded door beneath a low-pitched roof. Four barred windows looked out on a square flanked by stocks and whipping posts. The gallows stood at the far north end, blanketed by untouched snow.

Rylan tugged sharply on Magnus's sleeve and dropped to the ground. Magnus followed suit as a saccharine voice and crunching footsteps reached them.

"Their tracks came from the north. At least two, maybe more."

Pine needles scratched the scarred side of Magnus's face. He flinched away.

Three Paladins strode down the road. Two were younger—one stout and pale as sour milk, the other lean and dark as pitch. The tallest man, in the middle, was Roseheart himself.

"The others will crawl out under cover of darkness as rats and roaches do." Roseheart cinched down the strap of one vambrace and flexed his gloved hand. "Tighten the north end and city hall with mages as the sorceress suggested. I want clergy on every wall from dusk till dawn."

Roseheart's Ryostian drawl grated. Magnus tracked them to the jailhouse door through the branches. Both younger men paused at the foot of the steps.

"We'll see it done, sir."

Wood creaked under Roseheart's boots. He reached for the door and threw one last look at his minions. "Prepare yourselves, men. Soon, we will cleanse this unholy ground of Anordis's brood and bring peace and security back to the good people of Eidosinia. Our survival depends on you."

The Paladins touched their fists to their abdomens, their foreheads, their chests, then bowed.

"We serve with honor, Archeph," came their unified response.

Roseheart entered the jailhouse and the door banged shut behind him. As the other two departed, Magnus touched Rylan's forearm and pointed toward another barred window above them. Rylan nodded and levered himself up with the easy grace of a chaagra while Magnus stood watch.

Roseheart's drawl carried through the jailhouse walls. "We found the catacombs under the school, Governor. You might as well tell me where your other saphyrum caches are."

A slew of Syljian curses followed in an accent barely distinguishable from the snarls of a cornered bear.

Eris.

She was alive. Praise Silonas.

Rylan dropped back to the ground. He was grinning from ear to ear. "They're in a cell on the east side. Eris looks pretty rough. Serreth, Gamiil, and Luthen are with her."

Magnus let out a breath. That meant at least three of Eris's four officers had survived.

"That saphyrum is not yours." Eris spoke with all the defiance of a woman who had nothing left to lose. "You do the work of Chaos himself by perpetuating your hatred and lies."

"I suggest you don't utter that blasphemy again, blanker," Roseheart snapped in Eidosinian. "I don't need your ears intact for a prisoner exchange. Now, I'll ask again..."

*Deliver justice. Kill them all.*

With their exit blocked by mages, a new plan began to take shape. The governor's officers didn't have magic, but Eris did. She was a Guardian of some renown with the ability to Rift Bend; her help would be invaluable in their escape. Magnus eyed the grain mill cresting above the trees near the river.

A sharp crack and a cry of pain sounded from the jailhouse. Rylan flinched.

Magnus steadied him with a hand on his arm. "Come. There's nothing more we can do here."

Conflict showed in the archer's eyes. "We have to help them."

"We will," Magnus assured him. "But we must prepare first. While they're watching the walls, we'll get to work in the storehouse."

Rylan exhaled a slow puff of vapor. His expression bore a dangerous edge. "Then we take them out?"

Magnus set his jaw and nodded once. "All of them."

A booming report echoed across the city. Violet flames mushroomed into the sky, curling into red, orange, and fading to yellow before winking out in a cloud of smoke. Shouts and screams carried on the wind, coupled with the stench of Aether and burning timber.

The fireball illuminated Magnus's hands as he finished tying off the bundle of flares below the bakery window, summoned saphyric energy, and punched through the Aetherial Wall. Black mist ignited in his grasp.

Careful to keep the Aetherial flame away from the flares, Magnus pulled a short candle from the satchel and lit the wick, then tucked it into the bundle's center.

He was moving before the first drop of wax hit the bakery floor.

Another boom shuddered through the ground. He darted out through a hole in the bakery wall and down an alley. More screams gave way to frantic voices chanting and curt demands for order.

While mages tried to suppress the fire with magic, the Light Paladins would attempt to track the source of the devastation. Magnus was counting on the saph-bombs and sorcerers' spells to muddy the Paladins' aura tracing. As long as he and Rylan remained out of sight and used as little magic as possible, their enemies wouldn't find them.

The night sky erupted with Rylan's next bomb, signaling the destruction of the city barracks.

*Yes. Let them burn.*

Grim satisfaction tightened every muscle in Magnus's face.

Placed far to the east, north, and south, the bombs were meant to give the illusion of a city surrounded on three sides. The bomb Magnus had planted in the bakery would claim the west and hopefully divide the Guild forces enough to pull some attention off the prisoners. There was only one last place to rig before he met Rylan at the city hall.

White-violet flashes outlined the tops of buildings and evergreens—Rift Benders, or perhaps sigils of warding to protect the supply caches. He slid to a stop at the mouth of the alley and waited for a troop of Paladins to run past. When they disappeared into the thickening haze, he hurried toward the mill. His pulse pounded in his ears like cavalry hooves thundering across a battlefield. Smoke burned his eye and lungs.

Magnus dodged two more patrols and tucked himself between the mill's outer wall and an old water trough while he pieced together his next bundle of flares. Like most mills in this region, the building was constructed on piles to keep vermin and floodwaters out of the grain. He stashed the bundle beneath the floor and lit a longer candle for extra time before he dashed off toward the city's center.

A low whistle cut through the din as he passed a dark alcove near the jailhouse. Magnus took a sharp right toward it and ducked down to follow Rylan's signal, his nerves spiking hot down his spine. Had he been spotted? Was something wrong? His palm itched, and the phantom weight of Malediction triggered a longing so acute that he instinctively channeled saphyric energy. The Wall rippled in response.

But, no, it was not yet time.

*Patience.*

This wasn't where they'd agreed to meet, and Magnus's stomach sank. As he hunkered down beside his grim-faced companion and looked out, the reason became clear.

Standing guard at the base of the jailhouse steps were Guild Councilor Tallion, the blonde-haired sorceress, two other mages, and two Light Paladins. Their shadows wobbled in the torchlight. No smoke penetrated the area around them, and the breeze that whipped Magnus's hair from his forehead didn't seem to touch them at all. The Councilor's gnarled hands were raised, and sigils pulsed with white-violet light at his fingertips.

An air savant, capable of stealing the breath right out of a person's lungs. Magnus gritted his teeth.

The sorceress turned toward their hiding place. She squinted into the darkness, and Magnus stiffened.

Councilor Tallion glanced at her, lip curling. "Hear something else, Sorceress?" His tone dripped with condescension. "I don't know how you could hear anything over all this noise."

The woman scowled.

In that same moment, the bakery bomb exploded.

Fire and smoke roiled into the sky. Magnus ducked, pulling Rylan down with him, and distant screams filtered through the ringing in his ears.

"Chaos curse it! That was right next to Command." Tallion whirled on the Light Paladins, his sigils fading. "Where's your blasted Archeph? Why isn't he containing this mess?" Both men fumbled for a response, only to be dismissed with a flick of the Councilor's wrist. "Go. Find him. I want a status report immediately. And you"—he turned to the sorceress—"you want to make yourself useful? Go put out that fire before it destroys all our maps and information."

"But Councilor, the prisoners—"

"Not another word, Cameron Vika, or Gregory will have a very detailed report of your insubordination sent by Conduit tomorrow morning."

Magnus found himself grinning. As the sorceress and both Paladins departed, the smoke was already encroaching on the square in wispy, grasping tendrils. Tallion huffed and shook his head, muttering something that made the remaining sorcerers smirk. He returned to his sigils and pressed the smoke back.

Rylan shifted beside him. When Magnus turned, still not believing their good fortune, he found him with his bow in hand.

"Orders, *Amaa*?" He pulled an arrow from his quiver as if anticipating Magnus's command.

They'd have no greater opportunity to strike fear into the heart of the Guild than by killing a Councilor. But their enemies were all in a line at this angle. It wouldn't be a good shot. If Rylan missed—

Magnus's eye socket throbbed.

*Kill them.*

The command came swiftly. So, too, did Magnus's acquiescence.

"Take out the Councilor on my mark. Ready."

Rylan rose from his crouch and nocked his arrow.

Magnus rose, too, summoning saphyric energy. "Aim."

The bow creaked as Rylan drew back. All of Magnus's focus narrowed on the mage closest to them. He lifted his hands.

"Fire."

Rylan's arrow pierced the side of the Councilor's throat.

A shocked, choking sound carried across the yard. The Councilor dropped, and both younger mages startled. Invisible energy erupted from Magnus's palms, slamming the closer mage into his companion. They both crumpled into the sludge and went still.

"Go."

Rylan shouldered his bow and launched out of the alcove. He leaped over the bodies, took the stairs two at a time, and stormed inside. Magnus readied another blast and followed.

Councilor Tallion rolled onto his back, grasping for the arrow in his neck. Magnus started to step around him, but a choking sound snared his attention.

Torchlight reflected off Tallion's eyes. His foggy pupils nested in blue irises made gray by the fire; they dilated as Magnus's shadow fell across his face.

*Take it.*

Magnus's hand froze on the way to obeying that command, fingers quivering. The Councilor still lived, but not for long. He would bleed out here in the snow.

*Others will be on their way. Do it now, or lose your chance.*

Still Magnus hesitated. Blood and smoke mingled in his nostrils. The orange haze was closing in, no longer held at bay by the Councilor's magic.

*This is your moment. Show them they are* all *vulnerable, even in their highest ranks.*

A gurgle issued from the man's throat. Magnus's fingers twitched toward his dagger and stopped. He shouldn't—

Light flared at Tallion's fingertips. The air burst from Magnus's lungs as if he'd been crushed under a landslide. He clutched at his chest, and a sneer twisted the Councilor's face.

A similar sneer flashed before Magnus's mind—the straight white teeth of his torturer as spindly hands closed off the blood flow to his brain. Mounting pressure, dungeon walls, gleaming steel, the thundering of his heart, the stench of burning hair and flesh. Terror, blood, and bile on his tongue.

He would *not* be dragged into Baosanni's realm this way.

Lungs screaming, Magnus wrenched his blade from his boot and stabbed down into Tallion's eye. He sawed and pried until blood slicked his fingers and smoky air flowed freely into his lungs. The eye popped free with a rending snap.

Tallion lay still.

Heaving breaths raked down Magnus's throat. He stared long at the dead man before tucking his dagger away.

Voices carried toward him through the smoke.

"What is your will, Archeph?"

"Tighten our presence at the gates and ready counter-orbs. They might have gotten in, but they won't be getting out. You there—see what's keeping those mages from containing that fire."

That Ryostian accent further roused Magnus from whatever affliction had overtaken him. The Paladins' silhouettes grew darker as they closed in.

Magnus darted for the jailhouse door. Five relieved faces looked up when he entered. Rylan had already killed the remaining guard and unlocked the cells.

Eris cleared her throat. Though the top of her head barely crested Magnus's sternum, she still had an air about her that commanded attention. "We were beginning to think no one was coming, First Officer."

"Apologies for the delay, Governor," Magnus replied, forcing a similar casualness.

Serreth, Eris's Cintoshi advisor, snorted and adjusted his arm around Luthen's waist. "Don't let her fool you. We're all glad you're here."

Rylan searched through the keys and took one of Eris's wrists. "Are you well enough to rift us out, Governor?"

"I'll need saphyrum."

Her spellbinders clicked open and hit the floor. She and Gamiil had both been beaten bloody. Their robes of state hung in tatters and their lavender faces were so swollen they had lost all signs of feminine angularity. Bruises and dried blood hid their warriors' runes, and crusty scabs had formed where Gamiil's beautiful ear points should have been.

Gamiil gaped at Magnus. "Sweet Shavaan, what happened to your eye?"

His eye. Of course, they wouldn't have heard the news. They might not even know about Cheralach—

Magnus froze.

The eye. He still clutched Tallion's eye in his left hand. How could he have forgotten?

Rylan scowled, beads clicking in the bag at his hip. He pressed one into Eris's hand. "The Guild's work, Gamiil, same as you."

Gamiil winced. "Sorry."

The eye was still warm. To dispose of it right here would invite questions Magnus wasn't prepared to answer. If he was caught with it, they wouldn't all be as understanding as Rylan. They might assume he was unwell, and that was the furthest notion from the truth.

Yes. Yes, he should just let it go. Let it fall to the floor and kick it under that desk beside the dead guard. He should do it right now, while Eris was drawing her sigil for the rift, her attention out the window as she placed her exit rift.

He should...

Magnus's hand trembled, tightening around the eye.

No. Not here. Somewhere else. Somewhere he was sure to have the privacy to do so. When it felt right. It was such an accomplishment, killing one of the Guild's elite. Removing the eye sent a message, but *taking* the eye was a truer victory, like spoils claimed after a battle.

He tucked the eye into an inner pocket of his cloak.

Rylan glanced at him, blond brows furrowing. "You alright, *Amaa*?"

"Just finishing the job."

Eris's rift yawned black and misty before them. Wind snapped at Magnus's hair, pulling it toward the void. Eris waved toward Luthen, whose hairy-knuckled hand clamped tighter around Serreth's waist. "You first, Advisor."

The jailhouse door flew open.

Roseheart's hulking figure loomed over the pair of younger Paladins crowding the entryway. "There you are, Alliaansi swine."

Gamiil screamed and leaped into the rift. Serreth limped toward it, leaning heavily on Luthen. Eris held the rift open while Rylan drew his bow. Magnus extended his bloody hand, and the Aetherial Wall tore like wet parchment. Malediction gleamed in the lantern's glow, a blade of orange-streaked death that reflected light into the Reaper's face.

"Counter that rift!" Roseheart lifted his greatsword. "The one-eyed cur is mine."

Counter-orbs pooled in the young Paladins' hands.

An arrow flew over Magnus's shoulder and glanced off a Paladin's breastplate. Rylan swore.

"Go!" Magnus pushed saphyric energy into his blade, bracing for the clash of magic-infused steel as Roseheart charged.

He wasn't prepared for the savage onslaught that followed.

The Reaper's attacks rained down in a ferocious deluge that forced Magnus back. He blinked his eye clear, legs and arms screaming against the Paladin's greater strength. As their blades crashed over and over in his ears, he turned his attention not toward victory, but survival.

Counter-orbs soared, colliding with Eris's orbs in a shower of glimmering black mist. A window shattered, and Rylan's snaking vines lashed across one Paladin's throat.

Magnus parried a strike to his right shoulder, and Roseheart's teeth flashed. Too late, Magnus realized his mistake. With a limited field of view, he'd missed Roseheart's hand coming away from his sword. A gauntleted fist slammed into his left flank. As Magnus doubled over, the same hand seized the back of his head and shoved downward. Roseheart's armored knee crunched into his face.

Pain blinded him. Magnus stumbled, spitting teeth and blood. He threw himself away from the Reaper's blade and hit the ground. His hand clenched around a hilt that was no longer there. He rolled, panicked, bracing for the point of Roseheart's sword to plunge into his belly.

Rylan's war cry drowned out all other sound.

Red-gray haze still clouded Magnus's vision. Steel clashed, but no blows came. He shook his head to clear it.

"In you go, *Amaa*." Eris's cheery voice came from right beside him. Her tiny hands slipped under his arms and tugged upward, but did little to lift him from the ground. "Caelyn's wrath, why are you so heavy?"

A choked yelp cut off Magnus's bitter chuckle. His attention snapped toward Rylan. The Reaper's greatsword protruded from his back.

Malediction fell from Rylan's hand. The sword vanished into a puff of mist. "No!"

Roseheart kicked the archer's body off his weapon, stepped over him, and grinned.

Magnus lunged for him, screaming, only to be intercepted by Eris. She tackled him around the waist, and they both tumbled through the rift, landing in a heap on the wall overlooking the city.

Dread and anguish gripped Magnus's body like a vise. "No, no, no, Rylan!"

He scrambled for the parapet, hands closing on the stone just as the sky filled with fire and an ear-splitting boom echoed across the city.

The grain mill.

Another cry issued from somewhere behind him. He turned from the blooming cloud of smoke. Luthen knelt beside Gamiil's body, a hand over his mouth. A crossbow bolt jutted from her breastbone. Serreth glared up from Gamiil's other side, watching the mages on the wall closing in. Eris lifted her hands, fingers softly glowing.

Fire swept into Magnus's blood, and Aether rippled around him. He spun, looking out over the desolation that was once a beautiful city. His gaze locked on the storehouse containing the last of the Guild's saphyric flares. Embers had taken hold in the timbers, but it was slow in reaching the saph-bombs they had planted in and around the building.

He slammed his fist into the Wall, and fire ignited in his palm.

For what they had done, for everything they had taken from him, he would kill them all.

# Chapter Thirty-Six

## Ravlok

Every muscle in Ravlok's body ached.

Late afternoon sunlight spilled across the ornately carved Temple doors. He lugged himself up the last few stairs to the entrance with pain relief foremost on his mind.

He was fortunate Yonfé had been such an attentive mentor, developing both his mind and body. Without his early lessons in meditation, hand-to-hand combat, and swordplay, Ravlok was sure he wouldn't have survived the first several weeks of training under Kendi.

After the Fourth Legion left for Kuma'Kiir, the commander had equipped Ravlok with a new set of leathers, three daggers, and a bastard sword, as well as a short bow and a quiver of blunt-tipped arrows. He set aside time every day to address Ravlok's shortcomings with the weapon.

At the end of today's training session, Kendi had ordered him to see Orowen about some willow bark, but Ravlok planned to ask her for several other herbs as well. With winter solstice drawing near, he'd had no luck tracking down a few of the components for the Ritual of Ascension. The blue-veined talotiba mushrooms had been impossible to find, either in the forests surrounding the plateau or ground into powder at the local herbalist's shop. Saolanni's temple was his last hope for procuring them before they reappeared in the spring.

The delay would have been harder to stomach if Daeya hadn't come to an agreement with Tipori on her father's behalf. The Aetherian's knowledge of their half-baked escape plan had put to rest all talk of leaving. Daeya had promised Tipori good behavior, and she seemed reluctant to betray his trust. Despite how much he resented their captivity, Ravlok had ceded to her intuition.

A hush fell over him as he entered the sanctuary. Oil lanterns lit the smooth white columns flanking the main hall, and rows of infirmary beds filled the space between them. Roughly a third of the beds held patients, while white-robed healers wearing sashes of red, gold, or silver drifted along the aisles.

A soft male voice broke the silence. "Can I assist you, soldier?"

Ravlok turned to find a young man about Daeya's age gliding toward him on silent feet. His white acolyte's robe had a red sash, designating him a follower of Shavaan, the healing goddess. Faelocks tumbled down from a tie at the back of his head. When Ravlok offered a smile in greeting, the acolyte returned it, though muted.

Ravlok glanced down at the streaks of mud on his leathers and winced. "Forgive me, I didn't think to change before coming."

"It's alright. We accept all manner of dress here. Are you in need of healing, or do you seek sanctuary?"

"Commander Emaaris sent me to find Orowen. I hoped she could provide me with some herbs."

The acolyte's smile wavered. "The high priestess is with a patient. I'm afraid she's asked not to be disturbed."

"Oh."

"What herbs are you seeking? I can retrieve them for you."

Ravlok's first inclination was to refuse and return another day. He'd operated under the shroud of secrecy for so long that letting anyone else in on his plan seemed unwise. But it wasn't like the herbs he needed were forbidden substances, and the ache in his upper back would surely hinder sleep tonight.

"Thank you." He hesitated. "What was your name?"

"Bren, sir."

"Bren. I'm Ravlok."

The healer started. "You're the monk from Eidosinia?"

He ventured a nod.

Bren's bright laughter filled the quiet space. He took one of Ravlok's hands in both of his. "It's a pleasure. The high priestess has told us much about you."

Of all the scenarios Ravlok might have expected from this visit, this certainly wasn't one of them. Heat rose in his face as two more acolytes approached, their mouths hanging open.

"She has?"

"Oh, yes. She told us how you duped a mage for his keys, fought off dozens more, and carried her on your back for leagues to help her escape." Bren squeezed Ravlok's hand. "Thank you. Thank you for returning her to us. We are all in your debt."

Ravlok's discomfort mounted with each echoed sentiment as the room's collective attention settled on him. He stammered his reply with a dismissive wave. "There are no thanks needed. I was fortunate to be able to assist." After an awkward pause, he added, "About those herbs?"

"Right, yes, the herbs."

After listing off what he needed, Ravlok found a bench near the door and tried not to attract any more attention. He rolled his ankles, provoking a chorus of pops and cracks, and immediate relief from the long day on his feet.

Bren was on his way back with a parchment-wrapped bundle when a woman's distant cry shattered the stillness.

"No!"

Ravlok shot upright, all weariness forgotten.

"No, you don't understand! I have to warn her. It was important!"

Bren spun toward the passageway through which the voice had come. Ravlok was on his feet before he registered the movement; he stopped just shy of drawing steel in Saolanni's hall.

The sounds of a scuffle and more cries followed. Ravlok started forward, but Bren intercepted him.

"Apologies, Ravlok. We had no talotiba in storage. I'm afraid you must excuse me." He proffered the bundle of herbs. "I must attend the priestess."

As if on cue, Orowen's voice carried from the direction of the screams. "I understand, *neime*, but your father has asked me to keep you here. Please, let's get back to bed, and we can talk some more."

"No, I have to go. She has to know!"

A pale-skinned Syljian tumbled into the passageway.

Riisii.

"It was important. I have to tell her. I have to warn her."

Orowen stepped into view across the sanctuary, her expression pained, yet resolute. She gestured toward Bren, and he began to weave a sigil in his palm.

White tile streaked red under Riisii's hands. "It was important! It was important and she has to know!"

Orowen helped her to her feet, but held fast to her arm. "What, Riisii? Who has to know? Perhaps I can send a message—"

"Let go!"

Cringing, Orowen let go, and Riisii shot forward. The priestess nodded toward Bren, and he darted after Riisii.

The seer stopped dead, staring at Ravlok. "Bookkeeper."

Ravlok stood transfixed, snakes writhing in his gut. Riisii's eyes were bloodshot, and dark circles weighed beneath them. Her black hair was a mass of tangles falling over sunken cheeks and bare, muscular shoulders. More red smeared her right forearm.

Bren pressed his sigil forward, but Riisii spun back and snapped the amulet off his neck.

"Riisii, no!" Orowen cried.

The seer's palms flashed white-violet. Three acolytes converged on her with sigils of their own. Riisii thrust downward, and a powerful burst of energy shattered the tile, propelling her high into the air. She landed in a crouch in front of Ravlok, more tiles shattering underfoot.

Acolytes exploded into motion, drawing sigils to restrain her.

Ravlok glanced between her and the door, bracing to leap into her path. He might not have training in handling matters of the mind, but he could stop her from escaping into the city and endangering others.

Riisii rose, never looking toward the entrance. She seized Ravlok by the shoulders. "I'm sorry. I'm so sorry. I can't See him anymore."

Ravlok's heart leaped into his throat. "I—I don't understand."

"Chaos. You have to tell her about Chaos."

The seer had Seen Chaos. A pang of dread reverberated through him. Anordis had found them. Was he here in Starlight?

Ravlok swallowed hard. He had to warn Daeya. Without her magic, she was in grave danger.

*Calm. Breathe.* He couldn't help her if he panicked.

Healers surrounded them, glowing sigils at the ready.

Ravlok held up his hands. "Wait."

Uncertainty flickered across their faces. A few glanced toward Orowen, who frowned at Ravlok in silent question.

He returned his attention to the seer. "What about Chaos, Riisii?"

"He comes for the Shard."

"The Shard? What Shard?"

Her eyes blazed with clarity. "The one she stole from him."

# CHAPTER THIRTY-SEVEN

## DAEYA

Tipori paced the length of the *fursaan*—the Alliaansi's indoor training facility—assessing Daeya's form from every angle. He spun his staff and prodded her right foot to widen her stance.

"Tell me, what is the difference between sorcerers and aethermancers?"

Daeya made the adjustment and immediately felt the difference in the steadiness of her core. "Sorcerers shape Aether into one of four elements and rely on sigils and incantations for most spells. Aethermancers forgo elements in favor of raw Aether, punching through and destabilizing the Wall as they see fit."

Amusement colored Tipori's voice. "That's another Guild answer, and wrong on several points. Try again."

She bit her lip to stifle a groan.

Tipori's incessant quizzing and pacing was wearing on her. He'd said he wanted to test her for Aetherian potential, whatever that meant. She'd worked on balance, stances, and defense techniques during martial training with him, had indulged him in all manner of philosophical debate, but never once had he removed her spellbinders to see what she could actually do.

And as much as Daeya had craved mundanity before, over a month without magic was more than enough to put those desires to rest. *Everything* was harder without casting, from lighting a candle and reaching books on the high shelves to loading crates of supplies for the tent cities. She'd never realized how much she relied on it.

Across the *fursaan*, Zakaari leaned against the guardrail while two young women, one human and one Syljian, hung on the railing's opposite side. Both girls seemed utterly enthralled by the half-blood, and their fawning was making it hard to concentrate. Zakaari sidled closer to the human and brushed a lock of brown hair off her cheek. He murmured something, and she burst into giggles.

In her distraction, Daeya almost missed the tip of Tipori's staff whistling toward her face.

Daeya squeezed her eyes shut, bracing for the strike. She sucked in a sharp breath—

Only the imminent sting never came.

When she cracked her eyes open, the staff hovered less than a fingerspan from her cheek, held in unwavering hands. She found Tipori's disapproving frown on the other end.

Daeya growled and hurled her staff down. "This is stupid. If you want to prove how wrong the Guild is about everything, there are easier ways to do it."

The giggling stopped. All four pairs of eyes settled on her.

Tipori planted his staff on the wood floor. "What is the difference, Daeya?"

She threw up her hands. "Why don't you tell me?"

"Because you already know the answer."

"I obviously don't. You've asked me that question a dozen times over the last week, and I've been wrong every time."

"Three times," he corrected. His expression was a study in patience. "I've asked you three times, and each time you stray further from the truth."

"Then what *is* the truth?"

Tipori regarded her for a moment, then knelt to collect her staff. "We're done for today."

Something inside Daeya snapped.

She stomped down on the staff, and it cracked against the floor. "No, we're not."

Tension flooded the room so fast that the air around Tipori rippled. She'd glimpsed that effect before and recognized it for the stringently restrained power that it was. Daeya tasted metal on her tongue.

Stupid. *Stupid.* She knew better than this. She would have never acted out in front of Gregory. He would have switched her for such insolence.

Daeya lifted her bare foot from the staff and shrank away from him. "I'm sorry, *Amaa.*"

Tipori reclaimed the weapon and returned to his feet with the slow inevitability of a rising tide. His violet gaze snagged her like a crosscurrent and threatened to drag her out to sea. "You are impatient, distractible, and angry. Those binders will not come off until I trust you to control your temper."

She clutched her hands to stop their shaking. The tremor infected her voice, and she dropped her eyes to his feet. "Forgive me."

He stepped closer and tilted her chin toward him. Daeya stiffened, bracing for the sting of a rebuke, the bite of cold, calculated rage.

Instead, she found warmth. Concern.

Tipori's sternness evaporated. Brows furrowing, he glanced toward the others, then lowered his voice. "No one is going to punish you for being upset. I know things have been changing quickly for you."

She couldn't hold his gaze. No surprise, her parentage hadn't stayed a secret for long. The news had been met with mixed reception, from Jerinoch's glowing approval to Koraani's scathing denial. Only after being presented with her mother's pendant—the twin to his own—had her so-called uncle admitted the possibility. He'd barely acknowledged her existence ever since. To him, she was *Cheralach's* daughter, and his hatred for his late brother-in-law poisoned what little favor her Guild intelligence had gained her.

Tipori released her with a sigh. "The power I plan to teach you comes with responsibility. It's not just elements, rifts, and tavern tricks. To wield Aetherian magic demands discipline, humility, and temperance. I cannot stress this enough."

So, he'd already decided she had Aetherian potential. She wondered at which point in their mundane little exercises that had occurred, or if he believed the stories others told of her magic were proof enough.

"If it's so dangerous, why teach me at all?"

"Because before this war is over, our people are going to need you."

*Our people.*

His words hung heavy with expectation—with a truth Daeya wasn't ready to accept. These were her parents' people, yes, but she was still an outsider. Even with Sam, Orowen, and Niam's companionship, she wasn't sure that feeling would ever change. She was one of them, but she'd been raised human. Gods, she'd been taught to hate Syljians her entire life.

So many things made sense now: her ability to cast more efficiently than her peers, the sickness that had plagued her on the road when she'd sworn off magic, the reason her condition at Belden Abbey had improved only after Cam had replaced the mundane gem in her pendant with saphyrum. Gregory must have known Daeya wouldn't get far without it. Even half-bloods needed it in minute quantities to avoid saphyrum sickness.

That meant Cam likely knew, too. Maybe that was why Cam's brothers hated her so much. Maybe they'd all known, even Normos.

"Word's come back from Eidosinia." Tipori returned the staffs to the weapon racks. "The raids on the Cintoshi cache and the mine near Belden were successful. It's also been confirmed two convoys left Ferid on their way north using the routes you provided. Thanks to you, we'll have enough saphyrum to survive the winter."

Daeya nodded absently. "I'm glad to hear it."

Tipori padded closer. "I also have news of your father."

She perked up. Weeks with no word—which Tipori had apologized for repeatedly—had banished all hope of hearing anything. "Tell me. Please."

"He is well. My contact reports that there are mages tailing him, but so far they have left him and your cousin to their routines."

The tail was no surprise. Daeya had expected far worse—imprisonment, maybe, or house arrest. A shuddering sigh eased the tension in her shoulders. "Gods."

Tipori folded his hands behind his back. "Your father said he loves you, and he'll see you soon. Murtagh requested we bring Annie north as well, and I've agreed."

Any suspicion that he might have been making things up to keep her compliant vanished with the mention of Annie, Murtagh's partner. Another shaky breath couldn't stop the sting of joyful tears. "Thank you, Tipori."

"You're very welcome. I'm sorry it took so long. I've advised them to remain in the city and avoid trouble. My contact has standing orders to extract them if anything happens."

He'd kept his word. He'd actually kept his word. Daeya wiped her face. "I'm"—she shook her head and laughed, drawing a curious look from Zakaari—"I don't know what to say." No amount of gratitude felt like enough.

Tipori's smile was tender. "I pray it brings you peace."

Zakaari left his women and crossed the training floor, still wearing that curious frown. Things had more or less returned to normal between them since the memorial. Tipori's son was just as temperamental as the day they'd met, but the fact that he'd smuggled the last of Damiir's oranges into her room yesterday showed how thoughtful he could be underneath all that bluster.

"You alright, McVen?"

Daeya nodded. "Fine. Better, even."

"Good." One side of his mouth lifted. "I like when you smile."

Zakaari's near-flirting was another not entirely irksome change. Though he ran off with a different girl every night, he was always present when she needed him. It helped that he didn't live at the heart of an emotional void. Something that couldn't be said of Alar.

The sound of a door opening drew their attention. A girl of about ten slipped into the *fursaan*, her cheeks flushed a deep purple. "*Amaa*, there's a messenger for you."

Tipori stepped off the training floor, hands still clasped behind him. "Send them in."

"He's not here, *Amaa*. Finn's holding him at the perimeter." She cringed and glanced toward Daeya. "He's carrying a scroll from the enemy. Says he'll only deliver it to you."

Tipori frowned. "Tell Finn I'll be down shortly."

The girl bolted out the door in a whirl of white braids. Tipori pulled on his boots and gathered his cloak.

Zakaari started toward him. "*Peiaa?*"

Tipori paused at the entrance. "Stay here, *ennii*."

"But—"

"Run her through some hand-to-hand exercises. I expect a full accounting of her strengths and weaknesses when I return."

Zakaari deflated and rolled his eyes. "That won't take long. She couldn't throw a hook to save her life."

Daeya scowled. "Hey."

"A boy's last words." Tipori winked at her. "Go easy on him, Daeya."

Zakaari sighed as he watched his father depart. When he turned back, he gestured toward his partners still lingering against the guardrail. "I have plans tonight," he told Daeya, "so if you intend on getting injured, I won't fight you over getting healed. I'll drop you at Havensguard and you can be Sam's problem."

"I'd rather be her problem anyway." Daeya stretched her arms over her head, then twisted her back from side to side. "She's prettier than you."

Zakaari gave her an affronted look.

His partners giggled, their eyes bright with anticipation. Encouraged by their attention, he peacocked around the ring, pacing as his father did, before pulling off his shirt.

*Now, that's entirely unnecessary—*

Daeya's breath caught in her throat.

She'd seen plenty of shirtless men before, but none built like Zakaari, all supple lilac skin and corded muscle. Sunlight etched the valleys of his chest and abdomen in perfect shadow. His arms had that alluring fullness, purely masculine in nature, without being overly brawny or ill-proportioned. His trousers rode low on his hips, exposing a pair of dimples in his lower back that drew her eyes with magnetic precision.

Only the squealing and cheering from his retinue ruined the effect.

Daeya shook herself and dropped into a ready stance. No way would she allow him to see that lapse.

He turned from his admirers and leveled her in his haughty gaze. She tracked his movements, stilling her mind and body with deep breaths in through her nose, out through her mouth, as Ravlok had taught her.

Zakaari charged, overextending a punch. Daeya sidestepped and grabbed his arm. Using his own momentum, she hurled him into a front flip, and he went down hard on his back.

Daeya resumed her ready stance as he lay there dazed and gasping. Applause and laughter rose from his cheering squad. She cracked a smile and adjusted her stance, reminding herself to breathe as a heady rush swept through her.

Zakaari groaned and shoved back to his feet. Daeya anticipated anger or embarrassment, but when he whipped his dark hair out of his eyes, he was grinning.

"Alright, McVen." He settled into his own ready stance. This time, the look he gave her exuded discipline. Focus. "You have my attention."

Zakaari was a surprisingly good teacher. He challenged her in ways Ravlok had only begun, and he gave no quarter when it came to mistakes. She ended up on the floor so many times she lost count, but the bruising ache in her back and shoulders was a welcome one. They sparred well into the afternoon, breaking only for snacks and water, always goading each other into another round.

Daeya sat cross-legged on the floor, leaning against the cold guardrail. Zakaari slumped beside her, hair clinging to his face and shoulders. He passed her a strip of dried venison from a nearby satchel and kept one for himself.

She nodded toward the empty side of the room. "Your cheering section must have gotten bored."

"Huh." Zakaari looked up, chewing distractedly. He swallowed, then shrugged. "Must have."

She glanced toward the floor-length windows spaced in intervals along one wall. Slivers of light stretched toward them with the setting sun. "Didn't you say you had plans?"

"We should have left hours ago to make it in time." He shrugged again. "I don't think they'd have liked it, anyway."

Daeya snapped off a piece of venison and tossed it into her mouth. A smoky flavor complemented the salty crust. "Where were you going?"

"Nowhere. It was stupid."

Curious now, Daeya elbowed him in the ribs. "Come on. You owe me for that last throw."

"You left your right side open. I couldn't resist." Zakaari chewed a while longer, glancing toward her when he caught her watching him. "You really want to know?"

"No, I just asked assuming you'd ignore me."

Eyes narrowing, he considered her a moment more. "We were supposed to go to Sundance Falls down in the valley. It's a long climb over a rocky bluff, and neither of them like hiking."

"So, why take them there?"

"Because sunset on the falls is beautiful this time of year."

Whatever Daeya expected him to say, it wasn't that. Her surprise must have shown on her face because Zakaari winced and looked away.

"See? Stupid." He got to his feet.

Daeya wasn't about to squander that rare glimpse of vulnerability. The only other time she'd seen him without his guard up was when he'd spoken to her about Cheralach. "I don't think that sounds stupid at all."

"Well, you—" Zakaari spun on his heel, his tone instantly combative, before lurching to a halt. "You don't?"

"No. It sounds lovely."

"Oh." He cleared his throat. "Well, maybe we can go. When you can leave the plateau, I mean."

Daeya chuckled. "Are you asking me on a date, Zakaari?"

"No!" His horror might have stung if it hadn't turned his face a darker shade of purple. "I just—never mind."

He swiped his shirt up and jerked it on, then lingered in the middle of the training floor, raking his fingers through his hair.

A curious ache took root in Daeya's chest. She tucked the last of her venison into a pocket and rose, padding across the cold wood to meet him. She touched his elbow, and Zakaari turned, pressing his arm further into her palm.

Encouraged, Daeya let her hand close over him. Scents of citrons and lavender lingered beneath his layer of sweat. "I'd like to see the falls." When his brows furrowed, she added, "On a not-date, of course."

"A not-date," Zakaari echoed, his expression unreadable. He nodded with all the seriousness of forging some unbreakable pact. "I'd like that."

"As long as no one gets the wrong idea," she chided, releasing him. "The last thing I need is for one of your girlfriends to pick a fight with me."

He laughed. "They wouldn't stand a chance."

After a quick pass over the room to clean up, Zakaari tossed her cloak to her. "Where'd you learn to spar, anyway? You have good technique."

"Ravlok taught me."

"Monk training. That explains everything." He fastened his own cloak around his shoulders. As he guided her toward the door, his head tilted. "So, are you two together, then?"

"Oh, no. We don't think of each other like that."

"Really?"

"Mhmm. He's not really into anyone." A half-truth, but Daeya wasn't about to explain her friend's continued refusal to acknowledge his interest in Sam.

Outside, low clouds crept over the Alliaansi city. Snowflakes danced on the wind and dusted the landscape. Evenly spaced torches illuminated a strip of hard-packed soil sandwiched between the training circles and rows of benches. Daeya shivered, instantly regretting leaving her wool scarf at Havensguard.

She started when a layer of warm wool caressed her cheek.

"What about Alar?" Zakaari adjusted his scarf around her neck. He batted her hand away when she tried to protest.

His kindness muted her momentarily.

Since Alar left, she'd had some time to ponder their relationship—if there had ever been such a thing. Daeya pulled the scarf tighter. "I thought we had something at first, but it's clear he'll never trust me. And I can't say his psionics don't make me uncomfortable." A dark shape hurried toward them, rounding the farthest circle at a jog. She squinted into the space between two torches, her eyes fixed on the familiar outline.

"Masterminds make everyone uncomfortable. Even my father, and he's not afraid of anything." Zakaari tucked his hands into his cloak. "He warded our whole family against them."

She'd expected a scolding remark for her confession, not agreement. She tugged her hair out from under the scarf, distracted from the figure fast approaching. "And the other Alliaansi don't find that suspicious?"

"If they do, they like his money enough not to say anything."

She thought back to the Evallier family's home, sheltered away in its gardens. Even their most subtle displays of wealth would have been considered lavish in most Eidosinian abodes. Tipori had Rillanese connections, that much was certain, and his ability to command a room went beyond his skills as an Aetherian.

"Who is he, anyway?"

Zakaari hesitated. "He's—"

"Daeya!"

In the light of a nearby torch, the dark figure materialized into a man.

Daeya squinted. "Rav?"

"Thank Silonas," Ravlok breathed. Still dressed in his fighting leathers, he bent at the waist and rested his hands on his knees. Clouds of vapor puffed out of him, stirring the snowflakes that fell thicker by the minute.

She shared a look with Zakaari before stepping toward her friend. "What's wrong?"

"There's—" Ravlok held up a hand, taking another moment to catch his breath. When he finally straightened, the full weight of his harrowed expression settled over her. "There's something you need to see."

# CHAPTER THIRTY-EIGHT

## OROWEN

Orowen rolled the broken scalpel in a strip of leather and passed it to Bren. Then she spoke to the acolytes gathered in a loose circle around her. "Everyone should check their bags for missing instruments. No sharp objects or saphyrum beyond Riisii's basic needs should be brought within her reach. That goes for any casting jewelry or amulets as well."

"Yes, Devoted."

The Temple doors creaked open. Ravlok, Daeya, and Zakaari waded through the sea of beds and into the lantern light. Her acolytes shuffled aside for them.

Cooling relief soothed the tension in Orowen's spine. She embraced her nephew and kissed Daeya's cheek. "*Iiren'norvaa, neimen.* Thank you for coming."

Zakaari's brows furrowed. "What's this about, Aunt Wen?"

Orowen exchanged a look with Ravlok. He nodded once, his expression unwavering.

"Ravlok thinks Daeya might be able to help us understand what Riisii's been trying to tell us."

"Me?" Daeya shifted on her feet. "What can I do?"

Ravlok gestured toward the hallway of private rooms. "It's best if we just show you. May I, Devoted?"

"*Ciir*. You won't wake her." With Shavaan's blessing, Bren's double-layered sedative sigil would keep Riisii under for a few more hours. "Daeya, could you remove the bead from your pendant first, please?"

"Sure."

Daeya left the bead with Bren, and Ravlok beckoned to her. "Come on."

Zakaari stayed glued to Daeya's side while Orowen trailed after them. She gathered the panels of her robe around her as if to ward herself. Even now, the harrowing manifestations of Riisii's madness threatened to bring up the meager meal Orowen had choked down between shifts. Her niece had always been troubled, but there had never been a malady that she and Ashaara couldn't remedy. Until now.

Daeya entered Riisii's room with all the caution of a doe slipping into an open meadow. "Bleeding Aether."

Orowen leaned against the doorway while Daeya and Zakaari took in the room. Strange carvings covered all four walls, as well as the bed and side table. Some of the symbols resembled letters from modern Skriian or Aivenosian. Others had no recognizable correlation to any alphabet Orowen knew. Most disturbing were the runes shaped like eyes, gouged through with savage slashes and spattered with blood. The scalpel must have slipped during their making, which would account for the slices on Riisii's palm.

Orowen shuddered. She'd seen these symbols before, years ago, when she and Maralla tracked a string of sacrificial eye-gougings to a poppy den run by Chaos priests. The symbols had been carved into the priests' foreheads as part of a ritual believed to awaken their psionic talent. They'd kept rooms full of half-starved victims whose minds had been shattered by torture in preparation to become new vessels for their god.

Her worst fears had come to fruition; Chaos priests had returned to the north, and Orowen had no magic to fight them with. If she could only draw the warding sigils needed, she could call upon Saolanni's light to guard the Temple and at least create a haven against Anordis. None of the acolytes or junior priests could perform such powerful magic, and every master healer they could spare had been sent to Kuma'Kiir with Maralla's troops.

At least Riisii was still fighting his influence; it hadn't infected her yet. Ashaara's psionic therapy had healed most of the psychological wounds that had contributed to her madness. She'd also rebuilt the ward around Riisii's mind and assured them her Sight would repair itself with time. Unfortunately, Ashaara hadn't learned whatever it was Riisii so desperately needed to tell them.

Daeya approached one wall and traced the carvings. "Riisii did all of this?"

"*Ciir.*" Orowen bolstered her resolve and entered the room. She retrieved a candle from the bedside table to better illuminate the markings. "Ashaara said Riisii Saw the symbols in a vision months ago, but she couldn't translate them. I've seen a few over the years, but most are unknown to me." She glanced toward them. "Ravlok mentioned you had some training in the ancient languages."

One corner of Daeya's mouth twitched. "I suppose I do."

She examined a rendering of the pantheon's twelve-pointed star on another wall. One point had a jagged slash drawn through it.

Ravlok stepped up on her other side. "Can you read any of this?"

Daeya nodded. "It's an account. And a warning."

"What kind of account, *neime*?"

"One of a battle." Daeya frowned at a spot where several symbols repeated.

The room itself seemed to have borne witness to a battle. Orowen reached out to the mutilated pantheon star, her fingertips dipping into the jagged grooves. What in Mira's name had her niece gotten herself into?

"Can you explain what's significant about it?"

A thin, humorless laugh escaped Daeya. "I'm not sure you'd believe me if I told you."

"Try us," Zakaari challenged.

Daeya studied them both, then touched the pattern again. "If this transcription is accurate, it's the battle that destroyed Vintrios."

Gooseflesh prickled the back of Orowen's neck.

Vintrios. The Holy City.

Its name alone deserved reverence—a name Orowen had last heard over a century ago. Many speculated that Vintrios was once the seat of the entire pantheon—the place where all twelve gods, greater and lesser, walked among mortals. The city's fabled Temple of Saonis was said to be the birthplace of the nine lesser gods and their respective mortal races.

Fae tales abounded about the Holy City's fall. On these very walls, Riisii might have carved the answer to a puzzle that had eluded the most devoted Astenpori and Duerwisti scholars for centuries.

Overcome, Orowen swayed on her feet. Ravlok's warm hand steadied her. As a scholar himself, he seemed unusually calm about this.

She looked to Daeya. "Please, tell me what you know."

"There's so much here. I would need more time to translate it all. From what I can tell, they describe a coup that Chaos attempted on the Greater Throne. He meant to steal the seat from Saolanni."

She moved toward another set of runes. Zakaari followed like a shadow, though he seemed to be studying Daeya more than the walls.

"His attempt against her failed, and a sliver of his power was taken from him." Daeya touched a symbol resembling a pair of crossed swords. She spoke as if in realization. "He's vulnerable without that power."

"The Shard," Orowen recalled. Riisii had been raving about a shard all afternoon. Sparks of understanding began to smolder, but they produced more smoke than flame.

"Yes. And the warning here"—Daeya swept a hand toward their surroundings—"is that he's coming to take it back."

Just as Riisii had said.

Orowen shivered. "Riisii said 'she' stole this power from Chaos." She let her gaze linger on Daeya's profile, a blend of sharp lines and delicate curves so much like her mother's. "Does it say who 'she' is?"

"Yes." Daeya faced her fully. Conflict warred with the candlelight in her eyes. Her jaw tensed, as if she was restraining herself from saying more. Then almost as swiftly, she looked away.

Zakaari touched Daeya's shoulder. "What is it?"

An inkling of intuition seventeen years in the making itched along Orowen's nerves. Not far from this very room, outside in Saolanni's garden, she'd felt the press of her dear friend's lips on her forehead for the last time. A prayer answered. A divine task given. One Nerimoria couldn't speak about, even to a high priestess.

"It's okay, Daeya," Ravlok said. "She can help us."

It took Orowen a moment to realize Ravlok was talking about her. "Help with what?"

Daeya looked from Ravlok, to Zakaari, then to Orowen. "A ritual."

Orowen's gaze flicked toward the eye carvings, a hot stone dropping into her stomach. *That* ritual? Surely, they weren't afflicted... "What kind of ritual?"

"It's called the Ritual of Ascension." Ravlok nodded toward Daeya. "It's meant to help her control the new magic she's been manifesting."

Orowen remembered their scouts' reports of Daeya's scarlet fire and how it had devastated the Orthovian port. A vast swath of the forest southwest of Starlight Plateau had also been destroyed.

Orowen touched her fingers to her lips. "And how do we perform this ritual?"

Ravlok shifted subtly, his first sign of unease. "I've been studying the text for a while now. All we need is one more component and a space to perform undisturbed for several hours." He drew in a breath. "Devoted, if Chaos is coming for the Shard, Daeya must be ready. She needs her magic."

Zakaari held up his hands. "Hang on. Vintrios was destroyed, what, two, three thousand years ago?" He gave Daeya an incredulous look. "Is he seriously implying what I think he is? That you have part of a *god's* magic? How is that possible?"

Daeya cringed. "It's complicated. I don't quite understand it myself."

"The ritual should help with that," Ravlok said to her. "Based on my research, it should unlock your memories. I suspect it will all make sense once you've ascended."

Orowen slipped away to Riisii's bedside, her hand trembling as she replaced the candle. Her niece slept soundly under a nest of blankets, dark hair fanning across the pillow. She smoothed a lock that had fallen over her face.

There was more Ravlok was holding back. His and Daeya's discomfort wormed its way under her skin and left her battling a surge of guilt. Whether to trust the sorceress was still a contentious topic throughout the community, but no one had prioritized *Daeya's* trust in *them*.

Cheralach's visions had suggested his daughter was the key to the Alliaansi's survival. But if Chaos priests were also involved, then their problems extended far beyond the Guild.

Anordis's followers deployed smoke and illusion to carry out their master's will. What better time to infect Starlight's community than when it was fighting for its very existence? If the god of chaos reclaimed this Shard and was restored to the height of his power, what then? Would he make another play for the Greater Throne?

An icy hand clenched around Orowen's heart. What if the war was merely a distraction from an uprising of divine proportions? One as catastrophic as the battle carved into these walls? Not only Starlight, but the entire world, would depend on keeping the Shard out of Anordis's possession.

She looked toward the broken pantheon symbol. Sour heat filled her stomach. Whatever their enemy's intentions, a war among gods couldn't come to pass.

She fixed Zakaari with her most serious stare. "Riisii claims Chaos took her eyes from her when she tried to look into Daeya's future. That means there was something in it he didn't want her to See. She's been beside herself trying to remember what it was." Those ominous eye carvings loomed in her periphery. "If this business with the Shard has exposed a vengeful god's weakness, then we must prepare ourselves in every way possible."

If this ritual could provide answers and give them the power to defend against Chaos, it was perhaps just as important a task as defending their front line. Anordis had already targeted Riisii's Foresight; only Tiior knew when or how he would strike again. It was imperative then, that they safeguard the ritual space with warding sigils to keep him out.

Now, more than ever, she had to renew her vow to Saolanni and regain her magic.

Zakaari spared an affectionate look for his sister before turning back to Orowen. "But Riisii has never Seen into the past before. How could she have known all of this?" It was his turn to gesture at the walls.

"A question for Ashaara, perhaps." Orowen tucked her hands into her robe. "Your sister's Sight is rarely wrong. I've heard enough to believe it, no matter how it may have come about. Even if it's just Chaos priests starting trouble, we should speak with your father about having Daeya's binders removed."

"You know which way the council will vote on that. Koraani still doesn't trust her."

Orowen bristled. Baosanni take her if Koraani's prejudice put them all in danger. "Wilfau has been happy with her work in the orphanage. She's served in the tent cities without incident and provided all the information she promised. There's a quorum even without Magnus present, and I know Jerinoch will support his niece. If we can get your father to agree, we don't need Koraani's permission."

Zakaari ran a hand through his hair and looked at Daeya. He said nothing at first, but when she met his eyes with an expression that was equal parts hope and anticipation, something unidentifiable passed between them. His unease crumbled. "Alright. I'll help in any way I can."

Daeya smiled. "Thank you, Zakaari."

A gentle touch on Orowen's shoulder drew her attention back to Ravlok. "I've had some trouble tracking down the last component for the ritual. We need talotiba mushrooms, but I'm afraid they won't be available until spring."

"You've asked the healers to check our stores?"

He nodded. "I've checked every herbalist in town, too."

And the closest monastery—the largest producer of talotibas—was a hundred leagues south of the mountains in Guild territory. Orowen squared her shoulders. "I'll see what I can find."

She could ask Ashaara to send a message outside Starlight's ward to their contact in Ferid. But with snow hindering travel through the mountains, it could be well over a month before a carrier reached them. Perhaps Tipori would have a solution; his people overseas and all across Eidosinia possessed unique ways of transporting small goods.

In the meantime, she would return to her studies, finish her prayers, and practice drawing sigils in preparation for her oath. With Saolanni's blessing, she could ward the entire Temple against Anordis before the last component was delivered. If he came for the Shard—if he planned to harm Cheralach and Nerimoria's daughter to get it—he would have to go through her first.

Orowen folded her hands. "If Saolanni wills it, I can prepare a ritual space here at the Temple. For now, all of you go home and get some rest. I will speak with Tipori in the morning."

# CHAPTER THIRTY-NINE

## NORMOS

"If you can stitch the wound closed before you draw your sigils," Olivia explained, threading the catgut through the side of the laceration, "it will use less saphyrum to seal it."

"It will also heal faster," Normos recalled, watching her nimble fingers work the stitches into her fellow healer's forearm. Dona-Thal's injury was small but deep, and would hopefully serve as a lesson not to peel apples on the bench seat of a moving wagon. "And the potential for scarring is greatly lessened. Though stitches aren't always an option in the field."

Olivia's voice lifted with surprise. "Very good, Normos." She glanced up from the cut. "Someone's been doing his homework."

Heat touched Normos's cheeks. If there was one thing he'd always excelled at, it was his studies. He mustered his courage and gestured toward the needle. "May I?"

Olivia paused, looking from him to Dona-Thal.

The older woman eyed Normos distrustfully. Her lips pressed into a line. "I'd rather not be a pincushion for you, Sorcerer."

Normos inclined his head, willing to accept the healer's refusal with grace, but Olivia's eyes rolled skyward.

"Oh please, Dona. I've seen his needlework, and it's far neater than yours."

Dona-Thal scowled. "All the same, I'll not have it."

"How else do you expect him to practice?"

"It's alright, Olivia. I'll respect her choice." Normos placed his hands on his thighs and made to rise from the stool. He didn't blame the woman for her misgivings; he would feel the same if he'd been conscripted into the Guild's service, uprooted from his family, and sent north to a war zone. It was a wonder any of the healers chose to speak with him at all. "We should get moving soon. I'll let the lead driver know you're almost finished—"

Olivia snagged his sleeve. "Where do you think you're going? You still have work to do."

Normos jerked to a stop, bent awkwardly at the waist so he didn't knock his head against the wagon bows. He fumbled for words beneath those stern emerald eyes. "I was just—"

"Just nothing," Olivia snapped. "Now sit down until I say you can move."

Dona-Thal stared at Olivia as if she'd just used a dirty scalpel to lance a boil. Apparently, Olivia's lack of propriety around sorcerers was as much a surprise to the old healer as it had once been to him.

But a month on the road with the supply caravans had only whetted Olivia's tongue. She spoke to him now almost as sharply as she did to Gwen. The only difference was Normos didn't mind being bossed around. As long as Olivia continued teaching him healing techniques, he would do almost anything she asked.

He sat back down on the stool to await instruction.

Dona-Thal's eyebrows nearly met her hairline.

Olivia snorted and went back to her work, drawing a wince from Dona-Thal as she stuck her with the needle. "Don't look so surprised; they're easily trained if you use a firm hand." She winked at Normos, and he didn't bother to hide his sheepish smile. "Now, he's going to heal you, and I'll not hear a word out of your sorry mouth. Normos, prepare a grade two healing sigil and wait till I'm clear."

"Yes, my lady."

That drew another look from Dona-Thal, more curious now. Normos channeled a trickle of magic from Mira's amulet. With one finger, he drew the lines of a double-layered healing sigil. The disk of light hovered over his palm.

Olivia tied off the last stitch and leaned back. "Alright, ready. Remember grade two is stronger than your base sigil."

After a breath to calm the flutter in his chest, Normos held his sigil over the wound and relaxed his hand. Wisps of white-violet energy eddied around his palm. They sank from his sigil into Dona-Thal's arm and began sealing the wound.

"Slowly," Olivia coached. "That's it."

Normos took great care to maintain the steady trickle of power. Too fast, and the formation of new tissue would create excess heat, which could lead to wound cautery rather than healing. This, Normos had learned, was the true reason those considered weaker with magic were sent to study healing. It was easier to hone their talents toward more delicate tasks than train one such as he to use less.

Supple new flesh formed around the stitches. Normos's healing light continued its work, reducing the redness and swelling in the area.

Olivia held up a hand. "Pause just a moment."

Tensing his fingers to stop the trickle of magic, Normos waited for her to snip the first three stitches and examine his work. Pride swelled in his chest when she beamed.

"It's perfect," Olivia said. "I'll remove these last few stitches, and you can heal those, too."

Once the work was finished, Normos let his sigil dissolve into mist.

"By the gods." Dona-Thal tugged at the unblemished space where her injury had been. "Was that your first grade two?"

Another little smile tugged at his lips. "On someone else, yes." He'd been practicing on himself most nights when he could disguise the light in a wagon with saphyrum lanterns.

Olivia looked smug. "I told you he was good."

"He's amazing," Dona-Thal marveled. "Thank you, Sorcerer."

"It was my pleasure."

And truly it was. Nothing Normos had ever accomplished came close to the sense of fulfillment that healing brought.

Dona-Thal departed, leaving Normos and Olivia alone. He reached for a clean towel and doused it in spirits, then began wiping down Olivia's tools. The sharp smell of alcohol flooded the wagon.

It had become a ritual for Normos to clean the instruments after a lesson—a task normally allocated to a healer's apprentice—and he settled into it with the sort of contentment he'd only felt a few times in recent years. Olivia was one of the best instructors he'd ever had. She was straightforward like Gregory, but with the sympathy and patience his Councilor lacked.

"Good work, today."

He glanced up and smiled. "Thank you."

A short silence passed between them while he wiped down the scalpels. The journey north had afforded him a rare opportunity to interact honestly with another person, unguarded for once. It was a welcome change, despite the direness of their circumstances.

At first, he'd only humored Olivia's talk of conspiracy and Gwen's fae tale surrounding the School. Gwen worked for Sarikkian, after all, and Gregory's old rival had been trying to undermine his efforts on the Council for years. But the evidence Gwen and her people had collected got Normos thinking. Gregory wished to return Daeya McVen to his side, regardless of the laws that forbade it. Once touched by an imperium, a mage must be stripped of rank, spellbound, and isolated to ensure no harm could come to anyone else. If the Councilor was willing to overlook such safety measures, either he was compromised himself, or his affection for Daeya was making him reckless.

And Councilor Lucius Gregory was anything but reckless.

It was worth going along with them for now, learning all he could, if not to uncover the work of a blanker mastermind then to safeguard his mentor against a coup.

Olivia tilted her head. "Normos, have you ever given serious thought to studying healing? You're very good at it."

He chuckled. "You're very kind."

"I'm not just saying that. The control you demonstrate is remarkable."

Her praise was bittersweet. It validated his secret studies, but also added weight to the inevitable loss of them. By solstice, he would be at Gregory's side again, and his lessons with Olivia would have to end.

"I wish I could." He placed the last tool inside its case and slung the towel over his shoulder. "But that is not my calling."

She frowned. "That sounds like your Councilor talking."

Normos paused in fastening her tool kit. He could have lied and insisted he was a battle mage because he chose it. He could've boasted that his talents placed him among the strongest lightning savants on the continent. That he was slated to take his own seat on the Council someday—a seat no healer could ever achieve.

Instead, he straightened and met her gaze. "Because it is."

She crossed her legs and rested an elbow on the sidewall. "You feel like you owe him something?"

"He made me what I am. I owe him everything."

"Seems to me, if he had your best interests in mind, you wouldn't have to hide your desire to learn healing magic. Why not just ask him?"

"I have."

"And he said no? Why?"

Normos shifted on the stool. Floorboards creaked under him, sounding much louder in the cramped wagon than they should have. "He believes it's inferior magic."

Her eyebrows shot upward. "I'll keep that in mind the next time I save one of his idiot mages from a lethal knife wound."

The air in the wagon grew stifling, and his attention strayed toward the stripe of sunlight shining through the gate flap.

"Is that what you think, as well? That it's beneath you?" Olivia's hurt quickly reforged itself into a scowl. "That's why you want to hide what we're doing. Because you're ashamed of it."

"No." He cut his eyes back toward her. "No, that's not it at all."

"Explain it to me, then."

Where would he even start? Normos sighed and leaned forward, resting his elbows on his knees. Just as quickly, he straightened again with an involuntary growl. Joss's poor posture was rubbing off on him.

"I don't think it's inferior." Folding his hands in his lap, he searched the small sliver of floor separating the toes of their boots. "It's what I've always wanted to learn. But he believes it's a waste of time and forbade me from practicing so it didn't become a distraction. If he knew what I was doing, he would be very angry with me."

He winced in remembered agony as the echoes of his last correction stabbed through him.

Olivia's tight posture loosened. "Angry enough to hurt you?"

Her question came with a mask of neutrality, but there was a layer of something unidentifiable beneath it. Caution? Or perhaps disapproval? The sort one might use when questioning a child with a freshly blackened eye or a broken bone.

His urge to lie confused him, and he forced his own mask into place. "Never any more than necessary. He's always looked out for me, and he deserves my utmost respect."

The moment the words left his mouth, his hypocrisy was laid bare before him. Gregory deserved his respect, so why was he going behind his back to defy him? Wasn't that why McVen irritated him so much? Her blatant disregard for the Councilor's rules?

Normos stood so abruptly that he nearly brained himself on a wagon bow. He flinched back, cupping a hand over his head. "Forgive me, healer, I've wasted enough of your time."

To her credit, Olivia made no move to stop him, but her expression grew thoughtful. Normos hurried to the back of the wagon and lifted the flap. He jumped down, using one hand on the sidewall for balance.

Olivia's voice followed him out into the bright afternoon. "You're never a waste of time."

Normos's temples throbbed with the quickening of his pulse. For the last few weeks, he'd avoided the worst of his headaches, but now it seemed they might return with a vengeance. He resisted the thought of using a healing sigil to tame it. It was for the best that he curb his insolence now before their convoy reached the border.

He turned back toward the wagon and bowed, albeit with a stiffness bordering on impolite. "Good day."

"Good morrow, Normos."

The shade of the wagon obscured her face, but he could hear the disappointment in her voice. It lingered like an ache in his spine long after he'd left her.

A black cloud blotted out part of the horizon. It grew larger as Normos's caravan traveled along the road. He ordered his drivers to slow and remain on guard as he took point at the lead wagon. Super-charged white-violet static arced between his fingertips in anticipation of a fight.

They came upon the smoking wreckage of saphyrum carts near sunset. Gwen's caravan pulled up as Normos was interviewing witnesses.

"Gods-damned blankers." Joss pulled the bloody towel from the arrow wound on his shoulder. "Came out of rifts right outside the canyon."

Normos greeted Gwen with a nod, trying and failing to ignore Olivia as she drew healing sigils in his peripheral vision. A grade two to treat the spell burns, and a grade four for the arrow wound that had rendered Joss's casting arm useless.

"Ow! Bleeding woman." Joss jerked away from Olivia's stronger sigil.

Gwen scowled. "You couldn't handle a few blankers?"

Joss met her scowl with an equivalent look of fury. "There were too many."

And now they were armed with the Guild's own saphyrum—a supply that, though replaceable, could weaken their forces briefly while they awaited a new shipment.

Normos fought off a shudder. Gregory was going to be furious.

It was customary when using the secret supply routes to split a convoy over a league or two to draw less attention to the road. They'd broken this one into three parts with Joss in the lead, Normos at center, and Gwen in the rear to keep a strong caster with each group. Other lower-ranking mages and a few acolytes also attended each segment—more than enough to defend each portion from the usual rabble.

Looking around at the wreckage, there was little usual about this attack. Normos rubbed his chin. "They ambushed you at the end of the pass?"

"That's what I said," Joss snapped. "Bastards seemed to know exactly which wagons to hit, too. They were here and gone in minutes."

"It could've been worse," Gwen pointed out. "At least they didn't kill anyone."

Suspicion nipped at Normos. He looked back down the narrow gorge they'd just left, noting several windswept patches of bare rock that might suggest entry points through small rifts.

Everything was too precise. Too clean. And at the tightest bottleneck in their journey.

Gwen followed his gaze. "What are you thinking?"

"We chose this pass because it's one of few that have never been hit by the Alliaansi before. A coordinated attack like this means the route is compromised. I recommend tightening up the convoy. If they try again, we'll be stronger together."

She nodded, her headscarf shifting with the movement. "Agreed. We're nearing the Palisadics, anyway. There may be other attempts over the border."

Olivia resumed her work on the arrow wound, but Joss flinched again.

"Ow! Chaos curse you, you damned bi—"

Normos whirled on him. "Watch your tongue."

His sudden fury made even Gwen recoil. Joss's eyes narrowed, but in a miraculous moment of self-preservation, the idiot's mouth clamped shut.

Olivia gave Normos an appreciative nod, her forest-green lips curving. Gwen was watching him openly; her curious stare made his skin itch.

"We should let the horses rest," he suggested, turning away. "I'll see to—"

In his haste to get as far from the women as possible, Normos nearly collided with the Feridian boy, Peader, Councilor Sarikkian's young Conduit. A good-natured lad of about fifteen, he'd been assigned to Joss's portion of the caravan, allegedly to communicate with the other Conduits in the caravans. Normos suspected it was more to keep an eye on Joss.

Peader must have been hurrying to Gwen's side. His eyes squeezed shut, bracing for impact, and one furry hand covered his snout.

Normos stopped short, steadying him with a hand on his shoulder. "Watch it, acolyte."

One large brown eye opened, followed by the other. Both gleamed with tears. Peader kept his hand over his nose and whimpered.

Normos shot Gwen an uncertain look.

She closed the distance and crouched before the boy. "Peader? What's wrong?"

"I'm sorry. I'm sorry, Councilor. I tried—" Peader doubled over with a mournful howl.

The sound ripped into Normos. His flesh prickled as if it might crawl right off his bones. He dropped to one knee beside Gwen and cupped the boy's face. "Where does it hurt, Peader? If we're to help you, we need to see."

Peader shook his head, still holding his snout. Blood glistened in his fur.

"Oh no." Gwen covered her mouth. "No, Peader."

"Keep it together, Councilor," Normos scolded. "Your student needs you."

Her panic would only frighten the patient more. It was probably just a cut or missing tooth, something easily healed with a grade one or two. He tugged Peader's arm away.

But when Normos got a better look at the blood leaking from the boy's nostrils, he finally understood. Peader's large irises had disguised the burst vessels in his pleading eyes. Horror gripped Normos in viselike talons. He met Gwen's look of mingled anguish and fury with his own.

Words stuck in his throat. He forced them past a lump of sand and peeled his tongue off the roof of his mouth.

"He's been imperiumed."

# Chapter Forty

## Alar

Over four dozen barrels of saphyrum and cases of supplies filled the shallow cavern—the product of three successful raids on Guild supply lines this month—and Alliaansi of every race rejoiced. Alar took a few beads for himself, then retreated as his Syljian companions gathered around an open barrel. Flashes of arcane light preceded the return of healthier color, brighter eyes, and bigger grins. At least until spring, the threat of saphyrum sickness wouldn't plague his people.

Several distinct pops signaled the uncorking of bottles.

"Alar, where are you going?" Naruu asked. "Aren't you going to celebrate with us?"

Alar paused in his retreat from the festivities and turned back. His temples throbbed, and he needed somewhere quiet to sift through his newly imperiumed stream of thought.

"I'll be back in a few minutes."

Naruu's mouth turned down, as if he might protest. Then the scout shrugged and returned to the celebration.

Alar let the singing and cheering roll over him a moment more before resuming course. There would be time for wine later. He found a spot at the back of the cavern and sat, crossing his legs. The scent of Aether and sounds of his companions faded as he sank into the new river of thought.

Where once he might have struggled to translate the eddies and currents of another's thoughts, his imperium of the boy had given him a key to understanding. It was the first step in learning to read thoughts at will like Ashaara could. Much like how studying related languages improves comprehension of them all, the more imperiums Alar completed, the better he could translate the thoughts of those unknown to him.

He'd released the boy shortly after he finished the imprint of his memories. Ashaara had instructed him not to hold his first imperium in thrall; he was to copy the memories only and release the subject's mind. Later, when he'd mastered the basics of the technique, he could utilize the subtle methods of control to enthrall spies as she did. Attempting these things too soon, she cautioned, would only shred their minds apart.

After his mistake with Finn, Alar was less inclined to test the boundaries of Ashaara's direction.

His own meditative plane was a sea not unlike his mentor's, but without the branching river deltas that added scope to the power of her imperium. Only two branches flowed into his sea—his own, and Guild Acolyte Peader Fen-Ronl's.

The banks of the acolyte's river were steep, made in haste while the rest of his strike force rifted out supplies, distracted the mages, and set fire to the wagons. There were enormous gaps in the memories—jagged holes along the river bottom where the current was disrupted and eddies of incomplete thoughts swirled. Next time, Alar would have to be more precise.

Peader had been an easy target without wards to shield him. At first, Alar was disappointed he hadn't captured a mage with higher status. But as he waded through the river of the acolyte's thoughts, his pulse quickened.

Isa Sarikkian.

Shei-Gwen Mar-Pol.

Wastelands, even the imprints of Gregory's minions, Normos Beck and Joss Vika, were present in the boy's mind.

Maybe his choice had been a fortunate one after all.

Alar examined Peader's surface thoughts first: Sorcerer Vika, and his advances on a low-born healer; a note to report the mage's behavior to Mar-Pol; a rumbling in his stomach, and a longing for just one more pear; concern for the road ahead; the flash of light from what he swore was a rift.

Alar sank deeper, shivering. This cold and vacant imprint, in stark opposition to the warmth of a living mind, would take time to get used to.

More thoughts registered. The route they planned to travel, the waitress he'd met in Ferid—Alar smirked at the boy's curiosity about the way her skirts moved when she walked—a lingering worry for Councilor Sarikkian and his news about the ongoing investigation of the School.

He nearly passed over the last bit, scoffing and shaking his head, until Peader's next few thoughts yanked Alar to a halt.

Sliced piers. Burned beams. Rifting out evidence. And Sarikkian's message to stay away at all costs. Alar tossed aside the boy's concerns of possible mastermind manipulation in the Guild's highest ranks, certain he would know if such a thing had occurred. Instead, he focused on those two little words of speculation that kept spiraling through the acolyte's mind.

A set-up.

The School had been a set-up, and Sarikkian planned to prove it.

Alar shot out of his meditation so fast that his own body seemed foreign and cumbersome. Back in the main chamber, the celebration continued. He shoved himself to his feet, swaying.

*"Amiien!"* he called, still blinking his eyes clear. Their journey home would take weeks, maybe even months with so many supplies, but they had to get back. He had to tell the council. He had to tell Orowen.

*"Amiien,* we need to go!"

Gwen paced before the campfire, arms crossed through the slits in her sable traveling cloak. Her sleeves swayed down to her hips and tossed long shadows onto the hard-packed dirt.

"This confirms there are masterminds at work in Eidosinia." She glanced at Normos, who sat opposite her, his expression haunted as he stared into the flames. "We have to assume anything Peader knows is now known to our enemies."

"How much did he know?" Weariness accompanied the question. Normos wrung his hands between his knees.

Gwen hesitated. Peader had been the one to deliver Sarikkian's message about the School. He knew the route they planned to take through the mountains and which high-ranking Guild members they planned to observe for psionic tampering. Aetherial storms, *everything* they understood about the happenings in Ryost was because of Peader. She should have warded his mind. Why hadn't that occurred to her?

Her response came out barely more than a whisper. "Enough."

Normos seemed to blink himself awake, then leaned back and stretched his legs, wincing. "You know the laws regarding imperium, Gwen."

Her jaw tensed. Peader was fast-becoming one of the most talented Conduits in the Guild. He was supposed to follow Sarikkian in becoming an international ambassador.

"He said the blanker released him." She couldn't let a single encounter with a mastermind destroy Peader's life. Not like it had her father's. "He's worked so hard to get where he is. I can't just cast him out."

The look Normos gave her was surprisingly patient. "But he can no longer be trusted. He's a Conduit. That places him in the best position to spy for them."

Why did he have to be so logical? How could he stay so calm? Gwen scuffed her boot in the dirt.

"It's not fair to him."

"I agree."

Gwen tensed, preparing to argue, then paused. "You do?"

"I do."

Normos Beck disagreeing with a Guild decree was about as likely as snow in the Denorian Desert, but there it was. And the fact he'd been training with Olivia rather than turning her in for illegal magic use and harboring stolen saphyrum—

It gave Gwen an idea.

"Suppose we can prove he's no longer under the effects of an imperium," she ventured. "I could make a motion to amend the law and retain Peader as a student."

He shook his head. "An amendment like that takes time. More time than Peader has."

"Unless we don't report the incident right away." Delvin help her, what was she saying? She could be stripped of her rank for this. Imprisoned, even.

Normos gave her a dubious look, surely thinking the same.

When she'd accepted the white robe, she'd sworn to uphold Delvin's justice, to defend the laws of their realm. Laws made by mortals—people as likely to be influenced by their own desires and corruption as not. Laws she'd already broken to keep saphyrum in the healers' hands where it belonged.

Delvin curse her, she was a hypocrite. "I'll send him back to Ferid under guard to await orders."

Normos sighed. "There's one glaring issue with that."

"Which is?"

"Joss."

They both looked in the direction of Joss's wagon. He was right; Joss had witnessed Peader's confession. But if she made it appear like she was following orders, maybe Gregory's simple-minded minion would think nothing of it by the time they reached the border.

She turned back to Normos. "Don't speak with him about it. Just let me handle Joss."

"You assume we're even on speaking terms." He straightened, resting his palms on his thighs. "There aren't many ways to confirm what Peader claims as truth. A mastermind releasing an imperium makes little sense."

A shadow caught Gwen's attention. Olivia approached their campfire hugging her elbows, the pleats of her healer's robes framing her perfect figure.

"There are ways. Olivia has healing sigils that can detect imperiums. She"—Gwen bit back the truth about her father and pressed on—"she's used them before."

Normos followed Gwen's gaze toward Olivia as she settled beside him. "How is he?"

"Resting. I used a sedative sigil so he wouldn't be plagued by dreams."

He nodded and returned his eyes to his boots.

"Did the blanker release him?" Gwen asked.

Olivia nodded. "Far as I can tell."

*Thank the gods.*

Crackling wood and the distant howl of wolves filled the night as Gwen reconciled her plan with what she knew of Normos's skills. Olivia believed he had the makings of a powerful healer, and he'd demonstrated his ability to learn new spells quickly. They would reach Gregory's encampment sometime around solstice. It would have to be enough.

She stalked back to the campfire and sat on a log adjacent to him. "We can't afford to lose some of our strongest sorcerers to an unjust law. You're going to need some way to test Gregory and the other Councilors for psionic influence. What better way than to practice Olivia's sigils on Peader?"

Normos looked sharply at her. "You can't possibly expect me to—"

"You're closer to Gregory than anyone. If he's being controlled by a master-mind, do you really think he's going to let Olivia get close enough to test him? He trusts you."

Normos was shaking his head before she finished. "I can't do what you ask."

"What do you mean, you can't? I thought you wanted to help—"

"Shei." Olivia's quiet rebuke cut her off. "I think what he means to say is his Councilor will take any show of healing magic from him *very badly*." She stressed the last two words with a pointed look.

Normos's shoulders hunched, as if trying to make himself small enough to disappear. Shadows accentuated the hollows of his cheeks. He closed his eyes, so far removed from the cocky, self-inflated man Gwen knew that a wave of remorse cooled her ire instantly.

Olivia only used that tone with patients who had been mistreated by spouses or parents. That same haunted look had stolen the joy of many who had taken refuge at the Sanctuary. Normos wasn't just worried about his Councilor's opinion.

He was afraid of him.

Gwen leaned back on the log, shoulders sagging with the revelation. So many things made sense now: his strict adherence to the law, his immaculate behavior and pristine appearance, his need to excel at everything he did. Normos had been affixed to Gregory's side for as long as Gwen could remember. She would have never guessed he was being mistreated.

"Normos—"

He rose abruptly. "Excuse me."

"Sit down, Sorcerer!"

Normos flinched, all but confirming their suspicions. He sank back down and gathered his robe about him as if for protection.

Gwen smoothed her expression. Blankers aside, there was an opportunity here to remove their biggest opposition to the bill for non-adept healing *and* help Normos. She had to choose her next words carefully.

"Do you wish to report any unseemly behavior of your superior, Sorcerer Beck?" She adopted a formal tone and folded her hands. "Anything you say here remains confidential."

His breath hitched on his answer. "No, Councilor."

Shavaan help her, the stubborn boy.

Olivia put her hand over Normos's knee. "Has he ever hurt you or threatened to hurt you?"

"No!" Normos shook her away. "Mira's mercy, your concerns are unfounded."

He drew his robes tighter, retreating into himself, and Gwen gritted her teeth. "Has he ever harmed or threatened anyone else?"

"*No.*"

Gwen sighed. Obviously, something was going on. "Alright." She consciously relaxed her fists and opted for leaving the door open. "But if you think of something, Livvie and I are here to listen."

He glowered at her like a cornered chaagra. "We should get back to the matter at hand."

"Of course." There would be no winning with him tonight. Gwen looked at Olivia. "What would you suggest?"

Her partner thought for a while, using a twig to pick at her fingernails—an appalling habit Gwen might have scolded her for in any lesser circumstance.

"Your higher-ups are usually warded with enchantments, right? And a mastermind would have to bust through those to hold an imperium. What if we taught Normos the sigils to spot those wards?"

"It's not exactly healers' magic." Gwen considered the idea, watching as Normos came to the same conclusion.

Ward-seeking was a talent used to identify magic that could interfere with certain healing procedures, but it was also a skill Gwen used to expose elaborate illusions. Her disarming sigil to neutralize wardstones stemmed from the same magic.

"You think a blanker wouldn't rebuild a ward around a mind they've enthralled?" Normos sounded more curious than skeptical.

"They can't. Not without sealing their own minds inside the ward. What prevents entry also prevents exit." Gwen had studied psionic wards extensively after her father's mind had been taken. She'd since equipped herself and Olivia with some of the strongest wards she could build.

"So if their wards are still intact," Normos reasoned, "then we know they haven't been taken by a mastermind."

"Exactly."

Though what that meant with regards to the School didn't bring her any comfort. Gwen had never hoped for blanker involvement in a tragedy before, but the alternative was unfathomable. No more news had come from Sarikkian, and his silence was perhaps most troubling of all.

Normos looked between them. "Teach me the spell."

The next morning brought snow to the foothills of the Palisadics. Normos's fingers were painfully numb, but he kept practicing the sigil. Over and over, he drew the tiny loops and bends, channeling the magic until it became muscle memory. By fourth bell, he could draw it with his eyes closed.

He pushed the latest sigil toward Gwen, who sat beside him in the wagon chewing a slice of dried pear. The sigil bounced against her invisible wards and left a tiny trail of rippling energy as it shot back to him. It hovered over his palm, illuminating the space.

The information imbued within the sigil altered its shape. Olivia had shown him which alterations to look for to identify a psionic ward, a cloaking illusion, and an aura suppressant. She'd offered to show him the alterations for certain wards that countered sedative sigils and other healing spells, too, but Normos refused. It was best not to tread any further down that road.

Gwen glanced at him, amused. "I think you've got it, Normos."

"I'm just practicing." He frowned at a loop and knot that had been improperly placed and grunted with annoyance. He dismissed the sigil and began again.

Gwen clamped a hand over one of his, then flinched back. "Gods curse it, boy, has all that Aether addled your brain?" She swiped his woolen gloves from the seat and tossed them into his lap. "No more practice today. You'll give yourself frostburn."

"If I'm going to perform this work, then by Mira, I'm going to do it right."

"You've already done it right more times than I can count. I'm surprised you haven't burned through that bead already."

A sudden sheepishness stilled his tongue. She must not have realized when the last bead crumbled. There were still remnants of saphyrum dust on one knee of his trousers. As she looked away, he attempted to brush it off.

Gwen caught the movement. She turned back to him, eyeing the spot where his hand had stilled over the infernal smudge. "Seriously? You went through a whole bead with that tiny sigil?"

His jaw tensed. "Has it ever occurred to you the reason most mages can't layer more than two spells is because their work is sloppy?"

"No, it hasn't." She sounded affronted, as if he'd struck a nerve. He probably had, considering she was one of those mages. "Has it occurred to *you* that you hold yourself to too high a standard? That maybe there's more to life than pandering to a man who cares little for anyone but himself?"

Normos bristled. How dare she assume his efforts were so undervalued? Gregory had sacrificed years of his time to training him. Of course he cared. "I give nothing but my best, as the Guild expects of us all."

Shei-Gwen Mar-Pol didn't back down. "And when it's not your best, what happens then? You give yourself frostburn and lose the tips of your fingers? Put those gloves on before you say another word."

The pain in his hands was nothing compared to the pain of failure, which was exactly what would happen if he didn't practice until it was second-nature. Still, he pulled the gloves on. "There. Happy?"

Gwen's face twitched. "He's really done a number on you, hasn't he?"

Last night's conversation came barreling back. How close he'd been to ruining Gregory's reputation. The Councilor's punishments were harsh, true, but they were never unwarranted. If Normos had been a better student, a better mage, then such harsh tactics wouldn't have been necessary. Gregory knew he could excel—one day even sit on the Council himself—and he wouldn't allow Normos to settle for mediocrity. It was for his benefit, and nothing Gwen or Olivia could say to the contrary would change that.

"I know you're just looking for ways to discredit him," Normos seethed. "I assure you he's comported himself with the utmost attention to my wellbeing and growth as his student. You will not find a more dedicated mentor in all of Eidosinia."

Gwen fixed him with a stare as cold as hoarfrost. "Dedicated to what, exactly?" Before he could formulate a cutting enough response, she pounded the side of the wagon. "Excuse me! Driver! I'd like to walk a while."

Normos gripped his seat and winced at the pinpricks of returning sensation in his fingertips. Too many seconds delayed his answer, making it appear less certain than it should. "His students, of course."

Gwen was already moving toward the tailgate. The wagon lurched to a stop. She dropped to the snow and turned back, but where he expected anger or derision, he found something more akin to sadness. "I'm starting to understand your situation, Normos," she said, "and I truly pity you."

He scowled. More pain radiated from the sudden pressure at his temples, and his vision blurred, as if the heat of his anger caused a physical distortion of the air. "I don't want your pity."

"Of course you don't." Gwen pounded the tailgate twice, and the wagon pitched into motion.

# CHAPTER FORTY-ONE

## OROWEN

"No."

Tipori's curt response drew Orowen up short. "No?"

He stared out his study window at the white landscape, hands clasped behind his back. Thick gold drapery and darkly stained hardwood framed his figure. "No."

Until now, Orowen had kept herself as straight-backed and formal as she'd ever been with her brother-in-law, but his answer deflated all sense of decorum.

Had he not been listening to a word she'd said? It was obvious he was distracted by something—the latest news from Anya about his unborn grandchild, or Maralla's report about Guild forces near Kuma'Kiir, perhaps—but Tipori was never so out of sorts that he would ignore an official request. "You wanted me to ensure Riisii's safety and contain these Chaos priests. This is the way we do that."

"The council won't vote to remove her binders." Tipori glanced over his shoulder. "She's too unpredictable."

"You've been her loudest advocate on the council. What's changed?"

"I've gotten to know her." He turned back to the window. "Her temperament is as mercurial as a frost viper. I must be cautious when considering what calamities I'm willing to risk imposing upon this community."

His doubt in Daeya—Caelyn's wrath, the fact that he'd compared her to a venomous snake—might have been forgiven if it had come over a month ago. "Nerimoria was just as temperamental," she pointed out. It was hard to say whether it was a trick of the light or if Tipori actually flinched. "If it hadn't been for the council, you would have unbound her the day she arrived."

"Perhaps I, too, can make mistakes."

This was no time for self-deprecating humor. "You sound as paranoid as Koraani." He'd seen the damage of Chaos's influence on Riisii. How could he brush aside the solution as if the problem would go away by itself? Orowen folded her arms. "Tipori, I'm disappointed in you."

He had the nerve to chuckle. "You are not your sister."

Baosanni take the man. If her disappointment wouldn't move him as Maralla's did, then maybe her fury would. Orowen squared her shoulders, readying to give him a piece of her mind.

The door behind her opened, and soft-mannered Damiir slipped into the room.

He carried a silver tray topped with a tea kettle and three cups. His patient smile stayed her assault and disarmed her all at once. In the back of her mind, she wondered if Tipori had Seen him coming.

Damiir set the tray on the desk. "*Iiren'hyvaa, neimen.* I've brought tea."

"*Iiren'hyvaa,* Damiir." Orowen worked hard to return his smile while he filled the cups. She took the one he offered, letting the minty steam tickle the back of her throat. "*Taapad tiik.*"

"*Ushaar.*" He leaned against the desk with a cup in hand, side-eyeing Tipori over the rim. "Is he being surly again?"

"*Ciir.*"

"After how he came for me last night, I don't know how he musters the energy."

An indignant growl issued from their companion, and suddenly Orowen's smile came easier. If anyone could draw Tipori out of his foul mood, it was Damiir.

"You'll not change my mind," Tipori groused, turning to collect the last cup. He echoed his taller mate's posture against the desk and lifted the tea to his lips. "Is there anything else, Orowen? I'm afraid I have other business."

Her smile faded. "*Amaa*, Riisii's Foresight showed us this for a reason. If Cheralach believed Daeya's magic could be the key to our survival, isn't it worth investigating further?"

A shadow passed over Tipori's face. Damiir lowered his tea, uncertainty carving deep trenches around his mouth. The men shared an unreadable look.

Something was wrong.

Her gaze flicked between them. "She is Neri and Cheralach's daughter—"

"And Lucius Gregory's prized gem," Tipori finished, meeting Orowen's eyes with a new intensity.

The name sent a shiver down her spine. Lucius Gregory, the man who had doggedly hunted a rogue mastermind for decades. Who still used a crazed half-blood's evil misdeeds to justify the eradication of their entire race.

She hadn't forgotten Daeya's connection to him, but she refused to believe that sweet girl held the same prejudice.

Tipori set his teacup on the desk. "I want to honor their memory and trust her, *neime*, but she hasn't made that easy. This business with Chaos only confirms she hasn't been telling us the full truth."

"We haven't exactly been the most trustworthy people, either."

His brows furrowed. "Explain."

"Think about it. You're sixteen years old, running for your life from people you once trusted. You decide your sworn enemy is safer than the home you've always known, and you request shelter for your family's sake. Then that enemy takes your magic, assaults you, assigns you work, and tells you to behave while they consider helping your family, but only when it's most convenient for them. Saolanni's grace, Tipori, if a connection to powerful magic is all she's hiding, I would truly be surprised."

Tipori's expression grew more troubled. He leaned back, folded one arm across his chest, and stroked his beard. "You think that's all this is? Powerful magic?"

Something in the way Damiir tensed seized Orowen's tongue. She tried to catch his dark eyes in silent question, but he avoided her gaze, choosing instead to collect his husband's teacup and serve him again. Seconds ticked away with every swing of the costly pendulus behind her.

"Chaos priests crave power like wolves crave meat. I can ward the Temple once my magic is at full strength, but I'm afraid that won't be enough to stop what's coming." Orowen spoke slowly and from the heart, certain now that her answer could irrevocably alter their path forward. "If they've drawn arrows on both Riisii and Daeya, the Guild may not be the only force seeking to harm us."

Tipori's eyes slid toward Damiir.

"You should tell her," Damiir urged.

The fine hairs on the back of her neck prickled. "Tell me what?"

The room itself seemed to darken as Tipori's violet eyes snared her again. "This doesn't leave this room."

She nodded.

Tipori drew a breath. "I received a message from Gregory yesterday. He's requested Daeya's return."

A fierce surge of protectiveness brought warmth to Orowen's face. "That's unfortunate for him." But when the men shared another look, she hesitated. "You aren't thinking of honoring it, are you? Cheralach gave his life for her to—"

Tipori held up a hand, his jaw tight. "He has offered to exchange Daeya for Governor Eris Lathaarios and three of her officials from Willowmarsh."

The appearance of Chaos himself might not have caused her chest to clench any harder. They'd assumed them dead. With no word from Magnus or Rylan, rumors had already begun to swirl that they too had perished. But knowing Eris was alive brought a spark of hope—

And uncertainty.

"*Saonis miraar.*"

Conflict warred in Tipori's expression. "You see my predicament."

Her fingers curled into the wool of her cloak. "She belongs with us."

"I know."

Those two little words were loaded with so much pain and apology that it was clear he'd already made the obvious choice. A sorceress whom their community barely knew in exchange for a beloved governor and three high-ranking officials—to refuse the exchange would lead to social upheaval. The search for Chaos priests among their brethren was already sowing discord. They couldn't afford more of it.

But something wasn't right.

Damiir reached for Tipori's hand, squeezing it. The movement blurred into the background as Orowen tried to pinpoint the source of her nagging unease. Something...

"Why?" she whispered.

Tipori looked up, frowning.

"Doesn't it seem strange," she ventured, "that he would trade four prominent Alliaansi figures for one newly promoted sorceress?"

Both men stilled.

Foreboding crawled up Orowen's spine. "We all know Gregory. If he wants her back, there's a reason. One far more complicated than affection for his favorite pupil."

Damiir's eyes widened. "You're right."

Gears turned behind Tipori's gaze. "Whatever Eris and her advisors know has likely been extracted already. Their intel would be far more valuable than anything Daeya had access to."

"So what does Gregory know about her that we don't?" Orowen pressed.

Damiir rubbed the stubble along his chin. "Is it something about this magic?"

"It most certainly is." Tipori paced back to the window. Turned again. "Did Daeya tell you anything else about this ritual or what to expect from her magic?"

Orowen shook her head. "Ravlok said he's been studying the ritual. I'm not sure how much Daeya knows herself."

His jaw set with purpose. "Then it's time we find out."

Daeya matched Zakaari step for step, circling the *fursaan* floor. Every part of her body ached, but Tipori's surprise summons had returned her to the training grounds at third bell—*eighth hour*, rather—and Zakaari had offered to go a round or two with her while they waited.

They were on round four, and there was still no sign of Tipori.

Zakaari grinned, giving himself away a beat before he charged. He swept in low, aiming for her legs. Daeya blocked his grapple with her own. Their arms locked momentarily, then disengaged.

She grinned back at him. They settled into a rhythm, meeting and disengaging three times more before he caught her in a hold. She struck the pressure point inside his elbow, forcing him to release her arm, then went for his knees, using her head and shoulder to throw him sideways. He hooked his arm around her waist, and they both struck the floor.

Though she landed on top, Zakaari recovered faster. He rolled and straddled her. Daeya forced her forearm into his hips, bracing her wrist with her opposite hand to keep him from sliding higher. Muscles shaking, she tried to buck him off, tried to push him sideways, but managed little more than a frustrated growl at her waning strength.

His hand splayed against the base of her neck. She squirmed, torn between breaking the chokehold and keeping her arms locked.

Bare chest heaving, voice husky with exertion, Zakaari leaned down. "Got you."

Gooseflesh prickled her sweat-soaked skin. She laughed breathlessly and let her arms go slack. "Got me."

He eased the pressure against her collarbone, but his palm lingered as he gazed down at her. Time seemed to stutter right along with Daeya's heart. Suddenly, the thought of him pulling away, of him *not* touching her, produced such unbearable longing that she seized his wrist.

Zakaari's breath hitched. Surprise flickered across his face, his eyes searching hers. A sensation like fire and lightning intermixed in Daeya's belly. He leaned down again, close enough now that she could feel his breath against her lips. Strands of dark hair tickled her cheeks. Underpinnings of citrons and heady lavender overwhelmed her.

A throat cleared across the room.

Zakaari sat bolt upright, head snapping toward the sound. "*Peiaa*. We were"—he winced—"we were just sparring."

Gods, if only the floor could swallow her whole. Daeya followed Zakaari's lead and stood. Tipori leaned against the guardrail like he'd been waiting there unnoticed for some time. He quirked a brow at his son. "That's one way to do it, I suppose."

Fierce heat bloomed in Daeya's cheeks. She stole a glance at Zakaari, and he flashed her a sheepish smile before stepping away to retrieve his shirt. She straightened the neckline of her tunic, trying to ignore the low hum of anxiety that had settled into her limbs. No smiles or reassurances came from the Aetherian today.

"You wanted to see me, *Amaa*?"

Stupid. Of course he did. He wouldn't have summoned her otherwise.

"*Ciir*. Are you well enough for one more round?"

The temptation to lie—to assure him she hadn't exhausted herself to the point of failure only moments ago—weighed against the sheer force of will it took to remain upright. But lying to Tipori wouldn't win any favors. If anything, it would dig whatever hole she'd dug deeper.

"No, *Amaa*. I don't think that's a good idea."

Finally, a crack appeared in his neutral expression. "You recognize your body's limits. Very good."

A test, then. Thank the gods she'd choked down her pride.

Tipori withdrew something from his cloak and beckoned to her. She approached, side-eyeing Zakaari for some indication of what this might be about. His brows furrowed as he straightened the sleeves of his shirt, but he offered a nod that bolstered her resolve.

Tipori followed her glance. He frowned, eyes going distant as they sometimes did. Daeya was certain now he had some skill with Foresight; too often he could predict the outcome of a sparring match or conversation with uncanny accuracy.

Something unidentifiable flickered across his expression. "*Ennii*, I'd like to speak with Daeya alone, please."

Her stomach hit the floor.

Nothing good ever came from private conversations. She reeled against a wave of nausea, struck by phantom scents of leather and blood.

Bleeding Aether, this was serious. He'd likely spoken to Orowen by now. The priestess had assured her Tipori would agree to help them, but what if he blamed her for what happened to Riisii instead?

*Was* she to blame? Chaos was after her—after Baokryn and the Shard—but if Riisii had gotten in the way of a god's plans, then it was Daeya's fault the seer had been hurt. Tipori likely realized this, and when he started asking questions Daeya couldn't answer, he was going to get angry.

Zakaari looked between Daeya and his father, his jaw tight. As if he heard her silent plea, he stood taller and clasped his hands behind him—an echo of his father's formal posture. One she'd never seen from him before.

"I'd like to stay, *Peiaa*. I'm charged with her protection."

"And you've done an exemplary job." Tipori's face softened. "But I must insist. I'm just going to ask her some questions."

Zakaari hesitated, poised to argue further. Father and son studied each other until at last Zakaari folded under Tipori's steely gaze. His shoulders tucked inward, and he crossed the training floor, pausing at the entryway. "I'll be right outside."

Somehow, that little reassurance steadied her. Daeya nodded her thanks when words wouldn't come.

The door closed behind him.

Alone now with the most powerful man in the Northlands, Daeya summoned all the courage she still possessed and looked Tipori in the eyes.

He uttered an incantation in an unknown tongue—Rillanese, maybe—and cool air touched her wrists. Daeya looked down, her mouth falling open as the shiny spellbinders turned to black-violet mist.

"You—" She swallowed the frog lodged in her throat. "Forgive me, I thought you wanted to wait."

Tipori's smile eased some of the tension in her shoulders. "Yesterday, I spoke about trust, but I've since been informed that trust goes both ways." He took her hand and pressed something small and round into her palm. "So, I'm choosing to place my trust in you."

Daeya stared at the crisp white bead—patron's saphyrum, the purest and most magically potent form. She could perform hundreds of single-layered sigils and dozens of her most destructive six-layered spells with it.

"Why?"

Tipori didn't answer right away. Instead, he gave her his back while he removed his cloak. The significance of the move wasn't lost on her. With the binders removed and a bead of the most potent saphyrum in the world, an enemy captive could have attacked and seriously wounded or even killed him.

Daeya tucked the bead between the third and fourth fingers of her casting hand and waited.

Once he'd doffed his boots and stockings, he beckoned her toward the center of the *fursaan*, where they sat cross-legged, facing each other.

Tipori was straight-backed and steady as a mountain, palms resting on his knees. "You know, I have never seen anyone resist an imperium the way you did."

"What does that have to do with anything?"

"More than I originally thought." His head tilted. Sunlight caught the contours of one ear point. "You said you were meant to become Lucius Gregory's right hand. Tell me again, what changed?"

"I was chased out of Eidosinia by other sorcerers in Gregory's retinue. They framed me for treason because they thought I was a threat to them." She shrugged. "I suppose I probably was."

"Because of your arcane talent?"

"Yes."

His nostrils flared. "You're the youngest mage in Guild history. I verified your claim through several sources. Sessiri and Helenia said you wielded scarlet flames unlike any they had ever seen."

Where in the gods' names was he going with this? She forced herself to patience, shifting beneath that penetrating stare.

"I also heard you translated some disturbing runes last night. That your presence here could be connected to Riisii's malady. Orowen believes Chaos priests are involved, and this ritual you proposed will help us fight them. But before I agree to help you, I must know more about it."

It had been Orowen's idea to claim the ritual was to fight Chaos priests, rather than Anordis himself. Admittedly, it sounded less insane. "I don't know much."

"You know more than you're letting on."

She tried not to let her sigh become a growl and failed.

Trust. This exercise was about trust. He was giving her a chance, and she couldn't blow it. Not when Da's safety hung in the balance.

"I didn't know anything about the Shard until last night." Before the lines on Tipori's face became a full-fledged scowl, she held up a placating hand. "I know that sounds crazy, but it's the truth. I can read the ancient language it's written in, even though I never studied it in school."

Tipori leaned back, considering her. "What can we expect from the ritual?"

"Ravlok says it involves a bunch of chanting out of this book he has, and some spell components I'm supposed to burn."

"Hm."

It was clear her answer didn't satisfy him. It didn't satisfy Daeya either, but Ravlok hadn't been as forthcoming with his more recent transcriptions of the text.

Tipori reached into his cloak again and withdrew a small scroll. Placing it between them, he rested his elbows on his knees and steepled his fingers.

"Daeya, I'm going to say this as simply as I can. The information you've provided regarding the Guild's strategies and supply caches has been valuable. However, the council will likely not see you for the asset you are, even now."

She barked a bitter laugh. "Why am I not surprised?"

"Because you're learning." Tipori lowered his hands. "Your parentage aside, you realize you not only have to be useful, but irreplaceable to us."

His eyes strayed to the scroll.

A pit of foreboding opened in her abdomen. "What is that?"

Tipori hesitated before pushing it toward her. As parchment crackled beneath her fingers, he said, "Many years ago, I allied myself with a sorcerer for mutual gain. I knew little of the troubles between the Guild and the Alliaansi at the time. My wife had to educate me on just how deplorable conditions were for the Syljians here. When I joined them, this sorcerer and I had a falling out. But before that, I daresay we might have been friends."

Daeya scanned the familiar handwriting. It wasn't signed, but the scent of *his* favorite cologne still clung to the parchment. Tears welled, and the lines of the scroll blurred. "When did he send this?"

"It arrived yesterday."

The pit widened. "Has anyone else seen it?"

"Not yet."

*Not yet.*

Daeya rolled the parchment between numb fingers and placed Gregory's scroll back in the shaft of sunlight between them. She tried to retain her composure, tried to appear as calm and controlled as Tipori did.

But she couldn't.

"You're making the trade, aren't you?"

That was why he'd sent Zakaari away. He knew his son wouldn't agree to this. Daeya scrambled to her feet, her hand clenched around that bead.

They'd once been friends, Tipori claimed, but Gregory hated Syljians—even half-bloods.

Tipori followed suit in rising, his expression unreadable. The horrifying realization that he likely knew which way she would attack snaked its way around her throat. Daeya backed away, her fingertips sparking heat and light.

She could burn him. She could set the city ablaze and flee with Ravlok before anyone could stop them.

"Daeya." The scent of hot metal filled the air, and the Aetherial Wall rippled around him—a warning. "Look at me."

Power hummed inside her, begging to be set free, to rain destruction and render all the world to ash.

Tipori lifted his hands, looking at her—looking *through* her—with mounting alarm. "Don't do something you'll regret. I want to help you, but I need you to help me understand."

The way he said it made it seem like she still had a chance. But it wouldn't matter. None of it bleeding mattered. Gregory would just up the stakes, offer to trade them more. She was a caged animal—a caged, wounded animal that would be dragged back to her master and tortured all over again.

"*Amaa.*" Her knees went weak. All her bravery, all her resolve, every vow she'd made to confront the bastard without fear, evaporated. "Please, don't send me back to him."

Tipori took her by the shoulders. When she tried to jerk away, he grabbed her face. "Daeya—"

"I can't go back. I can't. You don't know what he'll do to me."

Her white-gold hands closed over his wrists, and he winced.

"*Look at me.*" Cloth smoldered between them. "I won't send you back. Do you hear me?"

Terror clawed at her insides, and she trembled so violently she risked rattling apart. He was lying. He had to be lying.

His grip on her face became steel. "You never have to go back to him."

"*Amaa*, please, he'll—" His fierce declaration pierced the tangle of Daeya's thoughts. At first, she was sure she'd misheard him. He couldn't refuse the trade. No leader would. "What?"

"Whatever he did to you, however he hurt you, I will never let it happen again." He brushed away her tears with his thumbs. "Say you understand."

She sobbed and released his wrists. "I understand." Eyes straying to his burning sleeves, Daeya cringed and lifted a hand. Blistering welts marred his wrists in the shape of her fingers. "I'm sorry."

Heat pooled into her palm and diffused back into the vibrant hum of magic coursing through her body.

"It's alright." He released her. "But, Daeya, I need to know why he wants you so badly. Why would he come to me with such a deal?"

She attempted a calming breath. This was her last bargaining coin. She'd wanted to save it in case the Alliaansi reneged on helping her father, but if they knew why Gregory sought her return, surely not even Koraani would allow the trade.

*Peiaa will believe you when you're ready to tell him.*

Daeya clenched the bead, turning Riisii's reassurance over in her mind.

"Because..." The words were a long time in coming. "Because I have the power to command dragons."

"You—" Tipori stopped. Stared at her. Opened his mouth and closed it again like he'd taken a slap to the cheek. "I beg your pardon. Did you say dragons?"

# CHAPTER FORTY-TWO

## DAEYA

Daeya told him everything.

Well, almost everything. She began with the storm at sea and ended with the warning from Caelyn. She even mentioned Dannicus's draegion story and her meeting with Tiior and Vortanis, but she left out Gregory's rune-carving fetish. That, she wasn't ready to explain.

Tipori took the existence of dragons and the involvement of gods surprisingly well, interrupting only when he had questions. When she finished, he replaced her spellbinders and promised to lobby for their permanent removal at the next council meeting. Then he escorted her and Zakaari back to his home, summoned Damiir, Jerinoch, Ravlok, and Orowen, and made Daeya go through everything a second time.

"Old boy was planning to obliterate us." Jerinoch slouched in one of three ornately carved chairs positioned around Tipori's desk, puffing on his pipe and filling the crowded study with the musky scent of dohanni. "Good thing he still doesn't know his head from his arse."

The empty chair beside him was meant for Daeya, but she couldn't bring herself to sit. She stood as far from the desk as possible, distracting herself with the costly pendulus in the corner. Her eyes followed the lines of beautifully etched metal up to the exposed gears of three clock faces. The polished case must have been Duerguardian olivewood; the swirling patterns in the grain could have been drawn by Caelyn herself.

Daeya looked at Tipori, brows knitting. Who was he, this man who dressed in silks and leather, who owned slave binders and a pendulus worth more than a year's income for most Eidosinian nobles, and who once allied himself with Lucius Gregory?

Tipori leaned forward, his palms on the desk. "If the legends are true, Starlight's wards won't mean much against a dragon, let alone an entire legion of them."

"Storm," Ravlok corrected. "That's what they call their legions, anyway."

Tipori shot him an impatient look, and Ravlok suddenly found something interesting about the bookshelves lining the back wall.

Damiir adjusted his three-year-old son, Aschiiq, on his hip and smirked at Ravlok. "Don't mind him. He could stand to be corrected more often."

One of Tipori's eyebrows lifted. "As could you, *nei ama're.*"

Zakaari groaned. "Can you two not? This is serious."

Orowen looked up from a side table where she'd been straightening Tipori's crystal decanters. "It must be, coming from you."

Zakaari sidled closer to Daeya, his knuckles just shy of brushing hers. He spared an indignant look for his aunt, then regarded his father with open defiance. "You're not giving her back. I don't care what they offer. She stays with us."

The fierceness in his tone warmed Daeya more than any fire ever could. She glanced down at their hands, so close to touching. Without giving herself a chance to overthink it, she let her forefinger skate across the webbing of his thumb.

Never breaking his father's gaze, Zakaari turned his hand into hers and interlocked their fingers in a strong, protective grip. A silent promise. Daeya's eyes closed against an unexpected sting.

"I agree," Tipori assured him, "but you must understand others won't." He shifted his attention to Jerinoch. "I will prepare a counteroffer for Eris and her officers to be sent back with the Guild messenger. We'll assemble an escort to ensure no Conduits are used to relay the message."

Jerinoch blew a smoke ring. "Buying us time. Excellent idea, my boy."

"And take his horse. Let him walk back to his master." Tipori straightened and addressed Orowen. "I'll put out feelers for talotibas while you ward the Temple for the ritual."

She nodded. "I'll start practicing this afternoon."

Finally, Tipori looked at Daeya.

She shifted beneath his scrutiny and lifted her chin. He was willing to help her, true, but now that he had all the leverage, including knowledge of both Telerion and her family, would he force her to be a weapon, just like Gregory?

It made her queasy just thinking about it.

Zakaari gave her fingers a reassuring squeeze. She returned it in silent thanks.

Eventually, Tipori said, "I will have my contact in Ryost begin extraction procedures for your family immediately."

Whatever she'd expected him to say, it wasn't that. Daeya's lips parted. "Really?"

Jerinoch's wheezing laughter ruined the effect of her surprise. "Looks just like Cheralach when she does that, by the gods."

Orowen grinned. "And she blushes like Neri."

Daeya's own laughter made her a full stone lighter. "You're really serious?"

"Gregory's going to be furious when he realizes you aren't coming back," Tipori said. "He'll use anything at his disposal to hurt you. We must mitigate his means."

This time, Daeya didn't hide her relief. "Thank you, *Amaa*."

"I made you a promise. You've held up your end. I intend to do the same."

"I promise you won't regret it. Da's the finest blacksmith the Guild has. He'll be an asset."

A calculated smile turned up one corner of his mouth. "So I hear."

Of course, he'd corroborated that information as well. His contact in Ryost was well-connected—of that, she was certain.

"We'll begin lessons in the arcane tomorrow. Draegion or not, some training in Aetherian control will do you well."

Daeya winced, recalling the burns on Tipori's wrists.

"And by the time Gregory's refusal comes through, we will see you on the way to find your dragon." He hesitated. "I pray you will both choose to ally with us."

That caught her off guard. She'd already agreed to swear her allegiance upon delivery of her family. "You're giving me the choice?"

He nodded. "We need soldiers who'll fight for our cause not because they are bound to it but because they believe in it. We are not the Guild, and I'm not Gregory. I won't hold you to a vow made in desperation."

What that meant to Daeya couldn't be put into words. She looked at Zakaari. "He's doing that thing he does, isn't he? Where he gives a rousing speech and sways people to his side?"

Zakaari's lips twitched. "Is it working?"

Her hand tightened on his. "I don't need to be swayed."

"I'm glad to hear it." A suspicious light flickered to life in his eyes.

Daeya touched her saphyrum pendant. "My mother was Syljian. That means I'm one of you. And if my father built this city for my mother's kind, and for others who would live free of Guild oppression, then I'll do right by them." She nodded once to Tipori. "I'll help defend it."

Tipori's look of pride was almost a reflection of her da's. "So you shall."

A soft pressure on Daeya's arm drew her attention. Orowen beamed up at her. "This is as much your home as it was theirs, *neime*."

Daeya started to tear up again, but her uncle saved her the embarrassment.

"I daresay that bastard could have at least warned me my niece would be bringing dragons home," Jerinoch chortled. He tapped his pipe on Tipori's desk and withdrew his pouch of dohanni.

Damiir wrinkled his nose. "Don't get ash all over my rug, old man."

Jerinoch ignored him. "At least your mother had some sense. Mira help you if you don't take after her."

Damiir snatched Jerinoch's dohanni and shook it at him. "Do you have wax in your ears? I said don't make a mess in my house."

As they bickered, Daeya leaned into Zakaari, who pressed close and murmured into her ear, "Careful, McVen. I'm starting to think you might like me."

"Wouldn't want you to get the wrong impression," she whispered back.

He chuckled, keeping his voice low. "Stay for dinner."

His breath against her neck sent a shiver down her spine. Still, she side-eyed him for good measure. "Ask nicely."

"Stay for dinner, *please*."

Daeya glanced at the others, still conversing among themselves. Ravlok was toeing the corner of the rug with a contemplative frown, which he swapped for a smile when he caught her studying him. Her brows furrowed in silent question, but he gave a subtle shake of his head.

Whatever it was, he wasn't ready to talk about it. Daeya wouldn't pressure him. She nodded once to him and looked up at Zakaari. "Dinner sounds lovely."

Ravlok's smile faded as Daeya and Zakaari slipped out of Tipori's office.

He was happy for her, truly. For once, she looked like her old self again—witty, playful, mischievous—before this business of war and Chaos had robbed her of joy. And to hear her laugh...

Odes of Ordeolas, it was all he wanted for her. To see her surrounded with all the love she deserved. To know she had a place among her parents' people, and her adopted family would be here soon. It made what he had to do a little more bearable.

He wouldn't ruin the moment. Especially not with this. There was nothing she could do about it, anyway. He couldn't tell her what was coming, or how her world was about to irrevocably change. She *had* to complete the ritual; it was clear now she would die if she didn't. Anordis would win and throw the world out of balance.

He only hoped, one day, she would forgive him.

Damiir and Maralla's son dashed out of Tipori's office with his father and aunt close behind him. Jerinoch wobbled after them, and Ravlok turned to follow.

Tipori's voice stopped him at the door. "Ravlok, a moment."

One hand resting on the polished wood frame, Ravlok looked back. "Yes?"

"Close the door, please." Tipori pulled out Jerinoch's vacated chair and beckoned for him to sit. "I have some questions for you."

# CHAPTER FORTY-THREE

## OROWEN

Sweat beaded on Orowen's brow despite the cold stone on which she sat. Icy wind whistled through Saolanni's garden and bit her ear tips. Woody vines arched overhead, sheltering her from heavy clouds that threatened snow.

Fatigue preyed upon her as the wolf to the hare, but Orowen couldn't rest. Not when her entire community was counting on her.

She tried to sink further into her meditation, seeking that plane of inner peace from which the wellspring of Saolanni's love flowed. If she could just reach that place again, if she could feel her goddess's light shining within her once more, then neither Mage's Folly nor her own fears could stop her from completing her task.

The world fell away after agonizing minutes. At last, the sharp pain of winter, the dull ache in her back, the itching of her nose subsided, and all was calm.

*But it's not as it was.*

This wasn't the restorative calm of her faith, but a hollow facsimile. One that had plagued her for months.

She shoved the thoughts aside. This had to work. It *had* to.

*Goddess, I am ready.*

There was no answer. No beacon of light filled her with warmth. No waters flowed from the font of magic. Where there should have been a vibrant pulse of life beating in time with her own heart, there was only stillness.

*I beg you, guide my hands as you guide my heart.*

Frustrated, she pulled magic from the amulet around her neck. Aether stung her nostrils and a spindly thread of light appeared at her fingertips. Heartened, she tried to weave it into a practice sigil. She imbued no warding or healing elements, but stuck only to the basic loops and knots that every acolyte knew.

More sweat trickled down her face. Hands shaking, she guided the light into the first loop, then the second, and finally a third. Orowen pressed the sigil closed, tied a secure knot, and leaned back to examine it.

Aschiiq could have done better, limited as her little nephew's magic was. The sigil's thickness varied, its loops were unequal, and there was no room to weave layers between them.

Orowen slashed through the sigil with a snarl. It tangled and burst with a *crack*, singeing her palm before dissolving into mist.

A novice's outburst. She clenched her teeth and sagged forward, cradling her burned hand. Bitter, angry tears crowded up behind her eyelids.

She couldn't do this.

If she couldn't even prepare a practice sigil, how did she ever think she could cast dozens of powerful warding spells over this entire temple? At this rate, the war would be over by the time she warded a single room.

She'd chosen to practice in the garden because it was once where she felt most connected to her goddess, where she used to find respite and guidance through prayer.

She had dedicated herself to Saolanni, championing temperance, honor, and mercy over all else, and one mistake—one horrific, deadly act of hubris—had undermined a century of loyal devotion. Now she couldn't even make it right.

Orowen closed her eyes. "What more must I do, Goddess?"

Foolishly, she'd believed accepting the challenge of warding the Temple would somehow fix her. That by having prepared herself for the oath with studies and prayer, agreeing to do what no one else in Starlight could might restore her magic out of necessity.

Orowen slumped further, her forehead nearly touching the stone, fingers clutching her white hair. "What am I supposed to do?"

Pressure forced its way up her throat. She tried to swallow it down, but a broken cry still slipped past her teeth

Saolanni had abandoned her. Never, in all her long life, had Orowen felt so alone.

Howling wind tore through the trees and shrubs. The sound rose again moments later, harsher and almost guttural in its fury.

Orowen forced herself upright and wiped her face.

When the howling came a third time, accompanied by the shattering of glass, she jolted to full awareness.

That was no wind.

She leaped off the stone and hurried toward the Temple doors. Bren burst out of them ahead of her, wild-eyed. Shavaan's acolyte stumbled to a halt, thick faelocks tumbling over his shoulders.

"Bren, what's—"

"It's Riisii, Devoted. She attacked someone!"

Another shriek spilled into the garden. Orowen took off at a sprint through the corridors, slippered feet sliding on the tile. When she burst into the Temple sanctuary, heart hammering, she found Riisii straining against the grasp of three older acolytes beside a broken window. A fourth acolyte picked herself out of the glass, bleeding from a cut on her arm, while a fifth hastily weaved a sedative sigil. The last acolyte on duty escorted a young man toward the front entry. The man cradled a small bundle under one arm, while his other hand lingered near the hilt of a dagger. He stole a glance at Riisii before quickening his pace.

"Aunt Wen!" Riisii cried. "Stop him!"

It took Orowen a full three heartbeats to recognize the sunken expression and sallow cheeks that belonged to the thief who had worked under Val in Ryost. "Jack?"

Red-rimmed eyes flicked toward her, flinging Orowen back in time. Back to Aon'In. Back to a den full of religious zealots and half-starved victims.

Very few things in life were as memorable as the bloodshot stare of a new Chaos priest—the product of their early fellowship, where night terrors and insomnia amplified their worst fears and drove them to the brink of sanity.

Jack's hand closed on his dagger, but the blade remained sheathed. Lip curling, he glared at Orowen. "You really should do something about her. She's going to hurt someone."

"He can't leave." Riisii wrenched herself out of the healers' hands and shot forward. "He's going to—"

"Wait!"

Too slowly, Orowen called out her warning to the acolyte whose sigil nearly took Riisii in the chest.

Her niece spun aside and dove for a set of surgical shears on a nearby table. She flung them at Jack, who leaped aside and rolled into a crouch before the entryway. His dagger flashed out of its sheath as the shears embedded in the wall.

Riisii ducked another sigil and slid beneath an empty infirmary bed. She came out on the other side clutching an amulet, its broken chain swinging around her wrist.

How she'd hidden the amulet was of little consequence. Right now, they needed Riisii's magic. Orowen made a cutting gesture toward the acolytes and pointed at Jack. "Riisii has the right of it. Detain him."

They exchanged bewildered looks.

Jack rose from his crouch and sneered. "So, they've both lost their minds." He backed toward the doors. "Face it; your high priestess has fallen from grace."

White-violet energy burst from Riisii's hands. It struck the last bed in the row closest to Jack, flipped the straw-stuffed mattress over the stairs, and set it ablaze. The bed smashed into the Temple doors.

Jack stumbled out of the way. With flames barring his escape, he turned and hurled his dagger at Riisii. It met her second arcane blast and careened off course. The blade clattered across the floor and disappeared beneath an offering table.

Protective fury alighted in Orowen's chest. She started toward Jack, tossing instructions over her shoulder. "Bren, prepare a sedative sigil. Nallia, Wyl, ready bindings. The rest of you, protect our patients."

Jack's glance toward the nearest alcove window betrayed his intent. "You're all fools. Following her will only lead you into ruin."

He made for the alcove, only to be blocked by Nallia, a junior priestess of Saolanni. Magic flared at her fingertips and reflected off the ceramic beads in her hair.

Pure malice twisted Jack's features. He recoiled from that light and, with a flick of his wrist, a smaller blade flashed in his hand.

Orowen strode through the rows of infirmary beds, her fur-lined cloak snapping in the wind through the broken window. "Saolanni's light reveals you, Chaos priest."

Jack whirled on her. In Orowen's periphery, Riisii cloaked herself in black-violet mist and dissolved into shadow.

"There is no light here, *oathbreaker*." Jack's snarl flung spittle. "Saolanni has deserted you. *Charlatan*."

Orowen drew up short. The same words echoed through her memory, haunted her dreams, bled together with sounds of falling stone and howling rifts.

To hear her own fears spat back at her, used to taunt her, jolted something loose inside her. The greasy film of Chaos's touch returned—a sensation just remembered.

*Saonis miraar.* How could she have missed this? Chaos preyed on mortals in their moments of weakness. The Guild dungeon had reeked of his corrupting influence.

She had been deceived.

Orowen's eyes narrowed on that treacherous face. "This is Saolanni's temple."

She focused on the rot beneath Jack's mask and let herself sink below the surface of her outrage, her fear, her desperation. She forced aside all the emotions Chaos preyed upon, resolved to give him nothing. Saphyric energy surged from her amulet and pooled in her hands. Stillness like the heart of a cyclone settled around her as she descended into that meditative space. She could sense it now, that slippery veil separating her from her goddess, reinforced all these months by layers of pain and self-doubt. She smashed through it and magic crackled inside her veins.

"And you are not welcome here."

Orowen wove light.

Jack shoved Nallia aside and bolted for the window.

Riisii exploded from the shadows, forcing him back in a blaze of arcane light. As he stumbled, he swiped outward and sliced a red gash across her cheek.

Nallia's binding took him in the left flank and threw him against the wall. Wyl knocked him to the floor with another.

Orowen's hands remained steady as she approached, holding a final binding sigil that would fully immobilize him. "Savii," she said to the nearest acolyte, fighting to keep her tone neutral at the sight of her niece's blood. "Fetch Tipori. Tell him we've uncovered a Chaos priest."

"Right away, Devoted."

More sigils took shape around the room. As the acolytes closed in, an eerie howl issued from Jack's throat.

"The witch will burn you all! You'll burn!"

Orowen gritted her teeth. A crazed gleam crept into Jack's bloodshot eyes. He thrashed against his bindings and red tears streaked his face.

"You'll all burn in the witch's fire!"

Bren appeared beside her, sedative sigil at the ready. "Devoted?"

Orowen lifted her chin and guided her binding sigil down. "It's alright, *neime*. It's over now."

"She'll kill you. She'll kill you all—"

Her magic settled over Jack, and he stiffened. Bren's sigil forced his eyes to close.

Orowen's shoulders drooped. Jack had long been a troubled man. His torturous beginnings must have provided fertile soil in which the seeds of Chaos's influence could grow. To see him fall like this, to see him succumb to Anordis's charm, made her chest clench. There were ways of helping victims cope with their trauma, but they required extensive emotional and psionic therapy. Most would never recover.

Dozens of citizens had been reported losing sleep or acting oddly since the search for Chaos priests began. None so far had appeared to have anything beyond mundane maladies like colds or common stresses, but if Anwic and Jack had succumbed, there would be more. Orowen would advise the council to redouble its search, despite what unrest it might cause.

Bren touched her shoulder; she looked up to find him beaming. "You did it, Devoted. Your magic has returned!"

For a moment, she stood there, not fully comprehending the words he'd spoken. She turned her attention inward.

The steady pulse of magic—of *Saolanni's light*—that had long felt absent now flooded her mind and reverberated through her body with every beat of her heart. Her eyes stung with barely restrained euphoria. Saolanni had been there all along, veiled by Chaos, suppressed by her own doubt.

Bren squeezed her arm. "I just knew it would."

The smell of smoke reached her; the fire was blackening the Temple doors. The nearest patients began to cough and struggle from their beds.

"Wyl, Thallios, bring water. Bren, help the others escort the patients out through the garden. Quickly, now."

"An accident," Riisii said as the others rushed to obey. Blood rolled across her cheek and down her neck. "I'm sorry, Aunt Wen."

Orowen turned to her niece and pulled her into a hug. "It's alright, *neime*. I'm just glad you are safe."

Acolytes bustled about, assisting patients, carrying buckets, or channeling magic to quell the flames and heal minor injuries. Doors and windows were propped open to vent the smoke. Two acolytes wrapped Jack in blankets and brought him out to await Tipori on the veranda. Orowen tucked the bundle of herbs he'd requested into her cloak, certain the council would want to inspect it later.

They mopped up the water around the ruined mattress. As Orowen helped push the charred remnants onto the front steps, raised voices and the distant crunch of footsteps carried across the plateau. She squinted into the twilight, across the deep layer of snow through which uneven paths had been carved.

"What is that?" Nallia asked.

On the road to the west, a crowd flanked a horse-drawn wagon carrying several cloaked figures. Their whistles and cheers became more distinct, along with dozens of joyful, tear-streaked faces, but the man sitting beside the wagon driver didn't smile at the welcoming party as he once would have.

Scarcely believing her eyes, Orowen drew her cloak tighter and minded her steps down the Temple path.

"Magnus!" Wyl dashed past her and slid to a stop beside the road. Still grinning, he turned back to Orowen. "It's Magnus!"

"Baosanni's breath," Nallia gasped. "What happened to him?"

A stone lodged in Orowen's throat. New burn scars marred the left side of his face. Much of his black hair had been burned to the roots. The rest was shorn to within a fingerspan of his scalp. As if Laangor and the Guild hadn't made the poor man suffer enough, he was barely recognizable from the gentle boy he'd once been.

Riisii drifted to her side. "He saw the Reaper's face."

Orowen shivered, but not from the cold. Still, the return of her niece's cryptic speech was almost comforting in a way. "Has your Sight returned?"

"It's all jumbled." Riisii still clutched the amulet. "Nothing makes sense."

The driver reined in beside the Temple path. Magnus climbed down, his arm wrapped in bandages that desperately needed changing.

Serreth Blackburr's gruff Cintoshi accent rose from the other side of the wagon. "By Delvin, Eris, just let an old man be! I can do it myself."

Short, stubby legs swung from the wagon, dangling in the air briefly before Serreth fell to the ground with a curse. Governor Lathaarios and her other advisor, Luthen, soon followed.

Mira's mercy, the sight moved her to tears. They were free from the Guild's clutches. Magnus had brought them home. And if Eris and her officers were here, that meant the Guild could no longer barter them for Daeya. Nerimoria's daughter was safe, and there was no need for all the scheming and subterfuge Tipori had planned.

She started toward them as they rounded the wagon, a smile tugging at her lips.

Nallia's voice brought her up short. "Riisii!"

Orowen spun in time to see Riisii meld with the shadows.

"*Neime*?" Her voice cracked in her rising alarm. She scanned the darkness, searching for unnatural movement. Riisii was still not fully recovered, and in the darkening night, she would be nearly invisible beneath an Aether Cloak. "Riisii, where are you going?"

"Ward the Temple quickly, Aunt Wen." Black mist kissed Orowen's cheek. Riisii's voice was a whisper in the wind. "I must go see the dragons."

# CHAPTER FORTY-FOUR

## MAGNUS

Three cloudy eyes bobbed in the viscous honey filling Magnus's jar. He tipped the glass to one side and examined the shriveled organs, each one harvested from a mage or Paladin he'd killed.

Councilor Tallion's eye wasn't among them. That prize had putrefied in his pocket long before they reached the village apothecary in Gii'Evaar. The stench alone had nearly exposed him. Eris had an excellent sense of smell, and if not for Luthen's wounds succumbing to fleshrot, Magnus wouldn't have been able to deflect her long enough to dispose of the remains.

He wouldn't suffer such terrible loss a second time. No, when he claimed his next prize—Archeph Elfred Roseheart—he would be ready. Rylan's killer may have escaped at Willowmarsh, but he wouldn't evade his end at Magnus's hands forever.

He placed the jar in a drawer beside Jack's bundle of herbs—evidence collected from the Temple of Life yesterday—and leaned back in his chair.

Foxhollow. Nettlesbane. Merisander.

Painkillers, all. When combined they produced a powerful sedative used to treat insomnia. They also comprised three of the five components the voice had instructed Magnus to collect. His search of Jack's belongings yielded the fourth component, xiranthesium, a toxic plant used to coat assassins' blades and arrow tips.

That left only poppy wine, easily obtained from the Temple healers. When he went to check on repairs to the sanctuary later, he would request some.

A knock came at the door. Magnus spared a final look at his jar and slid the drawer closed. "Enter."

Tipori Evallier stepped into the room, his keen eyes sweeping the space that once belonged to Cheralach. Magnus had kept the office largely the same, finding comfort in the familiar desk and low table. Shelves and scrolls lined one wall, and a map of the Eidosinian continent dominated another.

Magnus rose and offered his hand to the Alliaansi leader—now his equal. "Governor. To what do I owe the honor?"

Tipori's amusement turned up one side of his mouth. "Come now, there's no need for such formality." His callused hand closed on Magnus's. "Congratulations, *nei amii*. Cheralach would be proud."

As promised, the council had appointed him to Cheralach's seat as soon as he'd completed his report on Willowmarsh and delivered Eris, Serreth, and Luthen to the Temple. He'd finally fulfilled Cheralach's greatest wish for him.

His pride faltered when the voice slipped between his thoughts.

*He taunts you.*

Magnus considered the words, and Tipori's good-natured expression, then ultimately dismissed them. Tipori had always been a friend to him—an uncle, much like Kendi.

Dull pain throbbed behind his eye socket.

*He stole his position.* The ache built steadily until it crept across the new burn scars on his scalp and into his ruined left ear. *Now he sits a seat that should have been yours.*

Tipori's brows furrowed. "Everything alright?"

"Yes. Forgive me, it's been a long few weeks." He gestured toward the chair opposite him. "Please, sit down."

They both took their seats, Magnus straight-backed while Tipori lounged like a sated cat after a meal.

*He's gloating even now.*

Magnus's face twitched. He hadn't seen it before, but he did now. Tipori had usurped Cheralach's seat as governor the moment he'd left for Ryost. Now he touted his position like a crown atop his head.

Tipori's expression sobered. "I was sorry to hear about Rylan and Gamiil."

"Thank you."

Magnus forced the words out around the sudden tightening of his chest. He didn't want to discuss Rylan's loss with him or anyone else. Like Cheralach's death, it shouldn't have happened at all.

They sat in tense silence before Tipori spoke again. "News of Willowmarsh's destruction is already spreading. I fear what it will do for morale."

"I understand you're still planning a solstice celebration to help with that."

"I am. I think it's important for those here at home, especially the children, to have at least some sense of normality."

Magnus nodded. "You didn't come here to talk about the color of our streamers."

Tipori chuckled dryly. "No, I'm afraid I'm here to discuss a more serious matter."

Magnus had heard the rumors of Riisii's continued disturbances and Chaos priests in Starlight. The priests should have demanded no more concern than any other group of religious zealots, but Orowen had taken particular offense to their presence. Life priests and Chaos priests had been at war with one another since Tiior began recording history, and no meager skirmish between Starlight's clergy would change that.

He'd heard about the incident at the Temple. The council had already decided Jack would remain in the pits under heavy guard until after Orowen's reaffirmation tomorrow, when they would discuss what to do with him.

Whatever Tipori was here for, it likely didn't require this much suspense.

"Out with it, Governor."

"Maralla's troops were delayed by snow on the way to Kuma'Kiir," Tipori finally said. "It allowed Guild forces to slip past the city's northern defenses and blockade our supply line from Zeo'Taaron. The city is surrounded, and I fear it may fall the moment the snow melts." His fingers drummed on the arm of his chair. "I have a potential solution, but I need to know you will support it."

Wary, Magnus waved him on. "I'm listening."

"It has to do with the sorceress." The chair creaked under his weight as Tipori leaned forward. "The monk speaks of a ritual said to awaken immense power."

*NO.*

The voice's intensity startled Magnus. It took an act of sheer will not to flinch openly.

Tipori went on. "Riisii has Seen its necessity. It should push the Guild back over the border. Daeya has already agreed to help us."

*He is a fool, trusting the prophecy of a broken mind. Entertaining the promise of an enemy.*

Even without the voice's urging, he sensed the logical fallacy in Tipori's suggestion. "You trust the sorceress will offer tactical advice for defeating her own people?"

"She's gained us much in the way of supplies already," Tipori argued. "She has reason to stand against them, and I would honor her service by ending her trial early and offering her a place among us."

*She will be your undoing.*

"The agreement was six months." Magnus's jaw tightened. "You've had too little time to ascertain the integrity of her character."

A muscle ticked just below Tipori's left cheekbone. "We don't have six months. Maralla is out there right now with thousands of Guild troops breathing down her neck."

"As commendable as it is to put your family first, Governor, your personal concerns are affecting your judgment."

Darkness crept into Tipori's gaze. "This isn't just about her. If they're cut off from Zeo'Taaron, there will be no reinforcements from the Third Legion. No more supplies or saphyrum. No more food. The city will starve, and the Guild won't have to lift another finger."

Assured of his decision, Magnus let out a slow breath and held his chin high. "I'm sorry, *amii*. Unbinding our enemy hostage and setting her loose with the hope she'll kill her own people is something I can't support. Even Cheralach wouldn't make that gamble."

"She's Cheralach's daughter, Magnus."

"She... What?"

The syllables made as much sense as if the man were speaking Rillanese.

"It's true. Her mother was Nerimoria."

Magnus shook his head. He remembered Nerimoria. She'd disappeared only a few years after he joined the Alliaansi. "That's impossible."

"She wears Neri's necklace, and she is of an age that would suggest Neri was pregnant when she disappeared."

"She's"—a sour feeling rose in Magnus's gut—"she's really Cheralach's daughter?"

Tipori nodded. "Orowen thinks that's why he was having visions of her. Why he went to Ryost to find her."

Knots formed inside Magnus's abdomen. He sagged in his chair, blinking his eye against the pain that speared his skull.

Cheralach's daughter.

*He has forsaken you, Magnus.*

The whispered words of his torturer snaked through his mind, shed their skin, and exposed a new layer of meaning. Cheralach had gone to Ryost against all reason to save her. He'd risked the mission, risked his troops, risked *Magnus*, for a girl he didn't know.

*See how you have become unworthy?*

The only father he'd ever known, the one person Magnus trusted above all others, had been willing to see him tortured, to see him sacrificed. To give *his own life* for her.

How easily she'd usurped his father's love from him.

The thought pierced the armor around his heart like a lance. His pulse pounded in his temples, his ears, his chest, until no part of him could escape the insistent ache that betrayal left behind.

Tipori sighed. The sound seemed loud in the quiet room, despite the cotton in Magnus's ears. "Cheralach was once a Guild sorcerer, too. I see more of him in her every day. She has his heart, and her mother's fire." He hesitated. "I'd hoped you might find some kinship with her."

*And now she moves to usurp your place here, as well. See how he dotes on her. The fool.*

She'd taken his father from him; he wouldn't allow her to take anything else. Magnus's voice came out a rasp. "I've made my decision. She may be his blood, but she's still a sorceress. It's too risky."

The darkness in Tipori's gaze returned, but it was merely a shadow of its former ire. Some part of him might still listen to reason. He rose from his chair. "We have already lost Fawn's Breath and Willowmarsh. We cannot lose Kuma'Kiir as well."

Magnus stood. "Then we'll find another way."

Ever the diplomat, Tipori offered his hand. "I pray Silonas provides us such fortune."

They shook hands as before, but there was no warmth in it. Magnus remained standing until Tipori stalked out the door. Once it closed, he sat heavily, opened the drawer, and gazed in at his jar and the bundle of herbs.

This wouldn't be the end of their discussion. The sorceress and this ritual would come up again in council tomorrow.

*We must not allow the ritual to succeed.*

Cheralach's daughter was a threat to his people. She'd already proven that by luring Cheralach away to be murdered by their enemies. Now she had swayed Tipori. This power she promised would prove too alluring for the others to ignore.

*Take it.*

His head tilted. Could *he* use it to drive the Guild back? Would it still save his people?

*With this power, you can destroy* all *who oppose you.*

Magnus's palm itched. His fingers closed around the herbs. How?

*Listen closely.*

# CHAPTER FORTY-FIVE

## OROWEN

Orowen stood in gauzy white, unadorned by the silver sash and embroidery that would have marked her for a high priestess of Saolanni. The hallway tiles chilled her bare feet, and her stomach knotted around an empty void. She'd never been one for fasting, and the scent of mulled cider and sweet rolls drifted cruelly through the makeshift curtain.

She swallowed against her hunger and straightened her spine. This discomfort was as much a practice in discipline as it was a purification to receive her goddess. She would bear it with grace.

On the other side of the curtain, voices carried through the Temple sanctuary. The infirmary beds had been temporarily relocated, and hundreds of Starlight citizens were crammed beneath Saolanni's roof to witness Orowen's reaffirmation.

"...just a moment." Kendi's voice rose above the rest a beat before the curtain pulled back and sunlight spilled across her face. The commander was beaming, and he held a squirming gray kitten under one arm. "I've brought someone to see you."

Orowen grinned despite her nerves. In the weeks since she'd returned to Havensguard, the little creature had refused to sleep anywhere but tucked into her side beneath the blankets. She took her from him and scratched behind the kitten's ears. "I can't believe she let you catch her."

Kendi's smile turned roguish. "I bribed her with milk." He stroked beneath her chin, and her purrs rivaled the commotion outside the hall for noise. "We just wanted to wish you luck."

The kitten settled into Orowen's arms as if she planned to ride out the entire ceremony there. Her warm body steadied Orowen more than any other calming technique she'd tried in the last few hours. By the knowing spark in Kendi's eyes, he'd likely expected as much.

Warmth rose in Orowen's cheeks. He really was too good for her. "Thank you."

"Anything for you, *nei ama're*." The look he gave her was utterly tender. "You should name her. She's chosen you."

As if to prove Kendi's point, the kitten stretched up and butted Orowen's chin. She chuckled. "What makes you think that?"

"Call it intuition." He winked.

She planted a kiss between the kitten's ears, then extracted the tiny claws from her sleeve and passed her back. Kendi tucked her into his cloak, where she mewed indignantly for her freedom.

Orowen tilted her head, considering. "Panuu."

Light. It seemed fitting after all.

Kendi leaned close and tipped her chin up. "Panuu." He pressed the softest kiss to her lips, and Orowen's eyes closed. "It's perfect."

Another figure swept aside the curtain. Orowen blinked against the bright glow that silhouetted Bren's faelocks.

"Are you ready, Devoted?"

Though her mouth went dry and she twisted her hands into her sleeves, Orowen nodded. "*Ciir*."

Bren buzzed with excitement. "I'll order everyone to their seats." As if immediately regretting his choice of words, he glanced at the commander and hesitated.

Kendi spared him the awkwardness of ordering a senior military officer around and bowed his head. "That's my cue. I'll see you for the reception."

The two of them departed and Orowen resettled into a pattern of meditative breathing. It seemed silly to be nervous—certainly *this* nervous—but the feeling didn't ebb simply because it was nonsensical. If anything, it redoubled.

Not even the return of Saolanni's light had brought Orowen back to full strength. She could heal simple wounds and draw double-layered sigils, but every attempt to ward the Temple thus far had failed.

She prayed the reaffirmation would restore her. It must, or there would be no safe place for the ritual. Her community's survival hinged on her ability to protect them.

Sounds of shuffling feet and scraping benches followed Bren's orders, and a harp quelled the din. Savii pulled aside the curtain, revealing a long aisle between seats that led to an ornately carved altar. The acolyte of Mira smiled, her pale blue eyes shining with unshed tears.

Orowen returned the smile, then stepped from behind the curtain. Her breath caught as all eyes turned to her—their disgraced priestess come for absolution. Folding her hands, Orowen lowered her head in submission and forced her jellied legs forward.

With no other priests sitting higher than her to administer the oath, Orowen had enlisted Nallia to read from the Book of Life. The junior priestess of Saolanni stood behind the low altar with the book in hand, her expression serene.

On the altar itself were four unlit candles, a casting amulet, and a ceremonial dagger. Nearby, Daeya fidgeted with her black robe and cast an uneasy glance around the room. Absolution required the participation of a wronged party, or a representative of such, willing to stand before the goddess and her witnesses. Though a priestess of Mira could have represented the children, it meant so much more to Orowen that Daeya had agreed to this.

Zakaari and Ravlok flanked Neri's daughter, both having refused to leave her standing alone before an audience in sorcerer's black, even if it was only symbolic of her former alliance. Ravlok had wisely asserted that adorning the cuffs, hem, and collar with silver—Saolanni's color—wasn't enough to distinguish the garment from a real mage's robe.

The walk toward the altar seemed to go on forever. By the time she reached it, Orowen's knees were shaking, and cold sweat trickled down her ribs. Her shins struck the kneeling pillow, and a wave of dizziness blurred her vision.

What if this didn't work?

Nallia began the sermon, her voice the embodiment of a sun-warmed stream. "Good morning, friends and followers of the greater pantheon. Today we gather to witness Orowen Evallier's reaffirmation of faith to Saolanni, Bringer of Light and Goddess of Life..."

What if she couldn't be whom they needed her to be?

What if she was truly broken?

What if—

*No.*

Orowen retreated inward, away from her doubts, away from the self-loathing. With each breath, she descended to the place where Saolanni's light shone brightest. It steadied her, and she lingered there until a warm hand closed on her wrist, turned it, and pressed something cool and flat into her palm.

"It's time, Devoted," Nallia whispered. "Are you with us?"

A choked sound issued from Orowen's throat—half laugh, half sob. She'd been with her goddess, and that knowledge alone brought tears. "*Ciir, neime,* I am."

Nallia's dark gaze sparkled. "Then draw your sigil and repeat after me..."

Orowen slipped the amulet over her head and tucked it beneath her robes. The metal warmed against her breastbone as she channeled saphyric energy. Saolanni's light flowed freely into the Aetherial loops and knots that formed a simple cautery sigil.

"I, Orowen Evallier, who strayed from the Path of Saonis, humbly return home seeking the light of my goddess..."

The words of reaffirmation came easier than she'd expected. Her voice, despite the thickness in her throat, rang throughout the Temple, and as she held her sigil poised over the first of three small candles, she forged ahead without Nallia's guidance.

"In honoring Saolanni, I also honor her daughters." Orowen dipped the sigil and set the golden candle aflame. "I vow to hold sacred the art of creation, the miracle of birth, and give thanks to Mira for the safe delivery of all babes conceived with the Mother's blessing."

She moved to the emerald candle. "I vow to hold dear all of Caelyn's creation, never to harm or disrespect it out of malice, for it is her masterwork—the plants and animals of her vision—that nourishes our minds, bodies, and souls."

Then the third candle, crimson. "And I vow to honor the healing arts, practicing them in accordance with Shavaan's precepts: integrity, humility, and compassion for all in spite of prejudice or wrongdoing."

Orowen allowed her sigil to dissolve. Nallia beckoned to Daeya, who took her place at the altar. Orowen had given Nallia free rein to design the ceremony for her absolution. Anticipation sat uneasily in her lower back.

"Before you may retake the Oath of Saonis," Nallia continued, "our goddess demands absolution from those you have wronged. Sorceress Daeya McVen stands ready to hear your request."

Trembling though she was, Daeya straightened. The sight of her, a perfect blend of her mother's fierceness and her father's regal bearing, brought forth such a powerful surge of emotion that, for a moment, Orowen couldn't breathe.

The audience shifted collectively behind her, and murmurs arose as the silence dragged on. What could she say that would fully encompass the depth of her guilt? How could she pay her respects to every life she'd stolen that day? Daeya had already forgiven her informally, but Orowen owed it to her and to Saolanni to make this count.

"I beg your forgiveness, Sorceress," she began, her voice maddeningly tremulous, "for taking the lives of so many little ones. It was an act of—" Orowen stopped. Shook her head. It sounded like an excuse, and that wouldn't do. "When I opened the rift that destroyed your home, I was ignorant of the consequences that would follow. Had I known so many would die because of it, I would have gladly taken their place at Baosanni's Gate. I started the war between our people, and I would give anything for the chance to undo it."

Daeya blinked several times, knocking loose tears that she quickly swiped away. Zakaari started toward her at the sight of her distress, but Ravlok held him back.

Nallia gestured toward the altar. "The dagger between you represents forgiveness," she said. "Orowen, please pass the blade to Daeya."

Pressure built in Orowen's chest as she collected the dagger in both palms. When Daeya took it, louder murmurs rippled through the crowd. Worry creased the girl's brow, and Orowen followed her nervous glance toward Nallia. Surely she didn't intend for Daeya to use that blade.

Unfazed by the room's collective unease, Nallia smiled. "Sorceress, if you believe Orowen is unworthy of absolution, you may take this blade and leave Starlight immediately with what belongings you own. The governor has agreed to ensure your safe passage and reunion with your family if you choose this course."

It was like taking a sphere of frost to the abdomen, the way air rushed out of Orowen's body. Her shock reverberated through the crowd as voices lobbed protests behind her. Daeya stiffened.

"However," Nallia went on, "if you believe she is worthy of your forgiveness, you need only pass the blade back to her, and your place among our people will remain unchanged."

But it *would* change. There was real incentive behind keeping the blade, escaping Starlight, and traveling south to meet her father. If Daeya chose to leave, Ravlok would go with her, and whatever tasks they had to complete would go on without the Alliaansi.

Forgiveness, then, was a sacrifice and true admission of her willingness to stay. The entire community would bear witness to Cheralach's daughter accepting her place among them.

Orowen exhaled sharply. Tipori's heavy hand was all over this. Convincing the council to allow the offer must have been a feat for the ages—if he'd spoken with them at all.

Uncertainty wriggled into Orowen's bones. Absolution alone stood between her and her oath now, but only Daeya—the one person in their community most affected by her transgressions—could make the act truly meaningful.

Daeya stared at the dagger. Her gaze drifted over the audience, to the candles, aside to Nallia, and finally settled on Zakaari and Ravlok. When the sorceress returned her attention to the blade, Orowen was shivering. The smallest movement of Daeya's hands placed the dagger back in Orowen's grip, and all the tension and tears she'd been holding back sprang loose in a crushing torrent.

Daeya's eyes—her father's pale green eyes—also shone in the candlelight. "Orowen Evallier, High Priestess of Saolanni, I grant you absolution for the School, but I think you're mistaken about the war."

Murmurs rose again. Orowen swallowed hard. "What do you mean?"

As if she couldn't bear to stand any longer, Daeya knelt before the altar. "The Guild framed the School as an act of terrorism. They framed the fire at the Orthovian port like that, too—the fire *I* caused. They knew I'd done it, but they blamed the Alliaansi anyway." She sat back on her heels and shrugged. "My guess is the Councilors who've sought war for years finally had enough support to flip the dissenting votes on the Council. If it hadn't been the School, it would have been something else."

Tipori and Maralla had said the same. Orowen had been drowning in her grief for so long, she'd struggled to see it. She wiped her face and nodded. "My burden is lesser now. Thank you, Daeya."

Daeya reached between the candles and squeezed Orowen's shoulder. "Thank *you*, Devoted. For trusting me with this."

Orowen put her hand over Daeya's. "You have your father's heart. He would be so very proud of you."

Red-faced and teary-eyed, Daeya smiled, then rose.

Nallia, beaming, reclaimed her space at the altar. "With absolution granted, you may now renew your oath to our goddess." She gestured to the tallest candle, which bore three wicks at its center—one for each lesser goddess.

Orowen reached for the gold candle as Nallia continued. "Using Mira's candle, you will light the first wick, and repeat after me..."

The reception following Orowen's reaffirmation was a boisterous affair of music and celebration. Eager to retreat from all those curious eyes, Daeya slipped into the safety of a Temple alcove and pressed herself against the wall. Static buzzed through her, and her pulse feathered in her veins.

When Tipori had presented his plan for the absolution, Daeya hadn't expected it to affect her so much. She'd gone off script at the last, praying that it wouldn't get her stoned to death later. Fortunately, it had seemed to garner a modicum of respect from the masses.

Zakaari swept into the alcove after her, grinning. He leaned in to be heard over the noise. "You were amazing."

His breath against her ear made her cheeks bloom with warmth. She probably should have been embarrassed by such closeness in a room full of people, but right now she didn't care.

Choked laughter bubbled out of her. "I was terrified."

"You made it look natural." He pressed an orange into her hand. "Just don't eat it here. *Haalii* doesn't know I took it."

"Passing off your illegal contraband?" She glanced toward where Damiir stood playing mediator between Tipori and Koraani. Apparently, Starlight's governor hadn't informed the rest of the council about his plan. "Foolish of me to think it was a gift in earnest."

Zakaari's deep chuckle sent shivers down her spine. "Foolish, indeed."

He withdrew and cleared his throat. Daeya noted the gaggle of raised eyebrows that turned in their direction. It struck her as odd—Zakaari was affectionate with half the girls and even a few boys around the city; his behavior should be nothing new to them.

Nor should it have felt so significant to her.

She trained her attention on Tipori's conversation. As she watched, Ashaara drifted to Koraani's side and his posture relaxed. The mastermind thrust her chin toward the alcove.

Daeya froze.

For once, Koraani didn't look upon her with contempt, but with guarded interest. He shared a glance with his mate, exchanged a few more words with Tipori, then moved off with Ashaara on his arm.

"I... have a date tonight," Zakaari said, "but if you need some company, I can cancel."

Daeya blinked. "I won't ask you to do that."

"You sure?"

It almost sounded like he wanted her to say no, to ask him to stay, but Daeya shook herself. She was just imagining things. "I'm sure. You should enjoy yourself."

He frowned. "Alright."

Even so, Zakaari made no move to leave her side. For the rest of the party, he kept snatching glances at her and opening his mouth, then closing it again.

At one point, between adjusting her lapels and fidgeting with the orange in her pocket, Daeya looked up to find Tipori watching her. He caught her staring back and smiled with the sort of approval Da always wore when she returned home. The reminder of him was so strong it made her ribs ache.

With the return of Governor Lathaarios and two of her officers—the third sadly having perished—Tipori had assured her she was safe from Gregory. He'd promised her family was on the way and that soon the components for her ritual would arrive as well. They would be safe. They *all* would be safe.

She was almost starting to believe him.

# CHAPTER FORTY-SIX

## DAEYA

Daeya's spellbinders dissolved into black-violet mist. She rubbed her wrists and relished the cool kiss of morning air on her skin.

Tipori paced across the *fursaan* floor. "I wish I had better news for you"—he turned to face her—"but the council still holds firm on its decision to keep you bound."

Daeya shrugged. Even if Koraani seemed less hostile toward her after Orowen's reaffirmation, that didn't mean he'd be friendly. "So, what are we doing?"

Tipori's gaze grew distant. Between the war, Riisii's disappearance, and managing his network of spies, it was hard to imagine he had time for her at all.

He shook himself. "For now, we will work privately. Speak of this to no one." Tipori glanced toward Zakaari, who leaned against the guardrail. "Either of you."

"You're defying your own council?" Daeya's eyes widened.

That explained the absence of Zakaari's doting followers today. Though, with how little he'd seen his lovers recently, he would likely leave her to attend them early this afternoon, and Daeya wouldn't see him again until late tomorrow.

It didn't bother her. Not really.

"No." Few things in life were as calculated as the narrow-eyed look Tipori gave her. He waved his hand, and Aetherial mist bloomed over every window, shrouding the glass with veils so black they blotted out the sun. The only light in the room came from candles that sprang to life with another offhand gesture. "I'm testing you for Aetherian potential."

Daeya frowned. He'd already determined she was skilled enough when he'd unbound her the first time. If he needed the front of training her, that meant no part of his meeting had gone as they'd planned.

Warmth ebbed from her limbs. "They denied your request for the ritual, too, didn't they?"

"The vote was split. I met resistance from an unexpected source."

"Magnus?" Zakaari asked.

It had to be. With Jerinoch on their side, the only other dissent would come from the creepy one-eyed aethermancer. He'd swept into Havensguard like a storm on the day before Orowen's reaffirmation.

Somehow, Tipori maintained his enviable air of confidence. "He was especially combative when I mentioned the dragon. Both he and Koraani refused to accept one exists, much less one willing to aid us."

Daeya couldn't blame them. If not for Dannicus, she might have questioned if the whole thing with Telerion wasn't just a vivid dream. "I'm afraid I don't have any proof to offer them. Rav says the dragonbond may not be possible without completing the ritual first."

"It's a minor setback, only. By the time you have your talotibas, the matter will be dealt with."

She trusted him. Gods knew he'd earned it.

He clasped his hands behind his back and came to stand before her. "Are you ready to begin?"

"Yes."

Tipori tilted his head. "What is the difference between sorcerers and aethermancers?"

Daeya groaned. "If you're going to start there, can I change my answer?"

His laughter filled the air. "No, I'm afraid not."

She'd answered this question wrong so many times, it had become something of a game between them. But she wasn't in the mood for it today. Daeya lifted her hands. "I don't know."

He grinned. "At last, an answer I can work with."

"Wait—*that's* all you wanted me to say?"

"I'll take what I can get." Tipori started to pace again. "Sorcerers still layer their sigils to strengthen their spells, *ciir*?" At her nod, he added, "Show me what you can do."

She still had the saphyrum he'd given her in her cloak, but that was hanging on a hook by the door. Rather than retrieve it, she drew saphyric energy from her pendant.

A sigil of protection was the safest of her layered spells, and one she'd practiced to perfection. Gregory wouldn't have had it any other way; it was a battle mage's most important spell. She drew the first three layers within a few heartbeats, an intricate white-violet shield of knots and sweeping lines capable of deflecting arcane attacks. After tying off the third layer, Daeya began weaving the fourth—a more complicated series of knots to ward against physical projectiles.

By the fifth layer, which strengthened the ward against larger projectiles and most explosions, her hands were shaking. It was like trying to drag her fingers through molasses. Sweat broke out under her arms and across the back of her neck.

Normos was the only other sorcerer of her rank who could weave five-layered sigils; most couldn't layer more than two without risking Mage's Folly. Smaller sigils could burn if the light threads tangled, and three or more layers had a tendency to explode. She still remembered Normos's fury the first time she surpassed him with six. He'd nearly lost a hand trying to catch up.

Ribbons of light coursed from her fingers, weaving in and out among the perfectly spaced lines that made up the lower layers. They illuminated Tipori's face, but she resisted the urge to squint through the knots to see his reaction. Whether he was impressed or not, he wouldn't be pleased if she lost her focus and blew up the training room.

The sixth layer warded against more complex and powerful magic. It was rumored that elder magi once used the sigil to ward off dragon attacks.

Hands shaking, muscles protesting, Daeya threw all her weight into closing the sixth layer. She released the sigil and stood back, panting. Aether stung her nostrils and a bitter taste coated her tongue. Sweat rolled in rivulets down her face.

Tipori stroked his beard. "Impressive." He met Daeya's gaze through the sigil, then reached toward the sixth layer's last knot. "There's only one problem."

Dread shot through her as his fingers sparked white-violet. "Don't—"

Too late, Tipori wrenched the knot free, destabilizing the entire sigil. The magic pulsed with light and folded in on itself. Daeya spun away, throwing up a feeble fire ward as she dropped into a crouch and shielded her face.

A loud *pop* sounded, and she braced for the scalding heat and buffeting wind.

Only it wasn't an explosion. Several moments passed, and Daeya remained crouched, head tucked tightly between her arms. A cooling sensation caressed the back of her hands.

She looked up.

The light from her sigil was gone. Black-violet mist filled the space, spilling over her shoulders and enveloping her with the scent of hot metal. Beyond the shimmering haze, she found Tipori watching her. He offered his hand.

She took it numbly and rose, mouth agape. "How did you do that?"

"The problem with sigil-based spells"—Tipori waved through the mist, stirring it like smoke—"is they're easily unwoven."

"You just dissolved a six-layered spell as if it were a practice sigil."

Tipori chuckled again. "Everything is Aether, Daeya. Spellcasting is simply a matter of coaxing reality to your will."

It was the same thing Vortanis had said. It hadn't made sense, then. But looking around at all the ways Tipori used magic—the windows, the candlelight, the unwoven sigil—and without a single incantation, she was starting to understand.

He turned to his son. "Zakaari, demonstrate an aethermancer's shield, please."

Zakaari pushed himself off the guardrail and sauntered toward them. A ball of saphyric energy took shape between his cupped hands. The Wall undulated around the sphere and Aetherial mist swirled in inky tendrils, drawn to him by some arcane magnetism. Those tendrils penetrated the sphere and pulled away, trailing light in iridescent spirals and arcs much like the knots of a sigil, only made of dozens of strands rather than three or four. His shield didn't hold the same perfect symmetry as hers—in fact, it was terribly chaotic by comparison—but it formed effortlessly and without the obvious drawback of being one interwoven spell.

It was a masterwork. She could see now why one aethermancer might stand against several sorcerers at a time.

Zakaari's light sphere dwindled and the last tendrils spread like oil in water across the space. He smirked at her through the shield, two spirals framing his eyes. "You're going to draw flies like that, McVen."

Her mouth snapped shut. Heat bloomed in her cheeks, and she turned to Tipori to hide it. "Is it as strong as a six-layered sigil?"

He examined Zakaari's work. "A four-layered one, perhaps. But an Aetherian shield is as strong as you make it."

"Ancient castles used Aetherian shields to hold off invading armies." Zakaari stepped around his shield and joined Daeya at her side. The reverent way he spoke suggested he had a fondness for the subject. He'd been similarly enamored by the carvings in Riisii's room. "In some cases, the shields held long after the walls themselves turned to dust."

Daeya turned the information over in her mind. "That's why you need more Aetherians, isn't it? To strengthen your cities' walls."

For once, Tipori winced. "It would certainly help. I've trained Riisii, Zakaari, and their sister, Anya, in some Aetherian magic, but their skills are still developing. They won't be enough to hold the walls in Kuma'Kiir."

With Riisii gone, and no idea of when she might return, they were even weaker now. He'd already explained the worsening conditions in the city and his concerns that the Guild might starve them out before spring. And it wasn't just a matter of making more Aetherians. Only the strongest aethermancers and sorcerers—those who could cast beyond three or four layers—could learn to control Aetherian magic safely.

The path ahead took shape in her mind: break the siege, bolster their defenses, and, with Silonas's blessing, push the Guild back. She stared into Zakaari's shield, tracing the swirls of light with her eyes.

Finally, she looked back at Tipori. "Teach me."

✦

Daeya spent the next several days learning how to summon an aethermancer's shield.

It came easily, as all magic did. Daeya devoured the knowledge Tipori imparted with an eagerness she hadn't felt since she was an initiate, back when impressing Gregory and Normos was foremost on her mind.

She was surprised to learn that aethermancers recognized more elemental affinities than sorcerers did. In addition to air, wind, fire, and lightning, they had weaker affinities like earth, metal, light, and shadow. Some arcanists even claimed psionics functioned as a ninth affinity, making one element for each lesser god.

A week into her training, Tipori asked his question again: "What is the difference between sorcerers and aethermancers?"

Daeya sat cross-legged at the center of a cyclone of Aetherial mist. Magic sang through her limbs and pooled in her cupped hands. She looked up through the maelstrom and frowned.

Once, there were Aetherians and there were magi. The Schism broke the magi order into two factions: sorcerers and aethermancers. After two hundred years of Guild dogma and attempts to make sorcery more elegant and refined through the use of sigils, there was still no denying all their magic came from the same source.

The answer left her like a soft wind on a summer night. "Nothing."

Tipori smiled. "Now, you begin to understand."

By the end of the second week, Daeya could summon a shield that withstood four volleys of Zakaari's arcane blasts before shattering.

On the eve of winter solstice, she conjured one so strong that even his most powerful magic couldn't break it.

Panting, Zakaari bent at the waist and put his hands on his knees. His damp black hair fell in front of his eyes. "I'm starting to think there's something to all this talk of god-magic. You have an unfair advantage."

"Maybe if you take your shirt off, you'll have better luck," Daeya teased.

Zakaari straightened, grinning. "You'd like that, wouldn't you?"

She knew better than to admit how right he was. There had been little time for sparring recently, and arcane training didn't warrant the same close quarters that martial arts did. She was starting to miss the feel of his skin beneath her hands.

Tipori snorted. "Shall I come back later so you two can have some time alone?"

Daeya's cheeks burned at the reminder of his presence. She caught her lip between her teeth to stave off a sheepish smile.

Zakaari's ear tips darkened. "Sorry, *Peiaa*."

Tipori stepped around the guardrail and approached, studying Daeya's shield with a curious look. He held out one arm and Aetherial mist coalesced above and below his fingers in the shape of a curved battle axe. His hand curled around the haft as it solidified into a real weapon. "Stand aside, please."

Daeya stepped away, looking to Zakaari for some indication of what was about to happen. He only wiped the sweat from his forehead and guided her back even farther.

After a few practice swings, Tipori squared up to Daeya's shield and hefted the axe. He swung, and the sound of the collision was like a branch snapping in strong wind. White-violet sparks erupted.

The shield held.

A surge of pride swept through her. Only a five-layered sigil could have taken an axe like that, and she'd created this one in less than half the time without breaking a sweat.

Tipori drew back for another blow, throwing his entire body into the swing. The concussive force of the impact reverberated through the floor.

Still, the shield stood firm. Daeya's smile was so wide, it might have reached her ears.

Zakaari stamped out a tiny spark close by and elbowed her in the ribs. "I guess I don't feel so bad, now."

When Tipori drew back a third time, an intense violet glow suffused the blade of his axe, and the image of the man himself wavered as if from an Aetherial warp.

Alarmed, Daeya grabbed Zakaari's arm. "What's he doing?"

His palm closed over her knuckles. "Just watch."

A warp in the Aetherial Wall could tear open a rift wide enough to swallow this entire building. Daeya's grip tightened.

Tipori swung, his axe trailing black-violet mist. Blinding light seared Daeya's vision. She covered her face, blinking away spots, as a sound like a Mautori war gong drove the breath from her lungs.

She tried to suck in air while the familiar tang of metal coated her tongue. She dared a glance up and found the shield had burst into an even brighter cloud of white particles drifting out in all directions. Light winked out of the dazzling cloud like millions of stars before the rising sun.

Tipori turned, eyes aglow with magic, chest rising and falling in silent pants. He let the axe fall from his hand, and it vanished in a puff of mist.

"I think you've earned the rest of the day off." There was an odd note in his voice, as if he was just as stunned as Daeya felt. "We'll pick up again after the solstice."

She peeled her hand off Zakaari's arm and bowed.

Wood creaked underfoot as Tipori crossed the floor and clasped her shoulder. "Good work today."

Her heart soared. His firm grip kept her from bowing a second time, but she inclined her head. It was the same overwhelming sense of pride she'd once sought from Gregory, save for one key difference: the lack of crippling anxiety fueling her every move. "Thank you, *Amaa*."

Tipori resummoned her spellbinders and bade her and Zakaari good afternoon. He departed quickly, a frown appearing moments before he slipped out the door.

Daeya paused in lacing her boots and stared after him, concerned.

Zakaari knuckled the top of her head and plopped down beside her. His shoulder and arm pressed against hers. "You might have fancy god-magic, McVen, but I still outpace you in hand-to-hand and weapons."

It was hard to brood with his teasing smile lighting up the room. She tied off one boot and started on the other, trying to salvage an air of confidence that she no longer felt. "For now, maybe. Give me a few more years, and you might be in trouble."

"I hope so." A contemplative look stole over his face. "That you stay that long, I mean."

Daeya cinched down her laces. "This war won't be won overnight. I'll stay as long as it takes."

Zakaari's jaw worked. He tugged on his shirt collar and cleared his throat. "So, about the solstice dance tomorrow—"

She saved him the trouble of voicing his usual warnings about not getting underfoot. "Don't worry. I already told Sam I'm not going."

That drew him up short. "Why not?"

A one-shouldered shrug accompanied her practiced response. "I don't dance."

"Aethershite." Zakaari rose and offered her a hand. "Anyone who wields a sword can dance. I'll teach you."

His earnest expression stopped her usual follow-up excuse. She slipped her hand into his and let him pull her up. "Even if you could, I don't have anything to wear."

Parties and dances had never been a part of Daeya's life growing up. Keeping her runes hidden was impossible with the plunging necklines and backless dresses favored by Ryostian nobility. Even if she could've commissioned something more conservative from a tailor, Gregory would have never approved.

Zakaari didn't release her hand right away. He regarded her ill-fitting, stained blouse and baggy trousers, tilting his head. "I could borrow something from Riisii's closet. You're about the same size."

No doubt something overly revealing and inappropriate. Something that would have gotten her switched back in Ryost. Daeya swallowed. "I don't think she'd like that you took something without asking."

That should be the end of this. Daeya would be free from any obligation to attend, and Zakaari wouldn't have to play mage-sitter on a day meant for celebration. He'd be free to revel with his women, and she could keep her secret. That was what she wanted.

Wasn't it?

Zakaari scoffed. "She never wears any of the dresses *Peiaa* buys her. Believe me, she won't mind."

*Bleeding Aether.*

"I—Zakaari, I don't—" Gods, her hands were sweating. She needed another defense, but nothing came to mind. Nothing except how desperately she wanted to say yes.

Zakaari winced and released her hand, his black hair obscuring part of his face. "If you don't want to go with me, I understand."

Daeya blinked.

He was asking her to go *with* him? As if they were together? "Wait—"

Zakaari turned to collect his cloak. "Come on. Let's get you home."

The hurt in his voice might have been well disguised, had she not spent nearly three months affixed to his side.

Four paces already separated them by the time Daeya wrenched her feet into motion. She seized his wrist, and he stopped short, but refused to look at her.

"I'll go with you."

Tension pooled in the muscles of his arm, like he was about to pull away. "No, just forget I said anything. I misunderstood."

Daeya held him fast. "You didn't." She grimaced. "But I think I did."

Finally, he turned. His expression was not quite a scowl. "What does that mean?"

"I thought you'd be sick of me by now." Her grip went slack on his arm, but he made no move to retreat. Instead, he waited while she struggled to put her feelings into words. "I thought you'd want to spend the holiday with your lovers, not looking after me."

She averted her gaze. Her teeth clamped down on her lip, and she used the pain to ground herself. Somehow, she felt more foolish now than if she'd just let things be. He didn't owe her anything, least of all an explanation.

Zakaari reached up and gently extracted her lip with his thumb. His warm fingers curled under her chin with a subtle pressure that prompted her eyes back to his.

"You're scared." He said it as if it surprised him.

Those two little words rendered Daeya mute.

The truth was that she was terrified. She'd already made one mistake with Alar. With Zakaari, things were different. He never made her feel lesser for not being like him or tried to hurt her for the sake of duty or appearances, and that made her afraid.

Afraid of falling for him. Afraid of getting hurt.

Daeya's throat tried to close up around her admission. "I suppose I am."

His eyes misted over, and he made no attempt to hide it. "I am, too."

"You are?"

He nodded.

For once, there were no quips exchanged between them, no prodding questions or attempts at competition. There was just her, and him, and the certainty that whatever happened from here couldn't be undone.

But could she share him with the others? The concept was so foreign to her, she couldn't imagine it actually working. His other women had him first, and that made her the interloper here. Someone would get jealous.

That someone was likely her.

Chest aching, eyes stinging, she shook her head. It wouldn't be fair to him if she wasn't honest. "I'm not sure I'm ready."

His hand slid across her jaw to cup her cheek. "Then I can be patient."

A tear slipped down her face. Zakaari swiped it away with his thumb, then brushed his lips against her forehead.

She moved without thinking, pressing herself into his arms. She buried her face against his neck, the scent of citrons and lavender stirring feelings not unlike the joy of returning home. Her hands clutched the back of his shirt, anchoring her against the confusing maelstrom of emotions threatening to pull her under.

His fingers threaded through her faded red hair. "I'll wait as long as it takes. Alright?"

She nodded, the movement smearing tears against his collar. What it meant to hear him say that wasn't easily put into words. It was like that fae tale with the boy who was given the Mirror of Yearning, only if Daeya were to look into the mirror, it wouldn't lead her on any epic quest for untold riches or into a cave filled with destinies and dragon fire. It would show her as she was right now, with Zakaari holding her in his arms.

"I'll go," she whispered, selfishly holding him tighter. "I'll go with you."

He extracted himself just enough to rest his forehead against hers. "You don't have to."

"I know." Daeya's nose brushed his, and she smiled at how he sighed with his entire body at the gesture. "I want to."

Niam had taken a job with the local seamstresses. Daeya could ask her for advice on what to wear. Surely, northern fashion would favor sensibility and warmth over the risk of frostburn. She could delay the inevitable a little longer.

If not, at least she could explain the runes on her own terms.

Gods willing, Zakaari would choose to love her anyway.

# CHAPTER FORTY-SEVEN

## NORMOS

Normos pushed aside the canvas flap barring entry to Councilor Gregory's command tent. He blinked, willing his eyes to adjust to the dim space.

Saphyrum lanterns cast meager light across the ornate furnishings. A map of the continent dominated the tent's center. Scrolls and letters were piled atop a desk in one corner, and the scent of ink and sealing wax permeated the air. A half-filled wine glass stood beside a tome on another table; the white-clad sorcerer leaning over it didn't look up as Normos entered.

Gregory might not have reacted to his arrival, but the second figure did. The sight of blonde waves tumbling down black robes made Normos stop short. If his jaw clenched any tighter, he might have cracked his teeth.

But Daeya's hair was lighter, less curly. He forced his shoulders to relax.

Cameron Vika turned from the map and gave him a once-over. She had a deep scratch over her lip, and a burn marred her left temple. Both easily cured with a base sigil if—

No.

He was a battle mage, not a healer.

Normos secured the tent flap. "Good afternoon, Cameron."

One elegant brow lifted. "We weren't expecting you for another week, Sorcerer Beck." She inclined her head. "Welcome."

So cordial. Only Mira could explain how Cameron was related to Joss.

"We met less resistance through the mountains than we expected." They'd made excellent time once their smaller convoy split off in Trivvix. Joss had stayed behind to see to the distribution of resources there. "I've brought healers, if you would like to see them about your injuries."

Cameron's gaze flicked toward Gregory.

Their Councilor still didn't look up from his tome. "We will finish our discussion later. See that no one disturbs us."

"Yes, Councilor."

She bowed and made for the entryway, sparing Normos another glance. Outside of Gregory's field of view, she grimaced and gave the barest shake of her head, as if to say 'tread lightly.'

He nodded, careful to steel his expression into neutrality. She brushed past him and out the door, taking the rest of the tent's warmth with her.

His courage fell away as the tent flap closed.

He couldn't do this.

Ascertaining the integrity of Councilor Tressa Blake's wards had been easy. Her security was such that if Normos had been a blanker assassin, he could have slipped in and slit her throat in her sleep. Councilor Ferren would have to be tested later; he'd been sent to blockade Kuma'Kiir from the north. That left testing Gregory—a task that hadn't seemed so terrifying on the road. Now, Normos would have rather braved a dozen aethermancers alone on their choice of terrain than incur this man's wrath. Phantom echoes of crippling pain held him in thrall.

Truthfully, Normos deserved to be punished. The weight of Mira's amulet pressed against his sternum in silent accusation. He'd been a fool to wear it here. Gregory would surely see its outline through his shirt.

He should tell him. He should admit his indiscretions and beg forgiveness before Gregory had a chance to discover them. Things would be so much worse for him if he didn't.

Gregory turned a page. "I have had my fill of ill news this week, Sorcerer. I pray you have something better for me."

Rumors about the defeat at Willowmarsh and Freddick Tallion's demise abounded. Some claimed the savages had cut out Councilor Tallion's eyes before he died. One reported seeing his murderer devour the eyes in front of them.

Another said the same man had popped Tallion's eye into the empty socket in his own face and now wore it as a trophy. Ghoulish stories, all, but they spread around Guild campfires like lice in a Southgate brothel.

Normos squared his shoulders. If he wanted to speak with confidence, he had to look confident as well. "The saphyrum stipend for the healers in Ferid has been suspended, as you requested." Bolstered by the strength and steadiness of his voice, he continued, "Twelve of their best healers have been provided to aid the war effort. Joss and Toby are overseeing supply distribution in Trivvix and Sarton."

"And what of our pest problem?" Gregory turned another page. "I trust you have handled her as well."

Normos hesitated. "Councilor Mar-Pol insisted she come north with me to oversee distribution here."

Finally, Gregory looked up.

Normos braced himself. It had been a risk walking Gwen directly into camp, not hiding her on the outskirts until he could confirm whether any of the Councilors or their closest mages had been imperiumed. She'd insisted he would need help apprehending them if they turned hostile—a possibility he'd conceded, knowing the most powerful masterminds could control their victims from any-where in the world.

Gregory looked him over, his brown eyes hooded by shadow. His tone was razor-edged. "You have brought her here?"

Uncertainty welled in Normos like blood from a wound. Unable to hold that gaze any longer, he lowered his head. "Yes, Councilor."

"Excellent."

Normos stilled, disbelieving, afraid to move. Afraid to blink.

"Well done, Normos."

All thoughts of pain and punishment left him.

*Mira's mercy.*

Normos returned his attention to Gregory, searching. He'd expected disap-pointment, disapproval, or a firm correction with the back of his hand. Such a reaction might have even lent a modicum of weight to Gwen's concerns about the Councilor's so-called uncouth behavior with his students. But the man wasn't angry at all. He was *proud* of him.

A silent breath shuddered out of him.

Gregory smiled. Normos lived for that smile. The Councilor approached him and took hold of his chin, studying his face with a warmth reserved only for his most cherished students. "You have redeemed yourself, my boy. I knew you would."

Normos's chest swelled. "Thank you, Councilor."

"You will arrest her immediately."

There was no stopping the slack-jawed look that stole away any chance of passing off his hesitation as simple confusion. "Councilor, I—"

The whites of Gregory's eyes flashed like lightning before a thunderstorm. "Is there a problem with my directive?"

"No, of course not."

"Then you should have no trouble carrying it out." His eyes narrowed. "Unless you have taken a personal interest in the woman. It would be disappointing if such a brief exposure to her treachery has weakened you."

Gregory knew.

He *knew* Gwen had questioned him, tried to befriend him. He probably suspected her attempt to turn Normos against him.

Normos projected as much vehemence into his denial as he could. "No, Councilor."

Gregory lifted his chin. Though they were of the same height, Normos shrank beneath him. "Take Cameron with you. Mar-Pol is not likely to come quietly."

With that, he returned to his tome and the wine.

Normos stared at his boots, caked with dirt from his journey over the mountains. The journey that had provided a chance to explore his true passion. The journey that had made him question the justness of Guild law and ponder a conspiracy that might have caused the deaths of hundreds.

A conspiracy that still demanded answers.

If Sarikkian had really found evidence proving Guild sabotage collapsed the School, then demanding Gwen's arrest was exactly what an imperiumed Councilor would do. If left unchecked, the blankers could systematically destroy the Guild from the inside, felling the Towers next, or pushing for something even more ambitious, like another Vale's Hollow. Normos would never live with himself if he failed to safeguard his people.

It was just one sigil. A simple, harmless sigil.

While Gregory's back was turned, Normos slipped his hand beneath his robe and closed his eyes. Perfect knots and curving lines took shape behind his eyelids.

Saphyric energy trickled from the healer's amulet; it would have flowed too quickly from his casting chain. He pulled gently, as if sealing a wound, so he didn't give himself away with the telltale scent of Aether.

Holding two spells at once was a dangerous task, but with his casting hand, he prepared the ward detection spell and with the other, he drew the first three loops for a Rift Walk. If Gregory was afflicted by an imperium, the mastermind would compel him to attack Normos for discovering his secret. It was best to be prepared.

"Something else to report, Sorcerer?"

"N—" Normos's heart leaped into his throat. One thread of his spell snagged against another, and he seized it before it could tangle. Magic seared his fingertips, and he forced his pained expression into one of uncertainty. "Yes, Councilor. Well, a question, really."

Gregory sipped his wine, only half-turned toward Normos. "Stop stammering and speak."

An errant obscenity crossed Normos's mind as he fought the urge to shake off the spell burn. "Why shall I say Mar-Pol is being arrested?"

"Conspiracy to commit treason."

A charge that would ultimately lead to execution. Gwen deserved a short stay in prison for manipulating the saphyrum ledgers, true, but execution? It wasn't like his hands were any cleaner. "Treason, Councilor?"

"Yes." Gregory shot him an appraising look. "Did Mar-Pol discuss any plans involving Mardis Ulrich, Isa Sarikkian, or Lukas Derrover with you?"

Two knots left. Normos made quick work of them while he considered his answer. Once he'd tied off his sigil, he held it steady beneath his cloak and prayed the light wouldn't give him away. "No, but she did have some disturbing things to say about Sarikkian."

"What did she tell you?"

Normos struggled to come up with a benign enough lie. "She claimed he wanted to adjust his curriculum to include more blanker history." He hesitated. "From before the Saphyrum War."

The Councilor turned fully toward him, darkness creeping into his expression. "You have many talents, but lying isn't one of them."

Normos swallowed hard and bowed his head. *This* was why he obeyed orders to the quill stroke; it was why he'd never understood Daeya McVen's penchant for causing trouble. Why would anyone want to feel this sickening dread and self-loathing on purpose? "Forgive me, Councilor."

"Try again." Quiet contempt punctuated Gregory's words—a far cry from the praise he'd awarded only moments before.

"Sh-she said—" Gods help him, how had he failed so spectacularly in so little time? The truth. He had to tell the truth. "She said the School collapse was a set-up. That Councilor Sarikkian discovered Ignab's mages throwing evidence of the sabotage into the Aether."

Silence fell.

Normos flexed his hands beneath his robes. The incomplete Walker's sigil tugged at his awareness, tempting him to finish it. Tempting him to run. But running from Gregory's discipline never ended well. Normos had learned that lesson early in life. It was best to wait, best to bear whatever he had coming to him. He deserved it after all.

Sharp, humorless laughter broke that painful silence. "Of course she did. And you believed her?"

"I-I wasn't certain—"

"Stop stammering," Gregory snapped. "You're a mage, not an imbecile."

"Apologies—"

"And stand up straight. You have a spine. I expect you to use it."

Normos straightened, holding his head high despite his poorly masked terror. His hands shook so badly that the Walker's sigil tangled and burned his palm. The scent of charred flesh wafted up from beneath his robe.

Gregory sniffed, glancing down.

"Councilor, it wasn't my intention to deceive you." Normos panicked, anchoring his feet to keep himself from backing away. "It's my duty to ascertain the truth. Gwen made some serious accusations, and I had to give them their due diligence. For all our safety."

Gregory's pale lips curled back from his teeth. "I see you're on a first-name basis with her as well. Has she debased your loyalty so completely?"

"No," Normos hastened to say. "She presented me with an opportunity to betray your confidence, but I didn't take it. I would never."

Like the sharp lines of a cliffside eroding before wind and surf, Gregory's face softened. "They must have been compelling, the things she told you, hm?"

Shame seeped into Normos like ink spilled over cloth. The stains of doubt Gwen and Olivia had inspired would never scrub clean now. Beneath his robe, his hold on the ward detection sigil loosened, and its power faded. "Yes, Councilor."

Deep furrows lined Gregory's brow. "I must be honest; the Council made a dreadful mistake that day." For once, he looked torn. "We were to keep this secret, even from our most trusted mages, but you deserve a truthful explanation."

Normos shifted on his feet. The melancholy weighing on the Councilor's shoulders pressed upon him as well, as if, in a rare moment of vulnerability, Gregory trusted him to share this burden. He took the honor in stride. "I would hear it."

Resigned, Gregory folded his hands. "Four key Alliaansi members were captured outside Ryost the night before the School fell. One of them was Cheralach Bevausecc. Another was an Aetherian."

Having both rumors confirmed in the same breath staggered Normos. "What were they doing near Ryost?"

"What else?"

Normos grimaced. The answer was obvious: planning a raid on the capital.

Gregory continued without awaiting a response. "We took steps to contain them for questioning, but they escaped their cells, likely with help from the blanker spy, who was in league with Mardis Ulrich."

The Divination Master's betrayal didn't come as a shock to Normos. Gregory had always been suspicious of her, especially when it came to her prophesying. Ulrich was self-serving, and her so-called seer's skills bore a level of timeliness that couldn't properly be attributed to coincidence.

"That morning, Ulrich called an emergency Council meeting to warn us she had Foreseen the opening of a rift large enough to swallow the entire northern quarter. She counseled us to stop the rift early with a controlled collapse of the west wing—its origin point, or so she claimed. Councilor Derrover volunteered to submit the evacuation order, but we learned too late the order was never received."

The warmth drained from Normos's face. "The order was never received, but the School was leveled anyway?"

"As I said, it was a dreadful mistake."

Anger coursed like lightning into his fingertips. All those children, all that death, due to a miscommunication?

Normos fought to keep his voice steady. "It was a travesty. How could you"—*let this happen*, he nearly said, before biting back the accusation—"keep this from me?"

"For the same reason we amended the truth in our official decree. It is easier to explain the root of the problem." At Normos's questioning glance, Gregory added, "Sarikkian and Derrover were assigned to direct the collapse. Since then, both men and Master Ulrich have disappeared. We suspect they were all under the influence of blanker masterminds."

And now they'd come full circle. Masterminds were at work in the Guild, and Normos didn't know whom to trust. He sagged under the revelations and reached for the edge of the map table to steady himself.

The Northlands and greater Eidosinia stretched before him. He thought of poor Peader and the terror in the boy's face, knowing what must become of him now that he'd been tainted by psionics. How many others would suffer the same fate? How many of their best mages had already fallen?

A thought pierced his spiraling thoughts.

Gwen hadn't. Nor had Councilor Blake.

Normos had just tested Blake, and he'd thrown that sigil so many times at Gwen, he would have known if her wards were broken. She'd been so devastated by the sabotage that he couldn't believe she'd be complicit in such a treasonous plot. This emergency Council meeting must have occurred without her knowledge.

If it had occurred at all.

A treacherous notion. Gregory had no reason to lie.

Unless...

A wine glass appeared in Normos's periphery, filled with an aromatic red. He took it and washed down the tightness in his throat. "Gwen seemed truly distraught over her discovery. Is it possible she doesn't know Sarikkian could be compromised?"

All the softness in Gregory's face evaporated. "You let your personal feelings cloud your judgment. Mar-Pol is Sarikkian's creature. She would do anything—*say* anything—to protect him. Do not lose sight of this."

Normos bowed his head. "Yes, Councilor."

They sipped their wine in silence. Gregory turned back to his tome. Normos set his glass down and slipped both hands inside his robe. His amulet shifted, its warm metal steadying him for what he had to do.

"I expect her spellbound and rifted back to Ryost by nightfall."

The sigil took shape easily. "It will be done."

Gregory reached for quill and parchment, paying no mind to him. "Dismissed."

Normos tied off the light strands with quick, sure movements. His heart beat faster, but his conscience was clear. He started for the entryway and lifted the flap, letting a frigid gust of wind blow inward. As sunlight poured in and air stirred the Councilor's robes, Normos turned and flicked the sigil across the tent. Disguised by the rustle of cloth, the spell bounced off Gregory's back and returned to Normos's hand.

Without breaking stride, he tucked the sigil beneath his robe and departed. The canvas snapped in the wind behind him.

# CHAPTER FORTY-EIGHT

## SHEI-GWEN

Gwen paced the length of the tent, arms folded across her beaded bodice. Her rings caught the light from a saphyrum lantern and threw glimmers across the rickety cot she'd been issued. With her luck, the vile linens would be covered in lice or fleas or some other nasty parasite. She never thought she'd miss the cramped sleeping arrangement in their gods-cursed wagon.

Olivia sat on the cot, filing her nails into oblivion, unconcerned about the vermin feasting on her flesh.

Gwen reached the back of the tent and turned. "He's late."

The incessant rasp of Olivia's file stopped. "My offer still stands if you want to take your mind off things."

"How can you even think about that in a place like this?"

Olivia snorted. "I lived in a tree village for twenty years. I didn't get to be picky."

Footsteps crunched in the snow outside, staying Gwen's retort. She looked toward the entryway, readying to demand an explanation for Normos's long absence, but the tent flap only fluttered in the wind. Flashes of late afternoon sun shone through a tear in the fabric. Voices came and went, and the nagging itch that had plagued her since their arrival grew.

"Something's wrong."

"Oh, will you stop worrying?" Olivia's filing resumed. "Caelyn's wrath, Shei, sit down. You're going to carve a trench in the floor."

Gwen rubbed the base of her throat, ignoring Olivia's suggestion. *Her* people weren't likely to have been blanked by masterminds. *They* weren't possibly staging a coup to overthrow half their leadership. "He should have been back by now."

"Maybe he got hungry. He's probably as sick of living on rations as I am."

"Or he's planning to betray us."

Olivia's filing stopped again. "He won't. He's a good man, and he wants to do the right things."

She'd made the same argument before. They both agreed Normos was a troubled young man, clearly mistreated by his superior, but only Gwen feared he'd spent too long in Gregory's clutches to change sides.

"You really aren't worried about him? He wouldn't even practice with you these last few weeks."

Olivia twirled the file over her knuckles like a mercenary spinning a blade. Quiet contemplation replaced her exasperation, and for once, Gwen caught a glimpse of the perspicacious leader she might have been. "He still wears Mira's amulet."

"He can still pray to the daughters of Life without practicing their arts."

"You haven't seen how Mira's light shines in him." Olivia tucked the file away and rose, stretching like a leopard waking from a nap. She wrapped her arms around Gwen's neck. "He might fear the bastard he works for, but nothing will keep him from the Mother's call."

Gwen's hands slipped over Olivia's waist. Their foreheads touched briefly before Olivia turned her chin upward and captured Gwen's mouth in a kiss. She tasted of mint and lemongrass, and Gwen devoured it, chasing her lover's lips when they descended beneath her jaw.

Even lost in the heady taste of their kisses, fingers twined into Olivia's hair, that nagging sense tugged at the back of her mind.

"Promise me," Gwen breathed between kisses, "if things go wrong, you won't get involved."

Olivia hiked Gwen's skirts up. "Shut up, Councilor. It's time you forget your name."

Gwen protested only halfheartedly as Olivia shoved her toward the cot. She went down in a heap, abandoning her concerns about the cleanliness of the linens. Olivia disappeared beneath her skirts, and the world narrowed.

Just before nightfall, more footsteps drew Gwen from a boneless, blissful haze. Olivia was snuggled close, limbs heavy with sleep. Careful not to disturb her, Gwen extracted herself and retrieved her discarded robe.

A shadow moved across the canvas. "Councilor? Are you there?"

"Normos." Her breath left her in a cloud of swirling vapor. She hurried to unfasten the flap and ushered him inside. "Thank Delvin. What took you so long?"

Snow crusted Normos's blond hair, and his blue eyes were sunken. He brushed past her. "It's worse than we feared."

Cold swept through her. Gwen hugged her elbows and tried not to shiver. "What did you learn?"

He glanced toward Olivia, then lowered his voice. "When was the last time you heard from Mardis Ulrich?"

Gwen frowned. "A few months ago, before I left for Ferid. Why?"

"Did you speak to her the day the School collapsed?"

"No, not that I recall."

"So, she didn't call you to an emergency Council meeting to discuss what to do about the rift?"

"No."

His tone grew more urgent. The questions tumbled out one after another. "Was Sarikkian? Did you see him that day? Had he been having headaches?"

"I don't remember any emergency meeting." Gwen's eyes narrowed. "You think Sarikkian's been imperiumed?" A knot of foreboding tightened within her. "Did Gregory tell you that?"

Olivia stirred, drawing another uneasy look from Normos.

He rubbed his face. "He claimed Ulrich advised the Council to collapse the School and prevent the rift from growing. He said Derrover was supposed to issue an order to evacuate, but he never delivered it."

Ulrich. Sarikkian. Derrover. They all had one thing in common.

Of *course* Gregory would try to frame them for the collapse. She should have seen this coming.

"Normos, listen to me." Gwen struggled to keep her voice steady, not wanting to spook him. "Whatever Gregory told you, Sarikkian and Derrover have always been his loudest opposition on the Council. And Master Ulrich—"

"They're missing."

"They're—what?"

Normos fixed her with a harrowed stare. "And Gregory's wards have been broken."

Gwen's mouth fell open. "You're sure?"

Normos nodded.

It was just as they feared. Her thoughts turned toward Peader and her father, their eyes and noses bleeding, minds stricken or shredded. The blankers hadn't held either of them in thrall, but neither sat in a position of power. With the strongest sorcerer in the country under the masterminds' sway, the damage they could do was unfathomable.

Knees weak, she staggered to the cot and sank down at the foot. Olivia groaned and sat up, wiping sleep from her eyes.

"What's going on?" she croaked.

Gwen balled her fists to stop their shaking. "We have to remove him." She looked up at Normos, who regarded her with an expression made of stone. "We have to stop him before he destroys us all."

"We're no match for him. Not alone," Normos pointed out. "Do you know where Sarikkian and the others might have gone? We're going to need their help."

She pressed the heels of her hands to her forehead, willing herself to think clearly. "Assuming Gregory didn't quietly execute them?" The thought provoked a bitter pang of heartache. He couldn't have. Surely she would have known.

But Sarikkian had told her to stay away for a reason. He'd known something like this could happen.

"He would have made a spectacle of it if he'd killed them, to scare everyone." Normos knelt before her in the dirt. "Where would Sarikkian go? I can Walk there tonight, and we can have this done by morning."

Gwen looked sharply at him. "If they see you coming, they'll think you're there for Gregory. There's no way to get word to them safely without Peader."

He regarded her with patience worthy of Miriam Serrasiva herself. "Then you'll have to come with me to explain it to them. Just tell me where to go."

Sarikkian had entrusted her with the location of three safehouses—two in Eidosinia and one in Aivenos—with the stipulation that she never divulge their location to anyone. In any other circumstance, telling Gregory's right hand would be the ultimate betrayal. Gwen was willing to put herself at risk, but she hesitated for her mentor's sake.

Heedless of her state of dress—or lack thereof—Olivia swung her legs over the side of the cot, provoking a bright flush in Normos's cheeks.

"It's alright, Shei. Sarikkian will understand. Just tell him."

Gwen squeezed her eyes shut. Gregory surrounded himself with the strongest mages in the Guild. Any of those loyal to him would come to his defense. Normos was right; they couldn't do this alone.

"He has connections in Aarilon and Clysterna," she finally said. "There's a safehouse in the Aivenosian capital as well, but he can't Walk. He wouldn't have made it there yet."

Normos nodded. "We'll try Aarilon first. It's closer to Ryost, and I've Walked there before. Are there any others who can help us? Other students or mages you trust?"

Gwen chuckled humorlessly at the hopelessness of this situation. "No. Not when we don't know who's under blanker control. The bastards can communicate across distances. Even if we tested them all, it would only take one to warn Gregory we're coming."

Normos sat back on his heels and looked up at Olivia. "You should get dressed and prepare to flee in case we're discovered." He shifted his gaze to Gwen. "I'll wait outside for you. We can leave as soon as you're ready."

Nervous energy flooded Gwen as he departed. She twisted a bead on her casting bracelet while Olivia pulled one of Gwen's linen smocks over her head and shook out her hair.

Something itched at the back of Gwen's mind—a disturbance she couldn't quite identify, like the feeling of being viewed through a scrying mirror. Her eyes strayed toward the tent flap.

"Livvie," she whispered.

Olivia turned, brows knitted.

Gwen switched to Aivenosian, using the uncommon dialect of Clan Naranathia, Olivia's people. "Did he seem off to you?"

Olivia followed Gwen's stare and frowned. "You think he should have been more distraught?"

That was it.

He was too calm, too cool, after just learning his Councilor had been imperiumed. Once a blanker got inside a person's head, psionics could alter a mind forever. Even if they could free Gregory from the mastermind's control, the devastation the blanker would cause on the way out would be irrevocable. Normos was either resigned to the possibility, or he was fooling himself.

Gwen retreated into her thoughts while Olivia pulled on a champagne-colored dress and swiped at the wrinkled fabric. There was little to be done about Normos right now. Perhaps he was only distancing himself from the emotional weight of the task to come.

Before they left, she checked her casting bracelet one last time.

"Normos?" she called through the canvas.

Only silence answered.

Gwen called again, louder this time. "Normos?"

In her periphery, the glint of steel flashed, and a dagger appeared in Olivia's hand. Gwen tensed, trusting her partner's sharper instincts, and summoned saphyric energy as she peered through the tear in the tent fabric.

Campfires and torches dotted the night. Thick snow, still falling, blanketed the paths crisscrossing the field. Gwen looked one way, then the other, for a wider view. No shadows stirred. Not even the sway of a branch.

Something was wrong.

Movement, then blackness enveloped the sight. The scratch of fabric right outside the tear nearly sent her into the ceiling.

There was the sound of rustling, footsteps, and then, "Gwen? Liv? Are you ready?"

Normos's voice.

"Mother save me," Gwen choked out, shoulders sagging. Behind her, Olivia muttered a curse. Gwen stifled an embarrassed laugh and reached for the stays to the tent flap. "Aetherial storms, Normos, don't do that again—"

She tossed the canvas aside and white-blond hair streaked across her vision. A black-clad figure crashed forward, and rough cloth rasped against her cheeks. Gwen shrieked, reaching for the sack over her head, but it cinched tight with the tug of a string. Cold magic crackled at her fingertips, but colder metal snapped shut around one wrist, and the hold on it slipped away.

Double-crossed.

No. No, no, no, *no.*

Normos had double-crossed them.

The bastard had been scheming all this time. He was still Gregory's creature.

He knew Olivia was Oran Osa. He knew how to find Sarikkian.

Gwen howled and stumbled backward, catching someone with her elbow on the way to the floor. When she tried to breathe again, her mouth filled with dusty fabric. "Livvie, run!"

Strong arms wrapped around her, dragging her back upright. Juxtaposed against the sound of Olivia screaming, Normos spoke gently into her ear. "I'm sorry I have to do this."

"Delvin curse you, you conniving snake!" Propriety be damned. Gwen tore her unbound wrist from his grip and smashed it into some part of the wretched boy she couldn't see.

He was more solid than she realized. A rush of air and a grunt was all the blow afforded her. "Gwen—"

"Let go of me! Let go!"

Still holding fast, he incanted and the scent of Aether flooded the sack. She tried to stomp his feet, tried to kick, bite, and scratch, but a sudden weightlessness and a rush of air left her hollow and shaky.

Warm cobbles smashed into her knees. Familiar sounds of city nightlife added to her disorientation. Her fight resumed when the second binder closed around her wrist.

She launched herself at Normos, fingers hooked into claws, aiming for where his face should be. One nail caught the curve of his cheekbone, and he gasped. She slashed again, heartened by the sound.

White-violet light flashed through the holes in the sack, silhouetting every thread in fine detail.

"Say nothing."

Heat bloomed in her chest. A void both peaceful and insistent seized hold of her.

Then darkness.

# CHAPTER FORTY-NINE

## DAEYA

Daeya tugged the chemise over her head and watched it tumble to her knees in the mirror. It covered most of the runic spirals, blocks, and concentric triangles, but dipped too low to hide the runes below her collarbones. Her fingers traced the ugly scars and she sighed.

This was never going to work.

A knock came at the door. "You can't hide in there forever, Daeya." Jessie's voice carried wry amusement. "Come out and let us see."

"It's too big—" The door swung open and Daeya spun, clapping both hands over her chest. "Jessie!"

Jessie strode into the room, her own voluminous crimson skirts brushing both sides of the doorframe. She looked Daeya over, then reached for the emerald dress Zakaari had sent over. Niam stood outside the washroom in a much more sensible sable dress, a calming breeze to Jessie's whirlwind.

"No, that fits just right." Jessie examined Riisii Evallier's embroidered gown and whistled. "Chaos damn me, but the boy chose well." She lowered the dress and scowled when she caught Daeya slinking toward the only doorway with her hands still clutched to her chest. "Oh, don't be so modest. A little cleavage is nothing any of us haven't seen before. Just look at mine."

If a person could die from embarrassment, Daeya was certain she would have. Jessie gave herself a shake, and the tops of her ample breasts bounced against her beaded neckline.

Daeya tore her eyes from the sight. "Isn't there something a little warmer I could wear? Furs or wool?"

She looked toward Niam, silently pleading.

Jessie scoffed. "Look, if you want to hold Zakaari's interest for more than a fortnight, you have to stop dressing like a homeless woman who'd trade her last tooth to a fae for a loaf of bread."

Self-consciousness seized Daeya in a chokehold. "He's never complained about the way I dress."

"Only because he's being polite. Everyone knows he likes girls who—"

Niam knocked loudly on the open door, sparing Daeya from whatever crass assumption Jessie was about to make, and with a scowl, gestured to someone outside the washroom.

Sam poked her head around the corner and glared at Jessie. "That's enough solstice punch for you. Why don't you go downstairs and help get ready for lunch?"

Jessie rolled her eyes. "Fine. At least call me up to do something about her hair when you're done. We really should have touched up those roots with henna."

She continued grumbling, swaying on her feet, as Sam shooed her out of the room.

Daeya resisted the urge to reach for her blonde roots and offered Niam a smile. "Thank you."

Niam touched her arm, then beckoned her into the bedroom. Sam's bunk was covered in linens Niam had brought from the seamstress. She held up a different smock, frowned at it, and tossed it aside.

While Niam sorted through the stack, Sam shoved the ill-fitting door to their room closed. "I swear, she's worse now than she's ever been."

Daeya fidgeted with the chemise, keeping her runes covered with a deft adjustment of the neckline. "She was friends with that one archer who died, wasn't she?"

"Yeah, they were really close." Sam plopped down on her bunk. "He never would've tolerated that attitude."

"We all grieve in our own ways, I guess." It wasn't exactly helpful, but Daeya didn't know what else to say.

"Still," Sam said, "it doesn't give her permission to be an arse."

Niam examined another chemise, then approached Daeya and held it up for size. She nodded eagerly and pushed Daeya back toward the washroom, thrusting the fabric at her.

"Alright, alright, I'm going." Daeya laughed.

She closed the door and changed quickly, relieved to find this one had ruffles sewn into the neckline that hid the runes from view. Daeya gathered the emerald gown next, balking at all the ribbons, pins, and boning needed to give the garment its shape. It was a beautiful piece, but she had no idea how to put it on. Swallowing her pride, she draped the gown over one arm and cracked the door.

Sam rose from the bed. "Well?"

Daeya grimaced. "I need some help."

Niam's lavender eyes sparkled with mirth. She waved Sam back down and slipped inside the washroom, closing the door behind her. What felt like hours and hundreds of fastenings later, Niam spun Daeya toward the mirror and beamed over her shoulder.

Daeya gaped at the image staring back at her.

Gone was the formlessness that had plagued her since she'd discarded her tailored mage's clothing to the bottom of her satchel. Beads and silver thread glittered in the morning light. Ruffled sleeves matched the high neckline of her chemise, and the emerald fabric set off the green in her eyes. Boning in the bodice accentuated the curve of her waist, and modest petticoats traced the flare of her hips.

For the first time in her life, she looked... pretty.

She touched the bodice with a reverent hand. "Do you think he'll like it?"

Niam's expression soured in their reflection. She left Daeya standing before the mirror and searched the small washroom until she found Daeya's discarded blouse and baggy trousers. Holding them up in one hand, she used the other hand to flick her left ear point—her name sign for Zakaari—pound her chest twice, and poke Daeya in the sternum.

In the few months since Daeya had started her informal reading lessons at the orphanage, she and Niam had grown close enough to work out their own system of communicating. Daeya observed the series of gestures and puzzled out their meaning. "You're saying Zakaari liked me when I dressed in rags?"

Niam tossed the clothes over her shoulder and repeated the gestures, poking Daeya more firmly.

"Zakaari likes me no matter what I wear?"

She nodded.

"But what if Jessie's right? What if he's just being nice?" The possibility constricted her chest so tightly that Daeya could barely breathe. Or maybe that was the corset. But after their conversation yesterday—his promise to wait until she was ready—he was all she could think about. "I don't want this to be temporary."

Niam's smile was both tender and patient. She took her by the shoulders and turned her back toward the mirror. She gestured to their reflection, nodded decisively, and kissed Daeya's cheek. No matter what, she seemed to say, she would be here.

Emotion overwhelmed Daeya, then.

Niam released her and reached for the washroom door.

Daeya gazed at her reflection, then turned to address the Syljian girl. "Niam?"

She looked back, white eyebrows lifting.

There weren't enough words in the trade tongue, Eidosinian, and Syljian combined to express the immense gratitude Daeya felt. She settled for a simple, inadequate, "Thank you."

Niam gave her another soft smile, then opened the door.

A familiar male voice carried in from the main room. "Come on, Sam. I just wanted to see her."

"Well, that's too bad. She's not ready yet. Now, kindly march your arse back downstairs and wait like everyone else."

Early this morning, Sam had kicked all the men and boys out of the second floor so only women and girls could get dressed upstairs. She'd even sent Ravlok away, despite his protests that this was his room, too.

Daeya paused at the washroom door. She wasn't ready for this. What if he didn't like the gown? Or worse, what if he liked it so much that he pressured her to dress more like the other women he chased all over Starlight? Runes aside, their flowing skirts and revealing necklines were even less sensible up here than they were in Ryost. And as nice as it was to wear clothes that fit her properly, she had no funds to get an entire wardrobe tailored.

Niam narrowed her eyes and gave Daeya's arm a firm tug with surprising strength. Daeya stumbled into the room.

"I—" Zakaari stopped.

Cheeks burning, Daeya righted herself and wrung her hands inside her long sleeves. She stole a glance up from her stockings.

Zakaari's white doublet with emerald accents complemented his lilac complexion. His dark hair was slicked behind his pointed ears, and kohl lined his eyes.

Gods, he was so handsome, it hurt.

"Good morning," she said, more to her feet than to him.

"Morn—agh." Zakaari cleared his throat. "Good morning."

She should say something else. Compliment him. That's what people did in these situations, right? If she could only get her mind to communicate with her mouth.

Heat crept up her neck. Daeya smoothed a hand over her faded hair, certain now Jessie had been right; they should have at least touched up the roots or something. Next to him, she was going to look like an urchin caught playing dress-up in a noble's bedroom.

"By the gods," Sam swore, "I've never seen you struck speechless before, Ari."

Daeya looked up in time to see Sam elbow Zakaari hard enough to knock him off balance. Was it possible that, even with all his experience, he was nervous, too?

Sam turned an appraising eye on her. "Our sorceress cleans up well, doesn't she?"

"Don't be ridiculous." Zakaari approached Daeya, throat bobbing once, and touched her cheek. "She's always beautiful."

He said it not as if it were flattery, but an inarguable fact. It caught Daeya so unprepared, she couldn't even summon the instinct to deny it.

Her eyes closed at his touch. She shoved Jessie's disparaging comments to the back of her mind.

"I'm sure the smell is an improvement, at least," she quipped to break the silence.

He offered his hand and winked. "You won't hear me complaining."

The tension that had been building inside her all morning vanished. Fancy clothes aside, he was still the same boy who brought her oranges, dared her to leap off buildings, and sparred with her in the training hall.

She placed her hand in his. "This is your last chance to back out before you've committed to bruised shins and broken toes."

He chuckled. "If I'm that bad of a teacher, I probably deserve them."

Sharing his mirth came easily, like drinking wine from the same flask. It had the same richness, the same heady buzz, as the finest vintages she'd ever tasted.

"Alright, you two," Sam interrupted, "there'll be plenty of time for doe eyes later. Daeya still needs her hair braided, and Ari, a gentleman would get his date something for lunch."

Zakaari resisted Sam's attempt to usher him out the door. There was a giddiness about him as he brought Daeya's hand to his lips. That same energy sparked hot across her knuckles and planted firmly between her ribs. His violet eyes held her captive, and it was a good thing, too. If he hadn't anchored her there, Daeya's feet might have left the ground.

Sam inserted herself between them and tried to shove Zakaari toward the door. "Out with you. Out!"

Hand straining to hold Daeya's a moment longer, Zakaari finally released her. He caught the doorframe against Sam's final push and laughed heartily. "I'll see you downstairs."

"See you soon," Daeya said with her widest grin.

By the time he disappeared out the door, not even Niam could hold back her wispy laughter.

⁂

Winter solstice was one of the biggest celebrations in the world. Most countries hosted festivals honoring Mira for the start of a new year, Caelyn for the return of the sun, and Silonas for good fortune and prosperity in the months to come.

Starlight was no different. Every communal house was decorated with strings of crimson ziima berries, braided evergreen boughs, and towering candle displays. Green and gray streamers tumbled from every entryway, and some doors were thrown open to visitors in staunch defiance of the cold. People from all over Starlight Plateau could enter any of the communal houses today and be welcomed with food, entertainment, and goodwill.

After they'd feasted in Havensguard with Ravlok and Sam for lunch, Zakaari led Daeya somewhat successfully in her first Syljian dance. The dilapidated couches had been pushed to the walls, and he twirled her around the space, grinning like the biggest, most handsome fool.

By early afternoon, she could follow one pattern of steps with only the occasional blunder, and the number of times she stepped on his feet tapered off. Zakaari pressed his cheek against hers to be heard over the lutists and drummers. "You're a natural."

Face flushed, Daeya laughed and shook her head. "You're ridiculous."

He spun her again, and her skirts whirled. "I have something to show you."

"It's a little early for that, don't you think?" she teased, surprising herself. It didn't stop her from spreading her fingers across his chest, acutely aware of the lean muscle beneath his doublet. Too much wine with lunch must have loosened her tongue.

Zakaari's dark brows shot into his hairline. "You're going to make it very hard for me to behave myself, tonight, aren't you?"

"Maybe."

"I meant what I said." His tone turned serious, but his eyes remained playful. He leaned close and kissed her forehead. "I'll wait for you as long as you need."

The gesture didn't go unnoticed by the others around them. The gossip mills were already churning with speculation. Cupped hands and quiet words would spread the news that Tipori's son planned to add a sorceress to his growing harem.

Daeya ignored them. In some ways, the Alliaansi were no different from the Guild.

She smiled, content in his arms. "So, about this surprise."

"It's going to take a leap of faith."

"I'm not sure I should jump off a building in a corset."

He chuckled. "No actual jumping, I promise."

Zakaari glanced toward the nearest trio of women, whose narrowed eyes had been threatening to burn holes in his nice clothes for the last half hour. They turned away quickly when they caught Daeya looking.

Mental calculations ticked away behind Zakaari's eyes. "Do you trust me?"

Her brows pinched. "You're expecting trouble."

"More like avoiding it. Come on."

Zakaari spun her one last time and pulled her through the crowd and out through the foyer.

Daeya squinted against the light reflecting off the snow and breaking into rainbows through the icicles overhead. "Where are we going?"

"Just trust me."

Arm in arm, he led her through the bustling holiday traffic, their boots sliding occasionally on patches of ice. Beautiful parchment lanterns lined the pathways carved between the houses. They would remain lit all afternoon and into the night to greet the dawn on the first day of the year.

When they turned onto the path leading toward the one usually inhospitable portion of town, Daeya skidded to a stop. "Baani'anii?"

"Trust me." He turned to her with a look so earnest all the reasons she *shouldn't* enter Koraani's communal house froze on her tongue. "There's something you need to see."

"*In* Baani'anii?"

"It's the solstice. No one's going to turn us away today."

As she considered, a mixed group of humans and Syljians passed them on the street. Clearly drunk, and laughing so hard they had to hold each other up, they stumbled into Baani'anii ahead of Daeya and Zakaari. Indeed, no one tried to stop them.

Koraani's house was almost exclusively inhabited by Syljians and those few half-bloods he deemed trustworthy. Seeing humans boldly enter his domain lightened the weight of Zakaari's request. Knowing Alar still hadn't returned helped a little more.

"Please, Daeya." Zakaari didn't let go of her arm, but he didn't pull her toward the door either. "Leap with me."

She squeezed her eyes shut and readied to jump. What was the worst that could happen, anyway? "Alright. Lead the way."

His snow-white smile gleamed. "You won't regret it, I promise."

Inside, the place was packed. All races mingled together in their finest dresses, tunics, and furs. Soft lyre music played over the din of airy voices and clinking silverware. Scents of woodsmoke, savory sausage, and incense created an atmosphere of luxury so far removed from the Starlight she knew that they might have stepped into another world.

No one spared them a glance. Zakaari swept her into the foyer and through the buffet lines spilling out of the dining hall. Heartened by the inattention, Daeya followed him into a side corridor lined with paintings of Syljian men and women, sprawling landscapes, and a city of crystal spires.

"Astenpor," Zakaari said when her attention snagged on the last painting.

Daeya slowed to take it in. The fall of Astenpor had been the Guild's final blow to Old Syljia before its people were scattered to the winds and hunted nearly to extinction on the Eidosinian continent. Staring now at the bridges and buildings of saphyrum-laced stone, the reason why they took it seemed obvious. Ryost had been built in Astenpor's ashes, the remnants of the Crystal Towers drowned in the redirected flow of the Falcon River, and all those beautiful buildings torn down and mined for their saphyrum, silver, and gold.

Simmering anger bubbled to the surface.

"Daeya."

Zakaari gently pried her fingers out of their death grip on his arm.

"I'm sorry."

"It's alright." Quiet curiosity settled in the crease above his brows. "Come on. It's just a little farther."

He took her to the end of the hallway, only crossing paths with a few people going the opposite way. Zakaari stopped to peer around a corner.

The creeping sense he was leading her into some ill-conceived mischief made her heart beat faster. "Zakaari," she whispered, "where are we going?"

Pressing a finger to his lips, Zakaari checked around the corner one last time and beckoned her forward. They slipped down another hallway and arrived at a door no more or less conspicuous than any others.

He waved a glowing hand over the lock, and magic rippled in its wake. A subtle manipulation of the Aether banished the enchantment, and a second spell unlocked the door.

She'd promised Tipori she'd stay out of trouble, but the man's own son was leading her into temptation. The promise of secrets and mischief was simply too great to ignore.

Muted but tasteful decor greeted them. Curtains were drawn to keep out the light, the desk meticulously organized and centered along the far wall. Low bookshelves lined a second wall beneath a mounted sword and shield. A set of plate armor—Light Paladin steel—claimed one corner, and scents of ink and tallow permeated the air.

The last wall held a large portrait flanked by empty sconces. Rather than light them, Zakaari stepped toward the window and drew back the curtains. Rays of light spilled across the painting.

Daeya's entire body went numb.

The purple-skinned man in the portrait stared accusingly back at her, his eyes deep pools of amethyst. He wore a gray soldier's uniform, neatly pressed and covered in medals and ribbons, with a rounded square cap sitting perfectly parallel with the floor over his braided white hair. He stood with a woman wearing a similar hat knocked askew, whose shoulders drowned in a mane of white hair as fierce as her expression. Warrior's runes slashed diagonally across her left eye, and a thin scar traced her right cheekbone.

"This is Koraani's study." She stepped back, her heart in her throat, and groped for the door handle. "I can't be found in here."

Zakaari lifted placating hands. "Wait, Daeya. This will only take a moment."

She shook her head, anger rising in her. "You don't understand. He hates me. We need to leave right now." Her fingers closed on curved metal. Daeya tugged hard and threw the door open. "I can't believe you would jeopardize—"

"The woman in the painting is your mother," he blurted.

"My—" The heavy door slammed into her shoulder. Her eyes darted between Zakaari and the painting. "My mother?"

A new voice spoke up behind her. "*Ciir.*"

"Koraani." Daeya spun to face her uncle, nearly choking on his name. Silonas himself must have cursed her to have such ill luck. "*Amaa*, this isn't what it looks like."

The Alliaansi leader wore a plain white tunic and charcoal trousers, as if in defiance of the holiday. He held a long-stemmed glass of red wine, and a lazy smirk stained his lips. "Isn't it?"

He stepped inside his study, forcing Daeya back toward Zakaari. Caught between the two men, she bristled like a cornered chaagra. Koraani's appearance was too timely to be a coincidence; Zakaari must have set her up.

But why? She thought of her father, of Murtagh, of Ravlok, and all the progress they'd made getting the Alliaansi to trust them. Zakaari knew how much it all meant to her, and one stupid mistake was about to ruin everything.

"It's not." The sting of betrayal was too potent to ignore. "If I'd known—"

"Exactly." Koraani almost sounded remorseful. "That is why I asked him to bring you."

"Why not just ask me to come on my own?"

"Would you have?" When she hesitated, Koraani clicked his tongue. "I didn't think so. At least on solstice, no one will question your being here." He glanced over her head. "Zakaari, I would like a word with my niece."

She stilled.

He didn't say 'the girl' or 'the sorceress.' He didn't even speak with derision. For the first time, Koraani had acknowledged her.

As family.

Zakaari touched her shoulder. "I'll get us something to drink."

All she could do was nod. He kissed her cheek, and a stone formed in her stomach, but she didn't protest his departure. If she'd learned anything about Koraani, it was that he disdained shows of weakness, and begging Zakaari to stay would only wound his already fragile opinion of her.

As the door closed, she planted her feet and clasped her hands, adopting a posture not unlike the severe poise Gregory preferred.

In stark contrast, Koraani relaxed further, as if the wine afforded him the loose-boned fluidity of an alley cat content to rule over his domain.

He broke the silence first. "I never thanked you for participating in Orowen's ceremony."

"Why would you?"

"It took courage." He nodded toward the painting. "I saw your mother in you, that day. Just as I see her now."

Hunger rose in her at that. It was the same feeling she had each time Da spoke of Neri, as when Jerinoch and Orowen told her stories of her parents. Koraani would have a unique perspective on her mother that Daeya wouldn't get anywhere else.

"Will you tell me about her?"

In another stunning first, Koraani smiled at her. "Her favorite color was blue. She loved glazed sweetcakes topped with strawberries, and always favored a palm-heel strike in lieu of a closed fist. Once, she got her whole squadron stuck in mud so deep it took half a day to dig them out. She told me later it was a team-building exercise." He chuckled. "Looking back, I suppose it was."

His laughter brought forth a new lightness in him, tinged with sorrow, that afflicted Daeya, too. "She had a good sense of humor?"

"*Ciir.* It was infuriating at times." Koraani grimaced. "Your mother was a fierce spirit as well. I'm sorry I didn't see it sooner."

"I'm sure it was quite the shock," Daeya offered carefully, "learning you had a niece."

"A niece who was a sorceress, no less."

The remark came without venom, almost as if he were teasing her. She followed his gaze to the portrait, taking in the stubborn set of Nerimoria's jaw, her pinched brows, the barest smirk. "I wish I'd known her."

"I miss her." Pain clouded his gaze. "For nearly eighteen years, I have been searching, seeking answers for what happened."

Daeya shifted on her feet. "My da could tell you some. He and Ma took care of us for a few days before she died. He buried her on his old farm."

Koraani sobered and lifted his chin. "I hear he cleared the capital without incident. The snow has delayed him in the mountains, but he should be here within the month. If you will introduce us, I would tell you more of your mother."

A truce. A chance to know her birth family and reconcile with one of the most influential leaders in Starlight. Daeya seized the opportunity with both hands. "I would like that, *Amaa*."

One corner of Koraani's mouth lifted. "There need only be formality between us in council. Here and elsewhere, you may call me *haalii*."

Uncle.

Daeya swallowed sand and attempted a bow, but the dress forced her into an awkward curtsy. "Thank you, *haalii*."

The word tasted strange on her tongue, but there wasn't a chance in the Wastelands she would refuse him the name if he wanted it.

"It's what she would have wanted." His eyes strayed to the painting and grew distant. "Family was always very important to her."

"I can understand why." It was the whole reason she was here.

"Indeed." Koraani seemed to hear her unspoken thought. He frowned into his wine, then cleared his throat. "You should return to the festival. Enjoy yourself. We will speak more later."

Daeya still had questions, so many questions, but now wasn't the time to press him.

"*Iiren'hyvaa*," she said.

Her use of a Syljian farewell brought forth one last smile—a sight she didn't think she'd ever get used to.

"*Iiren'hyvaa*."

Daeya left Koraani's study in a fog, marveling at what had just occurred. It was a turning point, surely—one that boded well for the weeks and months to come.

She steadied herself against a nearby window and breathed, allowing herself to regroup before going in search of Zakaari. She owed him an apology for her accusation. He'd never earned that kind of suspicion. Facilitating this meeting was one of the kindest things he could have done for her, and she had to tell him how much it meant.

Except, when she descended the stairs and looked toward the sitting room, she found a crowd gathered in the corridor. At its center, Zakaari was pinned against the wall beside the painting of Astenpor, his lips locked on the mouth of another woman.

# Chapter Fifty

## Ravlok

Ravlok escaped Havensguard's festivities with the excuse of delivering food to Orowen. He shuffled through the snow to the Temple's front entrance. The infirmary was crowded when he slipped inside, but the warmth after his long walk was a gift from the divine. He maneuvered around visitors and patients, checking the bundle of food twice to ensure it didn't break open after stray shoulders and elbows jostled him.

Nallia found him searching the crowd for the high priestess. Gray and green beads clinked in her hair. Her dark eyes sparkled, and she held a glass of wine in each hand. "*Iiren'hyvaa*, Ravlok. Care for a drink?"

If he only had room for anything else in his stomach. "No, thank you. I was just looking for Orowen."

Nallia nodded toward the private rooms. "She's still working. Maybe advise her to rest, or come out and enjoy the party. She might listen to you."

It was as the rumors claimed, then. Orowen hadn't stopped working since her reaffirmation.

"I'll do my best."

Ravlok dodged a dozen other attempts at conversation as he threaded through the crowd. He'd never expected to achieve this kind of fame. How did Kendi make this look so easy?

He found Orowen in the room Riisii had occupied. The walls were still marred by carvings, many of which he recognized from his studies of the tome. There were whole sections of this room he could translate now; he'd even begun to record the story of Vintrios for the priestess.

Orowen sat cross-legged, eyes closed, before an altar adorned with incense and holy water. Ravlok placed his bundle on a side table and sat before her, content to wait until she finished.

Her hands weaved sigils so intricate the edges of the magical knots seemed to sink into the Aether before weaving back into the material world—a tapestry that stitched both realms together. The ward was supposed to keep Chaos from breaching Saolanni's temple, making it the safest place in the world for Daeya to complete her ritual.

Only, wards could be broken.

Ravlok shoved the thought aside. Daeya had wards even Ashaara couldn't break. He had to trust that Orowen could build something equally strong to deter a god.

If he wasn't a man of faith, he might have laughed. Ordeolas provided balance even to the greatest extremes, it seemed.

Magic washed over the room, and a flicker of longing rekindled in him. Once, he'd dreamed of possessing magic, as if the arcane could provide the purpose and direction he'd never found with Madame or Laerin's crew. But not even Tiior herself could bestow upon him such a gift, and he'd tried to content himself with protecting Daeya. Now, with the cost so high...

No. He wouldn't consider backing out. She'd chosen him, intentionally or not, and Ravlok would do this for her.

Light faded from Orowen's hands. For several moments, there was no sound, as if the world held its breath. The sigil shimmered away in an evanescent cloud of mist.

An icy wind slashed outward from the sigil's origin point.

Shards of light speared the Aetherial Wall. All along those arcs, the web strained like a seam stretched to bursting. A keening wail sounded through the rushing wind, and Ravlok tensed, ready to launch himself into movement. Toward what, he didn't know.

The room returned to an eerie calm. Ravlok blinked away scarlet and rubbed at the oily feeling on his skin.

Orowen pressed her face into her hands. Her sniffle pierced him right in the heart.

The ward had failed.

Uncertainty constricted the words of comfort in his throat. What could he say, anyway? Encouragement felt hollow, and pressuring her to keep trying as she had for weeks would only amount to frustration.

He shifted onto his knees. Ravlok didn't bestow blessings often, but it was something he'd practiced with Yonfé. He dipped his hands into the holy water, then rubbed his fingers into the ashes of incense blown about the altar. Cleansing fire was Tiior's symbol and ash was fire's remnant, so a blessing with the goddess of knowledge in mind would have to do.

"Tiior, daughter of Order, goddess divine," Ravlok began. Orowen wiped her face and looked up. "I invoke your blessing of knowledge so all that is unknown may become known as befits your will." Sleeves trailing water, ash clinging to his skin, he reached out to draw Tiior's flame upon Orowen's forehead. Her eyes closed again.

Ravlok dipped his hands a second time. "I beg for your blessing of wisdom, so peace may be found where hope has faltered, and clarity may come to a quiet mind." He drew the draconic rune for tranquility—two diamonds superimposed over a circle—on her left cheek. Already, she seemed calmer, her shoulders drooping as the tension left her.

"I ask for your blessing of strength, bestowed upon Saolanni's servant, so she may weave the mighty dragon scale that shields our hearts and minds from Chaos." Three dragon scales glistened on her right cheek.

Ravlok sat back. "May Tiior's radiant fire consume your doubts, Devoted."

"Thank you, servant of Ordeolas." Her voice was thick with emotion.

"Your acolytes demand that you rest." He smirked. "I suggest you stop being so stubborn."

A weak laugh rasped out of her. "Chaos never rests, I'm afraid. He's built his web so thick, I can't get any wards to hold." She looked stricken, her eyes shadowed by dark circles. "I may not be strong enough—"

"You are."

*You have to be.*

Orowen dropped her gaze. "I hope you're right."

Ravlok pushed to his feet and offered his hand. "But you'd be stronger after a nap."

With a heartier chuckle, she allowed him to help her up. "*Ciir*, Devoted," she teased.

He grinned and tucked her hand under his arm. He'd helped move her belongings into a spare room at the Temple for her year of self-confinement and service following her oath. Ravlok reclaimed the food from the table and escorted her there without delay.

"Oh, a package arrived for you this morning." Orowen halted outside her room and took the bundle. "I suspect you'll want to be in charge of it. Wait here."

The door squeaked open, and a sparsely furnished room with a messy bed and one cluttered table flashed into view before she disappeared inside. Orowen emerged a moment later with a tiny brown package.

It settled into his hands with the weight of destiny.

Ravlok swallowed hard. He didn't have to pull those twine knots apart to know what was inside. Drawing breath became as great a feat as lifting a carriage off his chest.

Before now, his task had been frightening, but he could rationalize every step. It was a process that could be broken down and studied. Now that the reality was upon him, he regretted the fullness of his stomach. The corridor swam and he squeezed his eyes shut to stop the walls from spinning.

Warm fingers closed on his arm. When he opened his eyes, Orowen's frown sewed her white brows together. "Are you alright, *neime*? You look pale."

He willed his quaking aura to stillness with a series of calming breaths. "I'm fine. Thank you, Devoted."

"Are you lightheaded?" She rose on tiptoe to feel his forehead.

"I was a little, but I'm okay now."

"How much solstice punch have you had? You wouldn't be the first to suffer from Jerinoch's recipe."

Distracted by the package in his hands, Ravlok almost missed her humor. "I'm alright. Really."

"At least let me send you off with some cannaberry tea." When he started to protest, she took his arm again and steered him toward the sanctuary. "Just in case."

There was no deterring a healer who had already decided on a treatment plan. Ravlok allowed himself to be led. Cannaberries also caused drowsiness, and he wasn't against a sleeping tonic that would allow him to dodge the rest of the solstice celebration.

Only, the sounds of festivities in the main hall had changed. There was no more laughter, and friendly chatter had been exchanged for hushed, urgent tones. Ravlok tucked away his package and shared a look with Orowen. She frowned and quickened her pace.

Tipori stood at the center of a panicked ring of patients, acolytes, and visitors, directing them with a voice of steel. He supported a half-conscious guard in dark green livery, while two more guards lay in wheelbarrows beside them. One bore a swollen head wound and the other had a crossbow bolt protruding from his knee.

"...and send runners," Tipori commanded the nearest healer. "I want every lift shut down immediately. No one in or out until we find them."

The crowd parted for Orowen as she strode toward him. Ravlok followed in her wake, unease tickling the back of his throat.

"What's going on, *Amaa*?" Orowen asked.

"Someone attacked our guards stationed at the pits." Tipori relinquished his charge to an acolyte. The air around him wavered like a pond disturbed by a strong wind. "Jack Orrin and Anwic Inillios have escaped."

All the blood drained from Ravlok's face.

Tipori's steely gaze settled on him. "Where is Daeya? She may be in danger."

# CHAPTER FIFTY-ONE

## DAEYA

Hurt stabbed deep between Daeya's shoulder blades. Zakaari had only been away for a few minutes. She'd known she wasn't his only interest. She'd known what she was getting into. They might have attended the solstice together, but they weren't *together*. She shouldn't be upset he'd found one of his lovers to distract himself—one that would give him what he so obviously wanted.

*If you want to hold Zakaari's interest for more than a fortnight...*

Jessie's assertion soured the wine in Daeya's stomach, and her hand tightened on the railing. She wouldn't allow this to break her. This was nothing compared to Gregory's torment, Alar's trickery, or Ashaara's psionics. She wouldn't allow him a single shred of her heart—

Zakaari wrenched his mouth away, growling. "Cirra, stop—"

"Shut up and kiss me, Ari." Cirra released his wrinkled doublet and grabbed him by the chin. Shadows pooled in the trenches left by her nails against his cheek. "I know it's what you want."

She pressed her body flush against his, and he put both palms flat against her shoulders to push her away. One of her hands disappeared between them. The small circle of onlookers tittered with laughter, egging Cirra on. Zakaari winced and started to speak, but her mouth smothered his attempts with another kiss.

The memory of Joss touching her in a similar way ignited rage so bright, Daeya saw red. Her voice carried over the din. "Get your hands off him."

Faces turned, both amused and uncertain. Some quietly slunk away with their drinks. Daeya stormed down the stairs, and the crowd parted as if her skin radiated flame. Zakaari had pulled away again and was trying to uncurl Cirra's fingers from his shirt.

"Let go, Cirra." He glanced Daeya's way, his ear tips darkening.

Cirra held fast, turning her scathing glare on Daeya. "Get lost, *ashaan*. Can't you see we're busy?"

Daeya chuckled at the half-blood slur. The subtle recognition of her parentage prompted ripples in the crowd like a stone skipping over the surface of a lake. "It's good to see I've moved up in the world." She stepped closer, keeping her hands deliberately loose at her sides. "Now, he asked you nicely. Let. Him. Go."

A saccharine smile spread across the Syljian's face. Her golden earrings flashed. "You obviously haven't bedded him if you don't know what he likes yet." Her hand cupped him between his legs again, provoking another wince.

Zakaari averted his eyes. "Stop."

The tremor in his voice inflamed Daeya further. He could have extracted himself with ease, given the way he could fight. Why wasn't he standing up for himself?

The memory of how she'd frozen at Joss's hands surged forward, and Daeya tasted bile. She eyed the crowd surrounding them. Were they really content to stand by and let this happen? "He obviously doesn't like that. Let go of him. *Now.*"

Cirra rolled her eyes. "This is a game we play. One you'd better learn if you want to compete with the rest of us."

Zakaari's face darkened. He shoved her hand away. "She doesn't have to compete with you."

The implication behind that statement, more than the returning strength in his voice, gave Daeya pause.

Cirra rounded on him, open-mouthed. "You'd choose the carrion feeder over your own kind?"

He squared his shoulders, a storm building as he reclaimed mastery over himself. "I would choose five minutes with her over a lifetime with anyone else."

Daeya's heart stuttered. She touched a hand to her bodice as murmurs filled the corridor behind her.

Cirra recoiled. "You don't mean that." Her painted upper lip curled. "Ari—"

Zakaari pushed past her. His warm fingers interlocked with Daeya's, and his body formed a protective wall as he tugged her toward the edge of the crowd. "Come on, McVen. Let's go."

His scent enveloped her. She looked up into his face, searching for something, but uncertain exactly what. Zakaari kept his gaze forward, glaring at anyone who didn't clear the way fast enough.

Once they'd made it outside, he led her around the building and off the main paths into the snow. In the shadow of a twisted evergreen, he took her face in his hands. Daeya started at the tears in his eyes.

"I'm so sorry you had to see that. It must have been the wine. She's not usually so—"

"Don't you dare apologize for her. What she did to you was wrong." A disturbing thought occurred to her when he cast his gaze to the side. "You know that, right? Male or female, it doesn't matter."

"I know."

"Then why tolerate it? At least report her or something."

He grimaced. "It's embarrassing. Please, can we just drop it?"

Daeya pressed her lips together and nodded grudgingly. Gods knew she never would have told Gregory about Joss.

Zakaari ran a hand through his hair. "That sort of threw a wet blanket over everything, didn't it?" He sighed. "I should take you home."

"I don't want to go home."

But the chagrined look Zakaari shot in the general direction of the festival told her he wasn't ready to face the rest of Starlight. Word of his humiliation would spread like sickness.

Daeya took stock of the sun's position and fashioned a playful grin.

"You know…" She slipped her hands into his again. "You still owe me a trip to Sundance Falls."

Technically, she still wasn't allowed off the plateau, but they would probably get there and back before anyone noticed they were gone.

It took work, but the allure of mischief coaxed a smile from him. "I haven't forgotten." Zakaari wiped his eyes. "We'll want to change, first."

She nodded. "Lead the way."

They were fifty paces from the base of Starlight Plateau, the snowy treeline growing taller with every step, when the cliff lift operator called out, "Hey! You there! Wait a minute—"

Daeya stiffened, but Zakaari tugged her on, grinning. "Faster. Don't look back."

She returned the grin and quickened her pace, feet sliding on packed snow. They'd both changed into dark tunics, trousers, and thick cloaks. Simply raising their hoods had gotten them this far, and Zakaari had assured her the guards wouldn't look twice at them on solstice.

"Hey! Wait!"

So much for that.

Hoofbeats sounded, and a bolt of fear cut through her, but Zakaari's defiant laughter banished the feeling as swiftly as it came. Her own laugh burst from her. They set off for the forest at a run, their cloaks snapping behind them.

"Stop!"

Zakaari kept firm hold of her hand and tore off his glove with his teeth. "Get ready to jump."

Her eyes snapped toward him. "What?"

He summoned a sphere of energy and hurled it in front of them. It broke through the Wall like a tiffleball through glass, opening a rift four paces away. Three, then two. One.

"Jump!"

Daeya jumped.

Light and color streaked by, the tang of Aether thick in her nostrils and bitter against her tongue. Her scream of mingled victory and terror disappeared into the void, swept away by the fierce current of magic hurtling them through space.

They tumbled out of an exit rift, still carrying the same momentum. It sent them rolling down a slope, and they crashed to a stop in a snowdrift as deep Daeya was tall. She lay there dazed, staring up at the jagged edge of the snowbank and the gnarled trees clawing into the sky. The sounds of hooves and angry lift workers were farther off, replaced by her ragged breathing and the creak of compressed snow.

A shift of Zakaari's body beneath her brought the rest of the looming snowdrift cascading down. He wrapped both arms around her and threw her sideways, rolling clear. Daeya came to a stop on top of him, sheltering her face in his neck.

Zakaari's laughter rumbled through her chest. His husky voice filled her ears. "Got you."

Every part of her became acutely aware of every part of him. Wherever their bodies touched, embers sparked and threatened to ignite. Magic more potent than draegion fire burned through her veins.

She looked into his eyes. "Got me."

Zakaari's lips parted. Conflict and questions danced in his expression. He brushed his fingertips across her jawline, up to her ear.

Daeya's own questions begged to leap forth, to demand an explanation for what he'd said to Cirra, but she couldn't form the words. Not when his touch left trails of static across her face. Her gloved hand splayed against his chest. Through wool and linen, his heart pounded almost as hard as hers.

Voices broke the stillness. "I saw a flash over this way."

"They can't have gotten far."

"Chaos curse that boy. Tipori's going to kill us."

With no small effort, Daeya extracted herself from Zakaari and sat back on her heels. Surely, their little outing wasn't that serious. She'd already sworn herself to the Alliaansi's cause. If Tipori really thought she would try to escape, he wouldn't have taught her Aetherian magic or petitioned to have her binders removed. He trusted her, and the last thing she wanted was to break that trust.

"Maybe we shouldn't—"

Zakaari's lopsided smile turned devious. He retrieved his glove from the snow, then rose, pulling her up beside him. "I'll take care of *Peiaa*. Don't worry."

Snow crunched somewhere off in the trees, signaling a sentry's approach. Daeya pressed closer to Zakaari, nodding silent acquiescence. After all, if they were already in trouble, they might as well enjoy themselves before begging forgiveness.

Zakaari pulled her flush against him and produced a bead of saphyrum. "We'll Bend a few times and lose them. Just hold on to me."

"Okay."

As if she was going to complain about those instructions. She wrapped an arm around him.

Zakaari tossed the bead into his mouth and swallowed. The first rift flashed open as movement caught Daeya's eye. A short-haired Syljian woman—Alar's friend Finn—strode from the trees.

Her scowl could have melted all the snow in the north. "Ari, wait. Your father has ordered y—"

Zakaari tugged Daeya into the Aether. She didn't have time to ponder what Finn had been about to say before Zakaari rifted again, and again in quick succession. Without sigils, he could Bend so fast she wasn't even sure how he could lock onto an exit point between rifts. The dizzying thrill of not knowing where they might land mingled with the terror of Bending into a tree or a rock and eviscerating themselves. Her stomach rolled with every lurching rift, until she dropped to the snow overlooking a valley of white mist. Zakaari fell beside her, his expression stuck somewhere between dazed euphoria and reeling sickness.

At least that made two of them.

He flopped onto his back, chest heaving. Daeya waited until she was sure her lunch wouldn't end up painting the snow before she crawled the short distance between them and looked down. "Are you alright?"

He grinned up at her. "That was incredible. I've never rifted this far so fast."

Her shoulders shook with laughter. "You're absolutely insane."

Zakaari tugged his glove back on and put one hand behind his head as if he planned to lounge in the snow for the rest of the afternoon. "You've met my sister. That shouldn't surprise you."

"Careful. I happen to like Riisii."

"I guess that makes us both crazy."

Cheeks aching with her smile, she took in their surroundings. They'd rifted onto a rocky outcropping, uncomfortably close to the edge of a cliff and a sharp drop into the misty valley below. Barren trees and snowy evergreens marched away in all directions to similar rises in the distance. Starlight Plateau was much farther to the southeast than she expected, and the northwestern horizon was a jagged array of snow-smothered mountains.

"Do you know where we are?"

"*Ciir.*" Zakaari sat up and pointed into the valley. "The falls are about an hour down that rise. We rifted through the worst of the hike, but I can't Bend us safely through the mist."

"What causes it?" There was something familiar about it, but she'd never seen its like in Eidosinia.

"Hot springs." He pointed to the mountains on the horizon. "Mount Eisekii is there, a few days' ride to the northwest. It creates all the volcanic activity in the area. Steam vents on the north end mark the Alliaansi border with Mautor. There's a place on the south side of the In'Jasuu made impassable by mud pools and geysers."

"The In'Jasuu?" The Shattered Mountains. Daeya's eyes widened. "I didn't realize we were that far north."

Zakaari smirked. "If we're lucky, we'll see the aurora tonight. They say seeing one on the solstice means you'll find love in the year to come."

It wasn't the thought of the aurora that made her return his smile.

Her eyes traced the peak of Mount Eisekii. It, too, felt familiar. The shape of it was seared into her memory as clearly as Da's profile. She knew this place. She knew these mountains and the air currents that flowed around them. Places to avoid. Places that would lift her high above the clouds with a single beat of her wings—

A powerful tug on her mind pulled her toward that mountain. Ash coated her tongue, and smoke stung her nostrils.

Zakaari cringed. "That was too much, wasn't it?"

Her senses shot back into her body. She seized his wrist to keep him from rising. "And what if you've already found it?"

Stillness settled over him as he knelt in the snow. Wind blew his dark hair over his face. His violet eyes, made luminescent by his use of magic, searched hers. "It's still a good sign, I think."

She swallowed the taste of ash. "Did you mean what you said to Cirra?"

He didn't hesitate. "*Ciir.*"

Daeya hadn't dared to hope, but now it was all she could do not to throw herself into his arms. "What about the others? What will they think?"

A knowing look, bordering on sheepish, lifted the corners of his mouth. "There aren't any others. Not anymore."

It made sense. He'd stopped running off at the first sign of sunset. Women no longer frequented the training hall to fan themselves over his lack of dress. He even found reasons to meet with her earlier and stay longer every day.

Her heart lodged in her throat. "Why not?"

He gently extracted his wrist from her and took her hand. Their bulky gloves kept their palms from touching, but the pressure of his fingers was enough to anchor her in this moment. To remind her this was real.

"Because I'm waiting for someone else."

The words crashed into her, forcing her eyes to close. Zakaari could have had anyone he wanted; why would he settle for a runaway Guild sorceress?

"As it turns out," he continued, enunciating each syllable as if to banish all doubt, "I've been waiting for her for a long time."

"Zakaari." Her throat was so tight, his name came out a whisper. "I want to be with you. But I'm afraid I can't share you with anyone else."

Tears welled in his eyes. "You'll never have to, I promise."

"But you've always had others. If that makes you happy—"

"It doesn't. I thought that lifestyle was right for me, but it's not." He touched her chin. "Not if it costs me a single moment with you."

He could change his mind. Daeya couldn't ignore that thought, but she didn't voice it either. She studied him for a long time. "If you would choose me, I would choose you, too."

The tension in his brow softened, and he blinked once, long and slow. "May I kiss you?"

She nodded eagerly. "Please."

Zakaari tugged her into his arms and cupped her face. His lips were soft but insistent, and the feel of them coaxed little whimpers of need from her as he deepened the kiss. Light and color exploded behind her eyelids, rivaling the aurora itself.

When they finally broke apart, Daeya gasped.

Zakaari pressed his forehead to hers. "I love you, Daeya."

Tears flowed freely down her face. "Are you sure?"

He laughed. "Yes, you ridiculous woman. You're perfect for me in every way."

Overwhelmed, she kissed him again, so hard it forced him onto his arse. He grinned against her lips and held her tightly. Never, in all her dreams, had she imagined hearing those words from someone else. She sobbed into their kiss, climbed into his lap, desperate to be closer, the fabric between them be damned. Daeya rained more kisses on his lips, and he chased each one down like snowflakes on his tongue.

To separate herself enough to speak was agony. "I love you, too."

# CHAPTER FIFTY-TWO

## RAVLOK

Ravlok met Sam and Niam at the top of the Temple steps. Stones settled in his gut at the crestfallen look on the Syljian girl's face.

"They weren't at the orphanage or the stables," Sam said. She fell into step beside him. Niam trailed at their heels. "Whatever happened at Baani'anii must have really spooked them."

Rumors swirled around the attack inside Koraani's home. Ravlok had started his search there since it was the last place anyone had seen Daeya. A few people claimed she'd punched one of Zakaari's girlfriends in the face after finding them kissing in a hallway. Others claimed Tipori's son had been assaulted, and he'd fled the house with Daeya in tow.

The former seemed more likely, but the girlfriend in question hadn't appeared injured, and Ravlok himself had taught Daeya how to throw a punch.

"They didn't return to Havensguard." He yanked the door open harder than he intended, drawing the attention of several healers and patients.

A gentle hand touched his arm. Ravlok looked down. "Yes, Niam?"

She glanced toward Sam, already halfway to where Orowen and Kendi were speaking quietly in one corner. Niam sighed and looked back at Ravlok. She drew two fingers around her neck and down to her chest, following the path a necklace might make. Then she flicked one pointed ear, drew the shape of a box, and pointed to herself.

Ravlok frowned.

He'd seen Daeya communicate with Niam through signs like this. She'd once mentioned an ear flick was her designation for Zakaari. "I'm sorry. Can you repeat that?"

She did. Then, she repeated them once more, even slower. Ravlok focused on the first sign. A necklace? A pendant?

"Daeya," he realized. She was using Daeya's pendant as her name sign.

Niam nodded enthusiastically and flicked her ear.

"And Zakaari."

Another nod. She repeated the square and pointed to herself, then started toward the door and stopped, looking back at him.

"I think she wants to check the town square, *neime*," Orowen called from across the room.

Ravlok shot her a grateful look. "Is that it?" he asked Niam.

She nodded.

"Good idea." He waved her toward the door. "If you find her, send her back here immediately."

Niam curtsied and hurried out the door. Ravlok joined the others and saluted Kendi. "Commander. Any news?"

"*Ciir.*" Kendi grimaced. "Jack and Anwic had help." He nodded toward the one conscious guard of the three who'd been brought in. "Marvos says he was hit from behind by a figure shrouded in black. When he woke up, his fellows were all unconscious, and the cell grates were left open."

Ravlok's hands rolled into fists. There was no chance they'd resolve this swiftly. Even if they caught Jack and Anwic, there was still someone else out there who posed a threat to Daeya. Ever since Jack's outburst here at the Temple, their search for Chaos priests had become more of a witch hunt. Fingers pointed in all directions, and left the real dangers disguised.

The Temple doors opened again, and a shaft of late afternoon sunlight speared the floor. Tipori stormed in and beckoned them to the private rooms beyond the infirmary without breaking stride.

Ravlok shared a glance with the others, then made to follow.

"Zakaari and Daeya left the plateau right as the lifts shut down," Tipori said once they had all filed into Riisii's old room and closed the door.

Ravlok blew out a breath, certain Silonas himself must have had a hand in that good fortune. If Daeya couldn't return to the plateau and Jack and Anwic couldn't leave, that meant she was safe. "Thank the gods."

Tipori's granite-hewn face cracked. "I wouldn't thank them yet."

"But they can't get to her," Sam asserted. "With the lifts down, Jack and Anwic might as well be trapped on an island."

"I'm afraid not. Before I commissioned the construction of the cliff lifts, the Alliaansi used a hidden staircase carved in the rock. I posted sentries at both ends, but someone has already disabled the wardstones on the top side. The lower wards are still in place, but we can't rule out someone resetting them to throw us off."

The oversight—the Chaos-begotten *negligence*—made Ravlok bristle. "You mean there's another entrance to Starlight, and you didn't have it guarded?"

"At ease, soldier." Kendi's veiled warning didn't placate him in the least. "We didn't leave it unprotected."

"The lower entrance is shrouded by illusions and natural rock formations," Tipori explained. "A guard would have called undue attention to the spot. Neither side can be opened except by powerful aethermancy."

Ravlok frowned. "So whoever is working with Chaos's agents has to be an aethermancer."

It didn't reduce their potential suspects nearly enough. There were hundreds of aethermancers in the Fifth Legion alone, and after all the adversity they'd faced over the years, plenty had seen enough trauma to leave them open to Chaos.

That left only one option that made sense to Ravlok. He addressed Tipori. "You can give her temporary access to her magic, right? By manipulating her spellbinders?"

Tipori eyed him warily. "I can."

"From a distance?"

"*Ciir.*"

Hope sparked in Ravlok's chest. "Then you have to. It's her best chance if Chaos gets to them first."

"Chaos priests, you mean." Tipori shook his head. "But that's a risk I can't take. Not while she's running loose outside Starlight. Magnus has already demanded she be detained for breaking her agreement—"

"Delvin take the agreement!" Ravlok's face flushed hot. "You're a gods-damned moron if you let that stand in the way of Daeya's safety."

"Ravlok!" Kendi's eyes went wide.

Sam cringed, and Orowen covered her mouth. Tipori recoiled, blinking as if he'd been struck.

Ravlok wasn't finished. "She's your people's best hope for survival. She's willing to lead entire *storms* of dragons in your defense! If she dies because you had the power to help her and chose not to, then maybe you deserve what's coming to you."

Stunned silence greeted him in return. Tipori's mouth hung open until Orowen stepped closer.

"Ravlok is right, *neime*. She's proven her loyalty enough. Zakaari may be able to protect her, but if he's up against even one Chaos priest, his odds are better with her help." She smiled as Tipori's expression softened. "And really, you don't think Kendi noticed you taking over the *fursaan* to teach her magic every day? Don't think of this as any different."

Odes of Ordeolas, was that embarrassment darkening the Aetherian's ear tips? Some of Ravlok's anger cooled. Leave it to Orowen to know just how to cut the man down to size.

Tipori dipped his head and closed his eyes. He uttered a few words and Aetherial mist bloomed between his palms. A beat later, the open cuffs formed solid and gleaming in his hands. Snow crusted one edge, but it melted quickly against Tipori's skin. He stared at the binders a long moment.

"You're a wiser man than I, Ravlok." His fingers curled around the metal. "Let's just pray she doesn't need it."

Ravlok trailed after Niam to the town square, where the darkening night and the press of bodies made searching for anyone impossible. But with the lower wards on the secret stairs still in place, he couldn't help the nagging sense that Jack and Anwic were still in the city.

The square was nestled between the council hall, a row of communal houses, and the eastern community garden. He maneuvered toward a natural ledge overlooking the sea of braids and hooded capes.

Ravlok mounted the snowy steps carved into the ledge and squinted into the torchlight. Certain neither Jack nor Anwic would move about unmasked, he searched for figures hunkering in shadows or lingering near the edges of the celebration.

Someone tugged his cloak sleeve.

He turned, expecting Niam. She wouldn't have heard the news about Daeya, and the last thing she needed was a run-in with a Chaos priest. "You should go back to—"

The face staring up at him wasn't Niam's. Puffy, red-rimmed eyes stared out of a Syljian girl's face. Half-frozen tears streaked her dark cheeks. "Soldier, please can you help me?"

She could barely get the words out through her chattering teeth. Her cloak was little more than rags patched together, and her hair hung limply about her shoulders.

Ravlok pulled off his cloak, ignoring the blast of cold, and knelt to wrap it around the girl.

"What's wrong, little one?"

She sniffled. "I can't find my *miaa*."

The poor thing. Lost on a day like this, surrounded by all these people. Ravlok tucked the cloak tighter about her and looked around. None of the passersby noticed the missing child, and no panic-stricken faces suggested anyone nearby was looking for her.

He couldn't leave her alone with two trained killers on the loose. "What's your name?"

"Aadra, *Amaa*."

"Where do you live, Aadra?"

"That way, I think." She pointed between two communal houses. "We live in a tent."

One of the northern tent cities, he guessed, assuming she hadn't gotten turned around. Though Starlight wasn't as big as Ryost, the journey across town in the snow could be dangerous without proper clothing, and the temperature was dropping fast. The Temple would be a safe place to take her, and perhaps Sam or Orowen would recognize the child.

"I'm going to get you home, okay? But first we're going to visit Saolanni's temple. The high priestess will get you some food and warmer clothes. Maybe some hot cider, too. Would you like that?"

She sniffled again. "I want *Miaa*."

"I know. We'll find her." So many of Starlight's children had grown to fear even a well-meaning stranger's touch. He settled for gently squeezing her shoulders, then rose and offered his hand. "Maybe we can look for her on the way."

"She said to stay by *Amaa* Clem's house." Some of the strength returned to her voice. She took his hand without hesitation and tugged him toward the narrow space between buildings. "Maybe she's still there."

Ravlok frowned, but he let Aadra drag him along. Snow rose up past her knees in places where paths hadn't been carved, but she trudged doggedly on, tears forgotten. Uncertain which house was the blacksmith's, Ravlok forced her to slow.

"Aadra, where is Clem's house?"

"Just a little farther."

She turned off the lantern-lit roads and tried to steer him down a path between two greenhouses. Ravlok planted his feet and stared into the near-darkness. Sounds of revelry filtered through the walls of distant buildings, but none of the gardeners would be on the grounds tonight. There was no reason the girl's mother would have come this way.

Aadra tugged again. "This way."

"It's getting late," he countered. "We should get back to the Temple before they run out of pastries."

The girl turned, her lips pulling back in a snarl.

Ravlok recoiled. Gods spare him—he'd blundered into a trap.

Footsteps crunched in the snow behind him. He wrenched his hand from Aadra's and stumbled over a drift, falling to one knee. A blade passed within fingerspans of his scalp.

Ravlok didn't think, didn't hesitate. He threw himself into his assailant's knees and knocked the black-clad figure flat. Another shadow detached from the corner of a building. The slighter figure kicked him, but Ravlok pinned their ankle and rolled, dropping them onto his first assailant.

Ravlok reached for the dagger in his belt, but Aadra launched herself onto his back. Her hooked fingers gouged his cheeks, barely missing his eyes. He turned with her until her back struck the ground. The girl yelped as his weight crushed the wind from her.

Her grip on his face fell away. Ravlok scrambled up and drew his weapon, backing toward the greenhouses.

Two attackers, plus the girl. None had used magic, but he couldn't discount it. At least the larger figures didn't move with the instincts of fighters. His dagger's reassuring weight kept his nerves steady.

Metal pricked his lower back. "Give us the book, *bashiin*."

Ice slid down Ravlok's spine.

Anwic.

Outnumbered and on treacherous terrain, Ravlok swallowed his heart and glanced behind him at Kendi's former second-in-command. There was no sign of Jack, but the assassin could have a crossbow trained on him from the roof of any nearby building.

The other two figures disentangled themselves with uttered curses. Aadra still clutched her tiny chest on the ground. If he had any chance at all, it was now.

Ravlok lifted his hands as if to surrender. "I have to summon it first."

"Then do it." Anwic reached for the dagger to disarm him.

Before Anwic's hand closed on the hilt, Ravlok let his weapon slip from his fingers. He caught it in his opposite hand, spun, and plunged it into Anwic's side.

Anwic stumbled, but he snagged Ravlok's tunic on the way down. They hit the snow and rolled, grappling for the upper hand. Ravlok snarled as he came to a stop facing the night sky. Cold seeped into his back, and the weight on his chest pressed air from his lungs. He fought to keep Anwic's knife from sinking into his shoulder. Black, tarry fluid coated the metal. Poison? Whatever happened, he couldn't let him score a hit with that blade.

Ravlok's dagger still jutted from Anwic's torso, pinning his cloak to his side. Ravlok used the extra tension to wrench the fabric sideways.

Anwic was prepared for it. He drove his forearm into Ravlok's throat, cutting off his airway. The tip of that poisoned blade dipped toward his face.

"The book, *bashiin*."

Vision darkening, Ravlok attempted every hold-breaking technique he knew. But new weight came to rest on his legs and extra hands pinned him down. He raged against Baosanni's call, even as his body weakened.

This couldn't be how he died. He still had so much to do.

"Alright," he choked out. "Alright!"

Pressure lifted from his trachea. Anwic's sneer was made of pure malevolence.

Silonas willing, this would work.

Anwic pressed the dagger against Ravlok's throat. The two figures seated on his feet remained out of sight, and the little girl was still standing watch at the corner of the nearest building.

"Make it fast." Anwic couldn't disguise the wince of pain from the dagger in his side.

Ravlok held up both hands and swallowed against the knife. He had no magic, but he had the magic of knowledge. Eyes fixing on a point high above Anwic's head, he spoke the word that summoned the book.

"*Asokhovha.*"

Black mist coalesced in that spot, and Ravlok could have wept with relief.

"What is that?" one figure asked.

The pressure of the knife's edge lessened in Anwic's distraction. Ravlok seized his wrist in both hands and pulled downward, drawing the blade from his throat. He smashed his forehead into Anwic's nose at the same moment the Tome of Eolaan crashed down on the man's head.

A sickening crunch and a spray of blood preceded the cry that echoed off stone and glass. The tome tumbled into a drift, and one of the assailants holding his feet lunged for it.

Still holding the knife away from his neck, Ravlok dug his thumb into the nerve cluster near Anwic's wrist. His fingers went slack, and Ravlok snatched the dagger up, thrusting the point under the man's ribcage. Forcing him to one side, Ravlok wrenched the other dagger out of Anwic's flank and threw it into the attacker still pinning his right leg. They fell backward with a strangled gurgle.

Anwic slumped to the snow.

The figure holding the tome backed away.

"What are you waiting for?" Aadra hissed. "Grab him!"

Ravlok struggled back to his feet. He eyed the black figure with the tome, calculating his chances of immobilizing this one for questioning.

Multiple pairs of footsteps crunched through the snow. A smaller shadow darted from behind the greenhouses.

"Hurry u—" Aadra's demand cut off.

Ravlok started to turn, but froze when the figure before him bellowed a war cry, lifted the tome, and charged.

"*Asokhovha.*" Ravlok banished the tome and braced himself for battle.

The smaller shadow intercepted his attacker as the book vanished into mist. Wind whistled, and a weighty, metallic *gong* rang out. Ravlok sidestepped as his assailant dropped to the ground and lay still.

A familiar figure stood in the attacker's place. Panting hard, she lowered the shovel and met his eyes with an intensity that left Ravlok gaping.

"Niam?"

"Secure the area." Kendi's voice. "I want this whole neighborhood locked down."

"*Let me go!*" Aadra screamed.

Goosebumps traveled down Ravlok's spine, but he couldn't take his eyes from Niam. The fierceness in her expression ebbed the longer he stared, until finally she swallowed and looked down.

Kendi was closer now. "And someone send for a healer."

Ravlok was about to reach for Niam, to thank her, when the commander gripped his shoulder. "Are you hurt, *amii*?"

Others rounded the corner, bearing torches that exposed the extent of their battle in the snow. Anwic lay in a bloody pool at his feet.

Ravlok finally found his voice. "Their blades are likely poisoned. They nearly got me."

"We're fortunate they didn't." Kendi looked at Niam. "Good work, *neime*."

Niam planted the shovel on the ground and curtsied as Kendi excused himself.

The ladylike gesture was so ludicrous in the aftermath of battle that Ravlok laughed. "Remind me never to make you angry."

Her only response was a sheepish smile and a subtle darkening of her cheeks.

# Chapter Fifty-Three

## Daeya

As twilight descended over the valley, the cliffs down which the Taaru'Kallii tumbled came alive with dazzling color. Steam from the hot springs and mist from the falls caught fading rays of sunlight, scattering them into brilliant rainbows that arched over the vale. It was no wonder the Sundance Falls were Zakaari's favorite place in all the Northlands.

Daeya rested her head on his shoulder, relishing how her scalp tingled with the brush of his fingertips through her hair. She sighed, letting her eyes drift closed.

"You like that?" he asked.

"Mm." She grinned and laced her fingers with his. The spring-heated rock beneath them provided enough warmth for them to remove their gloves. "Almost as much as this."

"Even more than oranges?"

"Now, let's not get ahead of ourselves."

A throaty chuckle rumbled out of him. He tilted her chin up and kissed her. Daeya splayed her fingers against his chest and surrendered her mouth to his.

"Gods help me, I'll never get tired of kissing you." He came up for air long enough to murmur the words and run his hand over her flushed cheek before gently reclaiming her lips.

Daeya's heart fluttered against her ribs. His kisses left her lightheaded. She wanted to feel his skin beneath her hands. She wanted his fingers to skate across her shoulders, arms, and chest like they skimmed through her hair.

Breathlessly, she pulled her mouth from his. "Zakaari."

"*Ciir, nei ama're?*"

"There's something you should know."

He pulled back and examined her face. She bit her lip.

His thumb just as quickly extracted it. "What is it?"

How to prepare him for all the ways Lucius Gregory had mutilated her body? How to explain that beneath her clothes, Zakaari wouldn't find some unmarked beauty like his other partners, but a tapestry of scars whose purpose far surpassed her understanding? It had been her secret for so long. What if she was too broken? What if he thought her scars so ugly that he didn't want her anymore?

Pressure mounted behind her eyes, and her excuses and explanations crowded up against the knot in her throat.

His expression folded. "What's wrong?"

Wiping her eyes with her sleeve, she drew a shaky breath. "There was a sorcerer who—"

A soft *snick* traveled up Daeya's forearms. She paused, looking down as the spellbinders fell from her wrists. One slipped deeper into her sleeve, while the other hit the stone, bounced twice, and rolled into the snow.

The metal cuffs burst into Aetherial mist.

"What—"

Whatever Daeya was about to say was swallowed beneath a sea of arcane power so intense it crushed the air from her lungs. The faint tug on her senses she'd felt hours ago wrenched at her mind like a riptide. She caught herself on the stone and squeezed her eyes shut.

Memories of fire and destruction, smoke and ash, flickered by so fast that she couldn't lock onto any of them. She seized on familiar threads of magic to keep herself afloat, and they snapped taut like an anchor snagging the ocean floor.

Dragon scales glinted in the light of molten stone. A body unfurled from massive snout to whip-like tail, responding to her presence in his mind. Leathery wings stirred volcanic air so hot it was like trying to breathe in lava.

Slitted eyes gleamed like pools of luminescent gold, and thunder rumbled in the distance.

*"Come,* Nashanett.*"*

Stone shook beneath her feet. *"Telerion."*

*"Come, and face me."*

The call to battle was as fire raging through the undergrowth. *"I hear you."*

Gold sparked at her fingertips, the pull so strong that she didn't remember rising, didn't remember lifting her hands to cast—

"Something's wrong." Zakaari's voice barely reached her through the roar reverberating through her mind. "We have to get back."

She spoke, but not in the trade tongue nor in Syljian. Guttural and sibilant sounds rolled out of her mouth. "I have to go."

Zakaari grabbed her face and forced her to look at him. "Pull yourself together, McVen."

How dare he stand in the way of her prize? "Let go. He calls me—"

"Listen!" His fingers tightened. "If *Peiaa* has released you, then something has happened. He could be hurt or..."

The sight of Zakaari's desperation, more than his grip on her face, steadied Daeya against the sudden urge to set the entire outcropping alight. As he choked on the other unfathomable possibility—that the master of her slave binders no longer resided on this side of Baosanni's Gate—Daeya peeled his hands off her and clutched her head.

Centering breaths.

She took centering breaths, in and out, just as Ravlok had taught her, until the rage receded.

*"Come,* Nashanett.*"*

"Daeya?" Zakaari's voice still sounded far away. His eyes darted to her glowing hands. "Can you hear me?"

Her body trembled as if she'd just cast a dozen six-layered spells. Sound returned in an overwhelming torrent that threatened to split her skull. "I hear you."

*"Come!"*

Across the mental threads, woven strong with her returned magic, she sent, *"Be patient."*

And the pull vanished.

Daeya quivered like a released bowstring. Only Zakaari's grip on her arm steadied her. She gazed down at her hands, fingers curling around the fading web of golden light. There was no time to marvel at whatever in the Wastelands had just happened. Not if something had happened to Tipori.

As soon as the ground stopped spinning and twilight reigned once more, she reached for her gloves and took Zakaari's hand. "Get us home."

Night had fallen by the time Zakaari rifted them within a stone's throw of Starlight Plateau. Torchlight and campfires illuminated the area around the lifts. More guards were patrolling, and a growing crowd of new arrivals—refugees, mercenaries, scouts, and even merchants—congregated around the gates. None of the lifts were running, and those visitors who hadn't found a place around one of the fires were starting to grumble.

Daeya leaned close to Zakaari. They kept their hoods drawn and their heads down. "Do they normally shut the lifts down at night?"

"No." His hand tightened on hers.

They ventured deeper into the throng. Rumors around the fires suggested there had been an attack by some escaped prisoners up in the city. Others spoke of enemy sorcerers in the area.

"There's another way up if we can circle around the far lift," Zakaari whispered.

Daeya glanced toward him, but his face was shadowed beneath his hood. "Another way up?"

"It's a decommissioned tunnel. One from Starlight's early days."

Of course. There was always speculation among the sorcerers as to how the Alliaansi had populated the plateau before the lifts. The reigning theory—supported by decades of fearmongering and lies—had been the use of rifts, through which hundreds of non-adepts apparently died every year, lost to the Aether because their bodies couldn't handle the strain. A hidden entrance made much more sense with their limited saphyrum.

Zakaari steered her toward the edge of the light. "Come on, while that guard is looking the other way."

Their footsteps creaked on packed snow as they hurried toward the darker shadows along the far cliff face. Away from the crowd, away from the fire—

"Hey! You, there."

Daeya stiffened.

"Laangor's breath," Zakaari muttered. He wrapped his arm around her and turned them both to face the approaching sentry. "Yes, what is it? My wife really needs to relieve herself. She's pregnant."

Clever. Bleeding Aether, was he clever.

The curly-haired guard hesitated before planting his spear in the snow. He gestured the opposite way with his free hand. "The latrines—"

Daeya put her hand low on her belly and adopted her best airy northern accent. "You think I can make it another minute without pissing my linens?" She glared at Zakaari. "I thought you said these people observed a proper matriarchy."

"They do. They do, *nei ama're*," Zakaari stammered. "I'm sure this gentleman is just doing his job keeping us safe."

"*Ciir*, like you were just doing your job getting me with child. Last I heard, all the bastards on their council were men!"

The guard cleared his throat. "Uh, apologies, *ru'miaa*. I didn't mean to offend. Please, just be quick about it. It's not safe to venture far from the light."

Daeya scoffed and spun herself out of Zakaari's hold. "Be quick about it, he says, like I couldn't have been there and back without his meddling."

She stormed away from both men, stumbling twice in the snow for good effect. Zakaari caught up to her quickly.

Vapor left him in a cloud as he huffed quiet laughter and tucked her against him. "That was brilliant."

The somber tension that had plagued them for the last hour eased a fraction. "Just following your lead."

They hurried around the cliffside and squeezed into a fissure in the rock. Zakaari pulled out a bead and touched it to his exposed cheek for light. He led her along a meandering channel that dead-ended in a shallow cave.

Scents of mildew and rust hung thick in the air. Only a distant whistle of wind broke the stillness. Zakaari held the light up to the rock. "The wardstones should be here somewhere."

Footsteps echoed against the stone behind them.

The hairs on the back of Daeya's neck stood on end. She whirled, ripping off her glove to cast—

"Whoa, easy, firebug." A familiar female figure stepped into Zakaari's light with her hands raised. White runes lined both eyebrows, and one forearm bore faint scars where Daeya's fire had burned her. "I've no interest in becoming seared brisket again."

"Helenia," Daeya breathed, lowering her hand. "What are you doing here?"

Helenia wore the same unadorned leathers Ravlok did as part of Kendi's Fifth Legion. She gestured to them with a flourish. "Working. Tipori ordered this musty old cave guarded, so here I am. You two are in big trouble, by the way."

"My father," Zakaari started. "He's alright?"

Her smile faltered. "Last I knew. He's been worried about you both."

"When was the last time you saw him?"

"A few hours ago. Why?"

Zakaari ignored her question and turned back to the cave wall. He tucked his gloves away and skimmed his fingertips along the stone.

Daeya rubbed one bare wrist beneath her sleeve, certain her thoughts echoed his. It had been just over an hour since the binders had come off. She looked down at the glove in her hand, then pulled the remaining one off to flex her fingers.

Zakaari felt along the wall. "We have to get up there."

"I'm not supposed to let anyone use this tunnel." Helenia eyed Daeya warily. "And Tipori ordered both of you detained."

Wardstones flared to life in a wide ring, encircling a door-sized section of stone. White-violet light washed over them, highlighting the challenge in Zakaari's expression. "So try and detain us."

He turned back to the wardstones.

"Zakaari, wait."

He paused in channeling a pair of bright spheres of magic, his hard gaze leveling on Daeya. She held his eyes without flinching, narrowing her own until the crease in his brow finally softened.

"What is it?"

"We shouldn't just charge up there. Something is obviously wrong, and we have no idea what to expect. We need a plan." Daeya turned back toward Helenia. "What can you tell us—"

Metal flashed in Helenia's hand. She lunged.

"Get down!" Zakaari commanded, and Daeya dropped.

Helenia's savage scream tore through the cave. Zakaari's answering snarl pressed Daeya tighter against the rock. Aether coated her tongue and flooded her nostrils. Two arcane bursts exploded over her head, and something struck one side of the tunnel. Boots scraped beside her, and then Zakaari hauled her to her feet.

"Come on." His voice shook. "We have to go. Now."

From where she'd fallen, Helenia's wild eyes gleamed in the light of the ward-stones. Bloody spittle flew in streams from her mouth. Her tongue moved errat-ically, speech slurring as if she'd bitten it. "*Thhhieving* witch!"

"No." Daeya backed into Zakaari and his arm closed around her. Tears pricked her eyes. "No, Helenia."

Chaos had taken her. When? Gods, had she been hiding it all this time? How had their search parties missed this?

"He's coming for you, witch." Helenia's smile oozed malice. "Then you'll pay."

"No, she won't."

Zakaari thrust his hand toward her. Colorless energy burst forth, distorting the space between them, and stone shattered as Helenia dove out of the magic's path. Another burst caught the cave mouth, spraying dust and shrapnel into the air.

Helenia leaped forward, blade slashing, and Zakaari spun to the side, shielding Daeya.

He gasped.

The sound jolted Daeya out of her stupor.

Rage kindled in her core, brighter with every breath. She twisted around Zakaari and caught Helenia by the throat. Golden light flared across Daeya's skin and magic sang in her blood. The bead inside her pendant shattered, and her body became a conduit for the full force of her element.

Helenia burst into scarlet flames.

Her screams sent heady vibrations down Daeya's forearm. They died too soon as the woman's windpipe turned to ash in her hand. The feeling of vengeance exacted curled like smoke inside her, stoking some primal part of her she hadn't known existed.

"Daeya."

Zakaari's choked voice pierced the fog of fury around her mind.

Horrified, Daeya thrust Helenia's body away. It broke into glowing cinders on the floor. The stench of burning flesh made her gag.

Daeya stumbled away from the remains, her knees shaking. It had happened so fast. How could she have—but she hadn't meant...

Gods, she'd killed her friend.

"Daeya," Zakaari wheezed. "The door."

Distantly, she understood the smoke was venting too slowly out of the cave and if they didn't leave soon, they would suffocate. She turned to face Zakaari. Behind him, a passageway stood open, framed by wardstones. He cradled his forearm close to his chest, blood darkening his cloak.

A sob tore free of her chest. He'd been hurt because of her.

Zakaari grabbed her sleeve and hauled her toward the opening. "Keep it together. We're not out of this yet."

Whatever *this* was, the thought of facing it any longer, of drawing closer to that darkness looming just beyond the fringes of her awareness, filled her with dread. Using her fire, taking a life, had produced an intoxicating miasma of sensation. It was as if she stood before a chasm so deep that she could see no end, and yet something at the bottom called to her, beckoned her to leap into the void and find euphoria at its heart. Her limbs quaked with the need to dare the fall, to chase that sensation and revel in the art of destruction.

What could she become with the power to shake the skies and level mountains? If the world should fall to its knees before her?

What would she become if no one was there to pull her out of the void?

She let Zakaari lead her into a room behind the gateway, where a set of stairs had been carved from the stone, winding up into darkness. Zakaari lit the way with a bead, still holding his injured arm close. Breathing became easier the higher they climbed, but soon the burn in Daeya's legs replaced the burn from the smoke. Her thighs shook from the strain.

Hundreds of steps later, they collapsed onto the floor of another circular chamber. A ladder led up to a solid slab of rock. Sweat rolled down their faces, and their discarded cloaks pooled in a heap between them.

Zakaari drew his knees up around his injured arm and hissed. His eyes were glassy and rimmed with gray.

Daeya wiped her forehead and reached for his bloodstained sleeve. "Let me see."

Reluctantly, he relinquished his arm. "It burns."

She pulled back his sleeve and clenched her teeth. The wound was small, but its edges were black and weeping. Dark lines traced the veins in his forearm.

No.

"That's way too fast for fleshrot. Her blade must have been coated in poison."

"Aunt Wen's going to kill me." Zakaari sighed and looked down at the wound. "This is not the date night I imagined."

She forced a chuckle, sniffling as she held back tears. "I wouldn't blame you if you're second-guessing things."

"Are you kidding?" He tried to smile, but it was more a grimace. "God-magic or not, I wouldn't trade you for anything."

Emotions tumbled over themselves and, overwhelmed by joy and guilt, Daeya grabbed his face and kissed him.

"Was it something I said?" he mumbled against her lips.

Earnest laughter and tears mingled. She pulled away. "How do I open this stupid door?"

"There should be two runes: one to disable the illusion, and one to activate the ring of wardstones marking the exit."

Zakaari leaned against the wall while Daeya started her search. She found the ring easily and frowned. "There's no illusion warding it. It's all right here."

"Then activate it. Here." He offered his softly glowing bead to her. "It's my last one. You'll have to use aethermancy. Just envision the stone turning to mist. You're strong enough; it should be easy."

It was like he'd placed his life in her hands. This was the last bead they had until they could reach the Temple or find Tipori. Without magic, they didn't stand a chance against Chaos's minions.

Daeya dismissed the light spell, inserted the bead between the prongs of her pendant, and tucked it against her skin. She triggered the ring with a surge of saphyric energy, then summoned the twin spears of light as she'd seen Zakaari do.

Tipori had taught her that magic was all about intention. About bending reality to one's will. Daeya closed her eyes and envisioned the stone above her weakening, the spaces between the rock growing. It dissolved in her mind's eye, as if superheated and turned to liquid, then to mist, in the fraction of a second. She brought the twin spheres to bear on the circle between wardstones and exerted her demand on the false ceiling.

The stone vanished.

The light winked out and Daeya was left night-blinded for several moments. Stars slowly came into focus, and cloth rasped in the silence. She looked toward the sound as Zakaari's warmth enveloped her.

"Nice work." He tucked her cloak around her shoulders and nudged her toward the ladder. "After you."

Daeya almost argued he should go first, but she was their only arcane defense now, and they couldn't waste precious time. The poison in his blood could be shutting down vital organs already, and she had no idea where in Starlight this tunnel would spit them out.

The metal rungs were mercilessly cold against her bare hands as she climbed toward the night. She'd lost her gloves somewhere along the way.

A dark figure leaned over the edge and leveled a crossbow at them. "Who's there?"

Daeya froze.

She recognized Sessiri's voice, but it was impossible to know if she was afflicted by Anordis as Helenia had been. Worse, a twitch of Sessiri's finger could bury a bolt through Daeya's eye. If she tried to weave a protective sigil with her free hand, the light from her magic would give her away before she could ever complete a spell. Tipori's Aetherial wards made rifting impossible.

But they didn't stop an Aetherian shield.

Even subtle magic could give off light in darkness. She took a risk and envisioned her intentions before drawing from her pendant.

"Speak!"

"I'm sorry, Sessiri," Daeya said, and opened herself fully to the flow of magic.

Light swirled and solidified with a sharp burst of Aether. A shield just wide enough to cover her and Zakaari formed over her head.

"Daeya? What—"

Daeya summoned raw energy and hurled it into the shield, propelling it skyward. It slammed into Sessiri's crossbow, snapping the mechanism and blowing her back. With a mighty burst of magic directed into Daeya's feet and hands, she leaped the rest of the way to the top of the ladder and swung herself up.

They appeared to be near a stable on the outskirts of one of the cliffside towns. Distant fires from the tent cities lit the way to Starlight.

Sessiri was doubled over in the snow, holding her face. Daeya darted for her, wrapped an arm around her neck, and closed off her carotid artery.

"Forgive me." Remorse sat heavy on Daeya's heart as Sessiri's movements slowed, then stopped. By the time Zakaari pulled himself over the ledge to stare forlornly at the far-off campfires, Daeya had rolled from beneath the unconscious woman and started to drag her toward the stable. Whether Sessiri was working for Chaos or not, Daeya wouldn't let her freeze to death out here in the snow.

She called back to Zakaari. "I hope you know how to ride."

After cursing the wards that kept him from Bending the distance, Zakaari helped her open the stable doors and saddle a pair of horses. They left Sessiri nestled in a bed of straw and set out across the plateau.

Solstice revelry was still in full swing when they reached the tent cities. Most partygoers were too inebriated to shy from the danger of galloping horses, so Daeya was forced to slow their pace to a crawl. The need to move itched along her skin. When the crowd finally thinned enough to canter again, they were well into Starlight's rows of storage sheds, just past the orphanage. Dense fog crept between buildings and scattered the light from the parchment lanterns lining the roads. Within moments, they were alone in a haze of white.

Zakaari slumped over his saddle.

"Bleeding—" Daeya snatched his cloak before he fell, nearly falling off her horse in her haste to catch him.

He mumbled something incoherent and struggled to right himself. Beneath his hood, his skin was pallid. Black veins crawled up one side of his neck. He swayed, made a grab for the horn of his saddle, and missed.

Fog swallowed Daeya's cry of alarm. Zakaari hit the snow with a muffled grunt, and she scrambled down after him. Hands trembling, she rolled him onto his back and shook him.

"Zakaari? Zakaari, wake up."

She shook him again, her tears freezing on her eyelashes. He couldn't. That blade had been meant for her. She wouldn't let him take her place. She just wouldn't—

Zakaari coughed himself awake and groaned. "Silonas slay me."

Daeya folded herself over him and sobbed into his chest. "Gods, you scared me."

He blinked up into the fog. "Why do I feel like I fell off a horse?"

She managed a laugh before dissolving into more sobs. Getting him back to the Temple like this seemed more impossible by the moment.

"You have to get up. We have to get you to Orowen."

"My house isn't far." He held out a hand for her assistance and slowly sat up. "If *Peiaa* or *Haalii* are home, they can help."

Gods, they still didn't know if Tipori was okay. But surely solstice wouldn't go on if he wasn't. Maybe Chaos's minions were deliberately trying to confuse her.

She shouldered Zakaari's weight and used her aching legs to lift him out of the snow. "And if they're not?"

"Our house is warded against unwanted entry. We'll be safe there."

"You still need a healer."

Zakaari winced. "I won't send you out alone."

That was the answer, wasn't it? Without him, she could move faster, and there'd be no risk of dragging him into greater danger. She could bring back help and give him a chance to rest.

They stumbled through the garden gate and along the trail meandering toward the Evallier home. There were no lanterns here, and the fog was so absolute she couldn't see the path beyond a few steps.

"I won't be gone long," she promised. "What matters is—"

Fiery agony exploded across Daeya's chest.

Her scream echoed through the fog.

Magnus turned to the others.

And smiled.

# CHAPTER FIFTY-FOUR

## DAEYA

Pain.

Gods, the pain.

"Nashanett?" Telerion's voice.

An otherworldly cry pierced her skull. Razors tore through her throat.

"Daeya!"

Each breath, each heartbeat, was like a thousand flaming knives stabbing her at once.

"Nashanett."

Hands pulled at her, shook her. "No. No, please, I just found you. Don't leave me."

Light blinded her. She squinted into the fog.

Foreign pressure. Something near her shoulder, above her left breast. She groped for it, but something stopped her hand from moving.

"D-don't pull it out."

"But it hurts." She had to make it stop.

"You'll bleed more if you do. *Haalii*!" Zakaari's voice broke on the word. "*Peiaa*, help!"

Daeya tried to move, but more fire exploded through her torso. The ground beneath her trembled.

"*Summon me.*"

"*Telerion?*"

"*Summon me, and I will come.*"

"*How do I...*"

Thought slipped from her. Darkness closed in.

"Come on, McVen. I need you to—"

Zakaari's snarl jolted Daeya back to full awareness. His warmth disappeared. She blinked her vision clear. Her bare hands glowed like the broken crust of a lava flow. A crossbow bolt jutted from her shoulder, and golden light throbbed as if trying to force it out.

Another bolt slammed into her. Light flashed and pain screamed through her body. A third bolt struck her lower. Daeya gasped for air. She clutched her injuries, distantly noting the absence of protrusions there. Two projectiles tumbled to the snow beside her.

A scream shredded the night.

Zakaari.

She strained to sit up. The world spun, and her left arm refused to obey. Cloaked figures approached, blades drawn.

Zakaari lay in the snow, a dark shape blurred by fog. He groaned weakly as an assailant crouched beside him and withdrew a gleaming blade.

Thunder rolled through her.

Daeya's hands sparked magic. Red-tinged flame scorched snow into steam.

What happened to her was of little consequence. Chaos's priests could come at her with everything they had.

But they wouldn't take Zakaari.

Daeya's last saphyrum bead cracked in its setting. Reality bent to her will, and she shrouded Zakaari in a dome of Aetherial light.

The attackers hesitated.

It was their final mistake.

Alar *seized* the falling stone as another earthquake dislodged part of the hillside. He guided it away from the campsite and dropped it on the other side of the supply wagons. The impact shuddered through the ground.

Trembling and coated in sweat, Alar braced his hands on his knees. They had worked too hard to gather those supplies. He wouldn't allow another intractable act of nature to ruin things for them only hours from home.

Their journey had been fraught with perils the farther north they traveled. Avalanches and rockslides in the Palisadics had given way to Guild patrols and Paladins in the pine forests. No fewer than three blizzards had caught them between villages, and they'd spent the last two days digging themselves out of a cave.

And now these cursed earthquakes.

"Alar."

An insistent tap on his shoulder forced his attention upward. "What, Naruu?" His tone was sharp.

Covered in small cuts and dust, Naruu tried to suppress a grimace and failed. The young sentry's aura roiled, and his thoughts were so loud, Alar could almost make them out.

Naruu pointed north. "Is that going to be a problem?"

Alar straightened, swaying when the world bucked again.

A towering column of flaming ash and steam belched from the In'Jasuu.

Warmth drained from Alar's face. Mount Eisekii, the Northlands' long-dormant volcano, had just awoken.

Mulled wine tremored in Ravlok's glass. He frowned into it and steadied his wrist with his opposite hand.

Odes of Ordeolas, his nerves hadn't been this bad since he'd worked for Laerin's crew.

Solstice festivities continued around him. Many Temple patients were starting to lag, but others were still bright-eyed as they conversed with their visitors.

They all acted as if no one had died that night. Anwic and the two unknown attackers had succumbed to their injuries right there in the snow. The little girl, Aadra, had been heavily sedated and put under guard.

Ravlok flexed his hands around the warm glass, his fingers still tingling. He'd spent too long in the cold without a cloak, and Sam had demanded he return to the Temple to rest and receive healing while she carried on the search for Jack. Divination magic had failed them, and Ravlok's mood darkened with each passing hour. He should be out there helping, not sitting idle.

The tremor came again. This time, it rattled all the way through his boots.

Conversation faltered.

Ravlok looked up. A few healers exchanged uncertain glances. They'd felt something too.

When the quake came a third time, exclamations and gasps rippled through the infirmary. Decanters shook and silverware rattled. Something clattered to the floor.

Tipori appeared from the back corridor, brows furrowed as he scanned the crowd. He settled on something near the front entry, his gaze growing distant. His power of Foresight wasn't nearly as strong as Riisii's, but it was far from useless. Ravlok lowered his wine.

The Temple doors burst open. Niam squeaked to a stop on the wet tile, her frantic eyes fixed on Ravlok. She dashed across the infirmary to get to him.

Ravlok rose. "What's wrong, Niam?" His voice was muffled beneath the ringing in his ears.

With trembling hands, she made the motion for Daeya's pendant and pointed toward the door.

Tipori drew up alongside Ravlok. "You found them?"

Niam grimaced and started for the door, motioning for them to follow.

Something terrible had happened. Daeya was hurt.

Or worse.

The thought rooted itself in his bones and grew until it threatened to splinter him apart. No magic in the world could stop an attack Daeya couldn't see coming, and Jack was an excellent marksman. He'd killed dozens of sorcerers in Ryost alone.

Ravlok balled his fists. He should have stayed closer to her. He should have been more vigilant. It wasn't even a question of Anordis's influence; Jack had always had it out for Daeya.

They stepped into the night. Violent bursts of lightning lit the fog. In a way, it seemed fitting, like Caelyn was taunting him. She'd known how badly this would end.

An orange glow burst in the northwest. The ground trembled under their feet. Fine snow collected in Tipori's hair, on Niam's cloak, in Ravlok's lengthening beard.

Niam tugged Ravlok's sleeve and pointed not to the glow in the distance, but to a closer one. A brighter one.

Ravlok took a half-step toward that scarlet light. "No."

Niam's grip on his arm tightened. There were tears on her face, her eyes glassy with remembered terror. More snow collected in her eyelashes and swirled in the warm breeze. Only, it wasn't snow.

It was ash.

The smell of smoke carried on the wind. The world bucked again and stone shuddered. He remembered what Caelyn had said about draegion fire. How it could consume everything in its path.

Ravlok spun to Tipori. "Rally every water and fire savant you have. Quickly."

Charred lumps of flesh encircled the small patch of garden left untouched by draegion fire. Blackened bones jutted from the corpses, smoldering like logs in a hearth. Bright embers rose with the smoke like fireflies on a summer wind. Snow melted and mixed with blood and ash, turning the once white landscape macabre shades of red and gray.

It was beautiful.

It was terrible.

Daeya's left arm was useless. The crossbow bolt still lodged in her shoulder throbbed with fresh agony, reminding her she was still alive. None of Chaos's priests stirred.

She dragged herself toward the Aetherian shield sheltering Zakaari. Her saphyrum was gone, and the shimmering dome wouldn't hold much longer. She buckled beside it and gazed into the inferno she'd created. It defied all laws of magic, but even without saphyrum, the fire sluggishly, reluctantly, obeyed her, and it strayed no closer to the dome. Her hold on it wasn't enough to put it out or pull it to her, but it would be enough to keep Zakaari safe.

Rain fell, and steam rose like the souls of the departed. Two dark shapes emerged from the haze, and Daeya stiffened. One wore a black scarf over its face and stood in shadow. The other was the most stunning Syljian man she'd ever seen.

He was built of lithe muscle and long limbs, and his white hair fell in loose waves past his elbows. Despite the long scar cut through his left eyebrow, his face boasted an excruciating sort of beauty that even a god might envy. Shadows obscured his eyes, but his supple lips curled upward in a smile that set Daeya at ease.

She struggled to rise, but the Syljian shushed her and crouched down, brushing her rain-soaked hair from her face. "It's alright, *niish amaar*. I'm here to help you."

The term of endearment struck her oddly, but his touch reduced the pain in her shoulder to a dull ache in an instant. "You're a healer?"

"In a way. You've sought comfort in my arms before. Don't you remember?"

Her brows tensed. "No, I'm sorry. I don't remember."

"Such a shame." His fingers stroked soothing trails down her face. Over and over across her temple. "You were so happy back then. I can help you remember. Would you like that?"

Maybe she was delirious. He wasn't making any sense. Each stroke of his fingers lulled her a little more toward sleep. Blissful, painless sleep. "How?"

"Just trust me. I'm going to take away your pain first, and then I will help you. Is that alright?"

Slowly, Daeya nodded. "Okay."

His fingers settled against her temple, his palm cupping her cheek. "I need you to lower your Shield, darling."

Her shield? Daeya glanced toward the dome. The energy she'd poured into the Aetherian shield was nearly spent anyway. Zakaari had been too still for too long. "Please, if you're a healer, help him first. He's been poisoned."

The man shook his head. "He is already lost, I'm afraid."

"No, he's..." The subtle rise and fall of Zakaari's breathing steadied her. "He's still alive. Please, you have to help him."

The Syljian's lip curled. "There is nothing anyone can do."

Daeya recoiled from that look, that tone of thinly disguised malice. Pressure mounted behind her eyes, and tears mixed with rain.

Zakaari couldn't die because of her.

"Please. I love him."

The man leaned forward, tsking her, and the light shining through her skin finally banished the shadows around his eyes. One was deep violet, the color of magic. The other, below that terrible scar, was cloudy white.

"Oh, Nahariim, you must let him go. He is a fragile mortal, destined to die sooner than you could blink. He is undeserving of your tears."

All thoughts of sleep vanished like fog before the sun. The fire, which had ebbed with the rain, flared hotter and brighter. Zakaari *was* worth every tear she'd shed tonight and more.

*She is no mortal.*

Caelyn's words returned to her like a dream. Not even Tiior had explained that little nuance of Daeya's ancestry. How did this man, whom she'd never met before, come to know it?

Lightning flashed, illuminating the person behind him. Clad entirely in black, silent and unmoving, the figure looked too much like the spectral Aetherman said to rift into children's bedrooms and steal them away in their sleep.

Perhaps it was waiting to do the same to her.

Tremors shook the ground like distant thunder. The threads connecting her to Telerion quivered, as if in warning.

The Syljian caressed her temple again. "Lower your Shield for me. There isn't much time."

Daeya narrowed her eyes. "Who are you?"

With her question came a fresh pulse of pain from her wound. Starbursts exploded behind her eyes. She gasped and might have doubled over had he not seized her by the chin.

"You will remember very soon. Come, *niish amaar*, you are suffering in vain."

Daeya shivered. The black-clad Aetherman shifted on its feet. Scarlet light glinted off a blade partially drawn from its sheath. Her gaze flicked toward it, then back to the Syljian, whose good humor had vanished, replaced by a jealous hunger.

Pieces settled into place. Daeya tore herself out of his hold and fire swirled around her, forcing him back.

"Anordis," she spat.

He sneered. "Baokryn."

Anordis reached through her flames and clamped onto her temples as if to crush her skull like an overripe melon. She grabbed his wrist and called fire again.

Acid scorched her bloodstream. The scream it tore from her seemed to go on forever.

Tiny white fissures splintered across the blackness in her vision. A tearing sensation inside her mind left trails of lava in its wake.

"You will return what is mine!"

It was unbearable.

"Give it to me!"

Like he was shredding her soul apart.

Blinded, unable to force him off, unable to focus her fire, and without saphyrum for her magic, Daeya reached up. Her fingers closed around the crossbow bolt still lodged in her chest. She tore it out.

And stabbed deep.

The voice's scream resonated like a Skriian war horn. Magnus hit his knees, clutching his head. Pain spiked through his neck. The corporeal form of his benefactor—Anordis, god of chaos—dissolved into mist.

This wasn't supposed to happen. The sorceress should have been spellbound. She shouldn't have had the strength to fight off so many. To resist the poison. Their army should have overwhelmed her.

"Zakaari!"

"Daeya!"

Others called through the flames. He couldn't allow anyone to find him here, surrounded by steaming corpses. Magnus pushed himself to his feet. The instinct to flee pulled at him, but a greater urge to look upon his enemy won him over. He approached the sorceress, his shadow falling across her face.

Her Shield faded, leaving her skin pallid and damp. Without that web of light, nothing could stop his blade from ending her life and saving his people. It was tempting. So tempting. But Anordis's instructions were clear: she couldn't die before they excised that power from her.

*Patience*, Anordis rasped. *There will yet be time. The poison still binds her.*

Time. Yes, just as it had taken time to accept his role in Anordis's plans. Putting his faith in Chaos meant having a god on his side to ensure his people's survival against the Guild. It was a sacrifice he made gladly.

Magnus crouched, observing how her blood pooled around that black wound.

The sorceress whimpered. Half-lidded eyes the color of molten gold fixed on him. "Magnus?"

He started.

"Daeya!"

"*Ennii*!"

The others were closer now, and the flames nearly extinguished. She'd recognized him; she could place him here at the scene when questioned later. He made a split-second decision and unpinned his cloak, pressing the fabric to her wound. "It's alright, Daeya. I'm here to help you."

"Daeya!"

The monk stepped into the clearing and coughed, fanning smoke from his face. Tipori appeared behind him. Magnus's jaw tensed; Anwic must have failed as well.

Pressure built in his chest. The bookkeeper's tome was paramount to their success.

*Patience.*

Patience. Yes, yes, patience. He shook his head to stop the mad feathering around his eye socket.

Swallowing the taste of smoke, Magnus called out, "They're over here!"

# CHAPTER FIFTY-FIVE

## OROWEN

Orowen swept the sheets back from the infirmary bed and beckoned Ravlok into Riisii's old room. He placed Daeya on the mattress, then helped Tipori maneuver a second cot supporting Zakaari through the door. Four others followed with bowls of steaming water, bundles of healers' tools, and clean linens.

Orowen replaced the blood-soaked cloak over Daeya's injury with a folded towel. "Ravlok, keep pressure here. Bren, Nallia, get Zakaari comfortable and start cleaning his wound."

Over a century of experience guided her movements. She couldn't allow her own emotions to cripple her. She ordered sigils prepared for Zakaari while weaving one for Daeya.

Tipori, however, wasn't so adept. Her acolytes tiptoed around him, too intimidated to demand he leave.

"Tipori," she called, tying off her sigil. He turned to her with tears streaking his face and thunder in his eyes. "I have need of you."

Reluctantly, he released Zakaari's hand. Nallia shot Orowen a grateful look and filled the space Tipori had left.

"*Ciir*, Devoted?"

His formality, acknowledging her skill and superiority in this matter, wasn't lost on her. "I need you to cut away her shirt—"

"*No*. Please."

Daeya's vehement jolt back to lucidity startled them all.

"Daeya, you have to let Orowen work." Ravlok's voice trembled.

"No! I can't." Barely conscious, Daeya tried to further cover the towel in Ravlok's hands. "Please, don't."

"I need access to the wound, *neime*. I need to see where to heal you." Orowen's heart wrenched for the poor girl. "There is no shame in being exposed here."

"Yes, there is. You don't understand."

Ravlok looked up at Orowen helplessly. His hands, already slick with Daeya's blood, trembled against the linen.

They were running out of time. "Daeya—" Orowen began.

Tipori seized the girl's chin. He spoke with an intensity not meant to comfort, but to command. "Look at me."

Gooseflesh prickled the back of Orowen's neck. The echo of Tipori's former life resonated in those words. He leaned down until his nose hovered within fingerspans of Daeya's—a gesture that might have been intimate but for the way his grip tightened on her face. "Whatever you're hiding, it's not worth your life. Now, lower your hands."

Orowen might have intervened if, after a moment's hesitation, Daeya hadn't let her arms fall to the mattress.

Tipori straightened and withdrew a dagger from his belt. "I'm going to use this to remove your shirt. You will let me work, and then you will let Orowen heal you. Say you understand."

Daeya stared up at Tipori like a scolded child. "I understand."

"Good girl." He softened and wiped the tears from her cheeks. "You'll feel better soon."

"I swear I didn't want them." Daeya squeezed her eyes shut. "Please don't hate me."

Orowen exchanged glances with Tipori and Ravlok. Normally, she would address concerns like this before a procedure, but only a small miracle was keeping the girl conscious. "It's alright, *neime*. We just want you well again."

Tipori sliced the fastenings of Daeya's outer tunic and parted the inner layer in the direction of the wound, allowing Ravlok to retain pressure. Orowen let the pulse of the sigil in her hand steady her for the work to come.

"Devoted," Bren called from Zakaari's bedside. "Whatever malady this is, it's not responding to a grade two."

Her jaw tightened. Zakaari's fleshrot had set in impossibly fast, and none of her acolytes could cast a grade three safely. "I'll be right there. Nallia, see if your combined sigils have any effect."

"Yes, Devoted."

Tipori paused in his work. "Gods be damned."

Certain the man had cut himself, Orowen opened her mouth for a weak jab, but the retort died on her tongue. "*Saonis miraar.*"

Daeya turned her face away, eyes pinched tighter.

Ravlok paled. "What are those?"

"Runes," Tipori murmured.

Hundreds of them. So many they completely altered the texture of her skin. A void formed in Orowen's chest as Daeya sobbed into Ravlok's arm.

*She didn't want any of them.*

The patterns were too deliberate, the cuts too precise, to have formed naturally. Someone had carved them into her. But who? And why?

Storm clouds gathered behind Tipori's expression, reflecting Orowen's own anger. Baosanni curse the monster who could do such horrors to a child.

She forced the feeling down. Right now, her patient was bleeding out. "Tipori, talk to her. Keep her calm. Ravlok, I may need to heal this in stages. Once you remove the linen, have another one ready."

*Saolanni, guide my hands.*

Tendrils of healing energy coursed from Orowen's fingers. She worked for several moments, guiding the light into the wound, trying to coax new tissue growth, but the same blackness in Zakaari's arm penetrated Daeya's injury. It resisted Saolanni's light like oil repelling water.

An enchanted toxin.

"*Caezo,*" Orowen cursed. This couldn't simply be cleansed from the body with magic or herbs. They had to break the ward first. "I need a counter-sigil for a warding enchantment."

Wyl hurried over, the sigil floating over his palm. He paused and stared at the runes on Daeya's skin. "Devoted?"

"Focus, Wyl. I need you to target the poison."

Wyl worked until his face flushed with exertion, but in the end, the ward proved too strong to break with an acolyte's counter.

"Savii," Orowen tried, noting the blue tinge to Daeya's lips. She'd slipped back into unconsciousness while Tipori whispered reassurances in her ear. "Try a stronger counter. Add your efforts to Wyl's."

When even that failed, Orowen banished her healing sigil and brought her own counter to bear. The ward didn't budge.

Orowen clenched her teeth. This was the work of Chaos priests, and only Tiior knew what kinds of magic they had at their disposal.

Her own talent still wasn't what it should be. But if she couldn't break this ward, both young ones would die.

*Tiior, grant me wisdom.*

"It resists Saolanni's magic." Brows knitting, Ravlok looked toward Zakaari.

The acolytes had removed her nephew's clothing so they could see the full extent of the poison's damage. Coal-black veins snaked up Zakaari's arm and across his chest. For all her poise, the sight of them creeping along his jaw stole her breath. The wound had already begun to putrefy.

Laangor have mercy, he was just a boy. The thought of failing him, of failing their family, had never crossed Orowen's mind. She'd delivered him into this world; she wasn't meant to see him out as well.

"Devoted, I have an idea."

Orowen forced herself to meet Ravlok's gaze. "What is it?"

He nodded to one of the walls on which Riisii had carved her runes. "During the Battle of Vintrios, Baokryn's dragonbond sustained a similar injury. Chaos speared her wing with a poisoned lance." Ravlok gestured for Tipori to trade places with him. "If I can remember the translation..." He stepped to the foot of the bed and uttered a guttural word. A massive leather-bound tome appeared in a swirl of Aetherial mist.

Orowen blinked. When had he gained magic?

Ravlok spoke to the tome again and opened to a blank page. His eyes danced for several seconds, as if reading something only he could see. "Copper healers... the lance... Corrupting eyes? No, that's not right. Psionics. Of *course*, psionics. And the wards"—he looked up—"the wards! That's it." He turned toward a spot on the wall. "A warding sigil."

Her hope and curiosity turned to irritation. "Yes, the poison is warded—"

"No, no, that's not what I mean." Ravlok hurried over to tap one of the gouged eye symbols. "The ancient healers discovered Chaos imbued the poison with his psionic magic. It allowed him to control how it affected a body." He touched another symbol—a pair of concentric circles with a jagged line tangent to their outer edge. "When they warded their infirmary against Chaos, it broke his hold and destroyed the enchantment, allowing them to save the dragon."

"Then, we need to ward the Temple." Tipori's gaze was on his son; Daeya's blood reddened his fingertips.

"Or at least this room," Ravlok amended.

Orowen's lips parted. They knew of her failures. Ravlok had witnessed it. "I've tried—"

"I know." Ravlok turned back to her. "But you have to try again."

Protests rose up at the futility, the wasted time, the utter hopelessness.

Tipori silenced the spiral of her thoughts. "We don't have time for doubts. I will help you in any way I can."

Wyl gently touched her shoulder. "We believe in you, Devoted. I will help as well."

"And I," Bren said.

"And I."

"And I, as well."

Nallia and Savii repeated the sentiment. Orowen took them in, one at a time, until the confidence she found in their faces bolstered her own. Maybe she'd failed before, but she didn't have to be alone in this. With all of them calling on the gods together, united against Chaos, perhaps it would be enough.

Ravlok returned to Daeya's bedside. He touched Orowen's forehead, where only hours ago, he'd bestowed upon her Tiior's blessing of knowledge. Ash still clung to her cheeks where he'd placed the blessings of wisdom and strength. She hadn't been able to wipe them away. Now she understood why.

"You have everything you need, Devoted. We're with you."

She drew a steadying breath and nodded. "Alright. Tipori, I need you to stabilize the Wall as best as you can. Ravlok, take over for him with Daeya's wound. Acolytes, I need marrow stimulating sigils on both patients, as well as holy water and incense."

A flurry of activity followed Orowen's commands. She walked Bren through the complicated sigils that would buy their patients time while the others retrieved spell components and pushed the beds together. If all they could manage was a small sphere of safety, she wanted the young ones close. Gods willing, if the ward could hold for even a few seconds, the enchantment should be broken.

Once all was prepared, the acolytes linked hands over the two beds. Bren and Nallia gripped Orowen's shoulders to keep her hands free for casting.

They channeled saphyric energy through their amulets, bathing them all in white-violet light. Orowen closed her eyes, let it permeate her senses like the incense smoke drifting through the room. The magic pulled her along through the eddies and rapids of each acolyte's ability like a leaf carried downstream, until they all flowed into one swift-moving river.

Holy water chilled her skin up to the wrists. Orowen reached that meditative point deep within her—a place that still bore inky black reminders of Chaos's machinations, like the shadows left in the runes made by Riisii's blade—and opened herself fully to that divine current. Light flashed behind her eyelids as if they'd summoned the sun itself inside the room. Chaos's shadows evaporated, leaving only love and warmth behind.

Orowen opened her eyes. The basin of water glowed beneath her fingers. Tendrils of magic wavered around them. She lifted her hands and began to cast.

In and out through the Aetherial Wall, she weaved those luminous threads, steadily building a barrier that penetrated both the gods' realm and the realm of mortals. The magic came easier, truer, stronger, than it ever had before. She tied off the first layer and began the second, letting the ribbons spread like watercolor through the space until they vanished into warding mist.

A black force slammed into the Wall around the heart of her sigil. Tremors shook Orowen to her core.

Tipori staggered, thrown into Zakaari's bed by the ripple that passed through reality. He caught himself on the mattress, eyes aglow as he harnessed the Aether and forced the Wall to calm.

He bared his teeth. "I think we have his attention."

No other event could have confirmed the rightness of their course so completely. Jaw set with purpose, Orowen resumed her casting with renewed fervor. She tied off the second layer and pulled more from the basin to begin the third.

The force came again, tearing a gasp from her brother-in-law. The Wall bucked and writhed like snakes in a sack. Tipori's bloodied hands balled in Zakaari's sheets. Aether poured off him in black-violet clouds—a stark counterpoint to Saolanni's light.

Wyl whimpered.

"Steady." Orowen traced the path of the next few knots, carefully timing their creation with the wavering Wall.

Sweat rolled down her back, and her arms trembled as she finished the third layer. The fourth and final layer of the warding sigil began with a series of loops and knots that cinched the spell tightly against the Wall. It was delicate work and prone to mistakes. Orowen worked as quickly as she dared.

Trails of sweat glistened against Tipori's skin. The next blow to the Wall nearly bent him double, and Wyl cried out in terror. Fissures broke open around them like tiny exit rifts leaking black mist. They burgeoned wider with every passing wave.

Savii's fear bubbled over, and the flow of her magic snapped. "It's going to warp!"

"Savii, no!" Bren reached for her too late.

Time seemed to slow as Savii ran headlong into the path of a new fissure. White-violet light burst through the room and the yawning void swallowed her whole.

Wind blasted the room apart. Loose objects tumbled into the Aether. The basin of water, healers' tools, bloodstained linens, and bits of shrapnel were all thrown about while Tipori strained to close the warp.

A sneering face appeared from beyond the void. One violet eye fixed on Orowen; the other was chalk-white. The visage grew larger and larger until a presence took shape inside her mind—

—and *screamed*.

Orowen went down clutching her head, the pain like white-hot spikes thrust into her brain. Hot blood gushed from her nose and eyes. Other voices echoed that scream.

Distantly, she registered pressure beneath her arms.

"Get up, Devoted." Bren's voice.

"Come on," Nallia added. "You're so close."

Tipori roared in agony. So close. So close, and yet...

*Oathbreaker*, a voice hissed. *You cannot save them.*

Orowen opened her eyes. Blood distorted the light of her sigil. The three-layered ward still stood firmly against the monster threatening to tear them apart. The hole through which Savii disappeared had been closed. Tipori had drawn his axes, and he stood facing the next widening fissure.

"Hurry up, Orowen," he growled, as if sensing her eyes on him. "He's breaking my rift wards."

*I will relish your fall, Charlatan.*

Anger poured into her at the invasion, but Orowen forced it back. She needed steady hands to cast her last layer, and she wouldn't be goaded by the likes of Chaos. She reached for the stabilizing knot of her third layer and dove headlong into that deep well of inner peace. With Saolanni's light surrounding her, she projected her thoughts toward the oily presence slithering through her mind.

*I am no charlatan.*

Light burst upward, carrying Orowen with it into the current of magic still trickling from her terrified acolytes. The river swelled, overflowed, and Orowen opened herself to it, drinking in every shred of power granted to her by her goddess. She spun Saolanni's light like threads on a loom.

Another scream tore through her mind, quickly drowned by the rush of magic. The last loops of her fourth layer spilled from her fingertips, and Orowen wrenched them taut.

Then everything fell silent.

# INTERLUDE III

## GREGORY

The rift appeared at half past first bell.

Gregory turned from the blood-tinged sky, expecting Normos, but the shape of the rift lacked finesse. His protégé wouldn't dare demonstrate such despicable form. It could be the Walker from Nash Ferren's army reporting in, but—

His source's emissary emerged from the mist.

Gregory stiffened.

It was the sort of creature out of a fae tale. Gray skin stretched taut against unnaturally sharp cheekbones. Its chin came to such a fine point that it looked like portions of its jaw were missing. Needle-like teeth filled its mouth, and fan-like ears clung to the sides of its head. A clicking sound issued from the hairless monstrosity's tongue.

Scarred, sightless eyes settled on him. "The mistress summons you."

Gregory touched the ebony dagger beneath his cloak, disallowing the tremor in his fingers. He had a debriefing at third bell with the spies from Aon'In, but they could wait. It wouldn't do to deny this summons.

The creature gestured to reverse the rift still standing open behind it, then reached its spindly claws toward him. Gregory grimaced, but took the thing's hand and let it guide him into the misty Aether.

Its precision left much to be desired. The Walk jostled him twice, and nausea turned his stomach. When at last they stepped out of the rift into his source's domain, Gregory was already lamenting the return journey.

A castle built of black stone rose before him. Behind him, a dense swamp stank of decay, stale water, and fae magic. He didn't need to see the hundreds of eyes staring out from the trees; he could feel their slimy weight on his back.

Gregory kept his chin high and smoothed the front of his cloak. None would dare trifle with him here, not while he carried the Oracle's blade.

"This way," the creature hissed, as if Gregory hadn't gone up the rise to the front door on his own many times before. It proceeded to make its aggravating series of clicks to guide itself across the muddy lawn.

Gregory's face twitched. He'd have preferred to slay the abomination where it stood, but the Oracle was fond of it. Unwilling to offend her, he stifled his annoyance and allowed himself to be led.

Into the castle, through the foyer, and up an unlit staircase, the emissary went, clicking the whole way. The twitch in Gregory's jaw took on a similar cadence, and the appeal of running the creature through began to outweigh his reservations.

Light at the top of the stairs stayed his hand. Legs burning from the climb, Gregory paused a few seconds, preparing himself. Then, he dropped his gaze and entered the room.

False tranquility numbed his senses. Gregory's hands clenched without due fervor. His wards were still not strong enough to evade her influence.

A voice worthy of bard song caressed his ears. "The draegion has reawakened."

It was not a question.

Her displeasure sent a chill through him. Gregory lowered himself to one knee and kept his gaze trained on the saphyrum-inlaid floor—the source of the white-violet glow.

"So, why do you delay our bargain?"

The silk-clad nightmare drifted toward him as he formulated a response. His emotions were still suppressed, but even if they weren't, fear had no place inside him. "I have not yet—"

"Wait. Don't tell me." Her bare lavender toes encroached on the sliver of floor he could see. "Let me guess."

Gregory jerked as her icy fingers closed on his chin. "That is not—"

"Necessary? Oh no, it isn't." She tipped his face up, and he cinched his eyes shut. "But I do love playing your little game. Open your eyes, Lucy."

Anger fractured the fog around his mind. "You will have what I promised when it is finished and not a moment sooner."

*"Open your eyes."*

The Oracle's psionic command threaded through his wards and *squeezed*, shattering them like glass. His will usurped, his body no longer his, Gregory found himself staring into such catastrophic beauty, he would sooner gouge out his own eyes than ever look upon a face less fair.

The truth spilled from him like blood from a wound. "We were defeated in Willowmarsh, and her family has fled. I await word from an acquaintance and pray he sees reason. Else I must obtain a new hostage to bring her home."

Amusement turned up the corners of her perfect lips. "You're getting better, at least. It took me longer to get through this time."

She patted his cheek and released him, rebuilding his wards as she left his mind. Gregory's fury at the intrusion poured forth in ripples of Aether that swayed the tower walls. He gathered the magic to him, fully intending to blast the room apart.

The Oracle brushed the wavering Wall as a musician would strum a harp. His magic drained away, soaked up by the wards that kept her bound.

"Beware the hand of the healer who seeks your heart. I still See a Devoted of Mira in my dreams."

Gregory had taken precautions to avoid healers whenever possible. Teeth clenched, body quaking, he rose and once more trained his eyes on the stone. "As you say, Oracle."

"So formal." She scoffed. "Vengeance has made you boring, Lucy."

His lip curled. "I beg your forgiveness."

"Mm, what is it you say? 'All is forgiven'?"

The Oracle turned, and Gregory denied his impulse to look upon her face again.

"My patience is not endless, Sorcerer. I will have what is mine within the year, or I shall withdraw my protection. Remember, the new Wasteland begins with you at its center."

It wasn't the first time she'd made such a prediction, but it was the first time he heard it as a threat. Gregory raged against his pact, *cursed* his younger self for his foolishness, but only for a moment. This was for Addy.

"I understand."

It was all for Addy.

"My lady."

# Part Four

# Chapter Fifty-Six

## Aliri

Mount Eisekii still trembled from the aftershocks of the young gold's anger. Fractured stone crashed down, echoing through the labyrinth of tunnels carved into the mountain. Magma pools churned at Aliri's scale-clad feet.

Her *draekhei*'s fire had melted the walls and widened the trenches of molten rock striping the cavern floor. He'd been so certain of the draegion's peril, he would have burned through the mountainside itself to get to her. But without a summons or a fully formed dragonbond to ascertain the extent of the danger or Daeya's intentions, Aliri couldn't allow it. Young dragons had been killed by unbonded draegion for much less in millennia past.

After she'd barred Telerion from leaving, the centureon had stormed off down an old lava tunnel and left Aliri alone with Vorsere. Falla remained on the surface, too uncomfortable with the close heat and constant clouds of vapor pouring off her frigid skin to remain. A brief telepathic exchange confirmed she'd taken to the skies to watch for Telerion's escape from another part of the mountain.

Vorsere lounged on her belly beside a magma pool, clawed humanoid fingers stirring it as if it were no hotter than the reflection pools inside Qiiseraan's

Platinum Palace. "I must admit, his fire is *impresssive* for a wyrmling. Almost worthy of a steel." She snickered. "Are you certain he's of Mertysian's brood?"

Aliri growled. Leave it to Vorsere to compliment and insult her in the same breath. "A gold mates for life. You know this."

Vorsere responded with a too-human roll of her eyes. She pushed herself up and gazed off in the direction Telerion had gone. Her hair fanned over her shoulders like striated obsidian. "What will you do if he refuses to return with you? The Gold Court has already demanded *vhessskhanash*. They will not wait forever."

No, they wouldn't. If Telerion refused to reclaim his birthright, she and Mertysian had just over four centuries to secure their throne by producing another heir. Hardly enough time to incubate an egg, much less spawn one without a draegion's magic to bolster them.

"He will come." She traced a safe path through the pools and trenches to the mouth of the tunnel. If she had to drag her *draekhei* back by his wings, he would come, not only for their family's benefit but for the draegion's as well. Daeya McVen would need instruction in containing and controlling her power, and a bookkeeper must be chosen to access her soul's memories. For the next several centuries, at least, the safest place for her would be Draeconis. "He will do what is best for his dragonbond."

"For once, I agree with Caelyn. The wyrmling is too young and *impulsssive* for the mantle." The Lady of Flame flicked magma off her claws before retracting them into her fingertips. "Better to end this now and pair the girl with an ancient who can *counsssel* her in wiser choices."

Heat rose in Aliri's throat. "She chose him. He views it as the honor it is, and I will not strip that from him."

"He would have heeded her call and exposed us all had we not been here to stop him."

"He was willing to defend her even if it meant his death." Aliri almost regretted holding him back when the words left her mouth. Laangor's breath, she was a hypocrite. "That is the mark of a true dragonbond."

"You speak as if they are already bonded. Nothing has been forged in steel yet."

"His quiescent bond with Daeya McVen is the strongest I've seen. Can *you* remember a time when a dragon reported seeing through the eyes of a draegion not yet bonded?"

"Assuming I believed him?" Vorsere bared her teeth. "Perhaps it is the Shard's magic."

An ominous thought, and all too plausible. This was the first time Baokryn's soul would pair with a dragon since she'd stolen the Shard from Chaos. Things were bound to go differently with a god's magic involved.

Aliri started across the cavern toward the tunnel. Assuming Daeya could access the Shard as Baokryn had, she could only pray for the girl's wisdom in its use.

"You remember the *controversssy*." Vorsere leaped a magma channel to join Aliri. "There are those among us who still see it as enslavement. We will not be bound like that again."

"I know, Vorsere." Aliri closed her eyes at the memory. The battle, the bloodshed, the frustration on both sides as Baokryn brought twenty thousand dragons to their knees. "I know."

# CHAPTER FIFTY-SEVEN

## RAVLOK

Ravlok sat alone beside an altar to Shavaan. Incense twirled between candles that flanked the healing goddess's symbol—a lotus, carved from marble and polished to a mirror shine. He shut his eyes against it.

*I know you will do your best.*

Tiior's words, spoken months ago.

He'd been a fool then, believing he could protect Daeya, and tonight served as proof. His arcane impotence had never been more excruciating than when the healers had clamored to save her life and all he could do was hold her wound and pray she didn't bleed out before the ward against Chaos snapped into place.

Ravlok threaded fingers into his hair and rested his elbows on his knees. The package inside his tunic pressed close—for once, a comforting pressure. He may have failed her tonight, but he wouldn't fail again.

A door opened and closed, followed by hushed voices. Two shadows darkened the corridor, their edges made soft by the predawn glow.

"...is there truly no other way?"

"We've tried everything, *neime*. It's just too far gone."

Tipori and Orowen, the true heroes of the night.

Eavesdropping was unbecoming of a man of faith, but Ravlok couldn't help himself. It had been hours without news.

"But you've restored limbs before."

"Ones that were severed, yes, but the poison accelerated the fleshrot beyond our ability to cure it. If we don't act soon, we risk further infection."

"You're saying his wound could still kill him."

Ravlok flinched at the bite in Tipori's tone—the product of a father pushed to his limit.

"I—well, *ciir*."

Truthfully, Ravlok had thought Zakaari dead when they found him. Magnus told them Daeya had been half-crazed and delirious, trying to guard the boy from enemies who weren't there.

Tipori's shaky sigh made Ravlok's heart ache. "Do what you must. Just save my boy."

Ravlok curled his fingers around a wisp of incense.

Zakaari could learn to live with only one arm, if he could be patient with himself. Ravlok had once trained with several men and women who'd lost limbs. One went on to remaster the sword, while others discovered ways to adapt their hand-to-hand technique. Another found passion in the gods' work and joined the monastery herself.

"If I didn't know better, servant of Ordeolas, I would think you were sulking."

Ravlok looked up at Bren, who'd slipped into his periphery. Warmth touched his cheeks. "I suppose I was."

Bren gestured to the bench. "May I sit?"

Certain he was about to get a lecture, Ravlok resisted the urge to groan. "Of course. Though I'm afraid I'm not easy company right now."

Bren smoothed his robe and sat. "That makes two of us."

Ravlok winced. One of Bren's fellow acolytes had died tonight. Who was he to think his pain outweighed the healer's?

Bren lit more incense and silently tended the altar of his deity. He bent his head in prayer, then lifted weary eyes to the infirmary before them.

A few minutes passed before the itch to speak won Ravlok over. "Thank you." When Bren frowned, he added, "For saving her."

Mirthless, broken laughter accompanied Bren's response. "That was mostly the high priestess. Her connection to Saolanni is unrivaled."

Orowen was indeed the most skilled healer Ravlok had ever known, but he didn't relent in his gratitude. He nodded toward the altar. "Your devotion to Shavaan is remarkable, too. When the high priestess began to doubt, you were right there, supporting her."

"So were you."

The acolyte's words gave Ravlok pause.

Bren glanced sideways. "Your quick thinking saved them both. No one else would have solved the mystery of that poison, and we'd be preparing bodies for the pyre, rather than making plans for their extended stay."

Ravlok swallowed once, twice. How much he'd learned of Draconic hadn't been apparent until that moment when Riisii's carvings stopped being madness and became an instruction. An index.

What would become of the book when his part in this was done? The thought left an odd taste in his mouth. Tipori had an entire organization to run. Orowen was bound to the Temple for the next year, and Riisii was too unpredictable. Perhaps Zakaari could take over. He'd already shown some interest in the ancient cities, and he possessed magic enough to be the partner Daeya deserved.

There had to be a way to transfer the book's ownership. He would have to research it later.

"Your mind is always turning, isn't it?"

He'd been quiet too long. "Something my mentor would be ashamed of. Makes for poor meditating."

"I can imagine."

Nallia appeared in the doorway. "Bren, we're ready for you."

Bren sighed. "I'll be right there."

Incense stirred in his wake as he rose. Ravlok followed suit.

"Is there anything I can do?"

"Just keep reading, brother."

*Glass shattered. Lantern oil spilled, and fire flared. The smoke made her eyes burn.*

*Da was going to be so mad. She knew she wasn't supposed to play tiffleball in the barn.*

*"Nashanett."*

*Her ma was outside, screaming for help.*

"Where are you, little one?"

*The fire ate at her dress—her prettiest dress with the lace on the collar. The one she'd begged Da for at the market. Flames flickered scarlet against her white-gold skin. Now she wouldn't have anything nice to wear.*

*Fire should hurt. Why didn't it hurt?*

*The barn door creaked wide, and a blast of hot air stirred the hay. A shadow moved through the smoke. She stepped backward, remembering what her ma said about talking to strangers.*

*Eyes like melted gold and slitted like a snake's. Blond hair that brushed his pale shoulders. He reached out, wearing that serious stare that reminded her of Da when he'd found her pet turtle in her sock drawer.*

"Do not be afraid."

*"Telerion."*

*He was no stranger. Daeya ran to him. Her friend wrapped her in his arms and scooped her up.*

"You are safe, *Nashanett.*"

*Wood splintered above them. Telerion folded his wings around her, sheltering her from the falling timbers. Embers spiraled upward as the walls came down. Outside, a scream rent the air.*

*Why was Da crying?*

*Sunlight. She peeked through Telerion's wings and sucked in cooler air. It didn't taste as much like ash. Daeya hid her disappointment.*

"Can we go flying again?" *she asked Telerion as he stepped over the broken barn door.*

*His golden eyes darted toward her parents. Sorcerers' rifts opened on either side of them. Daeya had never seen Da scared before.*

*Telerion set her down on the grass and pushed her toward Ma, letting his wings unfurl.* "Soon," *he promised.*

*He was a bad liar. Daeya turned and scowled at him, but he wasn't looking at her. She followed his eyes to a familiar human man and a Cintoshi woman who stepped through the rifts.*

*Telerion growled. His emotions were a cyclone inside her mind. They made Daeya queasy, like she'd tried to eat sugared ice too fast. He looked between the sorcerers and her parents, making a decision.*

"You're leaving me?"

"You belong with your family."

"But—"

"Do not worry, little one. I will wait for you."

*Crashing timbers made Daeya jump. She spun to face the plumes of smoke roiling into the sky.*

*It was so pretty.*

*A heavy hand settled on her shoulder. She looked up to find the old sorcerer studying the light on her skin with a weird look on his face. She leaned away from him, uncertain, but he smiled kindly and bent to look her in the eye. "There you are, my sweet. Your parents were so worried about you."*

*The Cintoshi sorceress appeared behind him. Her beard was woven with gold thread and white saphyrum beads that swayed with each step. She stared past Daeya at Telerion.*

*A burst of excitement chased away her misgivings. The sorceress could see him. Finally, she would get to introduce someone to her dragon friend—the one Ma insisted was just pretend.*

*Except, when she looked over her shoulder, Telerion was gone.*

⁂

Daeya shot upright, heart racing as she swept the room for Gregory, Anordis, or the Aetherman. Walls covered in runes swam into focus. The surface beneath her crackled like straw.

A thought filtered through her panic.

Telerion had known what she was. He'd known from the beginning.

More memories cascaded over themselves—memories of flight on dragonback, of Telerion playing hide-and-seek with her in the forest, of him warning her away from the man who offered her a ride on his pony if she but followed him to his wagon. Memories of extraordinary stories not even her Da could tell with such enthusiasm—stories of epic battles and falling kingdoms and terrifying monsters.

*Telerion knew.*

How had she forgotten him so completely?

And why hadn't he told Tiior about her?

The blanket fell to her lap, and cool air greeted her bare skin. She scrambled to cover herself. Bleeding Aether, why was she naked?

"Where—"

Pain lanced down her left arm, an abrupt reminder of the bolt that had been lodged there. Her cry shattered the quiet room. Daeya cupped her shoulder and breathed through the spasms. She tried to stretch her arm, but her elbow was slow to respond, and her two littlest fingers were numb.

When the twitching finally subsided, she looked down. The skin where the bolt had pierced her was almost perfectly smooth. Even the runes in that spot hadn't grown back. Other discolored runes surrounded it; they were normally white, but now they were as pink as the healed tissue, like they too had been damaged by the poison.

And when the runes had broken, her memories of both her dragon and her power had flooded back. As if they'd been another means of control.

As for Mardis Ulrich—had she seen Telerion that day? Was she just as complicit in all of this?

Movement caught her eye. Daeya stiffened.

"Doesn't look bad at all. Silonas smiles on you, McVen."

Daeya clutched the blanket and stared hard into her lap. Naked *and* in the same room as Zakaari? If she hadn't died in Anordis's attack, she'd surely die from embarrassment now.

"I—"

The runes. He could see them. They had all seen them.

Tipori had worked out in moments where they'd come from. She'd fallen asleep to his whispered promises of retribution, assuring her it changed nothing, that they could discuss the runes when she recovered.

It didn't change the fact that these ugly, horrible scars covered nearly every fingerspan of her body, and soon everyone in Starlight would know it.

*Gods...*

If she could only crawl under the blanket and disappear. Maybe there was a closet or a pantry she could sneak off to—one like in the stories she read to the children, with the little door on the other side that led to the Fae Realm or the Plains of Gray. Anywhere. Anywhere but here.

But there was no more running from this.

Daeya turned toward Zakaari, readying a hundred excuses on top of a thousand apologies. Only, nothing came out. All she could do was stare.

Zakaari was propped up by pillows in the other bed, so close Daeya could have touched him. White lines spiderwebbed up the side of his neck and across his chest, following the path of the poison. His left arm ended at his elbow.

He looked away, his gaze shuttering. "It's gruesome, I know."

"No." Her denial was reflexive, for lack of anything else to say. What *could* she say? He'd lost his arm because of her.

He snorted. "Your face says otherwise."

Right, staring at it wasn't helping. She tried to school her expression into something more stoic.

He wouldn't want an apology. 'Sorry' wouldn't fix his arm. She wouldn't say she understood because, of course, she didn't, even if she was ashamed of her own scars. They were nothing like losing a hand.

*Better his hand than his life.*

Daeya recoiled, but she couldn't shake the thought. Selfishly, she would rather have him without a hand than lose him entirely. But how to convey that without sounding callous?

Zakaari retreated further into himself as she formulated responses and tossed them aside until there was only one thing left she could do. If this didn't work…

She couldn't think about what that meant for them.

Slowly, Daeya lowered the blanket, letting it pool against her thighs. Her runes were on full display as she gathered her courage and carefully swung her legs over the side of the bed. Her nakedness mattered little. Her scars, even less. She could do this. Cool wood creaked under her feet. For him, she would do anything.

His attention pointedly fixed on her face. He started when she grabbed the edge of his blanket and pulled it aside.

"What are you doing?"

"Scoot over."

He did, speechlessly, allowing Daeya to climb into the bed. Every fingerspan of her rune-scarred torso fit flush against his side on the small mattress. Rather than settle her head on his pillow, she cuddled into the space between his chest and shoulder.

"Daeya—"

She scowled. "If you're going to demand I go back to my own bed, you can forget it."

Zakaari stared at her, studied her face. His eyes filled with tears and he curled his right arm around her. His left arm moved as if to wrap around her, too, and a frustrated sob shook his whole body. He buried his face in her hair. "I don't think I can do this."

"It's not going to be easy." Tears stung her own eyes. She snuggled tighter against him and pressed her hand over his heart. "But I'm here to help you in whatever way you need."

His composure cracked further. Soft cries came in waves that broke over him, on and off, for the next few hours. But even when the healers came to check on them and Nallia tried to chase Daeya back to her own bed, she refused.

At least for now, the crisis was past. Orowen assured her the ward against Anordis was in place and they were safe inside this room. She and her acolytes had already begun warding the rest of the Temple.

Telerion had been waiting over ten years for her to find him. He could wait a little longer.

# CHAPTER FIFTY-EIGHT

## ALAR

"Alar!"

Alar's feet slapped against half-melted slush. Ash dusted his hair, his cloak, even his eyelashes. He shook his head to knock it loose.

Smoke still poured out of Mount Eisekii, even though the aftershocks had tapered off sometime in the early hours of this morning. But the clouds over the mountains were nothing compared to the smoke still rising from the smoldering garden. Part of Tipori's house had gone up with Daeya's fire, and they'd lost several supply sheds on that side of town.

"Alar, stop!"

Alar's jaw tensed. Finn could wait. The supplies, the troops, all the intelligence he'd learned could wait until after he saw Daeya. He should never have left her alone.

Ashaara had been wrong about her, and Alar was certain he could make her see it now. He'd heard about how Daeya stood up for Orowen at her reaffirmation—how she'd all but dedicated herself to the Alliaansi's cause right then. It

496

had only taken a few months to reverse her prejudices. Daeya wasn't like Leah; she wouldn't so carelessly break his heart.

He took the Temple steps two at a time and wrenched the door open with his mind. It crashed against the wall, startling acolytes and patients alike.

Finn flew in behind him, her fur-lined hood blown back. "Gods damn you, pigeon-head, stop! She's moved on."

That brought Alar to a stumbling halt.

He'd heard the rumors, in a way. Whispers of thoughts had filtered through his awareness and begun to take shape as he'd traveled through Starlight. His ability to decipher psionic language had grown with each new imperium he'd performed. Half a dozen new rivers fed his sea of thought, and they acted as templates for piecing together the words in others' minds.

It was no surprise that someone as pretty as Daeya had attracted that kind of attention. If it had helped her make friends here—the sort of friends she'd always deserved—then he was glad for it. But Finn clearly misunderstood. Daeya cared for him, and he for her, and now that their people were provided for, he could give her his full attention, at least until his next mission called him away. Maybe next time, she would be free to come with him.

He turned on his heel, holding up a hand to stop the human acolyte encroaching on his periphery. "What?"

Finn winced. "He's been with her day and night. It was bound to happen."

"You mean Zakaari?" Alar couldn't stifle the laugh that crawled up his throat. If that was the case, Finn's concerns were truly unfounded. "That's ridiculous."

"I've seen them together, *amii*."

He fought the urge to roll his eyes. Finn couldn't know Daeya had a tendency to pick at scabs when she got bored. "It's only her forced proximity to the man-child that gives any illusion of interest. She has more discerning tastes than that."

Other healers approached. He turned to search the infirmary for Daeya.

Finn seized his wrist in a vise. "I'm serious. People are saying he left his other women for her."

Alar wrenched away from her. "And you believed them?"

Tipori's son was little short of a whoremaster. He was the kind of man mothers warned their daughters away from and fathers banned from their doorsteps. If he had any interest in the sorceress at all, it was because she was a novelty. A conquest. Daeya would see through him like a pane of glass.

"They went to solstice together. And I caught them running off into the forest." Finn's aura stilled. "Alone."

Alar frowned. He studied her surface thoughts for signs of uncertainty or deceit, though she had nothing to gain by lying. She'd encouraged him to mend things with Daeya in the first place. For the last three months, he'd thought of little beyond acting on Daeya's intelligence and crafting an ironclad argument to convince Ashaara they could be together. He *would* make things work with her. For all she'd done for their people, he would give her nothing less than his best.

But now Finn was accusing her of disloyalty. The only way to find out the truth was to speak with Daeya herself.

"Acolyte," he barked to no one in particular.

"Yes, *Amaa*?"

He turned to face the human, whose aura rippled with apprehension. "Take me to the sorceress."

The sandy-haired boy hesitated. "She's not prepared for visitors—"

Patience gone, Alar *pressed* the command into his mind, snatching his name as he went. "Now, Wyl."

Wyl's reservations folded easily under Alar's psionic touch. "Y-yes, *Amaa*. This way."

"Alar," Finn tried one more time.

His name lingered behind him as he followed the healer to the private rooms. Wyl knocked at a closed door, and Alar finally breathed to center himself.

Daeya's soft giggle broke against the door. One side of his mouth tugged upward. She was in the care of some of the best healers in the world. He'd been worried for nothing.

"Enter."

Zakaari's voice. Alar's smile faltered.

He shook off the doubt that lifted the hair on the back of his neck. Of course Zakaari would be standing guard. Alar entered the room behind Wyl.

It was like stepping into a waking dream. His senses deadened, ears filled with wool. No matter how many times he blinked, he couldn't force the sight before him to change.

Finn was right.

"Apologies, Sorceress—" Wyl began.

Daeya shot upright, holding a blanket to her chest. "Alar."

Never had his name carried so much mortification and guilt. Alar blinked again, looking between her and Zakaari, whose expression turned to stone. The boy was missing an arm, and Daeya's skin was covered in odd white markings, but those details refused to stick in his mind while the pair shared a bed, quite obviously naked beneath that single blanket. As if she were comfortable that way. As if they'd been this way before.

No. No, this wasn't happening.

The silence stretched into eternity before Daeya stammered a weak excuse. "I didn't know you'd come back."

There had been days where he'd thought of nothing but returning to her. Of holding her in his arms. Promising her that things would be different now that she was one of them.

But this...

Zakaari's remaining forearm flexed at Daeya's side. Alar followed the subtle movement to their joined hands. Her eyes darted toward Zakaari for reassurance.

It was too much.

Anger black as pitch welled inside him. "When I heard you were making friends, I must admit I never expected this."

Daeya's brows furrowed. "What's that supposed to mean?"

"Of all people, you choose him?"

"You left, Alar."

The accusation drove the blade deeper and twisted. Was this her way of punishing him, then? For putting his people first? He'd had no choice but to leave her, but for her to go running to someone who wouldn't appreciate her the way she deserved—

His hands curled into fists.

"What did he promise you? Power? Riches?" Alar scoffed. "Sorry to say, you'd have to bed his father for those things."

She recoiled with such perfection, it almost looked like real surprise. "It's not like that at all."

He couldn't see Zakaari's aura through his ward, but he didn't need to. The storm darkening his expression was telling enough.

"Get out."

Alar ignored him. His attention fixed on Daeya. Pressure mounted behind his eyes and forced his fury—his pain—higher. "You'll never be special to him. Whatever he's told you, you're nothing but a novelty. A tryst."

"Alar—"

"He'll toss you aside when he tires of you, just like all the others."

"No." Her expression steeled. "He wouldn't."

The healer tried to speak up, but Alar sidestepped his reaching hand and glared at Zakaari. "You just don't know when to quit, do you? How can you take advantage of someone you're supposed to be protecting?"

Zakaari struggled to sit further upright with the stump of his left arm. "I would never—"

Alar rounded on Daeya again. "You know you don't have to be with him just because he got hurt, right? You don't owe this courtesan anything."

Daeya wrapped the blanket tighter. "You're wrong about him, Alar. And you're wrong about me."

He carried on like a runaway cart full of saphyric flares, bent on destruction. "Maybe I am. Or maybe I didn't know you as well as I thought. Perhaps you'll enjoy being another one of Zakaari's whores."

"Enough!"

Zakaari threw himself out of bed, heedless of his nakedness, and fumbled for a bowl of beads on a nearby table. He tried first with his missing hand, making his efforts more comical than threatening; the bowl tipped and saphyrum scattered. By the time Zakaari downed a bead and summoned his sword from the Aether, he was swaying on his feet. Clearly, he hadn't fully recovered from whatever catastrophe Daeya had brought upon them.

Wyl darted toward the door. "Devoted! Help!"

Alar tracked Zakaari's approach, noting how he favored his right leg. He *nudged* several beads into Zakaari's path. Pity the boy stopped just shy of slipping on them.

"Say what you want about me," Zakaari snarled, "but you won't insult her again."

"What irony, the man-child defending a woman's honor," Alar spat back.

Daeya rose, the blanket trailing behind her as she rounded the bed. Light cast shadows across the strange texture of her skin. "You need to leave."

Those runic markings were too perfect to have appeared naturally. How had he never noticed them before? "Have you had those this whole time?"

She lifted the blanket higher, as if calling attention to them had made her uncomfortable. "Yes."

The impulse to hurt her swept through him like a cyclone. He wanted to make her feel some sliver of the pain he felt right now.

"That's unfortunate." The deadly gleam of Zakaari's steel didn't frighten him. Not when he could easily *seize* a scalpel from the mess on the table and plunge it into his good elbow. "You should see if Orowen can remove them."

His words struck their mark, and Daeya flinched.

Zakaari lifted his sword, readying to strike. Alar's eyes flicked to the scalpel.

Orowen appeared in the doorway, her face tight with fury. "Alaarios Felmani, remove yourself from this temple at once!"

Her use of *that* name stopped Alar cold.

Few still living had ever heard his true matriname spoken without venom, sullied as it had been by a man who had used his psionic gifts to harm their people, rather than help them. Alar would just as soon never hear it again.

Four more acolytes flanked her, lending silent support to her order.

Alar backed off. "Apologies, Devoted."

Orowen's expression didn't change. "I'm not the one who deserves your apology, *neime*."

Zakaari lowered his sword, sidled closer to Daeya, and hesitated. One hand couldn't do it all, it seemed. Alar's jaw twitched as Zakaari carefully placed his Aetherial blade on the bed and gathered Daeya to him. Light glinted off the tear streaks on her face.

His stomach clenched, but he couldn't force out an apology if he tried. He'd protected her, provided for her, and promised to return. And after everything they'd been through, she couldn't be bothered to wait for him.

He couldn't help himself. Alar thrust his chin toward the boy's mutilated arm. "Better you than me, I guess."

Zakaari stiffened.

"Aether take you," Daeya hissed. Her temper, at least, was something familiar. He noted with less trepidation than usual how her skin flickered gold.

"*Out,*" Orowen growled. "Now."

Alar backed toward the door, lifting placating hands toward her. "I'm to report to Ashaara." Duty came first, after all. "You may expect a summons from the council soon. I have news about the School."

# Chapter Fifty-Nine

## Shei-Gwen

*D*rip.
*Drip.*
*Drip, drip.*

The sound came from somewhere beyond the light of Gwen's tallow candle. She groaned and rolled over, thick chains and spellbinders chinking with the movement.

*Drip.*
*Drip, drip.*
*Drip.*

She sacrificed strips torn from her dirty shift to plug her ears, but the sound penetrated the fabric. It was an unusual form of torture, but an effective one. If she didn't freeze to death lying here on the unforgiving stone, the incessant dripping was going to drive her mad.

Time had little meaning when there was no sun to mark its passage. Her guards didn't replace the candle at intervals regular enough to track, and they delivered food and water just as sporadically.

None of them were magic-adepts. Their gray linen robes were unadorned beyond the black belts tied at their waists. Their bald heads shone in the candlelight, as if anointed with oils to ward off fae spirits. They never spoke, even to each other, and they always came in pairs.

Gwen had given up trying to interact with them. She simply observed their comings and goings through a barred window in the solid steel door. After sliding her meager portion of food through a slot, they would wait an indeterminate number of minutes before dragging the tray—empty or not—back through the slot by a rope and leaving her with only the rats for company.

Cursing Normos and worrying for Olivia became a sort of prayer each time she awoke, before every meal, and when she bedded down. It always accompanied a fresh wave of anger and self-loathing for allowing herself to have been so utterly deceived.

How she'd ever trusted Gregory's minion remained a mystery. To think, she had even entertained the notion of taking him on as her right hand. She'd entrusted him with her partner's safety and Sarikkian's secrets. Now, all she had to show for it was a measly candle and a pallet of flea-infested straw.

*Drip.*

*Drip.*

Gwen clapped her hands over her ears.

*Drip, drip.*

She didn't know where she was, or whether Olivia or Sarikkian still lived. What would become of them? Of Peader? Of the Guild?

*Drip.*

Why was *she* still alive? It was obvious there would be no trial.

*Drip, drip.*

Had Normos been telling the truth about Gregory's wards? Was it only a matter of time before they were all made slaves to the blankers?

*Drip.*

A horrible ache clawed up through her chest and lodged in her throat, threatening to become a scream.

*Drip. Drip. Drip, drip.*

She opened her mouth and drew a breath—

An acrid scent stung her nostrils, so far removed from the stench of the overflowing chamber pot that it jarred her from her manic spiral. It took a moment to identify the smell as Aether. Gwen rolled back toward the door. White-violet light blinded her, but sparked hope all the same. Magic meant saphyrum, and saphyrum meant escape.

At least, once she got these binders off.

"Good morning, Councilor." A pale face appeared through the barred window. The man's honey-sweet voice didn't match his hollow cheeks and sunken eyes.

Morning. She glanced at the candle, estimating how many hours it might last.

"I see you're adapting to your new living arrangement quite nicely." He looked toward something outside the door. "Open it."

As keys rattled and locks clicked, Gwen pushed shakily to her feet. Whoever this man was, she refused to meet him while kneeling. She might be filthy and dressed in rags, but she still had some dignity left.

Except, when she straightened fully the world turned sideways, and Gwen toppled back to the floor. Nausea churned her stomach and the distant *drip, drip, drip* was swallowed at last by the ringing in her ears.

"Sweet Shavaan," she breathed.

The man's polished boots appeared beside her. A frayed brown robe pooled around his ankles. "Ah, yes, that would be the torus root taking effect. It induces some dreadful vertigo." His boots creaked as he crouched beside her. "Merely a precaution, you understand."

He brushed the top of her head and Gwen jerked away, baring her teeth like an animal.

His laughter seemed to envelope her as the world listed again.

They'd drugged her food. Delvin curse them.

The thought provoked a sound of sick humor, not quite a laugh of her own. No god of law and justice existed here.

Gwen groped across the floor, seeking the wall to steady herself. If they were going to have this conversation, she was at least going to look her jailer in the eyes.

"What do you want?"

"Mm, I'm glad you asked. How thoughtful of you to consider your host's needs as well as your own."

Fantastic. Another creepy bastard who liked to hear himself talk. Gwen rested her head against the wall. The exertion left her breathless.

"You see, what I want is very simple." He snapped his fingers, and a pair of gray-robes entered. One remained by the door, while the other came forward on bare feet, holding a rolled bundle. Something clicked in the wall behind her. The room filled with a mechanical clinking, that of gears turning, and the slack in Gwen's chains was taken up into dark recesses in the walls.

Panic sliced through her. "Out with it, then."

She tried to sound strong, tried to thrust out her chin and grit her teeth, but when the man gave her a toothy, unhinged smile, gooseflesh exploded across her body.

"Oh, so eager, Councilor. You've not even seen my toys yet."

He rose from his crouch and motioned to the bald man holding the bundle, who set it down and unrolled it to reveal gleaming medical blades, scissors, and forceps. Gwen's horrified gasp slipped past her lips before she could stop it.

Every instinct screamed at her to flee, but she could only wrench at her chains until they were so tight she was forced to rise to relieve pressure on her wrists. With her arms extended to either side of her, she was completely at his mercy.

"Just tell me what you want!"

The winches behind the wall stopped. Her jailer stepped forward until she could feel his foul breath against her cheek. Gwen turned away, bile rising in her throat.

"First, I must apologize for my lack of manners. I haven't even introduced myself."

"You think I care who you are?"

His chuckle rumbled through the stagnant air. "Perhaps not, but propriety demands that you know just the same. My name is Nicolas, and I have some questions for you."

An interrogation? She had already told Normos everything. What more could they possibly need from her? Gwen tried to swallow, but her mouth was bone dry.

"If you provide me with truthful answers," Nicolas continued, "perhaps I can see about getting you some finer clothes. Better accommodations, even." His smile softened, as if he gazed upon a favored niece, not a prisoner. "Your discomfort here need not last long, Councilor Mar-Pol."

Her eyes strayed to the shining metal instruments. Obviously, Nicolas was lying; the only way Gregory was letting her out of here was in pieces. Still, she had little choice but to play his game.

"I have questions of my own. I'll trade an answer for an answer."

"A fine bargain. I accept." Nicolas regarded her and clasped his hands. "Dare I say, ladies first?"

Gwen tried to calm her pounding heart, but her voice edged higher. "Where's Olivia?"

His head tilted. "Who?"

Fear bled into annoyance. If this man was Gregory's creature, he had to know something. "Sorcerer Beck arrested her at the same time."

"I'm sorry, Councilor." Nicolas shrugged. "You are the only prisoner I possess. Logistics, you know. But I promise to find out for you, if you're amenable."

Maybe Olivia had escaped. Her screams hadn't followed Gwen through the rift that brought her here, and she would have known better than to stick around to be used as leverage.

"No," she replied, despite the pain it caused. It was best to distance herself from anyone the renegade sorcerers might harm on her behalf. Gwen dropped her gaze and channeled all her bitter anger into the next lie. "She betrayed me, anyway."

"I cannot imagine how terribly alone you must feel. Rest assured, I am on your side." Nicolas sounded sympathetic—the mark of a dangerous man. He gestured toward his implements of torture. "We need not dabble in further unpleasantries if your heart is already hurting. I will do whatever is in my power to have you moved to a room with all the amenities befitting a lady of your station. I just need to know where Isa Sarikkian is hiding first."

His placating tone blunted her anger, but her mind snagged on the last like a burr in a loom.

"I already—"

The words Normos spoke before she blacked out snared her tongue.

*Say nothing.*

Gwen floundered with the notion. Was it possible?

Surely not. Normos would have already betrayed her secrets to Gregory by now. While she didn't give him the exact locations of Sarikkian's safehouses, it wouldn't take the Guild long to root them out. With how quickly he'd found the tampered ledgers and the missing saphyrum in Ferid, Normos would have little trouble.

Unless they truly didn't know.

Which would mean Normos hadn't told them.

Nicolas studied her, dark eyes losing their friendly gleam. "You already what?"

Gwen peeled her tongue off the roof of her mouth. "I already told them I don't know."

Nicolas sucked his teeth. "You know, I've met worse liars, but I must admit I'm disappointed a Councilor isn't any better at it." From the instruments arrayed along the strip of leather, he took a long, thin knife.

"Now, wait a minute." Gwen needed to stall him long enough to think. If Normos hadn't told Gregory anything, then what was his plan? Why bring her here? "I really don't know where he is."

"That is a lie." Nicolas stepped closer, running his thumb over the edge of the knife. "And I do not appreciate lies. But I'm a reasonable man. I know revealing secrets is not easy, so I will give you another chance."

Cold steel traced her collarbone, then dipped to pierce her shift. Cloth parted beneath the knife, exposing her from shoulder to elbow. Shavaan save her; he was an animal.

Nicolas licked his lips. "Where is Isa Sarikkian?"

"I don't know."

The knife plunged in. Fire erupted across her elbow joint and scorched a trail along her arm. Gwen screamed.

"I must be honest." Nicolas watched the blood well. "I've been looking forward to this. You see, I made a mistake some months ago that has marred my reputation. I've been eager to get it back."

It took several moments fighting against the pain before Gwen found her voice. "Bastard."

"Yes, I am, indeed." He held the knife up for her to see. A trickle of blood ran down its length. "But the subject of my parentage is perhaps too gruesome to speak of here."

The Aether had clearly addled his brain. She averted her eyes as his tongue slid up the blade. Whether he savored the blood for show or genuine pleasure, her skin crawled either way.

Survival. Gwen turned her thoughts toward survival and enduring this man's interrogation. She had information he wanted. As long as she remained useful, he would keep her alive.

*Say nothing.*

She had to trust Normos. Maybe he knew something she didn't; maybe he was forced to bring her here to save face.

*He's a good man, and he wants to do the right things,* Olivia had said. *Nothing will keep him from the Mother's call.*

Gwen prayed her assessment proved true.

"I'm afraid I must amend our bargain." Nicolas tapped the flat of his blade against his lip. "Let's say a truthful answer from you will buy a truthful answer from me. Does that seem fair?"

She glowered at him through her eyelashes, refusing a response.

He smirked. "Excellent. Shall we try again?"

# CHAPTER SIXTY

## MAGNUS

Magnus's palm itched for his sword.

*He is the reason you failed.*

Tipori stood before the Alliaansi council, head high and hands clasped. Once, Magnus would have envied his confidence, or found it inspiring. Now it just made him angry.

"*Ciir,* I did remove Daeya's spellbinders against the council's wishes," he said in answer to Eris's question. "We suspected Jack and his conspirators were after her, and time was of the essence."

Others seated at the table shared satisfied glances, as if such a simple explanation for releasing their enemy after she'd defied their orders could mollify them. The fools.

*They play right into his hands. They don't see the danger he poses.*

"Forgive me, Governor," Magnus said, "but our scouts reported Daeya wasn't even on the plateau for several hours yesterday. You mean to say you released the sorceress while she wasn't in our custody?"

Tipori lifted his chin. "I admit I took a risk. But if I hadn't, both my son and Daeya would have died last night."

Sympathetic murmurs fanned the flames of Magnus's ire. Never mind his failure to excise Daeya's magic from her; endangering their entire community for a sorceress and a single boy was inexcusable. "You take too many risks with our people's safety."

"*Amaa* Gibbons, I have spent three months with that girl. I assure you she's no threat to us. She's pledged herself to our cause and defended our people on multiple occasions. If you're insinuating that I made an uneducated decision, you're wrong."

Pressure spiked into the center of Magnus's eye socket. "She destroyed the northern garden, four supply sheds, and nearly burned down the orphanage. So far, seventeen corpses have been found among the wreckage—"

"Then I was right to assume she would need her magic." Tipori's expression remained maddeningly cool. "Zakaari alone couldn't defend her against so many."

"The girl is a danger to us."

Serreth lifted his hand. "Magnus does have a point. She caused a tremendous amount of damage."

"And yet only one of the escaped prisoners was identified among the dead, and far from the fire in question," Eris added. "You say you were screening for these Chaos priests. There are upwards of thirty other civilians being detained for unusual behavior. None of them went on a murderous rampage last night. Where did these others come from?"

Jerinoch rapped his pipe against the table. Ashes scattered across the wood. "Seems obvious to me. A Chaos priest's influence spreads like a tumor."

"Four of those civilians *did* escape. We found them among the dead," Tipori informed them. "The high priestess says anyone with severe trauma in their past is susceptible. We had scouts watching for them in the community, but obviously we fell short in our efforts." He sighed. "As for the damage, the monk assures me the ritual he recommends for Daeya will grant a greater level of control over her magic."

"And control over a dragon, assuming one still exists." Magnus seized the opportunity to expose more of the danger. "Let's not forget how the dragons obliterated Denoria. That land is still a desert centuries later. If the sorceress can level a quarter-league in moments, imagine what a dragon could do to all of Starlight."

"Yes, but remember she fled the Guild," Tipori argued. "That girl was *trained* to level Starlight, and yet she came here requesting sanctuary for her family."

Jerinoch removed his dohanni pouch to refill his pipe. "If she wanted us dead, we would be already. You practically argued that point yourself, Magnus."

The bastards. Too blinded by her Shield to see. But Magnus couldn't let them gain the upper hand by losing control. There was still time to harvest Daeya's power before the Guild made its move in the spring. When Orowen's wards lapsed, or once Daeya stepped outside them, he could send Jack to try again.

"If both the sorcerers and the Chaos priests are after her, then it seems to me this dragon magic of hers has merit," Jerinoch mumbled around his pipe. His eyes crossed as he fumbled with lighting the bowl. "Imagine how she could aid us in Kuma'Kiir."

"With Daeya's magic and a fresh supply of troops, we could push our enemies back over the border." Tipori nodded toward Ashaara's apprentice, who stood beside the mastermind at the edge of the firelight's touch. "If Alar would brief us on their movements—"

Magnus's lip curled. "After her trial period has lapsed, you mean."

A muscle near Tipori's eye twitched. It was the first sign of his temper rising since the meeting began. "I insist we end this farce of a trial immediately. She is willing to do this for us. We waste precious time by not utilizing her skills."

"I agree."

Magnus's attention snapped to the other end of the table.

Koraani sat forward in his chair. "Make the motion, *ashaan*, and I will second it."

He couldn't. Koraani was the last to have any sense remaining.

Even Tipori seemed taken aback by Koraani's change of heart. No sound came out of his slack-jawed mouth.

Jerinoch guffawed. "Didn't See that one coming, eh, Tipori?"

No. This couldn't happen. Magnus rose, hands braced against the table. He fought with everything he had to keep his voice even. "We have discussed this matter, and it was already decided."

Koraani rose as well, straight-spined and sharp-eyed in his recklessness. "Then I motion to reconsider. She has earned the right to be a soldier like her mother before her."

"And her father, too, if you call what the old bastard did soldiering." Jerinoch lifted his pipe and coughed out a smoke ring. "I second."

Eris shared a guarded glance with Serreth before looking up at Magnus. "I don't like this either, but Serreth and I have no vote on Starlight's council."

It was true. His only allies sat in council merely as advisors.

*For now.*

Magnus lowered himself back to his seat. Pain pounded out a rhythm to the beat of his heart, straining at the confines of his skull until it threatened to crack.

*Perhaps it is time for new leadership.*

Yes. Maybe that *was* what the Alliaansi needed. All three of these men had some personal stake in the sorceress's wellbeing now, and they seemed determined to drive their people into the dirt for her sake. If they couldn't be trusted to make these decisions, they should be replaced.

A coup wouldn't be well received, even if it was best for the Alliaansi. Each man had a following, and martyrdom could get messy. But to discredit them systematically, perhaps, that could be done. Then, with their followers disillusioned, he could destroy them.

His vision narrowed to the man before the council, the usurper of Starlight's leadership. The source of his failure.

*He has undermined you at every turn.*

Tipori would be the first to go.

Further discussion blended into the background. The fools cast their votes and made the girl an official citizen of Starlight. When the monk's ritual came up again, Magnus remained silent. It was approved without contest.

Both the sorceress and the monk had taken shelter beneath the Temple wards, and Magnus had found he couldn't get through them. The opportunity for a swift resolution to this matter had passed.

*Her power grows, and so must ours.*

That meant rebuilding their secret army and reclaiming the governorship from Cheralach's usurper.

He would do what must be done.

"Light Paladins march on Kuma'Kiir," Alar informed the council. He stood in Tipori's recently vacated spot before them, the heat from the fire trench warming his back. "Archeph Roseheart is leading them."

Magnus bristled. "They come from Willowmarsh?"

"Yes, *Amaa*."

Using the honorific grated, but the way Magnus and Rylan had single-handedly routed the enemy forces in Willowmarsh was a story for the ages. Alar allowed himself a brief pang of sorrow for Rylan, then shoved it aside. There could be no more mistakes caused by his reckless heart.

Tipori's fingers stilled in their incessant drumming against the table. "They'll flank Maralla's forces and crush her between them."

Alar nodded. Memories from one of the scouts he'd imperiumed confirmed the maneuver.

"Ashaara will inform Saowen," Koraani said. Saowen was an accomplished mastermind whose telepathic abilities rivaled the best Guild Conduits for distance. "Retreat would leave Kuma'Kiir defenseless. If Commander Evallier can funnel her troops inside the city, they can lend extra support against invasion."

Tipori quivered in his chair, as if fighting the urge to storm out and defend his wife himself. "Tell Maralla to see it done before month's end. We'll need all the Aetherians and aethermancers on standby to construct shields for the city walls. Once we're in position, we'll rain dragon fire."

His fierce declaration sucked the air out of the room. The obvious question hung unspoken for a full five heartbeats.

Jerinoch leaned toward Tipori, cupped a hand over his mouth, and mock-whispered, "You might tell them where you're getting the dragon."

Tipori's gaze fixed on Alar. His silent demand needed no psionics.

Alar released a slow sigh. Just how much had Daeya told him? "Where the Three Sisters touch the mountain."

The words tasted sour on his tongue.

Alar would rather never see Daeya again, but if they wanted to keep Kuma'Kiir, she was their best chance. Light Paladins and sorcerers together would be a devastating force, but even they couldn't ward off dragon fire.

"We should assemble a small team to protect Daeya when she departs to find the dragon." Tipori shifted his focus to the others. "In the meantime, Ravlok and I will oversee the completion of this ritual."

The note of finality in his voice roused everyone from their rigid postures. Eris stretched her arms over her head, spine cracking audibly. Magnus shoved himself from the table.

"There's more." Alar waited until he had their collective attention again. "Before we returned north, I met an acolyte under the tutelage of Councilors Isa

Sarikkian and Shei-Gwen Mar-Pol. When I examined his memories, I discovered the collapse of the School wasn't the high priestess's fault."

He went on to outline all the information he'd gathered, from the burned beams to the disposal of evidence and the missing salvage crew. Everything in Peader's memories, including what the boy knew about the Feridian healers and the disappearance of both Sarikkian and his ally, Councilor Lukas Derrover.

"I also learned from another sorcerer that Councilor Mar-Pol was recently arrested for stealing saphyrum from the Guild inventory in Ferid." Whether that was true or not, the mage he'd ambushed near the border had seemed to believe it. "They think she knows the location of the missing Councilors, and plan to hold her until she reveals them." Alar hesitated. "Another sorceress, Mardis Ulrich, is involved somehow. She's now a fugitive."

None of the imperiums he'd performed offered insight into Ulrich's part in all this. One sorcerer believed she'd committed treason while under the influence of a mastermind. Another concluded she'd fled after being exposed as an Alliaansi spy. Peader thought she was working for Sarikkian to weaken Gregory, but the holes in his imperium had made it impossible to glean much beyond that. Whatever the case, people only disappeared like this when they knew something important.

By the end of Alar's report, Jerinoch's smile was so wide it exposed the gap from a missing molar. "By the gods." He elbowed Tipori hard enough to provoke a grunt. "Hear that? Councilors are mysteriously disappearing."

"It's a coup." Tipori's eyes widened.

Koraani grinned like a jackal. "Our enemy fractures from the inside. We can use this. Well done, Alar."

A wave of warmth broke over him at the praise. He dipped his head.

"If we expose their secret, it could mean civil war in Eidosinia," Serreth said.

"They'll claim masterminds are involved." Tipori looked thoughtful. "I've met Sarikkian. He is a diplomat, not a warmonger, and he is sympathetic toward Syljians."

That Tipori knew Sarikkian should have come as no surprise. There were few leaders who'd taken office in the last century he didn't know.

"If these other individuals disagree with the Guild's manufactured tragedy," Tipori continued, "perhaps we can offer them aid in exposing it."

Magnus's face darkened. "You would aid our enemy?"

"No." Tipori's mask of patience didn't fool Alar for a moment. "I would befriend our enemy's opposition. We have few allies up here, and it's time we make some."

"We'll have to find them first." Jerinoch puffed another smoke ring. "You can do that, can't you, my boy?"

Koraani didn't hide his annoyance at the old human's nonchalance.

"Yes, *Amaa.*" Alar leaped at the chance to dodge Tipori's team of babysitters. "I can have my affairs in order by first light."

Tipori frowned, but made no attempt to deter him.

"You will rest and recover first." Koraani's command brooked no argument. "Then we will discuss the specifics of your assignment."

"Perhaps we can send an emissary to the Mautori as well," Eris suggested.

Mautor was a nation built of warrior clans, and they'd aided the Alliaansi in border skirmishes with the Iceborn raiders before. Many of their chieftains remembered Syljia and Astenpor as they once stood, and distrusted Eidosinians as a result. Perhaps they would agree that a Guild presence in the Northlands was a threat to them as well.

"If they will join us," Eris added, "we could unite the continent against the sorcerers and declare our sovereignty once and for all."

Jerinoch chuckled. "I think you just volunteered."

"The hour grows late." Koraani rose from his seat. "We can discuss further details in the morning. Is there anything more, Alar?"

Alar bowed his head. "No, *Amaa.*"

"Anyone else?" When no one spoke, Koraani nodded once. "Then this meeting is adjourned."

# CHAPTER SIXTY-ONE

## OROWEN

Orowen sat heavily on the alcove bench, allowing the news to sink in. Panuu leaped up beside her and headbutted her hand. She scratched absently at the cat's neck as she looked up at Tipori. "You're certain?"

He nodded. "Ashaara confirmed Alar's interpretation. The Guild set us up."

She tried to reconcile what she remembered of that day with what Tipori was saying, but it didn't make sense. Ravlok's aid, Alar and Val's rescue, the battle, the rift. Their escape couldn't have been so deliberately timed to coincide with the sabotage. "How could they have known I would cast a rift?"

Kendi knelt beside her, stroking Panuu's dappled gray coat. "They didn't need to. Think about it. They knew exactly which beams to burn and which piers to cut to collapse the building. If they were discovered, they could have claimed Alliaansi spies got inside and created the diversion to get us out. Even if you hadn't cast that rift, they *planned* for the School to fall that day."

"Your presence might have been a catalyst," Tipori said, "but nothing you did or didn't do could have changed the outcome."

"Those children would have still died," Orowen whispered.

She put her hand over her mouth. Only the Guild would sacrifice its children to frame the Alliaansi and create a sympathetic platform for revenge. Only the sorcerers, who slaughtered her people indiscriminately, hoarded life-sustaining resources, and mutilated their own, could be capable of such evil.

After all these months of grief and remorse, after reconciling with her mistakes and renewing her vows to her people and her goddess, she should have been relieved. Instead, anger churned Orowen's stomach. Was their world so full of monsters that she should wish for tragedy over deliberate destruction?

A sob wracked her shoulders. Kendi had her in his arms in an instant, startling Panuu off the bench. "It's alright, *nei ama're*."

"No, it's not." None of this was right.

"It's only a matter of time until the world learns what they've done," Tipori said. "Eidosinia will have no allies after this. Not unless it makes drastic changes in its leadership."

"You sound like you have a plan."

"An inkling at best." Tipori's gaze strayed toward the corridor leading to his son's room. "My contact from Ferid has disappeared. I'm still waiting on a few channels to report in, but I fear she may have been compromised."

Pieces clicked into place, and Orowen grew still. "You're going to petition the Aivenosians." She shared an awestruck look with Kendi. Getting Aivenos involved with international affairs was challenge enough, let alone acknowledging a people without a nation currently at war with one of their strongest allies. "You really think they'll aid us this time?"

"I think High Chieftain Ithenor will be very interested to learn what has become of his daughter."

The ominous words hung in the air. Kallen Ithenor was not a man to entertain lightly. Maralla had once likened a meeting between Chieftain Ithenor and Tipori Evallier to one between two Rillanese bush lions—all fangs, claws, and bloodied manes. Whatever history the pair shared, it was best Orowen didn't get involved.

Nallia brought over glasses of watered wine for each of them. Orowen took hers in hand and drank long.

"What of your self-confinement?" Kendi asked.

Orowen cringed. One glass was perhaps not enough.

Kendi looked hopeful. "Does this mean you can return to Havensguard?"

One glass was absolutely not enough. Her relocation to the Temple had been hard on Kendi. How was she supposed to explain that her year of confinement was a necessary part of her reaffirmation, even now?

"*Neime*," she began, lacing the fingers of her free hand with his, "I still broke my oath to Saolanni, and I've promised her my unfaltering service. I've made peace with this. I ask you to respect it."

His lips formed soundless syllables and his grip tensed against hers but, eyes closing, Kendi nodded. "Of course, I will respect your choice." He lifted their joined hands and kissed her knuckles. "There's no one I respect more than you."

Warmth bloomed in her chest. "You really are too good for me, Commander."

"I beg to differ, priestess." A thought stole over his face. He turned to Tipori. "*Amaa*, I would ask—"

"For Silonas's sake, *amii*, you don't need my permission."

Orowen's brows furrowed at his sudden smile. Mira's mercy, his Foresight was unnerving sometimes. He stepped away from them, but lingered near the mouth of the corridor.

Kendi slid off the bench and knelt again. He set the wine glass down, then took her hand in both of his.

"Orowen Evallier, High Priestess of Saolanni, I have admired you from the moment we met. You continue to amaze me with each day that passes. It would be my honor to bestow upon you a fraction of the same devotion you show your goddess."

Breath was an essential part of life, but Orowen's lungs rebelled against the notion. Her eyes filled with fresh tears. "Kendi…"

"With a humble heart, I…" His throat bobbed, and the first tears slipped down his face, following the creases carved by his sheepish smile. "I, Varkendios Emaaris, ask to bear your name."

Orowen carefully placed her wine glass beside Kendi's. All around them, the bustle of the infirmary stilled. Dozens of eyes watched her lay shaking fingers over his. As if a fog had finally lifted from her senses, she gazed down at her oldest and dearest friend.

"Commander Varkendios Emaaris," she rasped, "I'm truly blessed to have earned such love and commitment from a heart as pure and noble as yours. I would gladly share my mother's name with you."

As cries and cheers erupted throughout the infirmary, Kendi extracted one hand and rose, capturing Orowen's mouth with his. Joy and love scorched through her veins, leaving her breathless once more.

In between tears and kisses, she whispered, "*Nei amaare tiik.*"

"*Nei amaare tiik.*" Kendi grinned. "You can't be rid of me now."

"I suppose you're right." Her smile was so wide it hurt. "If you plan to move in here, we may need a bigger bed."

He kissed her again. "I'll see it done."

Warm fingers skated across Daeya's back. Zakaari traced the whorls, blocks, and lines of runes with reverent care, as if they didn't disturb him at all. Warrior's runes, he'd called them, as if they mimicked the gods-given skills some Syljians were blessed with at birth. It was a much nicer way of thinking of them than mutilations.

Though his eyes remained closed in staunch defiance of the sunrise, occasionally the light caught a glint of violet, like he was checking to ensure she was still there.

He needn't have worried. Daeya could have lain beside him for all time. Static trailed in the wake of his touch, and only her arm draped across Zakaari's abdomen anchored her to the bed they shared. The heady feeling was so delightful and new she'd been slow to dress in the clothes the healers had left, despite being cleared to return to light activity today.

She turned her face into his chest, filling her lungs with his scent. His hand splayed protectively over the scarred patches on her hip.

"Daeya?"

"Yes?"

"Can we talk about what Alar said?"

She'd been trying very hard not to think about what Alar said. Every assertion he'd made had been carefully crafted to cut her, to punish her for not choosing him. But how could he have expected differently when he'd made himself so completely unavailable to her?

Still, she couldn't pretend his words didn't hurt. Zakaari's promiscuous reputation was no secret. He'd made a promise, true, but what boy wouldn't to get what he wanted?

Alar certainly had.

Zakaari shifted beneath her and struggled to sit up. The movement forced her up with him.

A jolt shot through her as he started to pull away. She put her hand on his chest. "Wait—"

"Before you say anything," Zakaari cut in, "just hear me out. Please."

Daeya steadied herself and nodded, resisting the urge to bite her lip.

He reached for something on the bedside table. Metal and ceramic clinked as he dug through the pile of personal belongings, cutlery, and breakfast dishes to retrieve a small wooden box. Daeya propped herself on one hand beside him.

Zakaari placed the box in his lap. "I know what other people say about me." He kept his eyes low, as if the admission brought him shame. "I know how it must look to you."

She attempted a smile. "My da would say I'm crazy to trust you."

His seriousness didn't abate. Piercing violet eyes leveled on her face. "I pray you believe me when I say I was never dishonest with any of my partners. My choices have hurt people, *ciir*, but I've always been upfront with them about the way I choose to love."

Daeya sobered under that intense look. She put her hand on his knee. "You don't owe me an explanation."

"But I do. I mean it when I say I've never cared for anyone the way I care for you. When I look at you, I understand the way *Peiaa* looks at *Miaa*—the way they both look at Damiir."

She remembered how Tipori and Maralla had kissed on the dais in front of thousands. She remembered craving the same love and affection all three of Zakaari's parents had displayed the night her entire world changed. If that was the kind of love Zakaari felt for her, then it rivaled what she felt for him. In no time at all, theirs had become the kind of love that conjured fire and leveled mountains. The kind for which kingdoms rose and fell.

"I want you more than anything else in my life, and if you say you don't want to share, then you don't have to." He nudged her hand with the box. "I know it's early, but if the last few days with you have taught me anything, it's that I'm right where I'm meant to be."

Daeya adjusted again to sit cross-legged, one knee over his thigh on the small mattress. Shadows filled the Rillanese carvings on the box. She took it and carefully opened the lid.

Inside a silk-lined interior sat a brightly polished ring, the one he normally wore on his left hand. It was platinum, she guessed, for silver was too soft to bear so few scratches when its wearer wielded a sword.

There was an inscription inside the band. Daeya tilted the box to get a better look. "What does it say?"

"Strength. Honor. Courage." Zakaari translated the Rillanese words. "*Peiaa* gave that to me when I turned fifteen. I'd never taken it off until..."

He looked down. Daeya caught his cheek in her free hand, every fingerspan of her responding to his pain with a fierce desire to protect him. She pressed her forehead to his and held him there even as the first wave of tears wracked his entire body.

Her own tears flowed silently alongside his. "You don't have to do this."

"I want to." His warm breath on her cheek cooled the stream of tears. He reached for the ring and brushed his knuckles against the back of her left hand. "I want you to have it. Keep it safe for me."

It was like he'd tasked her with guarding something sacred. She let him slip the ring over her middle finger. Her hand closed around the cold metal, and she sat forward to kiss him. "I will, I promise."

Daeya lost herself in his cascade of kisses. He wrapped his arm around her and fell back against the pillows with a muffled grunt. Heedless of their nakedness, she draped her body over his and reveled in the way his hard planes matched her softer curves.

Cheeks burning, she summoned her courage to address his growing predicament beneath their blanket. "Do you want to..."

"I'm sorry." Zakaari grimaced, ears darkening as he reached between them to adjust himself.

"It's okay." Heat scorched through her. That particular intimacy had been barred from her because of her runes, but now maybe she could see what all the fuss was about. "I want to."

"You do?"

She nodded.

Speech seemed to fail him. He started and stopped twice, searching her face.

"I thought I was supposed to be the blushing maiden," she teased.

The mounting tension in his body let go in a rush, and his smile was made of pure mischief. "Maybe tonight? When we're less likely to be interrupted."

As if on cue, the world outside their room reasserted itself with the sound of cheering, drawing Daeya's attention toward the door.

"Tonight," she confirmed with budding excitement and nervousness.

His smile faltered. "You can always change your mind. Don't think you have to."

This time, she took his face in her hands before kissing him. Her disheveled hair fell like a curtain over one shoulder and blanketed them in shadow. "I know."

A knock at the door sounded only seconds later, as if Silonas himself was validating Zakaari's self-restraint. Over the muffled roar of celebration came his father's voice: "*Enniien*, get dressed, please. We have matters to discuss."

"*Ciir, Peiaa.*"

He was probably here to talk about the runes. Daeya pried herself off Zakaari and eyed the stack of clothes with disdain.

Zakaari chuckled. "It won't be for long, *nei ama're*. Believe me. I prefer you without them, too."

There was no dodging the pillow she aimed for his head.

# CHAPTER SIXTY-TWO

## RAVLOK

A week after solstice, the ritual space was finally prepared. Carved pillar candles dotted each point of a twelve-pointed star drawn with crushed stone and saphyrum powder on the floor of the Temple's largest warded room. Inside the star nested a ring of salt and dried herbs. Vases of dried rosemary, dragon leaf, and cinnamon bark lined a smaller circle. Ravlok hadn't studied their arcane uses so much as the order in which they should burn.

Sparing the room a final glance, Ravlok sat back on his heels. He avoided Daeya's questioning glance, feigning distraction. They would only get one chance to do this right, and under no circumstances could she know how it was supposed to end.

Since the new year began, Orowen and her acolytes had extended wards throughout the Temple. Only the infirmary and the garden remained unprotected now.

Daeya stepped to the edge of the star and stared into its center, where the Tome of Eolaan awaited. "So, this is it, then?"

"Yes." The weight of his dagger tugged against an inner vest pocket. "This is it."

Ravlok had asked Yonfé many times throughout his training what Balance was supposed to feel like. His old mentor's response was always the same: he would know when he reached it. Some monks believed it was a trancelike state of otherworldly peace where pain could no longer touch them. Others thought it was the achievement of immortality. But Yonfé reminded them there could be no pleasure without pain, nor life without death, if each existed in Balance.

In the days since Anordis's attack, Ravlok had begun to understand. Balance, at least for him, wasn't an enlightened state of wisdom, nor was it a great awakening of his mind. It wasn't the abandonment of suffering and joy, but a blend of the two. It was the understanding that the sun couldn't rise without setting, and courage couldn't exist without fear.

The attempt on Daeya's life and Anwic's effort to steal the Tome had put things into perspective. Ravlok's prayers to Delvin, Anordis's natural opposition, had gone unanswered. As long as Daeya held the Shard, she alone stood in counterpoint to the god of chaos. It was Ravlok's task as a servant of Order to ensure she had the tools she needed to defend it.

"And you promise I'll have all the answers to my questions once I've ascended?"

Ravlok snorted, returning to his feet. "You'll get what you get, and I won't hear any complaints."

Jerinoch's wheezing laughter sounded behind them. "Listen to the monk laying down the law."

"He has a talent for it," Tipori agreed.

He stood with the other Alliaansi leaders, save for Magnus, who'd disagreed so strongly with the ritual that he'd refused to attend. His attention lingered on Ravlok while Jerinoch shuffled farther into the room and Koraani slipped away to confer with Orowen. With an almost imperceptible nod, Tipori confirmed his readiness for the part he was to play. Ravlok glanced toward Daeya.

While Jerinoch cuffed her on the shoulder and distracted her with small talk, Ravlok stepped into Tipori's space and withdrew three letters. One contained instructions for Zakaari's handling of the tome. One was an apology to Daeya for his deception and a long-winded monologue on his faith in her. The last was for Sam, also an apology, and a thanks for being a far better friend than he deserved.

All three disappeared up Tipori's sleeve. But before Ravlok could slip away, Tipori caught his elbow and pulled him close. Surprised, Ravlok let his hand close on Tipori's elbow in turn, recognizing the Rillanese gesture of friendship.

"Thank you," Tipori whispered.

Just as quickly, he released him and stepped away.

The nature of Ravlok's task didn't allow for proper farewells, so he hadn't prepared for them. Tipori's quiet acknowledgement carried so much more than simple gratitude, and for a moment, Ravlok couldn't breathe.

"Are you ready?" Orowen asked.

Ravlok scrubbed a sweaty hand over his vest and cleared his throat. "Yes, I think so. Daeya?"

"I'm ready." The sorceress lobbed a smile his way and stole another kiss from Zakaari.

Jerinoch whacked Zakaari soundly with his cane. "Plenty of time to crawl up each other's skirts later. Tipori, call off your boy before he makes a mess of the herbs."

Tipori chuckled and nodded toward Daeya. "You want to incur her wrath, be my guest."

Daeya kissed Zakaari again, and again, until Orowen dragged her nephew away by his ear tip.

"Come, *neime*, there's a spot over here for you."

"Just one more, Aunt Wen—ow!"

Warmth soothed the ache in Ravlok's chest. He might be leaving her in a few hours, but knowing she was surrounded by those who loved her made all the difference. He withdrew the package of dried mushrooms from his vest and portioned them out. "Eat these."

She made a face. "Gods, they stink."

"They taste worse."

He tossed his share into his mouth and chewed, doing his best to keep the bitter flakes off his tongue. As Orowen ushered the others away from the star, Ravlok led Daeya into its center.

"In about thirty minutes, you'll start to feel chills. That's the talotibas working." He sat cross-legged across from her with the tome between them. "You'll want to lay down your fire wards, then. After that, ignite the dragon leaf and breathe in. Then rosemary, cinnamon, and the circle of herbs, in that order."

"Right."

His jaw worked as he prepared himself for the last lie he would ever tell her. "Once that circle starts to burn, you must keep your eyes closed. If you open them for any reason, the ritual will fail."

She hesitated, but nodded once. "I understand."

Ravlok placed his hands on his knees. "Then let's begin."

Scarlet flames danced in Daeya's periphery, warming her against the chill. Colors brightened as the mushrooms set to work, and she got so lost in the patterns swirling through the smoke that she almost forgot why she was there. Ravlok's touch on her hand wrenched her focus back into her body, and he smiled.

Something in that smile felt a little sad.

"The dragon leaf, Daeya."

Daeya shook herself. "Sorry."

She lifted her hand and the dried plant caught fire. Ash sparked golden and puffed into smoke.

"Breathe in."

*"Breathe in."*

The command came from within, like an echo, except it wasn't Ravlok's voice. It wasn't Telerion's either, but Daeya *knew* it. A name lingered just out of reach, beneath the murky surface of time.

She filled her lungs with the dragon leaf's spicy scent, nose itching with the need to sneeze.

"Now the rosemary."

Fire leaped from her fingertips.

*"And the sinnas bark."*

The ancient term for cinnamon jolted her bodily. "Aristyn."

*"Yes, Bao?"*

*"You're not going to get all snobby once you've ascended, are you?"*

*The mautorosi monk threw back his horned head and laughed, tribal beads swinging from his braided mane. "No, I promise."*

Close pressure brought Ravlok's concerned frown into focus. His fingers tightened on hers, mimicking the feeling of Aristyn squeezing Baokryn's hands.

"Are you alright?"

Shadows formed on the wall behind Ravlok's shoulders: three lifeless trees in a barren plain. "Yes, I think so."

Ravlok believed the ritual was meant to unlock her memories. It made sense, then, that she might experience some of them vividly. She snorted. Apparently there was a reason Gregory had forbidden her from using mind-altering herbs.

"Rav?" Daeya blinked away the skeletal trees. "Are you sure this ritual is for me?"

"Of course it is." His frown deepened. "What made you think otherwise?"

"Something Baokryn said."

"When?"

She shook her head. "Just now."

Ravlok lifted his chin, as if he understood. "You're starting to remember. That's good. Now—"

*"—close your eyes."*

*Darkness closed in, and Baokryn's other senses came alive. Xosek's favored perfume wafted over her, filling the space with the smell of sinnas bark, nutmar, and apples.*

*Baokryn cracked an eyelid, and the other draegion glared back, folding her arms. Black braids tumbled over one armored shoulder, and her freckled human nose wrinkled with distaste. "Really, Bao? What are we, children?"*

*A smirk tugged at Baokryn's lips. She closed her eyes again. "As if you'd follow orders any better."*

*"The gods know to expect only the worst from me, not you." The smile in her friend's voice was unmistakable. "Now, hold out your hands."*

*Baokryn obeyed, and cool leather kissed her fingertips. Instinctively, her hands closed around the hilts of two well-balanced swords.*

*"Okay, open them."*

*The craftsmanship was unparalleled, with runes etched along the fullers and saphyrum inlay dotting the crossguards. The right-hand blade was longer and thinner than the left, which bore a serrated edge near the hilt.*

*"They're beautiful."*

*Xosek grinned. "I knew you'd like them. They'll need names to summon them properly."*

*Baokryn stepped away for a few practice swings. Magic hummed steadily, forged within the steel.*

Mischief and Malice.

Their names filtered into Daeya's thoughts as the circle of herbs caught fire and sealed her and Ravlok inside the ritual space. Something just outside her perception tugged at her, and the whisper of Aether ghosted over her ears. If she were to turn her full attention to it, she was certain those very blades would materialize from beyond the Wall.

"Keep them closed, now," Ravlok reminded her. "No matter what."

Daeya nodded.

A soft red glow bathed the room beyond her eyelids. The ruby world of geometric patterns soon distracted her as they spun and swirled like—

*—smoke.*

*It rose over the city in great clouds, blotting out the stars. Far below, and as far as Nahariim could see, towering fires illuminated the fruits of seven hundred years of careful planning.*

*Beneath her hands, golden scales quivered with fury. The great gold dragon rumbled,* "This goes against everything the Elders taught you, *mistress.*"

*Her dragonbond spat her preferred title like a curse. Nahariim sneered.* "The Elders are fools, Maratesh. In time you will come to understand this. We will rule this realm as we were meant to, before the gods usurped our reign from us."

"Your ambition will be your undoing," *Maratesh hissed.* "I cannot follow you."

*Deep laughter rumbled out of Nahariim's chest.* "You don't have a choice."

Dark, powerful magic thrummed across Daeya's skin and left her quaking with desire and dread. That memory harbored the same destructive force she'd felt days ago, standing before the chasm of euphoric power.

She shied from it and cinched her eyes tighter.

*"Why do you shy from our child, my love?"*

Daeya stiffened at the sound of that voice.

The wards. Anordis couldn't have gotten through Orowen's wards. Panic clawed up her spine, demanding flight.

Eyes closed. She had to keep her eyes closed. Ravlok's touch steadied her. Except the hand touching her shoulder wasn't Ravlok's at all.

*Two bright, violet eyes met hers. Anordis's teasing grin only stoked her rage further.*

*"It is an ugly thing," Nahariim snarled.*

*"She is exactly what you asked for. The first child born to a draegion vessel in twenty thousand years."*

*"You mock me. It might as well be mortal." She thrust the sickly syljoren monstrosity into its father's arms and wrenched herself off the birthing bed. "Here. Take your abomination if it means so much to you."*

*"She is a demigod." Teasing gone, Anordis's words were laced with venom. "She must grow to be strong."*

*"My breasts dry at the very sight of it. Now, go. Leave me in peace."*

The baby's scream wrenched at Daeya's heart, as if it cried for her across the eons.

A baby. Bleeding Aether, she'd had a *baby* with Chaos in a former life. A child that Nahariim had scorned.

As if responding to her heightened emotions, the circle of scarlet flames burned higher—

*—and encircled the battlefield.*

*Baokryn rolled from beneath her fallen dragonbond and pushed shakily to her feet.*

*Anordis's soul blight lance jutted from the membrane of Aliri's wing. Tainted blood leaked from the wound, and the dragon's golden eyes were closed.*

*Baokryn steadied herself against the dragon's snout.* "I'm so sorry, my friend."

*"So sad," Anordis crooned. "She was a mighty thing, wasn't she?"*

*Black rage clouded her vision. Baokryn summoned her blades.* "You coward."

*Xosek lay dying at the god's feet. Anordis planted his boot below the hole in her chest and feigned offense. The last of Xosek's tome crumbled to ash in his hands, ensuring her soul could no longer Shift.* "Surely you don't mean that. You once loved me, Bao."

*"Forgo your mind games, Anordis, and draw steel. It's time we finish this."*

The battle raged across Vintrios, and Baokryn and Anordis destroyed everything in their path. Ash lingered on Daeya's tongue and fatigue weighed down her limbs.

*Cold stone bit into her knees. Baokryn prostrated herself before the immortal creature and kept her eyes on the floor. The Oracle's devastating beauty was such that even Baokryn couldn't look upon her without jealousy and lust. She focused on the wound still weeping inside her from the broken dragonbond and stoppered her grief.*

*Eventually Aliri would understand.*

*Fingers curled into Baokryn's hair and wrenched upward. Hypnotic eyes like amethysts narrowed with beautiful, blistering hatred.* "Why have you come here, Traitor?"

*"The Traitor is no more." Baokryn winced, her tongue growing thick with enchantment. She didn't fight Jarrah's magic, and let the truth spill forth.* "Your father threatens the pantheon and wishes to enslave all mortalkind. I beg you hear my proposal."

Distantly, Ravlok began to chant. She tried to surface enough from the torrent to recognize the words, but the memories dragged her under again.

Daeya—

*—shivered.*

*Aristyn held the ceremonial blade in reverent, fur-covered hands. The words of power might have been poetry, so fine was his oration of the ancient tongue.*

*Baokryn's gaze shied from that bejeweled dagger. "How will I know what to do?"*

*Aristyn paused in his cant and opened first one eye, then the other. Where Raoghys the Wise might have scolded her for interrupting, Aristyn's long-suffering smile eased the tension in her shoulders. "Just as you learned to draw your first breath. Just as you learned to suckle. Just as someday, you will perform your Test and subdue a dragon. It's instinct, Bao. You need not worry."*

*"But if I fail—"*

*"Then you begin again."*

*"Baosanni is not going to let me try again. Not with you."*

*Ash, but the monk's smile never wavered. It even seemed to brighten, as if the prospect excited him. "Such is a brother's sacrifice. But I have faith in you. Now, are you going to help me ascend or not?"*

*Sheepishness warmed her cheeks. She dipped her chin low. "Vheth."*

*"Good. Now, close your eyes."*

*Her eyes drifted closed, and he began the chant again. This time, Baokryn remained silent despite the itch across her lower back and the ache in her legs. Their minds and memories merged over her tome. She tried not to flinch when the blade sank deep—*

Aristyn's strangled gasp sounded too close to Daeya, and she jolted from the memory with every muscle coiled to react.

Eyes closed, eyes closed, eyes—

"Ravlok!"

Orowen's cry of horror shattered Daeya's resolve. Her eyes snapped open.

Fire blazed around them. Scarlet-tinged smoke swirled and white-violet light illuminated the lines of the pantheon star.

One of Ravlok's hands rested on the open tome. The other disappeared beneath him as he bent double. His head bowed low, and when he listed sideways, steel flashed.

All the warmth drained from Daeya's body.

"No..."

This... this wasn't— How was she supposed to— He didn't prepare her for—

Daeya lurched toward him. Fire and light exploded outward.

"*No!*"

# CHAPTER SIXTY-THREE

## OROWEN

Mira's mercy, what sort of ritual was this?

Orowen darted for the flames spiraling around Ravlok, her eyes on the blade jutting from his chest. Light pooled in her hands as she wove her sigils. She had only seconds to heal that wound—

Her body struck an invisible wall at the edge of the pantheon star. She staggered, clutching her head.

"Orowen!" Daeya yelled.

This was wrong. So very wrong.

Orowen tried again, throwing her weight against the barrier. Ripples of white-violet light skittered across the dome and vanished.

Another cry tore through the flames. "Help me!"

Orowen slammed her fists against the wall, snarling. This couldn't end this way, not now that she had her magic back. She could save him.

A heavy hand clasped her shoulder. "Peace, Devoted." Tipori's expression was sad but stern. "We must not interfere."

Not interfere? Of *course* she had to interfere. "I can't just let him die."

"You must. The ritual demands a sacrifice."

"A sacrifice?" Orowen stared at Tipori, certain he'd lost his mind. "You knew about this?"

More arcane light burst forth, striking the barrier and filling Orowen's vision.

Tipori's attention flicked toward it in a flash of uncertainty, there and gone. "*Ciir.*"

Orowen forced herself to calm, though her fists clenched at her sides. "Lower the barrier, Tipori."

"I can't do that."

Zakaari ventured forward, voice shaking. "*Peiaa?*"

"She'll be alright, *ennii.*"

"But Ravlok won't!" Orowen insisted. "Please, Tipori. Let me help him."

Behind Tipori, Koraani and Jerinoch stared into the maelstrom, transfixed. Tipori took hold of her shoulders and turned her, pressing her back against his chest.

"Do you not see?" He pointed into the torrent of fire nearly blotting out the two white-gold figures in the center of the room. "Should I withdraw that barrier, we will all burn."

He was right. The air on this side of the wall was deceptively still, but inside the ritual space, only death awaited. Saolanni's grace, he was right.

Tipori hugged her tightly. "I know it's hard. But we must have faith that it's for the best."

Faith. *Ciir.* She'd never had more cause to have faith in the gods' will than now, when the monk she'd met in a Guild dungeon, who'd carried her on his back for leagues, who'd brought Nerimoria's daughter back to them, whose kindness and compassion knew no equal, had sacrificed himself for a cause he believed in.

Tears slipped down her cheeks. "What do you See?" she asked Tipori. "Tell me the truth."

He was quiet so long, she thought he wouldn't answer. Orowen looked over her shoulder.

His lips parted in wonder. "I See her steal a soul from Baosanni."

Everywhere Ravlok turned, gray greeted him. Dark gray ground stretched as far as he could see, hunkered beneath a lighter sky. Wisps of sickly clouds clung to the horizon, and twisted trees dotted the landscape. Their barren branches clawed upward like gnarled finger bones shattered by a giant's fist.

The Plains of Gray.

Ravlok was a gods-fearing man, but the existence of the fabled plane between the living world and the dead still surprised him. It was believed that all souls passed through here on the way to Baosanni's realm. Now, he had proof.

Disquiet snuffed out his scholarly excitement. He turned a full circle, but his feet made no sound against the packed soil. There was no one around to share his discovery. There was nothing around at all.

Some claimed those who acted poorly in life would be doomed to travel the Gray Plains forever in search of Baosanni's Gate—the only entryway to the Afterlife. A chill swept through him. Perhaps his service to Ordeolas hadn't balanced against his exhaustive list of childish mistakes.

Ravlok choked down his rising panic and steadied his aura with something akin to breathing. He was supposed to be dead, after all.

Gods help him. He was dead.

"Hello?"

The question squeaked out of him and gave life to all the uncertainty and fear he'd been holding back. Had the ritual worked? Did Daeya ascend? Was his sacrifice enough to protect her from Anordis?

*"You bleeding bastard. You lied to me."* Her voice came from everywhere and nowhere.

Remorse gripped him in a vise. "Forgive me."

Thunder rumbled across the desolate plain. A spark bloomed in his awareness and tugged on his mind.

*"Wake up. Wake up, or I swear to the gods, I'll..."*

The ambient light grew steadily brighter.

"Why do you linger, brother?"

Ravlok whirled.

Behind him stood a man with a long, bull-like snout and enormous twisting horns protruding from his head. Glazed beads swayed from his braided mane, and one bushy eyebrow quirked as he regarded Ravlok.

His name came easily, as if Ravlok had known him all his life.

Aristyn.

That tug on his awareness came again, but Ravlok resisted. "I'm sorry. I'm not sure what I'm supposed to do now."

A sad smile touched Aristyn's fur-lined lips. "Has so much time passed that the world has forgotten our order's greatest honor?"

*"Please, Rav. I need you..."*

In the sea of gray, Ravlok had failed to notice how similar Aristyn's robes were to those of his own monastic order. Aristyn's eyes began to glow, and a memory surfaced in Ravlok's mind. One that wasn't his.

*Hunger. Discomfort. Frustration.*

*Aristyn chuckled. "Be still, Bao."*

*The young warrior growled and batted at the vegetation shielding them from the cave entrance. "We've been sitting here for ages."*

*"Vheth. And we will sit here for ages more if we must. A draegion knows patience."*

*Baokryn's defiance sparked across their connection. He braced himself for the storm that would follow.*

*Sure as the sun rose, she frowned, creasing the emerald stripe across her golden eyes. Her scowl was fire incarnate. "A draegion is tired of sitting on her backside awaiting a dragon who probably smelled us from three leagues out. She's not coming."*

*He relaxed his hands on his knees and sent soothing waves of reassurance back through their bond. "She tests you in ways other than brute strength, it seems. Would you forfeit her challenge and admit defeat before she ever reveals herself?"*

*Baokryn's expression smoothed over as the fire inside her burned lower. One side of her mouth turned upward. "What would I do without you?"*

*Aristyn snorted. "I dare not consider it."*

*She smacked his arm. "Ashhead."*

The memory faded to the sound of their laughter. More knowledge flooded his mind—knowledge that staggered him. Ravlok might have fallen to his knees had the Mautori man not stepped forward and gripped his shoulders.

His order's greatest honor, the true purpose behind its formation thousands of years ago, wasn't to achieve Balance for the monks themselves, but to help others achieve it.

To help *draegion* achieve it.

"It is a bookkeeper's duty to guard his draegion's memories, to access them through her tome when she needs them, and to guide her when the power she wields becomes too great for her to contain alone." Aristyn gestured to the ground. "If you are to do this, your soul must ascend beyond its mortality and bind itself with hers."

Numbly, Ravlok followed the gesture down to the tome at his feet. It hadn't been there a moment ago; now it pulsed with guiding light. The tug came again, pulling him toward the open book. Tendrils of white-gold static spiked upward, as if searching.

*"Please..."*

Daeya's pain and grief cascaded through that plea.

Still, Ravlok hesitated.

"I don't understand." He lifted his eyes to the elder monk. "I thought this ritual was for her, to unlock her power and bring back her memories. I thought I was supposed to be the sacrifice."

"'A sibling's sacrifice to Ascendant divine,'" Aristyn recited. "*Vheth*, brother, you are making a sacrifice. To be bound to a draegion is to forgo death and renounce your place in Baosanni's Afterlife. Should you perish during your service, your soul will instead reside here"—he gestured again to the tome—"and become part of the great tapestry that is the last of all draegion magic."

"To forgo death..." Ravlok tried to break the explanation down into its smaller parts, like a complicated equation. "As in, become immortal?"

Aristyn nodded.

As if several decades of living a normal human existence weren't daunting enough. Ravlok stared out across the Gray Plains, as vast and endless as the years that lay ahead. His life so far had been an endless procession of lackluster experiences: bed warmer, thief, prisoner, monk. But Daeya's light had infused his most recent memories with splashes of color, as if through her he'd found a calling far bigger than he'd ever imagined for himself.

Could the rest of his years be filled with colors like that? If he got to be with Daeya and learn more about her power, about dragons, about all the civilizations lost to time, could he embrace that eternity with the reverence and commitment it deserved?

"And your soul is bound to the book as well?" he asked Aristyn.

"Yes. As all her bookkeepers are. We record the draegion's memories, and when a vessel suffers a mortal wound, the draegion's soul retreats to the tome until it can be born again. Storing memories here prevents her new vessel's mind from breaking under the strain each time her soul is Shifted."

Thunder crashed overhead, and Ravlok jumped.

Aristyn eyed the black clouds in the distance. "Baosanni grows impatient. It is still your choice, but you must make it soon." He frowned. "Yasuo should have been here by now. But I'm certain he'll be here momentarily to guide you on if you choose not to accept this task."

Ravlok shuddered. The god of death had taken a direct interest in him? And the Gatekeeper, fearsome Yasuo, the barbarian deity from which all horned peoples were said to have descended. According to Mautori lore, Yasuo defended the Gate from deranged souls and demons with a greataxe that stood over four spans tall.

Aristyn's image began to dissolve, trickling into the tome of light between them like sand blown from a dune.

"Wait." If Ravlok had possessed a heart in this plane, it would have lodged in his throat. He reached out, but his hand passed straight through the image. "How do I ascend from here? Isn't my"—he grasped for the term Aristyn had used—"vessel dead already?"

The finer details of Aristyn's form were no more. "Follow the draegion's call, and Saolanni will see you home."

*"Ravlok..."*

Daeya's broken whisper finally compelled his body to move. Ravlok reached for the tome—the source of her voice. Tendrils of light coiled around his arm and swept upward. Exultation and love doused him with warmth.

*"You arsehole."*

"I'm sorry."

*"You'd better be."*

That forceful tug came again, and Ravlok let it sweep him up and carry him away to the crash of thunder. He might have *become* light, for how it surrounded and suffused him, brightening until it became painful. Agony exploded, stealing his breath. He opened his eyes to a maelstrom of embers and blinked Daeya's tear-streaked face into focus.

Her memories of the experience tumbled into his mind along with all the tumultuous emotions they had endured together. The blade still jutted from between his ribs.

"Thank the gods." She kept a crushing grip on him with one hand and lifted the other toward the flames. Fire pooled in her palm. *"Amaa*, let Orowen in."

*"Well done, brother."* Aristyn's voice, much like Daeya's, came from everywhere and nowhere. *"But take heed. A draegion's power is a corrupting force, and our charge is the strongest of all."*

Ravlok might have scoffed, if not for the pain. Of course she was; Daeya never did anything in half-measures. He brushed the pages of the tome. *"Because she stole the Shard?"*

*"Not just the Shard."*

Orowen appeared above him. She touched his face, then his chest. "Foolish boy. What were you thinking?"

*"She stole back the power of every draegion slain by Anordis's hand."*

# CHAPTER SIXTY-FOUR

## DAEYA

"'And when the princess low… lowered her…'" Kalvus squinted at the page. "What's this word, Daeya? *Tay-nach*?"

Daeya choked on her mulled wine and clapped a hand over her mouth. Niam glanced up from her book. Other children tittered with laughter.

"That's…" Daeya cleared her throat. "Um, no, it's *tie-nach*." She exaggerated the pronunciation of the word *taenach*, a popular headscarf worn in western Eidosinia. "It's a Brogrenti word. Instead of 'ay,' we say, 'ie,' like in my name. *Die-ya*."

Kalvus sighed and rubbed his eyes. "Why does it even matter? Why can't I just say *tay-nach*?"

Two other children giggled again. Kalvus's cheeks darkened, and he slumped in his seat.

As funny as the mistake was, the library was a place of learning for children of all abilities, and Daeya wouldn't tolerate them laughing at another's expense. She fixed the girls with a warning glare. "Do you both want to help Wilfau skin the hares for dinner, or do you want to stay for story time?"

They winced. "Sorry, *Amaa*," the freckled redhead said. Her younger sister tucked her nose back into her scroll of traceable letters and dipped her quill.

Daeya put her hand on Kalvus's back and leaned in. "Because *tainach* means something very different."

"What does it mean?"

She grimaced, unsure how much she should tell the ten-year-old. The older redhead's eyes flicked upward. If Daeya didn't tell him, she certainly would later.

Daeya whispered into the Cintoshi boy's ear, "It's something adults do in private."

Owl-eyed, Kalvus spoke with a falsetto that attracted the attention of every child in the room. "Like sex?"

Oh, this kept getting worse. Daeya's cheeks heated. Even if talking about intimacy with Zakaari and Orowen had gotten easier over the last few weeks, speaking to a child was a different matter. And *this* topic specifically—her da and Murtagh would have been beside themselves. "Sort of. It's not something you need to know right now."

Niam came to her rescue and tapped the book in front of Kalvus. With a pointed look, she gestured: *read.*

Daeya tossed a grateful smile across the table, and Niam winked. She closed her own book and rose.

"Going to Sam's again?"

Niam nodded. She'd been training with Sam in hand-to-hand almost every day since she'd cracked a Chaos priest over the head with a shovel. When Ravlok told Daeya the story, she'd hardly believed it, but he'd passed his memory of that night through their new bond like moving sketches, providing all the proof needed. With a little more training, Sam often joked, Niam could one day join the order of mute assassins known as the Dasch'Kalliir.

"*Iiren'hyvaa, amii.*"

Syljian still didn't flow off Daeya's tongue, but it was passable. Zakaari's unorthodox lessons during their own private moments were certainly helping.

A heady shiver traveled through her at the thought.

After tucking the book back onto the shelf, Niam spared one last look at Daeya. Her smile came easily, as if nothing strange or life-altering had happened to either of them since solstice. As if Daeya wasn't leaving for war in a few days. For Niam, the look seemed to say, their friendship would always be as it was right now.

Niam signaled a farewell and departed. Daeya rushed through the last of her duties at the orphanage and kissed Ezra goodbye. Wilfau stopped her at the door with an enormous basket laden with bread and pastries. She surprised Daeya with a fierce hug.

"You stay safe, you hear me, girl? And bring back some new stories for the young ones."

Daeya returned the hug with a knot in her throat. Wilfau wasn't known for affection, and she never spared extra sweet rolls. "I will, *Amaa*."

The stout Syljian pulled away and dabbed her eyes with her apron. "Off with you, now. No one likes a dawdler."

Wilfau shooed her out the door and waved the gathering crowd of orphans back. Cries of protest followed Daeya down the walkway, and it was all she could do not to turn around, hug each one of them again, and promise to see them soon.

If only she could make such a promise. In several of her past lives, the Test of Flame had damaged her vessel beyond healing. And assuming she passed the Test, the Guild and the Church were still a threat. There were too many variables to make a vow to children who had already lost so much. She steeled her spine and hurried away.

"*Iiren'hyvaa*, Sorceress."

"Good morning, Daeya."

"Praise be, *amii*."

Daeya returned the greetings on her way to the training grounds, where the spark of Ravlok's aura burned brightest. She could always find him now, no matter where he was in the city.

After she'd officially sworn allegiance to the Alliaansi before a packed council hall, the collective mood of her parents' people—*her* people—had shifted. Though some still quietly muttered behind her back, Koraani's acknowledgement of her parentage and her part in Alar's supply heist had convinced most of Starlight to accept her. The Alliaansi now had enough beads to ward off saphyrum sickness and defend the city until midsummer. A considerable portion would be sent to aid Maralla's army.

Against all odds, Daeya had earned her place among them. And aside from occasionally scanning the shadows for Jack—who still hadn't turned up despite both mundane and magical efforts—she'd never felt more at home.

"Daeya." Kendi nodded to her as she entered the training grounds. He still wore the ceremonial paint of the recently wed: three white dots below his lip to honor the greater gods, and a stripe of white across his eyes for clarity of sight. The new ring on his finger glinted in the late morning sun.

"Good morning, Commander." Daeya scanned the snowy circles filled with soldiers and wooden training dummies. The steady glow of Ravlok's aura came from the *fursaan*, but she hesitated. "Is Zakaari inside?"

Ravlok had been training him in one-handed martial arts nearly every day since Orowen had released them. Zakaari hadn't asked Daeya not to attend the sessions, but it was obvious he didn't like her seeing him struggle.

Kendi's face fell. "He is."

"That bad, today?"

"He's improving, but it's hard for him to see it."

It had been difficult for Zakaari to adjust to life with only one hand these past few weeks. Some of his old flames were inescapably cruel about it, especially Cirra, whose influence on his social circle drove many of his so-called friends away. On more than one occasion, Daeya had been tempted to make good on the rumors from solstice and sock her right in her pretty face.

Only Tipori's offer for Daeya to move in with them had cheered Zakaari up. From a practical sense, it was easier to ward the Evallier villa than all of Havensguard, but more important was seeing Zakaari smile again.

"Tipori joined them some time ago." Kendi hefted a stack of training swords onto his shoulder. "They might be in need of rescuing."

Ever since Ravlok's ascension had awoken memories of Baokryn's past, Tipori had been eager to see what ancient martial arts Daeya could recall. Her muscles weren't fully attuned yet, but she'd accidentally disarmed him in their last session. He'd been itching for a rematch ever since.

She thumbed Zakaari's ring on her middle finger, ignoring the numbness still plaguing the last two fingers on her left hand. "I'll see what I can do."

Daeya crossed the grounds and slipped inside the *fursaan*. The proximity to Ravlok's brilliant aura loosened the knot in her spine instantly. She closed her eyes to savor it like sunlight on her face. It was no substitute for a dragonbond, but it went a long way to calming the tempest of magic inside her. After placing the basket of goods by the door and hanging her cloak, she turned—

—and stopped short.

Zakaari wasn't in the ring. He leaned against the guardrail in nothing but his trousers, watching Ravlok and Tipori circle one another on the training floor.

Tipori's back was to her, and for once, he was also shirtless. But it wasn't the man's chiseled, sweat-slicked torso or his right arm tied behind his back that gave her pause. It was the staggering network of scars crisscrossing his upper body.

Shadows dipped into trenches so deep they changed the way his skin moved against muscle and bone.

Bleeding Aether. What could have warranted such savagery?

"Make your hand their focal point," Tipori said as Ravlok grabbed him by the wrist, "and most opponents will be tempted to grab it. Let that be their mistake."

Faster than Daeya could blink, Tipori twisted his arm up and broke the grapple with an elbow to Ravlok's face. As Ravlok reeled, Tipori swept one leg outward and hooked his arm around his neck, dropping him into a pin with a knee squarely on his back.

Tipori released his chokehold, and a tiny dagger appeared out of black mist against Ravlok's throat. "And by quickening your ability to summon a blade, you can utilize the Aether as if it were a second hand."

The level of prowess in the moves was irrefutable. He hadn't earned those scars from just anywhere. Dozens of weapons contributed to that tapestry, not only a whip. There was an unmarked rectangle of flesh on his lower right flank, similar to her own patch of flayed skin, though his had clearly been healed by skillful magic. Thick white scars banded his wrists. He spoke Rillanese, observed Rillanese customs, and he was married to a man from Rillion.

Tipori rose smoothly and his blade vanished. "Now, if you want—"

"You were a pit fighter," Daeya blurted.

An extremely accomplished one, based on his wealth and obvious elevation in status. Rillion's rigid caste system offered little upward mobility for pit-fighting slaves beyond winning a Freedom Wager in the Durgostian Arena—a feat only a few men managed each decade. Tipori would have killed hundreds of men just to earn a chance at it.

If not for the horrors of Nahariim's cruelty still burning holes in her mind, Daeya might have shied from the realization. But she often awoke at night with the taste of smoke on her tongue, the stench of burning flesh in her hair. It was apparently something Baokryn had battled with for centuries.

Tipori's gaze settled upon her. He tugged at the rope that kept his arm bound, and the twisted fibers tumbled to the floor. "*Ciir*. One of the best."

There was no arrogance in his tone; he was simply stating a fact.

Ravlok rolled over and sat up, rubbing his jaw. "That explains a lot."

Tipori opened his mouth, then closed it. He cleared his throat and went to retrieve his shirt, as if to spare her the sight.

He'd been far less perturbed about her scars than she'd expected. Zakaari hadn't seemed put off by them either. Now she understood why.

*Our scars make us who we are,* Tipori had said. *You don't have to hide them anymore.*

Zakaari touched her arm. *"Nei ama're?"*

Gods, she'd come in expecting to help Zakaari, but here he was, concerned for her. "I'm okay." She squeezed his fingers and kissed his cheek, then ducked under the guardrail to approach his father.

Tipori paused in lacing his shirt. Uncertainty flickered in his eyes, and Daeya hesitated. Maybe they had more in common than she'd thought.

He might have once been a trained killer, but he was also the man who had taken a risk on her, mentored her, and welcomed her into his home. She had no more reason to fear him than her own father. Daeya stepped into his space and hugged him.

For all of two heartbeats, Tipori stood rigidly, until he returned the embrace with a fierceness worthy of Angus McVen himself.

"Thank you," Daeya breathed, eyes closing, "for everything."

Major repairs to the Evallier home were made swiftly, but parts of the turret's stonework still bore ridges where they'd turned to slag, cooled, and hardened again. All the priceless stained-glass windows had needed to be replaced with clear panes, and of the hedges surrounding the villa, not even ash remained. Fortunately, the interior rooms had taken only minor damage, and the lingering scent of smoke was easily combatted by Damiir's heavy use of spice in the kitchen.

Daeya was supposed to be setting the table for dinner when a knock came at the front door. Zakaari snatched her around the waist to keep her in his bed.

She giggled and tried to roll toward her discarded shirt. "Damiir is going to tan my hide if you don't let me up."

"Mm-mm." His mouth against her neck muffled the staunch refusal. "He'll have to go through me, first."

"Fearsome as you are, I fear his use of a spoon more." Her knuckles still smarted from when she'd tried to sneak an orange earlier.

Zakaari used his greater weight to pin her and continued the trail of kisses down her front. *"Peiaa* will get it."

Further halfhearted protests fell on deaf ears, and Daeya eventually gave in to the dizzying sensation of his mouth below her navel. Her fingers slipped into his hair.

The knock came again twice more with increasing insistence before Damiir called down the hallway, "Don't worry you two, *I'll* get it."

Zakaari paused in his work, chuckling, and Daeya's cheeks warmed. Gods bless his family, but their casual view of intimacy was still an adjustment.

Another voice came through the crack in the door. "Daeya?"

Zakaari groaned and turned toward the shadow of his three-year-old brother hunkered down outside his bedroom door. "Go away, Aschiiq."

"I play, too, Ari."

"For Silonas's sake, go!"

The mood broken, Daeya grinned and finally retrieved her shirt. "He's right, though." She pulled it over her head and combed out her tousled hair. "We're leaving soon. We should spend some time with him."

"I think you just like him more."

"He's easier to please, it's true."

Despite his grumbling, Zakaari pulled on his clothes. He swore under his breath when the knot tying off his excess shirtsleeve came loose. Daeya resisted the urge to tie it for him. Orowen had advised her to only help if he asked for it. Rather than watch him struggle, she slipped out the door and mock-raced Aschiiq to the dining room.

"Daeya, look at this!"

As Aschiiq balanced on one foot and hopped about, a familiar and irate voice drifted in from the foyer. Daeya paused in reaching for a stack of plates on the table.

Not even Baokryn's lingering memories of Rillanese could translate Damiir's rapid conversation with the newcomer. Still, the first man's anger and Damiir's exasperation were unmistakable. Daeya crept toward the foyer.

Only the sight of the squat, leather-faced bartender wrapped in animal furs could satisfy her disbelief.

"Po?"

Po Naftalli, the owner of Davy's Tavern in Ryost, took one look at Daeya and scowled. "Not now, Magelet. Po busy." And as if he hadn't just effortlessly acknowledged and dismissed her in a single breath, he went back to arguing with Damiir.

Finally, Damiir threw up his hands. He barked something that earned a smug look from Po and turned to Daeya. "Be a dear and fetch Tipori, please."

Perplexed, she started to turn away, but a hand on her shoulder stopped her. "I'm here, *neimen. Iiren'norvaa*, Po."

Po's scowl deepened. He snapped something else, and Tipori's grin sharpened.

"We can revisit the terms of compensation, of course. I know it was a mighty request. You've exceeded all expectations, as usual. My apologies about your tavern."

Tension left Po's shoulders and his hands uncurled.

Daeya couldn't hold back her curiosity. She'd spent a lot of time in Po's tavern, eating ham 'n' hash with Da and Murtagh. Ali McVen, her ma, was once dear friends with Nessa, Po's waitress. "What happened to Davy's?"

Tipori glanced at her. "There was an incident in the capital. Nothing of concern." Po puffed up again as if to disagree, but Tipori silenced him with a look. "Are you ready to see your family, Daeya?"

It took a few beats for the words to register.

They were here.

Sparks of anticipation and joy skittered across her skin. *Po* was Tipori's contact in Ryost; he'd gotten them over the mountains and out of Gregory's clutches. They were safe. They were *here*.

"Yes." Her chest tightened. She didn't know what to do with her hands. "Yes, please."

Tipori touched her chin and nodded toward the open door. "They're just up the garden path. Have a look."

Over Po's head, the familiar silhouettes of Angus and Murtagh McVen overshadowed several other figures. Tears welled in Daeya's eyes, and a shallow breath shuddered out of her.

For the second time that day, she caught Tipori in the biggest hug. "Thank you. Gods, I can't thank you enough."

"You're very welcome." He laughed as he returned the embrace. Tipori spoke to Damiir over her shoulder. "We'll put them up in the loft until more suitable arrangements can be made. It might be crowded, but we'll manage."

Damiir sighed again, but his exasperation ebbed when he smiled at Daeya. "We always do."

She released Tipori and seized Damiir next, breathing in the scent of red chilies, curry powder, and costly saffron. "And thank you for welcoming us into your home."

His deep laugh shook her head to toe. "Certainly, Daeya. I'll pull down a few more plates."

She stepped toward Po, but he crossed his arms and eyed her from beneath his fleshy brow. "Magelet not even think it."

For all Daeya's arcane skill, she still wouldn't dream of crossing Po Naftalli. She held out her hand instead. "Thank you, Po. I'm in your debt."

Po waved her off. "Agh, Axe Man pay debt. Shelter Needle and Mophead."

'Axe Man' must have been his nickname for Tipori. The last two names gave Daeya pause. "Nessa and Sorcha are here?"

"Daeya!"

Nessa's daughter Sorcha came tearing up the path, wild red curls bouncing against white shixxie fur. She clomped up the steps and pushed past Po, provoking an indignant grunt from him and leaving Damiir aghast as she tracked snowy footprints across the floor. She smelled of dirt and evergreens, and cold radiated from her cloak.

Daeya threw her arms around her. "I can't believe you're here."

"I can't believe *ye're* here." Sorcha squeezed her, then held her at arm's length, blue eyes sweeping Daeya up and down. "Rebellion's a good look for ye."

"Feels good too."

Wait till they all realized she was half-Syljian, and her parents were once Alli-aansi leaders.

Her smile faltered. Assuming Da didn't already know. She looked over Sorcha's shoulder, expecting a glimpse of him, but Nessa filed through the doorway next.

"Mira, Shavaan, and Caelyn, stop blocking the way, Po." Nessa's freckled face was rosy, and her tears gleamed in the torchlight. "Let me get a look at her."

"Nessa," Daeya breathed.

"Ye wee rascal." Nessa's fur-lined gloves framed Daeya's face. "Ye gave us all such a fright. We thought we'd lost ye."

"I'm fine." Bleeding Aether, any more of this and her heart might burst. "More than fine."

Murtagh knuckled the top of Daeya's head. "Getting all teary-eyed, are ye, crab-napper?"

Her cousin's bone-crushing hug squeezed the air from her lungs. *That* was a feeling she'd sorely missed, even if he stank like Perrig's tannery. "Murtagh, you orc-faced arse."

Murtagh stepped aside to make space for Annie in the Evalliers' crowded foyer. Daeya had only met the dark-haired woman once, but she still greeted her with a soft embrace. "It's good to see you, Daeya."

"And you as well."

But the hug she wanted most came from the enormous man who ducked through the entryway after them. His thick furs compressed against the sides of the doorframe, and tears were already collecting in his thick red beard.

Angus McVen's eyes met Daeya's, and the remnants of her composure crumbled like dry leaves in autumn. Her throat closed up and fresh tears blurred her vision. She took one step toward him, then another, fearing if she moved too fast, his illusion might disappear.

"Hi, Da."

His voice was made of gravel, as if he, too, was strangled by emotion. "C'mere, ye scrawny thing."

Daeya leaped into her father's arms, and the last shadow looming over her heart lifted. Though he'd been away from his forge for weeks, the scent of iron and hot coals was ingrained in her memory. She buried her face against his neck and powerful sobs ravaged her throat.

"I missed you so much."

"Gods, ye're a *breigh* sight for these old eyes, ye *kinnich*."

He lowered her to the floor, but didn't release her. Daeya held him tightly, relishing his warmth, his scent, his strength.

When he finally pulled away to wipe his eyes, Daeya reluctantly let go and followed his gaze across the foyer. Zakaari stood apart from the rest, having wrestled his sleeve into submission.

Angus looked back down and pinched her nose. "These lads must be treating ye well. Ye look happier than I've ever seen ye."

She sniffed, wondering once more how much he knew. "Da, there's someone I'd like you to meet."

His blue eyes lit up. "Aye, lass? Is it the young lad over yon?"

"Yes." A new emotion flitted about her chest, making it hard to stand still. "Zakaari." Gods, she hoped Da liked him.

Zakaari swallowed visibly. He dragged his fingers through his hair and crept forward, straightening his spine. "It's an honor, *Amaa*," he said, offering his hand. "You've raised a wonderful daughter."

"Twas mostly her ma's doing." Angus shook Zakaari's hand, assessing him from head to toe. "Ye've a *braugh* grip, lad. I take it ye can swing a hammer and wield a sword?"

"*Ciir, Amaa.*" Zakaari winced and lifted what remained of his left arm. "Though I've had some setbacks."

"Ach, that's why Mira gave ye a spare." Angus released his hand and put a heavy arm around Daeya. "And my Daeya, she's got a heart like a lion. If she chose ye, I suspect ye have one as well."

"He does," Tipori assured him. "They bring out the best in each other."

"Well, that's all a da can ask for, I *kinnich*."

Angus hugged Daeya close, and her jitters dissolved. Zakaari's shoulders sagged with relief.

Aschiiq squeezed between them to tug on Damiir's trousers. "Hungry, *Peiaa*."

"Patience, *ennii*." Damiir swung the boy up and perched him on his hip.

"So..." Sorcha glanced between Tipori and Damiir. "What's for dinner?"

"Sorcha!" Nessa scolded. "Did yer manners run off with the baker's son?"

Po muttered something uncivil about said baker's son, and Sorcha's cheeks bloomed scarlet.

Damiir wrestled Aschiiq's hand out of his pocket and peeled the boy's fingers from around a pilfered piece of candy. "Alright, alright. Everyone have a seat. Daeya, Zakaari, for the gods' sakes, finish setting the table."

"*Ciir, Haalii.*"

Zakaari offered his arm to Daeya. Angus gave her a shove when she looked between them, torn. His grin could have warmed her on the coldest night of the year.

"Go on, lass." He winked. "I'm right behind ye."

# CHAPTER SIXTY-FIVE

## NORMOS

"I understand you've been refusing to heal our soldiers. Let me remind you that is not in Gwen's best interests."

Normos maintained his indifferent tone with great care. He placed the dinner tray down on the desk, ignoring the hot pool of rage elicited by the sight of the chain binding Olivia's ankle to the tent's center post. It was something he expected to see in an Alliaansi encampment or a Rillanese slave block, not here. But right now he needed to keep his head. Others were listening outside.

Above the fading bruise on her cheek, Olivia's molten gaze burned into him like the lava flows still steaming along the Mautori border. Mount Eisekii's reawakening had coincided too closely with Gwen's imprisonment to be anything other than an ill omen—a quill stroke punctuating the hardest decision of his life.

"Don't pretend you care about Gwen's best interests, Sorcerer."

Normos glanced toward the tent flap, ensuring it obscured the cup he lifted from the tray. Beneath the cup was an iron key. Olivia's scornful glare dissolved.

"Believe me, I don't. And I expect once she tells us where Sarikkian and his accomplices are hiding"—he fixed her with a pointed look—"there will be little use left for her."

He couldn't answer the obvious question tugging Olivia's dark brows together—that, no, he hadn't told anyone about Sarikkian's safehouses—but he prayed she would understand. They only had so much time.

He'd lied to Gwen that night. Gregory hadn't been influenced by psionics, which meant the story he'd told Normos was free of blanker influence. Normos believed Gwen when she said she hadn't been called to an emergency meeting over a controlled collapse of the School. That left only two conceivable possibilities: either Gwen's companions kept their schemes from her deliberately, or Gregory was lying.

And if Gregory was lying, that meant...

Mira's mercy, he couldn't finish the thought.

The answers he needed could only be found with the two missing Councilors. However, Gregory had been keeping close eyes on him, preventing him from following the lead to Sarikkian.

"Unless, of course, you agree to cooperate. I know your talents far surpass the other healers from Ferid." He turned the dinner roll over to reveal the slit where he'd hollowed out the soft inners and stashed a saphyrum-laced seeking stone.

Intuition sharpened every line in Olivia's face. Her emerald eyes sparkled with pride.

Normos returned the roll to its proper position and revealed one final object from within a folded napkin. "I suggest, for Gwen's sake, you start acting like it."

She peered inside the napkin, then back up at him, lips parting. Surely, she understood the level of trust he was putting in her with both a seeking stone and a wardstone. The seeking stone would allow Normos to track her through its partnered scrying mirror, while the wardstone would hide her from everyone else. Should she discard the seeking stone, Olivia could disappear.

He prayed her love for Gwen was motivation enough to help him discover the truth.

Olivia shot out of her chair, chain clinking. Her open hand connected with his face, and he stumbled, catching himself on the center post. The resounding blow split his chapped lips and silenced the conversation outside the tent.

"Take your threats elsewhere, you ghost-eyed rat," she spat. "Where is your superior? I demand to see him."

For a moment, Normos held his stinging cheek, too stunned to respond. Olivia placed her hand over Mira's amulet, still hidden beneath his clothes, and stepped in close.

"I'll find them," she whispered.

Olivia stepped away just as the tent flap whipped open.

Cameron Vika's blonde hair glowed like a golden halo in the setting sun. "You know better than to put your hands on a mage, healer." She touched his arm. "You alright, Beck?"

"Fine." Normos dabbed his mouth and smoothed the collar of his cloak. "If she wants to see Gregory, I suppose she can do so after she heals our mages." He gestured to his lip. "Starting with this."

Fists trembling, Olivia sold her anger flawlessly. "Miserable wretch. I'd rather pray to Laangor."

Normos shrugged. "It won't be long before your lover breaks. Come, Sorceress."

"Wait." Olivia's uncharacteristically small voice stopped them from leaving.

Feigned smugness—a skill perfected over years in Gregory's service—came easily to Normos. He glanced toward Cam, who lifted one eyebrow and smirked.

"You're saying as long as you have my service, Gwen will live?"

Normos turned back to her. "If you comport yourself with the dignity of a Sanctuary healer, yes."

Conflict warred in Olivia's expression. She twisted the hem of her robe, then stepped forward, dragging the chain with her. She wove a base sigil and sealed the tiny wound on his lip.

Later, as he and Cam slogged through camp to reach Gregory's command post, the sorceress turned to him. "You really think he's going to allow that?"

"No." His stomach clenched. Gwen was as good as dead the moment Gregory's interrogator got what he wanted. Normos would need to free her before that, assuming they could find Sarikkian and prove the Councilor wasn't a threat. "But it would be foolish to tell her that."

Olivia already knew, anyway.

Gregory's tent was occupied when they returned. Standing before their mentor was a haggard soldier with weeks of beard growth and a stench that rivaled the worst tavern in Southgate. He leaned on a walking stick, one hand wrapped in dirty cloth. In the other, he held a mangled, wax-sealed letter.

The soldier hesitated when they entered. "Begging your pardon, Sorcerers. My instructions were to—"

"Your instructions were given to you by the enemy," Gregory cut in, taking the letter. "Now, be silent."

Normos fought the urge to shiver. This must be the emissary Gregory had sent to the Alliaansi. No one had expected the man to return. With too great a possibility he was afflicted by an imperium, there was only one way this meeting could end.

Gregory broke the seal on the message and scanned the parchment.

Cam fidgeted beside Normos, twisting a gold ring about her finger. He nudged her in silent warning. The last thing they needed was their Councilor's ire directed at them.

Gregory's face twitched. He turned away and held the note over a nearby candle. The parchment curled and smoke filled the room, making Normos's eyes water.

They stood in silence, watching the letter burn, until Gregory summoned a tiny rift and dropped it into the Aether.

"What is your name, soldier?"

"Carval Cerden, sir."

"Have you family, Mr. Cerden?"

"Aye, sir. A wife and three daughters."

Gregory's expression went carefully impassive. "Three daughters, you say?"

"Aye, and one more on the way." Cerden smiled. "We're praying to Mira for a boy."

A pang of regret struck Normos unexpectedly. They could change this man's fate. *He* could, with nothing more than a ward wrapped around Cerden's mind, as Olivia had done for Peader. No mastermind would allow himself to be trapped within the mind of one so insignificant. It was possible an inhabiting blanker might shred Cerden's mind apart on the way out, but it could also prove he wasn't imperiumed at all. He could be dismissed from Guild service and go home to his family.

But magic was forbidden on non-adepts.

*Not everyone's magic is strong enough to use as mages do,* Olivia had told him months ago. *But we all have it. Down to the last little ant and leaf, we are all created with Saolanni's light and Mira's love.*

Gregory approached and clasped the man's shoulder. His other hand slipped inside his white robe. "The Guild will see their needs met. They will want for nothing."

The soldier's eyes widened. "You'd do that for us, milord?"

*You've been lied to your entire life. You just refuse to see it.*

Normos tasted bile. He should speak up. He should stop this. "Councilor?"

Cam looked his way, alarmed.

Gregory kept his attention on the soldier. "Yes, of course."

Normos's heart hammered in his throat. Mira's medallion weighed against his neck. He had to step forward.

*Choose life.*

This man didn't have to die. His family didn't have to lose—

In one smooth motion, Gregory drew an ebony blade and thrust it upward beneath the soldier's ribs. A startled gasp burst from Cerden's lips. Gregory held the knife, supporting the man's weight as his knees buckled. "You have my word."

Horror froze the cry in Normos's throat. A grade four could save the soldier, but Normos hadn't trained beyond a grade two. His feet turned to lead.

Gregory spun a sigil and opened a rift in the floor. He let the body tumble into the Aether, then withdrew a handkerchief, wiped his blade, and Aetherial wind carried the bloody fabric away.

The rift closed with a *whoosh*, throwing Normos's hair into his face.

He'd seen people die before, but the cold efficiency shook him to his core. There wasn't even a spot of blood on the Councilor's clothes. No trace of the soldier's death at all.

The missing stonemason crew probably vanished this way, too.

*You've been lied to your entire life...*

"Is there something you wish to say to me, Sorcerer?"

Gods be good. Normos dug his fingers into his opposite wrist, focusing on the pain. "No, Councilor."

"Good." Gregory tucked his weapon away. "Let me remind you both, the blankers don't show mercy. Mr. Cerden wasn't returned out of goodwill; he was sent back as an Alliaansi spy. He served his purpose, and his family will receive a monthly stipend for his loss. Beyond that, nothing more could be done."

"Yes, Councilor," they replied in unison, though the half-truth rankled Normos.

"The spy should not have made it into camp at all. Cameron, see our saphyrum stores relocated and double the guard."

Cam bowed in acquiescence.

Gregory turned to his maps. "It seems my old acquaintance has decided not to return what is ours."

Though he didn't say her name, Normos stiffened.

"I have reports of a caravan traveling toward Kuma'Kiir, bearing a high-profile individual who could be just the incentive he needs." He moved a piccara chip far to the west, near Aon'In. "Normos, you will acquire this individual as a hostage."

Gregory's fixation with Daeya McVen, more than his unsavory demand, filled Normos with revulsion. It wasn't even blanker influence that kept his mentor coming back to the brat. It was negligence.

"Councilor, with all due respect, McVen is lost to us." Even if she wasn't enthralled, Daeya had been living among the blankers for months. "What good is trading a hostage?"

"She cannot be affected by psionics."

"Any wards can be broken; you've always said so."

"Not hers."

"Councilor." Gregory's cutting look might have frightened him once, but this time, Normos held his ground. "You would endanger us all just to have her back?"

Gregory moved to pour a glass of wine. "Your concerns are justified, though misplaced. I assure you, she is not under blanker control."

"Then it's so much worse." Normos caught Cam's gaze on him and looked her way. She winced, as if she knew something he didn't. "If she's not a thrall, she's a traitor."

"She is the key to winning the war." With a long-suffering look at Normos, Gregory poured two more glasses. "Now, enough of this. You will procure our hostage and return with her as soon as possible."

Numb fingers took the offered glass. Normos stared into the wine, his face reflected in its dark surface.

This wasn't right. None of this was right.

He washed down his anger with a gulp of wine. "Whom do I seek, Councilor?"

"Her name," Gregory said, "is Anya Evallier."

# Chapter Sixty-Six

## Daeya

Daeya's last two days in Starlight went by in a blur of heartfelt tears and drunken merriment. She showed off her new sword-fighting skills to Murtagh, who pretended to be unimpressed, and they played tiffleball in the snow with enormous drifts to cushion their falls.

The runes covering her body didn't come as a shock to Angus. Apparently, Gregory had visited him and Ali shortly after he'd taken Daeya from their farm. He'd told her parents she'd begun to show signs of psionics and offered an experimental procedure believed to suppress their development. This procedure, he'd promised, would hide her in plain sight of the Light Paladins while also protecting the world from her power. Of course, should they refuse, Gregory couldn't assure them Daeya's heritage would be kept a secret for long.

With their hands tied, Angus and Ali had agreed to never reveal her birth mother's true origins. Between Daeya's runes and her distinctly human features, they believed she was safer not knowing. She had to admit they were probably right.

As she'd promised, Daeya introduced Angus to Koraani, and they spent an evening in Baani'anii trading stories of Neri. Though Angus couldn't contribute much, Daeya still listened raptly as her da recounted her mother's last days on this side of Baosanni's Gate. There was still the question of why Neri was near Ryost the day she stumbled onto Angus's farm, but that was likely a mystery that would never be solved.

Tipori also had business with Angus. They took measurements of Zakaari's arm as the basis for a metal prosthesis. Tipori had these lofty ideas of a hinge that could function like an elbow using magic. Daeya had never seen its like, but if anyone could create such a thing, it would be Da and Tipori.

On the morning of the third day, Daeya hugged her father close, and he kissed her cheek. Saying goodbye so soon after reuniting left her heart in jagged pieces, but she knew he would be safe in Starlight.

"I'll be back soon."

"Ye just focus on taming that dragon, ye *kinnich*." Angus chuckled, always one to make light of things when he was nervous. "And give those sorcerers a piece of yer mind."

"I will."

Angus remembered her telling him about Telerion, too, though it was hard to tell if he'd truly thought the dragon imaginary when she was little. Apparently, Gregory had warned him that memory loss was common with this procedure, which confirmed Daeya's suspicions about the runes that had been broken by Chaos's poisoned crossbow bolt. Those few still hadn't grown back, and her memories of Telerion were clearer now than they'd ever been. She even remembered him training her in the use of her draegion Shield before he disappeared, leaving Daeya to believe Gregory's runes had also suppressed it somehow.

Murtagh cuffed her on the shoulder. "Don't let the scaly bastard eat ye, now."

She scoffed. "Take care of Da."

He put his arm around Annie. "We'll keep the ol' lout out of trouble."

Tipori, Ravlok, Zakaari, Sam, and Sessiri stood around the Evalliers' courtyard, checking their weapons, adjusting straps, and giving everything a last once-over. Damiir fussed with the collar of Daeya's cloak, then moved on to Zakaari and Tipori in turn. He kissed his husband with an urgency that bespoke the seriousness of their task, then stepped back to wave a final farewell, balancing Aschiiq on his hip.

"If you see Riisii, tell her she still has laundry to finish."

Tipori's grin could have cut diamonds. "I'll send her home straightaway."

Movement in Daeya's periphery drew her attention. Wrapped in a dark cloak trimmed with rabbit fur, Alar cut a stark figure against the freshly fallen snow. Daeya braced herself, uncertain how to greet him after their last encounter. Truthfully, she'd given up on salvaging their friendship. He would never forgive her for choosing Zakaari over him.

Alar spared her the awkwardness of acknowledgement. He let his eyes slide off her and addressed Tipori, "Everything is in order, *Amaa*."

"Thank you, Alar. See us as far as the mountain, and then you're free to go."

The shock of Alar's discovery concerning the sabotage at the School had largely worn off, but Daeya was still surprised the Alliaansi council would send him back to Eidosinia in search of the missing Councilors and Master Ulrich. Even one of them would make a powerful ally, true, but first Alar would have to convince them to trust a mastermind.

Unless the goal wasn't to convince them with words.

Daeya shivered.

Ravlok's soothing aura bloomed outward to envelope her. He watched Alar from under pinched brows.

Zakaari was at her side in the same breath, slipping his hand into hers.

"We have a ways to go before dark," Tipori said. "Best get moving."

When Paelic appeared in the sky, Ravlok knew they were headed in the right direction.

Caelyn's ancient godlings had existed long before Nahariim's time. They were the original Guardians of the forest. Some bookkeepers claimed they guided unbonded draegion through Caelyn's domain to ensure its safety, for the goddess's trust in their primordial power was sorely lacking, even in millennia past.

He hated to admit it, but her vigilance made sense.

The wealth of information in Daeya's tome was overwhelming. Tales of centuries-long battles, the rise and fall of empires, the birth of the lesser gods themselves—it was any scholar's dream. He could read Ancient Draconic and its earlier draegionic variants as if they were his native tongue. His initial plunge into the text had left him with something akin to a three-day hangover, and after that, he'd stuck mostly to Baokryn's seven thousand years of memories. There would be time for everything else; he was immortal, after all.

He was immortal.

It still didn't seem possible.

Alar halted their group with a raised hand. They stood on a rise overlooking the In'Jasuu. "The eruption must have altered the skyline." He turned to Daeya. "I don't suppose your dragon passed along updated directions?"

It was the first time he'd spoken to her since they'd left Starlight. Her easy posture turned defensive. "No. He's been quiet since solstice."

Alar sighed. "Why am I not surprised?"

Paelic alighted on a branch, bounced twice, and shrieked.

Sam sidled closer to Ravlok. "Tell me that's not the same bird we saw outside Ryost."

"It is." Ravlok squeezed her hand, then stepped toward the bird. He summoned a memory and spoke in the gods' tongue: "She seeks the dragon called Telerion. Will you guide her?"

Paelic shrieked again and leaped off the branch. He circled the air above Daeya's head once and shot off into the trees.

Alar looked at Ravlok, then turned in the direction Paelic had gone.

"Did he just ask directions from a bird?" Sessiri asked.

Tipori frowned. "I'm not certain that's any normal bird."

Daeya took the lead, brushing Ravlok's shoulder in thanks as she walked past.

For two days, they trekked along the mountainside, avoiding areas where steam vents and cooling lava flows melted the snow. Alar kept an eye on the Three Sisters, comparing a rough drawing Daeya had made to the shattered slopes of Mount Eisekii. Something about her connection to the dragon, she said, allowed her to picture the mountain as it once was.

Alar didn't question her. He kept conversation to a minimum and did his best not to fall back into the complacency her companionship once brought. He was here as a favor to Tipori, nothing more. It certainly wasn't because he felt guilty and wanted to make good on this one promise.

Twice more, Ravlok conferred with Crabby's bird in that melodic tongue. When Paelic finally gave a victorious squawk and perched atop a felled tree beside a pile of broken stone, Alar checked the lines of Daeya's drawing to confirm the placement of the three clusters of stars.

"It should be here."

Though, looking around, there was nothing but colossal boulders and trees torn from the ground. The others turned circles along the slope, searching what little they could see in the light of their torches, but Daeya approached the fallen rocks and placed one gloved hand against a boulder's cracked surface.

"Through here. I can feel him." She looked toward Alar and hesitated.

That hesitation speared him right in the heart.

Alar closed his eyes and took a meditative breath. He was here for his people, not for her. "Everyone, step back."

Stone shuddered beneath his telekinetic hold as, one by one, he lifted the boulders to expose a small tunnel in the side of the mountain. Sweat rolled down his face despite the cold, and he eyed the cloud of steam belching from the tunnel with growing unease. Surely, she didn't expect them to venture into an active volcano.

Daeya stepped into his line of sight. "Thank you, Alar."

He tucked away the biting comment that came to mind and nodded.

She turned to the rest of her guard, looking each of them over. "Ravlok and I will go the rest of the way alone."

"Daeya—"

"No, Zakaari." Her tone was firm.

Zakaari scowled and seized her in an embrace so tight, Alar had to look away. He sought Tipori.

"If that will be all, *Amaa*, I'll be going."

Tipori offered his hand with a knowing look that made Alar's jaw twitch. "Farewell, *amii*."

Alar shook his hand and made for the trees. No matter how big the knot in his throat grew, he refused to look back.

Alar disappeared over Zakaari's shoulder, and Daeya blinked back tears. There was so much she wanted to say, but it was clear he didn't want to hear it. So she held Zakaari tighter and relished his love for the pure and unconditional thing it was. Though her heart might ache, she'd chosen her partner wisely.

Telerion's call to battle sang in her blood, but she heeded Ravlok's direction and denied the dragon for now. A draegion was patient. Their bond would happen on her time, lest he gain the upper hand.

"I love you," she whispered to Zakaari.

"I love you, too." He kissed her hard enough to knock her tears loose. "You can do this."

With one final embrace, she stepped toward the tunnel, letting the lingering pressure of Zakaari's lips quell her rising dread. They hadn't discussed the deadly consequences of failing the Test, but she was certain he knew.

Ravlok walked beside her, dipping his chin toward Paelic. The bird remained like a sentinel before the steaming tunnel.

"Remember, he will test you mentally as well as physically," Ravlok said as the torchlight faded and Daeya summoned her Shield to banish the darkness.

The sweltering heat soon became oppressive, and they paused to discard their winter attire. Daeya concentrated on passing some of her protection onto Ravlok, and white-gold lines swept under his sleeves.

"They may call it the Test of Flame, but it's much more than that." Ravlok's furrowed brows relaxed as the Shield took hold. "It's pitting your will against his to prove you're worthy of his submission."

Daeya nodded. Fleeting memories of Baokryn's Test surfaced, along with knowledge as inherent to her as magic itself. Draegion who bonded gold or steel dragons took the Test of Flame, while bonding silver or cobalt dragons required a Test of Frost. Platinum-bonded draegion were once the rarest of them, and they took the deadly Test of Aether. They all served the same purpose: to ensure a draegion was worthy of their dragon.

"A young male will likely favor battle. If you engage him in a duel with weapons, he'll outpace you."

"What do you suggest?"

"Stay on the move. Use your size to your advantage, and don't be afraid to use magic. You want to force him into using his fire breath if you can. That's how you beat him. If he's cunning, he'll be reluctant to use it."

Daeya recalled the story Dannicus had told her months ago on the ship bound for Orthovia. When the Blight of Pananmai used his lightning breath against the draegion who came to stop him, the draegion turned the attack back on the drag-on and amplified it, ensuring it was strong enough to punch through his copper scales. Daeya could harvest fire in the same manner already, but only memories of Baokryn's Test assuaged the fear of actually standing before a dragon's breath and surviving.

Steam reduced their visibility to only a few steps in front of them. The drag-on's presence pulled her forward with the same bloodthirsty eagerness that had consumed her at the Sundance Falls.

*"Come,* Nashanett. *Come and face me."*

Her mouth filled with sand, and her muscles quivered with the need to bolt toward his summons. Soon, she was panting from the strain.

Daeya stumbled to a halt in the middle of the tunnel. Her hand pressed against hot stone. She stared long at the golden glow sparking from her fingertips. Mirror-like veins of obsidian reflected broken images of her face.

Ravlok's aura trickled into her awareness, soothing the ache inside her until it was manageable again. Daeya glanced aside to thank him, but he wasn't there.

Panic choked her suddenly. Violently. She whirled back toward the entrance, but only blackness greeted her. "Rav?"

Thunder rumbled through the stone. Searing heat whipped hair off her shoulders and into her face. The tunnel filled with the stench of smoke and sulfur.

"Ravlok!"

Her voice echoed into the darkness. He couldn't have just disappeared. Aristyn had been there when Baokryn battled Aliri—or had he? Once the Test began, it was all a blur of fire and motion.

Her heart hammered in her ears. The weight of the mountain pressed in around her.

*"Come, Daeya."*

She swallowed twice, but it did little to soothe her parched throat. She turned again and squinted down the path, where a familiar orange glow awaited.

A vicious tug on her senses set her feet into motion. Hesitant at first, then steadily gaining speed, Daeya hurried down the tunnel toward the sensation that set every nerve ablaze.

Her swords were in her hands, but she didn't remember summoning them. She sprinted around the bend and skidded to a stop at the mouth of a flame-scorched cavern.

Steam roiled upward, carrying a spray of molten rock with it. As the spray cooled and collapsed back into the stream of magma, a silhouette took shape through smoke and fire.

Golden, snake-slitted eyes contrasted sharply with the softer lines of his humanoid face. Toned muscle rippled along his bare torso. From his back stretched a majestic pair of spike-tipped golden wings, and though they stood half again as he was tall, he carried them as if they weighed nothing. Disheveled blond hair floated about his ears.

He was just as she remembered him.

Her grip tightened on her swords. "Telerion."

Telerion's eyes narrowed. Aetherial mist rippled, and a greatsword bedecked with gold and rubies manifested between his hands.

"I've been waiting for you, Daeya."

Too late, she realized her mistake.

The dragon charged.

# CHAPTER SIXTY-SEVEN

## RAVLOK

The world fell away from Ravlok, his name echoing off stone. He scrabbled for purchase on something, anything, like a swimmer caught in a current. Hot iron and void-chilled air replaced the close sulfuric heat of the lava tube. His stomach hung suspended. For the briefest instant, his mind must have been truly uncorked because he found himself sympathizing with Alar's disdain for Aetherial travel.

Then, everything righted itself with a jarring burst of firelight, color, and cold.

He landed hard in the snow and lay staring at the stars, wondering how in Ordeolas's name he'd gotten kicked out of another important test. He hadn't even insulted the instructor this time.

A pair of gray-and-black-striped eyes appeared above him. Their owner held a torch that illuminated similarly striped scales and plates that formed sharp points in place of her ears. The creature's nostrils flared, and she tilted her head. "What's this? A human morsel found its way into the volcano?"

Ravlok started.

Another face appeared opposite the first. Caelyn rolled her eyes. "This one is with the girl."

The goddess of nature reached down and hauled Ravlok to his feet. He might have murmured his thanks, had the sight of two more individuals not frozen his tongue. One studied him with shrewd golden eyes, her forehead crinkling around a pair of golden horns.

Ravlok recognized her, but his attention strayed to the mountainous, silver-scaled dragon that basked in the snowdrifts behind her. It tilted its sleek, serpentine head, its captivating blue eyes reflecting orange light.

The first woman took Ravlok by the chin. "It must not be very *sssmart*."

Claw-like nails pressed into his face, and a name filtered up through the mush of his thoughts. He had to project confidence, or these women—these *dragons*—would maybe-not-metaphorically eat him alive. "Release me, Vorsere."

Vorsere jerked back.

Aliri's laughter drew the steel dragon's ire off him. "Twelve thousand years old and you still underestimate humans." She regarded Ravlok with greater interest. "She must have learned to throw her Shield, or he would have burned before the sacred aura cast him out."

Caelyn snorted. "Silonas favors him."

A sacred aura. Of course. Once initiated, the Test wouldn't allow outside interference. Daeya and Telerion must remain within it until a bond formed, or a god's touch breached the sphere.

Dread wormed its way under Ravlok's skin. He'd prepared her all he could in such little time. Silonas willing, it would be enough.

"Fear not, Ascended." Even when spoken softly, the silver dragon's rumbled words shook snow loose from the mountainside. "You have gotten her this far."

"Ascended?" Vorsere and Aliri asked together.

Ravlok knew that voice. His sigh shuddered out of him. "Falla."

The Heart of Redemption, once bonded to Baokryn's best friend Xosek, had a tragic story of love and loss—one that made Ravlok's heart ache for her even millennia later.

Vorsere whirled on the silver dragon. "That's *imposssible*. It hasn't undergone the ritual."

He wasn't sure what grated more: being called a *bashiin* by certain Syljians, or having his humanity stripped from him by the word 'it.'

"I have, actually." Ravlok willed his aura to peace as he faced the two dragons in their humanoid forms. He unfastened his inner tunic to expose the scar and ceremonial markings.

While the dragons exchanged looks, Caelyn merely sighed. "So, you've chosen war, then."

The goddess's plan to lock Daeya away in Dromas, where not even Anordis could reach her, made more sense now. Without the Shard and all the draegionic magic said to have been woven into Daeya's soul, the god of chaos would have to devise another way to reach the Greater Throne.

"War is inevitable," Ravlok said. "Whether Chaos makes a play for it now or in ten thousand years, he won't stop just because you remove Daeya from the equation." He let his scowl fade. "She's already faced him once, and not at the height of her power. She can help you."

Caelyn's hand tightened on her staff. She looked at the dragons. "See that she is made ready."

Aliri bowed. "*Vheth, Saonivhatt.*"

The goddess glanced back at Ravlok. "Pray I do not regret this, Ascended."

The fact that even Caelyn recognized his new title bolstered him.

A distant roar rumbled through the ground. Ravlok turned, and more snow cascaded down the slope. Foreboding lodged in his gut.

*I pray I don't, either.*

Telerion leaped the river of magma, using his wings to glide half the distance. He landed lightly on his feet, sword flashing.

Daeya dove aside and channeled magic. Already, she'd put herself at a disadvantage. She needed distance, and she needed it *now*.

Her rift sprang open without a sigil, as Zakaari had taught her, but not before the dragon's blade swept down in a cutting strike that would have cleaved her in two if not for her Shield. She threw herself sideways, away from the rift. Pain exploded across her ribs.

Struggling for air, Daeya got one blade up to deflect the next blow and countered with the shorter one in a move Tipori had made her practice a thousand times.

Telerion's greatsword came with all the power and training of a centuries-old dragon behind it. Though Malice's serrated edge opened a jagged wound in his side, Mischief might have shattered if not for its infusion of magic. Daeya's arm went numb under the reverberating clash of metal. He hammered at her again and again, until he had her in full retreat.

Swallowing her heart, Daeya dropped Mischief back into the Aether and hurled scarlet fire at the dragon's face. He spun, snarling, and slammed his armored wing into her flank. The blow sent her careening over the magma and onto a blackened island between rivers of molten stone.

Daeya landed hard and rolled. Her Shield stuttered as she scrabbled to keep from skidding into magma. Every muscle screamed from the onslaught.

Bleeding Aether, not even Tipori fought like this. She released Malice to the mists, tensed to rise, and collapsed with the bright bloom of agony in her side.

A rift. Gods, she needed a rift.

Daeya struggled to blink away darkness. Hot wind and red embers whirled to the beat of wings. Telerion landed opposite her in a bright spray of magma.

He'd be on her before she could get to her feet, maybe even before she could summon an Aetherian shield.

Telerion lifted his sword.

Daeya imagined a rift cutting parallel to the ground beside her and rolled, ribs grinding, into it. She came out on a ledge overlooking an enormous pool of molten rock. The dragon spun a circle across the cavern, searching, then launched himself in the air.

A whimper escaped her as she shoved herself upright. She couldn't spring out of a rift and surprise him in mid-flight. Her right hand still buzzed from their brief clash of swords, and the pain in her ribs sapped her strength.

Magic. If she could keep her distance and use magic, she would hold the advantage.

Telerion flew over the magma, tugging on their connection in search of her. *"Come, Daeya, you can't hide forever. Let us finish this."*

His goading stoked the fire inside her. Daeya checked her casting bracelet and summoned an Aetherian shield.

The light gave her away.

Telerion spun, brows set with determination. His sword was gone, and in its stead he held a pair of three-bladed throwing weapons.

Vhalari. Sharpened on each edge, capable of decapitating an enemy from around a barrier, they were favored among native Skriian tribes.

The rippling shield in front of her would be about as useful as a child's snow fort.

Telerion's vhalari glowed softly, imbued by magic. He hovered over the magma, beating his wings in steady time.

Jets of fire coursed from Daeya's hands. Telerion swooped aside and threw his first vhalari. It chopped through the air in a wide arc around the Aetherian shield. Daeya ducked, unwilling to risk taking that magical edge even with her golden Shield still up. The vhalari whistled over her head and circled back to Telerion's hand. He threw the second in quick succession, though it went wide of its mark before returning.

"I expected more from the last draegion," the dragon taunted. "You want my submission? Stop playing games and fight!"

A frustrated snarl ripped from her.

His third attack whirled even lower. She dropped to the stone, and pain blasted through her. Pinned to the ground and with nowhere else to go, she braced for the bite of his fourth throw and tried one last defense.

Telerion's vhalari flew true. Daeya channeled magic and a rift sprang open half a span from where she lay. It sucked the vhalari in and snapped shut with a burst of light.

The dragon resummoned the weapon from the Aether and grinned. "You can do better than that."

He was toying with her. Daeya bared her teeth and started to rise, but Telerion changed his grip on the weapon and drew back. When he loosed the vhalari this time, it arced high and chopped low, directly over her Aetherian shield.

Two rifts opened at Daeya's command: one above her head to draw the weapon in, and the other to spit it back out.

The vhalari lodged in Telerion's shoulder. He plummeted with a roar before righting himself over the magma pool. Both vhalari dissolved into mist, and blood ran down his chest.

Daeya pressed her advantage. She didn't have to wait for his fire breath, not when she was in a room full of burning stone.

Not when everything was Aether.

Three beads crumbled as she dismissed the Aetherian shield and pulled saphyric energy from her casting bracelet. She turned her will upon the magma, and ribbons of fire coiled upward, snaking around Telerion in a scarlet tornado.

Magic stormed through her like lightning in a thunderhead. Golden sparks leaped from her fingertips, reaching for that column, greedy for more. The dark chasm yawned open before her, beckoning her to drink deep from the wellspring of euphoria at its heart.

This power—this *invincibility*—was her birthright. A magic unrivaled by even the world's greatest conquerors. Daeya lifted her hands and Aetherial mist responded to her like a faithful hound, swirling, twining, eager to please, and soft as the finest silk.

A smile tugged at her lips.

Telerion's roar of agony shook the mountain.

Daeya recoiled from the chasm and its wealth of power, roused from her dreamlike ecstasy by the dragon's pain. A blinding light flashed outward from the column of fire, and horror gripped her by the throat.

Gods have mercy. What had she done?

Light swelled, and the growing shape of the dragon broke her flames apart. Four jets of light burst outward, taking the shape of two wings, a serpentine neck, and a tail. A trio of horns topped his snout, and spikes lined his orbital ridges.

Islands of stone crumbled under the dragon's true form, sending up gouts of steam, sloshing magma over his enormous paws. His throat glands glowed white-hot, and a roiling ball of fire coalesced between his massive teeth.

All foolish thoughts of invincibility fled. The face of certain death leveled its gaze upon her, and Daeya's Shield was reflected in pools of molten gold. Her jaw clenched and she forced herself not to tremble.

Daeya remembered the ship's mast when it was struck by lightning.

She remembered the story of Pananmai.

She remembered Baokryn's Test, and Nahariim's, and dozens of other vessels before them. Daeya used them all to shape her own reality. She shattered every bead left in her bracelet and channeled magic.

Fire erupted from the dragon's mouth.

A tremendous roar drowned out the sound of her scream. Stone cracked like bone beneath her feet, and intense heat whipped her hair and clothing taut. For a small eternity, the sheer force of magic coursing between her and Telerion made it impossible to move, impossible to breathe. His fire pooled scarlet before her open hands. She willed it into Aether and pulled it inside her.

Like lantern oil poised to combust, the magic brimmed at her awareness, awaiting a spark. The last of Telerion's flames poured molten energy into her veins. She could kill him now with little more than a thought.

Daeya fought against the urge to turn that magic back on him like the draegion who'd killed the Blight of Pananmai. Like Nahariim, who'd leaped into the chasm of power and corruption to subdue the great wyrm Maratesh.

Instead, she spun the energy into the threads of her early bond with Telerion. Using Baokryn's memory as a guide, she pulled them taut and strengthened them with wave after wave of Aether. Telerion lowered his massive head, and Daeya stepped forward to place her palm against his snout. Golden light spiderwebbed outward across his scales.

She made her request telepathically. *"Bond with me?"*

The dragon's eyes closed. *"Vheth, Nashanett."*

Telerion's mind opened, and his thoughts and memories filtered into her like raindrops through a forest canopy.

A dragon prince scorned for his love of a mixed-metal from the lowest caste. Exiled for refusing to marry a pureblood for the sake of a crown. Finding a living legend in the woods, her knees scabbed and elbows scraped from climbing trees. Seeing the way forward, realizing the girl would be taken from him should he breathe a word to any *saonivhar*. Sheltering her, teaching her Draconic, always wary of the black-robes who came to the farm to harry the father about his taxes. The moment she was taken from him by the sorcerers; his urge to lay waste to the Eidosinian capital and expose all of dragonkind. A visit from a young syljoren seer who told him to go north, promising the girl would find him there soon. Then eleven long years of silence.

*"Riisii,"* Daeya supplied. When the seer appeared again, she was going to get the fiercest hug.

*"Riisii."* Telerion's outpouring of gratitude for Tipori's daughter flooded Daeya's mind, followed by a sea of remorse. *"I shouldn't have left you. If I'd known..."*

Daeya shuddered. The memory exchange had gone both ways. Her dragonbond knew everything that had happened to her in those eleven years.

*"We're together now."* She frowned. *"You kept me a secret from Tiior, knowing your people would demand I bond with an older dragon?"*

Telerion bowed his reptilian head. *"Vheth."*

Images of Telerion's father, Mertysian, flickered across her awareness, accompanied by phantom sounds of breaking glass. Daeya swallowed. *"You hoped a bond with me would circumvent your father and reunite you with your partner?"*

*"Forgive me, Nashanett. It was selfish."*

She could have been angry, but Daeya would have done the same thing for Zakaari. *"Believe me, I get it."*

He hesitated. *"Should you wish to bond with another, I understand."*

It was true, she didn't have to bond with him. Some Tests were only initiated to prove a draegion's legitimacy or prepare them to fight a stronger dragon. Now that she'd won his submission, she could call upon the gods to release her and walk away. But Daeya *knew* Telerion. He'd been a friend to her from the beginning, and that mattered more than anything else.

*"Honestly, I'd rather bond with you than some stuffy old wyrm."*

Telerion nodded once and became light as he transformed back into a man. He crossed the slag-strewn ledge and knelt, his wings folded behind him, arms outstretched. He summoned his greatsword and placed it at her feet.

He spoke aloud in the tongue of the ancients. *"Nashanett*, Daeya the Younger, for choosing to spare my life, I, Telerion Aethersworn, Prince of the Golden Court, pledge my sword into your service. Until my last breath, I will be your sworn shield and loyal servant. I will stand beside you, share the blessing of your joy and the burden of your tears. Should you accept my oath, I will cherish the title Dragonbond and place it before all others in my name. To do with as you will, my life is forever yours."

Heat blazed in Daeya's cheeks as she listened to his oath. His use of her full title for the first time settled like a mantle over her shoulders.

She knelt to retrieve his sword and offered it back to him. "I accept your oath, Prince Aethersworn, and give you mine in return. I promise to heed your counsel and honor your wisdom. I will respect your virtues and desires, even when they differ from mine. Above all, I will cherish your friendship and care for your welfare as if it were my own."

Telerion's hand closed on his sword, lips twitching. "You will make a good queen."

Daeya snorted. "Let's not be too hasty. Right now, I just need to get my friends out of a tight spot." She shared an abridged version of the situation in Kuma'Kiir, wincing and holding her ribs as they rose together. "Will you help us?"

"You're asking if I want to go to war against the people who mistreated you?" His expression darkened. "When I am through with them, they will be little more than ash."

# CHAPTER SIXTY-EIGHT

## RAVLOK

Ravlok slid down the mountainside, eyes trained on the pair of figures emerging from the lava tube. The light of dawn painted the snowdrifts in shades of pink and orange.

She'd done it.

She'd really done it.

"Daeya!"

Tipori and the others looked up when he called out. Accompanied by a cacophony of clattering rocks and snapping branches, Ravlok hastened the rest of the way, leaving Aliri, Vorsere, and Falla in their humanoid forms to climb gingerly down the slope behind him. He stopped short of sweeping Daeya up in a hug. She was holding her side and favoring one leg.

"You're injured."

"I'm alright," Daeya assured him. She gestured to the bare-chested, winged man standing beside her. "Meet Telerion."

Mouth gaping, Ravlok nodded to him. Telerion was nearly of a height with Aliri and shared the same golden eyes and shapely jaw, but he was much fairer both in complexion and hair color. Dried blood streaked his torso.

Telerion bowed. "Tiior's blessing upon you, Ascended."

Ravlok was never going to get used to that. "It's a pleasure, Telerion."

Zakaari approached, eyeing the ageless man. "You're really a dragon?"

His golden wings folded tighter. "I—"

Vorsere scoffed. "*Vhash*, he just wears the wings for show."

"Vorsere," Aliri growled.

Sam lobbed a questioning glance toward Ravlok.

Remembering his manners, Ravlok gestured to the three dragons. "Her Majesties Aliri, Falla, and Vorsere, queens of their respective courts."

Tipori blinked. "Dragon queens?"

As the rest of their party gaped, Ravlok rubbed the back of his neck. "They were here overseeing Daeya's Test."

Aliri spared a nod for Tipori. "Well met, syljoren."

"Tipori Evallier." He offered his name like an afterthought.

Aliri's attention slid off him like oil. She stepped forward to appraise Daeya. "It is an honor to meet you, Daeya McVen."

In stark contrast, Daeya's expression could have been mistaken for a scowl. "I wish I could say the same, Your Grace."

Waves of her restrained anger stormed across Ravlok's aura. He hesitated. Of all the dragons, he'd thought Daeya would find kinship with Aliri.

Aliri frowned as if she'd expected the same. Her gaze strayed toward Telerion. "You must share my son's anger with me. Let me assure you, I have lifted his exile order to honor his position as your dragonbond. You will both return home with us, where your training can begin."

That itching sense of foreboding returned. In Ravlok's peripheral vision, he caught Tipori's gesture to Sam and Sessiri. Both women drifted into flanking positions around their group. Zakaari slid one foot in front of the other in a ready stance.

Ravlok slipped closer to Daeya. Silonas help them if this ended in violence.

"You mean you lifted the order when you realized your son was about to claim the highest honor among dragonkind." Daeya stepped closer to Aliri. "With all due respect, we're not going anywhere with you."

Bitter laughter ripped through the clearing. Vorsere stalked forward to stand level with Aliri. "Ah, the *insssolence* of youth. Unfortunately for you, it has already been decided."

Sparks arced off Daeya's fingertips, and Ravlok tensed.

"You will return to Draeconis," Vorsere continued, "or you will—"

Ravlok didn't allow her to finish; any mention of Caelyn or Dromas would likely tip the scales toward bloodshed. He stepped between Daeya and the dragons, pushing his friend back into her dragonbond.

"Daeya and I both made commitments to the people of Starlight. I will not ask her to dishonor our vows." Dragons were all about their oaths and promises. "Once we've done our work, we can join you in Draeconis."

Falla, Tiior bless her, joined the dragons on Aliri's other side. "That is acceptable. When you're ready, Ascended, Telerion can show you the way to Tiior's realm."

It diffused some of the tension between the women.

"With one condition," Daeya said. "If we return, Telerion will not be forced into a marriage arrangement. His loyalty belongs to me first, and the Gold Throne second."

Her tone brooked no argument, and Ravlok had to bite his cheek to hold back his grin. She would yet rise to be their queen.

Vorsere cut a sharp glare at Aliri, who spread her hands. "The arrangement wouldn't interfere with his commitment to you. It is simply a means by which we unite the Gold Court's most powerful families. We strengthen our position on the throne this way."

"He doesn't need a mate to assure your family's throne," Daeya snapped.

Aliri bristled. "The Court has already called for *vheskhanash*. I would rather see our staunchest opponents made allies than risk war upon the crown."

*Vheskhanash* was how Aliri had gained the throne roughly three thousand years ago, before the Battle of Vintrios. It was a brutal and bloody affair in which an heirless ruler and three or four other dragons from opposing houses fought to the death for the right to rule. Aliri's injury would place her at a disadvantage. A political marriage would safeguard her family's position, but it wasn't the only way forward.

Ravlok held up a hand. "*Vheskhanash* may only be called when the ruling family has no successor to the throne. If you've rescinded Telerion's exile, you can also rename him heir."

"Telerion has made his stance on ruling clear. A mate dedicated to the task assures the Court a stable future."

Ravlok frowned. He glanced over his shoulder at Telerion, considering. "Baokryn refused to rule, too." He turned back to Aliri. "But she did her duty when it was asked of her."

Aliri narrowed her eyes. "Of course you would use Baokryn against me, bookkeeper. Her circumstances were much different."

"She was much older as well. Perhaps all Telerion needs is time."

Aliri regarded him grudgingly, then her gaze flicked to her son. "I would agree to the prince's freedom to choose a mate within a given timeframe."

"One thousand years," Daeya said without missing a beat.

Someone whistled behind them, but none of the dragons balked at the demand. A millennium for a dragon was akin to a decade for a human.

Still, Aliri hesitated. "Unless the crown's health declines. In such case, he should wed within the healers' prognosis. If he fails to choose, the king and I reserve the right to choose for him."

"*Vhash.*"

Hairs pricked the back of Ravlok's neck. He turned fully to Telerion. "No?"

The dragon's gaze was fierce. "I will agree to one thousand years. Should your health decline, I will ascend the throne without a *shavhar*." He dipped his chin toward Ravlok. "In honor of Baokryn."

Warmth spread through Ravlok's chest.

Aliri also nodded. "What say you, *Nashanett*?"

If Daeya picked up on Aliri's use of Baokryn's former title, she hid it well. Ravlok sucked in a breath and stole a glance at the other two wyrms. If Daeya was to eventually claim Baokryn's position as queen, the entire Circle of Nine would have to agree. The sage expression on Falla's face suggested she would support her, but Vorsere wore her distrust openly in her tight jaw and furrowed brow.

That one was going to be trouble.

"I agree," Daeya said.

"Then, the matter is settled." At last, Aliri's posture relaxed. "I think you'll do well in Draeconis."

Daeya's attention darted toward Zakaari, her uncertainty flickering through Ravlok's awareness like light from a guttering candle. He winced, sensing the thought as surely as if she'd spoken it aloud: going to Draeconis meant leaving Zakaari behind.

"We depart for Kuma'Kiir to help the Alliaansi defend against the Sorcerers' Guild," Ravlok ventured carefully. "We could get to Draeconis faster with your help."

Vorsere's painted black lips curled. "You would expose our existence to other mortals."

Falla rolled her eyes. "It's about time someone did. I've missed flying the northern currents."

"Unfortunately, I agree with Vorsere." Aliri winced as if the admission tasted sour. "Our brief presence in Caelyn's domain has upset her enough." With a cautious look at Telerion, she added, "There will be repercussions among the Circle, should you do this."

Telerion's wings flared with defiance. "I do as my dragonbond wills."

"I know." She smiled wistfully. "I'm proud of you, *draekhei*."

As the dragons exchanged farewells, Ravlok rejoined the soldiers and gave Tipori a halfhearted shrug. The other dragons' aid would have been a great boon, but at least Daeya had succeeded in gaining one ally.

Tipori squeezed Ravlok's shoulder. "Careful, soldier, or you're going to find yourself in command one day."

The notion was so ludicrous, Ravlok barked a laugh. But Tipori's knowing grin froze the retort on his tongue.

Odes of Ordeolas. He was serious.

"*Amaa*," Ravlok tried, but Tipori was already turning away, chuckling to himself. "*Amaa*, wait—"

# CHAPTER SIXTY-NINE

## DAEYA

Over the next week, Daeya honed her draegion magic into a force of nature. It was as if an integral part of her had been restored. There was no more wasting sweat on pretty sigils or fancy incantations. With her dragonbond, the veil had been lifted from her eyes and she could finally see.

"Alright, this time, channel his fire into Aether," Ravlok said, pacing a wide circle around them. The ages-old memory from which he pulled his instruction flowed through their bookkeeper's bond, and recalling the knowledge became as instinctive as breathing. "Then diffuse all the energy back into Telerion."

A move that could kill an unbonded dragon, but Daeya's magic bolstered him, too. Not only had Telerion gained in social status a hundredfold more than he'd lost in exile, he was now one of the toughest and most virile dragons yet living. Once skill and discipline were on his side—

*"I am disciplined,"* Telerion cut into her thoughts, his tone serious.

Daeya felt his indignation as if it were her own. She smirked. *"Of course you are, golden prince."*

His slitted eyes narrowed. Though the dragon rarely laughed, Telerion made up for his grave demeanor with endless patience. Unfortunately for him, his tolerance for her antics only made her work harder to crack his solemn shell. It was difficult to believe he was the same dragon who had spurned the Golden Court in favor of the coppers, whose whimsical way of life was seen as lecherous and uncivilized by his gold brethren. Exile from Draeconis had changed Telerion, and Daeya was determined to reunite him with his lost love and undo the damage his sire Mertysian had caused.

As for his impending marriage... They at least had a thousand years to work that out.

The Aether glands beneath Telerion's jaw glowed red, and flames curled between his teeth. Daeya summoned her Shield and reached out. Telerion cut loose a mighty stream of fire that pooled right into her hands. Powerful vibrations of Aether coursed through her. Sweat slid down her face and shoulders, and that euphoric sense of invincibility poured into her like a drug.

A mental nudge from Ravlok kept her from sinking further into that state. *Focus*, he seemed to say, though their bond was too rudimentary for true telepathy. It was a conduit for knowledge and balance, while the dragonbond was a conduit for power. Together, they rooted her against the tide of draegion magic like anchors in a storm.

*Everything is Aether. Spellcasting is simply a matter of coaxing reality to your will.*

All of Tipori's lessons made sense now. She'd learned them before as Baokryn, as Nahariim, as all the other vessels who had come before her. As Daeya stepped toward the dragon, limbs quaking, she imagined the Aether as a singular stream of energy, like wind through a keyhole or sand through an hourglass. Just as she'd forged their bond, she could diffuse magic through their connection and into the dragon, where it would dissolve harmlessly back beyond the Aetherial Wall over the span of hours.

Getting this technique right was vital to their success. Without it, Tipori's plan would see her either incinerate or warp the entire region.

Heat and wind buffeted her as she pressed her hands to Telerion's scales. Daeya's Shield flashed across his golden plates, and her magic funneled back into his body as she'd envisioned.

She didn't realize she was grinning until Tipori moved in her periphery; he'd been standing guard against any accidental warps. He inclined his head, a smile staining his lips.

"Well done, Daeya."

She steadied herself against Telerion until the hum of magic faded. "Thank you, *Amaa*."

Tipori still trained her in the sword—polishing the rust off her remembered techniques was no idle task—but he'd largely ceded his teachings in magic to Ravlok. If he found it strange that a non-adept should take point in her lessons, he hid it well.

Ever since his ascension, Ravlok had been calmer, more confident, and he carried himself with a regal bearing, like a man far older and wiser than his twenty-five years. The best part was he didn't seem to realize it.

Tipori looked to Ravlok. "I think she has it. Let's break for the evening."

"That seems wise." Ravlok approached and squeezed Daeya's shoulder. "I think there's one orange left."

Her mouth watered.

Zakaari and the others were huddled around the campfire. As she made to join them, Telerion vaulted upward and disappeared into the twilight.

"Where's he going?" Sam asked.

As if in answer, the phantom taste of blood coated Daeya's tongue. "Hunting."

They were still a week out from Kuma'Kiir—nine more days of agonizing anticipation and quiet dread for what they would find inside the city's walls—but they would be within sight of enemy troops any day now. After tonight, there could be no more practice or flight training if they wanted to maintain their element of surprise.

Daeya settled on Zakaari's left so he could still pick at his rations with his right hand. She offered him a smile as he passed the orange to her, but his attempt to return it seemed pained, like he'd stepped on a nail.

"Hey." She elbowed him. "What's wrong?"

Zakaari winced. He started to drag his fingers through his hair, but the chunk of bread in his lap overbalanced. He fumbled for it, only to knock it into the coals.

Their companions paused. Ravlok lowered his bread, while Sessiri and Sam shared an uncertain glance. Though he continued chewing, Tipori's eyes glazed with Foresight.

Daeya held her breath.

Zakaari had been increasingly distant since they'd left Mount Eisekii. He spent more time worrying the knotted sleeve of his cloak than looking at her. When she asked him to spar, he would deflect with claims of soreness or distraction. At first, she thought it was just concern for his mother or their people bothering him, but last night when they'd bedded down, Zakaari had stared at the empty space on one side of her, and the dragon on the other. He'd said nothing as he lay beside her, and Daeya hadn't pressed him, but she was starting to suspect the real issue.

Telerion moved when she moved, felt what she felt. He could sense her thoughts, her fears, her doubts. It didn't help that his humanoid form was obscenely handsome.

Zakaari's shoulders curled around his middle. He scowled at the bread as if it were the cause of all his heartache.

Daeya attempted lightness. "If you wanted toasted bread"—she reached into the campfire circle, Shield flickering, to retrieve the browned loaf—"you could've just asked."

Cautious grins caught the orange light like fireflies, but vanished just as quickly. None were Zakaari's. Daeya proffered the bread, but he made no move to take it.

If humor was lost on him, he'd truly retreated inside his head. She cringed and set the loaf between them, then returned to her feet. "Will you all excuse us?" Without awaiting a response, she reached for Zakaari and tried to pull him up beside her.

He resisted. "Daeya—"

"Please, Zakaari. Leap with me."

His lips parted, and he let out a shaky breath before nodding.

She led him through the snow and brush, over rocks and ravines until the campfire glow faded. They came to a spot where the ground dropped sharply, and at the bottom lay the glint of a half-frozen stream.

"What's this—" Zakaari began.

She pivoted on her heel and kissed him.

His eyes ringed white, and the palm he planted against her lower back was more a hasty attempt to remain upright than a sign of affection. He responded stiffly at first, but with each hungry demand of her lips, he ceded a little more.

He gasped when she finally broke away.

"I think I know what this is about." Daeya cupped the back of his neck. "Zakaari, you have nothing to worry about."

No bonds or telepathy were needed to understand the shudder that wracked him. "I can't be what you need."

"Aethershite." Her fingers dug into his nape as if letting go would allow their love to fall apart. "You're exactly what I need."

Sensing her distress, Telerion's voice rumbled through her mind. *Nashanett?*

*I'm alright.*

"You—" Zakaari swallowed. "You and Telerion work so well together. I don't want to get in the way."

"Telerion is my friend and my sworn protector. I will come to love him as I love Ravlok. But you *chose* me, as I chose you, and there's something incredibly precious about that."

Icy wind whipped his hair over her cheeks and knifed into her cloak. Zakaari was silent for so long that she had the creeping sense he'd already made up his mind. It threatened to strangle her.

"Please say something."

He pressed his forehead to hers. "You're immortal, Daeya. I can't protect you. I can't defend you. I can't *do* anything."

Someday, decades from now, would she allow the concern for his mortality to weigh on her, but not now. Right now, that didn't matter. "We protect each other. That's how this works."

He released her to wipe his cheeks, and the absence of his touch in those few seconds was more painful than any rune carved into her flesh. The agony only receded when Zakaari's gloveless fingers sifted into her hair, and he gazed into her eyes for the first time in days.

Daeya pressed on. "I see your pain. I know things seem dark right now, but the sun *is* going to rise, and I'm going to be right beside you at dawn, no matter what."

The last of Zakaari's poise crumbled. Vicious sobs wracked his body, and he buried his face in her neck.

"I love you," he said.

Unable to hold up the combined weight of his love and her relief, Daeya's knees buckled. She and Zakaari sank to the snow. His desperate kisses peppered her face and neck. She summoned her Shield and projected the golden lattice onto him as a barrier against the cold.

Again, no telepathy was needed. She unclasped his cloak. Zakaari let it slip from his shoulders. He lay back and pulled her with him, hands slipping beneath layers of fabric.

"I love you." He repeated the words like a prayer. "Gods, how I love you."

Soon, only the night stood between them. Daeya's Shield lit the trees, the rocks, the snow. They could be soldiers again tomorrow, when dragons, destinies, and imminent battles once more demanded their attention. Tonight, all that mattered were the soft kisses he sprinkled over her lips, chin, and chest, the way their soft laughter threaded through burbling water and whistling wind. The way their shadows danced among the trees.

When Daeya finally collapsed beside him, she was certain no more perfect harmony could exist. The gods had blessed her after all, it seemed, but with a different kind of magic:

Love.

Zakaari gathered her close, fingers splayed against the runes that had kept her isolated for so long. She buried her face in his hair, her grip tightening possessively on his upper back.

Theirs was a love not even Chaos himself would take from her.

She would make sure of it.

Ravlok's stomach turned over as Aetherial wind rushed past him. Streaking colors dazzled his senses, then the rift yanked him to a halt inside Kuma'Kiir's walls.

He might have severed his soul from his body once, but he would never get used to *that*.

Daeya and Zakaari stepped out of the rift behind him, followed by Telerion, Sam, and a queasy-looking Sessiri.

A female voice called out as Tipori emerged. "I hope you brought fresh clothes, *nei ama're*. You couldn't pay anyone enough here to wash those linens."

Three women dressed in forest-green tunics stood against a backdrop of snowy streets and blackened buildings. Ravlok remembered Commander Maralla Evallier from the memorial.

Tipori grinned. "I'm certain I could find someone for the right price."

Clearly an inside joke that was lost on Ravlok. Maralla broke formation and collided with her husband. Tipori swept her into his arms and spun her twice, kissing her as if the rest of the world could wait.

Instead of gawking or allowing his mind to wander toward Sam, Ravlok studied the two other Syljian women in their welcome party. One was older with unusual ice-blue eyes set in a face so severe it might have never seen a smile; the younger had two lines of runes running from her lower lip to her chin, and her demeanor was as bright as sunshine reflecting off a lake. The older woman—Saowen, he guessed—nodded to her apprentice, and the younger Syljian stilled with some difficulty, her gaze fixed on the wall behind Ravlok. As he turned, the rift snapped closed with a burst of wind.

For once, he wasn't met by screaming soldiers or falling stone.

Light Paladins had taken over the Fourth Legion's camp by the time he and the others reached the city. They'd relied on Saowen's team of psionists to get them inside. The mastermind's apprentices scouted the perimeter, opening and closing strategic wards to allow people in and out. According to Tipori, it was how Maralla and her troops had managed to withdraw inside the walls, leaving just enough arcanists to give the illusion of a fortified camp. When the enemy had finally closed its teeth around them, they'd taken minimal losses in their final retreat.

Starvation and disease were the more immediate threats now. The enemy seemed content to wait them out rather than attack the walls again. Taking in the destruction around them, Ravlok didn't need many guesses to ascertain the state of the city's morale.

"Tell me you have good news." Maralla's somber gaze took in each member of their small party until it settled on Zakaari. "*Saonis miraar.* What happened—"

"Later," Tipori said curtly. He fixed his wife with a pointed look.

Zakaari's ears darkened, and he looked everywhere except his mother's face.

She sobered, straightened, and tore her attention away. "Is this all you brought with you?"

"They are all we need." Tipori wrapped his arm around Maralla's shoulders. "Come, lead us to your command. We have much to discuss."

Commander Evallier's base of operations was a repurposed wine cellar bustling with soldiers and scouts. The air was crisp but not cold, despite the below-freezing temperature outside, and it smelled of soil and old parchment. A worn map lay in the room's center, laden with stones, chips, and wooden carvings to designate troop and enemy placements.

Maralla swiftly informed them of the city's predicament, worry framing her mouth. Guild troops had surrounded Kuma'Kiir on all but the western edge, where the sorcerers had begun razing the forest. The city's wells had been poisoned, and snowmelt had become their major water source. An emergency convoy bearing supplies and arcanists from Aon'In was nearly a week overdue, and food and saphyrum were running low. The overcrowded city was starting to feel the pressure, especially with many of her soldiers laid up by sickness.

Saowen's apprentice, whose name he learned was Isaan, elbowed Ravlok while Tipori was outlining his plan for reclaiming the southern perimeter. She regarded him with wide-eyed wonder. "Are you really immortal?"

Tipori paused mid-account and scowled at the young psionist. Taken aback, Ravlok searched for her presence in his mind, but found only Daeya's bright spark, which flared hot at Isaan's intrusion. In response to his dragonbond's anger, Telerion growled.

"Stop that," Saowen hissed. "Isaan, we have discussed this. We do not invade the minds of our allies."

Ravlok suppressed a snort. Funny how things had changed for them.

Isaan shrank under her mentor's chilling blue stare, but her attention bounced between the dragon and Ravlok. She looked years younger in that moment than Ravlok had originally thought. "Apologies, *Amaa*. His memories are just so fascinating."

Her curiosity softened him. Ravlok would have probably done the same if he could sift through others' memories at will.

"Yes. I'm immortal." Knowing what powerful beings existed in this room—ones who would defend him without hesitation—he opted for keeping the peace. He would research psionic wards for himself later. "The gods have tasked me with something very special."

Isaan's mouth fell open and the room's weight settled on him. Daeya's spark burned lower, and the tension in Telerion's shoulders lessened. Ravlok nodded to them and gestured for Tipori to continue.

Tipori returned the nod and reclaimed the room. "Once we have shields in place, Daeya can attack the southern flank. I will ride with her to keep the enemy at bay."

Maralla lifted a white eyebrow. "You? Ride a dragon? Tipori, you can barely ride a horse without turning a spectacular shade of green."

Quiet laughter rippled through the cellar. Ravlok cracked a smile as Tipori side-eyed his wife.

"Zakaari will ride with me," Daeya declared, taking her partner's hand. "No offense, *Amaa*, but I don't think Telerion would like you vomiting on his scales."

More laughter accompanied the dragon's rumbling assent.

Tipori deferred to his son with a look bordering on sheepish. "Very well. Zakaari, you will ride with Daeya. Keep her safe."

"*Ciir, Peiaa*." A meaningful look passed between Zakaari and Daeya, and for the first time in weeks, light returned to his eyes.

A curious ache took root in Ravlok's chest. He caught himself looking at Sam. Wind-tousled blonde hair framed her face and her cheeks were still rosy from the cold. As if sensing his attention on her, Sam glanced his way and smiled.

A smile that dazzled, despite the exhaustion weighing the corners of her eyes.

He *was* immortal. That meant plenty of time to decide what he really wanted. Maybe enough to work through whatever afflicted him. If he had the chance to be with Sam, maybe, just maybe...

But that would have to wait.

For now, it was time to break a siege.

The southern wind blew the stench of three-thousand-year-old death over the Isle of Maratesh, smothering the sweet scent of tropical fruit and natural decay. Aliri recoiled from it, held her breath until the wretched gust off the Wastelands subsided.

It was the first time in weeks Vorsere had shut her blightful mouth. She and Falla drew up short behind Aliri, holding their hands over their noses and staring solemnly in the direction of the Holy City some hundred leagues away.

The silence didn't last long.

"A petulant child and an even more petulant wyrmling," Vorsere grumbled. "They should not have bonded."

Aliri growled. Rising to the bait would do her no favors, though if she'd more often defended her *draekhei* from the likes of Vorsere and Mertysian, perhaps they wouldn't be in this position.

She shoved aside more tangled vines with a force that ripped loose bark from the branches overhead. She'd been so focused on keeping her crown—as if a throne could substitute for her lost purpose—that she'd let her ambitions tear her family apart.

"Disagreeable, reckless, ignorant. This does not bode well for *usss*."

A heavy metallic scent stung Aliri's nostrils, and the glint of light on still water shone through the vegetation. Only a few dozen paces more and they would pass through the portal into Draeconis, where Falla could shift again and they could spend the ride back to Tiior's palace in blessed silence.

"I thought she was very brave." Dear Falla had no qualms challenging their surly companion. "Aliri was right to honor her refusal."

Mud and leaf litter squelched beneath Aliri's feet. She tossed Falla a look of gratitude, and the silver winked.

"It was foolish. She entertains the *fantasssies* of a child."

Falla's conversational tone never wavered. "She made a promise to defend her people. I think Raoghys would be proud of his old pupil."

A belly shot. Aliri glanced over her shoulder.

Vorsere snarled. "But one must wonder, does she truly care for the greater good? Does she act with the nobility of Baokryn or the *ssselfishness* of Nahariim?"

"I think that's the nicest thing you've ever said about Baokryn."

Steel summer and silver winter. Aliri might have laughed if Vorsere's expression didn't threaten violence.

Aliri turned at a familiar tree and started down the stone path to the pool that would take them home. Sand rasped under her feet.

For tens of thousands of years, her brethren had tried to predict which personality traits of a draegion's soul would appear in any given vessel. But draegion magic was just as corrupting to any mortal vessel as it was to their original forms. Baokryn had struggled with her darkness for over four thousand years before the world saw her as anything more than the Traitor's shadow. Daeya the Younger would suffer the same prejudice and endure the same fight. Aliri could only pray her new bookkeeper would be as astute at handling her as Aristyn once was.

Movement at the pool's edge caught her eye.

She stopped at the base of the steps and let her pupils contract fully, taking in the clearing, the sandy soil, the forest greens and sky blues reflecting off the water. Her sharpened senses picked out a flicker of black-violet. A lone figure cloaked in Aetherial mist.

Before she could voice a warning, before the taste of smoke fully registered on her tongue, the mist coalesced into a young syljoren woman with eyes like amethysts and midnight braids stuck through with jagged twigs and evergreen needles.

Falla and Vorsere paused. The Steel Queen's rumbling growl prickled the back of Aliri's neck.

"Hello, Aliri Aethersworn," the syljoren said. "My name is Riisii."

Vorsere recoiled and Falla shifted smoothly into a defensive stance. Aliri stood her ground. This creature stood between them and home, and while no non-dragon mortal should know the location of this portal, the woman's scent sparked a memory: the man and the boy with Daeya McVen.

"Please, don't be alarmed," the creature said. "I know many things I'm not supposed to know yet, but it is urgent that I enter Draeconis with you."

Preposterous. The Circle would never allow it. Not when Chaos priests could wear any face. Aliri narrowed her eyes. "And why is that, Riisii of the Northlands?"

"I bear a message for Tiior."

No hesitation. Not even the flutter of an eyelid to betray an untruth. Still, Aliri remained wary. "If you present us with the message, we will deliver it for you."

"No." Riisii's expression grew pained. "I must go to Draeconis. It is important."

Falla relaxed almost imperceptibly at Aliri's side. "What could be so important?"

"It is about the Traitor's child."

For all her fire magic, Aliri's blood turned to ice.

Jarrah. She meant Jarrah.

Was it as they had always feared? Had the Traitor's child escaped Dromas?

"It is imperative that I speak with Tiior," Riisii insisted. Her eyes glazed over. "I know how this ends."

# CHAPTER SEVENTY

## DAEYA

The city of Kuma'Kiir was a dark stain across the landscape, smattered with snow-crusted rooftops and glowing campfires. Stone walls wrapped the perimeter, and a blanket of open ground stood between them and the enemies in the forest. Muddy streets teemed with shadows as soldiers and civilians made ready. Figures moved along the walls, carting crates and barrels filled with weapons and saphyrum.

It was only a matter of minutes, now.

Floating high above the treetops, the world was surprisingly peaceful. Only a low, musical whistle of wind sounded across Telerion's scales, reminiscent of Sorcha's flute.

Hunkered behind his cranial frills, Daeya adjusted her grip on Telerion's spinal ridge, grateful for the heat of his scales against the cold. Though dawn teased the horizon, it would bring no warmth to the killing field today.

Zakaari shifted behind her and pointed southeast toward a recently cleared stretch of land where over a hundred banners flew. "There."

Daeya passed along the instruction telepathically, and Telerion banked away from the forest filled with Guild encampments. They would take out the Paladins first—their deadlier foes, capable of tracking Syljians by the ripples they left in the Aether.

The dragon's powerful muscles flexed with the beat of his enormous wings. His descent still scattered moths through Daeya's stomach, despite all their practice. A gust dropped them sharply, and Zakaari started, clutching her middle. If not for the circumstances, she might have laughed.

White-violet light erupted along the city walls. Aetherian shields and protective wards swept across the horizon as far as she could see. Daeya's jaw set with purpose.

The signal.

Today, the Guild and the Church would regret ever stepping beyond their borders to harm her people.

War horns carried on the air, and the enemy camps exploded into movement.

Zakaari's hand settled against her abdomen. "This is it."

Daeya laced her fingers with his and held him tightly, fiercely, as if that alone could protect him from the world. "It's about time."

The first sphere of lightning shot into the sky. Zakaari tore his hand away and launched a counter-orb. Both spheres exploded, their dazzling light winking out in a cascade of mist.

Saphyrum casting jewelry weighed down Daeya's wrists, ears, and neck. She closed her eyes and focused. Her Shield warmed her from within, and gold-white light swept across Telerion's scales. It had been a fierce debate between them, which of her companions could benefit most from her limited ability to throw her Shield. Zakaari had insisted Daeya use it to protect Telerion. In the end, she had conceded if the dragon went down, they all would.

More spheres shot toward them. Zakaari knocked them out of the sky. Daeya's eyes narrowed on the white and gold banners. Paladins poured out of their pavilions, shrugging on shields and summoning weapons. Blue- and black-robed mages swarmed among them, some running in terror, others standing their ground.

"*Orders,* Nashanett?" The Aether glands beneath Telerion's jawbone already glowed in anticipation of her command.

Something in Daeya's stomach twisted as she watched the mages. The memory of broken bodies, terrified screams, and bloodied lavender knees sent spikes of anger into her fingertips. She curled her hands around them.

This was for Niam, Ezra, and Sessiri. For Zakaari and his family. For Orowen, Koraani, and Nerimoria. For all the Syljians and refugees who had lived with fear and persecution. For the Guild students who'd been murdered to start this war, and for the father she'd never known.

*"Burn them,"* Daeya said. *"Burn them all."*

Stars exploded behind Normos's eyelids, frozen trees blurring as he hit the snow. He curled around himself, breath fogging as he wheezed and cupped his groin.

Mira's mercy, he'd never been kicked so hard in his life.

The tiny blanker woman whirled in a tornado of white braids and shot off toward the creek. It was several moments before the pain receded enough for Normos to think clearly again, and a few more before he could stumble after her.

Anya Evallier wouldn't get far traipsing through the tangled undergrowth, spellbound and cloaked only in patched wool. Normos had missed the mark on his harried Walk back to camp by a few hundred paces, but his mistake, for once, wasn't the source of the churning void in his gut. Nor was the throbbing pain in his temples, or the sight of Gregory's saphyrum-lit pavilion through the trees.

No, somehow, this was much worse.

Normos tracked her uneven footprints until a sharp crack and a muffled yelp sounded off to his right. Mira's medallion hung like a noose about his neck. If the fool woman fell down an embankment in her condition...

It didn't matter. *Shouldn't* matter. She was a blanker. Normos gritted his teeth.

A pregnant blanker.

He didn't need to summon the Light Paladins to trace her. He simply followed the crunching and scrabbling noises to the shallow ravine she was desperately trying to scale with bound hands. When he topped the rise, she spun and snarled foreign curses at him.

"You're going to freeze to death out here." Normos channeled lightning and blasted the rock aimed for his face apart. "Do you really want to endanger your child?"

Her teeth flashed in the pre-dawn gloom. "Better she dies free than in your foul hands."

Why the words made Normos wince, he couldn't begin to explain. "You're not to be killed. You're to be a hostage."

The woman hurled another rock with surprising accuracy, given the chain connecting her spellbinders. Normos dropped it with another bolt of lightning. He growled and drew a sigil, Bending to the other side of the ravine. He seized her arm and hauled her out of the water.

"Your father has something we want." Why he bothered to reason with the purple-skinned creature was another mystery. A Paladin would have struck her unconscious and dragged her back to camp by her braids, but Normos couldn't bring himself to strike a pregnant woman, Syljian or not. Distantly, he considered whether she could have broken past his wards and used psionics on him. He still *felt* in control, but a nagging sense of... something... still plagued him. "As long as he returns it, you won't be harmed."

She shivered so violently that her pointed ears trembled. For the first time, Normos got a good look at her face. Trios of runes dotted her temples. Almond-shaped eyes regarded him from beneath thick white eyebrows, and a fresh scar marred the side of her nose.

Her expression buckled. "But my baby will be."

She tried to kick him again, but the combination of slick terrain and her growing belly nearly sent her tumbling back into the ravine.

Normos kept them both from sliding by snagging a low-hanging branch and tightening his hold on her arm. "If you're so concerned about the baby, then *stop doing that.*"

Still, he had to admit she had a point. Syljian gestation was twice as long as human pregnancy, and rumors claimed it was harder to maintain. Of course, those rumors had likely started during the Saphyrum War to justify the blankers keeping their stores to themselves, but the number of beads he'd taken off her almost lent credence to the idea. If Gregory planned to barter the governor's daughter for Daeya, he wouldn't need to ensure the baby's health for the exchange. The Paladins would demand it be destroyed.

Normos shouldn't care. What was one less potential mastermind in the world, anyway?

*Choose life.*

He swallowed against that churning sensation in his gut. Mira's touch on the woman didn't change how dangerous she was.

She cradled the swell of her belly, eyeing him with a mixture of defiance and disdain.

He shook himself. His task was to bring Anya Evallier to Gregory, and until he found Sarikkian and confirmed whether or not he was under blanker influence, Normos had to keep up appearances. The Councilor would send the message to Governor Evallier, who would come to collect Anya within a week or two, and then this pregnant terror would be the farthest thing from Normos's mind.

But then he would have to contend with the child prodigy.

His jaw tensed. He'd sooner release Anya back to her people than see Daeya again. He *could* release her, in truth, and Gregory would never be the wiser. Coming back empty-handed would cost Normos dearly, but in this case, the price for failure was maybe worth paying.

"Taking the blanker out for a walk, Sorcerer Beck?"

Normos stiffened. He bit the inside of his cheek to stifle the unseemly words threatening to leap from his mouth. Cameron Vika stood on the opposite embankment, head cocked and arms folded.

"It just needed a bath." Inwardly, he kicked himself. There would be no releasing her now. Perhaps he could sequester her away before the Paladins took stock of her condition. He tugged his struggling captive through a rift and stepped through beside Cam. "Is he awake?"

"I'm not convinced he ever sleeps." She shrugged. "Come on. This should put him in a better mood."

Anya dug at his fingers as they walked, then went for the nerves in his wrists. Normos steeled his grip on her hair, chastising himself for not taking the time to properly bind her hands behind her back.

One long, low peal of a war horn rolled through the valley, stopping them midstride. Normos frowned. There was no attack planned on the city walls today. That could only mean the enemy was moving to engage them.

"They're getting desperate." He started forward again, dragging Anya with him.

Cam stopped him with an upraised arm. Her brows furrowed. "Did they just say—"

"Dragon!" Cries from the Guild camp took the shape of an impossibility. "Dragon!"

Normos scoffed. "You'd think these idiots had never seen an illusion before."

A shriek split the air, followed by the crash of metal and splintering wood. "They've got a dragon!"

Cam hesitated.

Surely she knew better. The enemy's use of psychological warfare should be expected. Normos pushed past her, shaking his head.

More horns sounded. Anya's elbow jabbed at his stomach. Normos jerked on her hair and threw the blow off course. She struck his ribs instead.

He pulled her closer and channeled his element; sparks warmed his fingertips. "Another outburst ends with you unconscious."

Anya grumbled more curses under her breath. "Can't blame me for trying."

One side of his mouth lifted. "No, I suppose I can't."

The cacophony grew louder as they trudged through the snow. Normos stopped short at the edge of camp.

"The gods have cursed us!"

Acolytes fell over each other, running for their lives.

"They've summoned a monster!"

Sorcerers scrambled to contain the madness, barking half-baked orders even as their saucer-eyed gazes raked the horizon.

Councilor Blake bellowed in outrage, "Stand firm, you lot. Ready sigils!"

Normos dodged a flying cookpot and incanted a counter-orb to knock away a stray fire bolt. He'd have the head of whichever pathetic acolyte had lost control of their magic.

Cam drew up alongside him, mouth gaping. "I don't believe it."

"It's despicable," Normos agreed.

"No." She pointed. "That really is a dragon."

"Oh, for Mira's sake, Cam, dragons are ex—"

"Look!"

A burst of orange fire erupted in the sky.

All the warmth drained from Normos's face.

"Water savants!" Urgency pitched Councilor Blake's voice higher. "Water savants to the Paladins' camp!"

Numbness stole into Normos's body as a familiar scarlet glow bloomed at the base of the dragon's neck.

Impossible. This was impossible.

Ripples of heat and clouds of steam rose from the forest. Orange flames mingled with scarlet and consumed the horizon.

Blake stormed past them, snarling. "That means you, Sorceress Vika. Move! Now!"

Normos scarcely registered Cam's departure. Anya struck the nerve in his elbow and wrenched herself free. She made it six paces before he darted after her, arm still smarting.

Towering flames and screaming soldiers lent a dreamlike quality to his surroundings. Even as he threw both arms around Anya's diminutive frame and summoned a rift to take them straight to Gregory's pavilion, Normos was certain none of this could be happening.

Anya stumbled out of the rift and hit her knees in the snow. Normos paused in pulling her up as Gregory swept aside the tent flap, his face red with rage.

"What is—"

A thunderous roar drowned out his words. Gregory spun in a torrent of white and gold. Spined wings blotted out the morning light, and scorching wind swept ash over the pavilion.

The golden monstrosity dove straight for them.

Normos dropped to the ground, covering his head. Anya's body quaked beneath him. It was hard to say where her trembling stopped and his began.

Steam swirled and icy wind slammed into the gap made by the dragon's passage. Violent eddies plastered his cloak to his skin. Scarlet fire slashed across the Guild camp—a line of devastation that rendered everything in its path to ash.

Daeya's fire.

That unnatural color was unmistakable. Within moments, it could destroy everything.

Normos scrambled to his feet. "Councilor, we have to—"

Something in Gregory's face froze the warning on Normos's tongue. He stared in the direction the dragon had gone, his anger eroding into a look of intense calculations.

Spiders of dread skittered across Normos's skin. "Councilor?"

Slowly, implacably, Gregory's lips stretched taut against his teeth. A chuckle emerged, low and resonating, and morphed into full-bellied laughter. "See the governor's daughter secured and return here promptly." Another burst of dragon fire reflected in his eyes. "This will take but a moment."

Ravlok gripped the parapet and squinted into the smoke. The scarf around his mouth and nose filtered out the stench, but it still stung his eyes. Dragon and draegion fire lit the gloom, and bursts of white-violet silhouetted skeletal trees—an eerie echo of the Plains of Gray.

He shivered despite the heat. Caelyn was going to be furious.

Aristyn's warning was a permanent knot between Ravlok's shoulder blades, but he'd been carefully monitoring Daeya's emotions for the last quarter-hour. So far, she was channeling the excess power through her dragonbond appropriately, and there were no signs of her succumbing to corruption.

Movement beside him drew his thoughts away from the bright spot in his mind—the spark of determination and grim duty that was Daeya.

Tipori's head was similarly wrapped in a scarf, only his eyes showing. His voice was muffled. "How are they?"

"Daeya remains steady. Zakaari and Telerion are fine."

"Very good." He looked out over the fiery expanse. "Our shields are holding. We have fire and water savants at the ready to smother anything that gets too close."

A golden streak bolted across the sky. Bright flashes of red and orange erupted over the Guild camp, and a new swarm of black-clad figures erupted from the treeline.

Sam's voice rang out from somewhere beyond the smoke. "Fire at will!"

Bows creaked and Aether flashed. Archers and arcanists on the wall felled the sorcerers as they fled from one killing field into another.

Ravlok steeled himself. He was no longer a stranger to death.

"Tipori!"

Maralla Evallier's cry carried across the wall. Ravlok turned, bracing himself, as she hurried through the smoke, flanked by Saowen and Isaan.

Tipori stepped toward them. "What is it?"

Maralla seized her husband by the arms. "Tipori, the convoy…" She shook her head, struggling to catch her breath. "Anya was in the convoy. It was attacked. They took her." A sob nearly drove her to her knees. "They took our daughter!"

*No.*

Ravlok spun with the others toward the enemy camp. They stared over the wall as if they might catch a glimpse of Tipori and Maralla's firstborn through the smoke.

The stone parapet dug into Ravlok's palms. Hostages were as much an expected result of wartime as injuries or lives lost. But a hostage this valuable to the two highest-ranking officers in the city could undermine their entire operation.

Across the fiery landscape, Daeya responded to his unguarded emotion with a flood of concern. For now, he kept himself from relaying the information through their bond, lest he risk upsetting the delicate balance of her power.

A dangerous stillness settled over the wall. Maralla buried her face in Tipori's cloak. Tipori held her tightly, and looked over her head at Saowen. "Did he send a message?"

She wasted no time asking which 'he' Tipori meant. "He demands we cease fire and surrender the city, *Amaa*."

They couldn't trade the entire city of Kuma'Kiir for one person. They wouldn't.

"The city?" Tipori finally asked, as if the notion confused him.

Choking vines crept around Ravlok's throat.

Surrender the city. Not Daeya.

It was an oversight, surely. An assumption that she would be among the collective surrender. The Guild couldn't have captured her without his knowledge—

The bright spot in his mind flared like a star exploding. Daeya's crippling pain slammed into him, and Telerion's roar threatened to shatter the world.

Devouring flames rose from the remnants of Enlightened and Guild forces. Billowing smoke obscured huge swaths of evergreen forest. Daeya *seized* the fire, drew it upward, and hurled it back down in scarlet streams of destruction.

Power sang through her blood while Ravlok's neutralizing aura kept her focused on the mission, reminding her often to cast the excess energy into her dragonbond rather than lose herself to its tantalizing promise. The energy reverberated through Telerion's scales. His Aether glands glowed, and more fire thundered from his mouth.

Zakaari batted away their enemies' spells with counter-orbs, lessening the burden on Daeya's Shield. He blasted the Guild's siege towers apart with raw Aether and laid waste to the catapults rising through the smoke. Screams and splintering wood disappeared in the rush of wind and flame.

Daeya alternated between raining draegion fire and rebuilding the Aetherian shields that kept the city walls from turning to slag. As long as she kept the fire concentrated on the Paladins and sorcerers, the people inside the city would remain safe. She could withdraw the flames later to prevent them from spreading.

Then Ravlok's steadiness faltered. His anxiety seeped into their bond, and Daeya released the stream of fire she'd been holding. Telerion slowed and banked toward the walls, likely sensing her intentions before they formed.

*"What is it,* Nashanett?"

*"Something's wrong. Fly lower and scan the walls."*

The dragon dipped lower, and smoke whipped into Daeya's eyes.

Zakaari pressed close to speak into her ear. "What's wrong?"

"I'm not sure. I felt—"

Searing pain stormed across her body. Daeya bent double with a gasp. Her forehead pressed against a spike protruding from Telerion's spine. As if he shared her agony, the dragon lurched in the air, his thunderous roar echoing across snow and sky.

Something had gotten under her Shield.

"Daeya?" Zakaari gripped her shoulder. "Daeya!"

She couldn't speak, couldn't think. White-hot coals lodged under her skin, and the urge to dig them out consumed her. She tore aside her winter cloak, the leather cuirass, the layers of fabric, until she reached bare flesh.

Daeya froze.

An ominous black-violet glow suffused her runes. Between the golden lines of her Shield, darker magic pulsed. A familiar voice spoke inside her head.

*"Come, my sweet."*

No.

Icy horror writhed in her chest. The runes. Bleeding Aether, the runes—

A scream built inside her with the realization, the mounting panic. It raked vicious claws into her throat and burst from her unbidden.

Zakaari's hand tightened on her shoulder. "What's happening? Look at me."

But she couldn't. Instead, her eyes fixed on a point far below them, through the fire and smoke, where *he* stood. She couldn't see him, but she knew he was there. "He summons me."

"Who, *nei ama're?*"

*"Come to me."*

"Gregory," she rasped.

The compulsion to obey drew her in like a tracking hound to its master. She could no more resist him than she could stop the rain from falling.

*"Fight him, Nashanett."*

This wasn't happening. This was a dream—a nightmare. She had to wake up.

"Help." She clutched blindly for Zakaari, for Telerion. "Help me!"

She couldn't go back. She couldn't.

Zakaari wrapped his arm around her waist and pulled her close. "I've got you. Telerion, find somewhere to land."

"No!" They couldn't land. He would kill Zakaari and enslave Telerion. She conveyed the thoughts through the dragonbond, and the dragon soared higher, away from Gregory.

*"I will end him,"* Telerion promised. He banked over the city and circled back. His fury bled into their bond and pooled in his Aether glands.

Another wave of agony tore through her, another scream ripped from her throat. Each rune pressed into Daeya with the unforgiving heat of a branding iron.

*"Do not defy me, child. Come!"*

Broken sobs wracked her body. She writhed in Zakaari's embrace, tears streaming across her face.

*Obey, and the pain will stop.*

The knowledge was instinctive, immutable, like the burning in her lungs when she was underwater. If she could break the surface, if she could just draw breath, the pressure screaming inside her would end.

Telerion plummeted toward Gregory, steam rising from his scales. Flames ignited between his teeth. Daeya's ears popped painfully with the descent.

Smoke parted, and the white-clad figure grew steadily larger. Daeya clutched Zakaari's arm, bracing herself, enduring the agony just long enough for Telerion to destroy her former mentor once and for all.

*"Harm me, and Tipori's daughter dies."*

Riisii.

*"Telerion, stop!"*

Too late, fire erupted from the dragon's mouth. Magic poured into Daeya's veins, and reality warped to her will. Telerion strafed the Aetherian dome she erected around Gregory, pulled out of his dive, and circled higher.

Shock reverberated through their bond. *"Why?"*

But he knew why. She didn't have to explain it. Daeya sucked in hiccupping breaths of smoky air and tried not to choke as the pain continued to ravage her.

"*Surrender,*" Gregory commanded. "*Now.*"

Daeya trembled. No one had seen or heard from Riisii in weeks. It was a risk she couldn't take.

She struggled against the force of Telerion's upward momentum until he leveled off above the smoke. Blood pooled in her mouth from her ravaged lip. Gregory wouldn't stop. Not while she resisted him.

Her resolve eroded. She had to make it stop.

"*Telerion, take Zakaari back to Kuma'Kiir. Tell Tipori what happened*"—she winced—"*and give them all my love.*"

"*You can't—*"

Daeya pressed her will upon him and spoke with the power of command. "*Under no circumstances will you obey my summons while Lucius Gregory lives.*" Consciousness slipped from her, but she fought against the darkness with caged teeth. "*He will not use you to hurt anyone.*"

Sorrow and rage tore across the bond. Telerion reluctantly obeyed her wordless directive to circle back. "*As you command,* Nashanett.*"

As they sank back into the clouds, Daeya turned, slipping her legs free of Telerion's scales, and grabbed Zakaari by the cloak. She forced aside their scarves and kissed him hard. Where their lips met, the golden light of her Shield bloomed. She passed it to him in rippling waves, until only the black-violet glow of her runes remained. It would protect him long enough to get clear of the destruction before it returned to her.

Zakaari broke away, gasping. "What—"

"I love you." Daeya blinked against tears and smoke. "With all my heart."

"I love—" His dark brows shot upward. "No. Don't. We can fix this. Please, don't."

"I'm sorry." She pulled away and rose, her face damp. Telerion was close enough to the ground, now. "I can't let him have you."

Zakaari reached for her. "Daeya, *no!*"

She dodged his grapple, raced across the dragon's back, and flung herself into space.

"Sorcerer Beck!"

Normos kept walking, the key to Anya's shackles digging into his palm. He prayed to Mira the sigils of protection he'd built around her tent would hold. After all, what good was a hostage if the woman died?

"Sorcerer Beck, wait!"

He gritted his teeth and rounded on the soot-covered boy trailing after him. "You'd better have a damned good reason for the interruption, acolyte."

The boy flinched. "It's the healer, sir. She's escaped."

*Olivia. Thank the gods.*

He couldn't conceive of a better time than now to disappear in the confusion.

A flaming tree splintered and fell. Tremors reverberated up Normos's legs, and he shielded his face. Great clouds of scarlet embers spiraled upward. The acolyte flung his arms over his head.

When the boy looked up again, Normos gestured toward the tree and the fires. "If you want to go chasing after her in this, be my guest."

"But—"

"Truthfully, I think we have bigger problems." Normos spun on his heel. "See yourself southward, if you know what's good for you."

Gregory's pavilion rose from the smoke. Normos brushed past the fire and water savants battling the flames and reached for the flap stays.

A howl of rage from behind stopped him cold.

"Let go of me! Bleeding bastards!"

He turned to find Daeya McVen struggling against the hands of three mages. Councilor Gregory trailed behind them, his thunderous expression fixed on the wayward sorceress.

Satisfaction curled inside Normos. For once, it wasn't him on the receiving end of their mentor's disdain.

Dressed in Alliaansi furs and leather, with her hair woven into thick, cascading braids, she certainly looked the part of a blanker-loving rebel. Spellbinders encircled her wrists, and a set of manacles rattled at her ankles.

It was a good look for a traitor. Normos opened the tent and held the flap for the mages to shove her inside. Daeya hit the dirt with a gasp.

"Sorcerer Beck, attend me," Gregory ordered. "The rest of you, finish putting out those fires."

"Yes, Councilor."

"Right away, sir."

Normos followed him inside, and took up a position out of the way, yet in full view of the spectacle about to unfold. Finally, the child prodigy would get what she deserved.

Daeya rose onto her knees. "Where is Riisii? I demand you release her. Let this be between us."

Gregory whirled in a flash of soot-stained robes and backhanded her across her face.

A blow well-earned. She'd sent hundreds of their troops to Baosanni's Gate today. Normos shifted on his feet.

"It seems you have forgotten your place." Gregory circled her. "Let me be clear, my sweet, I have been patient with you because of your youth. But it is time to put your wanderlust aside. You will show respect, and you will obey, or you will suffer."

She bared her teeth like a savage. "Even when I obeyed, I still suffered."

Normos scoffed. She didn't know the first thing about suffering.

Daeya shot him a scathing glare. He held the look, pouring all the contempt he could muster into his answering sneer.

The Councilor circled her again. "If you have the dragon, then someone must have the book. Where is it?"

"What book?"

This time, Gregory struck her hard enough to drop her prone at his feet. "Do not toy with me. The tome. Where is the Tome of Eolaan?"

Eolaan. The Mother of Stories? What did Gregory want with a child's fae tale?

Daeya dragged herself upright, blood welling from her mouth. Haughty defiance shone in her face. Not shock. Not fear. Obviously, she'd experienced Gregory's displeasure so little, she had no idea what such petulance would bring. Normos almost felt sorry for her. Almost.

"I don't know of any tome."

Gregory's nostrils flared. Normos braced himself for the spell to surely follow.

But no incantation passed Gregory's lips. Daeya simply folded in half. Her scream punched into Normos's chest like a spike. She tore at her clothing until hooked fingers raked across her bare skin. An odd, violet glow shone through her hands. Normos tilted his head to get a better look, but he couldn't see what caused it.

"Stop," she rasped. "Please, stop."

"You can stop this any time you wish."

"I really don't know!"

Another scream pierced the armor of contempt around Normos's heart. Once, he and Daeya had been friends. A small piece of him still remembered that friendship, but she'd brought this on herself. Allying with blankers, killing her own people—he shouldn't pity her. She deserved this.

Gregory wrenched her head upward with such force that even Normos winced. "I will have that tome, and I will have that dragon. Until you come to your senses, you will remain in such agony that you will pray Baosanni takes you."

He tossed her aside, and Daeya crumpled, still writhing.

The scene turned Normos's stomach. It should have appeased him, seeing his rival brought low, but all he could think about was that horrible pain spell—the sensation of burning alive from the inside out, yet leaving no trace of injury. Was this how he looked when he displeased Gregory? Lying in the dirt, barely able to speak, body clutched as if to hold itself together—

Normos looked away, fighting off a shiver. The brat deserved it.

"Normos."

He straightened. "Yes, Councilor?"

"Find Sorceress Vika and Walk McVen back to Ryost. I want her guarded at all times. Take every precaution. I will send for you to collect me once I've dealt with the disaster here."

Normos bowed and turned for the entryway. "Your will."

"Does he know?"

Daeya's weak voice forced him to stillness. He looked back, pretending the sight of her didn't pain him. The tears in her clothes revealed the source of that eerie violet glow. He sucked in a breath.

Warrior's runes. Blanker warrior's runes, tainted somehow by dark magic.

She held his gaze with unusual gravity. "Do you know what he did to the School?"

Normos's blood turned to ice. She'd been far removed from the Guild for months. How could she know about that?

If death had a face, it likely matched the mask of rage twisting Gregory's features. "Breathe one word of that blanker heresy, and Anya Evallier will suffer for it."

Daeya's eyes unfocused in mingled pain and confusion. "Anya?"

*You've been lied to your entire life...*

If Gregory was willing to harm a high-profile hostage to keep Daeya silent, then she must know something important. But Normos couldn't let on that he doubted his story. Until he got Daeya alone to question her, until he found Sarikkian, he had to sell this ruse.

Normos crouched beside her. "Oh, I know all about the School. Usurping part of the Guild Council is no easy feat. Your blanker friends must be proud."

Her confusion only mounted. "What?"

The blankers trusted her to immolate half of the forest surrounding their city. Would they trust her enough to tell her if they held part of Eidosinia's leadership in thrall?

Normos's sense of foreboding grew. He masked it with another sneer and forced a laugh.

"Welcome back, Daeya."

# EPILOGUE

## GREGORY

Broken stone crunched underfoot. Moonlight streamed in from a collapsed wall, illuminating splintered benches and reflecting pools littered with rubble. The fallen abbey smelled of smoke and dust.

Fire and water savants had worked through the night, but in the end, Gregory had been forced to order the retreat.

They'd pulled back as far as Fawn's Breath and used the ravaged buildings to build a fast perimeter. The remnants of his and Blake's combined forces barely matched half of Ferren's untouched legion, and Archeph Roseheart's command had been destroyed. Only Gregory's capture of Daeya McVen and Anya Evallier had stopped the dragon from reducing the entire Eidosinian army to ash.

Gregory's face twitched. The Oracle had been wrong; Jarrah's runes didn't bind Daeya's will to him completely, as she'd promised. He was no closer to controlling the draegion and wiping out the blankers than he was to finding Draeconis. Though, the search for Tiior's city mattered less now. Daeya had successfully bonded a dragon, and someone, somewhere, possessed the tome. A few more days spent writhing in agony would pry the name from her tongue.

He strode to the front of the abbey and looked up. Wind whistled through the windows, whose broken panes gleamed like jagged teeth against the night.

It might have masked the killer's approach, had he not been expecting him.

"*Iiren'norvaa, amii.*"

He smirked. The sentimental old fool. Gregory turned, taking in those familiar vulpine features, the easy gait, and violet eyes. He paid no mind to how the man had gotten past his guards and into the heart of the Guild's temporary stronghold. He'd likely ghosted by the empty prisoners' tents, too.

"Mascha."

If the half-blood took offense to Gregory's silent refusal of his false name, Tipori, he gave no indication. "It's been a long time."

"Indeed. I wondered when you would show."

Mascha ran his hand along a polished windowsill and frowned when he reached a break in the stone. "I thought we had a deal, Councilor."

"I had to amend the terms." Stride for stride, they circled the shattered floor, appraising one another. "You took something of importance to me. It is only fair."

"I took nothing. She came to us after you mistreated her. I couldn't send her back to you in good conscience."

He lobbed the accusation with such self-righteous candor, Gregory laughed. "Your Alliaansi may not remember where you came from, Rorsch Hekkai, but I do. Your methods for breaking slaves were not so different from mine."

Mascha's voice lost its friendly edge. "I want both women and my grandchild returned unharmed. What's it going to take?"

"I would accept the dragon and the bookkeeper for Anya and the child she carries."

"I see," Mascha said, as if truly considering. It confirmed Gregory's suspicions: the tome was somewhere behind enemy lines. "And for Daeya?"

Gregory paused in a strip of moonlight, regarding his old ally. "I'm afraid nothing you possess is worth that exchange."

Mascha followed suit and folded his hands in front of him. He sighed. "Killing us won't bring Addy back, Lucius."

"No." The presumptuous mongrel had always been too forthright for his own good. "But it will bring me peace."

"Believe me, it won't. Addy wouldn't want this. She wouldn't want to see the man her father has become."

Rage blazed white-hot down to Gregory's fingertips and forced his hands to curl. "She could not *remember* the man her father was."

Mascha knew better than anyone what horrors had befallen Adelaide. He knew how every fond memory, every happy moment of her childhood, had been stripped from her and twisted into something wicked, torturous, or frightening. He knew how her love for her father had been so consumed by hatred, it had broken their family apart.

"Elsaar Felmani wronged us both," Mascha agreed. "For what he did to Riisii and Addy, I would have killed him a thousand times in a thousand ways."

The seer's name provoked an unexpected flood of memories. Gregory hadn't forgotten how they'd found Riisii, bloodied and broken by Felmani's experiments, at only five or six years old.

"But we have bigger problems than seeking revenge." Stone crunched beneath Mascha's boots. He closed half the distance between them before Gregory lifted a warning hand. "Problems that affect us all."

The Oracle had said the same. Jarrah was convinced her father's priests were proselytizing again, and she expected Gregory to settle his debt as soon as possible.

"I've seen Chaos's face."

That snapped Gregory out of his thoughts. Mascha's Foresight was legendary, and the possibility for a double meaning wasn't lost on him. "You've Seen it?"

"His priests infiltrated Starlight. Chaos himself appeared in the Aether before our priestess could cast him out."

It sounded ridiculous, but Mascha's serious expression never faltered. Gregory looked aside to the moonlit pews and frowned.

"You and I don't stand a chance against him," Mascha went on, "but Daeya is stronger than us both."

"I'm aware."

"Call off the war. Return Anya and Daeya, and let us work together to flush out his priests."

Silence settled over them like a shroud. They had reached an impasse; Mascha wouldn't send the dragon in for fear of hurting Anya, and until Gregory could break Daeya McVen, the dragon and the tome were out of reach. Moves and countermoves abounded, but he cared little for the machinations of the divine.

Still, Mascha's speech softened him. Gregory pressed his lips together and leveled his gaze on his old friend. "I'm willing to give you one last chance. Take your family and leave."

Mascha scowled. "You would have me overlook the greater threat?"

"I have it on good authority that particular problem is well in hand." He gestured dismissively. "If you will not leave, then let us draw a new line in the sand, hm?"

The man's pointed ears quivered with rage, but his lethal stare confirmed he was listening.

"Your daughter and her unborn will live, so long as you and your allies make no attempt to rescue Daeya McVen. Once the last mastermind has fallen, I will secure safe passage for Anya and the child out of Eidosinia. However, if I hear reports of a dragon on the horizon or catch any of your scouts snooping around my prisons, I will turn them both over to the Enlightened priests." He allowed the threat to sink in fully before adding, "Tiior only knows what horrors await them there."

Mascha's shoulders rose and fell with one silent breath. "Very well, Councilor."

Tension drained from Gregory's shoulders as the Aetherian turned to walk away. He remained on guard, but he breathed easier with every extra span between them.

"You know..." Mascha paused. "Addy and Daeya look a lot alike."

Gregory stilled.

"I wonder"—the blanker glanced over his shoulder—"could Addy have had Syljian blood as well?"

The accusation struck Gregory like a lance. Before he could splutter a response, Mascha wrapped himself in Aether and vanished.

# TIPORI

## A TALE FROM DESSOS

**A champion pit fighter crowned king of slavers.**
**A military leader collared and made to kneel.**
**An attraction of opposing forces that could topple an empire.**

Forty years before the events of *The Last Draegion Saga,* Maralla Evallier is taken captive and sold into slavery. On the shores of Rillion, she meets the infamous Mascha, leader of the Rorsch Hekkai, and inside the walls of his palace, she turns the slaver's world upside down.

**A spicy enemies-to-lovers romance set in a land where hedonism is law and deals are sealed with an exchange of flesh. Coming September 2nd, 2025!**

# THE TROUBLE WITH KNOWING

## A Seer's Story

### Not all those with Sight wish to See

A fae-touched seer and a clumsy dragon discuss the future of their world in this short story from Dessos. FREE to newsletter subscribers! Claim your copy today!

**WWW.THELASTDRAEGION.COM**

# Acknowledgements

They say writing is a solitary endeavor, perfect for introverts who would rather be at home snuggled up with a cat and a book than out socializing. But this book, this journey, simply wouldn't be possible without huge pushes from so many people—and especially those pushes and torch-wavings that kept some vicious imposter syndrome at bay.

Tim, my love, for never wavering in your support, even on the fifth read-through or the third-straight day solo-parenting our little gremli—I mean, children.

M.J. Lindsey, Alicia Leatherdale, and K.A. Herdt for being *the best* writer buds EVER. Y'all deserve gold medals, steak (or your favorite Ethiopian) dinners, and the nicest bottle of wine. But... after editing this chonk, I can only afford free books, shipping, and reciprocal cheerleading for your own projects, so get on them! My bookshelf is waiting for you <3.

Ellie Owen, Emma O'Connell, and Erynn Snel: the most fantabulous editing team I could ask for.

My ARC and street team for believing in me enough to shout about this series from those cursed social media rooftops. You guys make the most detested part of this introvert's job *so much* better.

Lastly, thank *you*, for picking up my second book! If you enjoyed the journey, pretty please leave those reviews, tell your buds, call those libraries—anything that helps get this story into the hands of more readers.

Join my newsletter and follow me on socials for updates on Daeya and co's next adventure, *Tides of Immolation*!

# PANTHEON GUIDE

### SAOLANNI, GREATER GODDESS OF LIFE

Mira, lesser goddess of creation and birth
Shavaan, lesser goddess of healing
Caelyn, lesser goddess of nature

### ORDEOLAS, GREATER GOD OF ORDER

Silonas, lesser god of fortune and trade
Tiior, lesser goddess of wisdom and knowledge
Delvin, lesser god of law and justice

### BAOSANNI, GREATER GOD OF DEATH

Laangor, lesser god of suffering
Yasuo, Gatekeeper, lesser god of the afterlife
Anordis, lesser god of war and chaos

# TRANSLATIONS

## ANCIENT DRACONIC (DRAEGIONIC)

*asokhovha* (aʒ-OH-ko-vah*): an incantation to summon or unsummon the Tome of Eolaan

*centureon* (cent-YER-ee-on): a dragon aged at least one hundred years

*draegion* (DRAY-jee-on): the original inhabitants of Dessos, once bonded to dragons in an effort by the Greater Gods to preserve draegionic magic in exchange for world dominion. Now believed to be dragon riders or tamers in some cultures.

*draekhatt, draekhei* (drake-AHT, drake-EYE): daughter, son

*mautorosi* (mau-tor-OH-see): ancient term for horned peoples who now live primarily in Mautor and parts of Skriia

*millenneon* (mill-EN-nee-on): a dragon aged at least one thousand years

*nashanett, nashanei* (nah-shan-ETT, nah-shan-EYE): (plural, neuter: *nashanar*) leader

*niish amaar* (NICHE ah-MAR): my love

*saonivhatt, saonivhei* (say-on-i-VAHT, say-on-iv-EYE): (plural, neuter: *saonivhar*) goddess, god

*shavhatt, shavhei* (shav-AHT, shav-EYE): (plural, neuter: *shavhar*) mate, spouse

*syljoren* (sill-JOR-en): ancient term for saphyrum-dependent peoples who now live primarily in the northern and central parts of the Eidosinian continent and in southern Rillion

*vhash* (VAHSH): no

*vheskhanash* (ves-kahn-OSH): the abdication of a draconic throne, usually prompted by a monarch's inability to produce an heir or a court's lack of confidence in its leadership

*vheth* (VETH): yes
*ʒ makes the same sound as the 's' in 'measure'


## BROGRENTI

*braugh* (BRAW): strong, strapping
*breigh* (BRAI): pretty, beautiful
*kinnich* (KEN-iç): (slang) know
*taenach* (tie-NAÇ): a headdress made to cover the neck, head, and face
*tainach* (tay-NAÇ): ...I see you, fellow dirty-minded friend


## SYLJIAN

*ama're* (AH-ma-re): beloved
*amaa* (ah-MAH): (universal) leader, teacher, master
*amaare* (ah-MAR-eh): to love
*amii* (ah-MEE): (plural, *amiien*) friend
*aon* (ay-OWN): no
*ashaan* (ash-AHN): (derogatory) half-blood
*bashiin* (bash-EEN): (derogatory) human
*caezo* (KAY-zoh): (derogatory) feces
*ciir* (SEER): yes
*ennii, enniia* (en-NEE, en-NEE-uh): (plural, *enniien*) son, daughter
*gesuu* (geh-SOO): dirty
*haalii, haaliia* (ha-LEE, ha-LEE-uh): uncle, aunt
*iiren'hyvaa* (EER-in hy-VAH): (both salutation and farewell) good morning/day
*iiren'norvaa* (EER-in nor-VAH): (both salutation and farewell) good evening
*miaa, ne'miaa* (MEE-uh, neh-MEE-uh): mother, grandmother
*miraar* (meer-AHR): above
*nei* (NIE): I, my
*peiaa* (PIE-uh): father
*ru* (ROO): little
*saonis* (say-ON-is): god or gods
*taapad tiik* (TAHP-ad TEEK): thank you
*torii, toriia* (tor-EE, tor-EE-uh): brother, sister
*ushaar* (yew-SHAR): you're welcome

# PRONUNCIATIONS

Aivenos: (AY-ven-os)
Alar: (ah-LAR)
Ashaara: (ah-SHAR-uh)
Baokryn: (BAY-oh-krin)
Baosanni: (bay-oh-SAW-nee)
Caelyn: (KAY-lin)
Cheralach: (SHER-uh-lack)
Daeya: (DIE-ya)
Eidosinia: (eye-doh-SIN-ee-uh)
Jerinoch: (jer-i-NOCK)
Koraani: (kor-AH-nee)
Nahariim: (nah-har-EEM)
Nerimoria: (ner-i-MOR-ee-uh)
Niam: (NEE-um)
Ordeolas: (or-DAY-o-lus)
Orowen: (OR-oh-wen)
Paelic: (PAY-lick)
Ravlok: (RAV-lock)
Ryost: (RYE-ost)
Sarikkian: (sahr-I-kee-in)
Saolanni: (say-oh-LAW-nee)
Tiior: (tee-OR, or TYOR)
Varkendios "Kendi": (var-KEN-di-os)
Vorsere: (vor-SEER)
Xavkavhosh: (zav-kav-OSH)
Xosek: (ZOH-ʒek*)
*ʒ makes the same sound as the 's' in 'measure'

# ABOUT THE AUTHOR

Cindy L. Sell supposedly lives in the Midwestern United States with a home full of furry critters, including her two boys and doting husband, but she really spends most of her time on Dessos battling sorcerers or negotiating trade deals with pirates.

She graduated from Washburn University with a creative writing degree, but didn't bother to do anything with it until COVID when she ran out of excuses. When she's not writing, she enjoys bowling, crochet, and riding her '82 Sportster.

Look for Cindy on Facebook, say hi on Instagram, and visit her website for upcoming events and shenanigans.

# WORKS BY CINDY L. SELL

## THE LAST DRAEGION SAGA

*Remnants of a Scarlet Flame:* September 2024
*Embers Rising:* August 2025
*Tides of Immolation:* TBD
*Aether and Ash:* TBD

## TALES FROM DESSOS

*Tipori:* September 2025

## SHORT STORIES

*The Trouble With Knowing:* August 2024

www.ingramcontent.com/pod-product-compliance
Lightning Source LLC
Chambersburg PA
CBHW061029310726
48969CB00004B/890